Introduction Summaries

The Sagebrush Bride by Amanda Cabot
1852 – Avice Longcope's parents have died on the trail, her uncle has confiscated all they owned, and now he wants her to marry his new business partner. When the wagon train reaches Fort Laramie, Avice is desperate to escape her uncle's plans, but she doesn't expect a sudden proposal from the widowed sutler.

Beckoned Hearts by Melanie Dobson
1856 – Recently widowed, Molly Goodwin has spent the winter as the only female in Idaho's Fort Hall, working for a shopkeeper as she waits to join a wagon train traveling East. When Payton Keller brings his ill sister into the fort, Molly saves the woman's life. Will she take another risk and follow her heart to Oregon with these new friends or return home on her own?

Shanghaied by the Bride by Pam Hillman
1851 – Blake Samuelson wakes up in the bed of a wagon lumbering west along the Oregon Trail. He remembers being attacked, but not how he got in the wagon. Cassidy Taylor sees Blake as an answer to prayer for a man to help her all female family on the trail.

Settled Hearts by Myra Johnson
1852 - Desperate to find her father in Oregon for her ill mother, Emma Clarke teams up with John Patrick, a loyal uncle who is determined to hide his niece and nephew from abusive adoptive parents. Will Emma and John find the hope they seek for their futures along the trail?

As Good as Gold by Amy Lillard
1851 – Ellis Hardy is headed to the gold mines of California when he takes up Trudy Johnson's proposition: pretend to be her husband and protect her and her daughter as they travel to meet up with her real husband in Oregon. Sounds easy enough, but Trudy is hiding something important.

Daughters of the Wind by DiAnn Mills
1851 – While Lane Walker is out scouting for a wagon train, a tornado destroys the wagons and kills everyone—except Deborah and seven little girls who had joined her on a hike to a rocky bluff. How is this little band of survivors to get through the wilderness without provisions?

His Frontier Family by Anna Schmidt
1851 – Captain Jason Campbell is not the marrying kind. So when yet another wagon train pulls into the fort he is unprepared for his attraction to the beautiful young widow, Emma Carson who comes to him for helping in finding her twelve-year-old son.

State of Matrimony by Ann Shorey
1858 – Diantha Bowers joins a family moving to Oregon, but when the husband dies, the wife wants to return East. Will Diantha lose her dreams of adventure, or will one of the two men vying for her affections convince her to stay the course?

Sioux Summer by Jennifer Uhlarik
1854 – Ellie Jefford is struggling after the death of her husband and son. Alone to serve Indians and immigrants at a trading post during her cantankerous father-in-law's illness, she welcomes a friendly face in Teagan Donovan, who declares he is on his last trip as a trail guide before settling down on his own farm.

THE *Oregon Trail* ROMANCE COLLECTION

Amanda Cabot, Melanie Dobson
Pam Hillman, Myra Johnson
Amy Lillard, DiAnn Mills, Anna Schmidt
Ann Shorey, Jennifer Uhlarik

BARBOUR BOOKS
An Imprint of Barbour Publishing, Inc.

Print ISBN 978-1-64352-176-3

eBook Editions:
Adobe Digital Edition (.epub) 978-1-63409-262-3
Kindle and MobiPocket Edition (.prc) 978-1-63409-263-0

Scripture quotations marked KJV are taken from the King James Version of the Bible.

This book is a work of fiction. Names, characters, places, and incidents are either products of the author's imagination or used fictitiously. Any similarity to actual people, organizations, and/or events is purely coincidental.

Published by Barbour Books, an imprint of Barbour Publishing, Inc., 1810 Barbour Drive, Uhrichsville, Ohio 44683, www.barbourbooks.com

Our mission is to inspire the world with the life-changing message of the Bible.

Member of the
Evangelical Christian
Publishers Association

Printed in the United States of America.

Contents

The Sagebrush Bride

by Amanda Cabot

Dedication

For Janet Ennis-Beard. Thanks for your continued friendship and especially for offering your family names for my characters.

Chapter 1

They called it Chimney Rock. Avice Longcope leaned against the side of the wagon and stared at the famous landmark, wishing she could join in the celebratory mood that seemed to have gripped so many others in the party. For days they'd talked about reaching this milestone in their journey, and now they were camped practically in its shadow. Some were headed toward the enormous limestone spire, hoping to climb it. Though they'd invited Avice to join them, she wasn't ready for any kind of celebration.

Tears trickled down her cheeks as she gazed across the prairie at what everyone else called Chimney Rock. If she were wise, she would think of it as a chimney, because she had no special memories associated with chimneys. But try as she might, Avice could not ignore the fact that Chimney Rock reminded her of the cake Ma had made for her birthday last year. That cake had had three layers, each smaller than the one beneath it, just like the rock. There had even been a candle on top, completing the resemblance to the wind-sculpted limestone just a few miles away.

The tiered cake hadn't tasted any different than an ordinary one, but its shape had made the day extra special. It was part of a birthday Avice would never forget, for that had been the day Pa had announced that he and Ma were thinking about moving west, building a new store and a new life in a new land.

Trying to tamp back the tears that threatened to turn into a river, Avice looked back at the tracks the wagons had left in the prairie, her mind picturing the single grave that marked the end of her parents' aspirations. Cholera had taken Ma and Pa, along with their dream of opening a mercantile in Oregon.

Earlier this spring they'd sold their home and store in Michigan in preparation for the move west. Avice had been almost as excited as her parents about their journey west, though she'd disagreed when they'd invited Uncle Eli to join them. Pa had claimed it was the Christian thing to do, to help his brother even though Eli had scant experience in a mercantile. He would learn, Pa had claimed. But now Uncle Eli was talking as if he'd been the driving force behind the mercantile. Though it had been less than two weeks since her parents' deaths, Uncle Eli had shown no sign of mourning. Instead he'd spent most of his time with Matthew Dempsey.

Avice shivered, even though the early evening air was still warm. She wasn't sure what Uncle Eli and Matthew Dempsey were planning, but she couldn't dismiss her misgivings. Though the man was older than Pa, when Mr. Dempsey looked at her, it wasn't the way an old man should. And then there were the times he brushed up against her, his hands making Avice feel as if something dirty had touched her.

Just because she was twenty-four years old and still unmarried didn't mean she was desperate for a suitor. Both Ma and Pa had agreed when she'd turned down the four men who'd offered to marry her. They knew that as much as Avice longed for a home and children of her own, she wasn't willing to settle for less than love. She hadn't loved those men, and she didn't love Mr. Dempsey.

Noticing a small rent in her skirt, Avice frowned then climbed into the wagon to retrieve her sewing kit. She was reaching for the cloth bag of supplies she'd placed in one of the inside pockets on the canvas top when she heard familiar voices.

"I tell you, Matthew," her uncle declared in his most bombastic tone, "this will be the best investment you've ever made. With your money and my know-how, we'll be rich. My brother claimed that a mercantile could support a large family. Think how much there'll be for just the two of us."

"The two of us and the girl." Avice cringed at Matthew Dempsey's words, for she had no doubt of the girl's identity. "It's no secret I've had my eye on her since I joined the wagon train. Her pa wouldn't let me court her, but the way I figure it, now that he's gone, you're the only one between me and her." His voice was softer now, as if he and Uncle Eli were walking away, and Avice feared she would not hear her uncle's response. But Mr. Dempsey continued. "The only way you and I've got a deal is if I get what I want—Avice as my wife."

Avice took a deep breath, trying to tamp down the anger that rose inside her. How dare they talk of trading her as if she were a team of oxen!

"It might not be that simple, Matthew," her uncle said. "Avice's got a mind of her own, and she's of age. I can't force her to marry you."

A moment of silence followed, as if Mr. Dempsey was searching for an argument that would persuade her. There were none. Avice would not agree to marry him any more than she had agreed to marry her other suitors.

"The way I see it, Eli, you give her a choice. She marries me, or you throw her out of your wagon. No one else on the train will take her in."

He was right. Now that Uncle Eli had appropriated all of the goods in the wagon, claiming they belonged to him as the surviving partner, there was no reason for another family to take Avice in. She would only be a burden.

The sound of her uncle's laughter sent chills down her spine. "You're a wily one, Matthew. I reckon that'll work. You two can get hitched when we get to Fort Laramie."

Though Avice wanted to scream, she remained silent. Screaming would accomplish nothing. She had four days until they reached Fort Laramie, four days to find a way out of this predicament. And she would find a way, for if there was one thing she knew, it was that Matthew Dempsey was not the man God intended for her.

Raleigh Bayne didn't need to look at the calendar to know that today was June 5. The date was etched in his memory. June 5 marked exactly one year since he and Dorothy had stood before the minister, smiling as he pronounced them man and wife.

Raleigh wasn't smiling now, and neither was his son. Jay was squalling, and nothing Raleigh did had made the least bit of difference. Jay wasn't hungry. Hannah had fed him only an hour earlier when she'd dropped off the day's milk. He didn't need a clean diaper. Raleigh had checked.

He looked around the building that had been his place of employment for the better part of a year. It was filling with customers and would become even more crowded when the wagon train arrived. He couldn't do anything now but let his son cry while he waited on the people who guaranteed his livelihood.

After exchanging quick commiserating smiles with the clerks at the other two counters, he greeted the woman who'd been standing in line, tapping her foot in annoyance. Rob or Tim needn't be subjected to Mrs. Taylor's legendary temper. Raleigh was managing the store, and that meant he should handle the most difficult customers.

When Mrs. Taylor left, harrumphing about crying babies, Raleigh looked up, his mood improving when he saw Farley making his way to the counter. By some small miracle, the store was experiencing one of the brief lulls that gave Raleigh and the clerks a chance to catch their breath.

"It sounds like your son's unhappy," Farley said, peering over the counter at the red-faced infant who was flailing his arms and legs in the flannel-lined basket Raleigh had placed on the floor.

"Tell me something I didn't already know."

Raleigh had met Lieutenant Farley Miller soon after he and Dorothy had arrived at Fort Laramie, and the two men had developed an instant camaraderie. Even Dorothy, who'd been critical of most of the soldiers, had liked Farley, and it had been Farley who'd stood at Raleigh's side as Dorothy's casket was lowered into the ground. Sometimes brash but always honest, Farley was a man Raleigh would trust with his life.

Right now his friend propped one elbow on the counter and leaned forward, lowering his voice as he said, "You want me to tell you something you don't appear to know? How about this? You've got to give up something. The way I see it, you have two choices. You can tell the sutler to find himself another manager, or—"

Raleigh cut him off. "I won't do that. You know I won't. This is the opportunity of a lifetime, a true godsend." Once his two years of managing the fort's trading post, more commonly called the sutler's store, ended, Raleigh would have the experience and the funds he needed to open his own store in the city of his choice.

Shrugging, Farley said, "Then there's only one thing to do—send Jay back to Dorothy's parents."

"Never!" Raleigh looked down at his son. Screams had turned to hiccups, and if today was like the others, Jay would soon fall asleep. Ogden and Flora Adams may have kept Dorothy fed and clothed, but they'd never given her love. There was no way on earth Raleigh would let them raise his son.

"Then what are you going to do? You can't go on this way. You don't sleep and everything's suffering—you, your son, the store."

Raleigh nodded. Farley was merely stating the obvious. "There's another answer."

"And what would that be?"

"I need a wife. I realized that yesterday." The thought had come to him when he'd been struggling to get Jay to sleep. Every time he'd laid his son in his crib, Jay had begun to scream, and even when Raleigh had tried to rock him in his arms, Jay had remained awake, his chubby cheeks red from all the tears he'd shed.

"A wife?" Farley didn't bother to hide his skepticism. "How are you going to manage that? Single women are as rare as roses around here."

"I know. That's why I asked God to send me one." When Jay had finally fallen asleep, Raleigh had spent an hour on his knees, pouring out his hopes and fears and begging for a way to keep his son with him. Through it all, the one idea that had refused to disappear was that of a wife, and so Raleigh had ended his prayer with a plea for God to send the right woman to Fort Laramie.

Farley's eyebrows rose so high that they almost disappeared under his hat. "And you think He will?"

"I do."

Chapter 2

It felt like home. Avice took a deep breath, astonished by the sense of belonging that swept over her as she entered Fort Laramie. This was the place where, unless God answered her prayers and showed her another way, she was to marry Matthew Dempsey. If for no other reason, she ought to hate it, and yet Avice couldn't help smiling at the sight of the fort.

The treeless prairie, dotted with blue-gray sagebrush and prickly pear cactus now adorned with pink and yellow blossoms, was far different from the fruit orchards that dominated the landscape in Michigan, but something about it filled Avice's heart with peace. Though this wasn't the verdant Oregon valley of her parents' dreams, she could not ignore the feeling that this was her destination, not merely a stopping point on the journey west. It made no sense, for she knew no one here and had no way of earning a living if she abandoned the wagon train, but Avice could not dismiss the idea that God had something in store for her here.

Grateful that the soldiers' inventory of their livestock kept Uncle Eli and Matthew Dempsey preoccupied, Avice slipped away from the wagon. Fort Laramie was busier than she'd expected, and that was good. With all the people milling around, it would be easy to lose herself in the crowds, if only for a few minutes. And as she did, perhaps she would find a way to escape from Matthew Dempsey permanently.

Though neither he nor Uncle Eli had spoken to Avice about the marriage, she'd heard their plans, plans that included Avice moving into Mr. Dempsey's wagon for the duration of the trip. She'd shuddered every time she'd thought of that, and each time she had offered another prayer for deliverance. At first it had seemed that there'd been no answer, but the way she felt now told her God was watching over her.

Taking another deep breath, Avice smiled. The wind blew the pungent smells of horses, unwashed men, and wood smoke toward her. Though many would consider the odors unpleasant, she found them invigorating, just as she found the sight of sagebrush and cactus appealing. The others on the wagon train had dismissed the prairie plants as ugly reminders of a barren landscape, but Avice found no ugliness in them.

She narrowed her eyes against the bright sunshine, grateful for the shade her sunbonnet provided, as she looked around. She'd expected Fort Laramie to be nothing more than a few crude buildings, but instead the variety of structures flanking the parade ground made it look more like a small town than an army post.

Rather than the uniform size and shape she'd expected, the buildings were a mixture of stone and frame. While many were only one story high, a large two-story white frame edifice with porches on both levels dominated one side of the parade ground. The sight of uniformed men emerging from one of the doorways confirmed Avice's belief

THE OREGON TRAIL ROMANCE COLLECTION

that this was Old Bedlam, the fort's famous bachelor officers' housing. Others on the wagon train had claimed that rowdy parties had led to its nickname. Avice had no time for such speculation.

While Old Bedlam was handsome, it was the long, low building to the north that caught her eye. Although it was one of the least imposing structures at the fort, Avice felt drawn to it. The number of people headed that way and the bundles in the arms of those who emerged made her believe it was the sutler's store. No wonder it attracted her. Avice's smile broadened at the thought of comparing this frontier trading post with the mercantile her parents had owned back home.

She hurried along the edge of the parade ground, careful not to disturb the soldiers who were marching, their faces as solemn as if they were leaving for battle. When she entered the store, Avice stopped, amazed by the sight that greeted her. The building itself was ordinary, with wooden counters lining three walls and a wide variety of merchandise displayed on shelves behind the counters. What wasn't ordinary was the chaos.

Three men stood behind the counters, trying to satisfy more customers than her parents' store would have seen in a day. Indian men, women, and children, their garments ranging from beautifully tooled skins to what appeared to be little more than rough blankets, mingled with soldiers, a few white women, some in fashionable dress, others wearing faded and patched calico, and rough-hewn men who might have been fur trappers. Everyone looked and sounded disgruntled. The muttered curses made Avice cringe, but those were more easily dismissed than the baby's wailing.

She looked around, wondering who was responsible for the poor service that was causing such problems. Two of the men behind the counters were little more than boys. In all likelihood the tall dark-haired one was in charge. Though he was more handsome than any man she knew, it wasn't the man's good looks that snagged Avice's attention but the rigid set of his shoulders and the obviously forced smile that left no doubt that he was as frustrated as his customers.

Avice's moment of sympathy faded as the baby's screams intensified. Where was the poor child? Her gaze moved quickly around the crowd. None of the Indian children were crying, and there were no white babies in sight, but the wailing continued. She tipped her head to one side, listening until she determined that the cries were coming from behind the counter. Someone had to help that child, and it looked as if that someone was her.

Avice made her way through the crowd then strode behind the counter. There he was. Her instincts told her that the squalling baby who'd been stashed behind the counter in a basket as if he were a sack of flour was a boy. Reaching down, she gathered the infant into her arms. Though she was no expert, the baby was so tiny that she guessed he was only a few weeks old.

"There now, it'll be all right," Avice said as she patted the child's back and began to croon softly. "It'll be all right."

As if he understood, the child ceased his cries and stared at her, his brown eyes widening in surprise. He was far from the most beautiful baby she'd ever seen, with his face red and blotched from crying, but as she traced her finger along his downy cheek and smiled at the now silent baby, Avice knew why she'd been drawn to the sutler's store. This child needed her.

—⁓—

Something was different. Raleigh handed the woman the dishes she'd ordered along with a teakettle and three bars of soap. Her frown turned into a grudging smile when he added two peppermint sticks for her children, explaining that they were a small thank-you for her patience. The truth was, she hadn't been patient, but there was no point in aggravating a customer, especially a customer who bought as much as she did.

Though the next few sales went smoothly and quickly, Raleigh couldn't dismiss the feeling that something was different. He glanced at Tim and Rob. Nothing different there. The two young men who helped in the store appeared just as frazzled as they had a few minutes ago. Suddenly Raleigh identified the difference: Jay was no longer crying. His wails had continued for so long that Raleigh had managed to tune them out while he attempted to earn a living for both of them, but somehow the screams had stopped.

He looked down, and for a second his heart stopped. Jay was not in his basket. Fear deeper than anything he had ever experienced made him grip the edge of the counter as the blood drained from his head and his legs threatened to buckle. Where was Jay? What had happened to his son?

Please, God. Keep him safe. Raleigh closed his eyes for an instant as he implored the Lord to protect his son. When he opened them, he blinked in disbelief. There was Jay, on the opposite side of the store in the arms of a lovely young woman. Perhaps five and a half feet tall, she had blond hair and, if Raleigh's instincts were accurate, blue eyes. He couldn't tell from this distance. What he could tell was that she held Jay as easily as if she'd done it every day of his short life while she moved through the crowd, speaking to a few of the women. Raleigh's fear disappeared at the realization that she meant Jay no harm, but merely sought to comfort him. Still, he studied her, wondering why she was speaking to the customers.

As he watched, a woman turned to leave the store, her anger palpable even across the room. Though the other customers continued to murmur among themselves, he heard the beautiful blond address the irate woman.

"I don't like to wait, either," she said, her voice clear and calm, "but I saw some yellow calico on the wall that would be perfect with your hair and eyes. I wish I could wear that color."

To Raleigh's surprise, the dark-haired woman stopped and gazed at the wall of fabrics. "Which one is it?" she asked.

The blond pointed to the shelf behind Raleigh. "Would you like me to get it down so you can see it?"

When the woman nodded, Jay's savior approached the counter. "Will you excuse me for a moment, sir?" she asked the man who'd made his way to the front of the line to ask Raleigh for a pound of nails. "It'll take only a second."

When the man inclined his head, the blond looked up at Raleigh. Her eyes were the deep blue he'd expected, and he saw the lightest sprinkling of freckles on the bridge of her nose.

"Can you help me?" she asked, pointing to the bright yellow calico that he'd despaired of ever selling. "I believe this lady will buy the whole bolt once she sees the quality."

Bemused by the way this stranger had so quickly assumed control not only of his son but of one of his customers, Raleigh pulled the calico from the shelf. "Certainly, Mrs. . . ." He let his voice trail off, inviting her to give him her name.

"It's Miss. Miss Avice Longcope."

Taking the fabric, Miss Avice Longcope returned to the customer, letting her finger what would become a new dress. As he turned back to his own customer, Raleigh was unable to hear what the lovely blond said, but five minutes later when the dark-haired woman reached the front of the line, he realized that Miss Longcope had been right. Not only did she purchase the entire bolt of fabric, but she also bought twenty yards of ribbon.

And all the while Jay rested in Miss Longcope's arms, quiet and apparently content. It might not be a miracle, but it was feeling very close to one. Raleigh took a deep breath, letting his gaze rest on the woman who held his son, and as he did, hope surged through him. Jay accepted her; she was better at handling customers than Raleigh himself; and she was unmarried. Could she be the answer to his prayers?

Raleigh had never been an impulsive man. He'd known Dorothy for years before he'd married her, and yet—impulsive though it was—this felt right. He continued to watch Miss Longcope, and as he did, his conviction increased. She was part of God's plan.

When the store emptied during one of those unpredictable lulls he never failed to appreciate, he walked toward the woman and extended his hand.

"We haven't been properly introduced, Miss Longcope, but I'm Raleigh Bayne, and that's my son, Jay, you're holding."

She shook his hand briefly then touched Jay's nose, making his son gurgle in delight. Truly, the woman was a miracle worker.

"I'm managing the store for the sutler," Raleigh continued, praying for the right words to convince her. "I appreciate all you've done, not just for Jay but for the customers."

She nodded, as if comforting his son and turning unhappy shoppers into satisfied ones was insignificant. "You're welcome. It was my pleasure."

As she smiled, Raleigh felt his heart pound with the certainty that it was not coincidence that she'd come here today.

"I know this is sudden," he said, trying to keep his excitement under control, "but I believe God sent you here for a reason. Will you marry me?"

Chapter 3

Avice stared at the man, unsure which shocked her more, that Raleigh Bayne, a complete stranger, wanted her to marry him or that she was considering it. She took a deep breath, trying to slow her racing pulse. Was it possible that this was the answer to her prayers? Was this the reason she'd felt so peaceful since she'd arrived at Fort Laramie? Was it true that God had been leading her to this man and his child?

Her heart continued to pound at the enormity of what she was considering. She, the woman who'd refused four suitors because she did not love them, was entertaining the idea of marrying a man she neither knew nor loved. And yet it would be a lie to say that there was no love involved, for as Avice looked down at the now sleeping baby she held in her arms, she felt tendrils of love wrap themselves around her heart.

Mr. Bayne touched her hand. It was the briefest of touches, little more than a brush, and yet it sent a shiver of excitement through Avice's veins. "You and I need to talk," he said. He turned to address the two clerks. "Miss Longcope and I will be in the office. I know you can handle everything." As the men's chests puffed with importance, Mr. Bayne led the way to a small room furnished with bookshelves and a desk, then pointed to one of the two chairs in front of the desk. When Avice settled into one, he took the other, turning it so he was facing her.

"I doubt this is the way you envisioned a proposal of marriage, but when I saw you with Jay, I knew you were the answer to my prayers."

Avice nodded slowly. That he was a praying man was a point in his favor. She had turned down two suitors not only because she didn't love them but because their faith began and ended at the church door. Raleigh—she couldn't continue to think of him as Mr. Bayne when they were discussing marriage—was different.

"I haven't known what to do ever since my wife died giving birth to Jay," he continued. "I don't want to send him back East to her parents, but as you could tell, I need someone to care for him." A tender smile lit Raleigh's face as he gazed at the child in Avice's arms, and in that second, she knew he had not been neglecting his son by allowing him to cry but had simply been overwhelmed.

"I wanted to hire someone to care for Jay," he continued. "Unfortunately, there are no women on the post who are willing and able to do that."

Avice wasn't surprised. She'd heard there were few women on army posts. "But to marry someone you don't know or love seems. . ." She broke off, not wanting to pronounce the word *desperate*.

He had no such compunctions. As if reading her mind, Raleigh said, "I'm desperate, Miss Longcope. I will do anything to keep my son happy and well. Even though it's been only a short time, you've proven that you can do that. But there's something even

17

more important to me. I've see the way you look at Jay. You may not know or love me, but I believe you're starting to love my son."

"I am." And the more time she spent with him, the more she admired Raleigh Bayne. He was an honest, God-fearing man who loved his son. Those were all important qualifications in a husband.

Tiny lines formed at the corners of Raleigh's eyes as he smiled. "I know you were headed west, but if you could agree to stay, it would only be for a year."

Avice felt the blood drain from her face. Whatever she'd expected Raleigh to say, it wasn't this. "A year? What do you mean? Marriage is a lifetime commitment."

He leaned forward, placing his hands on his knees as he said, "Our marriage would be in name only. Nothing else would be fair to you. I don't want to mislead you, Miss Longcope. No one can take Dorothy's place in my heart, but I want you to have my name to protect you from gossip here at the fort. When the time is up, I'll give you an annulment and enough money to move anywhere you want."

Avice took another deep breath, trying to digest everything he'd said. If she agreed to the proposal, she would not have to marry Matthew Dempsey. And, when the marriage ended, she would be independent. Both were important, but as she looked down at Jay, tracing the curve of one cheek with her finger, Avice realized there was a far better reason for becoming Raleigh's wife: she would have a child, even if for only a year.

Though she already knew that she would accept his proposal, Avice was still puzzled. "Why would our arrangement end after a year?"

"That's a good question." Raleigh crossed his ankles and settled back in the chair. "I told you I was managing the store. My contract will expire on July first of next year. At that point, I plan to head west. California, Oregon—I'm not sure yet where I'll go, but I know I want to open a mercantile wherever I settle."

He looked at his son and smiled again. "Jay will be sleeping through the night by then. In a larger city, I should be able to find someone to care for him during the day."

Raleigh's expression turned to dismay. "Here I am, talking about myself and what I need. I haven't asked about you and whether you'd be willing to leave your family for a year. Perhaps there's a man on the wagon train that you want to marry."

Avice shook her head. "I have no family. We were headed to Oregon to open our own mercantile, but my parents died of cholera last month. As for a husband, my uncle expects me to marry one of his cronies today."

Her tone must have betrayed her feelings about Matthew Dempsey, because Raleigh raised an eyebrow. "You don't look like a happy bride-to-be."

"I don't want to marry that man," she admitted, "but until today, I didn't know how I could avoid it. Like you, I've been praying for a solution." Avice gave him a small smile. "Mr. Bayne, I believe you're the answer to my prayers."

"Then you'll marry me?"

"I will."

⁓

Half an hour later, Raleigh and his new bride emerged from the chaplain's office. Though Reverend Collins had to have been surprised, he'd said nothing, merely asked both of them if they were ready to make a lifetime commitment. To her credit, Avice had simply nodded, saying her vows with so much emotion that, if he hadn't known better, Raleigh would have believed this was the marriage of her dreams. Then when he'd slid the wide gold band that had once been his grandmother's onto her finger, Avice had given him a smile that told him he had not made a mistake. This was the woman God had sent him.

As he blinked to let his eyes adjust to the bright sunshine, Raleigh transferred Jay to his left arm, bending his right so that Avice could place her hand on it. They were halfway across the parade ground when he felt her stiffen.

"It's them," she said. And in that instant Raleigh knew the two men who were approaching them, the scowls on their faces leaving no doubt of their anger, were her uncle and the intended bridegroom.

"Avice! There you are. I've been looking for you everywhere." The first man was an inch or so shorter than Raleigh with hair more gray than blond and a sour expression. "Where have you been?" he demanded. Then, as if he'd suddenly become aware of Raleigh's presence, he pointed at Raleigh. "Who is this man?"

Though he could feel a slight trembling in Avice's fingers as she gripped his arm, Raleigh was proud that her voice did not quaver as she said, "Uncle Eli, this is my husband, Mr. Raleigh Bayne."

So that was the uncle. Raleigh saw no sign of love or caring on his face. For a second neither of the men spoke; then the other one found his tongue. "Your husband? But I—"

Unwilling to let the man whose clenched fists made him look like a school-yard bully continue, Raleigh interrupted. "I'm sure you both wish to give Avice your blessing, but we're in a hurry to get her settled into my house. Good day, gentlemen."

Without waiting for their reply, Raleigh looked down at Avice and smiled, making sure both men heard him. "Come along, Mrs. Bayne. We need to unload your wagon." Though she'd told him her uncle had appropriated the goods destined for the new mercantile, Raleigh had no intention of letting him steal Avice's personal belongings.

When they were out of earshot, she slowed her steps and looked up at him, her expression solemn. "Thank you."

"For what?"

"For handling them."

"It was nothing." Though Raleigh could dismiss what he'd done, he could not ignore the way the obvious approval in her gaze warmed his heart. For better or for worse, Avice was his wife, and right now, there was no doubt that it was for better.

"It's a lovely house, isn't it, Jay?" Avice wasn't sure why she was talking to the baby, since she knew he couldn't reply, but when he gurgled as if he understood, she was glad she'd continued the one-sided conversation.

Though the house was perhaps half the size of the home she'd grown up in, after weeks of living out of a wagon and sleeping on the ground, Avice felt as if she were in a mansion. The first floor contained a parlor, dining room, kitchen, and small storeroom, while two bedrooms and an alcove that held Jay's crib were on the second. All were simply furnished.

Her foot moved slowly, keeping the rocking chair in motion as she thought of the man she'd married. It was thanks to Raleigh that she was able to soothe his son in the same chair where she had once been rocked to sleep. His displeasure at her marriage evident, Uncle Eli had supervised the unloading of the wagon, insisting that the furniture from her parents' home was now his and that all Avice owned was her clothing. He'd grudgingly allowed her to take the sampler her mother had stitched, although she knew he had no use for it, but had refused her request for her grandmother's rocking chair, claiming it belonged to him. To Avice's dismay, tears filled her eyes at the thought of parting with the chair that her mother had cherished.

Once again, Raleigh had come to her rescue, speaking so clearly that several other members of the wagon train had come to investigate. "Avice, I fear you've misunderstood your uncle. He wanted to be certain you knew that the chair was his and that it was his wedding gift to you." Before Uncle Eli could respond, Raleigh continued. "Both Avice and I thank you for your generosity."

With half a dozen witnesses watching the interchange, Uncle Eli could do nothing but nod as if it had been his idea, and before he could change his mind, the rocker was loaded into the cart Raleigh had borrowed.

Avice smiled as she looked at the baby in her arms. "You like being rocked, don't you?" By the time they'd unloaded her few belongings, Jay had been crying again. Knowing the store was undoubtedly filled with customers and that Tim and Rob would need assistance, Avice had insisted that Raleigh return to work. She'd heated milk from the icebox, then once Jay was fed and burped, she'd brought him into the parlor, hoping he'd drift off to sleep as she rocked him.

While her foot kept the chair moving, Avice studied the room. A horsehair settee and two matching chairs were separated by a small table. Though the furniture was adequate for the room, the parlor still felt empty. The reason, Avice decided, was the absence of personal touches. No pictures graced the wall, and no crocheted antimacassars adorned the furniture. No vases decorated the table, and even the towels in the kitchen were utilitarian, unlike the ones she and her mother had embroidered for their own use. Other than Jay, there was no sign that Raleigh's wife had ever lived here.

Avice bit the inside of her lip, wondering what had happened to the evidence of a happy bride. Perhaps Raleigh had packed everything so there would be nothing to remind him of what he'd lost. Avice wouldn't ask. Though she would do everything she could to make his life and Jay's easy, she would not pry. This was, after all, a business arrangement, not a true marriage. And yet. . .

As Jay's eyes blinked open for a second before he settled back to sleep, Avice stroked his cheek, smiling at the unfamiliar weight of the ring on her left hand.

"Can you believe it, little one? I'm a wife and mother."

Chapter 4

The sun was setting when the woman entered the house without knocking, her eyes widening at the sight of Avice sitting in the rocking chair with Jay in her arms.

"Who are you?"

When the stranger's voice registered both surprise and apprehension, Avice offered her most reassuring smile. The woman was about her height with carrot-red hair, green eyes, and roughened hands that bore witness to her occupation.

"I'm Avice, and you must be Hannah Dorchester. Raleigh told me you would be coming." He'd explained that one of the laundresses brought fresh milk each morning and evening and stayed to feed Jay. Though feeding was no longer necessary, Avice was grateful for the fresh can of milk, since Jay had drunk the last of the morning supply an hour ago.

"I've taken care of feeding him, but if you'd like to stay, I'd welcome the company." Avice was certain there were aspects of life at the fort that only another woman would know.

Hannah eyed her suspiciously. "What are you doin' here?" she demanded as she settled herself on one of the horsehair chairs. Before Avice could respond, Hannah's eyes focused on Avice's left hand. "You're wearin' Dorothy's ring."

Avice shook her head. It wasn't Dorothy's ring any longer. "Raleigh told me it was his grandmother's." He'd offered to buy her a new ring, but Avice had refused. The band he'd slid onto her finger was more beautiful than any she'd seen, wider than the one her mother had worn and engraved with a delicate filigree pattern. The fact that it had belonged to two other women did not bother Avice. Instead, she knew she'd enjoy wearing it for the year she'd be at the fort.

"But. . ." Hannah started to speak then broke off, saying only, "I don't understand."

"Raleigh and I were married this afternoon." It was the first time Avice had pronounced those words, and to her surprise, the simple act of telling another person about her marriage made it feel real.

"Married? Why?" Hannah flushed and ducked her head. "I'm sorry. That was rude of me. Everybody's got different reasons for gettin' hitched. They oughta be private. I just didn't reckon Raleigh would marry so soon." She shifted slightly then looked at Avice. "I never seen a man who doted on a woman like he did Dorothy. He was plumb heartbroken when she died. Gave away all her belongin's the day after the funeral."

That explained why there were no personal items in the house. Taking a deep breath and exhaling slowly, Avice willed herself not to be upset. She had gone into this marriage knowing it was not a love match, and yet she couldn't help wishing someone would love her as much as Raleigh had loved his first wife.

"Raleigh's a good man," she said softly. "Any woman would be proud to be his wife." She was. Even when they were together for only a few minutes, she learned something new about the man she'd married, and each revelation deepened her respect for him.

Supper had not been as awkward as she'd feared. They'd talked about Jay and the store—nothing personal, but Avice had felt the same sense of homecoming, of belonging, that had swept over her when she'd first entered the fort.

"I agree. Raleigh's 'most as good as my Sam." Hannah shifted in the chair, as if uncomfortable, and Avice wondered if she'd said something wrong.

"Raleigh told me you have a daughter. I hope you'll bring her with you sometimes when you come with the milk."

"That wouldn't be proper." Hannah appeared shocked by the suggestion.

"I see." She didn't, but Avice didn't want to ask about something that was making Hannah uncomfortable. Instead she said, "What can you tell me about Fort Laramie?"

To Avice's relief, Hannah seemed to relax once she admitted she'd been worried about how to tell Raleigh her cow was going dry, and for the next half hour, she entertained Avice with tales of the fort and its inhabitants.

As Avice had suspected from Hannah's earlier reaction, there was a strict code of conduct that dictated that laundresses and enlisted men's wives did not fraternize with the officers' wives. Though Raleigh wasn't part of the army, his status in the sutler's store was such that he was regarded as an officer. But, though convention might frown on it, Avice had no intention of avoiding Hannah's company, for by the time the woman left, she felt as if she'd made a friend.

—※—

Raleigh opened another crate of blankets. Today's sales had been better than he'd expected, and the shelves needed to be restocked. Normally Rob and Tim helped, but he'd sent them home early. It was the least he could do after they'd had to cover for him while he was getting married and settling Avice into his home.

Married! Raleigh chuckled as he plunked the blankets onto the shelf. He could hardly believe it. One year ago he'd married Dorothy, never dreaming that today would mark another wedding. Today had been filled with surprises, the greatest of which was Miss Alice Longcope, now Mrs. Raleigh Bayne.

Raleigh pried the last crate open, thinking about his new wife. Avice could not have been more different from Dorothy. While Dorothy had been a petite brunette, barely reaching five feet, Avice was at least six inches taller with blond hair and eyes as blue as the summer sky. The differences didn't stop there. Dorothy had not enjoyed cooking. Oh, she'd prepared good meals until she'd become so ill, but she'd made it clear that it was a chore. In contrast, Raleigh had found Avice singing while she cooked. She'd turned simple ingredients into the best food he'd eaten since he'd arrived at the fort. And then. . .

"I thought I'd find you here," Farley said, interrupting Raleigh's thoughts. His friend must have come in the back door, knowing that Raleigh left it unlocked until he retired for the night. "Tell me it's not true."

Raleigh raised an eyebrow as he leaned against the counter. Though he suspected the reason for Farley's visit, he wasn't going to make any assumptions. "What do you want me to deny?"

"That you married a total stranger today."

It was what he'd expected. The grapevine at the fort was as active as ever. "It's true that I was married today, but she wasn't a total stranger." Raleigh had learned a surprising amount about Avice in the few minutes they'd been together before the wedding.

Farley shook his head in dismay. "You're crazy, Raleigh. Plumb crazy. You could have hired her to help with Jay. You didn't have to marry her."

"Yes, I did."

The look Farley shot at him was filled with disbelief. "I suppose God told you that."

"He did." And the way Raleigh felt when he saw Avice in his home—their home, he corrected himself—told him their marriage was no mistake.

Chapter 5

"Breakfast will be ready in a minute." Avice couldn't stop smiling as Raleigh entered the kitchen, his face freshly shaved, his hair still wet from his morning ablutions. This was the second morning she'd cooked breakfast, and though she tried to remind herself that this was a temporary business arrangement, she couldn't ignore that she was beginning to feel as if she were part of a family.

The unexpected sense of homecoming she'd experienced when she first saw Fort Laramie had only increased in the hours since she'd traded an uncertain future on the wagon train for life as Raleigh Bayne's wife—his pretend wife. The problem was it didn't feel like pretend. After services yesterday, they'd walked around the post, Raleigh pointing out everything from the bakery and laundresses' area to the commanding officer's headquarters and the guard house. Then they'd returned home and had spent the rest of the day talking and playing with Jay, just like a real family. Now they were starting the workweek like every other couple—with breakfast.

"It smells delicious." Raleigh made a show of sniffing then grinned at the sight of the eggs Avice was scrambling with bits of ham left from yesterday's dinner. "What can I do to help?"

She looked up from the eggs, startled by his question. Pa had never done a thing in the kitchen. That was women's work he'd declared, yet here was Raleigh, offering to help. Avice nodded as she realized that since Raleigh had been alone after Dorothy's death, he'd probably learned the rudiments of cooking.

"Would you mind setting the table? The plates are..." As she started to point toward the cupboard, Avice laughed. "Of course you know where the dishes are. This is your house."

"Our house."

How good that sounded! Avice wrapped a towel around her hand and opened the oven door, pulling out the bread she'd been toasting.

"Where's Jay?" Raleigh asked as he removed two plates and cups from the cupboard then gathered silverware.

Avice placed the toast on a platter before she spooned the eggs into a bowl and met Raleigh in the dining room. "Jay's still asleep," she said as Raleigh held out the chair for her. "He woke twice for feedings, so I decided to let him sleep now."

Raleigh gave thanks for the food and looked up at Avice, his expression reflecting surprise. "I can't believe I didn't hear Jay cry."

The reason was simple. "I moved his crib into my room so he wouldn't bother you. You need your sleep." Though Raleigh had not helped with feedings the first night, she heard him pacing the floor until she'd gotten Jay back to sleep and had decided to do whatever she could to ensure that his slumber was uninterrupted.

"Thank you," Raleigh said when he'd swallowed his first bite of eggs, "but I still feel guilty. Two days ago you hadn't met either of us, and now you're the one losing sleep over my son."

Our son. Avice bit back the words, contenting herself by saying, "He's a wonderful boy. No one could help loving him." And she did. Though she hadn't thought it possible, in less than forty-eight hours she'd fallen in love with Raleigh's baby.

She spread jam on a piece of toast as she said, "He and I'll go to the store as soon as I get dinner on the stove. I know it's your busiest time of the year with all the wagon trains coming through, so I thought I'd make enough food for Rob and Tim, too. If only one of you leaves at a time, you won't have to close the store." Ma had often brought the midday meal for Pa then waited on customers while he ate.

Raleigh paused, his coffee cup halfway to his mouth. "We don't close. The rule is, we don't eat unless we have a lull."

"And you probably get as cranky as Jay when you're hungry."

His eyes twinkling with mirth, Raleigh nodded. "You're right, we do." He took another swallow of coffee. "I forgot to tell you. The household money is in the top drawer of my dresser. Take whatever you need."

Perfect. While feeding Jay, Avice had realized there was only one good solution to the milk problem; now she knew how to pay for it. With the dishes washed, dinner on the stove, and Jay fed, she settled him in his buggy and headed toward the wagon train that arrived early this morning.

An hour later, her mission complete, she entered the store. Nothing had changed from Saturday. There was still the same chaotic milling of customers, the same disgruntled comments as people waited in line. Keeping Jay cradled in her arms, Avice walked around the store, helping as many of the women as she could. And as she did, an idea took root. It would work. She knew it. The only question was whether Raleigh would agree.

"I wondered who arranged the shelves," she said as she dished out a bowl of stew for Raleigh three hours later. The clerks had already eaten, and though he protested, she insisted that Raleigh take a break. "You're getting cranky," she told him. She smiled to take the sting from the words, but when she'd seen his lips purse in annoyance as a customer vacillated between two blankets, she had known it was time for Raleigh to eat.

He chewed slowly, looking as if he was considering her question. "I don't know who's responsible for the merchandise arrangement. It was that way when I took over, and I didn't see any reason to make changes. Why did you ask?"

"Because I think you'll sell more and make it easier for both customers and staff if you reorganize it." As far as Avice could tell, the arrangement was purely random, a fact that contributed to the customers' frustration. If a woman wanted both calico and thread, she had to go to two different counters.

"How would you change it?" Raleigh asked.

"You've got three counters and three sets of shelves. I'd suggest the one on the left be used for items women buy—yard goods, notions, children's clothing. The one on the right would hold men's needs—their clothes, tobacco, things like that. That would leave the center one for everything else—blankets, buffalo robes, dishes, teakettles."

Raleigh snagged another biscuit from the plate and split it open. "I can see where that would make sense. I'll ask the boys to stay late tonight so we can move things after the store closes."

That had been easier than she'd expected. Though Raleigh seemed like a reasonable man, Avice hadn't known how he'd react to her suggestion. Pa had always insisted that the store was his responsibility, and while Avice and her mother had worked there, they'd had little say over what merchandise was offered and how it was arranged. But Raleigh was different.

Thankful that he'd accepted her suggestion, Avice smiled. "I can help you."

He spooned the rest of the eggs onto his plate and looked up at her, his expression serious. "You already have. But if you want to make sure we put everything in the right place, you're welcome to be part of the process."

That was what Avice wanted. The truth was, she wanted to be part not just of rearranging merchandise in the store but of every aspect of Raleigh's life. She couldn't—and wouldn't—take Dorothy's place, but for as long as it lasted, she was determined to do everything she could to prove that their marriage was not a mistake.

"Jay and I will be there."

"I don't know what to do with you, Avice," Raleigh said, his tone clearly joking. "You've only been here for two days, and you're already changing things. What else do you have in mind?"

"I bought a cow."

─ ∞ ─

A cow. Raleigh grinned at the sound of milk pinging into the bucket. Avice had a better head for business than any woman he'd met. When she'd heard that Hannah's cow was going dry, she'd bought one from a family on the wagon train who'd worried that it might not survive the trek through the mountains. Now, for less than he'd been paying Hannah for a month's supply, Avice had more than enough milk for Jay. She'd mentioned selling the extra eventually, but in the meantime she wanted to give Hannah a couple quarts a day until her cow resumed production. It was a kind and generous offer, but as Raleigh had come to realize, Avice was a kind and generous woman. She was what his mother had called a giver, someone who thought of others and rarely if ever asked for something for herself.

The cow was a perfect example. Avice had insisted that she would take full responsibility for it and had protested when Raleigh had volunteered to do the morning milking. She'd finally agreed when he'd explained that it was the least he could do, considering all that she'd done for him. In the week since she'd come into his life, Avice had made more changes than he'd dreamed possible.

Jay was happier, and so was Raleigh. Sleeping all night had made a huge difference at the store. He was no longer tired and irritable. Avice was right: regular sleep and good meals were essential. What he didn't know was how she found the energy to do everything she did. Dorothy could never have done it.

Waves of guilt and sorrow washed over Raleigh, and he wondered for what felt like the millionth time if he'd been wrong to marry Dorothy and bring her here. She'd always been fragile, reminding him of a delicate flower, and she'd found the prairie harsh and forbidding. But they'd been so much in love that they'd believed they could overcome every obstacle. They'd been wrong. The almost constant illness that had plagued Dorothy while she was expecting Jay had left her able to do little around the house, and then she'd died.

When the cow grunted, Raleigh realized he'd been so lost in his memories that he'd tugged too hard. Perhaps Avice was right and he should leave the milking to her. The woman was incredible. She cooked, cleaned, cared for Jay, and still found the energy to help in the store. Women customers gravitated toward her. They'd ask for her advice, then buy more than they'd originally intended.

Raleigh's mood lightened as he thought about this week's receipts. The sutler would be pleased. Raleigh already was. The woman he'd married had given him more than he'd bargained for—much more.

Raleigh raised his eyes toward the heavens. *Thank You, Lord.*

Chapter 6

Avice was humming as she fastened the red cummerbund around her waist. When Raleigh had encouraged her to make some new clothes, claiming it would be good advertising for the store, she'd sewn a navy skirt and a variety of printed shirtwaists. Then when he'd mentioned that Fourth of July was a major celebration at the fort, she'd made a white waist and red cummerbund to turn her ordinary blue skirt into a patriotic outfit. It might have been foolish, but she'd even sewn a little navy cap for Jay, trimming it with red and white ribbons.

Though he wouldn't remember it, Avice would. Today would be another day that she added to her memory box. Since the day she'd arrived, she'd begun storing up memories, knowing that when her year here ended, those memories would be all she had left of her time as Raleigh's wife and Jay's mother.

"Are you two ready?" Raleigh called from the first floor. He'd appeared amused when Avice had told him that both she and Jay needed a change of clothing after breakfast, noting that while Jay had spit up on his shirt, Avice had not. It was probably foolish, but she'd wanted to make what her mother would have called a grand entrance.

"Almost." Gathering Jay into her arms, Avice descended the steps, trying to still the pounding of her heart. This was a business arrangement, she told herself, but no matter how many times she reminded herself of their agreement, Avice could not stop herself from wishing theirs was a true marriage.

"Look at you!" Raleigh let out a low whistle and gestured toward Avice's clothing when she reached the first floor. "There's no doubt that you're proud to be an American. And what's that on Jay's head? It seems my son is as patriotic as you." Raleigh gave her a roguish smile. "I can guess who's responsible for all this fine apparel."

Avice smiled, hoping the blush that stole onto her cheeks wouldn't turn her face as red as the cummerbund. While it was true that she wanted Raleigh to appreciate her clothing, she hadn't expected to feel so flustered by his whistle and his obvious pleasure at Jay's hat.

"I'm afraid I don't belong in this party," Raleigh said, frowning at his dark gray pants and jacket.

Avice's smile broadened at the realization that he'd reacted as she'd hoped. She'd known that if she'd asked, he would have told her not to bother, but she'd wanted to do something special for him, something to make it clear that at least for today, they were a family.

"Oh, but you do belong," she countered. Handing Jay to his father, she headed for the storage room, returning a few seconds later with Raleigh's hat, which now sported a red, white, and blue ribbon over the hatband. "I wasn't sure you'd want to wear it," she said as she showed it to him.

"It's perfect, Avice." It was only a hatband, but the smile Raleigh gave her made Avice feel as if she'd presented him with a priceless gift. "Of course I'll wear it." He laid Jay on the settee so that he could settle the hat on his head. "Thank you, my dear."

Avice's breath caught, and for the second time this morning she blushed. The endearment was so sweet, so unexpected, that she felt frozen in place. Her parents had called her their dear. So had several of her suitors, but never had the words felt so personal, as if they'd been invented for her and her alone.

She looked up at Raleigh, and as she did, his expression changed. His eyes focused on her lips, and for a second, she thought he was going to kiss her. Instead, he raised his hand and brushed her cheek. Delight speared through Avice as the tender touch set every one of her nerve endings to sizzling. This was the first time Raleigh had touched her deliberately. Oh, their hands would brush in the ordinary course of a day, but that was always accidental. This was different. This was special. And like the endearment, it made her feel as if she'd been caught in a whirlwind. Was it possible that her dreams would come true?

Trying to act as if her head weren't spinning, Avice slipped on her gloves, but as she and Raleigh walked toward the center of the fort for the parade that marked the beginning of the festivities, she felt as if her feet were barely touching the ground. Smiling so much that her cheeks hurt, she looked at the baby in her arms. How much her life had changed in a month!

A month ago, Avice had been a single woman mourning her parents and dreading Uncle Eli's plans. Now she was a wife and mother, at least in the eyes of the world. Though she suspected that the sorrow over her parents' deaths would never disappear, the initial overwhelming sense of loss had been replaced with regret that Ma and Pa had not lived to see her married.

Avice took a shallow breath as she realized that if her parents had lived, she wouldn't be here with Raleigh and Jay. She would still be on the wagon train, headed for Oregon. Her new life was proof of the truth of Romans 8:28. God had brought something good from her sorrow. He'd known that no one could replace her parents, but He'd given her a new family to love. What wonderful evidence of His love!

When they reached the parade ground, Avice and Raleigh found a spot on the side closest to their home. Though Raleigh had explained that the best views were from the other side, Avice had worried that Jay might become fussy and that she'd need to take him away from the crowds. So far, he'd rested quietly in her arms, seemingly content to watch the passersby, but she knew that could change in an instant.

"Avice!" She looked up and smiled when she saw Hannah heading toward them with a man who must be her husband, a toddler clutching their hands.

"I wanted you to meet Sam," Hannah said with a smile for the man with the private's stripe on his shoulder. "He needs to join his company, but he's heard so much about you that he said he had to meet you."

Sam Dorchester appeared to be a jovial man who, judging by the fond looks he gave them, doted on his wife and daughter as much as Raleigh had on Dorothy. Once the introductions were complete, he and Raleigh spoke briefly before Sam kissed his daughter and laid his hand on Hannah's cheek. It was the same kind of caress Raleigh had given Avice less than half an hour earlier, but to her surprise, Hannah turned her face and pressed her lips to Sam's palm. What would Raleigh have thought if Avice had done that?

"You've got a good wife," Hannah told Raleigh as her husband marched toward his company. She touched the cummerbund that Avice had made for her when she realized Hannah would have no time to sew anything for herself. "She's mighty good."

"I know." The words were simple, but the warmth in Raleigh's eyes as he said them made Avice's heart expand with pleasure. What was good was how she felt being here with him.

The parade began soon after Hannah rejoined the other laundresses at the opposite end of the parade ground. At first, Avice was amazed at how well Jay reacted to the sounds of the band and the men's marching. He seemed content to watch the activity, gurgling occasionally as if he found something amusing. All that ended when the first cannon was fired.

Jay jerked in Avice's arms and began to scream.

"It's all right, little one," she said as she took a few steps away from the crowd. "You're safe." The screams continued. She turned him so he was facing her and began to stroke his back, but Jay wailed as if he'd been injured. Avice murmured reassuring words, she offered him a bottle, she did everything that normally quieted him, but nothing worked. If anything, Jay's crying only intensified.

Turning her gaze to Raleigh, she said, "I'll take him home, but you should stay. There's no need for you to miss the festivities."

He raised one eyebrow. "Is that what you want?"

No! Avice wanted them to be together, not just today but forever. Knowing she couldn't say that, she nodded. "It's probably best."

It happened so quickly that afterward she wasn't sure she'd seen it, but for an instant Raleigh's expression changed, and he looked disappointed. Avice felt a kernel of hope embed itself inside her. Was it possible that Raleigh felt the way she did? Was that the reason for the endearment and the caress he'd given her? Oh, how she wished it were true.

For a second, Raleigh said nothing. Then his lips tightened as he laid his hand on Jay's head. "It'll be all right, son. Everything will be fine."

The baby turned to look at Raleigh, hiccupping once before falling silent. And though another cannon boomed, Jay did not cry. Avice stared at him, astonished by the sudden change. When she raised her eyes to Raleigh, he smiled and said, "It seems he needs both of us."

─────

Raleigh strode toward the river. He wasn't running away—not really—but he needed time to think. Now that the fireworks were over, the crowds had dissipated, leaving the post relatively deserted. Solitude was what he needed.

He and Avice had decided not to take Jay to the fireworks, fearing that the noise would frighten him. Instead, they'd stayed inside with the doors and windows closed, speaking softly while the display continued. Jay had flinched a few times, but he'd never cried. Instead, he'd looked up at Raleigh with brown eyes like Dorothy's. If Jay grew up to resemble his mother, he'd be a handsome man. But no matter what he looked like, Raleigh knew he couldn't love him more than he did right now. Every time he thought of his son, his heart filled with love, and he knew that Jay was his own private miracle.

Raleigh slowed as he reached old Fort John. Built by the American Fur Company to protect their trading interests, it was the second fort on this bend of the Laramie River, replacing the original Fort William. Now Fort John was crumbling. When the army had taken over, they'd abandoned all except the hospital. Though it was in no better shape than the other buildings, with disintegrating walls and ground squirrels and other vermin taking up residence along with the patients, for some reason the army had decided not to build a new hospital.

His lips curled in disgust at the sight of the once proud fort, and Raleigh left, intending to circle back home. Home. He paused in midstride, startled that he'd thought of the sutler's residence as home. He'd never used that term until Avice had started calling it that.

So much had changed since Avice had arrived. Staring down at the water that had already receded from its spring high, Raleigh reflected on the differences in his life. The house was prettier. Avice picked wildflowers for the table almost every day. She'd hung her mother's sampler in the parlor and put some of those frilly white things ladies liked on the backs of the chairs and settee. Since they weren't for sale in the store, she must have made them, though Raleigh couldn't imagine where she'd found the time.

Thanks to the cow, not only was Jay well fed, but they had fresh cream for Raleigh's coffee and butter for the biscuits. Somehow Avice managed to find the time to churn butter and whip cream to top canned peaches.

Raleigh plucked one of the tall grasses that grew next to the river and bent it between his fingers. There was no doubt about it. His life was both easier and more pleasant since Avice had arrived. But the differences were deeper than that. There were times when he felt as if they were a family—he, Avice, and Jay.

He broke the grass and hurled it away. That was wrong. He and Avice weren't a family. Dorothy was his wife. She was the woman he loved.

Chapter 7

Avice folded the tablecloth and napkins, carefully placing them in the bottom of the basket. They might be wrinkled by the time they were taken out, but at least they were perfect now. Not that it mattered to anyone other than her. Raleigh wouldn't notice.

She tried not to frown at the realization that she felt like a bouncing ball. Up, down; up, down. Her moods vacillated between euphoria and despair, all because of Raleigh. He'd seemed so caring at the Fourth of July celebration, but when he'd returned from his walk that night, he'd been distant, barely speaking to her. Ever since, though he'd been unfailingly polite, there had been no hint of anything deeper. No endearments, no caresses, nothing but common courtesy.

Reaching for the salt and pepper shakers, Avice took a deep breath, trying to calm her nerves. She shouldn't have expected anything more than courtesy. They'd agreed that their marriage was a temporary business arrangement, and Raleigh was keeping his part of the bargain. It was only Avice who wanted more.

As the milk began to simmer, she pulled the saucepan from the stove and filled two bottles, wrapped them in flannel, and stood them inside the basket. By the time Jay was ready to eat, they would have cooled enough that he wouldn't burn his mouth.

Avice smiled, thinking of the little boy who was still sleeping peacefully in his crib. He and his father brought so much joy to her life that each day Avice found herself wishing this were a true marriage. Hannah claimed that Raleigh was happier than anyone had seen him and that everyone who came into the store commented on it. Though her heart had leaped with excitement when she'd heard that, Avice reminded herself that—much as she hoped otherwise—she might not be the reason for the changes.

Now that the last of the wagon trains had passed through and there were fewer customers, she was spending less time in the store. The slowdown was good, because Jay demanded more of her time. He'd begun rolling from his stomach to his back, but then he'd become frustrated because he couldn't get back to his familiar position on his tummy.

When that happened, he'd wail until Avice rescued him, and once she arrived, he'd decide it was time to play, grabbing for toys and giggling when she held them out of reach for a second. He was such a dear baby—happy, healthy, and growing so rapidly that she could almost see the difference from one day to the next. And today he was four months old.

Avice wrapped half a dozen biscuits in a towel, adding them to the items in the basket. When she'd seen the Bible in the parlor, she'd opened it to the family history pages and had discovered that Jay had been born on April 15 and that his mother had died a day later. Seeing those entries helped explain Raleigh's somber moods on the sixteenth of each month. But today was the fifteenth, and Avice was determined to celebrate Jay's milestone.

It would be a surprise for Raleigh. Since it was Sunday, the store was closed, leaving Raleigh with his traditional day of rest. They would attend mid-morning services, and then instead of their usual meal at home, she had planned a picnic. Realizing that if she hired a wagon so they could travel a distance from the fort, Raleigh would hear about it, Avice had decided that they'd go only as far as they could manage on foot. It didn't have to be far to give them a change of scenery and a break in their routine. And, if all turned out the way she hoped, the picnic would turn the day into a special one that she could add to her memory box.

"Good morning." Raleigh entered the kitchen moments after she'd finished loading the picnic basket and had stowed it in the storage room. "You're up early."

"I wanted to get an early start." For a number of reasons, one of which being that it took longer to feed Jay now that he thought he should be eating the same food·as she and Raleigh. "Would you like two or three eggs?" she asked, her hand poised over the bowl of eggs she'd bartered for two quarts of milk.

"Three."

They ate in companionable silence until Jay's stirring sent Avice upstairs. By the time she returned, Raleigh had soaked the dishes and gone outside to milk the cow. So far, it was a normal Sunday for him, and it continued that way until they returned from church services.

When they entered the house, Raleigh made a show of sniffing the air. "I don't smell anything cooking."

Avice nodded. "That's because I cooked yesterday. I thought we'd celebrate Jay's four-month milestone with a picnic."

She watched carefully, hoping he wouldn't dismiss the idea as foolishness. Instead, although he looked surprised, Raleigh smiled. "All right. What should I do?"

Avice brought out the basket and placed the remaining items inside it. "You can carry this, and I'll take Jay. I thought we'd eat near the river somewhere outside the fort."

Though Avice knew the entire fort quite well, she'd been reluctant to explore beyond it. While there had been no problems with the Indians since last year's treaty, she wasn't willing to take Jay into unknown situations. She'd seen enough prairie dog holes and rattlesnakes on the journey west to know that hazards lurked everywhere.

Raleigh nodded his approval. "It's the perfect day for a picnic."

And it was. The sky was the deep blue of summer, highlighted by several puffy cumulus clouds. And though wind was an almost constant force here, today it was lighter than normal, keeping the day from feeling too hot without threatening to blow their picnic away.

They found a spot along the river where Avice could watch the now slowly moving water. She'd looked for a place without cacti. Though the short grass that everyone called buffalo grass, because its curly blades reminded them of buffalo hides, was soft, prickly pear cactus was not, and it seemed to be everywhere on this stretch of land.

Once they'd selected the site, Avice fed Jay and then set out the food she'd brought for herself and Raleigh. His enthusiasm over the simple meal of fried chicken and biscuits with a dried-apple pie warmed her heart, but nothing pleased her more than the smile he gave her when their hands met as they both reached for the same piece of chicken. It was a simple touch, and yet it sent shivers up her arms and down her spine. Had he felt it, too?

They spoke of ordinary things—the store, Jay's progress, the old timers' prediction of an early winter. There was nothing special about the conversation, and yet the whole day felt special to Avice because she was sharing it with Raleigh. She sighed in pleasure.

Raleigh leaned across the blanket and touched her hand. "This was a good idea, Dorothy."

—m—

He'd hurt her. Raleigh clenched his fists, wanting to hit something to relieve the pain that welled up inside him at the sight of Avice's stricken expression. Her face had blanched, and for a second he'd thought she would cry. She hadn't, but her rapid blinking made him fear that tears were closer than he'd like. It was all his fault. He hadn't meant to wound her, but he had.

"I'm sorry, Avice. I was just—"

She shook her head, not letting him continue. "There's no need to explain. I understand."

But he knew she didn't. How could she when he didn't understand himself? When Avice began to repack the basket, her normally smooth motions jerky, Raleigh knew she was trying desperately to maintain her composure.

"You don't understand," he said, hoping she'd let him continue. Instead, she gave him a look that told him he'd best remain silent.

He thought back, trying to comprehend what had happened. Today had been one of the best days he could remember. He'd been basking in the realization of what a perfect day it was when he'd felt a moment of sorrow that he and Dorothy had never gone on a picnic. He'd always been too busy, and she'd been too ill. That was the reason—the only reason—he'd pronounced Dorothy's name. It had been an honest mistake but a costly one, for he'd hurt Avice.

As they walked back toward the fort, he tried again to make amends. "I enjoyed the picnic, and I appreciate everything you've done for Jay and me."

She kept her gaze focused on the ground. "It's what we agreed on." Though Avice smiled at Jay as she carried him, there were no smiles for Raleigh. And when they reached their house, she nodded toward the stairs. "Jay needs a nap, and so do I."

When she came downstairs to prepare supper, though she sounded like her old self, Avice was unable to hide the sadness in her eyes. It was sadness he'd caused, Raleigh knew, and that made him feel like a heel. If only he could take back those careless words, but that was impossible. He could only pray that she'd forgive him.

—m—

A bolt of lightning woke him late that night. Raleigh sat up and stared at the window. Seconds later the sky opened, spewing out fat raindrops and what the soldiers dreaded more than almost anything: hail. Marble-sized chunks of ice pummeled the roof, making it sound as if the house would collapse under their force, the pounding so loud that Raleigh could scarcely hear his own breathing.

Was Jay crying? Did Avice need help? Pushing himself out of bed, Raleigh hurried into the hallway and found Avice standing in her doorway. Another flash of lightning revealed her face white with terror.

"What is it?"

"Hail." It was no wonder she was so frightened, for if they had hail in Michigan, it was unlikely to have been this intense. "As long as you're inside, you're safe."

"I don't feel safe."

Raleigh winced at the sound of Avice's voice. Though normally strong and confident, now it was little more than a croak. Instinctively, he moved to her side and drew her into his arms. "It'll be all right," he crooned, trying to reassure her as he would have his son. By some small miracle, Jay had not wakened. Raleigh didn't know what he would have done if Jay had cried out, for it was all he could do to comfort Avice. She stood as rigidly as a soldier at attention, as if that would protect her from the storm that raged outside.

"It'll be all right," he repeated. The roof would hold, and her fears would subside. When they did, somehow Raleigh would find a way to recapture the joy they'd shared on their picnic. Avice had looked so happy sitting on the blanket, smiling as she rubbed a twig of sagebrush, and then he'd spoiled it. Now was his chance to make amends.

Raleigh wasn't sure how long he held her, how many times he murmured reassurances, how often he stroked her hair, trying to soothe her. All he knew was that he didn't want this wonderful woman to leave his arms.

"It's stopping," he said when the ferocious pounding began to lessen. "We're safe."

He should be grateful that the storm was ending; instead, disappointment stabbed Raleigh. Now there was no reason to hold Avice. But though the immediate danger was over, she did not move away. Instead, her posture softened and she wrapped her arms around his waist. When she laid her head on his chest, he smelled rosewater and the faint scent of sagebrush. Sweet and savory like the foods she served him, like the smiles she gave him.

Raleigh entwined his fingers in her hair, delighting in its silky softness, drawing her close enough that he could hear her heart beat. As the hail subsided and only rain hit the roof, Avice's breathing returned to normal. The danger was over.

Raleigh closed his eyes and pressed a kiss on the top of her head. He should probably release her, but he couldn't, not when it felt so good—so very good—to hold Avice in his arms.

Chapter 8

A vice stuffed the last shirt into the bag and headed outside. Jay was taking his morning nap, which would give her enough time to get the laundry to Hannah before he woke and wanted to play. She took a deep breath as she stepped onto the ground, inhaling the scent of clean air. The sky was so bright and cloudless that she could almost believe she'd imagined the storm until she saw the piles of still-unmelted hail next to the house and stepped onto the damp earth. The storm had been real. She hadn't imagined it any more than she'd imagined Raleigh's arms around her.

She smiled, remembering those magical moments. At first Avice had simply felt comforted, but as the minutes ticked by and her fear disappeared, that had changed, and she'd felt cherished. What a wonderful feeling!

"That was quite a storm last night," Hannah said as Avice entered the laundresses' area. Avice cringed at the smell of soap and lye whenever she brought dirty clothes to her friend.

"I've never seen or heard anything like it," she agreed.

Hannah looked up from the shirt she was scrubbing and narrowed her eyes. "You look different this morning. Is that a new dress?"

Avice shook her head.

"You done your hair different?"

"No." Instinctively, Avice touched her chignon, her face flushing as she remembered how good it had felt when Raleigh had run his fingers through her hair last night. Though Avice ducked her head, hoping that Hannah hadn't noticed the blush, she was too late.

"That's it!" Hannah propped one fist on her hip and grinned. "Your eyes are different. They're sparklin'. Why, you look just like I did when I fell in love with Sam." Her grin turned into a chuckle. "It happened, didn't it? Your marriage turned into a love match."

There was no reason to deny it. "It's true that I love Raleigh."

"And he loves you. It's perfect."

But it wasn't. Raleigh wasn't ready to love anyone other than Dorothy, and he might never be.

"Are you sure the missus won't mind if I come to supper?" Farley leaned against the counter, his blue eyes reflecting doubt.

Raleigh shook his head as he handed his friend the cribbage board he'd ordered. "Of course not. She always makes plenty." The truth was, Raleigh had felt awkward at breakfast and wanted a buffer between himself and Avice tonight. "I'll mention it to her when she comes in."

"Of course it's all right," Avice told him three hours later. "Farley can come whenever he wants."

Raleigh was paying more attention to Avice herself than her words. Surely it wasn't his imagination that she looked especially pretty today, even prettier than she had yesterday. Or was it only that he'd begun to notice everything about her? A tendril of hair had come loose from the knot at the back, reminding Raleigh of how soft her hair had felt last night, how it had smelled like fresh air and sagebrush. Fisting his hands below the counter to keep himself from reaching forward and touching the lock, he forced himself to chuckle.

"Don't tell Farley that unless you want him at our table every night." Suddenly the thought of Farley joining them any night, even tonight, seemed wrong. Raleigh should never have invited him. He didn't want to share Avice with anyone, not even his best friend.

Oblivious to the direction Raleigh's thoughts had taken, Avice said, "Maybe once a week. I want your friends to feel welcome." She glanced at the shelves then pointed to one behind him. "I'd better take another tin of peaches. I was going to make a cobbler and want to be sure we have enough."

At dinner that evening not just the cobbler but the entire meal was a success. Farley was more animated than normal, regaling Avice with stories of his life as a soldier, causing her to respond with anecdotes of her adventures on the Oregon Trail.

Both Raleigh and Farley had laughed at her tales of the pioneers' reaction to their first jackrabbit sighting. According to Avice, amazement at the animal's enormous ears had been followed by wonder at the speed with which it could run in zigzags. Raleigh and Farley had laughed so heartily that Jay, who'd been playing contentedly in his basket, had cooed more loudly than normal, as if he wanted to join in the laughter.

When Jay became fussy, Avice excused herself to put him to bed, and Farley rose to leave. "I wasn't exaggerating when I told your wife that was the best meal I've eaten in a month of Sundays," he said, patting his stomach as he walked out the front door.

"I owe you thanks and an apology," Farley continued. "I know I said you were making a mistake marrying her, but I was wrong. Avice is the wife you need. I hope you realize that you're a lucky man, Raleigh Bayne."

He was, and yet Raleigh couldn't dismiss the feeling that he was being disloyal to Dorothy. He'd loved Dorothy for as long as he could remember, and even though death had parted them, his love remained as strong as ever. What Raleigh felt for Avice was different. He admired her, he cared for her, but he couldn't love her, because he'd given all his love to Dorothy.

Feeling more restless than he had in days, Raleigh started to walk. He wouldn't head out of the fort. No indeed, he wouldn't, for that would remind him of the picnic he and Avice had shared. Instead he strode toward old Fort John. Normally the place held no appeal for him, but tonight he felt drawn to it.

"You look troubled, Raleigh."

Raleigh blinked, wondering how he'd missed seeing Reverend Collins until he was practically on top of the man. The minister must have just left his office, probably headed for his rooms in Old Bedlam, but Raleigh had been so lost in thought that he'd been oblivious to everything else.

"Is there something I can do to help?" the minister continued.

Shaking his head, Raleigh stared into the distance, not wanting the other man to see the uncertainty in his eyes. "I don't think anyone can help. I've prayed for answers, but God hasn't given me any."

A soft chuckle greeted his words. "Perhaps He sent me."

This time Raleigh looked directly at the man who'd buried Dorothy and married Raleigh and Avice. Was it possible that he was God's messenger? "I'm confused," he admitted.

"About your wife?"

A light breeze carried the familiar scents of the fort—horses, dirt, men. It was only Raleigh's imagination that he smelled rosewater and sagebrush and felt the softness of Avice's hair beneath his fingers. He nodded. "How did you know?"

"It seems logical. You've been married for a couple months. It's natural that your relationship is changing and that she's making a place for herself in your heart."

Though the sun was setting, it appeared that Reverend Collins had no trouble seeing inside Raleigh. Somehow he'd managed to express what Raleigh had only sensed, that Avice had found her way inside his heart.

"But I love Dorothy," he protested.

"And you don't think you can love Avice, too." It was a statement, not a question.

"How can I? It would be wrong." That was the thought that haunted him, that had driven him out of the house tonight. He couldn't let himself love Avice, for that would be a betrayal of everything he felt for Dorothy.

The minister laid a hand on Raleigh's shoulder as he shook his head. "It would be wrong only if love had limits. It doesn't. Love is a gift from God, and like His love, it has no boundaries. Love expands our hearts."

The words sounded like part of a sermon, and like many of the reverend's sermons, they gave Raleigh pause for thought. If what Reverend Collins said was true, it changed everything. "I want to believe you, but how do I know that's true?"

Instead of answering him directly, the minister posed a question. "You love your son, don't you?"

Of course he did. "More than I ever thought possible."

Reverend Collins tightened his grip on Raleigh's shoulder. "If you had another child, would you love it?"

Picturing a little girl with Avice's golden hair and blue eyes, Raleigh nodded. "Of course I would."

"Would you love your son any less?"

The idea was unthinkable. "Of course not."

"Then why is it wrong to love Avice? What you feel for her doesn't diminish your love for Dorothy. Believe me, Raleigh."

And as he closed his eyes in silent prayer and felt the peace that could come only from God sweep over him, Raleigh did.

Chapter 9

It was silly to be so scared. Raleigh wrenched a crate open with more force than necessary. He wasn't facing an Indian attack or bandits. Still, he'd never before courted a woman. He and Dorothy had grown up together, and from the time they'd been old enough to know what love was, they'd had an understanding that they would marry. It was different this time. He and Avice had an understanding, but it was a far different one. According to their agreement, their marriage would end next July.

Raleigh frowned as he brushed the straw packing out of the way, uncovering the fancy china the company commander had ordered for his wife's Christmas gift. Even though it was only the middle of September, the shipments were starting to arrive, and Raleigh was thankful. Last year he'd waited too long to place the special orders, and some had been delayed by snow. He wasn't going to make the same mistake this year. No more mistakes allowed.

Courting Avice wasn't a mistake. Of course it wasn't. The arrangement they'd made the day they'd married had been a good plan at the time, but that had changed as Raleigh had gotten to know her better. Now he didn't want their marriage to end. He wanted Avice to remain as his wife—his true wife. He wanted her to love him the way she loved Jay. He wanted the three of them to be a real family.

But Raleigh couldn't simply announce that he'd changed his mind. That wouldn't be fair to Avice. She deserved what every woman wanted: a proper courtship and a proposal of marriage based on love, not convenience. He was determined to give Avice that. There was only one problem: he wasn't sure just what courting involved.

Raleigh checked each of the dishes, paying special attention to the tea cups. Ladies were particular about their cups, and if a single handle was broken or even chipped, some would reject the whole set. He hoped Avice would be more tolerant of his efforts to court her.

When the last piece had been inspected and returned to the crate, Raleigh slid it onto the special orders shelf and wrote the CO's name on the side. Organizing merchandise was easy. Beginning a courtship was not. He entered the store's main room, hoping for inspiration.

Pa had once said that ladies liked sweet words. Unfortunately, Raleigh wasn't good at sweet words. Perhaps ladies liked other sweet things. He snapped his fingers. That was it. He'd give Avice some of those fancy chocolates that had come in the last shipment. As he wrapped the chocolates, Raleigh grinned. This would be the perfect beginning to his courtship campaign.

"For me?" Avice blushed as he handed her the package after they'd finished supper and Jay was asleep. Raleigh might not know much about courtship, but he knew it shouldn't be interrupted by a crying infant. Though he'd been impatient, he was glad he'd waited, because now he had Avice's undivided attention.

"Who else?" Though he pretended to be nonchalant, Raleigh's heart was pounding with worry that she wouldn't like the candy. Trying not to think about that, he focused on the way the heightened color in her cheeks made her prettier than ever. Surely she was the most beautiful woman at Fort Laramie, perhaps in the whole territory.

Avice's gaze dropped down to the box then returned to meet his, and he saw confusion mingled with pleasure in her eyes. "It's not Christmas or my birthday."

Her birthday! Raleigh frowned as the magnitude of courtship assailed him. A man who was courting a woman was supposed to know things like his intended's birthday, but he didn't. "When is your birthday?" he asked.

"May twenty-fifth."

To Raleigh's dismay, Avice's lips began to tremble, and he sensed that she was trying not to cry. Once again he'd made a mistake, hurting Avice when that had not been his intent, but for the life of him he couldn't figure out what he'd done wrong. He would never understand women, not if he lived to be a hundred.

"What's wrong?" he asked. "Birthdays are supposed to be happy, aren't they?"

Avice blinked furiously in an effort to keep the tears from falling. "Not this year. It was two days after I buried my parents."

Raleigh wanted to kick himself. He'd certainly blundered that time, hadn't he? All he wanted was to make Avice happy, and now she was on the verge of crying. He closed his eyes for a second, saying a silent prayer for guidance. This was new territory for him, and he didn't want to make another mistake.

He thought quickly, wondering what would make her smile again. Perhaps she needed to talk about her parents. She'd been here for over three months and had said very little about them.

"Tell me about your parents." Though Avice looked startled, the tears did not fall. That was a good sign, wasn't it?

"Why?"

"Because I want to know more about you." Raleigh wanted to know everything there was to know about Avice, but he wouldn't say that, lest he frighten her.

She nodded slowly. "All right, but only if you tell me about Dorothy."

—⁂—

She was a fool. Avice gripped the side of Jay's crib and stared at the baby she loved so dearly. Only a fool would have wanted to know more about the woman Raleigh loved. She should have taken Pa's advice and let sleeping dogs lie, but she hadn't. Now she knew.

"She was just a little bit of a thing, barely five feet tall." Raleigh's eyes had darkened as he'd begun to speak. His lips had trembled ever so slightly, as if the words were painful, but then he'd smiled. "She might have been tiny, but her smile was so bright that she lit up the room. Folks would forget that she wasn't the tallest or the prettiest girl there. All they'd see was Dorothy." Raleigh had stared into the distance for a second, his memories clearly focused on the tiny woman with the outsized smile.

"All the fellows were crazy about her," he continued, "but I was the lucky one. She loved me as much as I loved her."

Avice tried not to cry. Tears solved nothing, but even though she shed no tears, her heart ached at the memory of Raleigh's expression when he spoke of Dorothy. Even more than the words, it told her how deep his love was and how no one would ever be able to take Dorothy's place in his heart.

Avice reached into the crib and drew Jay into her arms, hugging him to her breast. "I love you, little one, and I love your father." She pressed a kiss on his forehead, breathing in the sweet smell of a freshly bathed baby. "I know it's hopeless, but oh, how I wish he loved me."

She carried Jay to the window and looked out, her eyes focusing on the prairie that stretched for miles in every direction. The gently rolling hills with their sagebrush cover never failed to bring her peace, and they did not fail tonight. Minutes later, she laid Jay back in his bed.

"Why do you suppose he gave me candy?" she asked the baby.

The gift had been both sweet and unexpected, but though she'd asked, Raleigh had not given her a reason. "I thought you might like it," he'd said. She had, but Avice still wondered why Raleigh had given it to her today.

When her suitors in Michigan had courted her, they had brought her flowers, books, and candy, the only gifts Ma had said were suitable for a courting couple. But Raleigh wasn't courting Avice. So why had he given her candy?

―⁓―

"You look like you've got a burr under your saddle," Farley said as he entered the store. "What's wrong?"

Raleigh glanced at his friend. Today was one of the quietest days in weeks, so he'd set Rob and Tim to work cleaning the back room while he manned the store. Though normally he welcomed Farley's visits, Raleigh was in no mood for casual chatter this morning.

"Nothing you can help me with." The man was a bachelor and, as far as Raleigh knew, had never courted anyone. How could he counsel Raleigh in the art of wooing a woman?

Farley folded his arms as he leaned against the counter. "That must mean you're having trouble with the missus." Tipping his head to one side, he stared at Raleigh. "You probably don't want my advice, but I'm gonna give it anyway. Don't let her get away. I saw too many officers let their wives go back East. It made them miserable."

"Avice isn't going back East." She wasn't going anywhere until July, and then if Raleigh could figure out how to do this courting stuff, everything would be different. Avice would go wherever he and Jay went. She'd help choose their new home, and she'd show Raleigh how to arrange the goods in their mercantile. They'd be a real family. If only he could get the courting right.

―⁓―

"Close your eyes, and don't open them until I tell you."

Avice looked up, surprised to see Raleigh in the parlor doorway, even more surprised by his words. He'd left soon after supper, and once Jay had fallen asleep for the night, she'd retired to the parlor to work on the tablecloth she hoped to have finished by Christmas.

"All right," she said. She laid the crocheting aside and closed her eyes. Seconds later she heard Raleigh's footsteps, felt him place something in her lap, and heard the crinkling of paper.

"You can open them now."

Avice stared at the three crudely wrapped packages in her lap. "Oh, Raleigh, what's this?" It had been a week since he'd given her the chocolates, a week where he'd acted as if he hadn't opened his heart and revealed how deeply he loved Dorothy. And now he'd brought Avice more presents. She wished she understood why.

For some reason, Raleigh looked ill at ease, and his expression was serious as he said, "It's for you. I know it's not your birthday or Christmas, but I wanted you to have this because..." He paused, leaving her anxious to hear the explanation for the gifts, but said only, "Well, just because. I hope you like it."

The packages weren't flowers, books, or candy. Avice knew that from the shapes. That meant this wasn't a courtship, and yet what was it? Why was Raleigh suddenly bringing her gifts? She reached for the smallest of the trio and unwrapped it carefully, revealing the finest silver-handled comb she'd ever seen.

Avice's heart began to pound with surprise and pleasure. Not even during the years the mercantile turned a particularly good profit had she received such costly gifts, and Raleigh giving them to her today rather than waiting for Christmas made these presents extra special.

"They're magnificent," she told him when she'd opened the matching brush and hand mirror. "I've never owned anything so beautiful."

A lump settled in Avice's throat, making speech difficult. The chocolates had been a wonderful surprise, but this was overwhelming. It wasn't simply the expense, although the set was extravagant. Avice knew that from having seen similar items in catalogs. Even more than the cost, she was bewildered by the gifts themselves. They were very personal items, something a man bought for his wife. The lump grew. Was it possible that Raleigh was beginning to view her that way? Oh, how she hoped so!

"Thank you, Raleigh."

Without considering the consequences, Avice jumped up and pressed a kiss to his cheek, savoring the faint bristle of whiskers beneath her lips. She had never before touched him that way, but she'd never before received a gift like this. When she stepped back, Avice saw that Raleigh looked startled, as if he was as surprised by her forwardness as she was. Though he didn't return the kiss or so much as touch her, he smiled.

"I'm glad you like it." There was a hitch in his voice, one Avice could not explain. "I ordered it months ago, thinking one of the officers would buy it for his wife for Christmas, but when the set came in, I knew it was perfect for you." His smile broadened as his gaze rested on her hair. "Your hair is like silk."

Joy and hope fought their way past the lump in Avice's throat then bubbled throughout her body. There was no doubt about it. Raleigh remembered the night of the hail storm and how he'd run his fingers through her hair. Though they'd never spoken of it, it seemed as if he cherished the memory as much as she did. It had been the single most wonderful moment of her life. In Raleigh's arms, Avice had felt as if she was where she belonged.

She touched her chignon, wishing she had the courage to let her hair down and ask Raleigh to brush it, but she couldn't. That would be too forward. Ma had been firm in saying that a lady never took the first step. Avice had already broken that rule by kissing Raleigh, so the next step would have to be his.

But as the weeks passed, she began to wonder if she'd been mistaken. Raleigh was friendly. He smiled more than he had when she'd first married him. His hand brushed hers more often, and at times it lingered on the small of her back a bit longer than necessity demanded when he guided her past a group of soldiers. Occasionally he'd look at her with a twinkle in his eye, as if he had a secret he wanted to share with her. Little touches, little looks. They set her heart to pounding, but there were never any words to accompany them. If he loved her, he would say so.

Avice took a deep breath and let it out slowly as she tried to quell her disappointment. She needed to accept the truth. She and Raleigh were friends. He was grateful for her help with Jay, but that was all. No matter how she wished it were otherwise, Raleigh did not love her.

Chapter 10

Avice had never seen snow like this. Though it was only mid-October, this was worse than the January blizzards everyone in Michigan dreaded. The snow itself was different. Back East, flakes were fat and soft. Here they were tiny, nothing more than pinhead-sized pellets of ice. And then there was the wind.

She shivered as she watched the blasts of air drive the snow sideways. When Raleigh had left, Avice had picked up her crocheting, hoping to make progress on the tablecloth, but she'd been unable to concentrate on the tiny stitches. Instead, she'd paced from the rocking chair to the window and back.

That did nothing to comfort her, for each time she looked out the window, she was reminded of the storm's ferocity. It was so intense that she could see only a few feet beyond the house. How could anyone find his way through a blizzard like this? Could a man even remain upright in wind that howled at more than forty miles an hour?

Though the stove kept the house warm, Avice shivered again as ripples of fear made their way down her spine at the thought of Raleigh struggling through the snow. She glanced at the clock for what seemed like the hundredth time since he'd left. Though she'd protested when he'd told her he had to go, Raleigh had been adamant. Mrs. Thomas needed her nerve tonic, and nothing Avice had said would dissuade him.

She gave the clock another glance. Even with the snow, he should have been back by now. Perhaps the Thomases had convinced him to stay with them until the storm abated. Avice shook her head, rejecting the thought. Raleigh would not leave her and Jay alone in a storm like this. No matter how bad it was, he'd come home. But he hadn't.

She shivered. Her teeth chattered, and she felt cold seep into her bones. It made no sense, for the room was warm, and yet as Avice closed her eyes, she pictured Raleigh's face turning blue, then white, and she began to tremble uncontrollably. Raleigh was in danger. She knew that as surely as she knew she had to save him.

Please, God, she prayed, *keep Raleigh safe. Help me find him.*

Avice raced up the stairs and into her room, hurriedly throwing on her warmest clothes. After she fastened the last of the flannel petticoats and slid her arms into a third long-sleeved waist, she moved to the crib, gazing at the child she loved so dearly. Though she hated to leave him alone, there was no choice. His father's life was at stake. Jay was asleep, and if tonight was like the past week, he'd sleep for several more hours. Surely Avice would be back before he woke for his middle-of-the-night feeding.

Sliding her feet into the heavy boots Raleigh had bought for her, Avice looked around the small storeroom. She already had her warmest cloak, mittens, and hat. When she spotted a coil of rope, she nodded. That was what she needed. She headed for the front door before stopping and reversing direction. Though she could not explain it, she knew she was supposed to leave from the other side of the house.

As she closed the back door behind her, she tied one end of the rope to the knob, the other to her wrist, keeping the rest of the coil firmly in her hand. Pa used to do that when he went to the barn in the winter, saying the rope ensured that he could find his way back to the house. Avice looked at her rope, trying not to frown. It wasn't very long, but it was the only thing she had. She couldn't risk getting lost, especially with Jay depending on her.

As she took a step away from the house, the full force of the wind assailed her, almost knocking her over. She righted herself then looked around. Which way should she go? The Thomases lived on Officers' Row, to the left. That was the direction Raleigh would have gone, but when she started to turn left, Avice felt something tugging her to the right. So she turned to the right.

"Raleigh!" she shouted as she trudged through the snow. "Raleigh!" There was no answer. The wind muffled her voice, convincing her that shouting was futile. No one would hear her, and it would only tire her. She needed to save her strength for finding Raleigh.

Moving was more difficult than she'd imagined. The snow was up to her knees in places. In others the ground was almost bare, scoured by the wind, but that was worse, for the thin layer of snow had turned to ice, making each footstep precarious.

Avice narrowed her eyes, searching for something—anything—that would lead her to Raleigh, but she saw only unrelieved white. No footprints were visible. If the snow hadn't filled them in, the wind had blown them away. She gripped the rope, trying to tamp back her fear of reaching the end of the rope before she found Raleigh.

"Raleigh, I know you're out here." Though the words vanished into the storm, she couldn't stop herself from uttering them. And then she bowed her head, knowing there was One who would hear her, even if the wind howled. "Please, God, show me the way."

Avice wasn't sure how long she walked. All she knew was that her feet had begun to turn to ice and each step took more effort than she had thought possible. But she couldn't stop. Not now. Not before she found Raleigh.

A particularly fierce gust of wind toppled her, sending her headfirst into a snowdrift. As she struggled to regain her balance, her hand touched something solid. Could it be? Avice's heart began to pound as she felt the unmistakable contours of a human body. Raleigh! Frantically she brushed the snow away from his face and laid her cheek next to his nose. "Thank you, God!" He was breathing.

"Wake up, Raleigh." Avice shook his shoulder, but he didn't respond. Somehow she had to waken him. She placed her hand on his face. Though she knew he couldn't feel her warmth through the mittens, she hoped the touch would rouse him.

"What...? What?" Raleigh's words were slurred, and he looked confused, but Avice gave a silent prayer of thanksgiving that he was alive and awake.

"Stand up, Raleigh. You've got to stand up." She tugged on both arms, struggling to get him to his feet.

"Feet." He looked down then up at her. "Can't feel."

Avice nodded, not surprised that his feet were numb. The cold was so piercing that her own had started to ache. "Lean on me." She hooked Raleigh's arm over her shoulders and wrapped her right arm around his waist to support him. "We're going home."

They moved slowly, gingerly taking one step at a time as they followed the rope back to the house. Raleigh's legs collapsed repeatedly, and each time Avice forced him back to his feet, praying that he'd remain upright. Just when she thought they'd never make it, she saw the lights of the house. Minutes later they stumbled through the back door.

"We've got to get you out of those clothes," she told Raleigh as soon as she'd thrown off her outer wear. His clothes were stiff with snow and ice, her fingers cold and unresponsive, but somehow she managed to get his coat, boots, and mittens off.

"Can you climb the stairs?" She needed to get him into a warm bed.

Raleigh's shoulders slumped with defeat. "Don't think so."

"All right. We'll bring the bed to you." Perhaps that was for the best. If she kept him in the parlor, he'd be closer to the stove. Within minutes, she'd brought every blanket downstairs and made a pallet in the parlor. She had to do more. There were no hot bricks to place around him, so once Raleigh was settled under the covers, Avice boiled water to fill bottles.

When she returned to the parlor, she discovered that Raleigh was unconscious again, looking even worse than he had when she'd found him in the snow. His shivering had stopped, and he was barely breathing. Though she didn't want to admit it, Avice knew that he was near death, that the effort they put into getting him home might have been in vain.

She knelt beside him, bowing her head as she prayed. "Dear Lord, I beg You to save Raleigh. Jay needs him, and so do I. You know how much I love him. Please, Lord, if it is Your will, let him live."

There was no answer, nothing but Raleigh's labored breathing, proof that he was still alive. It was up to Avice to do everything she could to keep him from slipping away.

The night seemed endless. Avice couldn't count the number of times she'd refilled the bottles or the number of prayers she'd offered, but there was no change in his condition. Though he continued to breathe, each breath sounded so tortured that Avice feared it might be his last. Afraid to leave Raleigh for even the time it took to feed Jay, she brought the baby downstairs and settled him in the kitchen. Fortunately, Jay woke only once to be fed, but by dawn Avice was exhausted and unsure how much longer she could go without sleep.

Reaching over, she touched Raleigh's face, her fingers tracing the contours of his cheeks, lingering on his lips. "You can't die, Raleigh. I won't let you die without knowing how much I love you." She raised her eyes heavenward. "Please, God, spare him."

Avice wasn't sure how long it was before she heard the difference in his breathing.

Afraid to hope, she kept her eyes closed in prayer until she heard him stir. When she opened her eyes, she saw Raleigh looking up at her, confusion clouding his expression.

"Where am I?"

Chapter 11

R aleigh stared at Avice, wondering why there were tears in her eyes, why she looked so haggard.

"You're home," she said, her voice breathless. "God has answered my prayers, and you're going to live."

He looked around, his mind registering that her hair had come out of its knot and was hanging down her back, and that for some reason he was lying on the floor of the parlor covered by a mountain of blankets.

"What happened? The last thing I remember is giving Mrs. Thomas her tonic."

Though she'd been kneeling, Avice settled back on her heels and stared at him, as if she were feasting her eyes on him. "You must have gotten lost in the storm." She gestured toward the window. As best he could tell, dawn was breaking, and the storm continued to rage. Somehow he'd lost more than twelve hours.

"When you didn't come home, I went out to find you," Avice continued.

As her words triggered a dim memory of being colder than he could remember and then wanting nothing more than to sleep, Raleigh realized that he must have become lost on his way home from the Thomases. "How did you get me back here?"

The way Avice bit her lip told him it hadn't been easy. "You walked," she said. "Most of the time, but let's not talk about that. All that matters is that you're alive." Obviously fighting tears, she rose. "I'm going to get you some hot broth."

Fragments of memories flitted through Raleigh's brain. There had been prayers and more prayers. He thought he remembered Avice saying she loved him, but perhaps that had been only a dream. As he'd drifted into sleep in the snow pile, Raleigh's last thought had been regret that he'd never told Avice he loved her. He might have imagined her declaration of love. It didn't matter now. What mattered was that he couldn't wait another day, not even another hour.

He pushed himself onto his elbows and called to Avice. "Forget the broth. We need to talk."

At the sound of Raleigh's voice, Avice rushed back into the parlor and saw him struggling to rise. "What's wrong, Raleigh?"

He shook his head, but he didn't protest when she helped prop him against the edge of the settee and sat on the floor next to him. "Nothing's wrong. We just need to talk."

Avice's heart began to pound as she worried about what he wanted to say. She couldn't remember ever seeing Raleigh look so serious, not even when he spoke of Dorothy. "About what?"

He took a shallow breath, as if he were trying to compose his thoughts. Finally he said, "We had an agreement. I want to end it."

No! Though she wanted to shout her refusal, Avice forced herself to act as if his words hadn't cut her to the quick. It had been a long and emotional night, leaving her with no energy to fight Raleigh.

"You want me to leave?" Somehow she managed to keep her voice even, though her heart was breaking. She had grieved when her parents had died, but this was worse, much worse, for in just a few months, Raleigh Bayne and his son had captured her heart. How could she face life without them?

Raleigh stared at her as if she were speaking a foreign language. "Leave? No!" The words came out like bullets from a rifle, and he shook his head. "I'm going about this all wrong. I didn't want to simply ask you. I was afraid you'd say no."

Ask her what? Raleigh wasn't making any sense. Perhaps this was what happened when a person came as near to death as he had. Before Avice could suggest that he rest and continue this discussion later, he continued. "That's why I decided to court you."

Avice wasn't certain she'd heard him correctly. Her mind must be playing tricks with her, making her imagine things. Just moments ago she'd believed Raleigh wanted her to leave, and now he was speaking of courtship.

He nodded. "That's why I gave you those chocolates and the hair set. I know ladies like pretty words, but I was never good at words." He looked almost ashamed as he admitted it. "I didn't need them with Dorothy."

Though part of her wanted to remain silent, Avice could not. "I know you love her." Raleigh's love for Dorothy was part of what made him the man he was—strong, honorable, and capable of deep love.

Raleigh nodded again. "I always will. At first I was afraid to love again, because I thought I was being disloyal, but Reverend Collins helped me see the truth. He told me that love has no limits, and that loving you does not diminish what I felt for Dorothy."

He loved her! The words embedded themselves deep inside her, and Avice's heart skipped a beat as she looked at the man she adored. Though his face was pale from the ordeal he'd experienced, his skin chapped by the elements, his chin rough with whisker stubble, Avice had never seen anything so wonderful. This was Raleigh, the man she loved with all her heart, and by some miracle, he loved her.

As he took her hands in his, his eyes glowed with such intensity that Avice felt almost burned by his gaze. And then he spoke, his words filling the empty spaces inside her.

"I love you, Avice. I think I did from the minute I met you, but I was too stubborn to admit it." Raleigh's fingers entwined with hers, and he looked down at their hands for a few seconds. When he raised his eyes to meet hers, she saw love shining from them, a love as deep and pure as the love she felt for him. "I want ours to be a true marriage," Raleigh said, his voice husky with emotion. "Will you do that? Will you be my real wife forever and ever?"

There was nothing she wanted more. "I will."

Though the storm continued to rage, Avice's heart filled with warmth as Raleigh drew her into his arms and pressed his lips to hers. Her prayers had been answered, for she'd found a home, a family, and most of all, love on the sagebrush prairie.

Beckoned Hearts
by Melanie Dobson

Chapter 1

Fort Hall, Idaho Territory
July 1856

Lightning slashed a jagged streak through the dark clouds that settled over Fort Hall. Seconds later a clap of thunder shook the log walls inside the sale shop.

Molly Goodwin pressed her fingers into the coil of rope looped through her hand, fighting off the familiar panic that surged through her with the onset of every summer storm. She was safe here, as long as she stayed inside the store.

"Ma'am?"

Molly blinked and refocused her gaze on the middle-aged emigrant man standing on the other side of the counter, a long list of supplies clutched in his hands. Stubble flecked his sunburnt face—and he smelled as if he hadn't bathed in weeks—but he didn't have a long braid of hair nor did he wear a shabby fur coat like the traders who wintered here.

She set the rope he'd requested on the wooden counter. "Where are you headed?" she asked, trying to calm the racing in her mind.

"To Oregon."

Sighing, she slid the lid off a barrel filled with Cuban coffee beans. Dozens of wagon trains had camped outside the fort's walls this summer, a few of them traveling to California but most to the territory known as Oregon.

Isaiah Dupuis, the man who owned the sale shop, said every July at least one cluster of wagons came through traveling in the opposite direction. She asked every new customer where he was headed in hopes that someone would say they were going east instead of west.

As she dipped her measuring cup into the beans, the man scanned the shelves filled with lanterns, blankets, and medicines like essence of peppermint and camphor. "It must be difficult to live inside a fort like this."

She shrugged. "I won't be here much longer."

He studied her face in the fading light. "Are you going west with your husband?"

Frustration replaced her fear of the storm for a moment. She didn't like the look in his eyes, like he was shopping for a wife along with supplies for his journey. What happened to her husband wasn't any of his business.

"I'm going home," she said simply as she twisted the simple wedding band on her finger. He didn't need to know she was going alone. "How many pounds would you like?"

"Three."

As she filled the scale on the counter with coffee beans, the acrid smell mixed with the dampness in the air. Light flashed through the room again, and she shivered. The rain hadn't started yet, but it would begin soon, probably around the time the dark storm clouds folded into the night sky.

She poured the coffee beans into one of the burlap bags he'd placed on the counter, and then she skimmed his list again, trying to distract herself.

Vinegar, flour, coffee, gunpowder, flints, rope.

She looked back up at him. "I'll have to go back into the storeroom to get the gunpowder and flints. How much gunpowder do you need?"

He glanced down at his list. "It depends on how much it costs."

When she told him the price, his eyebrows knit together with concern. "I suppose you should tell me the cost for all these supplies before I decide how much I want."

She reached for her slate and slowly totaled what he'd need to spend to supply his wagon for the second half of his journey.

When she turned the slate around, his face blanched. "That's atrocious!"

Anger flashed in his eyes, and she empathized deeply with his plight and the plight of every emigrant, man or woman, who stopped at the fort for supplies.

"It is atrocious," she said as she erased the numbers on the slate. "But unfortunately I don't set the prices, nor do I have the authority to negotiate them."

He retrieved his list. "We paid less than a third for these things in Missouri."

"My employer paid a high price to obtain these supplies," she tried to explain.

Isaiah still gouged the pockets of the emigrants who came to Fort Hall, but her job was to sell the supplies to people who needed them, not tell Isaiah how to run his business. Even if she asked him to change the prices, he wouldn't listen.

The man glanced at the door behind the counter. "Where is your employer?"

Instead of answering his question, she lowered her voice, just in case Isaiah or someone else from the fort was near the front door. "You're about two weeks from Fort Boise. They'll give you better prices there."

Uncertainty crept into his eyes, as if he wasn't sure whether or not to trust her. "We can't reach Fort Boise unless we cross the Snake River. . . ." His voice trailed off.

She nodded, glancing back at the scale on the counter. The journey west was all about weighing hundreds of risks while carefully calculating for the future. If an emigrant overloaded his wagon, it might be too heavy to navigate the rocky passes through the mountains. And he risked losing his entire investment if the wagon overturned in a river like the Snake. But if he didn't pack enough food, he and his family could starve to death in the wilderness.

This man would need to cross the Snake River in the next two weeks if he was going to travel north to Fort Boise, but if he didn't buy supplies at this shop and the river was too high to cross near the fort, he wouldn't be able to obtain fresh supplies until he reached Oregon. And if he pushed his wagon and animals too hard, he might lose someone he loved before he finished the journey.

Lightning flashed again, and thunder pounded so hard the lanterns clattered on the shelves. Molly gripped her hands together, trying to stop the terrible memories that flooded back with every storm.

She would be gone from this fort soon, leaving behind these frightening storms.

Her father had given her and Adam an old farm wagon to use for their trip west, but since she was no longer traveling to Oregon, she would use the farm wagon and the supplies she'd saved over the past year to journey back East instead.

The man stepped back from the counter.

"Do you still want the gunpowder?" Molly asked.

"Not until I speak with the proprietor of this store."

She pointed at the window. "He lives in the cabin to the right of the main gate."

The man left the coffee beans and rope on the counter. "I'll return."

"Of course," she said, though she knew he wouldn't get anywhere with Isaiah. If anything, Isaiah might raise the prices just to spite him.

After the door shut, she lit a lantern and dumped the coffee beans back into the barrel before returning the rope to the small storeroom behind the counter. The shelves were beginning to look bare, but Isaiah didn't seem to care one whit about the dwindling of supplies. He had one more warehouse outside the gates, though there wasn't much left there either. Fort Hall was closing at the end of the summer, and he was planning to relocate to Fort Laramie before September, taking any remaining supplies along with him. He didn't particularly want to travel with a lot of supplies, but he wasn't going to give them away either.

The citizens of Fort Hall had a reputation for their questionable and sometimes downright dishonest business practices, but she'd spent the past year trying to be honest—with her customers and Isaiah. From the time she'd arrived at the fort last year, heartbroken and afraid, she'd told Isaiah she was going home as soon as possible. And she'd waited for the company of eastbound travelers he said would arrive.

What would happen if no one came?

She began to tidy the shelves inside the shop, keeping her hands busy to help prevent her mind from wandering too far.

All of her personal supplies were stacked in crates back in the storeroom, ready to pack into her wagon when it was time to go. After almost a year living among coarse fur traders in this small fort, she longed to be among friends again. To talk to another woman about the conflict raging in her heart.

Somehow she would have to find a way to go east before the fort closed.

The clock over the counter ticked with every minute, but the emigrant man didn't return. Perhaps with the rain, he'd retired back to his wagon train. It was possible he'd return in the morning, but after speaking with Isaiah, she guessed he might wait to replenish his coffee and gunpowder at Fort Boise after all.

His decision shouldn't be any concern of hers, but she couldn't help worrying about the people who came through here. The overlanders may have their trusted guidebooks in their pockets, coins in their moneybags, and wagons full of food—just like she and Adam had when they left Indiana—but no amount of worldly goods could rescue them from the diseases, accidents, and heartache on the trail.

It wasn't her job to commiserate with her customers though. Isaiah said she was the first honest person he'd met in a long time, and he trusted her with this position to help outfit emigrants and their wagons for the remaining seven hundred miles of their journey.

Her own dreams to go west were crushed the night Adam died, but as long as she remained in this fort, she would help other people achieve their dreams. The cost for supplies may seem great, but she'd learned it was nothing compared to the toll of losing a loved one on this quest.

Rain pelted the glass on the front window, but mercifully the lightning seemed to have stopped. As much as she tried to fight it, her heart began to ache again, the dull pain that lingered long after it had been crushed. She no longer knew what to hope for in this life. For so long, all she had desired was to go to Oregon with her husband, but now, no matter what she wanted, she had no choice except to return home.

She locked the front door and extinguished the lantern so she could retire to her room above the shop for the night. This job kept her hands and her mind busy during the day, but nights were agonizing. No matter how she tried to stop the memories, they always seemed to color the darkness.

When it wasn't raining, she would spend her evenings walking the perimeter inside the fort walls, distracting herself from her thoughts. No other women lived in the fort, but the traders who lived here feared Isaiah's wrath, so no one even spoke to her on these evening walks.

Someone jostled the front door, and Molly jumped. Turning back, she eyed the latch, debating for a moment whether or not she should unlock it. Then her visitor knocked on the glass, and she decided to embrace the interruption along with the hope that Isaiah and the emigrant man might have come to an agreement after all. She may not know this man, but she appreciated the company for a bit longer. And the steady busyness of gathering his supplies.

Quickly she relit the lantern and carried it over to unlock the door. But when she opened it, the man with the dark stubble wasn't standing on her stoop. It was a taller man standing before her, water dripping off the edges of his rubber overcoat. And in his arms he held some sort of bundle under a wet blanket.

She lifted the lantern. "I'm sorry, I'm clos—" she began. Her words ended with a gasp when he peeled back the blanket and she saw the limp body of a woman clutched to his chest.

"Where can I find a doctor?" the man pleaded.

Fear paralyzed Molly for a moment. It had been pouring rain as well the night she lost Adam, almost as if the skies joined in with the sorrow of her loss.

"Please!" the man begged again.

Molly opened the door wide, ushering him inside. It had been too late to save Adam, but perhaps there was still time to save the woman in this man's arms.

Chapter 2

"Come this way," Molly urged the man back toward the storeroom.

He followed her through the maze of barrels and crates before moving up the steps to her room above the shop. As he ducked under the low rafter, she placed the lantern on her bedside table. Then he laid the woman—his wife, she assumed—on Molly's bed and sat down on the straw mattress beside her, reaching for her hand.

Water dripped off the man's coat, soaking the bedcovers and puddling on the floor below him.

"Can I take your coat?" she asked.

This man didn't seem to hear her question. Instead he mumbled softly, his attention focused on the woman before them, words and perhaps prayers blending with the pattering of rain on the tin roof.

The woman's wet hair clung to her forehead, and her face seemed gray in the flickering light, the color of ashes bleached by the sun.

Molly leaned forward. "Was she injured?"

He shook his head. "She's ill."

Molly pulled a wooden chair to the other side of the bed, and after she sat, she placed her hand on the woman's forehead. In spite of the cold rain that soaked her clothes, her skin was burning. "How long has she been sick?"

"I don't know," he said, his voice broken. Unlike the emigrant man who'd arrived earlier, this man's face was shaven, and he spoke like a gentleman. "She seemed fine when we broke camp this morning."

Molly nodded slowly. Some of the diseases on the trail could steal away a life in a single day. Someone might seem perfectly fit at breakfast and then be gone before supper.

"We traveled all morning, and then she collapsed when we stopped for our noon meal. I couldn't wake her." When he looked up, his dark eyes implored Molly in the candlelight, the fear in them raw.

She stood. "We have to work quickly to help her."

He glanced toward the door. "Where is the doctor?"

"We don't have a doctor in the fort, but sometimes one arrives with a wagon train. In the meantime, we need to take off her wet clothes and—"

He interrupted. "Do you know what's wrong?"

"It's impossible to say for certain," she said, afraid to tell him that she thought it was cholera. "After we get her dry, we'll give her some camphor and lots of clean water."

"We ran out of camphor back in Nebraska."

"I have extra downstairs," she said as she moved across the room to open the shutters. There was no glass on this window, but the downpour of rain had turned into drizzle and she hoped the fresh air would mollify the woman's fever.

As the cool air drifted into the room, Molly lit a candle and handed it to the man, giving him directions about where to find the tincture of camphor and the bag of salt in her crates along with a pitcher to fetch water. He began to stand, seemingly glad to have an occupation.

"What's her name?" she asked.

"Faith."

"I'll do my best to care for her."

He thanked her before he hung his coat on a peg and rushed downstairs.

Molly swiftly removed Faith's wet clothing. The woman was so thin that Molly could see her ribs pressed through her skin, but most of the women were too thin by the time they arrived here. After walking about twenty miles a day, along with the lack of food and all the hard work on the journey, a good trail wind could almost blow them away.

She examined Faith, searching for telltale patches of red splotching as she dried her skin with a towel. She wasn't a doctor, but she'd spent hours helping the doctor who had traveled with them from Missouri. A rash would indicate mountain fever or measles instead of cholera.

If it was mountain fever, Faith might be able to fight it, but unfortunately Molly didn't see any sign of a rash.

Faith was blessed to have a good husband to care for her. Molly just hoped he was a praying man as well. And she hoped God would answer his prayers.

She placed a dry blanket over the woman, and when the man returned with the pitcher, she mixed salt into the clean water. He lifted Faith's head so Molly could spoon the camphor and then salty water into her lips. Faith moaned before swallowing both the medicine and water.

"Are you going to Oregon?" Molly asked as he carefully lowered Faith's head back down on the pillow.

"Yes," he replied. "We're starting a school there."

Molly twisted the lid back onto the camphor bottle. "There are several wagon trains camping outside the fort tonight. Perhaps one would have a doctor."

Standing, he reached for his coat. "I'll be back as soon as I can."

Minutes after he was gone, Faith's eyes fluttered open and searched the room before resting on Molly's face.

"He'll be back," Molly whispered. "You're safe here."

The woman didn't say anything, but Molly thought she saw the faintest smile on her lips before she slept again.

As the night passed, Molly continued rousing Faith to spoon more salty water into her mouth.

Far too many people lost their lives on the Oregon Trail.

She would do everything she could to keep this woman alive.

—⁓—

Wagons congregated in two large circles outside Fort Hall. As Payton Keller rushed out the gates, toward the first circle, he prayed a doctor there could help save his sister's life.

Faith had been so strong the entire journey from Ohio and then in their wagon train from Missouri. With a heart full of faith and joy, she lived up beautifully to the name their mother had given her when she was born.

He couldn't let anything happen to her now. Samuel was waiting for his wife in Oregon City, and Payton couldn't fathom telling his best friend that Faith was gone.

Charley Lewis, the captain of their wagon train, had said Payton would get neither help nor sympathy at Fort Hall, but the woman at the mercantile proved Charley wrong. She seemed both concerned and capable.

And Payton didn't even know her name.

Perhaps she'd told him, but he hadn't been thinking straight since their wagon stopped for their noon meal today. When Faith collapsed, he panicked and handed over his oxen and wagon to Charley to guide the remaining distance to Fort Hall. Then he'd carried Faith on horseback to the fort. During the three-hour journey, his sister never once cried out in pain.

The entire company should arrive sometime tomorrow, and as he moved toward the circle of wagons, he also prayed that their company would wait for Faith to get well again before they continued their journey west. It would be impossible for him and his sister to finish this trip alone.

Many people called Oregon *paradise*, but he'd discovered the road to paradise was riddled with trouble. Faith said that every worthy goal was difficult to achieve, but his sister saw goodness everywhere, even in the hardest times. If she were coherent, she would probably even find some sort of silver lining in her illness.

When she was well again, she could tell him exactly what it was.

In the moonlight, he saw a hedge of wagon canopies in front of him, each wagon pieced closely together to form a corral to keep the animals inside. He couldn't see beyond the canopies so he squeezed between the bench of one wagon and the rear of another.

Even though the ground was still wet from the storm, a half-dozen campfires glowed in the darkness, and he smelled the aromas of stew and brewed coffee as he scanned the people milling near the campfires. He hadn't eaten since breakfast, but food didn't matter at this moment. He had to find a doctor.

"You sure are tall, mister."

Payton turned quickly to see a boy standing below him. There was a red bandana knotted across the boy's head and what he hoped was a toy pistol in his hands, though he'd seen younger children carrying guns on the trail.

"Are you lost?" the boy asked.

Payton shook his head. "I'm looking for a doctor."

The boy stepped closer and quickly eyed him down and then back up again. "You don't look sick."

"It's my sister," Payton replied.

"My sister's been sick since Nebraska," the boy said sadly.

Payton leaned down and put his hand on the boy's shoulder. "I'm really sorry." "She'll be better soon."

"Do you have a doctor traveling with you?" Payton asked.

The boy shook his head. "My mom's taking care of her."

"You're blessed to have a good mom."

The boy turned and galloped off on an imaginary horse. For a moment, Payton watched him ride around the campfires. When he was a child, he'd craved adventure and his imagination had pioneered across the country for him. He'd wondered at all the people traveling to wild places like Oregon and California, vowing that he would travel west as well when he grew up. Reality had dulled his imagination as he matured and began managing all of his father's responsibilities at the bank where they lived in Mansfield, Ohio.

Perhaps he and Samuel and Faith should have stayed in Ohio after all.

He rushed out of the circle, toward the second cluster of wagons. In Mansfield, he knew exactly where to find a doctor.

The second circle was smaller than the first. About fifteen wagons made up the walls around the camp, and a woman standing outside the circle said they didn't have a doctor either.

Dejected, he turned back to the fort, and he prayed for his sister as he hurried back in the darkness. Faith had given away all the medication they'd packed along the journey to care for other people—until there was none left for her to use.

They'd need a miracle instead of a doctor this time.

He prayed that God would give an extra dose of wisdom to him and to the woman caring for Faith at Fort Hall.

Chapter 3

At first Molly thought she was dreaming. Her eyes closed, she savored the rich voice of a man singing "Rock of Ages" near her. She hadn't heard anyone singing a hymn in a year, since the nights she and Adam had sat around a campfire with people who'd become like family to them.

She refused to open her eyes this morning, savoring the music and her memories with Adam before the daylight stole them away. It had been a blessing to be loved completely, but in his love, she'd given her entire heart away.

On the trail, many widows married quickly after they lost a spouse, but she hadn't been able to even consider marrying another man in the past year. It felt like there was nothing left within her to give someone else. Even when the captain asked her to continue traveling west with them, she couldn't go on without Adam. The company had to leave her behind at Fort Hall.

She and Adam had dreamed together for two years about marrying and then going west, but the dream that had bonded them also took his life. She'd been angry at God for months after her husband died, for taking Adam at first and then for not taking her, too. And she'd been angry at herself for championing a dream that killed the man she loved.

The singing stopped, and her eyes fluttered open. She stared up at the rafters from her makeshift bed, a pile of fur blankets on the wooden floor. Instead of a dream, she was in her little room, the early morning light stealing through the window. And Faith's husband was sitting on the bed beside his wife.

The events of last night flooded back to her, and she sat up quickly on the floor and rearranged the fabric of her green calico dress around her legs. Since the man hadn't been able to find a doctor, he'd taken over her work administrating the salty water and camphor. He was supposed to wake her hours ago so she could take over, but she understood him wanting to care for Faith himself.

She quietly studied his wide shoulders, bent slightly over the bed. Had his wife passed away during the night?

She silently pleaded with God, praying that Faith was still with them this morning.

As she stood, the man glanced back at her, his eyes bleary. Thankfully she saw only exhaustion instead of grief in them.

"How is she?" Molly asked.

"She seems to be better."

Molly leaned over, putting her ear against Faith's chest. "Her heart is stronger."

"Where did you learn about medicine?" he asked.

"We had a doctor in our wagon train, and I helped him care for those in our company who were ill."

His gaze fell back to the woman on the bed. "Do you think she has cholera?"

She took a deep breath. Even though she needed to be honest with him, she didn't want to tell him the truth. "I believe so," she finally said.

The man's shoulders drooped, his voice broken when he spoke again. "Our captain said there's no cure for cholera."

"There may be no cure." She forced a spoonful of water through Faith's lips, and the woman swallowed it. "But if we caught it early enough, we can help her fight it."

Hope flickered in his eyes. "You think she has a chance?"

She nodded slowly. "If we keep washing the cholera out of her body. And if she can rest here for a few more days," she said, though most wagon trains couldn't afford even a single day to wait for someone to recover from an illness.

"I don't want to impose on you."

She fed Faith another spoonful. "It's no imposition."

"Thank you, Mrs.—" He stopped, and his eyes flashed again as if he just realized he didn't know her name.

She glanced down at the simple gold band around her finger. "Around here, people just call me Molly."

"I'm Payton, Payton Keller," he said. "And this is. . ."

Before he formally introduced her, Faith's eyes opened, and she glanced back and forth between them before smiling at Payton.

"Where are we?" she whispered.

He brushed a strand of hair out of her eyes. "We made it to Fort Hall."

"I was hoping we were in Oregon."

"Not yet," he replied.

She sighed. "Samuel is waiting for me."

"Yes, he is," Payton agreed.

Molly wondered who Samuel was, but it wasn't really her business to ask questions like that. She dipped the spoon back into the water, and Faith sipped it willingly this time. Payton fidgeted with the blanket around Faith's shoulders as if he wanted to care for her but wasn't certain how.

When Faith's eyes closed again, Molly glanced over at the man beside her. "You must get some rest now."

He didn't move. "That was a good sign, wasn't it?"

She didn't want to fill him with false hope, but they all needed hope in their lives along with faith to press forward. His wife needed him to be strong. "It's a very good sign."

He sighed with relief.

Before she went downstairs, she told him he could use her bedroll to sleep. And she promised to check on Faith every half hour until he woke. Minutes after she flipped over the OPEN sign on the front door, an emigrant man and woman walked into the shop, ready to purchase supplies.

Even as Molly worked, she kept thinking about the man and woman resting upstairs. Oddly enough, for a few hours, she almost felt as if she were part of a family again.

Payton left Faith early the next morning to fetch her a change of clothes from their wagon that arrived with the company last night, and to retrieve more food for himself and for Faith when she woke again. His sister's fever had begun to subside yesterday, and Molly said if Faith recovered, it would happen almost as quickly as the illness had come upon her.

It seemed as if Molly was right.

Faith had awakened again this morning, drank her water, and then ate a few spoonfuls of Molly's porridge. She was exhausted, but at least she was able to speak with him again.

Their company was circled up near the fast-moving river, and his four oxen and horse were drinking in the threads of streams that crept away from it. Payton glanced across the twenty-five wagons that surrounded the livestock.

When the company arrived last night, Charley announced he wasn't planning to stay any longer than a day camping near the fort. The place, he said, was full of thieves, and he didn't want any of his members corrupted by the filth here.

Payton didn't know why a jewel of a woman like Molly was living among thieves, but he was grateful that God led him directly to her. She'd cared well for his sister, and he prayed her water and medicine really had overcome the cholera.

He untied the canvas on his wagon and climbed over the backboard. The inside was filled with trunks and barrels. Their food supply had dwindled over the past two months—the trunks were mostly filled with schoolbooks and slates for Samuel and Faith's new school.

He opened the one trunk with Faith's personal items and removed a simple yellow dress for her to wear after she recovered. He didn't touch the blue dress at the bottom, the one wrapped in cloth to protect it from the dirt. That was the dress Faith had sewn for their arrival into Oregon City. It had been a year and a half now since Faith had seen her husband, and she hadn't wanted to greet him in her dusty traveling clothes.

He folded the faded yellow dress into his satchel and turned toward the center of the circle to check on their oxen and the quarter horse that Faith had named Sunny.

Faith's husband had been his best friend for a decade. Samuel was a teacher at a boys' school back in Ohio, and several years ago, he'd read about the need for schools in Oregon. Faith was thrilled about the idea of teaching a group of children who had limited or even no access to an education.

Two years ago, Payton had been settled into his father's former position at the bank and was planning to marry Ketura Hamilton, the youngest daughter of his employer. Payton wasn't a teacher, but Samuel said he needed a good manager for the new school to succeed. Samuel wanted the children of Oregon to become educated business owners and teachers and even doctors—at the time, Payton had no idea how much they needed doctors in the West.

When he told Ketura about his desire to help Samuel start this school, she kindly but firmly explained that she wanted to marry someone who could offer her stability, near her family in Ohio. Payton almost changed his mind, but he felt as if God was calling him to this grand adventure.

He'd been so proud when he and Faith left Ohio, thinking he would never make the same foolish mistakes as some of the unprepared pioneers before them. They weren't even halfway there yet, and with every mile, and every mistake, it seemed that God picked apart a little more of his arrogance, forcing Payton to rely solely on Him.

But in spite of his errors, he prayed that God would spare Faith's life. Samuel had made it safely to Oregon last summer to begin preparations for the school, and by the grace of God, Payton and Faith would join him before the autumn snows began to fall.

Chapter 4

At six minutes past noon, Molly finished supplying an order for an older couple who planned to spend the final years of their life farming in what they called the Promised Land. With their enthusiasm, the familiar desire blazed through Molly's heart.

Ever since she was a child, she'd wanted to go to this strange, beautiful land called Oregon, a country purported to flow with milk and honey. She'd dreamed about pioneering a new place like her ancestors had done when they came to Indiana, of working hard to build her home and harvesting all manner of food from her garden in the Willamette Valley.

It was a dream that would no longer be fulfilled, but still she sometimes found herself being swept away in the dreams of others. She had to stop and remind herself of the realities that ended her journey.

Some nights this dream still flickered in her mind, though she couldn't fathom continuing on this journey without Adam. But no matter what she did, no matter how hard she tried to lock that dream away, it often haunted her in the hours she tried to sleep.

After the couple loaded their wagon, Molly flipped the store's sign back to CLOSED so she could check on Faith. She may not be able to travel west, but she could help Faith and her husband achieve their dream.

When Molly entered the room, Faith's eyes were open, her face turned toward the window as if she wished she could be outside among the bustle of wagons and people.

Her face brightened when she turned back toward Molly. "I'm so glad you've come."

In the sunlight, Molly saw Faith was a beautiful woman with warm blue eyes and long brown hair draped over her shoulders. It seemed as if the salty water and medicine were fighting off the cholera, and Molly was glad for her and even more glad that Payton wouldn't have to suffer through the loss of his wife.

Molly sat in the chair beside her. "Are you hot?"

"Oh, no. I feel almost well again, but Payton said he'll have my head if I get out of this bed for any reason except to use the privy. And I'm only allowed to do that with your help."

"He's a wise man."

"Indeed."

Molly filled a glass with clean water and held it up for Faith to drink. After Faith sipped it, she rested back on the pillows. "Thank you," she whispered.

"Can I get you anything else?" Molly asked.

"No, you've done more than enough already."

Molly sat back in her chair, her eyes heavy from the lack of sleep. Another wagon train arrived yesterday, and by ten this morning, there had been a line of emigrants out the door of the shop, waiting for her to supply their orders. Her feet ached from rushing back and forth between the main store and the storeroom until everyone had what they needed to press on.

Isaiah must have seen the line from his cabin, but he didn't come help her. Even though he owned the sale shop, he didn't tolerate travelers very well. The emigrants were his only customers, the shop his livelihood, but he only wanted to obtain the supplies, not sell them. Often he talked about the years before the wagon trains started coming, when the beavers and buffalo were plenty and fur trading was a lucrative business. He could roam the mountains for months, returning only to sell his wares to the British at a significant profit.

She wasn't exactly sure how he ran this shop before she arrived last year, but she'd heard stories about his legendary temper and verbal explosions when someone dared inquire about the exorbitant prices. Isaiah was not someone who appreciated accountability.

Faith scooted up on her pillows. "Where's my brother?"

Molly tilted her head, trying to understand her words. "Your brother?"

"Yes." Faith studied her for a moment. "You met Payton—"

"Of course." She swallowed, glancing over at the open window before looking back at Faith. "I just didn't realize he was your brother."

"The best brother in the world," she said with another smile. "My husband is waiting for us in Oregon."

Molly slowly contemplated her words. "Payton left to check on your wagon."

"Did the rest of our group arrive?" Faith asked.

She nodded. "They came last night."

Faith's smile started to fade. "I've caused so much trouble. . . ."

Molly took her hand to try and comfort her. "I'm sure they'll be quite relieved when they find out you're feeling better."

Faith smiled again. "Are you going to Oregon?"

She shook her head. "I'm returning east."

Faith's forehead wrinkled with concern, and Molly silently chided herself for making the woman worry.

"Why are you going back?" Faith asked.

Molly hesitated. Even though she wanted to be honest with this woman, she didn't want to make her even more worried. "The journey didn't turn out quite like I expected."

Faith's gaze settled on the sunlight streaming across her bed. "Does it turn out like anyone expects?"

"Probably not."

"Are you married?" Faith asked.

The pain cut fresh through her heart. She'd become an expert at dodging this question from the unmarried men who traveled through here, but no other woman had asked her about Adam. She'd longed for a friend to help her share this burden. "I was married," she said slowly. "My husband died about twenty miles west of here, and I returned to the fort last August."

"I'm sorry," Faith said in earnest. "One's heart can only bear so much sorrow."

"I fear the loss has punctured my heart for good."

Faith took her hand. "It will heal, Molly."

"I'm not so certain—"

Faith scanned the small room, her gaze lingering on a carved wooden box along the wall and then the clothing lined up on six pegs. "You should travel west with us," she said. "We have room for your things in our wagon."

"Oh no, I couldn't—"

"Payton won't mind," she insisted.

"But his wife might."

"Oh, he's not married." Faith smiled, seemingly lost in her own thoughts. "You and I could pretend we're sisters."

Her words sparked inside Molly. Her entire life she'd wanted a sister—when she was a child, she used to wish she could trade in all three of her brothers for one. She'd loved those first months along the journey west, walking with the other women during the day and then working alongside them each night.

She started to thank Faith for her kindness, but before she spoke, she heard Isaiah shout her name from outside the open window. Sighing, she stood. "I must go."

Faith inched herself farther up on her pillows. "Payton needs my help, too."

"Payton needs you to rest," Molly said, trying to assure her. "You can stay here as long as necessary."

Faith slipped back against the pillows.

"Molly!" Isaiah's voice rumbled again, and she moved toward the stairs.

"I'll try and come up again in the next hour," she said before rushing downstairs to unlock the front door.

"Why is this door locked at"—Isaiah pulled a timepiece out of his pocket, fumbling with it before he spat out the time—"almost half past twelve?"

"I'm tending a sick woman upstairs—"

He stopped her words with a wave of his hand. "I don't care one bit about your personal business, Molly."

"Of course not," she replied, gritting her teeth.

Surely a wagon train going east, even a small one, would be headed through here soon. Only another week or two, and she'd never have to see Isaiah Dupuis again.

He flipped the sign in the window back to OPEN. Then he tapped it. "This is where it will remain until dark."

Her shoulders cramped with frustration. "Yes, sir."

Isaiah didn't pay her a wage for her work, but he did provide her with a place to live and an allotment of supplies so she'd had plenty of food along with wood to burn for the winter. Sometimes she was as angry as many of the travelers at his stinginess until she recalled how destitute she'd been when she arrived here last year. Isaiah wasn't a compassionate man, but he'd needed someone trustworthy to help him with his shop.

Instead of using all the supplies he'd given her over the winter, she'd stored many of them and saved every coin that she and Adam brought with them. It was extremely kind of Faith to invite her to travel with her and Payton, but there was no reason for her to go to Oregon now. Her money and supplies would take her back to Indiana.

Two emigrant men stepped up onto the stoop, and she motioned them into the store. The man who'd come last night hadn't returned, and she guessed he'd sent someone else to obtain his things to avoid the humiliation of facing her again.

If nothing else, the trail humbled all of its pioneers.

After she gathered beans, lard, and loaf sugar, the customers paid her with silver coins. The door opened again as they left, and she glanced up, expecting to see a new emigrant, but Payton Keller stepped into the room.

Some of the worry had been washed from his face, and he looked quite handsome in his clean white shirt, suspenders, and denim trousers. For some reason, as he moved toward her, the small shop seemed even smaller.

He glanced toward the door behind her. "How is she?"

"Much better the last time I checked."

"We're both grateful for your help, Molly."

She returned his smile. "It was my pleasure."

"May I see her?"

"Of course," she said, opening the door to the storeroom. He ducked under the frame and moved toward the stairs, but he stopped before he went up.

"Could you join us?" he asked.

She considered his question for a moment. If she didn't flip the sign back to CLOSED, Isaiah wouldn't rush over here in a rage. "I can't stay for long."

Faith's eyes were open, and she greeted them with another smile. For someone who'd been so sick two days ago, Molly marveled at the woman's resilience and the grace she'd maintained through her ordeal.

Payton sat beside his sister. "Molly says you're feeling better."

"The pain is gone," Faith replied. "And I feel like I should be walking or working instead of lying here."

Molly stepped forward. "You need to rest a little longer."

Faith looked back at Payton. "When is our company leaving?"

"Tomorrow morning."

Her eyes grew wide. "We can't let them go without us."

Molly reached for the glass and helped Faith drink a few sips. "You need to rest for at least two more days."

Payton glanced back at Molly as if he were considering her words. "Is it critical to stay here?"

"It's critical for her to keep resting," she replied. "We have plenty of clean water to drink here, and she can continue using my bed."

"I can rest in the wagon," Faith insisted.

Molly shook her head. "You'll never recover with all that jostling."

Tears welled in Faith's eyes, and Molly wished she could tell the woman that she'd be fine on the trail, but Molly had learned from their company's doctor that if a victim of cholera survived the first days, she must continue drinking plenty of clean water and rest until her energy resumed. Right now Faith couldn't even stand up on her own.

"Then we must wait," Payton said firmly.

Molly's heart lifted at this man's respect for his sister and even more at the thought that Faith would get well again under his care.

"But what about our wagon train?" Faith asked.

"They'll either wait for us or we'll find another company to travel with."

Faith reached for her brother's hand. "I've invited Molly to go to Oregon with us."

"What?"

Molly heard the surprise in his question, and she shifted uncomfortably beside them.

"We have room in our wagon," Faith insisted.

"It's more than just the room."

Faith released his hand. "We'll talk later—"

Molly couldn't blame him for not wanting her to go. Even though she could care for herself, he would think it a tremendous burden to be responsible for another woman—a stranger—for almost three months.

"It's no matter," Molly told them both. "I'm not going west."

Payton turned toward her, and the look in his eyes startled her. Instead of frustration, she saw concern in them. "Where will you go?"

"Back to my family in Indiana."

"Hello," she heard someone call from the shop downstairs. "Is anyone back there?"

"Excuse me," she said as she backed toward the steps.

Before she descended the staircase, she heard Faith's voice. "You offended her."

Molly paused on the top step to listen to Payton's response.

"You and I should have talked about it before you invited her."

"She wants to go west. I can see it in her eyes."

"But where will she go when we get there?" he asked.

"Hello!" the customer called again, louder this time.

Molly didn't hear Faith's response, but it didn't matter what she said. She would never let her dreams sweep her away again.

—⁓—

Payton lifted his skillet off the sheet-iron cooking stove and dished up the fish he'd purchased from an Indian man outside the fort. As he seasoned the fish with salt, he chided himself for his outburst when Faith suggested that Molly travel west with them. After all she'd done for his sister, he must have sounded incredibly ungrateful.

But what if Molly decided to join them? How could he care well for two women, especially if Faith's sickness returned?

Then again, Molly could help him care for his sister.

Other emigrants in his company cooked their evening meals around him, and as he ate fish and fresh huckleberries, he scanned the circle until he found Charley Lewis.

Back in Missouri, he and Faith had searched for more than a week for a competent leader for their wagon trip. They felt like Charley was the one, but he, like every good captain, required payment up front for his work. If he and Faith stayed behind, they'd have to pay someone else to guide them on the rest of their journey.

Charley might appear callous at times, but he was smart and reliable. And he'd been honest with them from the beginning. The road to Oregon was a dangerous one. It was impossible for him to control every variable, but Charley had assured him and Faith from the beginning that he would do everything in his power to keep them safe.

Charley had instructed and directed them for the past two months, negotiating with the Indians and guiding them through the prairies and across the rocky paths. When Faith collapsed, he'd encouraged Payton to ride ahead to Fort Hall, but even Charley hadn't been able to save Micah Bates, a twenty-two-year-old married man with a daughter.

A rattlesnake bit Micah just three weeks into the trip, and their company surrounded his wife, Rose, and their daughter with assistance after his death. Faith had tried to convince Payton to marry Micah's young widow, but even though he'd do just about anything he could to help the woman and her daughter, he didn't want to marry anyone out of sympathy.

Faith felt sorry for Rose, but she also thought Payton needed a wife. He would never tell his sister, but he did desire to marry one day. To a woman who loved him as he did her.

Fortunately, another bachelor in their company—William Smith—asked Rose to marry him a few weeks later, and William asked Payton to stand in as a minister. He'd sung at quite a few weddings, but he'd never conducted a wedding ceremony before. He'd been more than happy to accommodate them, glad to be the minister and not the groom.

Tonight he found Charley sitting beside the red coals of a campfire, a pipe in his hand as he stirred a pot of stew. As far as Payton knew, the only thing their captain had purchased at the sale shop was more tobacco—he seemed to survive on jerky and whatever meat they shot on the trail along with the berries and roots they picked along the way.

Charley motioned for him to have a seat on one of the felled logs by the fire. "How's Faith?"

"Recovering quickly, but she still needs to rest. Molly Goodwin is caring for her."

"The woman from the sale shop?" he asked.

Payton nodded.

Charley tapped his pipe on the side of the log. "I never expected to find such a pretty gal in a pitiful place like this."

Payton supposed Molly was a beautiful woman, but he'd seen her more as a partner than a pretty gal. And Faith's guardian angel. "She saved my sister's life."

"I reckon she did." Charley took another drag on his pipe. "Are you and Faith going to be ready to break camp in the morning?"

Payton tossed a stick into the coals as he measured how to present his request to the man across the campfire from him. He knew Charley was obligated to guide the rest of their company to Oregon before the first snow in the mountains, but he couldn't risk losing Faith's life by pushing too hard. "Molly says that Faith needs to rest a bit longer before she can travel."

"Exactly how long did she say we should wait?"

"At least two more days."

Charley considered his words. "That'll put us at least forty miles behind schedule." Two days less on the other side to find shelter before the winter.

"I know it's asking a lot. . . ."

Charley ladled his steaming stew into a bowl. "Your sister's been awfully kind to Rose and her kid."

He nodded. "She has a huge heart for anyone in need."

Charley's gaze wandered over to the cottonwood trees that canopied the river, at the shadows beginning to fall. Then he looked back at Payton. "I reckon we can wait until Friday at dawn, but we can't leave an hour later."

"I understand," Payton replied calmly, though he wanted to slap the man on the back. "Thank you."

"I'll be telling the rest of the company that the animals need more time to graze."

"I won't say anything different." Payton paused before he spoke again. "What would you think about bringing one more person with us?"

The man's eyebrows climbed. "This Molly woman?"

Payton slowly nodded.

"Is she ready to travel?"

"She would accompany Faith and me."

Charley took another drag on his pipe, his gaze roaming across the circle and the people in his care. "I can't be responsible for her."

"I'd be responsible," Payton assured him.

Charley finally shrugged. "I suppose one more person won't hurt. As long as she's ready by Friday before dawn."

Payton thanked the man as he stood. Then he walked back toward the fort. He wasn't going to talk to Faith or Molly about this conversation, but if Molly changed her mind, he'd let her know she could travel with them.

What would happen if he tried to change her mind?

The thought startled him.

Even though Molly had said she wouldn't travel with them, Faith was convinced that she really wanted to go to Oregon. With her knowledge of medicine, she would be a tremendous help to Faith and their entire company. And he also knew that Faith craved a good friend—both on the trail and once they reached Oregon.

He glanced up at the log walls in front of him.

Perhaps he would try and convince Molly Goodwin to travel west with them after all.

Chapter 5

Customers flowed in and out of the sale shop all day on Wednesday, and as Molly worked, she mulled over Faith's invitation again. Payton slept in a tent last night, by his wagon, and she and Faith spent the evening hours talking about Faith's ideas to help educate the children of both settlers and missionaries in Oregon.

Faith fell asleep around nine, but Molly couldn't rest. Even though she'd dreamed again and again over the past year about the possibilities of going west, she'd never thought it could be a reality. As a single woman, she wasn't eligible to obtain free land, but neither did she want to spend the rest of her life working for a man like Isaiah.

Minutes before she closed the shop for the night, the front door opened one last time, and a man and woman stepped inside. The man was much more stout than most of the emigrants who came through Fort Hall, and his wife was dressed in a bright yellow calico dress.

"Good evening," the man said as he handed her a short list of supplies.

"Where are you folks headed?" she asked as she perused their list.

He sighed. "We're traveling back to Missouri."

Molly's gaze lifted slowly as she processed his words. "Did you say Missouri?"

"I did." He glanced back toward the woman examining a case with glass beads and mirrors. "My wife is ready to return to civilization."

She lowered the paper. After all this time, someone was finally going the direction she needed. "Were you in Oregon?"

He nodded. "For three years."

Molly began to slowly scoop cornmeal onto her scales, her mind racing. "Is it as beautiful as people say?"

He lowered his voice, seemingly so his wife couldn't hear him. "It's the best land I've ever seen."

That's not what she wanted to hear. She wanted him to say it was all a lie—the land was ugly and dry and nothing would grow. She wanted him to tell her that she was making the right choice in traveling the opposite direction as well.

"Why are you leaving?" she asked.

"Ruth says we need refinement in our lives."

Molly almost laughed. At one time, she might have been concerned about refinement as well, but after a year living among fur traders, she wasn't even certain she'd know what to do with refinement.

"We're expecting our first child this fall," he continued, "and she doesn't want him or her to grow up without manners or a decent education."

Molly poured the cornmeal into his burlap bag. "Aren't there schools in Oregon?"

"Not many, and I don't think any of them would be called good."

Molly glanced back at the door. "How long are you staying here?"

"We're resting a few nights before heading out on Friday morning."

She didn't need her slate to do the numbers. It was already almost seven in the evening. If she hurried, she could be packed and ready to leave in thirty hours.

She lowered her voice, leaning back against the counter to ask one more question. "Would you have room for one more person in your party?"

He eyed her warily. "It would have to be someone equipped to travel."

"Of course."

"My name's Joshua Hubbard," he said, stretching out his hand to shake hers. "I'd have to talk to our guide, but I think he'd be agreeable to it."

She quickly assembled the rest of the supplies for the Hubbards. It would take her a full day to pack her wagon, but she had all the supplies necessary to travel. Isaiah could manage the shop for the rest of the season, and she'd be back with her parents in Indiana before the end of the year.

Back to the life she'd had before she met Adam.

She tried to evoke some sort of excitement over this opportunity to go east, but there was no fire inside her. She'd known this was coming, the end of her and Adam's dream, but she couldn't remember a time at home when her mind wasn't ablaze with plans to go west.

But even if she didn't want to return home in her heart, she had to press through it. Traveling to Oregon was no longer a viable option for her.

Joshua Hubbard didn't complain about the prices for the cornmeal, tea, or the tools he ordered, and as he and his wife left, he promised to check with their captain about taking one more traveler with them.

She stood at the counter as if she were in a trance, the summer heat settling over her as she slowly twisted the gold ring that Adam gave her when they married. Finally this was what she wanted, what she'd been praying for all year, but still she felt empty inside.

Four years had passed since her oldest brother brought Adam home to meet their family over dinner. Adam had spent the evening trying to convince her parents and her married brothers to go west, telling them about Oregon's new land act that granted every married couple 640 acres of land. Free.

Her father wanted to head west, but Molly's mother had no interest in spending five months in a wagon. In the end, her brothers hadn't gone either, but Molly had been dreaming about going west since she was a girl. She was seventeen when she met Adam, and while she wasn't particularly excited about continuing to work on a farm—either in Oregon or Indiana—she'd fallen hard for her brother's friend.

The land act expired last year, months after Adam died, but he'd once told her that if anything happened to him, he wanted her to continue on to Oregon alone. And the opportunity and adventure still beckoned her, but each time her heart called her west, she muffled it. Not only did it feel impossible to travel without him, she couldn't imagine achieving this dream without Adam at her side.

Their wagon was stored in one of Isaiah's warehouses, and the oxen were waiting for her in a corral by the river.

She would begin preparing her wagon tonight, praying the Hubbard's captain would let her join the company going east.

She flipped her sign over, but before she stepped outside, she heard a movement behind her. Turning, she saw Payton in the doorway behind the counter.

For a moment, she'd forgotten that she had company upstairs.

———

Payton hadn't meant to eavesdrop. Once Faith fell asleep, he'd planned to retire to his tent and talk to Molly first thing in the morning. But when he stepped into the storeroom and heard the conversation between Molly and her customer, he decided that they needed to talk right now.

Did she really intend to go east with a company of strangers?

As Molly leaned back against the door, he saw tears in her eyes. Even though he was still practically a stranger to her, they'd battled hard together for his sister's life. He wished he could take away her pain as she'd done for Faith. "Are you finished for the night?" he asked.

She nodded. "I was just leaving."

"Can I join you?"

"I suppose," she said with a shrug.

A tin lantern glowed from her hands as they stepped outside, into the crowded courtyard of the fort. Horses and oxen roamed freely between the log buildings, and carts filled with supplies moved in and out the main gates. The air smelled like tobacco and linseed oil.

"Do you want to return east with them?" he asked, shoving his hands in his coat pockets as they walked toward the gate.

"I do," she said, her voice sounding more resigned than resolute.

Perhaps he should leave her alone to her thoughts and her determination to return home, but it seemed Faith was right—Molly didn't want to go back. "You know what I think?"

She walked faster. "I'm not sure that I want to know."

"I think you still want to go to Oregon."

"It doesn't mat—"

He interrupted her. "It seems to me that you might be running away from the place you're supposed to be."

She stopped, freezing for a moment before she slowly turned toward him. Instead of tears, her eyes flared with frustration. "You don't know anything about me, Mr. Keller."

He lowered his voice. "Then tell me."

A cart rumbled by them, and she started walking again until they passed through the gates. Outside the fort, the night glowed orange from the patches of campfires near the riverbank. He didn't want to be harsh with her, but if she went back to Indiana, he doubted she'd ever have the opportunity to travel to Oregon Country again. While he could never pay her back for how she'd helped Faith, perhaps he could do exactly what he'd done with his customers at the bank—encourage her to do what was best for her future.

Molly slowed her walk beside him, but she didn't turn again. "My husband and I came west together last year. It was his dream to start a farm in Oregon."

"Was he a farmer in Indiana?"

She shook her head. "Adam never farmed a day in his life, but he was passionate about learning new things."

"Passion can make someone successful."

"But it can't keep them alive." Her voice trembled when she spoke, and for a moment her words hung between them.

"No, it can't," he replied slowly. "Was this your dream as well?"

She nodded. "Ever since I was a girl."

"Then perhaps you can still keep his dream alive."

She finally turned toward him, her gaze fixed on his face. "I can't do it. . . ." Her voice faltered. "There's nothing for me in Oregon now."

"You have friends in Faith and me," he said. "And perhaps there might be a position for you to work at the school."

"But there's no guarantee—"

"No." He paused. "Only a guarantee about the friendship."

She stopped at a corral and draped her arms over the wooden fence. Away from the campfires, the stars sparked like fireflies in the sky and several animals grazed in the shadows, on the other side of the fence.

"What will you do if you return home?" he asked.

She shrugged. "Help my parents on their farm, I suppose."

"Adam was a wise man to marry you."

"Because I know how to work a farm?"

"No, because—" Suddenly he felt uncomfortable as multiple reasons for Adam's wisdom popped into his mind: Molly was smart, kind, resourceful, pretty, and apparently knowledgeable about farming.

Adam Goodwin had been a blessed man indeed.

In the awkward silence, Molly managed a lopsided smile. "I don't know why he married me either."

Payton tugged at his collar, not certain of what to say. He didn't want to insult her, but it didn't feel right either to list off the many reasons why her husband must have loved her.

"You can't give up on your life, Molly."

"I know." Her voice cracked again. "But only God knows how I'm supposed to live it."

He put his hat on his head. "Then I suppose you and He have some talking to do tonight."

She hopped over the fence. "I have to make sure my oxen are ready to go."

"Come west," he said again, pleading with her as she walked away.

But she didn't say anything in response.

This was a decision Molly had to make on her own, but as he watched her moving across the field, he realized he didn't just want her to go west.

He wanted Molly Goodwin to go west with him.

Chapter 6

Wagon wheels rattled near the riverbank, and several oxen bellowed in the early morning fog that veiled the water. The smell of wood smoke mixed with the cool air, and while Molly couldn't see anyone along the river, she heard people calling to each other as the two companies prepared to leave—one headed east and the other traveling to Oregon.

She sat on the bench of her wagon in the darkness, holding the reins for two oxen as they awaited her direction. The little she owned was packed tightly in barrels and crates behind her, and under her dress, she'd hidden a money belt filled with the last of her coins.

Her heart seemed to rattle like the wagons, and she felt the pull of both companies, like two powerful magnets tugging her in opposite directions. In these minutes before dawn, she had to decide for the final time between left and right, between fulfilling her dream or locking it back inside her heart forever.

She squinted, trying to scan the darkness to the west, but fog concealed the entire company.

After their discussion near the corral, Payton hadn't tried to convince her again to go west with them. Faith had regained enough strength to walk without assistance so he'd escorted her back to her tent last night, but before they left, Faith had pleaded with her one more time to travel with them.

She'd been up most of the night, praying and thinking and even allowing herself the pleasure of dreaming one last time what it would be like to start life over again in Oregon. On her own. And then she'd dreamed about traveling west as she slept.

What if she did journey with friends and had a potential job at the end of the trail? It was one more big risk—if Faith's husband hadn't accumulated enough students to pay tuition, there might not be a job for any of them. But she might be able to find work someplace else.

If she decided to go east this morning, she wouldn't allow herself the freedom of mulling over the possibilities in Oregon any longer. Her dreams would have to end right here.

She clicked her tongue and prompted her oxen toward the west.

Even if she didn't leave with them, she wanted to say good-bye to Faith and her brother one last time. They'd both been kind to her, and she would simply—

"Whoa," she commanded, slowing the oxen near the river. Her insides seemed to crumble again with the view.

The wagons were already gone.

Climbing off the bench, she scanned the trampled grass along the bank. Smoke from the abandoned campfires curled up into the fog as a wave of nausea swept through her.

Then grief curled up from her heart like the smoke. In that moment, she felt the agony from another loss. This death of a dream.

Tears flowed down her cheeks, and she collapsed back against the sideboard of her wagon. She knew she must hurry if she was going to travel with the other company, but her legs felt as heavy as her heart.

Before Payton and Faith arrived, she'd been resolved to the idea of returning home, but when Faith invited her to join them, her dormant heart felt as if it were coming to life again. Payton had been right. This was her dream as much as it was Adam's, and she wanted to finish this trip for both Adam and for herself.

But it had taken her too long to decide. There was no longer a choice for her to make.

Behind her, she heard the pounding of horse hooves, and she turned, squinting again in the emerging daylight until she saw a tall man riding toward her.

"Payton?" she whispered.

He dismounted, and as he led the horse toward her, her heart sparked in spite of herself. Payton Keller had come back for her.

A laugh escaped her lips—relief—and she quickly wiped the tears off her cheeks.

"Faith and I were hoping you'd change your mind," he said.

She swallowed hard, trying to stop the tears. "Who said I changed my mind?"

"Just a hunch." He smiled. "The others have gone ahead of us, but we can catch them when they stop for the noon meal."

She glanced into the cloud of fog behind him. "Where's Faith?"

"I made her a bed in the back of the wagon, though I doubt she'll get much rest. Charley's making sure our oxen are staying on course."

Strength simmered inside her again. Maybe she really could go to Oregon. Not on her own entirely, but alongside a competent captain and new friends.

Perhaps she wouldn't thrive in Oregon. Perhaps, in two or three years, she would have to return home like Joshua and his wife, but in this moment she knew—if she didn't go west, she would regret it for the rest of her life.

Her gaze traveled back to her right one last time, and as the fog lifted, she could see the last of the wagons beginning their journey east. They were leaving without her. . . and she bid them well.

When she looked back at Payton, she saw questions in his eyes. Then she climbed back up to her bench and nodded to the west. "Oregon or bust."

He smiled again. "I have no intention of busting."

She clicked her tongue, and the oxen began moving.

For the first time in a year, the fire in her heart flickered again.

—⁓—

Payton stood on the edge of a canyon and watched a powerful chute of water cascade down a cliff, crashing into the river below. The company had stopped for the night, but as he watched the waterfall, he wondered again how they were ever going to cross the

Snake River. Right now, they couldn't even get their wagons down into the canyon.

Charley assured them that they'd be able to obtain water from the river tomorrow, but tonight they kept both oxen and children away from the steep cliffs.

After their long journey today, Payton had set up tents for himself and Faith and then watered their animals from the little that remained in their barrel. As he worked, he could hear the thunder of the waterfalls from their campsite, and before it was dark, Faith urged him to visit the falls.

The land in Idaho was more beautiful—and more wild—than he imagined. The raw power of the water intrigued him—it was strange to be standing so close to a river and not be able to drink from it.

Almost like traveling alongside Molly Goodwin every day and not being able to tell her about the feelings that were stirring in his heart. They'd been traveling almost two weeks now—God help him, he didn't know how he was going to survive the next two months until they reached Oregon City.

It had been a courageous decision she'd made to come west with them, and he knew her heart was closely entwined with the memory of her husband as she pressed to fulfill this dream for both of them. If Payton even hinted at the emergence of his own feelings, he would scare her.

Molly still hadn't told him what happened to Adam last year, but perhaps one day she'd reveal some of the secrets she held close to her heart. And perhaps one day he could be honest with her as well about the emerging feelings inside him.

But in the meantime, it was akin to torture to be in such close proximity with her.

He'd planned to help Molly along the way, but she didn't need his help. She managed her oxen well and could easily set up her own tent and prepare a fire each night from the buffalo chips the children collected for them. The only thing Molly didn't do was hunt. Her gun was stored in the back of her wagon and she refused to take it out, so when he shot an antelope or quail, he shared the meat with her and Faith. Thankfully, his sister's health had rapidly improved, and instead of riding now in the wagon during the day, she'd been walking alongside Molly.

Some days the heat seemed unbearable, and then the cold night air swept in with the darkness and the entire company circled up around the campfires before they went to bed. But they all pressed through it together. He and Faith and Molly Goodwin.

Faith seemed to sense his growing discomfort around her friend. When their group stopped for the night, she often asked him to do tasks outside their circle. But every night he had to return to camp, and when he arrived, he did everything possible to avoid being with Molly. He didn't regret inviting her, for Faith's sake, but he wished he had better control over his own emotions.

As the sun began to set, he walked back to their makeshift village of campfires and tents. Molly was grinding coffee beans near his tent, and as he hurried past, she looked up and motioned him toward her campfire.

He stifled a groan as he stepped over the rocky terrain. "Can I help you with something?" he asked.

"No," she replied and then motioned to the flat rock beside her and her camp stove.

"Please sit down."

Reluctantly, he complied.

"Where did you go?" she asked as she poured the ground coffee into her coffeepot.

"To see the waterfalls."

"Would you like some coffee?"

"Very much," he said even as he silently rebuked himself for his weakness. He should be doing about anything else except having a cup of coffee with her.

"It'll be ready in a minute or two." She leaned back against the spokes on her wheel. Nearby William Smith's fiddle harmonized with the steady sound of working hands—women scraping dishes clean over the fires, men pounding their tent pegs into the hard ground.

"Before we started our trip from Missouri, I used to wonder what I'd do out here in the evenings." Her gaze swept over the dozens of people surrounding them. "But there's something special about working hard together all day and then resting as a sort of family in the evening. . . ."

Her voice trailed off, and he wondered what she was thinking. He didn't tell her, but even as he tried to distract himself, he was enjoying his evenings a lot more now that she'd joined their company.

She poured him a cup of the steaming black coffee. "I have plenty of sugar if you'd like some."

When he nodded, she pounded the sugar in a mortar and then spooned it into both of their cups.

"What's the first thing you'll do when you get to Oregon?" she asked.

He took a sip of the sweetened coffee. "Slap my brother-in-law on the back and then unload this wagon as soon as possible so I can get to work at the school." He glanced over at her. "What will you do if you don't work at the school?"

She shrugged. "Perhaps there's a sale shop in need of a clerk?"

He smiled. "I think you should start a farm."

She shook her head. "That was Adam's dream."

He slowly stretched out his legs. "What was your husband like?"

She wrapped her hands around her tin cup. "He loved trying new things. I don't know if he would have made a good farmer, but he would have been quite creative in his pursuit of it. I, on the other hand. . ." She took a deep breath. "Sometimes I don't know if I can do this without him."

His eyes locked on hers. "Molly, you are a strong, competent woman, and I have no doubt you'll succeed quite well in Oregon doing whatever you choose to do."

She rewarded him with a smile. "Thank you."

There was much more he wanted to say, but he harnessed his words.

Someone stepped next to her stove, and he looked up to see William Smith. "Will you lead us in a song?" the man asked him.

"Of course." Payton glanced back at Molly as he stood. "Do you like to sing?"

She slowly set his cup beside her. "I used to enjoy it."

He held out his hand. "Come join us."

She glanced down at his hand, and for a moment he thought she might take it, but she shook her head. "I need to prepare for the night."

He didn't press her any further. Perhaps one day he could tell her about his new dreams. And perhaps one day she would sing again as well.

Chapter 7

Molly dipped her fingers into the rapid current of the Snake River and watched the cool water rush through them. There were three small islands in the river where the oxen could rest between channels, and she stood at the edge of the third island, waiting for Payton and Faith to finish their crossing.

The guidebook she'd studied religiously said to avoid this treacherous area if possible, and she'd heard stories over the past year of emigrants who'd lost everything in this section of river. But it was the only place they could cross to reach Fort Boise, so Charley insisted they try. The water was low, he said, and they needed supplies from the fort since most of them had avoided buying anything at Fort Hall.

The wheels of Payton and Faith's wagon groaned and teetered as they passed by the skeleton of an abandoned wagon tipped over on its side. Molly studied the weathered sideboard of the wagon for a moment, wondering what happened to the people who'd been riding inside it. The river probably stole their supplies from them, but she hoped it hadn't taken any of their lives.

She didn't know how to swim, so she tied her dress up far above her knees in case she fell off the bench, hoping she could wade to the far side. Last night she'd spent hours brushing tar on her wagon so her food and other supplies wouldn't get wet during the river crossing either, and she'd harnessed all four of her oxen to the wagon to fight the current.

A barrel rolled out the back of Payton and Faith's wagon as they neared the river-bank. The current carried the barrel a few feet west before it crashed against the rocks and broke apart, the swarm of dried beans swirling in the water. But even though they'd lost a barrel, her friends' wagon made it safely across, and as it rolled up onto the bank, Molly thanked God they hadn't lost anything else.

Once Payton's wagon was safe, he rode his horse back across the stream. She'd told him earlier that she didn't need his help, but as she eyed the river, she reconsidered.

"I thought Sunny and I would just stroll along beside you," he said.

She glanced over at him from the bench. "I'll be fine."

"Of course." He scanned the side of her wagon. "Are you ready to go?"

"I'm ready to be on the other side," she replied, trying to sound much more light-hearted than she felt.

He led her two pairs of oxen into the water, and she didn't argue again with his assistance. The river dipped quickly, rushing past the knees on Payton's horse, and she clutched the board beside her as the water rose quickly to the bellies of her oxen. "Get up," she commanded, urging her team forward.

Her animals fought the current slowly, and the old farm wagon trembled each time it rolled over a rock or dipped low into a hole. The right side of the wagon turned up at an angle as they climbed over a large boulder, and she slid to the edge of the bench. Then the wagon crashed back down into the riverbed, and Payton commanded the oxen forward for her.

Her animals pulled on their chains, straining against the yokes attached back to the wagon, but they didn't take another step toward the shore. Her wheels had stopped moving.

The current swirled around the oxen, and Molly felt the left side of her heavy wagon settling into the mud. Charley had said not to panic if they got stuck, but she couldn't stop the feeling of panic that surged inside her.

If her wagon tipped here, she would lose everything she owned to the river.

The oxen bellowed again, shaking their heads as they tried to pull the wagon out of the hole. They had been so faithful to her on this journey. She prayed they wouldn't tire now.

"Get up," Payton shouted as he slapped the haunches of the animals. She joined him in the shouting. If the wagon didn't move, not only might she lose her things, she might lose her oxen as well.

The wagon began to tip again with the current, the water swirling about a foot below her bench. Charley Lewis and two more men joined Payton on horseback, pushing the wagon, urging the oxen forward.

"Come on," Molly whispered.

Payton rode up beside her. "Can you climb onto my horse?"

She knew what he was really asking—he was asking her to abandon her wagon and things. She'd given up so much on this journey, and now she had to give up her medicines and food and everything Adam had left for her.

Slowly she climbed off the bench and mounted the horse behind Payton. She wrapped her arms around his waist at the same time Charley lifted one of her wooden boxes out of the back of the wagon and tossed it into the water.

She squeezed her eyes closed before she saw what happened, but she heard the box splash in the water.

When she and Payton reached the riverbank, he helped her to the ground and then quickly turned his horse to head back into the river. Faith put her arm around her shoulders, and they watched the men continue to push and prod her oxen. And dump another one of her precious boxes into the river.

She closed her eyes again, twisting her wedding band back and forth around her finger, until Faith let out a cheer. Opening her eyes, Molly watched one of her oxen take a step forward and then another followed. She clasped her hands in front of her chest, praying that God would give them the strength to haul the rest of her supplies across.

Payton shouted again at the animals, and they slowly pressed forward. Molly bit her lower lip as they plodded, one slow step at a time, through the current and then up the bank. Rushing forward, she put her arms around the damp necks of each of her animals, kissing each of them as they huffed for air. Then she released them from their yokes.

Payton rode up beside her, and she looked up at him. His eyes were shaded by the wide brim of his hat, but his smile was wide.

"We did it!" she whispered.

He nodded. "We did."

"Thank you, Payton."

He tipped his hat before turning the horse toward his wagon.

Chapter 8

Silhouetted against the pale sky were the Blue Mountains—the gateway to Oregon. The guidebook said that Mount Hood wasn't far beyond this mountain range. Once they saw the snow-coated mountain peak, towering by itself above the hills, they would be about three weeks away from Oregon City.

Home.

Her legs no longer ached like they did in the weeks after they left Fort Hall. Every day, she and Faith walked side-by-side, forging up sagebrushed hills and climbing over the rocks on their path. Their bonnets covered their heads but failed to keep the rays of sunshine out of their eyes.

Instead of feeling tired from the heat and exercise, she was exhilarated. She never thought she'd be able to finish this trip without Adam, but she was doing it. She'd lost her sugar and cornmeal in the Snake River, and she traded some of her dried beans with Faith in exchange for cornmeal. Ever since the river crossing, she was learning to rely more on those traveling with her.

Beside her, Faith shielded her eyes from the midday sun, and Molly silently thanked God again for bringing her a friend. Faith's husband hadn't died, but she missed Samuel terribly and the company, it seemed, was a gift for both of them.

Faith moaned. "My feet are about to revolt."

Molly nodded toward the dirt-stained canopy beside them. "You could ride in my wagon."

Faith shook her head. "My entire body will revolt if I have to ride in a wagon again."

Molly opened the lid of the barrel hanging alongside her wagon and used the ladle to drink some of the clean water. Then she held out the ladle. "Would you like some?" she offered.

Faith nodded and took a long sip as well then hung the ladle back onto the side of the barrel.

"I'm so glad you are well again," Molly said.

"I'm grateful, too." Faith paused a moment before speaking again. "But sometimes I feel guilty that I'm well while so many other people are sick or have lost their lives on this trail."

Molly contemplated her words before responding. "Perhaps we'll never understand why the lives of people we love are stolen away much too early," she said slowly. "But I'm trying to rejoice for the lives of those who are saved even as I honor Adam's life."

"What do you think Adam is doing right now?" Faith asked.

Molly clutched her hands together, cradling her wedding band between them. "I like to think he's working on 640 acres of heaven's farmland."

Faith lifted her plaid skirt to climb over a boulder in their way. "Perhaps he has an orchard, too?"

"A huge one with cherry trees and apples and peaches and plums."

Faith sighed. "I'd trade the entire contents of our wagon for an apple."

According to her guidebook, Oregon was akin to a cornucopia stuffed full of fresh fruit, and it was one of the many things that propelled her feet forward. They hadn't even found berries on the trail since they'd left Fort Hall. "Maybe there will still be apples on the trees when we arrive."

"And grapes on the vines," Faith said. "I think we need to walk faster."

"Indeed," Molly replied. "Especially since Samuel is waiting for you on the other side."

Faith glanced back over at her. "Do you think you'll marry again when we get to Oregon?"

Payton's face flashed into Molly's mind, and she silently chided herself for it. Ever since they'd left Fort Hall, she no longer dreamed about going west. Instead, after Payton helped rescue her and her wagon from the river, he'd been wandering into her dreams when she tried to sleep. And sometimes she found herself thinking about him during the day as well.

It seemed the more she tried to stop herself, the more she failed.

"I can't imagine marrying anyone else," she said.

Faith shielded her eyes again and glanced across the clusters of people walking together before pointing toward the only man walking by himself. "Charley Lewis seems awfully interested in you."

Molly groaned. "Charley Lewis is much more interested in himself."

"I suppose you're right," Faith said. "You need to be with someone who loves you more than himself."

"I don't need to be with anyone," Molly protested.

Faith didn't seem to hear her. "Someone who serves God, of course, and is kind and determined and will take excellent care of you."

She fiddled with the tie on her bonnet. "I don't need anyone to take care of me."

Faith studied her again. "Do you think Adam would want you to remarry?"

The question had entered Molly's mind multiple times in the past year, but she'd refused to answer it. Still it was a question she needed to answer. "I know he would," she finally said.

"Then he truly loved you."

"Yes, he did," she said quietly. "But I need to fulfill this dream for him before I even think about marrying again."

"What happens after we arrive in Oregon City?"

"I don't know. . . ."

"Perhaps in time there will be someone else"—Faith glanced sideways at her—"other than Charley, of course."

Molly didn't take the bait. Faith had been hinting about Payton since their river crossing, but it didn't matter what she said. Her brother had been kind to help her that morning, but for the most part, he'd avoided her on this journey. She'd enjoyed his singing with the rest of the company around the campfire, but he only spoke with her when absolutely necessary.

Not that it mattered. . . .

She glanced over and saw Payton walking beside William Smith. When she caught his eye, she quickly refocused her gaze forward. Even though he rarely spoke to her, it seemed that his eyes kept meeting hers, and she wasn't certain how to react to his gaze.

"I hope you'll spend the winter with Samuel and me," Faith continued, oblivious to the turmoil inside Molly.

She blinked. "I can't intrude on you."

"Intrude?" Faith said with a light laugh. "You saved my life, Molly. I may not be able to save your life in return, but I hope you'll live with us until you decide what's next."

In front of them, Charley signaled that they would stop to camp for the night, and the oxen beside them began to slow.

"My feet thank you," Faith called out.

Molly turned to unyoke her oxen even as Payton stepped up to care for his animals in front of her. As they tended their animals, she couldn't help but wonder—was Payton also planning to stay with his sister and Samuel when they arrived?

Perhaps it was good that he'd been ignoring her. She wasn't quite sure what she'd do if he wanted to spend time together.

—〰—

Lightning flashed above Payton's tent, and rain poured down the sides of the canvas, traversing into the tiny streams around his bedroll. He tried to sleep, and then he tried to sing quietly to clear his mind, but he was too worried about his sister and Molly to rest.

Staring up at the canvas, he prayed quietly for guidance. Molly said she enjoyed being with the company in the evenings, but being close to her each night had become torture for him. He'd done everything he could to avoid her, but as much as he tried, he couldn't avoid her for long in their small company. Nor should he avoid her tonight.

Sitting up, he buttoned his rubber coat over his flannel shirt and trousers then shoved on his hat before he unhooked the canvas opening. The oxen were huddled together nearby, and no one else seemed to be roaming around the circle. The storm should keep any wild animals away from their wagons tonight as well.

Rain soaked his coat as he stepped toward Faith's tent first and peeled back the top of the flap. In the flash of light, he saw his sister sleeping soundly, exhausted after their fifteen-mile walk today. Perhaps Molly was resting as well.

If she was asleep, he wouldn't startle her. If she was awake—he didn't know exactly what he would do.

"Molly?" he whispered outside her tent, loud enough for her to hear above the storm but not so loud that their neighbors might wake and wonder what he was doing. Charley said a few people were already whispering about them. He didn't need to give anyone else in their company a reason to talk.

When Molly didn't respond, he took a deep breath, relieved she was able to sleep through this storm.

He took a step away from her tent, his boot splashing into a puddle, but before he turned back toward his tent, he heard her voice.

"I'm under here," she said.

Payton leaned down, and in the next flash of light, he saw Molly and her bedroll hidden under her wagon, her eyes wide with fear. His hands sinking in the mud, he ducked low and scooted in beside her, his long coat dragging behind him. Then he took off his drenched hat and set it beside him.

He couldn't see her in the darkness, but he knew she was close as he stretched out his legs beside her. "Terrible storm," he said, struggling to focus on why he was there.

"I hate lightning."

His hand brushed her side, and he moved back toward the edge of the wagon. "For good reason." He paused, trying to order his racing thoughts. "When I was a boy, my mom used to sing to me during the storms."

"Faith told me you lost your mother three years ago in a carriage accident."

He nodded in the darkness. "And my father gave up on life not long after she passed away."

"She was a good mother, wasn't she?"

"An amazing one," he said. "She was a lot like Faith in that she always seemed to care more about the people she loved than she did about herself."

Her arm brushed his coat this time, and he realized she was rocking. "Sometimes it seems that all I can think about is myself and my fears."

"God doesn't want you to be afraid, Molly."

Thunder shook the wagon above them. "Then He shouldn't send a storm."

"Maybe He wants you to learn how to rely solely on Him during the storms."

Seconds passed before she spoke again. "I'm not as afraid of the storm, as I am of the memories."

His chest clenched. "What memories?"

"The night of the accident." She rocked again. "The men in our company were out hunting for buffalo when it started to storm. It began to lightning—I thought I could cure any sort of ailment with my medicines, but there was nothing I could do for my own husband when the lightning struck him. He was gone before they got back to camp."

For a moment, he felt her grief deep inside him—the loss of her husband without being able to say good-bye. "It's heartbreaking to lose someone you love."

She paused. "I don't want to think about that night anymore."

"Then let's not think about it."

"I can't seem to stop myself—"

"Sometimes the only way I can stop my own thoughts is to start singing."

"I haven't sung in over a year," she said.

He eased himself up farther on his elbows, his head bumping the wagon. "Do you mind if I do?"

Silence drifted between them for several seconds before she spoke again. "I suppose not."

So he began to sing a hymn like his mother had done when he was a child, like he did around the campfires almost every night now to encourage the others in their company.

"Abide with me; fast falls the eventide;
The darkness deepens; Lord with me abide.
When other helps fail and comforts flee,
Help of the helpless, O abide with me."

He sang the entire hymn quietly, the lyrics mixing with the cadence of the rainfall, so no one except Molly could hear it. As he sang, he realized that she stopped rocking. Though the lightning didn't cease, he prayed her soul was calming.

The last lines he sang a bit louder, words he hoped would embolden her.

"Heaven's morning breaks, and earth's vain shadows flee;
In life, in death, O Lord, abide with me."

The song ended, and Molly shifted beside him. In another flash of lightning, he realized her head was turned, watching him.

His chest clenched again so tightly it felt as if it might strangle his breath. How he wanted to take her in his arms, tell her how much he loved her, how much he wanted to be the one to make the shadows and the storms flee.

But he wasn't God. He might be able to help protect her, but he couldn't direct her steps, nor could he even really protect her from the travesty that could happen on this trail.

She had to cling to God first, and then perhaps—

Perhaps God would allow him to love her one day. Payton couldn't keep her from the storms, but he could comfort her in the midst of them.

He leaned back to rest his head on his hat, trickles of water running around his neck. Right now, he needed God's strength most of all to remain beside Molly.

They spent hours hidden under the wagon—talking about their childhood and their dreams, about their losses and what they missed most about the people they loved.

The rain stopped an hour or so before dawn, and he snuck out from under the wagon before Charley sounded the morning bugle.

The storm had passed in the sky, but a new storm raged soundly in his heart.

Chapter 9

Molly hated being alone at night. During the days and the early evenings, she had plenty of company with Faith and others, but when everyone retreated to their tents on nights like this, she often lingered by the campfire, watching the dark clouds creep across the starlit sky like they were searching for a place to rest for the night as well.

She rubbed her hands over the dying fire. The days were much shorter and cooler now that they were nearing the end of September. The coolness was a relief, but not the shorter hours. They were only a reminder that autumn was upon them, and Charley often reminded them that snow came early in Oregon.

But they'd made it through the Blue Mountains, and Charley announced this morning that they'd see Mount Hood soon.

Once they descended into Oregon City, most of the company would go their separate ways. Everyone, it seemed, had a solid plan except for her.

Something moved on the other side of her wagon, and she crawled into her tent. One of the men guarded the outside of their encampment tonight, but coyotes and other animals still snuck into their circle sometimes to hunt for food or harass the livestock inside. She didn't want to confront a wild animal by herself tonight.

Inside the tent, she draped her warm afghan over her dress and bedroll, her rifle lying on the ground beside her. She wrapped her arms around her chest, not wanting to feel alone, but she couldn't seem to stop the ache in her heart again. Most of the people in their company traveled with members of their family, and both Faith and Payton had Samuel to welcome them on the other end. Faith was like a sister to her during this journey, but she couldn't stay with her if Payton decided to live with them as well.

It had been more than a week since Payton had crawled under the wagon beside her, and their night together replayed over and over in her mind. She'd felt foolish, having him know that she hid under the wagon, but instead of ridiculing her, he'd been so kind to share his story and the songs with her. In the midst of it, with him singing beside her, she'd almost forgotten her fears.

The day after the storm, she thought it would be awkward around Payton, but he continued to avoid her, so she reciprocated. She hadn't felt nervous around him that night, but she'd been nervous ever since.

She blushed again at the memory of him singing beside her.

Faith had asked her about remarrying. If she ever married again, it would be to someone like Payton.

Most nights she slept well from exhaustion, but when she couldn't sleep, her loneliness felt like it might smother her. Did Payton feel lonely as well? He'd said that singing was the best way to stop the thoughts that tortured her, so she began to softly sing the lyrics that he'd sung to her during the storm.

"When other helps fail and comforts flee,
Help of the helpless, O abide with me."

She wasn't completely alone. God was here with her in the darkness, and she prayed for help. Comfort. In those first months after Adam's death, she'd been angry at God, but her anger subsided into sorrow. When she was a girl, she had loved the story about God creating a beautiful garden for his children. A perfect place. God wanted beauty and peace for this world, not death and destruction. He didn't want any of his children to suffer.

She didn't want to be like clouds, chasing one dream to the next. She wanted to be like the mountains. Stalwart and strong. She had nothing left except this wagon of supplies—and no one really who was required to care for her—but she prayed He would never leave her. Just like so many emigrants refused to let the trials on this trail stop them, she didn't want the trials in this life to stop her from journeying forward.

She began to drift to sleep when an oxen bellowed near her tent. Then a gunshot echoed outside. Leaping up, she reached for the rifle beside her and moved to the opening of her tent. Outside were two of the men in their company, and in the lantern light, she saw a dead cougar at one of their feet.

She shivered. Perhaps it was time for them to finish this journey.

Payton hurried up to her tent. "Are you okay?"

"I'm fine." She stepped outside. "How is Faith?"

"Safe in her tent. Molly—" he started.

"What is it?"

"I'd feel a whole lot better if you started pitching your tent on the other side of mine."

"I don't want to be an obligation, Payton."

"You're not an obligation."

He looked as if he was prepared to argue his case, but she wasn't going to fight. She'd certainly feel better pitching her tent closer to him and Faith—tomorrow night. There wouldn't be any use in trying to sleep again tonight.

Inside her tent again, she quickly folded up her bedroll and then tore down her tent. After the men hauled away the cougar, she began stirring batter to make johnnycakes by lantern light.

As she ate breakfast, dawn broke with brilliant shards of light over the hills. Faith called her name, and Molly rounded the side of the wagon to find her friend.

Faith was standing up on the bench, her eyes focused west. "You have to see this."

All Molly could see from the ground were terraces of yellowed grass on the bluffs in front of them. "What is it?"

Faith pointed toward a small cliff that rose above their wagons. "Come this way." She hopped off the wagon and reached for Payton's arm. "You have to come as well."

The three of them scurried up the rocks, and Molly looked down below at a blue thread of a river. Then she lifted her eyes, and before them, rising above the hills and valley, a giant white peak pierced the autumn sky.

"Mount Hood," she whispered.

Faith took her arm. "And Oregon City will be on the other side."

Payton reached for his sister's hand, and then he reached for one of Molly's hands as well. Faith prayed first, thanking God for bringing them to Oregon. Then Payton prayed and asked for protection for the remainder of their journey.

Molly's heart was filled with a strange mixture of sorrow and joy. Sadness that Adam wasn't with her to enjoy this beautiful site. Joy that she was able to see it for both of them, along with the hope that this new world was filled with beautiful mountains.

Neither Faith nor Samuel asked her to pray, but she paused to thank God out loud for bringing her west with her friends.

Charley blasted his bugle, signaling it was time for them to begin rolling toward this great mountain, and Molly's feet felt light as she guided her oxen away from the cougar who'd threatened them—and from the loneliness of the night.

She would complete Adam's journey, and then perhaps she could start a new journey on her own. Like the thousands of miles she'd walked to cross this country, she would take it one slow step at a time.

She would never forget her husband, but she could feel God slowly stitching back together her shredded heart.

—m—

Payton stared at the row of wooden and brick buildings as they descended the western slope of Holcomb Hill into the valley before them. After five months of traveling, they'd finally arrived in Oregon City.

A waterfall spanned across the entire Willamette River above town and then spilled into the river coursing through the valley. Their company's livestock milled by the riverbank, behind George Abernathy's general store, and in that moment, he felt overwhelmed with gratitude that they'd made it.

But life as they'd known it on the trail was about to radically change.

Faith had been ecstatic the past week, her pace quickening, while it almost seemed to him that Molly lagged behind on this last stretch, reluctant to finish their journey. Now that they'd arrived, Faith's attention would, of course, turn to her husband and the new school. He knew Molly well enough to know she'd be thrilled for Faith, but it would also be hard for her to rejoice when her husband was gone.

Charley led their company to a grassy meadow, but this time, they didn't circle up. Instead he stood up on the back of a wagon to speak, holding his rifle at his side. "It's been a pleasure bringing you all to Oregon," he announced. "You're on your own from here, but no one's gonna stop you from camping in this meadow until you find something more permanent. I wish you all luck in God's country."

Someone started clapping behind Payton, and they all joined in the applause as Charley climbed down from the wagon and shook each of their hands. Then he hopped on his horse and rode north.

And their company began to disband.

Molly stood beside her wagon, petting one of her oxen, and Payton knew she was trying to be strong. Faith was inside their wagon, changing into the fancy blue dress that she'd reserved just for this day.

"Molly—" Payton started, and when she turned toward him, he could see the questioning in her eyes. "I'd like to talk to you this morning."

Faith emerged from the back of the wagon looking quite proper in her dress of ribbons and lace and a clean white bonnet. Payton helped her step down onto the dusty ground, and she looped her arm through Molly's. "You're coming to stay with us, aren't you?"

Molly scanned the bluffs lining the river valley. "I don't know."

"But you must—"

Molly nodded back toward the general store. "I was going to check and see if Mr. Abernathy needs help for the winter."

"You're staying with us," Faith insisted.

Payton stepped up beside them. "Give her a little time, Faith."

Molly's smile looked strained when she spoke again. "Samuel's waiting for you."

Faith glanced back and forth between them before nodding her head. "Will you meet us back here?" she asked.

Molly nodded, and when she turned away from them, Payton watched her walk toward the waterfall.

Faith nudged him. "You should go to her."

He shook his head. "Not quite yet."

"But soon—"

"Let's go find your husband." He extended his arm, and she looped her arm through his as she'd done with Molly.

They left their livestock and wagon tied to the cottonwood trees before moving down the street, past clapboard and brick buildings. Instead of talking, Faith scanned the faces of the men walking along the street, searching for her husband among them.

A group of school-age children were throwing sticks into the river, and Faith stopped to speak with them. "Could you please tell us where your school is located?"

One of the older boys stepped forward. "Which school do you want?"

"What are the options?" she asked.

The boy shrugged. "An old one and a new one."

"Is the new one run by a man named Samuel Lancaster?"

"Dunno," he said as he threw another stick into the fast-moving current. "My pa don't send me to school."

She sighed at his response. "Where is the new school?"

"Down two streets, to the left," the boy said. "Right next to the church."

"Very good," she said before thanking him. As they walked away, she muttered, "I'm going to talk to his father."

Payton smiled. "I'm sure you will."

"All those boys should be in school."

He glanced up at the sky and saw dark clouds forming in the west. If they didn't hurry, Faith's new dress might be ruined in a downpour.

His sister didn't seem to notice the looming clouds, but her pace quickened as they turned the corner. They found the clapboard school building beside the church, like the boy said, and across from the school was an apple tree, the branches heavy with fruit. In spite of all her talk about the apple trees in Oregon, Faith ignored it now. She stared instead at the door for the school.

Payton nudged her forward. "Knock on it."

She took a deep breath before rapping on the wood.

When no one answered, she pounded harder. "Samuel?"

Seconds later, the door opened, and his old friend stood before them, dressed in a black waistcoat and trousers. The surprise in his eyes turned to pure joy as he engulfed Faith in his arms. Then he lifted her up and spun her around. "I didn't think you'd ever arrive."

He turned to shake Payton's hand. "We weren't certain ourselves."

Samuel pulled his wife close to him. "I'm so glad you've come."

Payton cleared his throat, and Samuel opened the door wide for both of them. Inside the building were rows of roughly hewn benches with a blackboard hanging from the whitewashed wall in front of the classroom. Windows lined one side of the room while the other displayed a world map and an American flag along with a shelf of books. "I can help you build desks," Payton said.

"We're going to need quite a few of them," Samuel told them, his arm around his wife's waist. "We have twenty-five students registered, and I'm getting at least one new pupil a day."

"We're both ready to work," Faith said as she smiled up at him. "And we brought someone with us whom I'm hoping can help as well."

Samuel's eyebrows glanced back at the open door behind them. "Who did you bring?"

"Her name is Molly Goodwin," Faith explained. "She's smart and good with medicine—she helped save my life when I got cholera."

"Cholera?" He studied her face, his eyes distraught as he seemed to search for any trace of the disease.

"I'm fine now."

He pulled her close to him again. "I could have lost you."

She nodded solemnly. "Molly lost her husband on the trail."

He glanced back toward Payton as if he wanted to ask a few questions, but he didn't probe. "We could use the help if Mrs. Goodwin doesn't require much in the way of a salary yet."

Payton nodded toward the steps. "I think she'd be quite satisfied with meals and a good place to sleep for now." Surely she'd take that over a job at Abernathy's general store.

"We can offer her both of those," his friend said.

Samuel's gaze rested back on his wife, and as they smiled at each other, any time lost between them seemed to disappear.

Payton stepped back toward the hallway. "I think I'll go check on Molly."

Samuel glanced back over. "You don't have to leave," he said, though his words lacked conviction.

"I believe I do," Payton said as he placed his hat back on his head. Now that they were in Oregon, there were a few things he'd like to say to Mrs. Goodwin.

Chapter 10

Molly sat on a flat rock at the base of the waterfall, the droplets spraying her face and hands. Above her, storm clouds were weaving together like blue and gray patchwork across the late afternoon sky, but she refused to let the impending storm stop her.

As she untied her bonnet, she leaned back against another large rock. Every crevice around her seemed to be ablaze with life, and she soaked in all the details—the autumn leaves that colored the trees, the steep cliffs on the far side of the river, the ducks that paddled far from the splash of the falls. To the east, Mount Hood stood as a memorial of sorts in the distance, its snow-flanked peak soaring above the storm clouds.

She and Adam had dreamed together for so long about coming west, and she'd done it. For both of them.

Glancing down at the gold band around her finger, she slowly slid it off. She'd been faithful to her vows to Adam, and she'd been faithful to their journey. Death may have parted them, but she'd never forget the man who'd been her husband. And she'd never forget his dreams for life in this beautiful country before her.

It was time for her to let go of Adam's dreams and start anew now. She needed to cling to God's faithfulness as she stepped fully into this dream He'd given her.

"Good-bye, my love," she whispered as she lowered Adam's ring into the cold water. The gold glistened in the fading sunlight, and she watched it for a moment before she let it go. The ring twirled in the current, and then it was gone.

Lightning flashed in the distance, and she turned away from the river. The fear in her heart was subsiding, but she didn't want to be here alone in this storm.

Now that she was in Oregon, she was ready to work as hard as any other woman here. Even though she wanted to work at the school with Faith, she knew now it would be impossible for her to continue alongside Payton.

He had been so kind to her, allowing her to accompany him and Faith to Oregon City and helping her along the way. He treated her as he did Faith, as a faithful brother in caring for her needs when necessary, but her heart had begun to long for more.

Hopefully, one of the general stores would have a position for her. She was in Oregon, and she would do everything she could to embrace this new adventure on her own.

—◆—

Payton stood beside the lumber mill as he watched Molly release her wedding ring to the river. She had honored Adam by traveling so far and completing this dream for both of them. Even though the ring was gone, Payton hoped she would hold on to the good memories forever.

Before they began this trip, he'd promised her friendship, but he didn't know how

BECKONED HEARTS

he could fulfill that promise now. After their long journey together, he couldn't imagine living in Oregon without Molly, as much more than a friend. God had used her to put hope back into his heart—hope that he might love again in the future. Hope that he would have someone to share his own heart and dreams. Hope that perhaps she would start a new adventure with him.

But even though she'd fulfilled Adam's dream, it didn't mean she would want to remarry. Nor did it mean she'd want to marry him. Still he had to ask—

He stepped up beside her in the meadow. "Are you okay?"

She nodded, though her gaze was still on the river.

"I'd like you to meet Samuel," he said, holding out his hand.

She looked down at his hand for a moment before taking it, and they quietly walked through the town. It hadn't started to rain, but the streets were empty now. It seemed as if everyone had retreated back into their homes before the storm.

Across from the school door was a bench, under the apple tree, and he motioned Molly toward it. He plucked off a piece of fruit from the tree and handed it to her as they sat, but instead of eating it, she rolled it between her hands. He'd admired her for her strength and wisdom from the beginning. And her beauty. She was much more than a pretty gal, as Charley once called her. She was an absolutely stunning woman, both inside and out, and he loved her deeply.

She glanced over at him. "Is something wrong?"

"No. I—" He stopped.

"What is it?"

"I don't think I can do this, Molly."

Her eyes widened. "Do what?"

"Live in Oregon without you."

She fiddled with the apple again. "It was kind of you to bring me here, Payton, but you don't have to care for me anymore."

He took the apple from her hands and then enclosed her fingers with his. When she looked up at him again, he saw tears rimming her pale blue eyes. He knew her heart was still tender, but if he didn't ask her now, he feared she would leave here soon, journeying farther into the wilderness beyond them. God was the only one who could heal her heart, but perhaps, if she'd let him, he could help her love again.

"I don't want to press you." He studied her face again, the sun-kissed freckles on her slender nose and the waves in her soft brown hair. "But I want you to stay here with Faith and me."

She shook her head. "I can't—"

"I know you can live on your own, Molly." He hesitated. "But I don't know anymore how to live without you."

Her lips trembled. "What are you saying?"

"I'd like it—" He took a deep breath. "I'd be honored if you would marry me."

A breeze rustled the leaves above them, and a chill swept over his skin. What if she said no? What if she left this evening and he couldn't find her again?

She glanced back at the schoolhouse across the street. "My heart is still broken."

"I want to help you put it back together again."

Rain began to fall from the dark clouds, but neither of them stood. Instead her gaze returned to meet his. "Do you love me, Payton?"

He pulled her hands to his chest. "With all my heart."

When she smiled at him, he no longer noticed the rain.

"Then why have you been avoiding me?" she asked.

"I started loving you in those hours that you helped me fight for Faith's life, but I was terrified to tell you."

"And now?"

"I'm still terrified."

"You shouldn't be," she said softly.

Hope erupted in his chest, and he wrapped his arms around her, pulling her to him. Then he lifted her chin and kissed her lips, wet from the rain.

"It's about time."

Molly pushed away from him, and they both looked across the street to see his sister standing with her hands on her hips. Samuel slipped out the door behind Faith and put his hands on his wife's shoulders. "Faith was just telling me she hoped we might have a wedding soon," he said.

Payton glanced back over at Molly. "I'm hoping Faith is right."

Molly inched closer to him again. "Your sister is always right."

When she smiled again, he took her hand, and they crossed the street.

He'd thought his journey had come to an end, but he was wrong. He and Molly would begin a new journey of healing and hope, dreaming this time together.

Shanghaied by the Bride

by Pam Hillman

Chapter 1

Cassidy. . .he's awake!"

Blake Samuelson groaned as the high-pitched screech shot through his aching skull. *Who was Cassidy?* And why was his bed swaying from side to side? Was Missouri having one of those rare earthquakes he'd heard about? He struggled to open his eyes, to get out of bed and out of the ramshackle boardinghouse before it collapsed and buried him beneath a mountain of half-rotten boards.

The sound of jingling harnesses seeped into his consciousness, and his back jolted against something hard. He squinted at the off-white canvas top swaying above him.

Not a boardinghouse. A wagon.

Movement at the rear of the prairie schooner caught his attention, and shifting, he came face-to-face with a middle-aged woman wedged between boxes, crates, and sacks of foodstuffs, her arms wrapped securely around a little girl.

"Who are you?" Blake glowered at the woman. "And why am I in this wagon?"

The woman pulled the child closer, her gaze flickering to the front of the wagon. "Cassidy. . ."

The apprehension in her voice set Blake's teeth on edge. What was going on here? He needed answers and needed them fast. The Beecher party was due to hit the Oregon Trail at sunrise, and he still hadn't been able to purchase a dependable wagon anywhere in Independence. Beecher had been clear when Blake signed on: anyone who was late got left behind. No ifs, ands, or buts.

And Blake didn't intend to be late. He needed only to find a wagon.

A hazy memory of being slapped upside the head with something akin to a stick of dynamite and dragged into an alley assaulted him, but he had no memory of what happened after that. Worry slammed into his gut, and he ran a hand over his stomach searching for his money pouch. His groan had nothing to do with the pain in his head.

Gone.

He tossed one more disgruntled look at the woman and child and levered himself up, ignoring the white-hot throbbing at the back of his skull.

The jostling, jolting wagon attempted to throw him on his backside, but he focused on the man driving the wagon, floppy hat pulled low. He crawled forward over the tops of trunks, tools, and gewgaws and grabbed the man called Cassidy by the arm. "Mister, stop this wagon. Right now."

"Can't." The driver threw him a glance, and Blake did a double take. It wasn't a man on that wagon seat, but a pretty young woman wearing a floppy hat. And not just any hat. *His* hat. He raked his gaze over the familiar coat that swallowed her whole. And *his* coat.

"What is going on? Who are you?"

"Cassidy Taylor. And Beecher said we couldn't stop until he gave us leave." The wagon veered off the trail as the mules pulled left, searching for the fresh green tufts of grass by the wayside.

The woman called Cassidy turned back to the task at hand, slapped the reins against the mules, and struggled to pull the ornery beasts back on course. Blake squinted at the long line of wagons snaking along in front of them, the morning sun pushing them westward. Whole families walked alongside the wagons, and a girl swatted the haunches of a milk cow tied to the wagon directly in front of them. The discontented animal bellowed and strained against the lead rope, tail switching.

Beecher rode down the line, pointing and giving instructions to each driver. Blake rubbed the knot on his head, wondering if his senses were playing tricks on him. But no, that was Beecher all right, and the creaking wagons, jingling harnesses, and the dust churned up by fifty or more wagons heading west couldn't be ignored. Wagons-ho had been called, and he'd been out cold for the festivities. He climbed over the seat back and plopped down next to the woman.

"I don't care what Beecher says. You're going to turn this wagon around right now."

Eyebrows the color of coffee with a heavy dollop of cream lowered over robin's-egg blue eyes. "You signed on with the Beecher party, didn't you? Why would you want to turn around now?"

"Because this ain't my wagon, and those aren't my. . ." His mouth fell open, and he stabbed a finger toward the team of six. "Wait a cotton-pickin' minute. Those are my mules. Lady, you've got some explaining to do. And *give me my hat!*"

He jerked his hat off her head and plopped it on his own, satisfied that he was in control of something this morning. She blushed all the way to the roots of her honey-blond hair and looked mighty pretty doing it. Plumb disgusted at himself for noticing her eyes, her hair, or anything else about Cassidy Taylor, he made a grab for the reins, intending to stop the wagon and straighten this whole mess out.

Beecher swept toward them, his dappled-gray mare prancing along, anxious to move faster than the plodding pace set by the wagons. Blake nodded in the wagon master's direction. "Finally. Somebody who can give me some answers."

Panic swept over Cassidy's face, and she clutched his forearm, her long tapered fingers warming his skin through his thin work shirt. "Don't say anything to Beecher. Please? I can explain."

That knock on his head must have addled his brain because Blake stared into her sky-blue eyes, anxiously begging him to honor her request even as Beecher reined up beside them.

"Morning, Samuelson. I see you found a wagon after all."

Blake scowled at Cassidy before facing the wagon master. He gave the man a clipped nod. "Yes, sir."

"Good." Beecher nodded. "It woulda been a shame to miss the last train out of

Independence. We'll keep moving until the noon hour. Let the animals work out the kinks. They'll be ready for a slow, leisurely stroll this afternoon." He tipped his hat, his attention on his horse and his responsibilities. "Ma'am."

As soon as Beecher moved on, Blake settled his hat more firmly on his head and glowered at Cassidy.

"Start talking."

Chapter 2

Cassidy wanted to snatch the hat back if for no other reason than to have something to hide behind.

"Well. . ." She squirmed on the wagon seat, unsure how to begin. "We found you unconscious behind the livery this morning—"

"Who's *we*?"

"My mother, and my sister, and I."

"So you just decided to kidnap me—"

"It wasn't like that!" Cassidy peeked sideways at the man Beecher had called Mr. Samuelson. His large, capable hands—scarred and nicked—held the reins with ease, in contrast to the clenched tightness of his blunt jaw, shadowed with a week's worth of dark stubble. "I'll explain, if you'll listen. It was almost daylight, and Mr. Cummins—"

"The liveryman, the one who sold me six mules but was fresh out of wagons?"

"That's the one. Anyway, when I found you unconscious, I didn't know what to do, so I ran to get help. I thought you needed a doctor, but Mr. Cummins said there wasn't time, that Beecher wouldn't wait."

Cassidy's face flamed anew at Mr. Cummins's assumption that the unconscious man was her husband. Without giving her a chance to explain, the liveryman had informed her that she'd better get a move on. Beecher waited for no man—and especially not a woman. As a matter of fact, it was common knowledge that Beecher wouldn't let women and children travel with his party without the provision and protection of an able-bodied man. Which was utterly ridiculous if you asked her.

Within minutes, the livery owner and his son had tossed the man in her wagon and took the liberty of hooking up his mules. Without thinking through the consequences of her actions, Cassidy had donned the man's coat and hat and fell into place in the long line of wagons headed to Oregon.

"Mr. Beecher was chomping at the bit, so I just, uh, brought you along with us."

"You just brought me along? Mighty convenient to use my own mules to do it." He snorted, sounding a lot like one of his ornery mules.

"Well, it would've been ill-advised to leave the mules behind, now, wouldn't it?" Cassidy didn't bother to hide her sarcasm as she crossed her arms, wishing she could have left *him* behind. But Beecher had her over a barrel, and she needed the man whether she liked it or not.

Brows drawn down into a dark storm cloud, he slapped the reins against the mules' backs. "What about your own mules?"

"Didn't have any." Cassidy shrugged. "Cummins sold you the last ones he had."

"And the wagon?" His gaze—as dark as day-old coffee left on the stove—slid toward hers, narrow and assessing.

"I bought it yesterday morning off an elderly couple who'd turned back." She chafed that she'd spent a chunk of her precious funds on the wagon before she'd found out Beecher's strict rule about women traveling alone.

"Figures." Samuelson grunted.

"I brought your plunder," she offered, the words an olive branch she hoped would soften the thunderclouds on his face. "What was left anyway."

"Mighty decent of you."

Tears pricked Cassidy's eyes and she turned away, pretending to watch the rolling hills and tufts of early spring grass that had sprung up overnight along the trail. Had she made a huge mistake? But what other choice did she have? There'd been no time to stop and think, no time to pray about her decision, or discuss it with Mama. Would Mr. Samuelson insist they turn around? Would he let his pride get in the way of the one chance they both had of making it to Oregon before winter set in?

"Why don't you tell me the real reason you shanghaied me?"

Cassidy sucked in a quick breath. "I told you why."

"No, you didn't. You told me why you brought my mules, and you told me why you had to do it in a hurry. But you didn't tell me why you brought *me* along for the ride. You could have given Cummins enough money for the mules and left me behind, but you didn't. Why?"

"Mr. Samuelson—"

"Why?"

"Because. . .because Mr. Beecher has a rule. Every wagon has to have a"—the reason stuck in her throat, and it galled her to have to say it, but she forced the words out—"a *man* along, or the wagon's not allowed to join the party."

His thick, dark brows slammed together like two fuzzy black caterpillars butting heads over the bridge of his perfectly straight nose. "What did you say?"

"I said Mr. Beecher insists—"

"I heard what you said. But I'm not sure I understood it. Are you're saying that Beecher thinks that"—he paused and blew out a long, slow breath—"that we're *married*? To each other?"

Cassidy squirmed. "Well, I didn't exactly *say* that. Beecher was in a bit of a hurry this morning, and we were the last wagon to arrive. He just glowered at me and growled out, 'Samuelson family?'"

"And you said yes?"

She nodded. "I didn't know what else to do, Mr. Samuelson. It all happened so fast."

He shook his head, the scowl on his face telling her that he thought she'd lost her mind. "Might as well call me Blake. No sense in standing on ceremony if all these fine folks think we're one big, happy family."

—⁓—

Blake clenched his jaw and focused on a spot between the lead mule's ears so that he wouldn't say or do something he'd regret.

How had his simple plan to start a new life in California unraveled so quickly?

When Mr. Kirkwood's brother had written that he could use help in his smithy, Blake had pulled up stakes and headed west. There was nothing left for him in Mississippi—there never had been, really, but with the old man dead and gone, now had been the time for him to start over. But since those thieves had taken his money and left him at the mercy of Cassidy Taylor and Beecher, he'd have to tread carefully. At least he still had his mules and, if Miss Taylor could be trusted, his meager supply of tools.

He tossed a quick glance at Cassidy, her slender form ramrod straight beside him. "Beecher's going to ask questions eventually."

She pursed her lips. "Well, you could be our hired hand."

"Beecher will never allow that. This is the Samuelson wagon—"

"Samuelson mules. Taylor wagon."

"As far as Beecher's concerned, the mules and the wagon are signed up under my name. There aren't any Taylors on this wagon train."

Her face paled a bit. "You wouldn't—wouldn't—throw us out?"

"Serve you right if I did." Blake shook his head. "But no, I reckon not."

They rode in silence for a few minutes, which Blake liked just fine. He needed time to think. Suddenly she faced him, the flame of blue fire back in her eyes. "What would you have done if I hadn't found you? If Cummins hadn't thought we were together?"

Blake propped one foot on the footboard and settled his hat more firmly, unwilling to air his financial straits with a woman who'd kidnapped him. Instead, he turned the tables on her. "What about you? The way I see it, you're riding my coattails on this wagon train. What would you have done without me? Would you have gone back to wherever you came from?"

Panic skimmed across her face, as quick and sharp as the flicker of a flame. She faced forward, and he thought she wasn't going to answer. After a moment, she shook her head. "No. There's nothing to go back to, and not enough money left to survive in Independence a whole year either. Joining Beecher's wagon train is my last hope if we're going to file a claim and get in a crop before next year."

Last hope.

A tight band of compassion clamped around Blake's chest. Cassidy Taylor and her mother and sister in the wagon were betwixt a rock and a hard place, much like he was. None of them could go backward.

The mules slowed, and Blake slapped the reins against their backs. "Well, looks like we don't have much choice but to keep going. We'll deal with Beecher when we have to."

"Giddyup, there!"

Chapter 3

Within an hour, the wagons strung out along the trail, the draft animals plodding along nice and easy-like. Cassidy and her sister joined those who abandoned the spine-jolting wagon beds in favor of walking.

Julene made fast friends with the girls from the wagon just ahead of them, and Cassidy smiled as her little sister skipped along, laughing and talking and gathering wildflowers. It wouldn't be long before she'd grow weary of walking and beg to ride again. But the more they all walked, the better off the mules would be in the long run.

Blake, Cassidy, and her mother took turns driving and walking throughout the day and didn't speak of their questionable relationship again. The sun hung low in the west by the time Beecher called a halt along a creek a good twelve to fifteen miles west of Independence. The stoop-shouldered farmer from the wagon they'd trailed all day started unharnessing his mules and nodded in Blake's direction.

"Howdy. The name's George Atwood." He motioned to the stout woman beside him. "And this is my wife, Gertie."

"Blake Samuelson." Blake nodded in her direction. "Mrs. Taylor and her daughters Cassidy and Julene."

"Where you folks from?"

"Mississippi," Blake replied.

"Indiana," Cassidy responded at the same time.

A frown of confusion puckered Mr. Atwood's brow, and his attention swiveled from Blake to Cassidy and back again. Blake recovered quickly. "Well, I'm from Mississippi. Mrs. Taylor and her girls hail from Indiana."

"I see." Mr. Atwood nodded. "What part of Mississippi? I've got kinfolk down that way."

The men led the animals away so they could graze, and the women started setting up camp. Within minutes, Gertie Atwood and Cassidy's mother were deep in a discussion about the quickest way to share chores. In the end, they agreed that a communal campsite would be ideal and would make cooking easier for all concerned.

It didn't take long for Gertie to pull a young mother named Eliza Ann into their circle. Eliza Ann clutched the hand of a gapped-toothed toddler while riffling through the contents of her wagon. Clucking like a mother hen, Gertie convinced the shy young mother to pass the child off to one of the girls.

"I don't know what hurts worse, my feet from walking or my back from riding." Gertie bustled to the back of her wagon and pulled out an iron kettle.

"Angus doesn't want me to walk." Eliza Ann pressed a hand to her stomach.

"Land sakes, child, are you in the family way already?"

Eliza Ann blushed and nodded.

"What is that man of yours thinking?" Gertie tsked, tsked as she bustled about the campsite.

"He's thinking of our future." Eliza Ann's face glowed with excitement.

Gertie harrumphed and wagged a finger at Cassidy. "Now, I hope you don't end up with child, too. One baby on this trip will be quite enough, thank you very much."

"But, Mrs. Atwood—"

"Call me Gertie. I daresay we're gonna get to know each other real well before this trip's over."

"Yes, ma'am—Gertie. Blake and I aren't married. He's just..." Cassidy tried to think how to explain the situation. "We combined resources to make the trip, and we'll part ways as soon as we reach Oregon."

Eliza Ann gasped, and Gertie's mouth opened and closed like a fish left too long on a creek bank. "Not married, you say?"

"Who's not married?" Cassidy groaned as Beecher strode into their midst. She opened her mouth to explain, but nothing emerged but a squeak. With Gertie and Eliza Ann staring at her like she'd grown two heads, it didn't take Beecher long to figure out exactly who wasn't married to whom.

His face blanched as recognition dawned. He wagged a finger at her. "You...you're the young lady who came to see me yesterday, the one who wanted to go to Oregon. The *single* young lady."

"Yes, sir." Cassidy took a deep breath. "I can explain—"

His gaze landed on their wagon. "And that's Samuelson's wagon."

Cassidy didn't think it was a good time to tell him that the wagon was hers. "Uh, yes, sir."

"Where is he?" He glowered at the group of women. "I'm going to get to the bottom of this. I won't have it. Pretending to be married so that you can travel on my wagon train, when I very clearly explained—"

"Oh hush, Horace." Gertie interrupted his tirade. "Nobody's pretending anything. Cassidy up and told me straight out that she and Mr. Samuelson aren't married. If they'd wanted to deceive you, do you think she would have told me that?"

"Gertie, now you just hush up. This ain't none of your affair."

"Mama?" Eyes wide, Julene huddled close to their mother.

"Don't worry. Everything's fine." Cassidy reassured her sister, praying it would be as she listened to the exchange between Gertie and the wagon master.

"It's just as much mine as it is yours, Horace Beecher. And don't you tell me to hush up."

Cassidy stepped forward, heart pounding. She didn't want Beecher to have it in for Gertie on account of her. "Mr. Beecher, this whole thing is my fault. Somebody knocked Mr. Samuelson out cold and stole his money. And this morning Mr.

Cummins thought we were together—" The whole sorry tale spilled out of her in one mad rush of words.

Beecher grimaced. "Figures that Cummins would be mixed up in something like this. The old codger's probably laughing his head off by now."

Chapter 4

One glimpse of the women standing like frozen statues around Beecher, and Blake knew the gig was up.

"Well, trouble's brewing already." George chuckled. "That didn't take long."

Blake frowned at the affable man, not finding one thing funny about the situation. Young Angus hurried to his wife's side, both of them acting like kids with their hands caught in the candy jar, and they hadn't done anything wrong as far as Blake knew. Nope, he suspected the thundercloud on Beecher's face was aimed directly at him.

"Evening, Horace. You and Gertie at it again?" George grinned, his voice tinged with laughter.

Without acknowledging George or the odd mention of his wife, Beecher's attention zeroed in on Blake.

"Samuelson! What is the meaning of this?" He shook his finger in Cassidy's direction, his face rivaling the red-and-gold streaks crisscrossing the horizon to the west. "How long did you think you could pull the wool over my eyes?"

"There was never any intention of deceiving you, Mr. Beecher. I was robbed, and—"

"I know what happened." Beecher held up a hand to stop the lengthy explanation. "*Miss* Taylor has already explained everything."

Blake glanced at Cassidy, standing guard over her mother and sister. Beecher jerked his hat off and jabbed a finger eastward. "I could send the entire lot of you back to Independence for this."

"Oh, Horace, don't be ridiculous." Gertie plopped her hands on her hips. "It's a day's ride back, and what are they going to do when they get there? Blake's already told you that he's in dire straits because of those no-account thieves who waylaid him. And besides, you're right."

"I'm right?" Beecher eyed Gertie as if he'd just stepped over a rock and found a rattler sunning on the other side.

"Of course you are." She smirked at him. "It certainly won't hurt for Cassidy and her ma to have a big, strong feller like Mr. Samuelson along to take care of them."

"Well, then, in that case, we'll just"—Beecher slapped his hat against his trousers—"we'll just go ahead and get you two hitched right now and be done with it."

"Now hold on." Blake held up both hands and backed away. "Nobody's getting married."

"Why in the blue blazes not?" Beecher rounded on Blake. "You ain't already got a wife, have you, Samuelson?"

"Of course not. But—"

"Then there's nothing to stop you from marrying Miss Taylor, and then we can all go on toward Oregon as one big, happy family."

Blake winced as the words he'd spoken so casually earlier in the day were thrown back in his face. He raked a hand through his hair. "There's just one thing about that, Mr. Beecher. I'm not going to Oregon. I'm going to California."

Beecher blinked, his attention swinging from Blake to Cassidy and back again. "Wal, I reckon there's plenty of time for you folks to decide your final destination before we reach Fort Hall."

"I'm not marrying Miss Taylor."

"Rules are rules, Samuelson. I'll allow you and the Taylors to stay until morning, but then you'll have to head back to Independence."

"Horace, can I have a word with you and George?" Gertie asked. "Alone."

"Not now, Gertie."

"Yes, now."

"This better be important." Beecher stomped off after Gertie. George grinned but followed along as if he was enjoying the show.

Blake squinted into the gathering twilight after the three of them. What was that woman up to? Whatever it was, it gave him some time to straighten things out. He turned on a boot heel and hurried toward Cassidy, grabbing her by the arm and pulling her into the shadows between the wagons.

She whirled on him. "Why didn't you tell me you were going to California?"

"I thought you knew."

"How would I know that? Everybody goes to Oregon."

Exasperated, Blake anchored his hands against his hips to keep from throttling her. "If everybody went to Oregon, there wouldn't be a California Trail, now would there?" A couple strolled by, giving them a curious glance, and Blake nodded at them. "Evening, folks."

When the couple moved on, he lowered his voice. "Besides, what difference does it make?"

"It'll make a lot of difference when we get to Fort Hall." Cassidy's eyes flashed blue in the reflection from the campfire. "So, you're determined to go to California?"

"Yes. And you?"

"Oregon." She lifted her chin. "So marrying each other is out of the question. And besides, I don't even know you."

"I don't know you either, so we're even." He sucked in a deep breath then slowly exhaled. Arguing wasn't getting them anywhere. "Beecher's determined to see this thing through or else. Are you prepared to go back to Independence?"

Worry churned his gut. Could he survive a year in Independence? The place was teeming with folks just like him—too broke to go on and too broke to go back.

"I promised Pa we'd go to Oregon. I can't—" Her attention flickered toward the fire where her mother and sister waited. She bit her lip, and he could see the indecision warring across her face. She squared her shoulders and faced him. "Oregon, and I'll marry you."

Blake's temper spiked like sparks from a forge. Cassidy Taylor had shanghaied him, used his own mules to haul him halfway across Missouri, and now she wanted him to roll over like a lapdog and trot along to Oregon with her.

"California," he gritted the word out, slowly, one syllable at a time. "Or Beecher can send us all back to Independence."

His heart slammed against his rib cage then shuddered like a trapped animal. What had he just done? Somehow he'd agreed to marry Cassidy Taylor if she'd go to California with him.

She searched his face, hers pale in the waning light. "I. . .I—"

"It's settled, then." Gertie's voice sliced through the tension between them. She came sailing back into camp, grinning from ear to ear, George right on her heels. There was no sign of Beecher.

"Horace has agreed to let Mr. Samuelson and the Taylor family remain with the wagon train, provided there isn't any hint of impropriety. George, Mrs. Taylor, and I will act as chaperones." She clapped her hands. "Now, isn't that just lovely?"

"But. . .but why?" Cassidy sputtered. "How?"

George laughed and tossed his arm across his dumpy wife's shoulders. "Didn't you know? Horace is Gertie's brother. He never could outsmart her."

Chapter 5

Cassidy struggled up the incline behind the wagon, careful of the steep drop-off to her left.

Gertie had joined her mother on the wagon seat, and the two women had their heads together plotting and planning who knows what. Hopefully something as innocent as supper. Gertie's laughter rang out, and Cassidy smiled. If she'd known the strong-willed woman was Mr. Beecher's sister, she would have befriended her before they ever left Independence.

It would have saved them all a lot of trouble.

Her *trouble* walked a few feet ahead of her, his long stride easily keeping pace with the mules. She swallowed, remembering Beecher's insistence on a wedding last night. Would she have said yes?

In the split second before Gertie had barged back into camp, Cassidy had spotted her mother and sister huddled around the campfire and known she'd do whatever it took to provide a home for them. Her pa had finally found his backbone and started making plans to go to Oregon after Grandma died. It had taken a year to sell their small plot of land, but then he'd died after no more than a week on the trail. Cassidy and her ma had made the decision to keep going. They'd worked too hard to get this far, and there was nothing to go back to even if they'd wanted to. But Gertie's intervention had given her a reprieve, and for that she was grateful.

She reached the top of the hill and started down the trail that snaked along the curve of the hill, watching her footing and the briar-lined drop-off to her left. The Atwood's cow jerked against the rope, bellowing as the wagon pulled her down the hill. Cassidy frowned. Where were the children? They'd had to switch the cow to keep her plodding along, but now she pulled against the rope, digging in every step of the way. She was going to break free if she didn't learn to accept being tethered to the wagon.

Even as Cassidy broke off a switch and urged the cow along, her thoughts and her attention strayed to Blake, his wide shoulders honed by years of pounding metal in a blacksmith shop, his confident stride eating up the miles. Would it be so bad to be married to Blake? Maybe. Maybe not. But physical strength wasn't everything. Her pa had proved that time and again.

Blake turned, his dark-eyed gaze catching hers. She took a deep breath and looked away, her heart fluttering against her rib cage. She wasn't opposed to marriage. She just didn't want to jump in before giving it a bit of thought. And maybe a bit of courtship. *Lord, if he's the man for me, show us both before we reach Fort Hall.*

George's cow dug in her hooves and strained against the rope. Cassidy swatted at the cow, one hand holding her skirt. "Get on up there, missy. You're making it hard on yourself."

Suddenly, the rope broke, and the cow, bellowing her displeasure, plowed backward toward Cassidy. She scrambled out of the way, tripped on the hem of her skirt, and tumbled over the edge of the steep drop-off, her skirts tangling around her legs as she rolled down the hill, her bonnet protecting her face from the briars.

By the time she rolled to a stop, she was covered in dirt, scratches, and cockleburs. She winced at the multitude of scrapes on her forearms and the backs of her hands. She pushed her hair back and saw half-a-dozen men scrambling down the hill to her aid. All strangers.

"Be ye hurt, lass?"

"Be careful now. She might have broken something."

"Yer hand, lass." The man with the Irish lilt reached for her and then pushed her ripped sleeve back. He shook his head. "Ye tangled wi' the blackberry bushes on th' way down."

"I'll be fine. Just a few scratches."

"Are ye sure?" He doffed his hat. "Flynn McGowan at your service."

"Yes, I'm fine. Thank you, Mr. McGowan."

"Flynn." He gave her a cocky grin, and if she didn't know better, she'd think he winked.

Cassidy spotted Blake in the sea of floppy hats and suspenders, his scowling face a welcoming sight among so many strangers. He pushed his way to her side and hunkered down.

"Cassidy, are you hurt?" Did she detect a hint of panic in his voice, in the way he shoved everybody else to the side like toothpicks?

"Her arms—"

Blake reached for her hand, his touch warm against her palm.

"It's just a few scratches." Cassidy spoke quietly, embarrassed at all the attention. "Can we just get back to the wagons? I don't want to hold everyone up."

He held her gaze for a moment then nodded. "Come on. Be careful now."

Blake and Flynn McGowan helped her to her feet, and she gingerly took a few steps. The rest of the men circled them like a bunch of mother hens around an injured chick. All the attention made her blush. The scratches burned, and she was certain she'd sustained even more on her legs, but she certainly wasn't going to share *that* with her rescuers. "I'm fine. Really. Thank you."

Everyone started back up the hill, struggling to make it through the brush and brambles. Blake grabbed her elbow on one side, and Mr. McGowan assisted from the other.

"Careful, lass."

Cassidy felt like a sack of flour being lugged up the hill as first Blake, then Flynn McGowan and a black-eyed man, who kept up an excited stream of Italian that she couldn't understand, manhandled her up the hillside. After what seemed like a lifetime, they neared the top. Cassidy cringed as her gaze scanned the trail. Half the wagon train had gathered to witness her embarrassing predicament.

"*Signorina?*"

Sighing, Cassidy took the Italian's hand and let him pull her toward him. Just a few more feet and she could slink back into obscurity. Suddenly, the dirt shifted, and the Italian lost his footing. Slack-jawed, he let go of her hand. Cassidy teetered on the steep hillside. Blake snagged Cassidy's waist and jerked her close against his chest with one corded arm.

In dismay she watched as the Italian pinwheeled, slammed into Flynn, and they both tumbled down the hill, landing in a tangle of arms and legs, boots and hats. The swarthy Italian jumped to his feet, gesturing with both hands, yelling at McGowan. Of course, McGowan gave back as good as he got.

A deep rumble vibrated in Blake's chest. Cassidy turned, spotted a twisted grin of amusement on his face, and bit her lip to keep from laughing out loud. His dark eyes met hers, the edges crinkled with amusement. His gaze swept over her face, from her forehead to her chin and back. Her stomach dipped, but she didn't think it had anything to do with the unstable ground underneath Blake's boots. She lowered her gaze, and he cleared his throat and shifted his hold on her. "Let's get you to the top."

Just as they reached level ground, Mr. Beecher rode up, reined in his horse, and took in the scene with an angry glare. McGowan and the Italian struggling up the hill, clothes torn and dirty, Cassidy clutched in Blake's arms, looking for all the world like she'd fought with a wildcat.

"What is going on?" Beecher ground out, edging his mount closer. "Samuelson, I warned you and Miss Taylor. . . ."

"Miss Taylor fell." Blake ripped off his hat and took his time slapping dust from his trousers. He settled the hat back on his head and lifted his chin, his square jaw hard as chiseled granite, his voice as cool as fresh-churned butter. "It's a good thing she didn't break her neck. Wouldn't you agree?"

The wagon master's gaze flickered, shifted from Blake to the crowd and back to Cassidy. "Yes, of course. All right, everybody. Show's over. Get back to your wagons and get moving."

"Watch your step from now on," Blake tossed over his shoulder as he stalked away.

Cassidy glared at his back. What bee had got under his bonnet?

It wasn't like she'd fallen on *purpose*.

Chapter 6

"Horace was fit to be tied today." George scarfed down a spoonful of beans and chased it with a bite of corn bread. "I thought he was going to have a conniption fit when he saw you and Cassidy on the side of that drop-off."

Blake arched an eyebrow. "It was your cow that started the whole thing."

"Yep. I shore was sorry about that. Ornery cow broke my rope, too. But the good news is that everybody's been mighty friendly tonight. Cassidy's bound to find herself a feller after this." George grinned and wagged his fork in Blake's direction. "You'd better step lively now."

"I've done all the stepping I plan to." For some reason Beecher—and now George—had gotten it into their heads that Cassidy Taylor needed a husband. And that he fit the bill.

Maybe she did and maybe she didn't, but that didn't mean Blake intended to be shoehorned into that role as well. He was already obligated to take care of the Taylors all the way to Fort Hall, but that didn't mean he was ready to make any lifetime commitments.

He stretched his legs and leaned back against a log, hat pulled low over his eyes as he surveyed the camp, quiet as all of Cassidy's admirers had finally ambled away to eat supper.

"Well, ladies, that was some mighty fine eating." George stood as Cassidy filled her plate and glanced around for a place to sit. "Here you go, missy. Take this spot. I 'spect you'd like to get off your feet after that tumble today."

"Thank you, George." She eased down onto the other end of the log, sucking in a sharp breath. Her dress, which had been light green this morning if Blake recalled, was streaked with dirt and ripped and torn in several places.

Flynn McGowan sauntered up, jauntily tipping his hat. "Ladies."

Somebody giggled, and Blake grimaced. Anybody with one eye and half sense could tell the man was up to no good.

"Flynn. Join us for a spell." George didn't miss the opportunity to invite him to sit, which Blake suspected was the reason McGowan just happened by their campsite in the first place.

"That's six. Or is it seven?" Blake muttered, low enough that only Cassidy would hear.

She glared at him.

He winked at her and ticked them off on his fingers. "Giovanni. Peter. And what was his name? That redheaded stick—"

"Hush up." She kicked a clod of dirt at him. "And the redheaded stick *is* Peter."

He laughed and pulled his hat lower. McGowan was the sixth man to come by to check on Cassidy since they'd made camp, and that didn't even include the ones who'd inquired after her while he was putting the mules out to pasture.

But McGowan was bolder than the rest. He sauntered around the campfire, stepped over Blake's legs without so much as a by-your-leave, and plopped down on the log close to Cassidy. Much too close in Blake's opinion.

McGowan tipped his hat. "Evening, lass."

"Mr. McGowan."

"I brought ye a bit of me ma's ointment. For yer hands." Flynn reached into his pocket and pulled out a small round tin. "Mrs. Atwood said ye might have need o' it."

"Thank you, but—"

Blake snorted. As if Mrs. Taylor didn't have plenty of salves to ease Cassidy's scratches. And they were barely noticeable. No, it was obvious the ointment was just an excuse for McGowan to come see Cassidy.

Cassidy smirked at Blake then held out her hand. "On second thought, I might need it after all. Thank you. And your mother."

Gertie dried her hands and glanced toward Mrs. Taylor before taking a step toward McGowan. "Flynn, dear, would you care to join us for supper?"

"Thank ye for the offer, ma'am, but me mam's got the pot bubblin' already."

"Some coffee, then?"

"A wee sip, then."

Gertie grinned as if she'd just found her long-lost son, and McGowan settled in as if he intended to stay for a while. Blake took another sip of coffee, studying Gertie and Mrs. Taylor from underneath the brim of his hat. What were those two up to? Was it possible they'd encouraged all these yahoos to stop by to check on Cassidy just to find her a beau? He bit back a smile. He wouldn't put it past Gertie, but Mrs. Taylor? He couldn't see her trying to pawn off her daughter. But Gertie was a force to be reckoned with when she made up her mind.

He rubbed a hand across his jaw, considering the situation. If one of these fellers started calling on Cassidy, then Beecher wouldn't have any reason to pursue his crazy notion of matrimony between Blake and Cassidy. With someone to take care of Cassidy and her mother, Blake could go on to California with a clear conscience when they reached Fort Hall.

He could see the merits of such a plan, and that might be Gertie's intention.

Then why did his stomach feel like the beans he'd just eaten for supper had been liberally doused with the cockleburs he'd plucked off his trousers after rescuing Cassidy Taylor today?

Chapter 7

Beecher called a halt on Sunday. After Sunday morning worship, the men repaired harness and shoed horses, and the women washed clothes.

Cassidy and her mother joined Gertie, Eliza Ann, and the other women at the riverbank, washing the week's worth of soiled clothes and draping them over bushes to dry.

Her mother shaded her eyes, frowning at the clouds gathering in the west. "I just hope it doesn't rain before all these clothes get dry."

"Johnnie, get back here." For the fourth time, Eliza Ann made a grab for her son as he headed toward the water. She finally tied a leather strip around his waist and tethered him to her.

Gertie hung the last of her family's laundry on the bushes. Plopping her hands on her hips, she eyed Eliza Ann with consternation. "Here, missy, let me help you."

Eliza Ann smiled, looking like a wilted flower as she tried to wash clothes and keep up with Johnnie at the same time. Without making much to-do, they'd all taken to coddling the expectant young mother. In no time, the three women had Eliza Ann's laundry spread out along with theirs, a colorful patchwork on the riverbank. Cassidy took Johnnie from her. "Why don't you go rest awhile? I'll mind Johnnie."

"Are you sure?" Eliza Ann looked hopeful. "A nap sounds wonderful."

"Pway." Johnny squealed and leaned toward the water.

Cassidy jiggled him on her hip and laughed. "I can't promise he won't be soaking wet when we get done."

"A nap is just what these old bones need." Gertie took Eliza Ann's arm and headed up the path toward the wagons. "We'll come back in a little while and help you fold the clothes. Coming, Elsie?"

Cassidy waved her mother away. "Go on. Johnnie and I'll be just fine, won't we?" She tried to keep from getting wet, but it was useless as she chased the rambunctious toddler. Soon the hem of her damp skirt was caked with mud from the river's edge. Sighing, she grabbed Eliza Ann's tether and tied it to Johnnie's waist. He never noticed, he was so busy squealing and splashing.

The other children, her sister among them, played and splashed in the shallows. The older boys swam downstream, and their whoops and hollers could be heard in the distance. It wasn't long before little Johnny tired. He'd pat the water, then his head would droop, but the splash would wake him up again. He'd squeal and play some more before nodding off again.

"Nap time for you, mister." Cassidy scooped him up in her arms.

"No. Pway."

"All right. Just a few more minutes. We need to wash all this dirt off you anyway."

As she cleaned him up, the clouds overhead blocked the sun, and a welcome breeze swept along the riverbank. A breeze that pushed the storm clouds closer and closer.

Cassidy decided not to wait any longer. The clothes were dry enough, and if the storm blew in they'd get wet all over again. She called out to Julene and the Atwood sisters. "Girls, I need some help over here."

"Ah, Cassidy."

"There's a storm brewing. We can't let these clothes get wet again." She handed the toddler to her sister. "Take Johnnie to his mother, and send Mama and Gertie to help us."

As soon as Julene left, Cassidy brushed the mud and muck from her clothes and washed her hands in the river. The other women collected their washing and headed toward the wagons, and Cassidy scrambled to gather the laundry for three different families, her attention on the approaching storm. The wind picked up, and the clouds swept across the broad sky. Cassidy hurried. She'd just sent the Atwood girls up the trail with two baskets of clothes when Angus and Blake came hurrying toward her. She thrust a basket of clothes at Angus as the first drops began to fall. "Here. Eliza Ann's."

"Thank you." He sheltered the basket against his chest. "Do you need help with the rest?"

"No, there's just one more basket."

Angus took off, and Cassidy rushed to the bushes and grabbed the rest of the laundry, tossing them into the remaining basket. Blake grabbed the basket and reached for her hand. "Ready?"

"Yes. Oh, wait, there's Julene's green pinafore." Cassidy hurried toward the dress, her boots sliding on the muddy bank. Suddenly, her feet flew out from under her, her arms pinwheeled, and she plunged toward the river, her scream cut off as the water closed over her head. As she beat against the water, trying to find her footing, Blake splashed toward her and plucked her from the shallows.

Cassidy stumbled up the bank. Grimacing, she lifted her skirts and peered at her shoes—her only pair—soaked. "Oh no."

"They'll dry." Blake lifted his face to the sky. The rain fell in sheets, drenching his head, face, and clothes, at least what hadn't gotten wet when he'd pulled her from the river. He plopped both hands on his hips, hiked an eyebrow, and grinned. "I don't suppose there's any need to hurry now."

"I suppose not."

He grabbed Julene's dress, draped it over the basket and hefted it with one hand. An amused smile lifted one corner of his mouth, and he held out his arm, crooked. "Let's try this again."

Cassidy blinked and took his arm. She lifted her skirt out of the muck, wincing at the sight of the mud. Hopefully the rain would wash most of it off before they reached the wagons.

She cast a sidelong glance at the water sluicing off Blake's hat along his shadowed jaw and soaking into his shirt. It wasn't fair that the downpour only served to mold his shirt to his broad shoulders and muscled forearms while she felt like a drowned prairie dog in comparison.

Falling in the river hadn't helped either. She seemed to have developed a habit of falling, and needing to be rescued. By Blake. She'd never hear the end of it if word got out. She bit her lip as the circle of wagons came into view. "Do we have to tell them I fell? Again."

He chuckled, his gaze taking in her drenched clothes, her disheveled hair, the mud-caked hem of her skirt. She didn't doubt she had mud and twigs and no telling what else in her hair.

"I suppose I can keep it a secret." His lips twitched in a half smile, and he winked, a slow intimate exchange that twisted her stomach into knots and brought a rush of heat to her face. "For now."

The rain blew through quickly, leaving a clean, fresh scent in the air. Puddles dotted the wide-open space inside the circle of wagons, but it wouldn't take long for the thirsty ground to soak up the moisture.

Blake had changed shirts and hung his damp one up to dry. He sat on a crate, his back propped against the side of the wagon, repairing a piece of harness. He stilled as Cassidy emerged from the wagon, her back to him, wearing a fresh dress. Blue, to match her eyes. Her damp hair, the color of corn silk in the fall after the leaves have turned, hung to her waist. He swallowed as she separated it into three sections and started plaiting, the damp strands forming a thick shining braid over her shoulder.

She turned and caught him staring. Roses bloomed in her cheeks, and then she looked down, her fingers nimbly finishing the task. "You were watching."

"Guilty as charged." Blake cleared his throat and rubbed a hand over his chin. He shouldn't have gawked at her, but what was he supposed to do? Jump up and do some kind of song and dance to let her know he was there? "It's just hair."

"But. . ." She huffed and spun away, her blue skirt billowing out like the flash of a robin's wing.

Blake opened his mouth to stop her, to call her back, to tell her. . .what? That her hair was the most beautiful thing he'd ever seen? That he couldn't stop thinking about how his heart had jumped into his throat when he'd seen her plunge into that water and how it had only climbed back into his chest cavity when he had her safely in his arms? He clamped his lips together and slammed the back of his head against the rough timber of the wagon.

Better to leave well enough alone.

Chapter 8

The sunny weather lasted all of two days before the late spring rains hit full force. Cassidy huddled on the wagon seat and slapped the reins against the mules' backs. "I am so sick of this rain."

"We all are." Her mother pulled a piece of canvas around the two of them, holding it over Cassidy's head as well as her own as the mules plodded along, heads down against the drizzling rain.

"Mama?" Her mama turned at the sound of Julene's plaintive cry from the interior of the wagon.

"Yes, sweetie?"

"My throat hurts."

"I know, darling. We'll be stopping soon, and I'll get you some water."

Julene mumbled something that sounded like agreement, and her mother faced forward, worry creasing her brow. Cassidy tamped down her concern and kept driving the mules forward, following close behind the Atwood wagon. Julene had a cough and had been running a fever all night. She wasn't the only one. The Atwood girls had been sick for two days. Was it just something the children had eaten, mountain fever, or the dreaded cholera? An elderly woman had died earlier in the week, and her funeral had sobered them all. Was the woman's death the first of many? It would be foolish to think otherwise on such a long, dangerous journey. She simply had to have faith and move forward one day at a time.

God, please heal these girls, heal Julene. Take the fever away. Please, Lord.

She wanted to stop to let her mother take care of her sister, but they couldn't. The rain and mud had slowed them down enough, and everyone understood the need to keep pushing forward, no matter what.

The wagons slowed to a crawl, and she craned her neck to see what the holdup was. A wagon had pulled to the edge of the trail, listing to the side like a broken table with three legs. Several men worked to repair the wagon, Blake among them. He'd been a godsend to the entire party as his skills as a blacksmith and a farrier became more evident the longer they traveled.

As Cassidy drove nearer, Blake glanced at her, his gaze raking over the mules, the wagon, then back to her. He gave her a slight smile and a short nod as if assuring her all was well with their belongings. Her heart gave a lurch.

Their belongings.

There was no them, no *theirs.*

But somehow over the past few weeks, even with the other travelers calling on him for assistance, he'd still managed to come back to them every night. Come back to unhitch the mules, rub them down, feed them, and lead them away to graze.

He inspected their wagon every day, making sure the iron tires fitted snug against the wooden rims, the axles were greased and ready to roll the next day. Would she have been as careful—or as knowledgeable—in taking care of the mules and the wagon? No. They would probably be broken down on the side of the trail like the wagon they'd just passed.

As much as she hated to admit it, Beecher had been right. Maybe she could have made it without a man, but it sure wouldn't have been easy.

Relief swept over her as the call came down the line to halt. Cassidy pulled her wagon in behind the Atwoods' and set the brake. Flynn materialized through the drizzle. "Gertie said ye might be needing a bit o' help."

"Blake should be here any time." Ignoring her objections, Flynn started unhitching the mules.

Flynn, Giovanni, and Peter had taken to stopping by almost every night if Blake was busy helping others, and Gertie and her mother seemed to encourage the lot of them. George was almost as bad, and after the men were gone, the three of them discussed the merits of each man as a marriage prospect as if they were at a horse auction. Since Julene and the Atwood sisters were too young to even think about marriage, she had to be the object of their plotting and planning. As much as she appreciated the men's help, the idea that they expected something in return didn't sit well at all.

"If that nosy Italian stops by, tell him he's no' needed." Flynn grinned and led the mules away.

Cassidy shook her head and moved to the rear of the wagon, her bonnet wilting under the downpour, intent on setting up camp as quickly as possible. She hurried to the far side of the wagon to grab the tent poles for the lean-to and found Giovanni unlashing them.

He doffed his hat. "Miss Cassi-dee."

"Giovanni. Thank you." Cassidy sighed. Honestly, she really needed to have a talk with her mother and Gertie.

Flynn returned, and amid much strutting around like two banty roosters, the men put up the canvas awning. Two additional pieces of canvas along with the wagon formed a three-sided tent for eating and sleeping. Cassidy coaxed a fire from the buffalo chips she'd managed to keep dry in the sling under the wagon and shooed the men over to help Angus and George while she brewed a pot of coffee.

By the time the coffee boiled, all three wagons were set up nicely, even if all four men, including George and Angus, looked like drowned rats. George stepped out of the rain, Flynn and Giovanni on his heels.

"Is that coffee I smell?"

"Yes, sir." Cassidy poured each of them a cup of coffee just as Gertie slipped under the canopy, a shawl draped over her head, her hands bearing a coffee cake she'd made the night before.

"You men have been lifesavers tonight for sure." She beamed, cutting a piece of cake and handing it to each of them. "Thank you for taking pity on us old folks."

"It weren't us they were helping, Gertie, old gal. Right, Giovanni?" George slapped him on the back.

"Sì, signore." Giovanni nodded.

"Good thing we've got pretty little Cassidy here to draw you fellers out of the wood-work. Otherwise, me and Angus would have to do all this work ourselves." George took another sip of his coffee. "By the way, where's Peter? I haven't seen him around the last few days."

"He's courtin' me sister, he is." Flynn grinned and toasted the others with his cup. "I'm a bettin' there'll be a wedding before we reach Fort Hall, or my name's no' Flynn McGowan."

"You wouldn't have had anything to do with that, would you, Flynn?" George asked.

"What kind o' low-bellied scalawag do ye take me for?" Flynn attempted a scowl, but the grin on his face all but erased any hint that he'd been offended by the accusation. "All I did was point out t' me dear wee sister that Peter would be a fair-to-middlin' catch an' she'd do well t' heed me advice."

"With Peter out of the way, that leaves less competition for you and Giovanni, doesn't it?" George laughed.

"Don't forget Blake," Gertie whispered, giving Cassidy a sly wink.

Cassidy frowned and said just loud enough for the older woman to hear, "I'm not interested in getting married, Gertie."

"That's what we all say, sweetie. One of these days you'll change your mind." She pulled her shawl over her head. "I'd better get back and check on the girls."

Cassidy winced. She should've asked about the girls first thing. "How are they feeling?"

"Much better. And Julene?"

"About the same."

"I'll be praying for her. You come get me if she gets worse, you hear?"

"Yes, ma'am."

As she left, one of Flynn's little brothers skidded to a halt at the edge of the lean-to, searching for Flynn. "Da needs ye to th' wagon. He thinks one o' the mules lost a shoe."

After the men left, Cassidy started making preparations for supper, the steady splat of rain against the canvas her sole companion. Her mother coaxed Julene out of the wagon just long enough to eat a few bites of stew before they both retired for the night.

The cloudy sky brought twilight early, and it was almost dark by the time Blake stumbled into camp, soaked to the skin. Cassidy turned up the lantern and motioned to his dry clothes folded neatly on the top of a crate. "I'll warm your supper while you change."

She stirred up the fire as Blake disappeared behind a canvas curtain. When he returned, she handed him a tin plate of rabbit stew. He cradled the plate in the crook of his left arm and shoveled food in with his right. Cassidy's gaze bounced from the bandage wrapped around his hand, to his face, and back again.

"What happened?" She motioned to his hand.

"Mashed some fingers." He shrugged. "It'll be fine."

Cassidy waited for him to tell her more, but he kept eating, taking several bites and washing them down with the coffee she'd kept warm. "Did you get the wagon repaired?"

"No." He shook his head. "It's been on its last leg for weeks now. They're going to have to abandon it."

Cassidy sucked in a breath. Another one. "I'd hoped we would be able to make the trip without having to abandon anybody's belongings and especially a wagon."

"Can't be helped."

Cassidy grabbed Blake's wet, muddy clothes and tossed them into a pot of hot water. She couldn't give them a good scrubbing, but at least she could rinse them out and hang them in the wagon tomorrow so they could dry while they traveled. When she'd wrung them out as best she could, she draped them over the wagon wheel and tossed over her shoulder, "What're the Graysons going to do?"

When Blake didn't answer, she turned around. He'd fallen asleep, the half-empty plate on the barrel beside him. She scraped out the leftovers, rinsed the plate, and stored it in the crate with the others.

Moving quietly, she found a light quilt and moved to his side, studying his face in the light of the lantern. His cheeks, darkened by long days on the trail, had grown leaner in the last few weeks. He hadn't shaved since Sunday, and dark stubble covered his cheeks. His hair, still damp from the rain, fell in disarray where he'd ran his fingers through it.

She reached out a hand to smooth back his hair but pulled back when he moaned, turned on his side, and folded his arms over his chest. She winced at the sight of the dirty, tattered bandage on his hand. She'd find some clean muslin strips and rewrap it tomorrow. Sighing, she covered him with one of the quilts she and her mother had pieced last winter and stood there watching him sleep, thankful he wasn't on guard duty tonight. They'd doubled the guards because they'd heard wolves howling for the last few nights, and the stock had gotten skittish.

"Miss Taylor?"

Cassidy pivoted as Mr. Beecher ducked underneath the edge of the canvas awning, hat in hand, his clothes drenched just like Blake's had been. Heart pounding, she wondered what she'd tell him when he insisted that it was improper for her to be alone with Blake like this. But, goodness, they were in plain sight of the rest of the party. Well, those who were still awake at least.

But he didn't even acknowledge that he'd noticed. "Where's Samuelson? A couple of horses need shoeing."

"He's asleep." Cassidy closed the gap between her and the wagon master, keeping her voice down. "It'll have to wait until morning."

He peered around her. "But I need—"

"Mr. Beecher, Blake is not made of steel, as much as you'd like to think he is. He's been going nonstop for weeks now, not only repairing all the wagons and shoeing the animals but taking his turn at guarding the stock as well."

"We're all tired, Miss Taylor, but Samuelson is the only one who can shoe these mules properly. He even built a bellows and a sling for the oxen out of some canvas. His skill with iron and that bellows is the only thing that's kept us moving as fast as we are."

"If he doesn't get some rest, he won't be any good to you or anybody else. You make sure the fire is good and hot in the morning, and I'll wake him at dawn. It won't take long for him to get the job done, and we can be on our way."

Beecher shifted his attention to her as if he was really seeing her for the first time. He let out a long, slow breath. "All right. I reckon you're right."

He plopped his hat on his head and turned away.

"Mr. Beecher?" Cassidy called to him. "What happened to Blake's hand? I asked, but he said it was nothing."

"He didn't tell you?" The man's face screwed up like he'd been eating persimmons. "The Grayson wagon slipped and caught his fingers between the axle and the bed."

Cassidy pressed a hand to her stomach, stopping its sudden roll. "Are they broken?"

"I don't see how they couldn't be. They were as flat as a silver dollar when we lifted that axle off 'em. But Samuelson just ripped off part of his shirt and told Angus to tie 'em up. He worked the rest of the afternoon with it like that. Didn't seem to slow him down much." He shook his head. "I'm telling you, Miss Taylor, that man of yours just might be made out of steel after all."

"He's not my man."

"You could do a lot worse, ma'am. Good night." Beecher planted his hat more firmly on his head and strode away, his boots splashing through the muddy mess that was the center of the campground.

All the starch wilted out of her when she turned. Blake lay on his back, his injured fingers cradled against his stomach, the makeshift bandage filthy and ragged. He'd been so exhausted he hadn't even roused during her conversation with Beecher.

She tamped down the urge to knock some sense into him, to—to do what? Wake him up and tell him that he needed to eat more, work less, and to be more careful. He wouldn't listen if she did. She took a deep breath, blew out the lantern, and muttered, "Men."

Chapter 9

The first thing Blake noticed when he woke was that it had stopped raining. Next was that his hand throbbed like he'd stabbed it with a hot poker. He flexed his stiff fingers and decided to ignore the pain. Wasn't much else he could do.

The third thing he became aware of was Cassidy stoking the fire against the backdrop of the rising sun. He could count on his fingers—the uninjured ones—the number of times he'd watched a woman cook breakfast.

Blake couldn't remember his ma, and he and his pa had sharecropped all over the south, picking cotton, mostly. When his pa died, Ezra Kirkwood had taken him in and taught him everything he knew about working a forge. Breakfast had been whatever the old man had on hand, sometimes leftovers from the night before, and sometimes nothing at all.

He remained still, watching Cassidy as the camp came to life around him. She bustled around, throwing together a pan of biscuits faster than he could beat a horseshoe into submission. Then she started frying bacon, deftly holding her skirts back from the fire while wielding a long-handled fork. His eyes drifted closed, and he breathed deep of the enticing aroma of coffee and bacon, barely holding in a smile as the sound of Cassidy's humming washed over him in soft, gentle waves. This was what it would be like to have a wife, a family, a home.

Early morning. With birds chirping. Coffee brewing and bacon sizzling. And the sound of skirts swishing along the kitchen floor. He'd never really thought about taking a wife, but a man could get used to waking up like this.

"Blake?"

Cassidy's soft whisper tickled his senses. Opening his eyes, he found her standing near, offering him a cup of coffee. He blinked, thinking she looked like an angel with the sun haloed around her wheat-golden hair. He sat up and propped his back against a wagon wheel, reaching for the cup with his uninjured hand.

"How's your hand?"

"It's fine."

"That's what you said last night. Beecher told me what happened."

"Beecher?" He sipped the coffee, enjoying the strong brew.

"He stopped by after you went to sleep. Some mules—or horses, I can't remember—need shoeing."

"How many?"

"Two, three. Maybe more. Giovanni's little brother said one of theirs lost a shoe yesterday. So, at least two."

"Why didn't you wake me earlier? Beecher'll want to be on the trail soon." Blake gritted his teeth and forced his fingers to cooperate as he pulled on his boots. The pain made him forget all about swishing skirts and waking up to the smell of coffee brewing and a hot breakfast.

"You needed the rest. You didn't even move when Beecher stopped by." She flipped the bacon and nodded at his hand, a frown of annoyance pinching her forehead. "And besides, how are you going to hold the iron with your hand all wrapped up?"

"I'll manage."

"I suppose it's too much to ask if you'd like a fresh bandage."

"No need. It'll be just as filthy as this one within an hour." He splashed water on his face and ran the fingers of his right hand through his hair before grabbing his hat and plopping it on his head. "As soon as I get done, I'll be back to help you break camp."

"I can break camp just fine on my own." Cassidy blocked his way, arms crossed. "What about your breakfast? You barely ate any supper. I dumped half of it on the ground because you were too tired to eat."

The feisty look on her face made him smile. First she'd chased off Beecher so he could sleep. Then she'd gotten all flustered over his hand. Now she insisted that he eat breakfast. He'd never had a woman so determined to take care of him. Shucks, he'd never had a woman take care of him at all.

He changed his mind again. Maybe he could get used to this.

"Blake?" Angus strode out of the darkness. "You ready? I've got the fire good and hot just like you showed me."

"Be right there."

Angus glanced between him and Cassidy then headed back out into the darkness. Cassidy whirled away, hunkered down, and used a bristly brush to remove the coals from the dutch oven. He heard what sounded like a sniffle. Was she sick? Or. . .*crying*? Blake stared at her back in horror. Torn between his duty to get the train moving as quickly as possible and doing as she asked, he stood rooted to the spot.

"Cassidy—"

"Go. I'll—I'll keep your breakfast warm."

Blake moved toward her, leaned over her shoulder. She blinked and lifted her chin, all but ignoring him. He took a whiff of baking bread when she lifted the lid, not sure why it was so important that he eat now while the food was hot, but for some reason it was important to her.

"Those biscuits ready?" he asked, his voice rough-sounding even to his own ears.

"Yes," she whispered.

"Maybe I could take one with me and some of that bacon."

Like a mini whirlwind, she sliced open a biscuit, popped bacon in it, and handed it to him. She stepped back, running both hands down her apron, then jerked her head in the direction Angus had gone. "You'd better get going. Angus is waiting."

"Yes, ma'am." He grinned. All she'd wanted was to feed him. Long strides carried him toward the makeshift smithy, and he took a bite of the flaky biscuit, the crispy, salty bacon tasting as good as it smelled.

But even better was knowing he'd made Cassidy happy by letting her feed him. He'd do well to remember that.

As promised, Angus had the fire stoked and had cleaned out the hooves on the first mule. He even had several buckets of water handy. Blake shoved his injured hand into a thick glove, clenched his jaw, and started to work, each blow against the iron shooting pain up his arm. Without making a fuss, Angus pitched in, holding the iron when he could, helping get the job done.

"You ever thought about being a blacksmith?"

"Thought about it but just haven't ever had the chance to learn much."

Blake grunted as he plunged a horseshoe into a bucket of water. Steam hissed as the metal cooled. "Looks like this is your chance."

They worked as fast as they could. One after the other, the travelers led the animals away to hitch them up as the group broke camp. Angus pumped the bellows as they worked to shoe Abram Oleander's mule, an ornery cuss if there ever was one.

Oleander, a wiry old man, stood over Blake's shoulder, watching every move he made. "Used to be a blacksmith," he said, flexing his gnarled fingers. "When my fingers got too stiff to do much more'n hold the horses and pump the bellows, I passed the reins to my son, Paul. He's waiting for us in Fort Hall. Ain't seen him and his young'uns in over a year."

"He'll be glad to see you and the missus. Hold still, boy. Almost done." Blake held the mule's hind leg between his knees and pounded in the last of the nails. His hand was throbbing by the time he finished. Just as he released the mule, two youngsters raced by, yelling at each other. The skittish mule lashed out, clipping Blake on the leg. He doubled over, almost passing out from the pain.

"You all right?" Angus asked, his brow knotted with worry.

Blake blew out a breath. "Yeah. He just nicked me."

He rubbed the knot on his shin, straightened, and took a few steps, grateful the mule hadn't broken his leg.

Oleander led the mule away then turned back, a quizzical look on his face. "Where'd you say you were headed, Samuelson? Californy or Oregon?"

"California."

The old man grunted. "Well, iffen you change your mind, they'll probably need a blacksmith in Fort Hall. My son was on his way to Californy last year and his wife got sick, so they decided to winter at the fort. They're going to join up with us and continue on. But I tell you, that gig in Fort Hall ain't bad at all. My Paul has had all the work he could handle what with all the wagons passing through and shoeing horses for the army."

Blake nodded, only half listening to Oleander as he gathered tools and tossed them into a pile. He'd swing by and load them on the way out of camp. "I'll consider it. Thanks for letting me know."

Chapter 10

Blake rolled his shoulders and headed toward the wagon. At least he wasn't nearly as weary as he'd been during all that rain, and he barely limped anymore from being kicked by that crazy mule. His fingers were a different story, but at least the swelling had gone down enough that he could grasp his tongs, at least for a little while. Angus was the only one who knew what the effort cost him.

When he neared the campsite, Cassidy's mother nodded at the campfire. "There's a fresh pot of coffee if you'd like some."

"Don't mind if I do." He hunkered down in front of the fire and poured a cup.

Eliza Ann hung diapers on a line stretched between the two wagons, while little Johnnie napped on a pallet in the shade, both arms flung wide. Mrs. Taylor stirred something over the fire then wiped her hands on her apron. "I'm so thankful the rain has moved on for a few days. It's almost impossible to cook or do much of anything in a sea of mud."

Blake couldn't agree more. Gertie rounded the wagon, a bucket in each hand. "Elsie, I'm headed down to the creek to get some water."

Mrs. Taylor frowned. "More water? I thought—"

"You can never have too much water on hand. That's what I say. When I get back, I think I'll make us a peach cobbler. I soaked some dried peaches last night." Gertie turned, her smile widening. She held out the buckets. "Blake. I didn't see you standing there. Would you be so kind as to fetch me some water?"

Blake's mouth watered. He hadn't had peach cobbler since—since—he frowned. He couldn't remember the last time he'd had peach anything. "Ms. Gertie, I'll be glad to, so you can get started on that peach cobbler."

"I knew that would catch your attention." She laughed and shoved the buckets at him. "And while you're at it, see if you can find that Cassidy-girl. She's been gone half an hour or more. She should've been back by now."

Eliza Ann giggled, and Cassidy's mother shushed her. Blake's attention swiveled between the women. What was that all about?

"Be off with you, then." Gertie shooed him away. "I've got a peach cobbler to make."

"Yes, ma'am."

As he walked away, he heard Mrs. Taylor say, "Three buckets of water, Gertie? Really!"

Blake spotted Cassidy down by the creek. Along with another bucket and Flynn McGowan. Gertie had hoodwinked him. She didn't need water any more than a drowning fish did, but for some reason, she *had* wanted him to see Cassidy with Flynn. As if she knew that seeing Flynn tugging the bucket out of Cassidy's hand would send Blake's blood pressure soaring into the wispy clouds hovering overhead.

Flynn held out one hand to Cassidy to help her up the steep bank. She hesitated before relenting and placing her hand in his. Flynn tugged a little too hard and she almost lost her footing. Blake gritted his teeth when Flynn said something about catching her if she fell.

"Thank you, Flynn." Cassidy reached for the bucket. "I can manage."

Flynn held it out of her reach, laughing as she grabbed for it and missed. Blake stalked forward, of a good mind to start swinging the buckets clanging against his legs. He stopped halfway down the bank, his gaze boring a hole in McGowan then shifting to Cassidy. "Is everything all right?"

Two spots of bright color flamed on her cheeks. "Everything's fine. Flynn was just offering his assistance."

"Mighty nice of him." Blake joined them, hunkered down, and dipped Gertie's bucket in the water.

"Yes, it was very nice." Cassidy picked up a pail of water and flounced up the path.

Blake watched her go. What had got her so riled up? It wasn't his fault that he'd interrupted their little meeting. But he was glad he had, and he was a good mind to tell her so. She didn't have any business being alone with Flynn McGowan, who flirted with every single girl on the train.

McGowan laughed, and when Blake finally pulled his attention from Cassidy, the loon laughed even harder. Blake flexed his hand, wishing his fingers weren't so sore that he couldn't make a fist. He forced himself to relax. "What's so funny?"

"Your face." He doubled over, both hands on his knees.

"What's wrong with my face?" Blake growled and took a step forward. He wasn't a fighting man and generally got along with most folks, but McGowan would try the patience of a preacher.

"Don't worry yerself, Samuelson." McGowan straightened and held both hands in the air as if to ward him off. But he still sported a grin a mile and a half wide. "If the lass means tha' much t' you, you can 'ave 'er."

"What in the blue blazes are you talking about?"

McGowan jerked his thumb in the direction Cassidy had gone. "Cassidy. It's plain as the nose on me face tha' you've staked a claim on her."

Blake clenched his jaw. "I haven't staked my claim on her or any other woman."

"Ah, ye didn't come bargin' down 'ere like a raging bull fer naught, lad." McGowan saluted and headed back toward the camp. Blake made a fist.

The pain felt good, almost as if he'd managed to land at least one punch after all.

Chapter 11

Cassidy stalked toward the wagon.

She didn't give a fig about Flynn, but him trying to make her fall into his arms and Blake seeing the whole thing embarrassed her to no end. She didn't want Blake to get the idea that every time she was around a man, she fell into his arms. She sloshed water on her skirt and slowed down.

Whistling reached her ears, and her heart fluttered against her chest, but just as quickly the sensation died as she recognized one of Flynn's jaunty Irish tunes.

"Lass, wait."

She kept walking, same pace as always. It wouldn't take long for him to catch up to her anyway. He drew abreast of her, his hands in his pockets. He tossed her a grin. "Odd, that."

Cassidy scowled at him. "Odd seeing Blake down at the river?"

"Why would Gertie and your ma send you t' get water then send him?"

"Especially since they sent you to the creek as well." Cassidy arched a brow.

"Ye think they sent me, lass?"

"Listen, Flynn, I know what Gertie and Mama are up to. And, to tell you the truth, I'm not interested."

"No?" His lips twisted in amusement, and Cassidy gritted her teeth.

"No."

They walked in silence for a bit, and then Flynn turned to her. "Did it never occur t' ye that I might enjoy your company in spite o' Gertie's matchmaking schemes?"

"Flynn, don't be ridiculous. I know you've got every girl in this wagon train on a string." She arched a brow at him. "Now, tell me, which one do you really have your heart set on?"

For the space of a heartbeat, she thought she caught a glimpse of something serious cross his face, then it was gone. He flashed her a wide grin and winked. "I'll never tell."

Cassidy laughed as they walked into camp. She'd learned over the last few weeks that Flynn McGowan's affections were as flighty as the wind. But one day some woman would steal his heart, and that would be the end of Flynn McGowan's carefree ways. Gertie glanced up from her mending, her gaze darting from Flynn to Cassidy and back again. "Oh, Flynn. Good afternoon. Where's Blake?"

"Told ye, lass." Flynn leaned down to whisper in Cassidy's ear as he passed. "We saw him, an' he was in quite a dither, 'e was. I thought 'e was goin' t' take me head off, for sure."

The sudden flurry of activity in the camp set Cassidy's nerves on edge. Gertie mumbled something about checking on a peach cobbler, her mother concentrated on the mending in her lap, while Eliza Ann knelt to move little Johnnie to a shadier spot. Cassidy turned away, more confused than ever. If Gertie wasn't trying to match her up with Flynn, then what was she up to?

George came barging into camp, grinning from ear to ear. "We're going to have ourselves a wedding. Gertie, old gal, where's my fiddle?"

"Who's getting married?"

"Peter and Willa McGowan."

The news spread like wildfire, and excitement filled the camp. Everyone hurried through supper so they could attend the wedding. When all was ready, Mr. Beecher quieted everyone, and Peter moved to stand beside him. As soon as the couple was pronounced man and wife, George hauled out his fiddle and played a merry tune.

Night fell, and the music continued. As the musicians played on, the more adventuresome of the party danced and asked for another song, then another. Peter sat beside Willa in two straight-backed chairs decorated with garlands of wildflowers.

Cassidy declined several requests to dance and headed back to the wagon to wash up the supper dishes, and Blake fell into step beside her. He hadn't said two words to her since barging in on her and Flynn down at the river. Well, if he didn't want to discuss it, she wouldn't bring it up. She wrapped her shawl close and glanced at the star-studded sky. "It's a beautiful night for a wedding. Peter and Willa seemed so happy."

Blake chuckled. "They looked scared."

Cassidy pursed her lips. "Well, who wouldn't be? Marriage is a big step."

"True." He cleared his throat. "Sorry about today. I wasn't spying on you and Flynn."

"Wouldn't matter if you were. There wasn't anything to see."

He didn't answer, and she wondered if he believed her. At the campsite, she started gathering dishes. Blake reached for a cup and poured himself some coffee, the filthy bandage on his left hand an eyesore if there ever was one.

"I'm changing that bandage right now." Cassidy stalked to the back of the wagon and rummaged around for the bandages she'd cut up.

—※—

Blake flexed his fingers. Or at least he tried to. He could feel the swelling inside the tattered rags Angus had wrapped around his fingers. The bandage probably did need to come off, but he really wasn't that interested in discovering that his hand looked like it had been mauled by a wildcat. As long as it wasn't bleeding, and it didn't feel like someone was jabbing it with a red-hot poker, he figured it was fine.

"It's fine," he muttered, his heart pounding at the thought of Cassidy seeing his mangled fingers, of her touching him. He swallowed, wanting to suggest letting her mother or Gertie take care of the chore but didn't know how to broach the subject without explaining why.

Cassidy pointed her scissors toward a chair. "Sit."

"Maybe we should return to the party."

She lifted an eyebrow. Blake finally did as she asked and plopped his arm on the barrel, steeling himself against her touch. Cassidy snipped through the cloth and then unwound the bandage. She sucked in a sharp breath when she saw his fingers, still sausage-like and a dark rainbow of purple, blue, and black.

"Oh, Blake, you didn't tell me it was this bad. Are they broken?" She turned his hand over and cradled it in the palm of her hand.

He forgot that he could barely move his fingers without nearly passing out, forgot that he'd kept the bandage on for days so he wouldn't see the damage, forgot the scars, the nicks, the burns from the forge. Forgot it all as her soft, gentle fingertips caressed his bruised skin.

"Can you close your hand?" She turned her face up to meet his, a worried frown puckering her forehead.

Deciding he needed to think about something other than Cassidy's soft touch and the way her hair shone in the light cast off by the fire, Blake flexed his fingers and, forcing himself to endure the pain, closed his hand into a clawlike fist.

Better than he'd expected. He relaxed his fingers, now throbbing with the movement he'd forced on them. But he was pleased. In a few days, or weeks, his hand would be good as new. He tried again, curling his fingers inward.

"No. Don't. You're going to make it worse." Cassidy winced and grabbed his hand, smoothing his fingers out, her touch like silk. "At least it's stopped bleeding."

The music stopped, followed by a flurry of activity, laughter, shouting, and the most awful sound of beating and banging he'd ever heard. Cassidy cringed as the racket drew nearer. "What in the world are they doing?"

McGowan raced by pushing a wheelbarrow, hauling his sister around the circle of wagons, his crazy antics in danger of tipping her over. She squealed for him to stop before he dumped her on her backside, but from the sounds of her laughter, Blake knew she enjoyed the attention.

Half-a-dozen young men carried Peter on their shoulders, his lanky arms and legs flopping like loose spaghetti. Half the wagon train followed behind, banging on pots and pans, ringing bells, singing and shouting good wishes to the couple.

"It's a shivaree."

"Where does Flynn come up with some of his ideas?" Cassidy laughed as she filled a pan with warm water and found a bar of soap. She washed his hand, her touch gentle as she cleansed the grime that had worked beneath the bandage. "I've heard of shivarees but not hauling the bride around in a wheelbarrow."

"McGowan doesn't have a lick of sense, but I reckon it's all in good fun." His heart rate slowed when she backed away, dried her hands on her apron, and watched as the noisy parade made one more circuit around the circle of wagons.

McGowan finally led the way to a wagon the younger girls had decorated with garlands of wildflowers. Blake half expected the man to dump his sister on the prairie, but instead he offered her his hand and lifted her into the wagon. Whooping and hollering, Peter's friends unceremoniously dumped him in the back of the wagon.

Cassidy shook her head and reached for the bandage. "Fun or not, it looks a bit dangerous to me, what with Flynn in charge of that wheelbarrow."

As she wrapped the dressing around his hand, Blake closed his eyes and concentrated on his breathing. If anything was dangerous, it was the way Cassidy's touch shot sparks up his arm, straight to his overworked heart.

Chapter 12

The horses!"

Blake had barely dozed off when the shout jerked him awake. Stomping into his boots, he grabbed his shirt and rushed toward the stock corralled outside the circle of wagons. The chilling howl of a pack of wolves carried across the prairie, sounding as if they were just over the next rise.

He scowled. Probably howling at the ear-splitting racket they'd been forced to endure half the night. That fool Flynn and his friends had serenaded Peter and Willa every few minutes into the wee hours, until Blake felt like his head was going to explode. They'd finally settled down after Beecher had ordered them to shut up and let everybody get some rest.

But apparently their antics had done more than agitate the newlyweds.

He squinted into the predawn darkness. The remaining stock milled about, the oxen gathering in nervous bunches, ears and attention on the predators. The men quickly rounded up the remaining animals and hobbled them. That's when Blake discovered that four of his six mules were gone. Borrowing a horse, he and several men headed out to round up the strays.

Mrs. Taylor and Julene were breaking camp when he returned. All around them, people were getting ready to head out.

"Two of our mules are still missing." He started harnessing mules. The four he had left would have to pull the wagon until he found the others. "Where's Cassidy?"

"As soon as it was daylight, she and Julene went to get a bucket of water. She spotted the mules and sent Julene back to tell me she was going after them."

Blake blew out a frustrated breath. Trust his mules to head off in the opposite direction to all the others. And trust Cassidy to take off after them alone. "Fool woman to go off by herself with a pack of wolves running around," he muttered.

"Wolves?"

"I heard wolves last night. That's what scared the animals."

"I thought I heard something, but what with all that caterwauling the revelers were doing, I wasn't sure."

"Don't worry. I'll find Cassidy and the mules." Blake harnessed the mules and then helped Mrs. Taylor load the rest of their belongings. He grabbed his rifle and patted the mules. "You shouldn't have any problem with these fellers. We'll catch up soon."

Mrs. Taylor's gaze fixed on the gun before her lips tightened into a firm line. "All right."

Blake headed toward the river. At the water's edge, he tried to determine which way Cassidy had gone, kicking himself for not asking Julene. The riverbank was a jumble of prints from washing and watering the animals and children playing in the shallows. It was impossible to tell what direction Cassidy and the mules had gone in. Taking a chance, he headed east.

Ten minutes later, he found the trail, but no sign of Cassidy or the animals. He trailed them for half a mile to a sandy stretch along the riverbank then hunkered down to get a closer look. Wolf prints crossed their path then joined and followed along Cassidy's trail. They weren't likely to attack, but the thought of them being so close worried him.

The farther he got from the wagon train, the more worried he became. He should've alerted Beecher and the others that Cassidy and two of his mules were missing, but he'd expected to find them down by the creek, not heading east and being stalked by a pack of wolves.

Lord, please help me find her. Keep her safe.

They needed the mules, but Cassidy's life was more important than finding the animals. Another mile and he lost her trail, only to crisscross back and forth until he found it again. Deliberately slowing his pace, he kept a close eye on the trail. If he lost it again, he might not ever find Cassidy in this desolate land. His heart lurched when he heard a rustling off to his left. He stilled, searching a grove of cottonwoods, then spotted half-a-dozen gray shadows waiting patiently, their attention caught by something upstream.

The wolves.

Blake heard a hoof strike stone and followed their line of sight. Cassidy appeared, leading the two mules with one hand while holding her skirt with the other as she picked her way along the river's edge. The hem of her blue dress was wet to her knees, a messy braid hung down her back as if she hadn't taken time to brush out her hair before she'd taken off on a wild mule chase.

Blake glanced toward the trees only to find that the wolves had quietly melted into the shadows and disappeared. He whistled and Cassidy spotted him. She waved, a smile blooming across her face. He grumbled low in his throat. At least one of them could smile. He met her halfway and held his tongue until he had a firm hand on both mules. Then he faced her. "Why'd you run off like that? You could've been killed."

Chapter 13

Cassidy plopped her hands on her hips and glared at Blake, forgetting how glad she was to see him. If he was itching for a fight, she'd give it to him. She hadn't slept a wink, hadn't eaten, and was hot, tired, and scared. And when she got scared, she got mad. "If I hadn't trailed the mules, they would have been long gone by now."

"If you hadn't chased them, they wouldn't have gone as far as they did."

"So it's *my* fault they took off, is it?"

"The wolves spooked 'em, but—never mind." He shook his head and led the mules up the bank, out of the cottonwoods toward open ground. "They've been trailing you."

"Wolves? I thought all that racket last night was the two-legged kind." Cassidy tamped down her unease, eyeing the underbrush along the riverbank. "Wolves don't attack people, do they?"

"Not likely, and even if they did, they'd be after the mules."

At the top of the incline, the mules snorted, their long, floppy ears perked up, their attention drawn to the shadows. Cassidy glanced back. Her heart lurched into her throat as she spotted the wolves following them, a good fifty feet away. "Blake? Look."

"Hold the mules." He handed her the reins, and she patted the animals to quiet them.

He strode confidently toward the wolves, rifle in hand. When he shot off into the air above their heads, they trotted away then stopped, watching. Blake turned back to Cassidy, formed a cradle with his hands, and gave her a boost up onto the back of one of the mules. "They'll give up if we put a little distance behind us."

He mounted, and they headed out. The mules didn't need any urging, and Cassidy grasped her mount's stubby mane and gripped its sides with her knees as she bounced along. She gritted her teeth and held on.

Blake let the mules have their heads, not that they got much above a fast walk, but at least they were moving, and in the right direction.

But so were the wolves. Not that he was really worried about the marauders. He'd never heard of them attacking travelers unprovoked, but having them on his trail was a bit unnerving. He was more worried about Cassidy staying astride her skittish mule bareback than anything.

If the situation weren't so serious, he'd laugh at her dogged determination to hold on as her mule kept pace with his, both animals making an effort to put a bit of distance between themselves and the predators.

After they passed through last night's campsite, Blake scanned their trail and didn't see any sign of the wolves. Maybe they'd give up the chase and expend their curiosity on the abandoned camp. He leaned over his mule's neck as the animal lumbered up a sharp incline. Hopefully the wagons weren't too far ahead. Suddenly, he heard Cassidy yelp and turned to see her tumbling off the mule. The mule clambered up the incline and disappeared in the direction of the wagon train.

He slid from the back of his mule and reached Cassidy before she stopped rolling. "You all right?"

"I'll live." She pushed her hair away from her face and shoved her skirt over her ankles.

He hunkered down beside her, grinning. "I've been waiting for you to do that."

"It's not funny." She flapped at her tattered skirt. One sleeve was ripped, and dirt smudged her face. "Ugh. Look at my dress."

Blake reached out to tuck a strand of hair behind her ear. "Don't talk like that. You saved the mules, and they're worth a hundred dresses."

His knuckles grazed her cheek, and he cringed at the sight of his rough, scarred fingers next to the perfection of her skin. Her clothes might be a mess, but she was still the prettiest girl on the wagon train and didn't need his battered, scarred fingers touching her. He motioned toward the remaining mule. "We'll have to ride double the rest of the way."

"Double?" she squeaked.

"I'll walk, if you prefer."

"No." She took his hand, the warmth of her fingers searing his skin. He tugged, pulling her up with him. Her eyes, as bright and clear as blue flames in the smithy, captured his, and his heart hammered against his rib cage. She lowered her gaze and disappointment shot through him like the sudden dousing of a light. "Double is fine. The sooner we catch up, the better."

He mounted the mule and pulled her up behind him. As her arms snaked around his waist, holding tight, warmth curled in his stomach, and he realized he didn't want her to ever let go.

Chapter 14

The rhythmic ping of Blake's hammer reverberated throughout the camp.

Cassidy's fellow travelers lounged inside the large circle of wagons, the aroma of frying bacon, biscuits, coffee, and the occasional scent of a sweet delicacy wafted through the camp. The clothes were all washed and dried and put away for another week, and the children were laughing and playing tag on the flat prairie that stretched as far as the eye could see.

She sighed and stretched.

"What was that all about?" Eliza Ann sat next to her, sewing a gown for the baby. Johnnie played a few feet away, piling rocks into a tin pan then dumping them out, only to squeal happily and repeat the process again and again.

Cassidy waved a hand at the camp. "This. Sometimes I wish we could just stay like this, here on the prairie, and not have to pack up and move in the morning."

"You didn't enjoy it so much when it was raining for days on end."

"True."

Eliza Ann smiled as claps and whistles rang out from the dozen or so men lounging around the temporary smithy as Angus finished making his first set of horseshoes. "Angus always wanted to be a blacksmith but didn't think he'd ever get the chance. God works in mysterious ways, doesn't He?"

"He sure does." Not for the first time, Cassidy's attention strayed to the group of men, her gaze seeking out Blake, head and shoulders above the rest. Memories of the short ride back to the wagon train over a week ago slammed into her thoughts as if it had just happened.

She'd been forced to hold on to Blake to stay on the mule, and even now the thought of being so close to him made her tingle with embarrassment.

"We almost didn't come."

Her attention shifted back to Eliza Ann. "Because of the baby?"

"Partly. But mainly because of Ma. My parents have never had anything to call their own. We moved every year or so, sharecropping, taking on odd jobs. Pa would come west, but..." Eliza Ann trailed off.

"But what? He's not sick, is he?"

"No." Her pale cheeks pinked, and she concentrated on her needlework. "Ma refuses to, and she runs roughshod over him. I don't know why he lets her, but he always has. He'd rather let her have her way than argue."

"My grandma was like that. She lived with us the last few years of her life, and she bossed Pa around something fierce. She was a force to be reckoned with, that's for sure."

"Sounds like my ma and your grandma were cut from the same cloth. But I determined that I'd never be like that." Eliza Ann's gaze sought out her husband, and a smile softened her features. "I promised Angus that I'd follow him wherever he wanted to go."

"Have you ever regretted that promise?"

"Never." Eliza Ann shook her head. "But I'm blessed that he wants to do what is best for me, Johnnie, and the baby."

Cassidy spotted Gertie and her mother headed their way, Gertie talking a mile a minute, waving her hands. Her mother just smiled and nodded, just like she'd done all those years when Grandma had made the decisions for their family.

She didn't want to be a doormat like her mother, but she didn't want to be as overbearing as her grandmother and Gertie either. Somewhere in between would be nice. She squirmed, unable to keep her attention off Blake.

How did he see her? Like her mother, or like Gertie? She *had* shanghaied him after all. And Beecher had almost forced him to marry her, and then on multiple occasions, she'd been more than a little bossy. She bit her lip.

Maybe that was why he'd been avoiding her for the last week.

Chapter 15

They'd made camp hours ago, and Blake hadn't returned. Probably repairing somebody's wagon or shoeing horses. But Cassidy couldn't help but worry that he might be deliberately avoiding her. Even if he didn't want to be around her because she was bossy, the man needed to eat.

Still a bit weak from her bout with fever, Julene climbed into the wagon and was asleep almost as soon as her head hit the pillow. Cassidy's mother brushed her hair and braided it as she readied for bed. "You coming?"

"Soon."

Her mother paused. "Are you waiting on Blake?"

Cassidy fidgeted, straightening the camp, packing away things they wouldn't need in the morning. "He hasn't had supper."

Her mother smiled and finished braiding her hair. "The man is capable of getting his own supper, Cassidy."

"I know, but. . ." Helplessly she looked at her mother. "Am I stubborn and bossy like Grandma?"

Laughing, her mother closed the distance between them and took her by the shoulders. Her eyes, a slightly faded mirror image of Cassidy's own, searched hers. "Now, why would you ask me that?"

"Because—" Cassidy plucked at the hem of her apron. "Because, well, I make Blake eat, I made him change the bandage on his hand. I kidnapped him, and I wouldn't let Mr. Beecher wake him that night he was so tired—"

"Oh, sweetheart, that's not being bossy. That's just doing things for someone because you love them." She smiled. "Well, except for the kidnapping part."

Cassidy sucked in a quick breath. "I don't love him."

"I think you do."

Did she? Was this feeling of wanting to be with Blake, to take care of him, love? She shook her head, miserable. "But it doesn't matter. He doesn't feel the same way."

"I think he does. It's plain as the nose on your face to everyone that the two of you are meant to be together, but you're both too stubborn to admit it."

Tears pricked her eyes. No, Blake didn't care about her, not in that way. He'd been avoiding her ever since she'd gone after the mules. Yet another time she'd taken matters into her own hands when she should have let him handle it.

"There's one thing you can do to prove to Blake and to yourself that you're not like your grandmother."

"What?"

"Tell him that you're willing to go to California."

"But Pa wanted us to go to Oregon. That's why he sold our place back in Indiana."

"Your pa's gone, Cassidy, and he'd want you to do what's best for you." Her mother hugged her then held her at arm's length. "Do you love him?"

"He's not going to—"

"That's not what I asked you. Do you love Blake?"

Warmth flooded Cassidy's chest, and suddenly she knew. She did love Blake. With all her heart. Tears pricked her eyes, and she nodded.

Her mother's tone softened. "And would you follow him wherever he decides to settle, whether that is California, Oregon, or right here on this very spot?"

Cassidy's heart pounded as she realized that her mother had opened the floodgates of her heart and exposed her deepest yearning. Yes, she would. She'd follow him to the ends of the earth. "I would."

"Then tell him. Follow your heart and fight for your dream. If your pa had started following his earlier, things might have turned out differently."

Chapter 16

Lightning flashed in the distance as Blake stumbled through the darkness to check on his mules.

He'd taken his turn as night watchman the night before then worked from sunup to past sundown making repairs that were becoming more difficult every day. Some of the wagons were falling apart, and he'd exhausted almost every spare piece of iron, even with the entire party rounding up lost horseshoes, flat bar, broken rings, chain links—anything they could salvage to keep the wagons moving.

Beecher predicted they'd make it to Fort Hall any day now, and Blake hoped to use the smithy there to forge some new horseshoes and repair the wagons. But after weeks on the trail, Oleander's suggestion of staying on in Fort Hall was sounding more and more appealing.

As soon as he checked on his mules, he wanted food and sleep, in that order. And if it wasn't for Cassidy hovering over him, determined to shove a hot meal inside him, he might even skip the food and go straight to bed. Not that he didn't enjoy her cooking, but tonight sleep beckoned him more than food.

That wasn't exactly true. And burning his candle at both ends wasn't as much about the need to keep the wagon train moving as it was to avoid Cassidy. Because he was afraid if he didn't avoid her, he'd be headed down the same slippery slope Peter had taken.

Suddenly, out of nowhere, a half-dozen shadowy figures rushed him, grabbing his arms and legs. Blake struggled against their hold, kicking and lashing out with both fists. He connected solidly with somebody's jaw.

"*Ahi!*" Giovanni's howl of pain brought him up short. *Giovanni?*

"Grab his arms!"

He pulled his punch when he heard Angus yell out. His surprise gave his attackers the upper hand, and within minutes they had him trussed up like a chicken ready to be plucked. He grunted as they lifted him and put him in the back of a rickety oxcart that should have been abandoned days ago.

"Angus?" Blake surged against the bonds, trying to see his friend's face in the darkness. "What's going on?"

"This is for your own good." Angus sounded plum miserable, but not miserable enough to untie him.

"We're gonna have us a little shivaree, eh, lads?" Flynn leaned close, and Blake could barely make out the wide grin of pure joy on the Irishman's face.

"Untie me," Blake growled, his narrowed gaze shooting daggers in Flynn's direction.

"That depends on ye, me lad." Flynn laughed. "Say ye'll ask Cassidy Taylor t' wife, an' ye'll be set free in a twinklin'."

Blake fumed in silence. If he wanted to marry Cassidy—and it was none of Flynn's business whether he did or didn't—he wouldn't be forced into it by the likes of Flynn McGowan.

"Well, lads, 'e's a stubborn un', fer sure." Flynn led the mule-drawn cart away, Blake bouncing in the back.

Angus leaned down and whispered, "They're determined to go through with this, so just go along. You don't want to scare Cassidy."

"Cassidy?" Blake surged up, his heart lurching along with the wagon. Angus pushed him down. "What are they going to do?"

"They're not going to hurt her. Just. . .uh. . .kidnap her."

"Angus—" Blake struggled against Angus's hold. "They can't do that."

"Sorry, but they just did." Angus let him go and scrambled out of the way.

"Angus!" But the yellow-bellied coward was gone, and the next thing Blake knew, a soft warm body in a flurry of skirts was lowered into the cart beside him. He struggled against the ropes holding him tight. If he could get his hands on Flynn McGowan.

"Let me go, you big—" Cassidy's screech was drowned out as Flynn's cronies rode around the cart, whooping and hollering, making enough racket to wake the dead.

Before Blake could reassure her that everything was going to be all right, she started kicking at him with her bound feet, the toes of her boots gouging deep trenches in his shins. He groaned as a well-placed blow landed smack-dab in the middle of where Oleander's mule had kicked him.

Blake shoved his face right up to hers and shouted her name.

Chapter 17

Cassidy broke off mid-scream.

"Blake?" She squinted into the darkness. Lightening zigzagged across the sky, illuminating his square jaw, dark eyebrows drawn down into a V, and chin jutted forward inches from her face. She winced as the cart jounced her against the hard flooring, throwing her against him. She grabbed his shirt with her bound hands and held on. "What's going on? What are they doing?"

Blake leaned toward her. His warm breath tickled her ear and goose bumps peppered her arms. "It's their idea of a shivaree."

"A shivaree?" She frowned. "But we're not married. We're not even *getting* married."

"I told them, but they wouldn't listen." He rested his forehead against hers. "We'll just let them have their fun, then they'll take us back."

His brown eyes pleaded with her, and what else could she do? Flynn enjoyed a bit of fun, and when he got carried away, there was no stopping him. "Where are they taking us?"

"Who knows?" Blake rolled onto his back. "We might as well get comfortable."

Just when she thought she couldn't stand the noise any longer, the men stopped hollering, but the cart kept bouncing along. North, south, east, or west? She wasn't sure.

"McGowan?" Blake bellowed. Cassidy winced. The sheer volume of his voice told her he'd had enough of Flynn's foolishness. "This has gone far enough. Turn around and take us back before that storm blows in."

"No' until ye say 'I do.'"

"Flynn, I'm warning you," Blake growled.

"Dis es far enough, yes?" Giovanni's accent had grown thick, along with the distance and the threat of another storm. "The lightning es bad."

"Aw, that storm's no' even close." The cart stopped, and the handful of riders reined in around them. Lightning flashed, and Cassidy caught a glimpse of the Snake River not far away. At least she had her bearings. If the river was close by, she could find her way back. "Well, Samuelson, what's it goin' t' be? Either yer goin' t' lay claim t' Cassidy, or you're no' gonna say anything when I do."

Cassidy sputtered and struggled to sit up. "Why, Flynn McGowan—"

"Or Giovanni, sì?" Giovanna stepped forward and thumbed his chest.

"Or me either!" Somebody yelled.

Snickers erupted from the ring of young men around them, and Cassidy plopped back down. It was no use arguing. She shifted, her gaze landing on Blake's rock-solid jaw just inches away. A muscle twitched in his cheek, and her heart sank. He wouldn't be bullied into marriage. She knew him well enough to know that.

Her thoughts slammed back to the beginning of the trip when Beecher had insisted they marry or go back to Independence. Blake had been willing then, as long as she went to California, but she'd dug in her heels and refused, too stubborn to give even an inch back then. But Mama had told her to follow her heart. And her heart was no longer set on a place, but a man. Had she missed her chance back when she didn't know what she wanted?

But to pick Flynn, or Giovanni, or even one of the others? Nope, she wouldn't do that either. Flynn had shanghaied the wrong woman if he thought she'd pick out a man willy-nilly just because he said she had to. She relaxed against the rough lumber of the oxcart and watched the lightning flash across the sky. "I guess I'll just stay right here, tied up and drowning in the rain."

A snort of amusement rumbled from Blake. "Untie us, Flynn, before we all get soaked."

"Miz Taylor was right." Flynn stomped toward the back of the cart and made quick work of releasing both Blake and Cassidy. "Too stubborn for your own goo', she said, and tha' we'd be wastin' our time, for sure."

Blake sat up. "You should've listened to her."

"Maybe we'll let you walk back. Tha' should knock some sense into yer thick—" He cocked his head. "What's that?"

Cassidy froze as she heard a rumble like thunder. But different, as if it came from the ground, not the sky. The roar magnified in intensity, and terror gripped her throat. "Blake, that sounds like—"

"Flash flood! Get out of here." Blake grabbed the reins and slapped them against the mule. "Hiya!"

Flynn swung up behind the nearest rider, and the mounted men raced away. Heart pounding, Cassidy held on as the cart lurched across the prairie, the roar of the water and the crack of breaking limbs drowning out the pounding hooves. The cart hurtled along, bouncing into the air, only to slam back to earth with enough force to splinter the thing in two.

Lightning flashed, and horrified, she saw a wall of water bearing down on them. "Blake!"

He let go of the reins, grabbed her, and pulled her to the floor of the cart, protecting her with his body as the floodwaters slammed into the cart.

Chapter 18

The cart flipped, dumping them into the raging waters of the flooded Snake River.

Blake kept an iron band around Cassidy's waist, even as the force of the water tried to rip her away from him. He slammed into a tree and sucked in a breath before wrapping his free arm around the trunk. He shoved Cassidy up and out of the water. "Grab hold of something. Anything."

She scrambled up, escaping the grasp of the deluge, and wrapped her arms around a battered sapling. A flash of lightning illuminated the sky, revealing her pale face, her hand stretched out toward him. "Take my hand."

"Go." He shouted, terrified that the water would suck him back down and her with him. "Get to higher ground."

"No. Please, Blake, hurry." A long tree branch slammed into him, the other end lodged against the tree Cassidy had anchored herself against. She held on to the limb, and Blake pulled himself out of the floodwaters toward her.

He kept moving, leading Cassidy farther away from the river toward higher ground. Only when the roar receded did he stop, collapsing to his knees. Cassidy fell beside him, gasping for breath. He grabbed her shoulders and raked his gaze over her, frantically searching for injury. "Are you hurt?"

She shook her head, her face awash in tears. "No. I thought. . .I thought I'd lost you. That. . .that the water was going to pull you under. I've never been so scared—"

"*Shh.*" He pulled her into his arms and let her cry. "It's over. We're safe."

Finally her sobs faded and she lifted her head, her face flushed from crying and her lashes spiked with tears. But she was the most beautiful woman he'd ever seen. Overcome with the realization that she could have died, he cupped her face in his hands and pulled her close, capturing her lips with his. Choking back a sob, she wrapped her arms around his neck and kissed him back, as if she never wanted to let him go.

Blake groaned as light exploded inside his chest, like sparks from the well-placed blow of his hammer. No matter what happened, he couldn't let her go. He'd come too close to losing her back there and couldn't bear the thought of parting ways ever again. He kissed her one last time then eased back and growled, "Cassidy Taylor, we've got some things to settle."

She hitched a delicate brow, her expression too enchanting to be threatening. "Oh?"

"Yes, ma'am." He stood, pulled her to her feet, and looped his arms around her waist. "I wouldn't be in this predicament if you hadn't shanghaied me back in Independence."

"Is that a fact?"

"Yes, it's a fact, and you know it. And you also know that Beecher's gonna be fit to be tied by the time we get back."

"Mm-hm." She bit her lip in an effort to hold back a smile.

His grip tightened, and he snuggled her closer. "So, I've been thinking. Maybe I'll just shanghai you until you agree to marry me and go to California."

The teasing smile dimmed, and she became serious. "I thought maybe you didn't want me, that I was too much like Gertie and—and my grandma."

Blake frowned. "What's your grandmother got to do with us?"

"She ran roughshod over the whole family, including Pa." She cleared her throat. "Some would say she was a bit contentious."

"Stubborn, maybe?"

"Yes, that, too."

"She ever kidnap anyone?"

"No." Cassidy replied on a half laugh as she swatted his arm. "You're not mad at me for what I did?"

Blake gazed down at her, thinking back to the day he'd woken up in her wagon. "Sweetheart, I don't think I was ever really mad at you, even from the beginning. But I guess I'm just as stubborn as you are and didn't want to be forced into doing something I didn't want to do."

She plucked at a button on his shirt, ripped and torn from their fight with the river, before lifting her gaze to his, a teasing smile tugging at her lips. "So, do you feel forced?"

He chuckled, lifted her off her feet, and twirled her around. She laughed and threw her arms around his neck. He slowed, claiming her lips once again. When he could breathe, he inched away and murmured, "Not by a long shot."

Smiling, she reached up and brushed his hair back, her fingertips soft and gentle against his skin. "Like Ruth, I'll go wherever you go. If it's California, Oregon, or right here on this very spot."

"Are you sure? Because you're my California. We'll go to Oregon if that's what you want. Or stay in Fort Hall. I hear they're going to need a new blacksmith."

Cassidy smiled. "Fort Hall seems like the perfect compromise."

"And you're not ever going to be contentious again?"

"Well, I didn't say *that*."

She stood on tiptoe and lifted her face to his, proving just how uncontentious she could be.

Chapter 19

They came across the mule a half mile from the floodwaters. There was no sign of the oxcart, and what was left of the harness had tangled in some mesquite bushes and held fast.

A mite skittish, the mule was otherwise unharmed. Blake cut him free, discarded the harness, and helped Cassidy onto the mule's broad back. He swung up behind her, and they headed in the general direction of the Oregon Trail.

The sun was breaking the horizon as they crossed the main trail, and Blake estimated they were somewhere between the wagon train and Fort Hall. So they headed east.

Cassidy wrinkled her nose at the pitiful state of her dress. "I must look a sight."

"You look mighty fetching, Miss Taylor." Blake tightened his arm around her waist and kissed her temple.

Cassidy blushed. "Behave yourself. You're going to have to act properly chastised, or Mr. Beecher's going to have a fit."

They topped a ridge and saw the wagon train in the valley below—the same spot they'd left it the night before. They'd broken camp, and the wagons were just starting to line up, but a party of riders had gathered and seemed to be arguing. A shout went up when someone spotted them, and Blake urged the mule forward. The riders hurried to meet them, Beecher's dappled-gray mare in the lead.

Cassidy spotted Flynn, Giovanni, and Angus in the group, and even though she was still annoyed at them for kidnapping her, she was glad they were safe. And, if truth be told, she was just a tiny bit glad they'd interfered.

Beecher reined in, his ruddy face looking like he was about to bust a gut. "Samuelson, it's about time you and Miss Taylor showed up. What do you have to say for yourself, man?"

"Good morning to you, too, Mr. Beecher."

"Samuelson, I warned you," Mr. Beecher blustered.

"Yes, sir, you did." Blake sidled the mule up to Beecher's mare. Cassidy found it difficult to look guilty when she was bubbling over with happiness, but she did her best. "I'd like to ask Mrs. Taylor for her daughter's hand in marriage. I figure it's the least I can do under the circumstances and all."

"Well, um—" Beecher sputtered, "I reckon that's a fine idea. I can't imagine Mrs. Taylor refusing, though."

Blake's chest rumbled with laughter. "I can't either."

He kicked the mule, and they rode past. The entire wagon train lined up to welcome them back in true shivaree fashion.

From behind her, she heard Beecher say, "Well, Flynn McGowan, that shanghai stunt was about the most irresponsible thing I ever heard of, but I suppose all's well that ends well. Mr. Samuelson and Miss Taylor are getting hitched before we reach Fort Hall. Just like you promised."

Settled Hearts
by Myra Johnson

Chapter 1

Emma Clarke fought the jostling crowds. She yelped as a brawny, bearded man almost knocked her into the street.

"Careful, little lady." He steadied her with a rough grip on her upper arm.

"Thank you." At least he recognized she *was* a lady. Many she'd encountered since arriving in Independence hadn't been so polite. Some seemed annoyed, others mildly curious, a few outright leering.

All of them, apparently, were gearing up for the trek west.

Emma ducked into a general store. She picked through a display of boots, trying to look inconspicuous while she studied the customers' faces. Surely she'd find one kindly soul among the emigrants, preferably a Christian family man with a wife and children. She could pay her own way, and she knew how to work hard. But as a woman traveling the Oregon Trail alone, she didn't stand a chance.

"Help you with some boots, miss?" The balding store clerk cast her a doubtful glance.

"Thanks, just looking." She turned her attention to bags of dried apples.

A meaty hand brushed hers, and she looked up into the yellowed grin of a man who'd ogled her on the street earlier. A stench of tobacco fouled his breath. "Sure hope my wagon's close to yours, pretty lady."

Lady on his lips took on an entirely different connotation. Backing away, Emma stumbled into the store clerk.

The clerk braced her elbow. "He bothering you?"

Nothing like looking the part of a helpless female. Emma stiffened her spine. "I can take care of myself, thank you."

The clerk steered her toward a quiet area near the counter. "I've been watching you for a couple days now, wandering up and down the street like a lost puppy. What exactly is it you're looking for?"

Emma loosened the drawstrings of her reticule and pulled out a ragged folder. She opened the stiff brown paper and showed the clerk a photograph. "I'm looking for my father. He and a friend left for Oregon two years ago. Maybe they were in your store?"

The clerk chortled. "With all the folks traipsing in and out, you expect me to remember a fella from two years ago?"

She knew it was a long shot. With a sigh, she tucked the daguerreotype into her reticule. "Then perhaps you know of a family going west who might have room for one more?"

"Most folks are already packed to the rafters." The clerk cast her a patronizing smile and nodded toward the door. "You should head on home, missy. A slip of a thing like you has no business on the Oregon Trail."

She stood her ground. "I *must* find my father. My mother is—"Tears threatened, but she wouldn't give in. "I have a room at the Mockingbird boardinghouse. If you should learn of a family who might let me journey with them, please send word."

John Patrick laid a pair of leather chaps and three rubber sheets on the counter. "I'll need three of those blankets behind you, too." While the clerk totaled the sale, John watched the pretty young blond march out of the store. "The girl you were just talking with— couldn't help overhearing. She's looking for someone to travel with?"

"So she says. I say she's only asking for trouble." The clerk took John's money and handed him a receipt. "You aren't thinking of taking her on, I hope."

"Just curious." Mouth flattening, John gathered up his purchases. Heaven knew he could use a woman's touch with the children. Not to mention he wasn't much of a cook. Like so many headed west, all he knew was farming, and the chance to claim free land in Oregon tempted him even more than the gold luring countless others to California.

After stopping at the blacksmith's to check on repairs to the wagon he'd purchased, John returned to the diner where he'd left ten-year-old Henry to watch over his little sister, Addie. His heart clenched at the sight of them huddled together at a corner table as Henry read aloud from Dickens's *The Old Curiosity Shop*. The story might be a bit over a seven-year-old's head, but Addie seemed enthralled.

As John neared the table, Henry glanced up, his eyes lighting. "Addie, look. Unc—I mean, Papa's back."

John gave a subtle nod and pulled out a chair. "You children been behaving?"

"Yes, sir." Henry straightened, looking every bit the responsible big brother. "Addie had to use the facilities once, but a nice lady helped her."

"That's good." There'd been similar awkward moments since they'd left Kennard, Illinois, and John had asked himself more than once whether he'd made a huge mistake. Traveling west with an adventurous young boy was one thing. It was quite another seeing to the needs of a growing girl.

He thought again of the young woman in the general store. Would it hurt to meet her and ask about her plans? Perhaps they could strike an arrangement beneficial to them both.

"Kids, can you mind yourselves here a little longer? There's one more stop I need to make before we head back to camp."

At the Mockingbird boardinghouse, a plump woman with a severe bun—the proprietress, he gathered—eyed him up and down. "This is a family establishment. There'll be no unchaperoned visits between a single man and a single lady."

"Ma'am, if you could just tell the young lady I'd like to speak with her." Hat in hand, John waited on the front porch until the door opened again and a pert blond head peered out.

"Hello," she said warily. The proprietress stood right behind her, arms folded.

Now that he saw her up close, John's nerves kicked in. How could he risk involving anyone else in his problems, least of all an innocent like this girl? She looked barely twenty, if that. The store clerk was right—she had no business on the trail with a bunch of gold seekers and land-hungry emigrants. "Sorry, this was a mistake. I shouldn't have bothered you."

Before he could step off the porch, the girl hurried out, halting in front of him. "Did the store clerk send you? Are you going west?"

"Uh, yes, but. . ." He flinched beneath her sharp scrutiny.

"Are you a family man, sir?"

"I am." He stood a little taller.

"Are you a Christian?"

A much harder question, and one he'd wrestled with often the last few years. "I was raised a Christian, yes." He gnawed the inside of his lip. "Just don't get to church much anymore."

She frowned briefly. "And did the store clerk explain my. . .situation?"

"Only said you were alone and hoped to join up with a family going west."

The girl shot a glance toward the steely-eyed woman watching from the doorway. "We should talk then. But not here."

John's gut said one thing, but his heart said another. He had to do right by those kids. "My children are waiting for me at the diner around the corner."

"Fine. Let me fetch something from my room and I'll be right along." She turned to go then paused and offered her hand. "By the way, I'm Emma Clarke."

He swallowed hard before enfolding her dainty hand within his own. "My pleasure. John Patrick, at your service."

—⁓—

Darting upstairs, Emma hoped she'd read the tall stranger correctly. He had an honest look about him, and he did mention children, which must mean he also had a wife. She'd prayed to find a Christian family man, and God had sent one right to her door.

After making sure the daguerreotype of her father was still safely tucked into her reticule, she threw a shawl over her shoulders and hurried down again. Mrs. Dill, the proprietress, cast her a disapproving frown, but Emma said a quick good-bye before the woman could lecture her on the dangers of consorting with men of dubious repute.

Mr. Patrick waited for her at the corner. As they walked to the diner, Emma kept a respectable distance between them, which she was grateful the man honored.

He showed her inside, where she spied a boy and a girl sipping milk and munching on cookies. Fairer in coloring than Mr. Patrick, they must favor their mother.

As they ambled over, the boy's brows shot up. "Hi, P–Papa." With a guilty expression, he wiped his mouth across his sleeve. "We didn't ask for the milk and cookies. The nice lady gave them to us."

"Did she now?" Grinning, Mr. Patrick ruffled the boy's hair. "I'll thank her later. In the meantime, I have some business to talk over with this lady."

Emma glanced around. "Your wife isn't here?"

"It's just me and the kids." Mr. Patrick pulled out a chair for Emma at an empty table nearby.

She remained standing. "Excuse me, but you stated you were a family man. I assumed—"

"Never meant to mislead you. And, as you can see, I do have a family. Just. . .not a wife."

"Oh, you're a widower. I'm so sorry." If he'd been married, he must surely know how to respect a woman. Besides, his children seemed quite well behaved. Emma edged closer to the chair.

A serving woman came over with mugs and a coffeepot. "Those kids are the sweetest things ever. You two must be wonderful parents."

"But I'm not—" The protest died on Emma's lips as the woman filled their mugs then bustled over to the next table.

"Please, let's sit and talk." Mr. Patrick motioned again toward her chair. When they were seated, he hauled in a deep breath and let it out again. "The thing is, I'm in kind of a bind, and I gather you are, too. Maybe we could help each other."

"If you're needing assistance with the children, I'm quite experienced. I'm the eldest of four girls." She glanced past Mr. Patrick's shoulder toward the handsome little boy. "I confess I have no experience with brothers, however."

"I do all right with Henry." He sipped his coffee. "It's Addie I worry about. She's only seven."

"Poor dear, so young to lose her mother." Emma's thoughts traveled back to St. Louis, where her own mother grew sicker every day. Urgency to find her father before it was too late had trumped common sense and prompted this journey westward. If John Patrick could help her. . .

Hands clasped on the table, she leaned forward, her gaze pleading. "Please, Mr. Patrick, you're my last hope. Take me with you on the Oregon Trail."

Chapter 2

John couldn't decide who was crazier—him or Miss Clarke. Scrambling eggs at their campfire the next morning, he had to wonder at the courage of a young woman willing to leave behind home and family and embark on such a perilous journey.

Henry held out a tin plate for the overcooked lump of eggs John served him. "I hope Miss Clarke cooks better than you, Unc—"

"Papa. Call me Papa." John cupped the boy's chin. "You mustn't forget, Henry. Ever. Everything depends on it."

"I'm sorry." Henry's brown eyes shone with regret.

"It's okay. I know this is hard, but it's the only way we can be safe." Quick glances toward the neighboring campsites assured John no one had overheard their exchange. In a few more days, the wagon train would set out, putting even more distance between John and his old life. For his sake, but even more for the children's, he hoped it never caught up with him.

He fixed a plate of eggs for Addie then sent Henry to the tent to wake her. Pale yellow hair in a tangle, she stumbled out rubbing her eyes. One look at the eggs and she wrinkled her nose in disgust.

John sat her down on a camp stool. "Come on, sugar, you gotta eat so you'll be strong for the trip. It's a long, long way to Oregon."

Addie peered up at John with eyes so like Sarah's it made his chest ache. "Will it be pretty there? With flowers and trees and a cozy house for us to live in?"

"Prettier than a picture, just you wait." Grinning, John tweaked one of her messy curls. Addie asked the same question every day, as if she needed reassurance they were headed to a better life. A happier life. A life where innocent children were cherished and kept safe.

John only hoped he could keep them all safe until they made it to Oregon.

And now, "all" included Miss Emma Clarke. Again, he wondered if he'd made a huge mistake. He should ride into town right now and tell her so. Tell her to head back to where she came from and forget about finding her father.

Except he'd seen the same stubbornness in her that drove him. If he turned her down, she'd likely keep on trying until she found someone else to take her west, and who knew what unscrupulous characters she could end up with? With a resigned sigh, John realized he could no more abandon Miss Clarke to an unknown fate than he could have left Henry and Addie to suffer abuse.

He washed down the last few bites of tasteless eggs with coffee stout enough to grease an axle. One thing for certain—Miss Clarke's cooking couldn't be worse than his.

They'd need more food and supplies for the journey though, so he'd best get to town and stock up.

With his mule hitched to the farm cart, he set off with the kids. When they pulled up to the Mockingbird boardinghouse, he had the children wait while he called for Miss Clarke. He could tell from Mrs. Dill's sour expression that she hadn't changed her opinion of him.

Moments later, Miss Clarke came out to the porch, her eyes filled with worry. "Please don't say you've changed your mind."

"No, ma'am." John removed his hat, mangling the brim with nervous fingers. "Not that I didn't come awful close. But it won't be an easy journey. Are you dead certain you're up for it?"

"Dead certain. I *must* find my father, or at least learn what became of him. Mama can't hold on much longer."

"All right then. The wagon train boss wants to leave early next week, so we'd best be ready. I'm pretty much stocked for myself and the children. With you coming along, we'll need more supplies."

Brow furrowed, Miss Clarke looked past John toward the cart. "Is that what we're traveling in?"

"Oh no. I already bought a wagon and a team of oxen to pull it. Henry can drive the cart with our extra gear for as long as it holds up." He glanced down at her dainty black boots. "I sure hope you can handle miles and miles of rough ground."

Doubt flickered in the girl's wide brown eyes then vanished just as quickly. Chin raised, arms crossed, she held herself erect. "I'm tougher than I look, Mr. Patrick. I'll keep up, don't you worry."

He should worry. He should worry plenty. But something about her unyielding attitude emboldened him, and he found himself looking forward to her company on this journey. "Then let's go get those supplies."

———

Though Mr. Patrick—John, as he'd insisted she call him—had suggested Emma stay at the boardinghouse until the wagon train left, she decided she may as well get used to life on the trail. They'd spent the last two days scouring stores throughout Independence for additional food and supplies. Flour, bacon, coffee, dried beans and fruit, molasses, cooking utensils, pails, blankets, tools, lanterns. . . Emma had never ventured farther than the outskirts of St. Louis and could only trust John to know what they'd need.

If she'd been born a boy, she might know a bit about camping. She might have gone west with her father instead of staying home to wait and worry. Now, with no word from Papa and her mother growing weaker every day, Emma felt torn in two. *Please, dear Lord, keep Mama alive until I can bring Papa home.*

Standing with the children near the rear door of the livery, Emma watched a man help John hitch up the team of four oxen to the long, canvas-covered wagon they called a "prairie schooner."

Addie slipped her hand into Emma's. "Those big oxes are scary-looking."

"Yes, indeed. We'd best stay out of their way."

With spare parts loaded onto the wagon and two more oxen tied to the back, John helped Emma and the children climb up to the seat. John walked alongside and urged the oxen forward, steering them with a "Gee!" or a "Haw!" as they headed to the campground. As they bumped along the well-worn road, Emma dreaded how much worse the open prairie would be. John had said she should be prepared to walk. She only hoped the four pairs of sturdy boots she'd purchased would last the journey.

It was nearing sunset when they reached John's campsite. He waved to two men seated at a campfire nearby. "Thanks for keeping an eye on our stuff," John called.

"Happy to oblige." The man wearing a plaid flannel shirt rose and ambled over. "See you brought your missus back with you. Glad to have you join us, ma'am."

Emma shot John a look of surprise.

"Just nod and smile, okay? I'll explain later." He reached up to help the children to the ground.

Emma stayed put, only to glance over and find the man in the flannel shirt offering up a hand to her.

"Howdy, ma'am. I'm Louis Finch, and that skinny fella over there's my brother, Barney. Looks like we'll be traveling together."

Reluctantly, she allowed him to help her down. "How do you do? I'm Emma Cl—" She snapped her mouth shut. Since these were John's friends, perhaps introductions were better left to him.

He'd already started unhitching the team. "We'll catch up later, gentlemen. I need to see to the livestock and get the family settled in."

"You betcha." Louis offered a friendly grin. "You can graze your animals over yonder with ours."

While the Finch brothers helped John with the oxen, Emma decided she should make herself useful and figure out something for supper. She spied the circle of stones marking John's campfire and sent Henry in search of kindling then hunted through the supplies in the farm cart. She found dried beef, eggs, cornmeal, and beans, and with Henry's help getting the fire going, she soon filled the air with the savory aromas of stew and corn bread.

Addie took a big sniff from her perch on a stool near the fire. "This sure smells better than what Papa cooks."

"I've had a lot of practice," Emma said with a laugh. Considering the lack of variety in their food stores, she'd need to be quite creative in finding new ways to serve dried meat and beans.

The men returned, and when Emma saw the hungry looks in the Finch brothers' eyes, she was glad she'd made extra. Though they'd already eaten their own evening meal, they weren't shy about polishing off the leftovers when the others had eaten their fill.

After helping with the cleanup, Louis and Barney thanked Emma again for the delicious stew and headed over to their camp. Fatigue catching up with her, Emma leaned against a wagon wheel. John had sent the children inside a small tent to get ready for bed, and now Emma wondered where she would sleep tonight. Remembering John's friends believed she was his wife—which he *still* had yet to explain—she certainly hoped he wasn't entertaining any ideas about shared sleeping arrangements.

John ambled over. "That's the best meal I've had since. . ." He glanced away briefly. "Well, in a real long time. You sure weren't lying about your cooking skills."

Arching a brow, Emma straightened. "Apparently, *one* of us is lying. Why would you let your friends assume we're married?"

"Think about it, Emma. Other men on the trail find out we're not married, and they'll think you're a loose woman."

Emma! sucked in a breath. "I most certainly am *not*! And if you think for one minute—"

"Lower your voice." Glancing right and left, John stepped closer, resting one hand on the wagon wheel near her shoulder. "Believe me, Emma, I have the highest respect for you. The only reason I let on we're married is for your protection, so other men will leave you be."

What he said made sense. Emma had been too anxious to leave for Oregon to consider how her traveling with John and his children might appear. "But. . .you might have told them I was your sister, not your wife."

He looked away sharply, his eyes mere shadows in the waning light. His tone hardened. "What's done is done. I'm sorry. I should have talked to you about it first."

"Yes, you sh—" Before Emma could finish, John marched off toward the children's tent. The air around her seemed suddenly colder, and not even her thick wool shawl could quiet her shivering. To play the part of a wife, when she'd never even had a beau? And despite her traipsing all over Independence with the man, John Patrick remained a virtual stranger. What did she really know about him beyond the fact that he was a widower with two good-natured children?

You did this to yourself, Emma Clarke. You and your stubborn, reckless determination.

Well, there was nothing to be done for it now. Turning, Emma eyed the canvas-topped wagon. Until they finished filling it with supplies, it could offer a bit of privacy and a protected place to sleep. She was about to hoist herself in through the rear opening when a muscular arm clamped around her waist.

She screamed.

Chapter 3

E asy, easy. It's just me." John held Emma firmly until she stopped struggling. "Didn't mean to startle you. Just thought you might need a hand up."

She straightened her skirt and glared at him. "Glory be, John Patrick! For all I knew, you were one of those unscrupulous types coming to take advantage of a *loose woman*."

He'd laugh if it wouldn't mean risking a slap. He bent down to retrieve the bedding he'd dropped while trying to calm her. "Brought you some blankets. Anything else you need before morning?"

"Not from *you*," she shot back, the bedding hugged against her chest like a shield.

John cast a wary glance toward the Finches' camp and hoped they'd assume the raised voices signified nothing more than a harmless marital spat. The first of many, unless he and Emma came to an understanding soon. He apologized again. "If you'd be more comfortable letting people think you're my sister, I'll think up something to tell Barney and Louis. It's just, with the kids and all—"

"It's too late." Emma's chin dipped. "No use compounding lie upon lie."

Her words stabbed John in the gut. How many lies had he already told since leaving Illinois? Not by choice, but certainly out of necessity. Would God forgive him for what he'd done? Would Sarah, if she knew?

I did it for the kids, he whispered in his heart, and hoped his plea reached heaven.

He realized Emma was staring at him. More like staring *through* him, as if she could see the layers of deceit blackening his soul. She pursed her lips. "I suppose your plan is best, although I can't imagine how you'll explain away our separate. . ." Her sharp sigh and quick glance at the wagon hinted at the blush the darkness hid.

"For tonight, anyway, we'll say the tent proved a bit too crowded for the four of us."

"And tomorrow, and every night after, when the wagon is filled with our supplies?"

Since tucking the children in for the night, John had thought of little else, and he'd come up with an idea. "You and Addie can have the tent. Henry and I will sleep under the wagon. Nobody will question that arrangement."

After a moment of thoughtful silence, Emma nodded. "Very well. Now, if you don't mind, I'm exhausted."

"Of course." John offered a hand to help her into the wagon. She took it reluctantly, gathering up her skirts as she climbed inside. He waited another minute or two to make sure she settled in then called a tentative "Good night."

She didn't answer.

—m—

"Unc—I mean, Papa. Wake up." Henry's urgent tone roused John from a deep sleep.

"What is it, boy?" John forced his eyes open, only to squeeze them shut as bright sunlight blazed through the tent opening. Heavens, had he slept half the day away?

Henry shifted, blocking the harsh light. "Miss Emma—I mean, *Mama*—" He grimaced, and John felt his pain. "She's been keeping your breakfast warm. And the wagon master's asking for you."

"Okay, okay. I'm up." Reaching for his boots, John scrambled from beneath the blanket. Aromas of coffee and sizzling bacon made his mouth water, and he couldn't get to the campfire soon enough.

A hint of concern in her eyes, Emma handed him a plate. "I began to wonder if you'd taken ill."

"Just overslept." No doubt because he'd tossed and turned until nearly dawn. Couldn't blame his restlessness on the hard ground though. It had everything to do with the fair-haired woman pouring coffee. If they'd met under different circumstances. . .

Emma sat across from him with her own steaming cup. "Did Henry tell you? The wagon master wants to head out at first light Monday morning." Her gaze swept their stash of supplies. "Can we be ready?"

Savoring Emma's hearty breakfast, John had to coax his mind back to business. He ran through his mental list and then gave a firm nod. "We'll take one more inventory before packing it all into the wagon."

"Mama, Mama!" Addie rushed over, cradling one hand against her chest. Tears streaked her sun-reddened cheeks.

Emma shared a look with John before gently spreading Addie's fingers. "What happened, honey?"

"I got a thorn. See? It's bleeding."

"Oh my, it's a big one. But I think I can fix you right up." Emma popped off the camp stool and hurried Addie over to the wagon.

Henry's chin quivered as he bent close to whisper in John's ear. "She's not our mama."

"I know, son. I'm hurting, too." Wrapping an arm around Henry's waist, John pulled him close. "But it has to be this way if I'm to keep you and your sister safe."

John noticed some other boys tossing a ball and shooed Henry off to play. The boy's slumped shoulders echoed John's own feelings about what had brought them to this point. But when he recalled the circumstances he'd found the children in, anger eclipsed grief. Getting far away from Kennard, Illinois, was all that mattered. Their departure for Oregon couldn't come soon enough.

—⁓—

By Sunday evening, Emma's back and shoulders ached from all the lifting, toting, and shoving as they packed the wagon. John had told her several times to let him handle the heaviest loads, but she refused to appear weak. John's male pride had caused her trouble enough when he balked at taking her money to buy additional supplies.

As she fetched water to wash up after supper, John hurried over to relieve her of the sloshing bucket. "I'll take it from here. You've worked hard enough for one day."

"But the dishes—"

"Henry and I will clean up." John's eyes held a softness that made Emma's throat clench. "Take Addie to the tent and get some sleep. We've got a long day of traveling ahead, and plenty more to follow."

"Will you and Henry be all right under the wagon? It looks like rain."

She'd barely spoken when the sky let loose. Fat raindrops pelted the ground, already muddy and rutted by wagon wheels and animals' hooves. A crack of thunder sent her flying into John's arms, and before she could collect herself, both Henry and Addie shoved between them.

"To the tent," John ordered, his arms around all of them.

Seconds later and drenched to the skin, they huddled beneath the canvas while rain sheeted past the opening and thunder rolled overhead. John gathered up blankets and wrapped one around each child then started to do the same for Emma.

She flinched as his hand brushed her cheek. "I–I've got it. Thank you." She tugged the blanket around her shoulders and scooted toward the corner of the tent. Even in the confined space, she could feel the warmth of his breath.

"Will you hold me, Mama?" Addie crept onto Emma's lap. "I'm scared."

Emma hardly knew what to make of the child's easy acceptance of the pretense John had concocted. But Addie clearly craved a mother's tender care, and for now, Emma was the closest thing these children had to a mother.

Even so, she sensed Henry's resentment. . .and something else. More than once, he'd seemed to stumble over calling John *Papa*. What was their story? And what had happened to the children's real mother?

With Addie snuggled beneath her chin and the toil of the last few days catching up with her, Emma began to relax. Soon the storm abated, and John and Henry crawled from the tent, giving Emma and Addie privacy to change into dry clothes. Emma burrowed deep into a nest of blankets with Addie at her side and fell asleep within minutes.

Hours later, she awoke to the sounds of men's voices and the bawling of oxen and mules. Dawn hadn't yet broken, but already the air was heavy with smells of quickly prepared breakfasts and strong coffee. This was the day Emma had been waiting for, the day they set out for Oregon. Somewhere along the way, she'd find someone who remembered her father.

Hold on, Mama. I'll bring him back to you, I promise.

"Emma?" John called through the tent opening. "We're leaving soon."

"Coming." She roused Addie then hurried them both into their boots and coats.

Outside, the whole encampment was abuzz with excitement. John already had his oxen yoked and the mule hitched to the farm cart. He thrust a tin of coffee into Emma's hands then gave her and Addie slabs of brown bread and dried meat. "Eat up quick," he said. "No time for cooking."

"I'd have fixed something. Why didn't you wake me sooner?"

"Same reason you let me sleep too long the other day." John smiled and winked before hurrying off to some other task.

After only a few days, had they come to care so much about each other's well-being? Despite Emma's growing questions about John and his family, she sensed he was a man she could trust, a man who'd look after her and keep her safe.

Henry came from the Finches' camp with a cup of milk for Addie. Emma had been glad to learn the brothers were bringing their dairy cow and had offered to share.

"You take such good care of your sister," Emma remarked, hoping to ease past Henry's reserve.

"Got to, since our ma—" He clamped his lips together, his gaze shifting nervously.

"Perhaps someday you'll tell me about her." Emma tipped her head toward the neighboring campsites and added softly, "When other ears aren't around to hear."

Henry answered with a shrug before darting over to where John gave the wagon another inspection. Apparently satisfied, John motioned Henry to the farm cart then strode to the campfire.

"Time to hit the trail," John said as he doused the fire and gathered up the remains of breakfast. "Henry will drive the cart. Emma, you and Addie can ride in the wagon seat. Enjoy it while you can, though, because the roads aren't going to get any smoother."

Emma's heart thrilled, as much from the hope of finding her father as from the spirit of adventure surrounding this journey. She'd so wanted to accompany Papa when he'd set out two years ago. They'd find fertile land in Oregon then send for Mama and the other girls, and they'd all start anew.

But today, Emma's excitement was tempered with worry. Though Emma had kept her plans secret until the last possible moment, Mama would know by now that her eldest daughter had left for Oregon and would worry plenty—not good for a woman growing weaker every day. In town last week, Emma had posted a letter assuring Mama she was all right and promising to send word again as soon as she could.

She could only pray her next letter would contain encouraging news about finding Papa.

Chapter 4

John had been right—within days of setting out, Emma was more than ready to walk. When others weren't looking, she'd groan and give her poor, bruised backside a rub. The prairie looked deceptively smooth, while beneath the undulating grasses lay ruts and gullies ready to snap axles and wagon wheels.

Most every evening a spring rainstorm blew in, and they were fortunate if it came late enough that the wagons had stopped for the night and John had erected their little tent. More often than not, the showers caught them on the open prairie, flooding streams and making passage treacherous.

Late one afternoon during their second week on the trail, they reached a stream crossing just as the sky opened up. Several of the other wagons made it across before the waters rose, but when the next wagon foundered, John opted not to take the risk. Working alongside him in the pouring rain, Emma helped set up the tent and hurried the children inside.

"You should go in, too," John said, water dripping from his hat brim. "I need to see to the livestock."

Emma pushed a sodden lock of hair off her face. "It'll be quicker if we work together. Then we can both get out of the rain."

When he looked as if he might argue, Emma spun around and waded through the puddles to the front of the wagon. She'd watched John unhitch the team often enough that she had an idea where to start.

"Emma—" John's shout came a split second before the nearest ox stepped sideways, its massive hoof crushing Emma's foot.

She yelped and fell backward into the mud. Blinded by rain and searing pain, she gasped for air while John shoved against the stubborn animal's haunches. After freeing Emma's foot, he knelt over her, shielding her from the downpour while he struggled to remove her boot.

"You fool of a woman! You could have got yourself killed!"

Now that she could breathe again, she pushed up on her elbows only to sink back in the mire. At least the pain had lessened. Looking down at her boot, muddied up to the ankle, she realized the rain-soaked earth had cushioned the impact, saving her foot from far worse damage. "Just help me up, will you? I'm fine."

Muttering under his breath, John gave up on the boot and turned his fiery gaze upon Emma. "Why couldn't you do as I said and wait in the tent with the children?"

"I only wanted to lend a hand. I thought the sooner we took care of the animals, the sooner we could make camp for the night and get some supper." Emma fought against the heavy mud clinging to her clothes and stumbled to her feet. If she stood in the rain long enough, she might eventually get clean.

Then, as quickly as it began, the downpour abated. John's stormy face mirrored the thunderclouds retreating in the distance, and Emma wondered what had fueled his anger. . .or was it fear? Had her accident stirred memories of how his wife had died?

Lowering her gaze, she wiped her hands on her wet skirts. "I'm sorry if I upset you, John. I'll be more careful."

"See that you are." With a frustrated groan, John slid an arm around Emma's waist. "Can you walk?"

Her injured foot felt bruised, and her ankle had twisted when she fell, but that seemed the worst of it. "I told you, I'm fine."

John didn't look convinced. He didn't remove his arm either as he led Emma away from the oxen. "All the same, you'll ride in the cart with Henry tomorrow. It'll be more comfortable than the wagon seat."

The other wagons on this side of the stream had circled up, and most of the travelers had their animals unhitched for grazing. The Finch brothers strode over, both of them in dripping rain slickers.

"We saw your missus go down," Louis said. "Everything okay?"

John's grip tightened around Emma's waist. "She got her foot stomped."

Barney whistled softly and shook his head. "Oxen ain't nothin' to be messed with, little lady. You best leave 'em to the menfolk."

Emma nodded silently, shooting John an awkward glance. Once she'd assured him she could walk unaided, she left him and the Finches to see to the livestock. Emma called Henry and Addie from the tent and had them fetch the dried buffalo chips they'd collected along the trail. With the campfire blazing, she started supper preparations.

The meal was a silent affair. Addie kept nodding off as she ate, until Emma finally carried her into the tent and put her to bed. Henry wouldn't admit how tired he was, but when John suggested he lay out their pallets under the wagon, he didn't argue.

When it was just Emma and John at the campfire, she poured him another cup of coffee and sat down beside him. "Are you going to stay angry with me forever?"

"I'm not angry." His tone said otherwise. He curled his fingers around the tin cup and stared into the flames.

"I honestly didn't mean to cause you trouble. I told you from the outset I'd pull my own weight on this journey."

"You have been, more than I ever expected." John slid his gaze her way, his dark eyes shimmering in the firelight. "I've come to depend on you in ways—" He broke off, swallowing hard. "I can't have you taking risks when the children need you so much."

"They need you, too." Emma glanced at his strong, work-roughened hands and remembered his firm but gentle hold as he'd helped her to her feet earlier. He must have been a good husband to his late wife. Emma hoped someday to find a man who'd be as good to her. . .or had she already found him?

No, she couldn't think of such things, not while she still searched for her father. Nothing must interfere with finding Papa and bringing him home.

Another week had passed since Emma's run-in with the ox. She'd limped a bit the first couple of days but stubbornly insisted on walking rather than giving the poor, tired mule more weight to haul in the farm cart. John admired her persistence, and he couldn't rightly blame her for declining to ride with Addie in the hard wagon seat.

Sometimes John could almost forget they weren't really married and that Emma Clarke was only a traveling companion. He'd awaken in the dark of the night and imagine holding her close and burying his nose in the sweet, rain-washed scent of her hair.

Heaven knew they'd had plenty of rain for washing since leaving Independence. But the spring rains would end soon, and then they'd have to search for clear water in rivers and streams. John didn't like thinking about the reports of cholera and other sicknesses they might face farther on.

Shifting in his bedroll, he squeezed back the rising panic in his chest. Was he crazy to bring those innocent children on such a perilous journey? Were they really better off with him than back in Illinois?

Then he recalled the welts on Henry's legs after the undeserved whippings and little Addie's tear-streaked face when she was sent to gather eggs in a henhouse full of sharp-beaked, ill-tempered chickens. If he'd realized how the Sleeths would mistreat the kids, he'd never have allowed them to be adopted.

Now he'd gotten himself into a mess of trouble. Worse, he'd brought an unsuspecting young woman along with him.

A woman who was slowly working beneath his defenses, and he couldn't allow it. If Emma learned what he'd done, kidnapping his niece and nephew and evading the law until they could get out of Illinois, she'd quickly lose whatever trust she'd placed in him.

A few days later, as the wagon train followed the South Platte through Nebraska, John needed a rest. He climbed up next to Addie to drive the oxen from the wagon seat, and they hadn't traveled far when his left front wheel hit a deep rut. The wagon tilted, Addie screamed, and before John could grab her, she toppled from the seat.

Terror shot through him. He yelled at the oxen to halt, but the beasts kept plodding forward. "Addie! *Addie!*"

"I've got her. She's all right," came Emma's voice from somewhere behind the wagon.

He leaped to the ground and finally halted the oxen. Then, spying Addie in Emma's arms, he ran to them. "Are you okay, honey? Does it hurt anywhere?"

"I bumped my elbow," Addie whimpered, tucking her head against Emma's shoulder.

The urge to scoop Addie to his chest and hold her close was intense, but he took a step back and breathed deeply until his racing heart settled. "This is my fault. If anything had happened to her—"

"John." Emma's tone was firm, matching the unwavering look in her eyes. "It was an accident. You can't bear all the blame."

"But I'm responsible. For the kids, for you." He whipped off his hat and slapped it against his thigh. Suddenly he remembered Henry. He spun around searching for the farm cart. "Henry!"

"He's up ahead, following the Finches." Stroking Addie's hair, Emma moved closer as other wagons pulled around them to pass. "We should catch up. Addie and I will walk for a while."

John nodded then took another steadying breath and marched back to the wagon. If Emma hadn't been there, if she hadn't reacted in time, he could very well be burying his little girl by the side of the road.

Forgive me, Sarah. I'll try harder to protect the children, I promise.

By the time he got the oxen moving again, they'd fallen far to the rear of the wagon train. It had been dry for a few days, so trail dust lay heavy in the air. This close to the river, insects were equally bothersome, and John looked back several times to see Emma shooing flies away from Addie's face and her own. How Emma managed to hobble along the rough trail with Addie clinging to her neck, John couldn't imagine. God may not have much use for John after what he'd done, but surely He'd shown His mercy toward those children by bringing Emma into their lives.

"I brought her for you, too, John." The thought drifted through his mind like a fresh summer breeze. Was it possible God really did care?

He dared another glance at Emma, who cast him a smile of reassurance as she shifted the dozing Addie on her hip. He could see fatigue catching up with her, but he knew she'd stubbornly refuse if he suggested she put the child down.

Tonight when they made camp, he'd make certain Emma got some rest, even if he had to do the cooking and cleanup all himself. She mothered his children. She'd saved his little girl. He owed her his gratitude and so much more.

———

As the sun lowered toward the horizon, Emma shielded her eyes and gave a sigh of relief that another day on the trail would soon end. Up ahead, the first of the wagons began their turn, leading the train into a circle for their nightly encampment.

Addie stirred. "Are we almost going to stop?"

"Almost." Emma kissed the curls at Addie's temple and wished she were hugging her sisters back home. She prayed that Dora, the second oldest, was taking good care of Mother and the younger girls.

If only she'd learn something soon about their father. Without so much as a letter from him since he'd left two years ago, she couldn't even be sure he'd made it to Oregon. What if he'd changed his mind and headed to California instead? Or was captured by Indians? Or died on the trail?

Lost in such thoughts, she startled when John appeared before her, his arms extended toward Addie. "I've got her," he said. "Go sit down and rest."

Emma was too tired to argue. She moved aside as the last of the wagons moved into formation, and then sank to the ground, massaging her aching arms. John laid Addie on the grass beside her and then strode off to unhitch the oxen. Watching Henry struggle with the mule's harness, Emma searched for the strength to get up and help. Then she needed to start a fire. She needed to put supper on. She needed to pitch the tent and lay out their bedrolls.

"Mama?" Addie crawled closer and rested her head on Emma's lap. "I'm hungry."

"I know, sweetie. We'll eat soon." If only Emma could find the energy to move again. They were still weeks away from Oregon, and some of the hardest stretches of the trail still lay before them. How would she ever make it? How would the children?

A shadow fell across her legs, and she looked up to see John standing over her. "I brought you some water." He set a pail beside her, a clean cloth draped over the rim.

"Thank you." Emma eased Addie off her lap then started to stand. "I'll get supper going right away."

"Not necessary. The Finches are cooking for all of us tonight." Kneeling at Emma's feet, John inched up the soiled hem of her skirt and began unlacing her boots.

With a gasp, Emma drew her knees up. "What are you doing?"

"I'm taking your boots off. What's it look like?" He grabbed one ankle and tugged off the boot, only to mutter a curse. "Look at this! Why didn't you tell me?"

Peering over her knees, she stared in shock at her bloody stocking. "I—I didn't realize."

"Your feet are covered in blisters, and you didn't realize?" Scowling, John undid her other boot, this time removing it gently. Carefully, he peeled off her stockings, revealing the angry, seeping sores. He wet the cloth, wrung it out, and tenderly washed Emma's feet.

She sucked in her breath as the cold water curled her toes, but quickly relaxed into John's soothing touch. Every few moments he glanced up with a reproachful frown, but his eyes held a glint of concern that made her heart do funny things.

When he'd finished cleaning her wounds, he rinsed out the cloth, tore it down the middle, and used the halves to wrap each foot. "I want you to stay right here and don't try walking. I'm going to check on Henry and the Finches, and I'll bring you back some supper. Afterward, you're going straight to bed."

Emma opened her mouth to protest, but Addie, her face pinched like a crotchety schoolmarm, stated crisply, "Now, Mama, you have to do what Papa says, 'cause he's in charge and he knows best."

Emma wondered how many times John had used those very words to convince the children to do something they didn't want to do. With a compliant smile, she tucked her skirt around her bandaged feet. "Well, if *Papa* knows best, I suppose I'd better obey."

"See that you do." John pushed to his feet, returning moments later with a camp stool and a blanket. After seeing to Emma's comfort, he took Addie with him to the Finch brothers' campsite, where it appeared supper was already under way.

A confusing mixture of emotions swept through Emma as she watched John dish up stew for the children and settle them around the campfire with Barney and Louis. Then he filled two more tin plates and carried them over to where Emma waited. After handing her a plate, he plopped onto the ground at her feet and began eating in silence.

After a moment, she said, "You don't have to keep me company if you'd rather be with the children."

"They're fine." He took a few more bites. "In case I didn't say it before, thank you."

"You don't have to thank me, John. I care very much for Addie. For both the children." Emma laid down her spoon. "I only wish Henry would accept me. It's clear he

THE OREGON TRAIL ROMANCE COLLECTION

still misses his real mother."

Instantly she regretted her choice of words. What had come over her, speaking as if she were the children's stepmother, as if she and John were actually married?

He set his empty plate aside and shifted to face her. "Emma, considering all you've done for me, for the children, I owe you the truth. Afterward, if you decide you no longer want to travel with us, I'll go from wagon to wagon until I find a decent family who'll take you the rest of the way."

Sudden dread stole the remains of Emma's appetite. When John Patrick had been so kind to her, when over the past few weeks her entire life had come to revolve around John and his children, what could he possibly tell her that would be horrible enough to drive her away?

Chapter 5

John wasn't sure why he'd picked tonight to confess everything to Emma. But he knew he couldn't live with the dishonesty any longer. He paced in front of her, casting quick glances toward the Finches' camp every little bit to make sure the kids were still enthralled by Louis and Barney's never-ending supply of tall tales.

Emma reached for his hand, stilling him. "Please, John, what is it?"

Cradling her palm, he took comfort in the reassuring look in her eyes. "I've lied to you, Emma. I'm not a widower, and the kids aren't mine. They're my nephew and niece, my sister's children."

Emma pulled her lower lip between her teeth. "I wondered why it sometimes seems hard for Henry to call you Papa. Your sister is dead?"

"She and her husband both. In a carriage accident back in Illinois."

"Oh, John, those poor children."

"That's not the worst of it." An ugly sound worked its way up John's throat as he recalled the abuse the children had endured. "A couple in town offered to adopt the kids, and me being single and struggling to make a living as a dirt farmer, what kind of home could I offer? I thought they'd be better off." Painfully, he described his discovery months later of how the Sleeths had mistreated Henry and Addie. "I didn't know," he said, his voice breaking. "I didn't know."

"So you took them." Emma clutched his clenched fist to her breast. "You did the right thing, John. You saved them."

"Yes, but for what? For a life of running from the law?" He searched Emma's gaze for understanding. "The Sleeths legally adopted the kids. I kidnapped them! That's why we're headed to Oregon." He jerked his hand free and stared into the darkness beyond the circle of wagons. "And now I've dragged you into our troubles."

With the buzz of insects and the murmur of other conversations filling the silence, John could only imagine what must be going through Emma's mind. She might pity him, she might feel a growing affection for the children, but how could she possibly want to continue west with a liar and a lawbreaker? For all he knew, when they reached the next outpost, she might even turn him in.

Filled with this new fear, he pondered his options. He and the kids could leave the wagon train and strike out on their own. Except what protection would they have against Indians, or what if John took sick and died, leaving the children utterly alone? Each new worry stabbed him like a knife wound—

Until Emma limped over to him and, with a palm to his cheek, offered up the tenderest of smiles. "You're a good man, John Patrick. I've believed it from the first moment we met. So, unless you're looking for an excuse to be rid of me, this doesn't change anything. I'll pretend to be your wife and the children's mother for as long as necessary."

He could hardly believe what he was hearing, and he couldn't have stopped himself from what happened next if a herd of buffalo had charged through the camp.

Slowly, cautiously, he scooped her tangle of blond curls from her neck as his gaze trailed to her parted lips. He'd imagined their softness so many times, and now he wanted—no, *needed*—to taste them for himself. His mouth lowered onto hers, her warmth and willingness fueling his longing.

"John..." Ducking her head, Emma pulled away. Her voice trembled. "Please. Don't."

"I shouldn't have done that. It's just..." He was falling in love with this woman, and the timing was all wrong. "I need you, Emma. I don't deserve you, but I need you."

When she looked up at him again, immense sadness darkened her gaze. "You're the kindest, most deserving man I've ever met. I prayed for God to send me someone just like you who'd take me west to find my father. But once I find him, I'm taking him home, and...and you'll be staying in Oregon."

He gripped her shoulders. "You could stay, too, Emma. You, me, the kids—we could be a family."

"My family is in St. Louis." Swiping a tear from her cheek, Emma shrugged off his hold. "I told you, John, my mother is dying. With or without my father, I have to go back."

—⁓—

Emma's feelings were confusing enough already. Why did John have to complicate everything by kissing her?

While her blisters healed, he refused to let her walk alongside the wagon. So up she climbed every morning to the wagon seat, with Addie planted securely next to her. Henry followed close beside them with the mule and farm cart.

Emma wondered how much longer the cart, or the mule, would last. John had already cobbled a rough repair job on one of the wheels, and a few days ago the mule had thrown a shoe. The blacksmith had replaced the shoe, but he'd expressed concerns about the mule's health. "If she makes it to Fort Laramie, I'll be surprised."

One night after the evening meal, Emma carried a pail of wash water to dispose of outside camp, and on her way back, she glimpsed Henry and the mule, nose to nose, in the shadow of their wagon.

"You just gotta hang on, Sadie," Henry pleaded. "I been movin' stuff little by little out of the cart so it won't be so heavy, and I know it's a long way, but once we get to Oregon, we're gonna need you." Giving a sniffle, the boy rubbed the tired old mule under her chin. "So please, please don't give up on me, okay?"

Heart clenching, Emma wished she could mother Henry the way she did Addie. *Oh, Lord, I love them both.* Loved them as she'd never expected or intended to.

Just as she'd never planned to fall in love with John. Yet she had, and there was nothing to be done for it.

Shoving aside such futile thoughts, she set down her pail and quietly walked over to Henry. She knew he'd recoil from her touch, so she stroked Sadie's neck instead. "She's having a hard time of it, poor thing. I can see her ribs sticking out more every day."

Henry replied with a noncommittal "Humph."

"I wonder if she's getting enough to eat."

"She grazes every time we stop," Henry said.

"Yes, but maybe the prairie grasses aren't enough for her." An idea formed as Emma recalled visits to her grandfather's farm. "Wait here. I'll be right back."

Emma retrieved her empty water pail, marched to the wagon, and climbed inside. There, she opened a sack of cornmeal and poured some into the pail. Then she pried the lid off a container of molasses and drizzled some onto the cornmeal, mixing it together with a wooden spoon. She lowered herself to the ground and carried the pail over to Sadie. "Here you go, girl. Try this."

The mule sniffed with interest before dropping her muzzle into the pail and slurping up Emma's concoction. When she finished, she nosed Emma's sleeve looking for more.

"She liked it," Henry said, a touch of wonder in his tone. "What was in there?"

"Cornmeal and molasses. I remembered my grandpa used to add a little to his mules' feed during plowing season." Emma scratched Sadie behind her ear. "Pulling a cart through country as rough as we've faced, Sadie's working as hard as any farm mule."

"If we give her some every day, will it help her make it to Oregon?"

"All we can do is try." Feeling as if she'd opened a small door into Henry's heart, Emma dared a quick tousle of his hair. "It's late. You should get to bed."

When he grinned up at her before darting off, a bubble of happiness rose in Emma's chest.

Boots crunched on the hard ground behind her, and Emma turned to find John striding over. He motioned toward Henry. "What was that all about?"

"He's worried about Sadie." Emma explained about the mixture she'd fed the mule. When a pained look contorted John's face, she feared she'd overstepped. "I know you didn't plan for feeding the animals from our food supplies, but I'll be frugal with meals until we reach Fort Laramie and can restock."

"Emma, it's fine. We'll manage." John sighed. "I only wish I'd thought of it. I've just been preoccupied with. . .everything."

Everything, Emma decided, must mean her. Them. What they'd each tacitly agreed to *not* discuss further.

A chilly gust of night air prompted Emma to tug up her coat collar. "I should check on Addie."

"Already tucked her into bed. She fell right to sleep." John made no move to go, and since he stood between her and the tent, and with Sadie blocking her other means of escape, Emma could only gaze up into eyes that mirrored the questions in her own heart. "Emma. . ."

He was going to kiss her again, and she wasn't going to stop him.

———

"Marry me, Emma. For real." Pulse racing from the kiss they'd shared, John held her close enough to feel the thudding of her heart against his chest. He prayed she'd say yes, because with each day that passed, he grew more and more certain he couldn't live without this woman.

"Oh, John, you know why I can't." Yet she clung to him as if she couldn't let go.

"We'll make it work. I don't know how, but we will."

She didn't respond except to nestle deeper into his embrace, and her silence spoke more than words. She loved him. Needed him as much as he needed her. They just had to figure this thing out.

Except he couldn't go back to Illinois without risking arrest, and once she found her father, or at least got word of what happened to him, she wouldn't stay.

Why, God? Why'd You bring us together only to tear us apart?

But God wasn't answering, and John figured it was his own fault. He'd failed as a brother, failed as an uncle, and this was God's punishment.

Chapter 6

Henry waved from the cart. "Look, Papa! Look up ahead."

Walking beside him, Emma strained to see past the long line of wagons. "What is it, Henry?"

"I think it's the fort. Do you see it?"

John craned his neck. "Yep, I think you're right." Laughing, he shouted, "Fort Laramie, here we come!"

Tears of relief pricked Emma's eyes. For two months they'd trekked through Kansas, Nebraska, and now Wyoming. They'd bounced through gullies and forded swollen streams. They'd fought off insects, struggled with broken wheels and axles, traded with friendly Indian tribes, and sadly, buried friends.

Here, at last, they'd have a chance to rest—*really* rest—because a grueling journey through the Rocky Mountains still lay ahead.

And perhaps Emma would find someone who remembered her father.

It was late afternoon by the time the last of the wagons halted outside the fort, its exterior wall of clay bricks topped with a palisade of slender stakes. As soon as they'd set up camp, John took the children to visit with traders and explore the fort, while Emma joined several other women down at the river to launder their dirt-encrusted traveling clothes. Though the water was cold, Emma couldn't resist wading in fully dressed to rinse the trail dust from her hair.

One of the wives she'd grown acquainted with, a fortyish German woman named Olga, handed her a clean, dry towel. "Sit here, and I will comb out your hair."

Heat from the afternoon sun still radiated from the flat, smooth boulder, and Emma soaked it up with relish. "It feels so good to be clean again. I'd almost forgotten what a luxury it is to bathe."

"It's no wonder that husbands and wives are choosing to sleep separately. Who can stand the stench?" Olga released a mischievous laugh. "Tonight though? I will remind Rupert why he married me."

Cheeks burning, Emma replied with a vague murmur. For the most part, she had avoided being drawn into such frank conversations with the other wives on the trail. *Other.* As if she were one herself.

"Marry me, Emma."

If only. . .

With her damp hair twisted into a bun and the laundry strung on a line between John's wagon and the Finches', Emma changed into her last clean dress, the prim blue calico she'd been saving especially for their stopover at Fort Laramie. Inside the tall gates, the fort bustled with activity. Emigrants haggled lustily with traders, some wanting to sell the excess furniture weighing down their wagons and others furious over the price of supplies that cost far less back in Independence.

Emma jostled through the crowd of emigrants, soldiers, traders, and Indians to the post commander's office, where an aide introduced her to First Lieutenant Richard Garnett, a distinguished-looking man with a full beard and mustache.

Garnett rose from behind the desk and offered his hand. "How may I assist you, ma'am?"

"I'm looking for my father. He'd have passed this way two years ago." Emma held out the daguerreotype.

The lieutenant studied the photograph for a few moments then sadly shook his head as he returned it. With a vague sweep of his hand, he stated, "You've seen for yourself what a madhouse we have when a wagon train comes through. I'm sorry, ma'am, but even if your father had been here only yesterday, I doubt I'd have remembered him. Feel free to ask around the post though. I wish you luck."

She preferred to put her faith in divine intervention. Apologizing for the interruption, she thanked the lieutenant and slipped out.

"Ma'am?" The young corporal who'd shown her in stopped her at the door. "Couldn't help overhearing. You might try a trader named Joaquim Domene. He's been around a few years, and I hear tell he's got a long memory."

Emma's hope surged again. "Where can I find him?"

"This time of day?" The corporal cast her a disapproving frown. "Most likely at the sutler's store guzzling beer with the off-duty enlisted men. And, ma'am, that ain't no place for a lady."

Even so, Emma had to try. On her way across the grounds, she spied John with the children and called out to him.

"It's crazy here, isn't it?" John shouted over the noise. He kept a firm grip on Henry's and Addie's hands. "Learn anything about your father?"

"I've been told to find a man named"—Emma fumbled with the pronunciation—"Joaquim Domene."

"I know who you mean. Louis and Barney were just talking to him outside the sutler's store."

Addie tugged on Emma's skirt. "And he was very scary. I didn't like him."

"Aw, he wasn't so bad," Henry said. "I'd like to hear more about his Indian adventures."

"Another time, son." Motioning Emma in the direction they'd come from, John showed the way to the store.

They found the Finch brothers guffawing over something a long-haired, rough-looking man in a leather coat was saying. The man's eyebrows rose appreciatively as Emma neared, and she instinctively drew her shawl tighter around her.

"Are you Mr. Domene?" She hoped she sounded more confident than she felt.

"*Oui,* and whom do I have the pleasure of addressing?" His courtly bow, combined with his odd foreign accent, only heightened Emma's discomfiture.

John stepped forward. He shielded the children with one arm and slipped the other possessively around Emma's shoulder. "My *wife* is seeking news of her father. We're hoping you might remember him."

"I have a photograph." Emma pulled it from her reticule. "He left for Oregon two years ago."

Domene opened the ragged paper folder and frowned. "Something is familiar about the eyes, but I can't be certain. The man I recall had not shaved in many weeks."

Forgetting her unease, Emma moved closer, the words gushing forth. "His name is William Clarke. Forty-two, light brown hair, about six feet tall. He set out with a friend, Abel Bertram. Abel is short and stocky—"

"Balding, with little round spectacles? Oui, oui. He was here. I remember them both."

An explosive sigh burst from Emma's throat. "Do you remember what happened to them? Did they go on to Oregon?"

"How far they traveled on from here, I cannot say." Domene's mustache drooped in a frown. "The tall man—your father, so you say—was not well. I did not have high hopes he would survive the rest of the journey."

Emma's knees threatened to give way, but John's strong arm held her firmly. Bracing against him, she murmured a breathy "*No.*"

"Thank you, Mr. Domene. Emma, let's get the children back to camp." John took the daguerreotype and tucked it in his shirt pocket. Never once releasing his hold on Emma, he steered her and the children toward the gate.

At their campsite, she collapsed next to a wagon wheel, the wild ride of her emotions leaving her weak and hopeless. "What if he's dead, John? How will I ever break the news to my mother and sisters?"

—⁓—

John would give anything for Emma to find her father alive and well, but after Joaquim Domene's grim report, he held out even less hope than Emma. Disease and death were all too common on the trail. Dysentery, cholera, measles—how many graves had they passed along the way? At least a half dozen from their own wagon train had already succumbed. Upon the death of his sister and brother-in-law, John's belief in the Lord had hit a serious rough patch, but out here in the wilderness, in constant worry over two innocent children and the woman he loved more every day, he was finding prayer his only consolation.

After a couple of days to rest and restock at Fort Laramie, the captain of the wagon train rounded everyone up to continue the journey. John decided the farm cart would never make it over the Rockies and emptied its contents into the wagon. He hadn't had the problem of so many who'd overpacked with furniture and household goods, figuring he'd build or make whatever they needed once they settled in Oregon.

Now, with the secret dream that Emma would someday consent to marry him, he wished he had something more substantial with which to furnish their future home.

His immediate problem, however, was convincing Henry to leave their mule behind. "Sadie's tired, son. Thanks to you and Emma, she made it this far. Let's leave her to a good life here with the soldiers."

Henry hugged the mule's neck. "If we ever get back this way, can we visit her?"

John never expected to see Fort Laramie again, but he agreed all the same. He and Henry walked the mule over to the hostler, who promised he'd treat her well.

Early the next morning, the wagons headed out. Concerned about Emma's despondency, John encouraged her to ride in the wagon seat with Addie. For several more days they followed the meandering path of the North Platte then left the river behind as they headed due west toward the Rockies. The ground, sloping ever upward, was hard and unforgiving, rutted from countless earlier wagon crossings. A fine, white dust hung in the air.

Nearly two weeks after leaving Fort Laramie, John heard a shout from ahead: "Independence Rock!"

So called because each year the emigrants strove to reach this point by the Fourth of July, the massive, dome-like outcropping was a welcome sight. Though they'd missed celebrating the Fourth here by three days, the captain had promised they could take a short rest. The oxen could use some extra grazing before they began the steep climb into the Rockies, and the Sweetwater River flowing nearby offered fresh water for drinking and bathing.

By midafternoon they'd formed up the wagons and loosed the livestock for grazing. Several emigrants wandered over to explore the rock, saying they'd heard previous travelers had carved their names on its smooth face.

"John, can we look?" Emma pleaded. "My father may have stopped here."

She hadn't shown this much optimism since their conversation with Domene at Fort Laramie, and John hadn't the heart to dash her spirits. "Sure. We'll all go over and take a gander."

With Henry and Addie racing ahead, John took Emma's hand as they walked toward the huge mound of stone. It had to be at least a hundred feet high, and John couldn't begin to guess its circumference—maybe a mile or more. As they drew near, he made out several names etched deep into the rock.

Emma rushed forward and trailed her fingers across the carved inscriptions. Her gaze swept the rock's scarred face. "Please, Papa, please be here. . ."

Henry asked what names they were searching for, and then he and Addie took up the cause. John looked, too, but he kept one eye on Emma as he worried how she'd react if she did find her father's name. . .or if she didn't.

"Over here, Papa," Henry called. "Is this it?"

He strode along the rock face to where Henry examined a spot several inches above his head. "What'd you find, Henry?"

"It looks like C-L-A-something, but it's too high for me to see good."

John leaned close to blow dust from the indentations then ran his fingertips across the roughly carved letters as he read:

ABEL BERTRAM WAS HERE 6-JULY-1850
BURIED MY FRIEND WILLIAM CLARKE YESTERDAY
HE DIED OF DYSENTERY, GOD REST HIS SOUL

Henry touched John's arm. "Is it her pa?"

"Afraid so." John set his hand on Henry's shoulder. "Let me be the one to tell her."

"Yes, sir." Mouth drooping, Henry blew out a noisy sigh. "I'm sad for her. When her sick mama dies, she'll be an orphan like me and Addie."

John knelt in front of the boy. "You and Addie are not orphans anymore, Henry. You're *my* kids now. I love you, and I'll always, always take care of you."

"I love you, too, Papa." Henry threw his arms around John's neck and squeezed tight.

It took John several seconds to find his composure. Swallowing with difficulty, he pushed to his feet. "You best run along and see to your sister. I'm about to have a hard conversation with Em—"

Henry stopped him with a tug on his arm. "You mean our *mama*?"

Brows furrowed, John looked the boy straight in the eye. "You okay with that?"

"She's been real good to us. Reckon if I had to pick a new mother, it'd be her."

Seeing Emma coming their way, John felt his stomach plummet. Once he showed her the inscription, how much longer would she stay?

Chapter 7

The sun had set hours ago, and Emma's tears had long since dried on her cheeks. But with her last hope dashed, she couldn't bring herself to leave the shelter of John's arms and head to bed. She wouldn't sleep anyway, not while agonizing over how she'd break this devastating news to her mother and sisters.

If Mama was still alive.

And now Emma must find some way to get back home. They'd come so far. How would she ever make it alone?

How would she ever leave John?

"Emma, Emma." John drew her closer, his lips brushing her forehead. "You've got to get some rest. We'll figure all this out tomorrow."

But the next morning brought no answers, at least none helpful to Emma. The officers of the wagon train had conferred with a scout and determined they needed to move out immediately. Otherwise, they might not make it through the mountains before winter set in.

Once again, Emma found herself bouncing along in the wagon seat with Addie. She tried to distract them both by reading from Addie's favorite storybook. Repeated use and one or two encounters with a mud puddle had marred the pages so badly that Emma had to rely on memory to fill in the missing parts. . .not unlike how time and distance had blurred the memory of her father's face.

As the miles carried her farther and farther from Missouri, Emma felt as if her heart were being ripped in two. John and the children had come to mean everything to her. Over these past two months they'd become a true family in every way but one—and *that* way wouldn't happen without a preacher and "I dos."

Although John hadn't forsaken his pursuit, he'd been careful not to pressure her. When he did speak of his hope for a new beginning in Oregon, she also sensed the shadow of misgivings, the guilt he carried for taking Henry and Addie from their legally adoptive guardians. No matter where they settled, could John ever rest secure as long as the threat of discovery hung over him?

"Come back with me, John," she pleaded early one morning as she watched him hitch up the team. "Come back and clear your name."

John sputtered a harsh laugh and fastened the yoke onto the hoop around the second ox's neck then moved the pair into position. "The county sheriff is Uriah Sleeth's cousin. Either one of 'em would probably shoot me on sight."

"But you have right on your side. The Sleeths mistreated the children. They aren't fit to be parents."

"Which is exactly why I took the kids." John brushed past her and ducked between the oxen to attach the wagon tongue. "Sorry, Emma, but I can't take the chance of losing them all over again. I've got no choice but to go on to Oregon."

When he eased out from between the oxen, she crossed her arms and stepped solidly in front of him. Her lower lip trembled as she asked softly, "But you'd take the chance of losing me?"

"Emma. . ." he growled. "No, I don't want to lose you." He seized her shoulders and gave her a rough but meaningful kiss then touched his forehead to hers. "I've come to need you more than life itself."

"I need you, too, John." Hands creeping around his torso, she ran her fingers along the lean, hard muscles of his back. "Have faith in us. Have faith in God. Don't make me go home alone."

His only answer was a soft, whispery intake of breath followed by one last kiss before he firmly guided her to the wagon seat. Calling for Addie, he boosted the little girl up next to Emma. Another day's journey began, and as Emma picked up the shawl she'd started knitting to pass the time, she felt her hopes for the future unravel even more.

The next morning at breakfast, Olga Volker and her husband, Ingel, approached. Emma could tell from their grim faces that something was wrong.

Olga lifted her chin. "We are turning back."

John rose abruptly and shot Emma an anxious glance. He certainly knew what such an announcement meant for her. Tensely, he asked the German couple, "Why? What changed your mind?"

"I'm not so young," Ingel stated. He looked toward the distant shadow of the Rockies. "The mountains make me afraid. I don't think we will make it over."

"You won't be alone." A desperate urgency tinged John's voice. "We'll all help. We'll make it over together."

Giving a sad shake of her head, Olga squeezed her husband's arm. "No, Ingel is right. This journey was too much for us. We should have stayed in Missouri."

"But—"

Emma rose to her feet, silencing John with a firm but sorrowful look. She turned to Olga. "If you've made up your mind, then I need to ask a great favor."

Within the hour, she'd moved her personal belongings and a small portion of food stores over to the Volkers' wagon. All that remained was to say a tearful good-bye to John and the children.

John clung to her fiercely. "Will I ever see you again?"

"You can still change your mind. We can go home together."

"I can't. . . . I can't." With a final, despairing kiss, John released her. Retreating a few steps, he drew the weeping children close to his sides.

"Mama, don't go!" Addie sobbed. "Don't leave us!"

Henry held himself rigid, silent tears streaking his face. Confusion and disbelief twisted his brows into knots.

Trembling fingers pressed to her lips, Emma shook her head helplessly as she backed away. "I love you. I love you all so much."

A callused hand gripped her shoulder, and Ingel spoke softly into her ear. "Emma, we must go."

She followed blindly as Ingel guided her to the wagon. As she climbed up to the seat, Olga pulled her into a hug and briskly rubbed her back. "So sad to leave your husband and children," the woman cooed. "You will see to your mama and sisters, and next year you will find another family to take you west."

Emma couldn't reply. She couldn't think, couldn't breathe, couldn't hope. As the miles slipped by and one day bled into another, anguish mellowed into numb resignation, and the searing pain in her chest dulled to an achy heaviness.

They stopped for two nights at Fort Laramie so Ingel could have a blacksmith thoroughly inspect the wagon and make repairs. Traveling on their own, he wanted to be sure it would last the journey. Emma used her own money to purchase additional food to round out their supplies, and soon they were on their way again.

Now the summer sun beat down mercilessly, and the insects along the rivers and streams were even more bothersome. Nearly every exposed inch of Emma's skin turned red with bites, sunburn, or both. So much thinner and hardened by the journey, she wondered if her mother and sisters would recognize her.

She didn't dare let herself wonder whether upon her arrival her sisters would take her straight to Mama's grave.

—⁓—

"Why'd you let her go?" Henry plodded alongside John upon a long, steep rise. "You could have *made* her stay."

With Addie propped on his left hip, John heaved an exhausted sigh and urged the oxen forward. He missed having Emma's help to watch over Addie. He missed Emma, period. "She needed to go home. I couldn't stop her."

Under his breath, Henry muttered, "You're just a coward, Uncle John. A big ol' yellow-bellied coward."

He halted and glared at the boy. "How can you say such a thing, when I risked everything to get you and Addie away from the Sleeths?"

"I can say it 'cause it's true." Fists nailed to his narrow hips, Henry glared back. "You had us a new mama, and we were all set to be a real family again, until *you* let her go!"

"That's enough, Henry." Shifting Addie to his other side, John swung his gaze left and right to see who might be overhearing their heated words.

At almost the same moment, Louis Finch gave a shout. "Mind your team, John!"

Only then did he notice his wagon had traveled several yards ahead, and the oxen were veering off the trail. "Blast it all! Henry, take your sister." John dropped Addie to the ground and plunged ahead, cracking his whip and yelling at the team to move back in line.

Louis jogged over. "Everything all right?"

"Yeah, just got a little distracted." John yanked off his hat and used his shirtsleeve to mop beads of sweat from his forehead. He looked past Louis to make sure Henry and Addie were following.

With a knowing laugh, Louis clapped John on the shoulder. "I'd say you been a *lot* distracted since your missus left. What's so important in Oregon that you'd let that pretty thing turn back without you and your young'uns?"

Ire boiled through John's gut. He was mad at Henry for calling him a coward, mad at Emma for leaving, and mad at Louis for pointing out the obvious. Yes, he was distracted. Seriously, appallingly, dangerously distracted.

Most of all, he was mad at himself, because he was terrified deep down to the toes of his smelly socks that Henry was right about him. Only a coward would steal his own sister's children. Skulk away under cover of night. Beat a path for Kentucky to throw his pursuers off the trail then take the long way around to Missouri so he could join a wagon train heading west. Kidnapping, lying, running from the law—what kind of example was he setting for those kids?

Keeping one eye on his wandering oxen, he waited for Henry and Addie to catch up. With a dismissive nod to Louis, he took Addie's hand and continued walking. He had some things he needed to say to Henry, but he had some hard thinking to do first. Heaven knew, on this rugged trail into the mountains he had plenty of time to think.

Heaven knew, indeed. If John had any hope of becoming the father these children deserved, it was time to quit pussyfooting around with the Lord and settle down to some honest-to-goodness prayer.

Chapter 8

E mma. . .oh, my dearest Emma!" Weak, pale, Mama strained to lift her head from the pillow.

Emma rushed to the bedside and buried her face against her mother's neck as their tears mingled. It had been five long months since Emma set out to find her father. "I'm sorry for leaving you, Mama. So very, very sorry."

"You're home now. That's all that matters." Mama's breathing relaxed, her happy sighs like a warm breeze across Emma's cheek.

"Emma." Her sister Dora's voice came from behind her. "She needs to rest."

Nodding, Emma kissed her mother's forehead and stood. "Sleep, Mama. I'll just be downstairs."

She followed Dora to the parlor, where their other two sisters waited, eyes wide with anticipation. Anxious to see Mama, Emma had scarcely said two words to them since she'd arrived home only minutes ago.

"Well?" Dora planted her hands on her hips. "Two terse letters in all the time you were away. Did you find Papa or not? Is he coming home?"

As exhaustion caught up with her, Emma sank onto the nearest chair. "No," she said, a choked cry closing her throat, "Papa isn't coming home. He—he died on the way to Oregon."

Her sisters gasped, the two youngest falling tearfully into each other's arms. Dora nodded grimly. "I feared as much. How did you find out?"

Emma described Abel Bertram's inscription on Independence Rock. "I couldn't bring myself to break the news to you in a letter. I just kept praying Mama would hold on until I could get home." She met Dora's gaze. "But now, how will I ever tell her Papa is dead?"

Dora perched on the arm of Emma's chair and wrapped her in a hug. "I think, in her heart, she already knows."

In the days that followed, Emma spent every possible moment at her mother's bedside. Her heart broke to see Mama so thin and feeble, declining more noticeably every day. It was as if she'd fought death for as long as she could, and now that Emma had returned, and knowing Papa wouldn't, Mama was ready to move on to her heavenly rest.

One day near the end of September, while Emma sat reading scripture to her mother, Dora interrupted. "Emma, there's someone here to see you."

Expecting their pastor to discuss Mama's final arrangements, Emma steeled herself for a conversation she dreaded. "Tell him I'll be right down."

Dora arched a brow. "Actually, you have three visitors—a man and his two children."

Emma's heart swelled. She bolted from the chair and flew downstairs in a whirlwind of anticipation. "John? Oh, dear heavens, John!"

Laughing, he snatched her up and swung her around. "Do you know how many Clarkes there are in St. Louis? I can't believe I found you!"

"And I can't believe you're really here!" Vaguely aware of her sisters' curious stares, Emma gave him a delighted squeeze before untangling herself from his embrace—*very* much against her will. She knelt to hug Henry then gathered Addie into her arms and stood. "Oh, I've missed you all so much!"

"Emma. . ." Hands folded at her waist, Dora offered a stiff smile. "Perhaps you might introduce us?"

"Of course. This is John Patrick and his children, Henry and Addie. We—" Emma bit her lip. She'd told her sisters only that she'd found a family to take her west with them, never mentioning the part about posing as John's wife. "We were traveling companions on the trail. John, these are my sisters, Dora, Katy, and Nancy."

The younger girls gave tiny curtsies while giggling behind their hands. Dora nodded politely, her expression doubtful.

Addie hugged Emma's neck. "We missed you, Mama. I was scared we'd never find you again."

Dora's eyebrows climbed nearly to her hairline. "Traveling companions? Apparently, you two became *quite* close."

"I—I can explain." Emma shifted nervous glances between John and her sisters. "Katy, Nancy, would you girls please go sit with Mama? We grown-ups need to talk."

Katy harrumphed. "I'm nearly fifteen. Can't Nancy—"

"Go." Emma pointed to the stairs. When she heard both sets of footsteps reach the landing, she turned to Dora. "Perhaps we'd all better sit down."

Ten minutes later, she'd poured out the story of meeting John in Independence and agreeing to mind his children in exchange for his protection on the trail. Explaining how they'd posed as husband and wife so other men wouldn't bother her, she assured Dora their relationship had remained chaste.

"You have my word," John stated. "Your sister's honor is intact. The truth is, though, that I'm in love with her, and as soon as. . .other things. . .are settled"—he reached for Emma's hand, his eyes darkening with silent affection—"I intend to make her my wife."

A quiver raced up Emma's spine. She'd given up hope of ever seeing John again, much less of their future together. Yet here he sat, and his words implied he'd come back to make things right. *Praise God!*

―⁂―

John didn't feel like talking. He felt even less like explaining himself to Emma's sister. All he wanted was to be alone with the woman he loved and drink her in.

Even so, some things had to be said, because he could sense Dora Clarke didn't quite believe nothing improper had happened between John and Emma on the trail.

Not so easy to discuss, however, with Henry and Addie in the room, and they didn't look at all like they'd willingly leave Emma's side. John couldn't blame them in the least.

"It's true, there's more to the story," John began, "but it has nothing to do with Emma, other than she's the reason I'm here." Hat in hand, he stood. "Emma, if I could have a few minutes alone with you. . ."

She drew her arms around Henry and Addie, who leaned close on either side of her. "Children, my sisters made some oatmeal cookies this morning. I'm sure Dora would be happy to take you to the kitchen for some cookies and milk."

Dora's pinched face suggested differently, but she started for a door across the room and invited the children to follow.

Alone with Emma, John scooted closer to her on the settee, taking both her hands in his. "I'm going back to Illinois to turn myself in and try to clear my name."

"Oh, John!" She pressed his knuckles to her lips as fresh tears flowed. "It's the right thing. I know God will bless this decision."

"I hope you're right. I've sure been praying hard about it." He shifted uneasily. "I wondered, though, if I could leave the children with you. I'm afraid if I take them with me, they'll end up back with the Sleeths, and all this will have been for naught."

Brow furrowed, Emma cast a weary glance toward the staircase. "I'd say yes in an instant if it weren't for my mother."

"Of course. I should never have asked. I can see how worried you are." John pulled her into his arms and dropped tender kisses upon her temple. "I wish I could help somehow."

"Just seeing you again has helped, more than you know." Straightening, Emma found a handkerchief in her pocket and dabbed her eyes. "Forgive me—I should have asked if you'd like something to eat, too. You must all be tired and famished after such a long trip."

True, it was nearing suppertime, and John hadn't wanted to stop long on the road as they'd traveled across Missouri. "I wouldn't say no to a bite of food. Must say, I've missed your cooking something fierce."

Emma cast him a demure smile. "Surely it isn't only my cooking you missed?"

"Not by a long shot." With a long, reverent kiss, he showed her exactly how much he'd missed her. "I think," he whispered, cupping her cheek, "you should introduce me to your mother now."

Understanding lit her eyes. She took his hand and led him to the stairs. As they stepped into the room, Emma excused her younger sisters then closed the door behind them. "Mama, I brought someone I want you to meet."

An ashen face turned toward John, and curious brown eyes so much like Emma's smiled up at him. Mrs. Clarke murmured a raspy "Hello."

"Honored to finally meet you, Mrs. Clarke." John edged closer, easing onto the straight-backed chair Emma slid his way. "I'm the one who took your daughter west to find news of your husband. I'm sorry. . .so sorry."

"Emma told me a kind man with two children had helped her. Thank you." The effort to speak brought on a cough. Lifting a handkerchief to her lips, Mrs. Clarke looked away until the spasm passed.

"The thing is, ma'am, Emma's come to mean a great deal to me." John leaned forward and rested one hand on the quilt next to Mrs. Clarke's arm. "I have some urgent business I need to see to first, but once that's done, Lord willing, I hope to come back and take your daughter's hand in marriage." He swallowed. "With your blessing, of course."

Mrs. Clarke turned watery eyes to Emma. "Is this what you want, dearest?"

Sinking to her knees beside John's chair, Emma clasped her mother's hand. "I do, Mama. More than anything."

Something akin to relief softened the woman's features. She let out a long, slow breath and with her other hand took John's. She squeezed his fingers, her grip amazingly firm for someone so ill. "Then you have my blessing."

—⁓—

With John close by, Emma sat beside her mother awhile longer, simply holding her hand. As Mama had spoken her blessing on their betrothal, Emma sensed a subtle shift in her mother's condition. She seemed more. . .restful, more at peace, as if she now had one less worry over her children's futures.

As her mother drifted off to sleep, Emma bent close to her ear and whispered, "It'll be all right, Mama. We'll all be all right."

Downstairs, they found Katy and Nancy in the parlor acting out a silly scene from their school play for Henry and Addie. Enthralled, Henry laughed out loud and Addie clapped with glee.

Watching from the doorway, John slipped his arm around Emma's waist. "It's been too long since I've seen the kids having this much fun. This feels right, like we're already family."

The wistful note in John's tone brought a catch to Emma's throat. She rested her head on his shoulder. "Once you've settled things in Illinois, we will be."

Unwilling to part with John again so soon, Emma insisted he and the children stay the night. After supper she made pallets for Henry and Addie on the parlor rug and gave John a pillow and blankets for the settee. Tomorrow would be soon enough for John to face whatever awaited him back home.

Since her return, Emma had taken Dora's place on the cot in their mother's room. Unable to sleep after the day's excitement, she listened to Mama's rhythmic breathing and the soft rustle of sheets.

"Emma?"

Startled, Emma tossed her covers aside and bolted to her feet. "Yes, Mama, what do you need?"

"Nothing, nothing. But since neither of us is sleeping, I thought you might want to talk."

Relief flooded Emma as she made her way to the bedside chair. She laughed softly. "How did you know I wasn't asleep?"

"Because I know my daughter. How could I miss how happy you are to see John again? And yet. . ." Mama sighed. "I'm not too ill to sense that something troubles you. Tell me, dearest."

During all the months she'd been away, Emma had missed having her mother to confide in. With only the briefest hesitation, she poured out the story of how John had taken his niece and nephew from the adoptive parents who had mistreated them. "I urged him to go home and clear his name, but now I can't help worrying. What if the law won't listen to his side? What if he's arrested and forced to give the children back to the Sleeths?"

Mama remained silent for several moments. "It seems you have but one option. You must go with John and speak on his behalf."

"But, Mama, how can I leave you again? What if—" Clamping a hand to her mouth, Emma swallowed the words she refused to utter.

With a breathy chuckle, Mama reached up to touch Emma's cheek. "My dearest, I have no intention of dying until I see my firstborn happily wed to the man she loves. Now get some sleep while you can. You and John should get an early start in the morning."

Heart overflowing, Emma sniffed back tears as she pressed her mother's hand. A powerful impression that could only come from the Lord settled over her. Somehow, by God's grace, all would be well.

Chapter 9

When Emma informed John she was going with him, he'd been both stunned and grateful, but with every mile they traveled, fear and foreboding gnawed a deeper hole in his belly. He'd rather die than see Henry and Addie returned to the Sleeths. He should have tried harder to convince Emma to keep the children at her house until he got things straightened out.

With less than half a day's ride yet to travel, John found himself easing his horse into a slower and slower walk. Soon, Emma and the children, riding in the buckboard he'd traded for his prairie schooner back in Independence, were far ahead.

Emma peered over her shoulder with concern. "John? Are you all right?"

Heaving a groan, he clucked softly to the horse and caught up. "I'm thinking I should go on alone."

"No, Papa." Henry's eyes reflected John's own fears. He tucked a protective arm around Addie. "You can't leave us."

"And I can't risk taking you with me." John motioned for Emma to halt the buckboard then rode up close beside her. "There's a little town not far ahead. Find the preacher and tell him who you are. He'll put you up until. . ." Gut churning, John glanced away.

Emma clutched his wrist, forcing him to look at her. "I have absolute faith this will all work out for the best. Just send word as soon as you can."

Emma's faith would have to be enough for all of them, because John's was running out. He clasped her to him and planted a rough kiss on her lips before spurring his horse forward. As he veered off through a copse of trees, the last thing he heard was Addie's tearful cry, "Papa! Come back!"

His heart splintered. *Lord, I'm begging You. Do what You will with me, but keep those kids safe.*

Choosing a route across open country rather than along the road, John hoped to avoid being stopped until he could voluntarily turn himself in to the county sheriff.

He hadn't even made it past the Kennard schoolhouse when someone recognized him and made a beeline for the sheriff's office. By the time he rode up, Sheriff Ted Tisdale stood waiting for him in the street, gun drawn and with two armed deputies backing him up.

John dropped his reins and held both hands aloft. "I'm unarmed, Sheriff. I came to turn myself in."

Tisdale motioned with his weapon. "Then you best get down off that horse and mosey inside to a jail cell. And you better tell me right quick where you took those kids."

John handed off his horse to one of the onlookers and walked up to the sheriff. Ignoring the gun pointed at his chest, he spoke in a voice loud enough for anyone in the immediate vicinity to hear. "Ted, if you can't figure out why I did what I did, then you're even blinder and stupider than I gave you cred—"

Wrong thing to say. Tisdale's left hand whipped around and slammed into John's gut. All his air whooshed out. Knees buckling, he sank to the dirt.

"Get him inside and lock him up," Tisdale barked.

The deputies seized John under the armpits and manhandled him into a cell. As he stumbled forward, the door banged shut behind him. Sick and dizzy, he whirled around and grabbed the bars. "Tisdale! You know good and well how Uriah abused those kids. Do the right thing for once."

Across the room, the sheriff glared. With a flick of his head, he sent his cronies outside then marched over to the cell, stopping a good three feet back. "I ain't the one who kidnapped two children from their legally adoptive parents. If you're so concerned about 'em, you shoulda taken 'em in right away after their ma and pa were killed."

The old guilt swamping him, John pressed his forehead hard against the cold steel bars. "It's a mistake I'll regret to my dying day."

"So where are the kids, Patrick? Turn 'em over right now, and when the circuit judge comes to town in a couple weeks, maybe I'll ask him to go easy on you."

John edged away from the bars. "They're in a safe place. That's all I'll tell you until I can talk directly with the judge."

"Have it your way." Tisdale snorted and gave John his back. "You can rot in that jail cell, for all I care."

Gulping down his anxiety, John prayed he hadn't just lost his children forever.

—⁂—

As John had promised, the preacher and his wife were more than happy to extend hospitality to Emma and the children. The elderly Pastor Higgins had known John and his sister when they were growing up in this tiny rural town. After learning last spring about John's absconding with his niece and nephew, the pastor refused to believed John would have done so without good reason.

Now, more than a week had passed since John had turned himself in. They'd heard he'd been arrested immediately, and Emma feared any day now someone would come to claim the children. All she could do was hope and pray.

As she helped Mrs. Higgins hang laundry one afternoon, the pastor returned home after visiting with some congregants. "Word is the circuit judge will be in Kennard tomorrow. John will get his day in court."

Emma dropped her corner of a bedsheet and covered a grateful gasp with both hands. "I want to be there. Can you take me?"

"Most certainly." The pastor climbed down from the buggy seat. "With the Lord's help, we'll convince the judge to set John free and grant him custody of the children."

Buoyed with hope, Emma found the children and told them the news.

"Really, Mama?" Henry asked. "Do you promise they'll let Papa go?"

Her heart twisted at how naturally the children had come to call them *Mama* and *Papa*, even after any reason for pretense had passed. She knelt in front of them and clasped their hands. "No, Henry, I can't promise, but God says in His Word that He hears the desire of the humble. Whatever happens, we can trust Him to take care of us."

The rest of the day crawled like molasses in winter, and despite Emma's encouraging words to the children, her growing anxiety made her useless for anything but the most menial tasks. Sleep was long in coming that night. Then, up before dawn's first glimmer, Emma bathed, dressed, and had breakfast on the stove by the time Pastor and Mrs. Higgins arose.

At half past seven, Emma and the pastor left for Kennard, while Mrs. Higgins traveled with the children in the opposite direction. Concerned Pastor Higgins's appearance in town would give away the children's location, he'd arranged for them to stay with friends until John's case was settled.

The buggy ride over to Kennard took nearly two hours, and Emma fought the whole way not to grab the reins from Pastor Higgins and whip his plodding gray horse into a gallop. When they reached the sheriff's office, the buggy had scarcely rolled to a stop before Emma leaped out and barged up the steps. Inside, she marched straight to the desk and addressed a gruff gray-haired man wearing a badge. "I'm here to see John Patrick."

"That so?" Slowly the man rose to his feet. "You wouldn't by chance be hiding a couple of kids for him, would you?"

Behind her, the pastor shuffled through the door. "Not a word, Emma. Sheriff Tisdale, we'll have our say in front of the judge."

"Emma..."

At the sound of John's voice, she whirled around to find him peering through iron bars at the other end of a short hallway. The discouragement in his eyes nearly undid her. "John, I'm here!"

Before she could run to him, the sheriff blocked her path. "Unless you want to tell me where those kids are, you can have your reunion in front of the judge. Trial starts at noon."

"And where will this trial be held?" the pastor asked.

"Over yonder at the boardinghouse, where Judge Nicholson is staying."

"Thank you, kind sir." With a fatherly arm about Emma's shoulders, he guided her to the door. As they stepped outside, he whispered, "Yes, indeed, the Lord works in mysterious ways. The sheriff may stand against us, but Judge Nicholson was once a young lad in my parish. I've never known him to be anything but honest and fair-minded."

Emma squeezed her eyes shut and sent up a prayer of thanks. If only she'd had the chance to tell John and kindle a spark of hope!

—⁂—

"Five minutes. You couldn't give us five minutes?" Resentment churning his belly, John paced behind his cell door.

Ted Tisdale sauntered into the hallway and leaned against the bars of an empty cell. An unpleasant grin twisted his lips. "Why, so you and your lady friend could pretend to whisper sweet nothings while plotting how you'll escape with those kids?"

"I turned myself in voluntarily, remember?"

"Yeah, but you still haven't told me where the kids are." Tisdale pulled the cell keys and a set of handcuffs from his belt. "Too late. You had your chance to come clean. Now you'll answer to the judge."

A few minutes later, with John's wrists cuffed behind his back, the sheriff quick-marched him across the street and down the block to the boardinghouse. From the foyer, John glimpsed Emma and Pastor Higgins waiting in the parlor. Emma jumped up when she saw him, but he silenced the cry on her lips with a subtle shake of his head.

Tisdale wheeled him through another door and shoved him into a chair at one end of a long, narrow room. A middle-aged man in a dark suit sat behind a table at the far end, while two other men stood before him pleading their case.

John had to wait through three more cases before the judge finally called his name. Tisdale yanked him to his feet and shoved him forward.

"Now, Ted," the judge drawled, "what call do you have for roughing up your prisoner?"

" 'Cause he's a kidnapper and a liar."

Scowling, the judge turned his attention to some paperwork. An eternity later, he looked up at John. "Mr. Patrick, these charges claim you willfully and unlawfully absconded with your niece and nephew. How do you plead?"

John hiked his chin. "It's not as simple as that, Your Honor."

"Under the law, I'm afraid it is. Do you admit to taking the children or not?"

"Yes, sir, I did, but—"

Judge Nicholson held up a hand. "You'll have your chance to speak once we get the preliminaries out of the way. So you're entering a guilty plea?"

Long seconds passed while John weighed his response. "Your Honor, the *only* thing I plead guilty to is rescuing my niece and nephew from the couple who mercilessly abu—"

"Judge!" Sheriff Tisdale stepped in front of John.

"Back off, Ted." Leaning around the sheriff, Judge Nicholson shot John a warning stare. "Very well, the defendant pleads not guilty to the charges as presented. And I think we can do without the handcuffs, Ted." Once John's hands were freed, the judge nodded toward the small, bespectacled clerk waiting at his left. "Bring in the witnesses."

The man strode from the room and returned moments later with Emma, Pastor Higgins, and the Sleeths.

The judge motioned Uriah Sleeth to approach. "Sir, you and your wife are the legally adoptive parents of the missing children?"

"We are. Took 'em in out of the goodness of our hearts after their ma and pa was killed. And this—this *hooligan* swiped 'em from right under our noses. The missus, she's been heartsick, missing those young'uns like crazy." Sleeth went to stand by his wife, who sniffed loudly and blotted cheeks that to John's eye looked dry as parchment.

With a stern warning about name-calling, the judge asked Sleeth a few more questions then instructed him to take his seat. "Pastor Higgins, are you here to speak on behalf of the defendant?"

"I am, Floyd—I mean, Your Honor." The pastor stepped forward. "Also with me is the young woman who mothered those children for much of the time they were...uh..."

Biting his lip, he angled John a nervous glance. "That is to say, she had no part in the abduc—" Once again, he choked on his words.

"It's all right, Pastor. The young lady is not on trial here." The judge motioned to Emma. "Miss, go ahead and speak your piece."

John held his breath as Emma rose and stood before Judge Nicholson. When she sent him a reassuring smile, warmth flooded him.

Facing the judge, she introduced herself then confidently described how she'd first met John in Independence and could tell at once that the children loved and trusted him deeply. "Exactly as I came to love and trust him as we traveled west. John Patrick is a good and decent man who wants only the best for Addie and Henry, and he never would have taken them had he not learned of their mistreatment—"

This time, both Sleeth and the sheriff shouted their objections. The judge banged his gavel to silence them. "Thank you, Miss Clarke. You may be seated." Referring once again to the papers in front of him, the judge pursed his lips. "Where this alleged abuse is concerned, it seems we have only Mr. Patrick's word against the Sleeths'. I'll need to speak with the children."

John burst to his feet. "No! They're scared enough already. You can throw me in prison or hang me if you want, but I'll make sure the Sleeths never get their hands on those kids again."

Pastor Higgins patted John's shoulder and urged him to quiet down. "I think this is for the best, John. The judge needs to hear from Henry's and Addie's own lips what their life was like with the Sleeths."

"Why, they'll lie just like their no-good uncle," Uriah snarled. "No, sir. You need to convict this man and give us back our kids."

Once again, the gavel slammed down. "John Patrick, the court orders you to present Henry and Addie Sleeth—"

"Henry and Addie *Meade*," John corrected loudly.

"Either way," the judge continued patiently, "the children in question are to appear before me at ten tomorrow morning, after which I will render my decision. Next case, please."

Chapter 10

Emma hugged the children on either side of her as Pastor Higgins drove the buggy. "Don't be frightened," she said. "The judge is a kind man, and all he wants is the truth."

Addie looked up, her eyes round with worry. "And then he'll let Papa come home to us?"

"I believe it with all my heart." *Please, Father, don't let us down.*

She shivered inside at the memory of John's terrified expression yesterday as the sheriff had cuffed him to return to jail. "Emma, don't!" he'd begged. "Just take the children and get as far away as you can!"

Which she couldn't, of course, and he knew it. There could be no more running. The children's future—and hers with John—was firmly in God's hands.

A crowd of townspeople milled about outside the boardinghouse as they drove up. Shielding the children between them, Emma and Pastor Higgins made their way inside. The judge's mousy-looking clerk showed them into a small sitting room off the kitchen.

Judge Nicholson uncrossed his legs and laid aside a sheaf of papers. "Come in, children. I've been looking forward to meeting you."

Bravely, Henry marched over and thrust out his hand. "I'm Henry Meade, and this is my sister, Addie. We're here to see to it you let our uncle out of jail so he can marry Miss Emma and we can be a family."

"Is that so?" One brow lifting, the judge quirked a smile.

Addie tugged on Henry's sleeve. "We're supposed to call 'em Mama and Papa."

"Your Honor," Emma began, fearing the judge would misunderstand.

"No need to explain." The judge nodded toward the door. "I'll speak to the children alone now. You may wait in the parlor."

The next half hour passed in agony while Emma carved a trench in the carpet with her pacing and tried to ignore accusatory looks from the Sleeths on the other side of the room. With one ear attuned to the room down the hall and one eye on the street hoping for a glimpse of John, she'd never been so frightened in her life.

Finally the judge emerged, spoke a few words to his clerk, and then disappeared again. Several more minutes passed while the clerk exited through the front door and returned shortly with the sheriff and John. Emma thought it a good sign that today John's arms swung freely at his sides. As he stepped into the hallway, he shared Emma's encouraging glance, while Sheriff Tisdale's sour look spoke pure contempt.

With the clerk clearing a path through the onlookers, the judge escorted Henry and Addie into the makeshift courtroom. The clerk then showed Emma, Pastor Higgins, and the Sleeths inside, and Emma's chest nearly exploded to find the judge had seated the children next to John in the front row. Arms looped through John's, Addie and Henry held on tightly, all three faces lit with hope.

"As I promised," the judge began, "after a most enlightening conversation with this bright young boy and girl, I am ready to render my verdict. John Patrick, please rise." His face hardened, and for a brief moment, Emma feared the worst. "Mr. Patrick, though you pled not guilty, you have freely admitted to kidnapping the children from their adoptive parents, and the law does not tread lightly in such cases."

John lowered his head. "I understand, Your Honor."

"However, after speaking at length with the children, I am convinced that abuse at the hands of the Sleeths did take place." Uriah's indignant protest brought a quick response with the gavel. "Therefore, justice must be tempered with mercy. While the court finds you guilty, it would not be in the children's best interests to incarcerate you."

A relieved sob burst from Emma's throat, prompting another rap from the gavel. She covered her mouth with both hands and forced herself to sit quietly as the judge continued.

"Mr. Patrick, your sentence will not be an easy one. Until each of these children shall reach the age of majority"—though his mouth remained firm, a mischievous twinkle lit his eyes—"you are hereby ordered to parent them with the utmost wisdom, unfailing kindness, and an abundance of love."

It was John's turn to cry out as he hugged the children tighter. Emma closed her eyes in silent thanks to God.

"*What?*" Again Sleeth's strident voice rang out. "What about *our* rights? We're the kids' legal parents, in case you forgot."

"Mr. and Mrs. Sleeth, your adoptive rights are hereby revoked." Judge Nicholson glared. "My personal choice would be to lock you both in prison and consign you to hard labor for the rest of your natural lives. However, child welfare laws have much catching up to do with today's society, so my hands are tied. Be advised, though, that as long as you reside in my jurisdiction, you will never adopt another child."

With a final, resounding rap of his gavel, the judge concluded the proceedings.

—⁂—

"It's over. It's really over!" Weak with relief and gratitude, John feared his legs wouldn't hold him if he tried to stand. He hugged Addie and Henry with all his might then reached for Emma and the pastor.

Emma squeezed in next to him and threw her arms around his neck. "I told you God would see us through."

"Excuse me, Mr. Patrick."

Seeing the judge standing before him, John found the strength to rise. He accepted the judge's outstretched hand. "How can I ever thank you?"

"It's the children you should thank. And this young lady, too." Grinning, Judge Nicholson tipped his head toward Emma. "What will you do now?"

John slid an arm around Emma's waist. "Well, Your Honor, the first thing I'm gonna do is marry this woman."

"Hmmm. Seems you have both a judge and a preacher present, so if you're in a hurry…"

John looked at Emma, and she looked at him. They both nodded. "The sooner, the better," John stated. "And afterward, seeing as how the kids are orphans again, my new bride and I would like to officially adopt them."

Judge Nicholson laughed. "I think that can be arranged." He turned to give his clerk some instructions.

Moments later, John and Emma stood hand in hand before Pastor Higgins, the children beaming on either side. John leaned close to Emma's ear and whispered, "Will your mother and sisters be disappointed we didn't wait?"

"Maybe at first. But when Mama realizes she's become an instant grandmother and my sisters learn they're aunts, I think everyone will be just fine."

Pastor Higgins cleared his throat. "John Patrick, do you take this woman. . . ?"

"I do."

"Emma Clarke, do you take this man. . . ?"

"I do."

"You may—"

John didn't wait for permission. Sweeping his beautiful bride into his arms, he planted his lips on hers with a kiss that spoke all the love he'd been storing up since she'd first laid claim on his heart.

Chapter 11

Arms crossed and a frown turning down her lips, Dora Clarke stood at the bottom of the porch steps. "Why do you have to go so soon? It's only been two months since we buried Mama."

The reminder brought a tear to Emma's eye. She glanced over her shoulder, where John and the children finished loading the buckboard. "We have to be in Independence by April so we'll be ready to leave with the next wagon train." She coaxed her sister into a hug then did the same with Nancy and Katy, waiting nearby. "I'll write often, I promise. And once we're settled in Oregon, you girls can come out to visit. As fast as the railroad is advancing west, it won't be long before it stretches all the way to Oregon."

"Not soon enough though." Dora sniffled and dabbed her eyes. "And it's still a long, long way."

No words could make this parting any easier. But Emma and John had talked at length about their future. With John's brush with the law behind them and Emma's mother now at rest with the Lord, they'd agreed it was time for a new start.

John came up beside her. "Emma, honey, we need to go."

She nodded, a lump rising in her throat. After giving each of her sisters one more hug, she cast a farewell glance at her childhood home before taking John's hand and striding purposefully to the buckboard. Love for her husband settled over her heart, while her spirit danced with anticipation for what lay ahead.

Adventure called to them on the Oregon Trail, and she wouldn't miss it for the world.

As Good as Gold
by Amy Lillard

Chapter 1

Trudy Johnson walked smartly down the planked sidewalk of Independence, Missouri. As smartly as she could, considering the number of creatures milling around the town, mostly men and mules. But she had a destination and a plan. It was a bad plan at best, but it was her last hope. She had a wagon, supplies, and everything needed for a trip west. Everything except a driver.

That wasn't entirely true. She'd *had* a driver, but last night she found out he'd lost the deposit she had given him in some back-alley card game. This morning he was nowhere to be found. It might be all right if she had another week to find someone else to drive her wagon west. But they had to leave tomorrow. A large group of five hundred or so left this morning. If Trudy waited much longer, she would run the risk of getting caught in early winter storms. It was a chance she wasn't willing to take.

She pulled her gloves from her hands as she neared the sheriff's office. He was surely the one person she could trust to help her find a new driver for her well-stocked rig.

"So you're not going to do a thing about this?" A booming voice met her ears while she was still a good five steps from the open door of the sheriff's office.

"Now, Mr. Hardy, what would you suggest I do?"

"I would suggest you get off your. . .chair and find the man who stole my rig."

"There are pert near four hundred wagons in this town right now. How do you suppose I find yourn in all that?"

Trudy stepped in front of the door, the lack of light filtering in alerting the men to her presence. Their conversation abruptly stopped. She was glad. From the look on Mr. Hardy's face, what he was about to say was not suitable for feminine ears.

"Gentlemen." She took one step into the room and stumbled over a loose floorboard. She caught herself before sprawling at their feet and completely ruining her composed air.

Sheriff Jacobs took one step toward her but stopped as she straightened. "Are you all right?"

"Yes, of course." She tugged on the bodice of her dress and smoothed back the unruly locks of her auburn hair that were struggling to work free of the pins she'd placed there just a few short hours ago. She much preferred a braid to this fancy chignon, but she knew if her plan was going to be successful, she had to present herself as a mature businesswoman.

She smoothed her hands down her skirts and stared at the two men. They looked back, each waiting on. . .something.

The sheriff cleared his throat. "What can I help you with?"

"Oh. Yes, of course." She gave a little cough. "But I thought you were helping, uh, Mr. Hardy here."

The big man's eyes narrowed. "Have we met?"

"I don't believe so, no." Trudy squirmed as he continued to stare at her.

He was just the kind of man she needed to avoid. Large, strong, and mistrusting. The last she could see in his eyes—blue, blue eyes as clear as the sky above the prairie before them. His hair, what she could see of it curling out from under his dusty trail hat, was as dark as day-old coffee, and his full beard of the same color covered the lower half of his face. She wondered what he looked like when he was smiling. No, she didn't. She was perfectly content with his scowl. After all, she didn't have business with him, just the sheriff.

"I can do no more for Mr. Hardy today," the sheriff said.

"I think you mean *won't*," Mr. Hardy countered.

"However you want to say it."

"You're darn right."

The two men started in again, raising their voices a little bit each round of the argument as to be better heard over the other.

"Excuse me," she said, the words a whisper in the wind. "Excuse me," she tried again. Neither man paid her any mind. "Excuse me!"

They turned to look at her.

She pulled on her bodice again. "Sheriff Jacobs, my name is Trudy Johnson, and I need a driver for my wagon."

The sheriff looked from her to Mr. Hardy then pulled the matchstick from his mouth as he smiled. "Well, ain't you two a sight. One needs a driver and one needs a wagon."

Trudy looked from the big angry man back to the sheriff. The stare Mr. Hardy gave her wasn't much kinder. "I don't believe Mr. Hardy is the driver I'm looking for." Trudy couldn't imagine trusting her life to those gigantic hands. They looked as if they could crush rocks. If it had been just her, she might consider it, but she had Molly to think about. "He's—" *Large? Scary? Handsome?* He was all three.

"I don't drive for people."

"—not right," she finished.

"Not right?" His face turned a dangerous shade of crimson.

"And argumentative." She should stop before he went from red to purple.

"I'll have you know—"

Trudy turned to the sheriff. She didn't have time to argue with the handsome oaf. She had to find a driver. A reliable driver who didn't tower over her and make her feel like a child in women's clothes. "Thank you, Sheriff Jacobs. You can find me at the livery stable if you happen to think of someone who can help me." She turned back to Mr. Hardy. "Someone else, that is."

She spun on her heel, and before she lost her nerve, she marched from the office. Once she was out of sight of the two men, she let go of the breath she'd been holding. Her shoulders slumped, and she practically collapsed to the ground as she walked.

So that wasn't as successful as she'd hoped. There had to be a good place to find a man in this town. There were hundreds. All she wanted was one.

Mr. Hardy's blue eyes flashed before her mind's eye. She shivered and headed back down the sidewalk. So the sheriff wasn't going to be the help she needed. She still had a few more ideas.

She quickened her pace, clipping along as swiftly as she could while still managing some sort of decorum. People were shoulder to shoulder in the town, even though many of the trail riders had left that morning. The last group was set to leave out first thing tomorrow, and she planned to be among them.

She had a few more stops to make before she could head back to the stable and Molly. They'd been lucky to get a room at the boardinghouse in the middle of such excitement and chaos, but people would do almost anything if a widow and a six-year-old child were involved. Anything but give them a free room. And money was getting tight.

Once she'd found out her driver left town, she let the room go and moved them into the wagon she had stored at the livery stable. It wasn't the safest place to stay, but it was a far sight better than the camp filled with a sundry of people preparing to leave the next morning.

Truthfully, she wasn't a widow. Not exactly. Well, not at all. She had never even been married. But due to their twelve-year age difference, when people saw her and Molly together, they automatically assumed that she was the parent and Molly her child, instead of orphaned sisters trying to find their way in the world.

She should have politely corrected their mistakes, but she didn't. And even though it was an error on their part, she still added the lie to her prayer list each evening.

Since she had failed with the sheriff, she would get with the pastors of the local churches, see if they knew of someone who was trustworthy that would be willing to drive her rig to Oregon.

She blew the wayward strands of her curly hair out of her face and tried to remain positive, but with each church she visited, she became more and more discouraged. And more and more exhausted from holding her head up and fighting her way through the crush of people.

Finally she stopped, leaning against one of the building's posts. She laid her head against the wood and closed her eyes. She would never find a driver this late. Traveling the trail could be a tricky venture. If they were going to make it there before the winter hit, they had to leave. . .soon.

Like tomorrow.

Where was she going to find a driver now?

"Why, lookit here."

Trudy spun around at the drawling voice. She smoothed her dress and patted her hair nervously. The man was big and tall with tobacco-yellowed teeth and a sweat-stained shirt. "H–hello." She patted her hair again and looked toward the crowd of people surrounding them.

"What's a purty thing like you doing out here all alone? You need some help?"

His tone suggested he had more than help to offer.

"I–I'm looking for a man," she said without thinking through the suggestion in her words.

He straightened and puffed his chest out like a bullfrog as a grin stretched the corners of his mouth.

"A *certain* man," she quickly clarified.

"What if I told you I was him?" His smile turned downright wicked.

Panic flashed through her, brief and heart-pounding. People surrounded them. He couldn't do anything to her right out in the open. She took a deep breath to calm her nerves.

"I don't believe you are, sir." She started to turn away.

"What's this man look like?"

Well, now there was the problem. "He's tall and dark and very muscular." That ought to deter the unkempt gentleman before her, but he seemed oblivious to the subtle warning in her words.

"And what do you, uh. . .need this man for?"

She stiffened her spine and met his bloodshot brown eyes. *Lord, forgive me this lie.* "He's my husband."

"You don't say?" His gaze flickered to her ringless left hand then back to her face.

She wouldn't be the only woman who had sold her jewelry to get money to travel west. "That's right." In for a penny, in for a pound. She had started the lie, and she would see it through. What choice did she have?

But the spark in the man's gaze called her out even when he said nothing. "Well, let's see if we can go find this husband of yourn." He wrapped his grimy hand around her arm and started to steer her away from the bustling people. "He's probably in the saloon."

Trudy dug in her heels hoping to stop him, but he was way bigger than she was. She only managed to slow him a bit. "Unhand me, sir. I think I can find my husband on my own."

He ignored her and continued pulling her toward the swinging doors of the saloon.

"I must insist that you let me go at once." She'd meant for her voice to be stern and unyielding, but the warble at the end ruined that plan. "Sir, please."

"Let her go."

The deep voice stopped the man in his tracks. He turned to stare at the newcomer. Trudy used his pause to once again attempt to free herself from his grasp, but he only tightened it.

A small gasp of pain escaped her. She hadn't wanted to resort to violence, but it looked as if that was inevitable.

"What business is it of yourn?" He spat on the sidewalk near the other man's feet, but Mr. Hardy didn't so much as flinch. Of all the people to try to rescue her, why did it have to be him?

She took a deep breath, preparing to administer a well-placed kick to the shin. And maybe an elbow to the ribs.

"Let her go."

"Or?"

"There's going to be problems. For you."

He looked from Mr. Hardy back to her. Trudy sensed the change in his stance. She raised herself up and tugged once again. This time he let her loose, mumbling something about her not being worth the trouble. He stalked off as if he'd been scalded. Ghastly man!

Trudy pulled on her sleeves and smoothed away the man's touch. She'd most likely be black-and-blue come the morrow, but she'd worry about that then.

"You're welcome."

She spun around, unpleasantly surprised to find that Mr. Hardy was still standing behind her. "Yes? For what?"

"For saving you from your admirer."

She waved a hand through the air in the direction of the departing man. "Him?" She sniffed. "I had that under control."

"Of course you did." The man's deep blue eyes twinkled. He smiled in a way that set her teeth on edge. He was smug, like he had truly done her a favor.

"I did indeed." She turned back to scan the crowd. She didn't have time for this man and his shenanigans. Today was the day. Tomorrow this wagon train was headed to Oregon, and she planned to be a part of it. And this man with his flashing dimples and condescending attitude would only hold her back the longer she stood there talking to him.

"Right."

"Are you saying that I can't take care of myself?"

He shrugged those broad, broad shoulders. "I'm saying you looked like you needed some help."

"Looks can be deceiving." She sniffed and started to turn away.

"I wouldn't go down that way if I were you. It only gets worse from here."

Trudy had been so intent in her search that she hadn't realized where she was. Not the best part of town. "I'm going back this way, but only because I want to." She turned with a swish of her skirts and started back toward the stables.

The way this day was going, she would have to drive the wagon herself. Was it too late to trade her oxen for mules? She might be able to control them a little better. She hadn't the foggiest idea on how to drive oxen. Surely she wouldn't be the only greenhorn on the trail. But where was she going to get eighteen mules this time of day?

Ellis Hardy watched the woman pivot and walk away like she were first cousin to the Queen of England.

Woman. He snorted. Slip of a girl was more like it. And whatever her story, he'd better not get involved. She was misfortune on two legs, a walking disaster. The last thing he needed was to spend the next five months or more making sure she stayed out of trouble.

But she has a wagon.

The one thing he did need. Ellis stroked his beard and watched her wind through the crowd. Her red hair was like a beacon in the crush of people. He shook his head. He'd always had a thing for gingers, and she was about as ginger as they came. In hair and spirit. All sass and freckles. She needed more than a driver. She needed someone to take care of her.

Which is exactly why he wasn't going to get involved.

A wagon. He didn't have the time or the money to buy more supplies. Why, oh why, did his only hope of getting to California have to lie with a woman like her?

With a shake of his head, he started after her. "Miss Johnson, wait up!"

He called her name three more times before he caught up with her. He suspected she heard him the first time but was ignoring him.

"Yes?" She turned and eyed him, her stance cool, her demeanor frosty.

"What are you offering?"

"I beg your pardon?" One rusty brow shot up her forehead, but otherwise her expression remained the same.

"You can't expect a man to drive you all the way to Oregon Country without some sort of compensation."

"Oh, yes, well, a share of the supplies, of course. And the trip itself."

"The trip?" Was she serious? One look in those bottomless green eyes and he knew that she was.

"That's no small amount. Surely you and I can agree on that, Mr. Hardy."

"Miss Johnson—"

"Mrs.," she corrected. "It's Mrs. Johnson." A flush of pink rose to her cheeks.

"Okay, then, *Mrs.* Johnson, that is a goodly amount, but a man such as myself, taking on a young woman"—he almost choked on the word—"would need to be compensated in other ways as well."

The pink turned to a shade of red that clashed horribly with her hair. "Mr. Hardy!"

"No, no, no," he said, only then realizing what his words implied. "I'm talking money."

"Oh." She pulled herself up to her full height, which was a fair amount below his shoulder, her color returning to normal. "And what amount would you suggest?"

"Two hundred dollars plus supplies."

She sputtered. "Two hundred dollars? That's pure robbery."

He crossed his arms and gave her a casual look. He'd had everything he owned in his wagon. Now, aside from not having a way to get to California, he was broke. He needed the money for the trail and to get started once he got to the mines. They said gold was as easy to find there as ticks on a hound dog, but he wanted a little in his pocket just in case.

She was still sputtering when he turned to leave. "Thank you anyway, *ma'am.*" He tipped his hat and started back down the sidewalk.

"Wait!" She was chewing her lower lip when he turned back around.

"Yes?"

"A hundred and seventy-five plus supplies."

He pretended to think about it a second then gave her a small nod. "All right. But I can only take you as far as Parting of the Ways. That's when I head to California."

"How do you propose to do that? Not in my wagon."

He shrugged as if it was no big deal. He surely hoped it wasn't. "Most of the people on the trail these days are headed for California. I'll find someone going that way and hitch a ride with them."

"How am I supposed to get to Oregon if you do that?"

"Easy enough. Somewhere on the trail there'll be a driver whose wagon breaks a wheel. You just hire him from that point forward." He watched as she mulled over the decision. But apparently she was as desperate to go west as he was. "Fine," she said.

"Good." He reached out to shake on their agreement. "Mrs. Johnson, you have a deal."

His hand enveloped hers like a horse blanket slung over a baby goat. She seemed so tiny and fragile, but there was a spirit in her eyes that eclipsed her small stature. He was glad. From the stories he'd heard, the trail was no place for a tenderfoot.

"I see you found your husband," a voice hiccupped nearby.

The man who had accosted her earlier was staggering toward them once again.

Her backbone went ramrod straight, and her chin pointed high into the air. "That's right."

"Now wait a minute—" Ellis protested.

She moved toward him, planting one tiny foot on top of his, effectively cutting off the rest of what he was about to say. "Yeow," he released under his breath. For such a puny thing, she could add on the pressure when she wanted to.

She looped her arm through his and gave the drunkard a smile that would melt butter. But she didn't get off Ellis's foot. "My dear, dear husband." Her smile widened until it was downright scary. But the warmth of her so close and the sweet smell of woman were doing funny things to his heartbeat. "Smile," she said out of the corner of her mouth.

"This is gonna be extra," he whispered in return then nodded toward the unkempt man. "That's right."

The drunk looked from one of them to the other then staggered away, shaking his head all the while.

"You can get off me now," he said.

"Oh." She stepped off his foot and released his arm. Despite the rising temperatures of the day, he felt almost cold as she placed herself in front of him again. "I will not pay you extra for that little charade."

"That's the second time I've saved you from him today."

"And I asked for your help neither time."

"Oh, really?"

"Really." Her chin tilted to a stubborn angle he'd seen his grandmother use countless times. She was not backing down. He knew a wasted cause when he saw one.

"We're back up to two hundred."

She started to protest.

"Two hundred or no deal."

"One eighty?" She looked up at him, the hardness gone from those eyes. They had turned a soft green, like a dewy meadow at first light.

"One eighty," he heard himself say. Only then did he realize this was going to be the longest five months of his life.

Chapter 2

She had done it! They were heading to Oregon and a fresh start. Just what they both needed.

After instructing Mr. Hardy as to where he should meet her in the morning and assuring him that he didn't need to look at the wagon, she made her way back to the livery stables. Despite everything, her stride was a bit lighter.

She stepped into the large barn that served as the stable. She had paid a pretty penny for the right to keep her wagon here, and after she heard Mr. Hardy's woes, she felt it to be a sound investment.

"Molly?" she called softly, but hopefully loud enough for her sister to hear. She didn't want to alert the stable master to the fact that they had moved into the wagon. She wasn't sure how the dour-faced Mr. McCartney would take such news, but she was certain it would involve tossing her out on her ear or charging her double for the boarding. Neither of which she could afford. "Molly?"

"I'm here." Her sister crawled over the top of the supplies and waited for Trudy to help her to the ground. Like her, Molly was small in stature, but she had a mature air about her that Trudy herself envied. Molly Johnson was a twenty-year-old trapped in a six-year-old's body.

"I did it." It took everything Trudy had to keep her voice at a normal tone.

"You found someone to drive us to Oregon?"

Trudy nodded. Molly threw her arms around her and hugged her close. "I'm so glad. I was so worried we wouldn't make it there."

"I told you God would provide for us, and He did. Just like I promised."

"God is good," Molly said in that downtrodden way of hers that made those around her wonder if she really meant it. Trudy knew Molly meant every word.

She might be a serious child, but that was only to be expected. The poor child had lost both parents in the span of eight months. After the death of their father and stepmother, Trudy was all Molly had left in the way of family. Well, Trudy and a wayward uncle in Oregon Country that neither one of them had ever met.

"Are we really going to sleep here tonight?"

"Of course we are." Trudy tried to make it sound like the best plan in the world. They were about to spend the next five months sleeping in the wagon, or perhaps under it. What was one more night being uncomfortable?

One night she would have stayed in a hotel room with a real bed and a hot meal waiting for them come morning. But this was a sacrifice they would have to make.

"It'll be an adventure. You'll see."

Molly nodded, her chin at a brave angle, though her green eyes—so much like

Trudy's own—had doubts.

Other than eye color and stature, there was very little the two of them had in common. Molly's hair was as dark as. . .well, as dark as Mr. Hardy's. Where Trudy's hair had a mind of its own and required constant taming, Molly's was smooth and straight, a beautiful curtain of deep brown. Their individual locks were gifts from their different mothers, while their father's eyes had found their way to the both of them.

"Now come on," Trudy said, grabbing her sister's hand. "We're going to have a picnic for supper."

Molly's eyes lit up in the happiest expression Trudy had seen since they had decided to make this trip. "Outside? We're going outside?"

The drunk man and his mean bloodshot eyes came into her mind's eye. "Of course not. There is way too much rabble out there. We will eat here. On the wagon."

"But Trudy—" Molly started.

"Absolutely not. Besides, you'll have your fill of outside soon enough."

Molly stared down at her feet. "I suppose you're right."

"That I am." Trudy sucked in a deep breath, trying to relieve some of the guilt she felt at corralling her sister this way. She was only looking out for her. For them both. Trudy didn't know what she'd do without her sister. "And remember," Trudy said, hoisting Molly back into the wagon, "if we're going to pull this off, you have to remember to call me Mother."

"Yes, Tr—Mother."

Trudy smiled. "That's my girl."

—m—

Ellis shifted from one foot to the other. The sun was just peeking over the horizon, and the day had begun. The wagon master had called "Roll out!" close to half an hour ago, and the train had headed west. But his. . .companion and her coveted wagon had yet to turn up. Surely she had to be out here somewhere. Or maybe they should have picked a more specific place to meet. He supposed that was partially his fault. Partially. He knew how many wagons were left in the prairie outside of town. But then again, she did, too.

"Whoa! Whoa! Hold up! Ho!"

That voice sounded more familiar than he cared to admit. He looked up to see his partner tugging on a leather strap connected to the team. The huge lead oxen seemed a bit cantankerous. Or maybe he just didn't want to take orders from a wisp of a girl that barely reached his chin.

The beast decided to stop, as did the rest of the team. And no matter how hard she pulled and tugged, he remained in one place. In fact, he seemed so interested in staying right where he was that Ellis wondered if he would have sat in the dirt had he been able to.

"Come. On." She tugged and tugged as the wagons continued to roll past. At least she was on the outside edge, otherwise she might be crushed under one of the wagons.

With that thought, he was spurred to action. "Hey-ho!" he hollered as she continued to struggle.

She turned toward him, releasing the strap and straightening up as if nothing was out of the ordinary. "Good morn to you, Mr. Hardy," she called over the rattle of the train.

"Where's your goad?" he asked, not bothering with a greeting. He had to get them on the trail. Then they could observe the social niceties.

"What?"

"The stick to direct them."

"Oh. On the seat."

That was when he noticed her. A small girl, no more than four or five from the size of her, sat on the wagon's seat, swinging her legs as she waited for them to start moving again.

"Who is that?" He gave a nod toward the lass.

Mrs. Johnson turned as if she wasn't aware anyone was in that direction. "That's Molly."

"Molly, huh?" He braced his hands on his hips. "And who exactly is Molly, and what is she doing on my wagon?"

Immediately Trudy Johnson puffed out her chest. She pressed her lips together, and he was surprised when smoke didn't shoot out her ears. "First of all, Mr. Hardy, Molly is my daughter. It's not like I can leave her behind. And second of all, this is *my* wagon. You best not forget that."

Didn't she know? Children had an awful way of getting hurt on the trail. Oh, some of the stories he had heard about young'uns falling off the wagons and being crushed under the wheels before anyone knew they were down.

He couldn't have that on his shoulders, too. The scrappy woman before him was more than enough for him to babysit for the next five months. But what choice did he have? He had to get to California and as quickly as he could. He wanted his share of the gold.

He snatched the goad from under the child's feet and stalked to the front of the team. "Hiyah," he called, whacking the pointed stick against the wooden yoke between the lead oxen. They dug in then strained against the tack, pulling the wagon. It inched forward a little at a time until the motion was steady.

Then he turned back toward his pint-sized employer. "It might be your wagon, Mrs. Johnson, but you need me to drive it. Best not forget that either."

—⁂—

Insufferable man! He was taking all the excitement out of the journey. But they were under way! She wanted to twirl around in a circle with her arms up high in the air, but despite her desires, she just kept putting one foot in front of the other. A new start was just five months down the trail, and she could hardly wait.

"You never told me what is in Oregon Country?"

This time she did whirl around to face the stern-faced Mr. Hardy. He had shaved since the day before. The absence of facial hair revealed a squared-off jaw and a dimpled chin that were even stronger and more handsome than she had previously thought. Why did he have to be so good looking? "Oh," she said recovering her thoughts as the world spun in a circle. "Oh, I. . .well, my husband is there."

He shot her a look, and she tried to act like she said these words every day. Or at the very least that they were the truth.

"He's in the military. And he, uh, went out there last year to serve at one of the forts." There. That was a good answer if she had ever concocted one.

"Really?" He raised his brows in apparent interest. Or maybe he was finally trying to be cordial. "Which one?"

Which one? Her brain scrambled around, but she couldn't even think of a good made-up fort name, much less any that actually existed in the Oregon Country. "Well, sir, it's not like I can remember every tiny detail of my husband's work." She pulled on her bodice. "Are you sure it's okay for Molly to ride up there?" Trudy was torn between letting the child ride high on the wagon seat or walk between them. Either way, she was worried about the safety of her sister.

A frown worked its way across Mr. Hardy's forehead just under the brim of his dusty hat. "It's as good a place as any as long as she doesn't climb around."

"She won't. I'm sure of it."

He had finally settled down about Molly being with them, though he raised his price another twenty dollars. She had no choice but to agree. Though she and Molly would have a long talk as soon as they could about staying out of Mr. Hardy's way.

By the time noon came around, Trudy thought her legs might fall off. Never had she walked so long at one time.

The wagons reached the designated camping spot, and the drivers pulled the wagons into a circle. The men took care of the animals while the women built fires and started cooking bacon.

"Is that what we're eating?" Molly asked. She had settled down on the ground near the fire, but not so close that she received too much warmth from the flames.

"Yes." Trudy flipped the bacon, wincing a little at its dark color. This cooking over an open flame was no easy task.

Molly made a face.

"You like bacon sandwiches."

"When Esther makes them," she said, referring to the Johnson's longtime housekeeper and cook.

"You know that Esther didn't want to go to Oregon with us."

Molly peered into the popping skillet and made another face. "I wish she had changed her mind."

Me, too. It was hard enough that they were going to Oregon alone, even harder that they had no friendly faces to meet when they got there. Trudy just kept praying that once they showed up on their uncle's doorstep he would change his mind about his brother's "brats."

Trudy forked the half-burnt, piping hot bacon onto a piece of bread and handed it to Molly. She made one for herself, and the two of them sat down. They thanked the Lord for their food and the beautiful day and asked that He watch over them as they traveled.

Trudy had just taken the first bite of her own sandwich when Mr. Hardy sauntered back to their lunch site.

"You got one of those for me?" he asked, flopping to the ground.

"Meat's in the skillet, and the bread's in the bag by the water barrel." She nodded in that general direction.

For a moment, he just stared at her as if she had grown a third eye in the middle of her forehead, then he pushed back to his feet and went to make a sandwich.

Surely he didn't expect her to serve him. He was a grown man and could get it himself. After all, she had walked every step with him this morning, cooked the bacon, and fed Molly.

He scowled at her as he returned to his previous spot, this time with a sandwich in one hand. "Looks like the bacon is well and truly done."

She sniffed. "If you feel you can do any better, Mr. Hardy, I encourage you to try."

"And you'll take care of the oxen?" All annoyance was gone, leaving a mischievous light in those blue eyes.

"No, I—I mean. . .no." The oxen scared her silly. After all, they were the biggest beasts she had ever seen.

"Now that we have that cleared up, just one more thing." He shot her a self-satisfied grin. "I think you should call me Ellis. After all, we'll be spending the next five months together. Day and *night*. I think that allows for a more familiar address, don't you?"

—⁂—

The sight of *Mrs.* Trudy Johnson swallowing hard, eyes wide as the intimacy of their situation settled in, kept Ellis chuckling under his breath for the rest of the afternoon.

Let her stew on that awhile.

They had started back up at two that afternoon and would continue on until they reached the Shawnee Mission. It was Methodist run, but with a little bit of luck, he wouldn't run into any men of God. He'd had enough preaching to last through this lifetime and into the next. Or maybe he'd had enough of scheming preacher's daughters who used people for their own purposes then tossed them away when they were no longer useful.

He pushed the thoughts away, not willing to let Nattie Mae ruin another day in his life. She had made her decision, and he had made his. Yessiree, it was the single life for him.

"Are you married, Mr. Hardy? I mean, Ellis."

"No, ma'am." Nor was he planning on ever being tied down. He was going to make a fortune in the gold mines and spend the rest of his days being waited on by beautiful women who felt their fortune lay in simply being close to him.

She cleared her throat. "I'm sure my husband will be very grateful to you for returning me to him unharmed. Perhaps even thankful enough that he offers you a bonus for my safe journey."

He tapped the lead ox on the rump just to remind him who was in charge then turned his attention to the scrappy Mrs. Johnson. "If you are so afraid of me, why did you hire me?"

"Who said I was afraid of you?"

He shook his head. "It's written all over your face. I make you very uncomfortable. So why did you hire me?"

"The train was leaving. It was my last chance to get west until next year."

He nodded.

"If you dislike me so much, why did you agree to drive my oxen?"

"Who said I dislike you?"

"So you treat all women this way?"

He felt those green eyes on him, steadily watching for any weakness. "I have treated you nothing but fairly."

"All women then. I understand."

He sighed. "Someone stole my wagon and all my supplies. Gold was discovered two years ago. Next year who knows how many panners will be in California looking for their share of the fortune? I've got to get there before there's none left to be had. I really didn't have much choice, now did I?"

"I guess neither one of us did."

It was only one thing they had in common, but it was a start.

—ɯ—

So many lies. She might have to write them down on a scrap of paper in order to keep track of them all. But it was purely to protect herself. Surely God wouldn't hold them against her. She wasn't just doing it for herself. She was looking out for Molly.

Just to be sure, Trudy kept repeating the lies over and over again in her head, committing them to memory. It wouldn't do to go around forgetting her own tales. She had a feeling Mr. Hardy. . .Ellis would remember every detail.

At six that evening, they finally stopped. As much as Trudy wanted to keep going, they had reached the mission, and she was tired. Bone weary was more like it. They had traveled fifteen miles if they'd gone a foot, and every part of her body ached.

"It'll get better." Ellis picked that moment to come up next to her. "Once we've been on the trail for a couple of days, you'll hardly notice how sore you are."

She seriously doubted that.

"Supper almost ready?"

"Getting close." When they stopped, she had taken a little more care with the bacon. This time it wasn't nearly as black as it had been during the nooning.

She scooped up some of the bacon and placed it on a slice of bread and handed it to Molly. The child had been especially quiet on the trip. Trudy supposed being jostled around on the wooden wagon bench was as hard as walking every step, but they had no other choice. They needed a fresh start, a new home, someplace they could call their own without memories and ghosts to haunt them. It wasn't their fault that their father had made some rather unfortunate business decisions. Yet, they were the ones paying the price—literally and otherwise. Almost all the money their father had left them was owed to creditors. After everyone was paid, Trudy had managed to scrape together what she needed to buy them a wagon and a new start in Oregon. It was imperative for them to leave before any more "associates" crawled out from the woodwork to claim their piece of BD Johnson's estate.

Trudy pushed those thoughts away as she fixed sandwiches for Ellis and herself. Then she settled down close to the fire, but not so close the heat became unbearable.

She bowed her head as Molly did the same. "Thank You, Lord, for our first day on the trail. For guiding us safely to the mission. Thank You for the food and the many blessings You have bestowed upon us this day. Amen."

She raised her head to find Ellis Hardy chewing. Half his sandwich was gone. Had he not prayed to thank God for their food? Come to think of it, he hadn't said a blessing at the nooning either. What kind of man had she hired to take them to Oregon? *Lord, please don't let me regret this decision.*

"What do you think, Molly?" she asked, turning her attention to her sister. It was better by far than trying to find something to talk to Ellis Hardy about. Or asking him why he hadn't prayed. "Exciting, huh?"

"Yes, ma'am." Molly shrugged and took a small nibble of her sandwich.

Trudy was so very aware of Ellis's steady gaze on the two of them.

"Do I have to eat this?" Molly asked.

"Yes." Ever since their father's death, Molly had been obsessed with what she was eating and if anything had to die for her meal. "We've talked about this. Bread is not enough food for a growing girl."

"But I ate the bacon at noon."

"Don't get fresh, Molly Sue," Trudy warned.

Molly ducked her head and nibbled at her sandwich once again.

It was going to be a long two thousand miles if she and Molly argued about their dinner every night. Trudy sighed and took a bite of her own sandwich.

"When we get to Oregon, can I have a kitten?" Molly asked.

"Of course," Trudy said automatically.

"And a dog?"

"Anything you want." Anything to put a smile back on her face. A girl shouldn't be orphaned at six. It just wasn't right. But as much as Trudy tried to make sense of their tragedy, she knew that God had a plan for them.

"Hi-ho!" A small voice called from the edge of their camp. A young boy hovered there waiting for permission to come closer.

"Good evening," Trudy called in return. Maybe this was what Molly needed: a playmate. A distraction from the sadness of her thoughts and the discomfort of their journey.

"My name's Joseph. But everyone calls me JJ. That's my wagon just there." He pointed to the wagon directly behind them. "Do you want to come play with us?"

Molly perked up a bit. "Play?"

Trudy was about to encourage Molly to finish her sandwich when JJ continued. "We're picking up dried buffalo dung."

"What?" Trudy hadn't meant to holler the one word at the lad. "I mean, excuse me?"

"Let her go," Ellis said from across the fire.

He hadn't said one word during the entire exchange and now he wanted to give advice? Encourage her sister to pick up. . .well, things that no little girl should be picking up.

"We'll need it."

"For what?"

"It's great for burning in the fire. Not a lot of wood around here. It may feel warm enough out here now, but once the sun goes down, it'll get mighty cold."

Molly looked from Trudy to Ellis then back again. Once she was satisfied that nothing terrible was about to happen to them, she pushed herself to her feet, half-eaten sandwich still clutched in her hand.

"Finish that before you leave." Ellis's voice rang with authority, and Trudy wondered how many people he'd bossed around in his lifetime. He was too good at it by far.

Molly shoved the remainder of the sandwich into her mouth.

"Don't go too far. And keep the wagon in sight," Trudy warned.

"Yes, ma'am." Then without another word, she followed the boy toward a group of children waiting to head across the flat field.

"Is she always so serious?"

Trudy turned her attention from watching Molly to the man sitting across from her. "Only since—" She had been about to say only since their father's death, but that would have ruined all her carefully concocted lies.

"Hi-ho to the camp." A man approached, his appearance saving Trudy from having to answer.

She breathed a sigh of relief until she saw who it was. The drunk man from town. But he had been so deep in his cup when they'd met, Trudy was certain he wouldn't remember either one of them.

"Well, lookit here. The happily married couple." His beady eyes narrowed even as his mouth continued to smile. Or maybe *sneer* was a better word.

Trudy stared, wide-eyed as Ellis slowly pushed to his feet. "There's no need for past troubles to follow us on the trail."

The man held up his hands as if surrendering, but something about his stance still looked like he was on the attack. "Oh, no. It was just so good to see a familiar face out here. And to think that we're neighbors."

Ellis made some sort of noise. Trudy couldn't tell if it was a snort or if he was agreeing with the man.

"Where are my manners? Joseph Kelley." He reached out a hand to shake.

Ellis took it into his own but much slower as if it were a snake about to strike. "Ellis Hardy. And this is Trudy Joh—my wife."

It took all that she had not to choke when he said the words. But wasn't that why she hired him? To protect her from questionables like Joseph Kelley?

"Isn't this nice? Now we can keep an eye out for each other."

"And your wife, sir?" Trudy stood, food forgotten. She ignored the pain that screamed in every inch of her body and went to stand next to Ellis.

Mr. Kelley turned toward her, flashing those stained teeth in an almost smile. "Oh, I'm not married."

"Pa, look!" JJ, the boy who had come to play with Molly, rushed up to Mr. Kelley, holding a pair of shoes high above his head.

"JJ, where did you get those?"

"I found 'em, Pa. Honest. There's a whole bunch of things over there. Crates of baking flour, a bunch of clothes, even a washtub."

Molly picked that moment to come back as well. Her cheeks were flushed from exertion, her eyes sparkling. "Look what I found."

That was when Trudy noticed her sister holding up the ends of her pinafore to make a sack. Molly let go of both ends and a multitude of dried buffalo patties tumbled to the ground at their feet.

Trudy resisted the urge to yelp in surprise and disgust. Were they really going to use those?

"Good job, Molly. From now on, you're our official dung gatherer."

Great, Trudy thought. Day one on the trail. The man at her side was pretending to be her husband, the man behind her was a miscreant, and her sister was collecting buffalo ordure. Could life get any better?

—⁂—

Darkness fell, and for the first time since they started off, Trudy realized they would be sleeping outside.

"You don't think there are wolves out there, do you?" Molly looked toward the darkening prairie with apprehensive eyes.

"Of course not," Trudy said.

"Of course." Ellis's words fell on top of her own and almost drowned them out.

She frowned at him.

"What?" he asked. "She'll be better off with the truth." He turned to Molly. "There are a lot of critters out there with empty bellies, but you stay close and everything will be fine. Do you understand?"

Molly nodded.

"Good girl." He patted her on the head.

Trudy squelched her annoyance. He was only trying to help, but she hated the way Molly looked at him. Like he was a savior come to take them to the Promised Land.

Maybe he was. But Trudy wanted to be her sister's hero, not some stranger who would leave them as soon as the trail split.

"We'll sleep under the wagon," he said, pulling out the blankets she had packed for the trip. It was something of a luxury she noticed as others around them began to settle down in the dirt without the comfort of a quilt or pillow.

Ellis chocked the wagon's wheels, and together they settled down on the earth. Molly was directly under the wagon with Trudy next to her and Ellis on the outside. She knew that he had done that to protect her and her sister, and despite all the cross words she had shared with the man, she was touched by his gesture. Or perhaps he thought he wouldn't get paid the remainder of his money if she died along the trail.

The night was filled with sounds: the rattle of metal, the various noises the animals made—the ones inside their makeshift corral and out. People stirred around, ready to rest for the night. And beside her, the man she had hired sighed into the night.

Lying next to him was. . .different. She had never been so close to a man. She had never even slept in the same room with her father, if she didn't count those Sunday afternoons when he fell asleep in the parlor. But BD Johnson snored so loud the windows rattled, and this man beside her didn't. She felt as if he was holding himself in check. Was he feeling the same closeness she was? Her heart pounded at the thought. She was safe, she told herself. But that didn't stop the wild beat in her chest.

There was nothing Ellis would do with her sister lying on the other side of them. That wasn't the issue. The problem was the intimacy of listening to him breathe, knowing that she could reach out and touch him if she wanted to. Not that she did or ever would, but the option was there all the same.

"Trudy," Molly whispered where only she could hear.

She *hoped* she was the only one who heard. Molly had once again forgotten she was supposed to call Trudy mother. She hated asking that of the child since her actual mother was not long in the ground, but it was necessary to keep up the charade they'd started.

"Yes?"

"I'm scared."

She pulled Molly into the circle of her arms and held her close. "It's going to be all right. There's nothing to be afraid of. You want to sleep in the middle?"

"Yes, please."

The girls traded spots.

Trudy was not about to feel guilty for the relief she felt at having a buffer between her and the handsome man. Not since it made the one person who meant the world to her feel safe and loved. Molly was her number one concern, now and always. But it was thoughts of the man and his blue eyes that invaded her dreams all through the night.

Trudy woke the next morning with sore muscles, an aching back, and tender feet. Oh, and fifteen more miles to travel that day.

The wagon master sounded the trumpet at 4:00 a.m. and everyone woke up. Trudy could never once in her life remember getting up that early and never once after sleeping on the hard ground. By seven, the men had the teams back in front of their wagons and the groups of wagons hitched together for protection. The women had breakfast cooked and everyone fed. Then the bugle sounded again.

"Wagons roll!" someone shouted, and they started off for the day.

At noon they stopped to eat and drink and let the animals rest while some people even took naps. By 2:00 p.m. everyone got back in line, and they started off again.

An hour before they were ready to stop for the evening, scouts rode ahead to find a good camping spot. Once that spot was reached, they pulled the wagons into a circle. The men took care of the animals while the women put up the tents, built campfires, and cooked the evening meal.

Come dark, they would go to bed. In the morning, they started the entire routine again.

Chapter 3

Trudy had been keeping track of the days in a journal. Each day after their noon-day meal, she sat while Ellis napped and Molly played with JJ Kelley. Trudy didn't completely approve of Molly's friendship with the ruffian's boy, but she reminded herself that everyone deserved a chance. It was not very Christian of her to hold the sins of the father against the son.

They had just begun their fourth week on the trail. Their pattern from the first day held steady, including the fact that despite all her encouragement and questions, Ellis refused to pray before their meals. All it did was increase Trudy's own prayers, as she had to add Ellis's spiritual health to her growing list. Ah, well, it gave her lots to think about as she rested her tired bones each night and waited for sleep to come.

"What's that?" Trudy pointed toward the horizon.

"My guess is Fort Kearney," Ellis replied.

"That's a fort?" It looked more like a shanty town on the edge of nowhere.

"It's a military fort, but that doesn't mean it has to be made of stone."

"If you say." But Trudy wasn't convinced, and her confidence in the place did not grow as they drew closer. The buildings looked as if a good wind would knock them into kindling. Their sod roofs sagged under the weight of bad construction.

"Regardless of how it looks, they have mail service. Very reliable from the rumors. Do you want to write a letter to mail?"

She shook her head. "I don't have anyone to write."

"What about your husband?"

Exhaustion and the trail were getting to her. "I wrote him before we left. He knows we're on the way."

"But you could still send him a letter letting him know where you are."

She lifted her chin in an angle that said she wasn't backing down. It was a look she perfected long ago seeing as how she had been smaller than everyone else around her. "I do not believe that is necessary, Mr. Hardy. But thank you all the same."

His eyes narrowed in apparent suspicion, but he shrugged. "Whatever you prefer."

She breathed a sigh of relief and began to set up their camp. They would be leaving in the morning. And, with any luck, Ellis Hardy wouldn't bring the matter up again.

—◦◦◦—

Ellis dropped the matter of Trudy sending a letter to her husband, but something about it didn't sit right with him. Even days on the other side of Fort Kearney, the matter plagued him. If his wife were out on a five-month trip with another man, he'd surely want an update as often as possible.

But that was never going to happen because he was never getting married. Never. He had big plans for his life that centered around living out his days on the gold he found in California, but that didn't include a wife.

Maybe her husband wasn't the jealous type. He tapped on the wooden yoke between the oxen and steered them back in the opposite direction. They were really okay going down the trail behind the other animals, but tapping wood to wood gave him an excuse to turn a bit and study her profile.

She was beautiful. Not in an untouchable fashion. But in a soft and simple way. Even with trail dust clinging to her clothes and her hair in two plaits that made her look no older than twelve, she was beautiful.

He shook his head at himself. The trail was getting to him. Watching families work together to make it on the hard trip west had softened his heart to the point of destruction. Beautiful or not, she belonged to another man. A military man who most likely wouldn't hesitate to shoot anyone who besmirched his wife's good name.

"Do you really think the men at the fort were telling the truth about Ash Hollow?" she asked as they walked along.

"I don't know any reason why they would lie," he returned.

"They just looked a bit disreputable. I figure someone like that. . ." She trailed off, leaving the rest unsaid—someone like that might not be altogether honest.

He shrugged. "We'll find out soon enough." And they did, a few hours later when they came upon the steep incline the men at the fort had told them about.

Getting down the hill that led to the hollow was no small feat. The wagons took turns. A dozen or so men tied ropes to the back of one wagon and pulled against the force of the slant as the driver slowly urged his oxen toward paradise at the bottom. Ellis lost count of the times the wagons got away from the men, but most were close enough to the bottom that the wagon was spared. One wagon slipped early on and a spectacular crash followed.

Ellis held his breath as they lowered their wagon—*Trudy's* wagon. But the longer they spent together the more invested he became in it all.

That was only natural, he told himself, but it didn't mean a thing.

"This is incredible." He turned as Trudy rushed up to him. She handed him a pot filled with water.

"Thank you," he said, taking it from her. Incredible was not the word. It had been weeks since he'd had fresh water.

"The wagon master says we're going to stay for a couple of days. Isn't that great?"

"Great." He smiled to prove the sentiment, but it wasn't in his heart. They all needed a rest, but staying on the trail kept his mind busy as well as his body. Lounging about with his pretend wife even for a couple of days might be more than his resolve could stand.

—⁂—

Ash Hollow offered the first trees they had seen in a hundred miles. It was a paradise, nestled on the trail as if God had somehow placed it there to give the travelers hope.

Ellis leaned back against the wagon wheel and closed his eyes. He tipped his hat for some extra shade, though the surrounding trees offered a good deal of respite from the summer sun.

Trudy was sitting on a crate of flour he had taken from the wagon for the sole purpose of serving as a chair for her while they remained in the hollow.

The more time he spent with Trudy Johnson, the more he wished he could give her some comfort on the trail. A soft bed instead of just folded-up blankets, a pillow instead of a rolled-up flour sack. But none of those things were his to give, and she belonged to another.

He opened his eyes, peeking from under the brim of his hat to look at her. She had finished writing in her journal and had picked up a sampler of sorts that she had been working on. He had never given much thought to women and their needlework. Nattie Mae wasn't much for such endeavors. But Trudy Johnson was not Nattie Mae Olsen.

"I hate boys." Molly flounced through their camp and plopped down on the ground next to Ellis.

He tipped his hat up where he could see her sweet face. "What's wrong?"

"The boys are playing leap frog." She made a face as she said the words as if it were a sin they would never recover from.

Ellis hid his grin over her theatrical ways.

Molly Johnson came out of her shell a little more each day. And each day Ellis waited on her smile. It didn't come at the same time of day, nor did it last very long, but it came all the same. With any luck, by the end of the trail she would be smiling all the time, and—

He shook the thought free. He wasn't going all the way on the trail. Just on the other side of Fort Hall the trail turned south, and that was where he was headed. California, the land of promise.

"Sorry about that." Girls didn't participate in such games. It just wasn't appropriate. The boys knew it, and whenever they wanted to exclude the girls, it was their game of choice.

"You should be engaging in more ladylike endeavors," Trudy said, sounding like the mother she was. Daily he had to remind himself that she was an adult and another man's wife, not a girl he'd just met.

But with her hair in those pigtails, she looked like a schoolgirl herself.

"Yes, Tru—Mother."

"Or we could blow soap bubbles." Ellis pushed himself to his feet, not bothering to figure out where the idea came from.

"Soap bubbles?"

He reached a hand down toward the girl and pulled her to her feet.

He could feel Trudy's inquisitive eyes on him as he led Molly away, but he didn't turn and engage. He didn't have any more answers than she did.

─⁓─

After watching Ellis and Molly blow soap bubbles for the remainder of the afternoon, Trudy's heart was as soft and mushy as an overbaked apple. She had just been on the trail too long, worrying about Molly high on the wagon seat, exhausted from walking nearly twenty miles a day, and plum sick of being dirty.

But there was plenty of fresh water in the hollow. She bathed and washed her clothes and hair. She felt better than she had in weeks, since she left Missouri nearly two months ago.

She ran a brush through her unruly hair. The tresses were almost dry now. She had washed herself first then the clothes, which had given her hair plenty of time to dry as she hung up their clothes to dry. She had pinned up one of Ellis's large shirts, only then realizing that she had never washed a man's clothing. Not even her father's. It was too intimate by far, but it was the nature of the situation she found herself in. Pretending to be a wife, twice over. Her prayers had grown so long she needed pert near an hour to complete them each night. But she knew in the end, she was doing the right thing. She needed to move on, to Oregon and her uncle's house.

She had received no response to the last letter she sent him, but she wouldn't let that worry her. She couldn't believe that he, too—their last living relative—was dead and gone like their father. She wouldn't believe that she and Molly were alone in the world.

She plaited her hair in one fat braid down her back and walked to the edge of the wagon. She looked out among the fertile valley where they found themselves. Fresh water, trees, grass for the livestock. She was happy here, content. Why couldn't they just stay right there in Ash Hollow and live out their days, just the three of them? She pulled those thoughts to a quick halt. Ellis had his own plans, and they surely didn't include a wife and daughter.

"Are you listening to me?" Molly tugged on her skirt.

"Of course," Trudy said.

"Were you thinking about Pa?"

"No." She shook her head.

"Mr. Hardy then."

Trudy whipped around and stared at her sister. Then she gave a nervous laugh. "Why would I be thinking of Mr. Hardy?"

"Because he's handsome." Molly shrugged. "And strong, and I see how he looks at you when he thinks you aren't looking."

He looks at me? "And how would that be?" she asked in the most disinterested voice she could muster.

"Like he wished things could be different."

"Why would he—?" Because he thought she was married to another man. "Don't be ridiculous." He had his life planned out. He took great pride in telling her that he was going to California and he wasn't ever coming back. And he was never getting married. Molly was mistaken.

"I know what I saw."

"It was probably just gas." She waved one hand in the air as if to dismiss the whole thing.

Molly burst out in a fit of laughter. Trudy began brushing her sister's hair, but thoughts of Ellis Hardy kept flying around inside her head.

"Look what I've got." Ellis held up a skinned carcass. Two of them actually, and Trudy resisted the urge to scream.

"Ahem, what exactly are those?" She did her best to make her voice even and interested.

"Rabbits. Mighty fine eatin'."

"Oh." She tried to put some enthusiasm in her voice. She really did, but the words came out a little more like incredulous than excited.

"I thought it would make a good change from bacon. Do you not like rabbit?"

"I'm not sure I've ever eaten it."

He eyed her as if trying to determine whether or not she was joking or serious. "I guess you were a bit pampered growing up." He hesitated before saying the word *pampered*, as if mulling over the best word to describe her upbringing.

"I guess you could say that. My father was very wealthy."

"That explains a lot."

She tilted her head to one side, trying to figure out what to make of that. "What do you mean?"

He shrugged but grinned, taking the sting from his words. "Hiring not one but two drivers, all the money you were throwing around, the burned bacon."

She laughed. "Sorry about that. We had a cook the entire time I was growing up. I never quite learned myself."

"You've more than made up for that."

Her heart warmed at his compliment, but she turned away before he could see the joy in her eyes. "What exactly am I supposed to do with these?"

"Heat up the skillet. Tonight we're having a mess of fried rabbit."

Not surprisingly, Molly refused to eat the rabbit. And just adding to his many fine attributes, Ellis had the forethought to realize this. He found some sort of greens and wild onions, and he bartered for a few potatoes. They would all eat a fine supper because of him.

"Did you tell Mr. Hardy thank you?" Trudy asked Molly.

"Thank you, Mr. Hardy." She graced him with a shy smile.

These days her sister was coming out of her shell more and more, but usually only around Ellis. Watching the two of them together this afternoon, blowing soap bubbles and laughing as they sailed into the air made her realize that Molly needed a man in her life, a father figure to care for her and guide her. Trudy wanted nothing more than to be everything to Molly, but she knew that the girl needed a father just as she had. That need would be assuaged if she were truly going to meet a husband and father in Oregon like her lies claimed. But in truth there might not be anything at all save heartache waiting for them.

"I think I'll go walk for a bit." Ellis pushed to his feet, and only then did Trudy realize that she had been staring at him.

He disappeared into the dark fray of wagons and bodies. This was their last night in the hollow. Tomorrow it was back to the trail. And tomorrow was a special day. It was her birthday, but there would be no celebration. The trail was hard and demanded all of their attention. She shouldn't be sad about it, but it wasn't every day a girl turned nineteen.

She laid her head back against the wagon wheel and tried to put everything in perspective. She wouldn't celebrate, in order to get a new start. Yes, it would be worth it.

"Someone down the way has a fiddle." Ellis materialized out of nothing. "Come on. Let's go dance." He grabbed Trudy's hand before she could protest and pulled her to her feet. She cast one look back at Molly where she sat playing with another little girl, then allowed him to lead her away.

A man she had seen many times on their journey had brought out a fiddle and was sawing out a lively tune. Some travelers sat on makeshift seats of various crates. They clapped their hands in time with his playing, all smiling and stomping their feet. More adventuresome people had started a dance, a variation of an Irish reel. Partners bowed and pranced toward each other, the ladies holding up the hems of their skirts as they skipped along.

Another man brought out an Ozark harp, and together they played the sweetest music Trudy had ever heard.

Ellis spun her around. Trudy laughed, really laughed, for the first time in a long, long while.

Her troubles and grief slipped away as she and Ellis danced. She forgot about her lies and the uncertainty that awaited in Oregon. She forgot about the rapscallion who traveled behind them and the feelings that were starting to develop for a man who had vowed to remain single. And she danced.

More instruments were brought out, some traditional but most makeshift. The more the men played, the more people joined in the fun. Pretty soon it felt like half the camp was dancing to the peppy tunes. The children joined in, swinging each other around and bowing to their partners, mimicking the adults. Even Molly joined in, her cheeks flushed with excitement and joy.

Trudy felt like she had danced for hours, and probably they did. But the wagon master brought an end to the festivities, reminding them all that morning came early to the trail.

The musicians put away their instruments, and everyone started wandering back to their tents and wagons.

Ellis looped Trudy's arm through his as they made their way back to their wagon. She resisted the urge to lay her head against his strong shoulder as they walked. Thankfully, Molly was with them, helping her keep her wits about her where Ellis Hardy was concerned. And she needed those wits more now than ever.

Tonight he had ceased being an oaf who was only interested in money and finding gold in California. If she was being honest with herself, that image of him had fled long ago. He was wonderful with Molly, steady, dependable, and unavailable. His heart belonged to the goldfields in California, though Trudy suspected that it had been broken before that. What else would make a man like Ellis want to hide himself away and vow never to get married? And his reluctance to abide by God's law. Oh, nothing big, just that refusal to pray before meals and bed. Though she had noticed that now he had at least been waiting until she finished the blessing before starting to eat. She smiled to herself. There was hope for him yet.

As Molly would say, *God is good.*

———

The feel of the woman beside him, her warmth and joy, was almost more than Ellis could stand. Dancing with her had been a little piece of paradise, completing the beautiful scenery around them. The two of them had been at odds since they met, but tonight had been different. It was refreshing to just walk beside her, listen to her hum out the tune of the last melody played and shuffle her steps as if she were still dancing. And dancing with her. . .that had been a dream.

"What are you thinking about?" she asked. She tilted her face toward him, and Ellis instantly measured how easy it would be to lean in and steal a kiss.

Thou shalt not and all that. . .stealing was exactly what he would be doing. All her affection belonged to another man. Her husband.

"That your husband is a very lucky man." He could have told her that he was thinking about the trip tomorrow, getting back on the trail. Or worrying that the wagon was too heavy and they would have to jettison some supplies in order to keep the oxen healthy. No sir, he had to go and say something like that.

"Ellis, I—"

"Ow," Molly cried, and immediately the sobs followed.

Ellis backtracked a couple of steps to where Molly had fallen, Trudy right behind him. "What's hurt?" she asked.

"My ankle." Molly sniffed, and Ellis could see how hard she was trying to be brave.

"Let me take a look." He knelt down beside her and turned her bare foot gently from one side to the other. As the summer had heated up, Molly and the other children had abandoned their shoes.

"I think I stepped in a hole," Molly said.

"It's swelling," Ellis said. "It'll probably be black and blue tomorrow."

"Is she going to be okay?" Concern laced Trudy's voice.

"Of course." He scooped Molly into his arms and carried her gently back to the wagon.

He deposited her on the crate and peered at her ankle. "I'm no doctor," he said, "but I think the best treatment is lots of rest and no games of tag. Agreed?"

Molly's eyes grew wide. "Forever?"

He chuckled at the innocence in that green gaze. But he did not notice how much her eyes were like her mother's. The girl must have gotten the dark hair from her father. A pity, really, considering the fetching flame of Trudy's locks. "How about three days," Ellis said. "Do you think you can manage that?"

Molly gave a solemn nod.

"And one more thing." He pulled a peppermint from his pocket and handed it to the girl.

"For me?" she breathed.

"Of course."

Molly flung her arms around his neck and squeezed until she almost cut off his breath. "Thank you! Thank you!" she squealed.

It was the most emotion he'd ever seen from her, and he was proud that he had brought it out. Deep inside she was as fun-loving as all children, but something had happened to suppress her spunk. As ridiculous as it sounded, he wanted to be the man who gave that back to her.

"Where did you get that?" Trudy asked.

Ellis shrugged as if it were no big thing that he had done. He didn't want Trudy making too much out of this. "At the fort. I traded some things I had for it and a couple of other things."

"What other things?" she asked.

He shot her a smile. "Oh, you'll find out soon enough."

And on that cryptic note he left them alone to get ready for bed.

―――

She should be ashamed of herself. Trudy willed her body to relax and her mind to do the same. How was she supposed to get any sleep tonight? She should be exhausted after all the dancing that she and Ellis had done, but she wasn't. She could have danced straight through till the dawn if he had been her partner.

Her thoughts were going in circles as well. First the softening feelings she was starting to have for him. She wasn't about to call it love. She couldn't be falling for a man like him.

What's wrong with him? that side of her challenged.

Not one thing. Except she had done nothing but lie to him since the first time she met him. He seemed forgiving enough, but he didn't seem the kind of man who would allow something like that to be easily forgotten. She had almost told him the truth, had even started to confess the real reason she and Molly were on the trail, when Molly had fallen.

It was beyond silly, the wave of jealousy that washed over Trudy when he picked up Molly and held her close to that strong chest. Envy was a sin, just one more item to add to her list of prayers. But she had wondered in that moment what it would be like to be held close in those arms, cradled in safety. It was something she would never know. The quicker she realized it, the better off her heart would be.

Aside from the lies out of her own mouth, he had declared his plans and dreams the first day on the trail. Never once had he mentioned a wife and a daughter. . .or rather a sister-in-law. She sighed under her breath. Even she was having trouble keeping up with her deceit.

"Having trouble sleeping?" Ellis's voice floated to her from his side of the wagon. Since that first night, they had taken to Molly sleeping between them. Trudy supposed that being in the middle gave her a sense of security that she hadn't felt in a long time.

"Yes. You?"

In the dark she realized how deep and strong his voice was. A voice that reflected the man himself. "I think I danced a little too much. Got myself all stirred up."

"It was fun though."

"That it was."

Trudy sighed again.

"I hear tomorrow the trail gets a little tougher for a while."

"Harder in truth, or because we've been lying about for three days?"

"Maybe a little of both."

"I guess we should try to get some sleep then."

"Yes. Goodnight, Trudy Johnson."

"Goodnight, Ellis Hardy."

But sleep was a long time coming.

Chapter 4

Happy birthday!"

Trudy returned from washing to find Ellis and Molly standing by the wagon. After a near-sleepless night, she had walked down to the water's edge to wash the tired from her eyes. Today they were back on the trail, and she needed all the energy she could get.

Ellis and Molly were side by side and seemed to share a secret. An exciting secret, if their barely suppressed smiles and sparkling eyes were any indication.

"How did you know today is my birthday?"

Ellis smiled in that way he had that made her heart beat a little faster in her chest. "'For a bird of the air shall carry the voice, and that which hath wings shall tell the matter,'" he quoted.

Trudy raised one brow. "Ecclesiastes, Mr. Hardy?"

He shrugged. "Is that a bother to you, Mrs. Johnson?"

Her heart gave a hard knock at the mention of her fake title. "I had the notion you weren't a God-fearing man."

"Wherever did you get an idea like that?"

"You never pray, for one."

"And that makes me not fear God?"

"What would you call it?"

His blue eyes grew stormy, but she knew he wasn't mad at her. "A man who has been hurt one too many times."

She wanted to ask more, but it seemed he was finished with the conversation. "I got you something at the fort."

"You did?" Her eyes widened as he pulled a small package from behind his back. It was wrapped in a piece of newspaper and tied with a scrap of cloth. And it was the sweetest thing she had ever seen.

"It's from me, too."

But Trudy knew the truth. Molly might have told that Trudy's birthday was coming up, but the present was all Ellis.

She took the package from him, her fingers trembling with excitement.

"Hurry," Molly said, bouncing up and down in her seat. She had promised to obey Ellis's order of rest and no play, but Trudy wasn't sure how long it would last.

Trudy tore into the paper to find two beautiful strips of green satin.

"Ribbons," Molly squealed.

"For your hair," Ellis explained. "They match your eyes."

He had noticed her eyes? Trudy pushed the thought away. Now was not the time to lose her head. "I don't know what to say," she whispered, lightly touching the beautiful gift. Out here on the prairie, so many miles from civilization, and she had received the most precious gift in her life.

"You're supposed to say thank you," Molly instructed.

"Do you not like them?"

"They're beautiful," she said.

"Like you," Ellis returned.

"Thank you." Trudy couldn't help herself. She lunged toward Ellis, throwing her arms around his neck and pulling him close. She pressed her cheek to his, stopping just short of kissing him on the cheek.

His response was slow, his arms barely coming up and around her before retreating and finally resting on her waist.

She pulled away before he set her from him. She didn't want to feel his rejection. And surely not a refusal based on a lie of her own making.

"Do you want me to tie one in your hair?" Molly asked.

Trudy blinked back her joyous tears and smiled at her sister. "When did you learn how to tie?"

Molly gave her a sly grin. "Maybe Mr. Hardy taught me."

She turned to Ellis. "Did you?"

"No."

Molly dissolved into a fit of giggles.

Trudy stared at her sister. What had happened to the sullen child? Not that she didn't love the changes she saw. She had expected the trail to take its toll on the young grieving girl. She had prayed and prayed for the good Lord to help them on this journey, and He had answered her prayer in the man before her.

"Here," he said. His voice was as rough as a cob.

He took one of the ribbons and tied it at the end of her braid.

Trudy suppressed a shiver and lowered her gaze to watch as he completed the task. His work-roughened fingers snagged a few strands of her unruly curls as he managed to tie a neat bow into the delicate ribbon.

"There," he said.

If she had thought his voice rough before, it was doubly so now. She looked up and caught his midnight gaze with her own.

In his eyes she saw his past hurts, but the future as well. The future he was denying himself and some lucky lady who would capture his heart.

She opened her mouth to tell him so.

"Wagons roll!" the wagon master called, effectively cutting off anything that Trudy might have said.

Ellis cleared his throat. "I guess we should get going."

Trudy nodded then swallowed hard. There was so much she wanted to say. So much that needed to be said, but all of that would have to wait until later. Another time. Maybe even never.

She folded the other ribbon back into its wrapping then turned to help Molly onto the wagon.

"Trudy?"

She looked up to find Ellis still staring at her. "Happy birthday, Trudy Johnson." Then he took up his oxgoad and prepared to get them back on the trail.

—⁓—

They fell into a different pattern as they continued west. Or maybe it was the same pattern and only *felt* different given the days they had spent together in Ash Hollow.

Then there were the times when Trudy would lean down and her braid would fall forward and she would catch sight of the green satin. Even though it had been days since Ellis had tied the ribbon and she'd had to retie it several times, that morning of her birthday always came to mind. How it felt to have him so close, all of his attention centered on her. Her sister laughing with glee. The smell of roses and jasmine floating on the breeze. She wanted to go back and hold that time forever. For in that moment she had almost told Ellis the truth. Still wished that she had. But the opportunity had flown away. And once again they were on the trail.

Yet things were different, on a more even field. She finally managed to learn how to cook bacon. Just in time for all of them to become so tired of bacon they would rather eat almost anything else.

"Trudy," Molly called from her place on the wagon. Her ankle was still a bit swollen, and Ellis insisted that she spend at least a couple more days on rest before she started back playing with the children she had befriended along the trail.

She turned and shot her sister a chastising look, though she knew Molly couldn't see her stern expression from under the brim of her hat.

"What's that?" Molly pointed off into the distance where two rock formations rose up from the ground.

"I don't know." She had heard talk of different sites along the trail, but she couldn't remember what they were called.

"That's Jail Rock and Courthouse Rock."

Trudy jumped as Joseph Kelley came up beside her. For a man who should be driving his own team, he seemed to get around. His horse was as black as sin and had the same wild look in his eyes as his rider.

"Mr. Kelley." She kept her voice as even as she could. The last thing she wanted was for him to know how uncomfortable he made her. Men like Kelley were not to be trusted.

"Where's your husband today, Mrs. Hardy?"

"He walked up ahead a ways."

"Is that so?"

"He should be back any minute." She hoped. Aside from having to deal with the unwanted attention from Mr. Kelley, she could only handle the team for so long before they realized she was driving and started to take advantage of her lack of experience.

"Aw." He made a face. "That's too bad. I was looking forward to getting to know you better."

"If it's all the same to you, Mr. Kelley." She quickened her pace until she was almost jogging. He could have easily matched her stride for stride on foot. With him on horseback, she had no chance to escape him, but thankfully, he took the hint and left her alone.

"Stop." Just then, her pretend husband came riding up, his roan shaking his mane as Ellis reined him in. He dismounted on a run and grabbed the goad from her, stopping the oxen before she could even ask what the matter was.

"What's wrong?" she called, but he didn't answer as he climbed into the back of the wagon. The next thing she knew, he had pitched out a crate of flour and another of fabric she had been saving. Two more crates and her mother's desk came flying out the back of the wagon. It splintered into a hundred pieces as it hit the hard, packed earth.

"What do you think you're doing?" Her vision turned red. He'd gone crazy! What happened to the man she had danced with just a few nights ago?

But he didn't answer her. "Molly," he called, "get back here."

Trudy pressed her lips together then stormed toward the back of the wagon. "What are you going to do? Throw her out the back, too?"

Whether it was her words or her tone, she didn't know. He ignored her and waited for Molly to climb over the supplies that were left in the wagon.

"That was my mother's desk," she yelled at him. "It wasn't yours to throw away." She wanted to cry, but tears wouldn't bring back one of the few things she had of her mother's. Nor would tears help her keep her anger, and right now she wanted to stay mad. "Are you listening to me?"

"No," he yelled in return.

"But you can hear me," she hollered.

"Half the trail can hear you, Trudy."

She crossed her arms and tapped her foot. She could hear him in the wagon talking with Molly and the soft murmur of her sister's voice in response. She'd give him right now for whatever bug was biting him, but once they were alone she was giving him a piece of her mind but good.

A few minutes later, Ellis emerged and retrieved the goad he used to drive the oxen.

"Ellis Hardy, what is *wrong* with you?"

He didn't answer right away. She knew he wanted to get the wagon started back down the trail. But she needed some answers, and she wanted them now.

He ignored her and tied his horse to the back of the wagon. Then, without another word, he started the oxen once again.

"I'll have you know, I'm taking this out of your money."

"Be quiet, Trudy, you don't know what you're talking about."

"Then tell me." She marched up beside him but didn't say any more. Something in the hardness of his eyes and the slant of his jaw kept the rest of her words at bay. She had never seen him look so. . .worn. Something had happened when he rode toward the front of the train. She turned back toward the wagon, but Molly was no longer sitting high in the seat. "Where's Molly?" Surely that subject was safe enough.

Ellis closed his eyes just briefly, then they fluttered back open. He heaved a deep breath as if preparing for a battle he couldn't win. "She's inside the wagon. I made her a place there. A safe place."

"I don't understand."

"You remember the man with the fiddle back in Ash Hollow? He had a son."

"Yes, of course." He was an adorable little fellow with tow-blond hair and a snaggle-tooth smile.

"The boy fell off their wagon."

It took a minute for the meaning to sink in. "Is he—?" She couldn't bring herself to say the word.

"Yes." The word was barely a whisper, rusty and choked. "They buried him a little while ago."

"And they are still going on?"

"What choice do they have?"

They could turn back, but Trudy knew that heading back East would not bring back their son or ease their pain. "And Molly?" she asked.

He shook his head. "She is one special little girl. I can't stand the thought of her getting hurt. If there is only one thing I do in my life, I'll get that little girl to her daddy safe and sound."

She should tell him now. Explain to him that she never meant to deceive him. She never meant to tell him lie upon lie, but one had led to another. She was sorry. There was no daddy, unless he wanted to fill the position.

"There." He nodded toward the side of the trail. A mound of freshly turned earth was covered with as many rocks as the family could find. Their wagon was pulled up a little ahead of the grave. A small cross of knotty wood marked the site. None of the family could be seen, but Trudy was certain she could hear their sobs even over the rattles, creaks, and noise of the trail.

"Will you pray with me?" she asked.

"We can't stop."

"I know. But I think God understands."

She clasped his left hand in her own. "Dear Lord above, I won't try to understand why a family had to lose one so young, but, Lord, please give them peace in this troubling time. Bless the family as they carry on their journey, let them know in their hearts that their son is now with You. I pray for them to have understanding and acceptance, peace and tolerance as they enter into their grief. Amen."

They walked in silence for several minutes before Ellis finally spoke. "Will you say another prayer? One for me?"

Trudy managed a watery smile. "Ellis Hardy, I pray for you every night, and have since the first time we met."

—※—

She prayed for him? The thought shouldn't have warmed him so, but it did.

After seeing the family's grief and loss and realizing the same could happen to them, he had no other choice but to make Molly a safe place inside the wagon. He didn't know what he would do without the girl.

He'd find out soon enough. In only another month or so, he'd be on his way to California while Trudy and Molly headed for Oregon.

The thought filled him with a sadness he didn't understand. California had been his dream for nigh on two years. Ever since he'd heard about the gold there. Or maybe it was ever since Nattie Mae had used him to get the man she truly wanted to marry to propose. It had taken him that long to save the money he needed to buy a wagon and supplies.

Despite what Trudy thought, he believed in God. Loved Him even. He'd just gotten a sour taste in his mouth where religion was concerned. But Trudy helped him to realize that religion wasn't God, and the good Lord shouldn't be blamed for the shortcomings of His followers.

That night, Trudy was very quiet as they sat around the fire. She had picked up her stitching, though he couldn't imagine how she could see in the dim light.

They'd eaten their usual supper of dry bread and bacon. What he wouldn't give for a big juicy apple right about then, but the fruit hadn't been in season when they left, and none that he could have brought with him would have survived this long.

"What are you thinking, Ellis Hardy?" she asked without looking up from her work. He felt like an old married couple that could read each other's minds with nary a word spoken.

"Just wonderin' if they'll have apples in California."

The lack of light must have gotten to her. She gave him a small smile then folded up her sampler and tucked it away. "I didn't know you liked apples."

"Not much call to find out such things out here is there?"

"I suppose not." She pulled her braid over her shoulder and studied the ribbon he'd given her.

He'd wanted her to have something special for her birthday, and it was all the fort had to offer. But the look on her face when he'd given it to her. . . He shook his head. He was only five and twenty years and was becoming a sentimental old coot faster than he cared to admit. And the way she flung herself at him, wrapping her warmth so close to his. It took everything he had not to drag her off to the nearest preacher and say binding vows before man and God.

Impossible, he reminded himself. She already belonged to another.

"Do you really believe there's all that gold in California like they say?"

"Sure." He said the word, but any fool could tell he had his doubts. And they grew daily as he talked with others along the trail. So many were going to California. Was there really enough gold there for them all?

"I've been thinking," she started, staring off into the setting sun. The sky seemed to go on forever, painted with the color of lilacs but streaked with blue and gold. "That if you wanted to, I mean, you could go with us. Me and Molly."

"To Oregon Country?"

She nodded. He couldn't read her expression under the shade of her hat, but he wasn't sure he wanted to see it.

"Why would I want to do something like that?"

She shrugged. "You just seem different, you know. From these other men. Like there's more to you than just wanting to strike it rich."

Anger filled him. She thought he would tag along behind her and her daughter, watch her reunite with her husband. *No, thank you.* "I can't imagine what."

"I don't know. Maybe the love of a good woman? A family. What most people want from life." She shrugged again, and he realized that she was uncomfortable talking to him about such matters. Well, maybe she should keep her nose out of his business.

"I tried that once before," he said, doing his best to temper his anger. He succeeded, but only just, and his voice held the hard edge of his annoyance. "I fell in love with a beautiful preacher's daughter. I was so smitten, so thrilled that out of all the men she could have chosen, she wanted me. We courted and went about, showing the town around us that we were in love. Come to find out, she wanted to make her ex-fiancé jealous."

"I'm sorry." Her voice was small and sad. But he didn't want her pity. He wanted her to understand.

"He came running back, and she dropped me like she'd picked up a hot poker."

He shook his head, the events of that day clearer now than they had ever been.

"I'm sorry she caused you such pain," Trudy murmured.

"You know, I loved her, yes. But what really hurt? That she lied to me. I was with her for pert near six months, and never once did she tell me the truth."

— ∞ —

His words stayed with Trudy for the remainder of the week and took some of the joy out of the sites. They passed by a curious rock formation called Chimney Rock that seemed to stretch a mile into the sky. They passed other oddities in Scotts Bluff, though Ellis explained that they would be going on an alternate route through Mitchell Pass.

The ruts were deep and the going rough. She heard the horrific tales of others on their journey who had fallen like the fiddler's son and died there in the pass. And every night she thanked God for sending her Ellis Hardy. He alone was the reason why they all survived. The protective hole he had made in the supplies kept Molly safe from the violently rocking wagon as they struggled along the way.

And every night she prayed for Ellis to find peace and happiness. It was one thing for a man to want to seek out riches for the sake of getting wealthy, but quite another when the man was running from his own life.

Not that she was one to say anything. She was running from her own life, her father's mistakes. She was telling her own lies and hating it all each step of the way.

Her thoughts became more and more clouded as her feelings for Ellis grew. Couldn't he see what a fine husband and father he would make? Didn't he realize that he had so much to offer a family?

Her only regret was that her lies would keep him from ever meaning more to her family than the man who drove them over the trail.

The thought saddened her beyond belief, but her excitement managed to take its place—if only for a little bit—when the call rang out. "Fort," someone shouted. "Fort!" And the word worked its way through the trail wagons. Civilization, the first in weeks.

Fort Laramie was up ahead.

Chapter 5

U nlike Fort Kearney, Laramie was an honest-to-goodness military fort. That the military needed a post to help protect the trail from the Sioux Indians was unsettling to Trudy, but she tried not to let those facts invade her thoughts too often. She knew this was a dangerous trip when she'd set out, but she worried about Molly and what would become of her if something happened to Trudy herself.

Yet the adobe fort did instill some confidence in Trudy, hope that the trail, though wild and untamed, was leading them on to a new life, a new civilization.

They rested there a couple of days, watching other travelers as they turned away and headed back East. Trudy didn't understand. They were a third of the way to their destination.

"Why are they leaving?" Trudy asked. One family had lost a grandmother and a child along the trail. She could understand why they felt the hardships too great to continue. But others it seemed were just giving up.

Ellis pointed off into the distance. "See that?"

She did. A mountaintop was outlined there, strong and daunting.

"That's Laramie Peak. The first we will see from the Rocky Mountains."

Trudy's eyes grew wide. "We're going to climb that?"

"No." Ellis shook his head. "But the going is about to get rough. Are you up for it?"

"Yes." She had come this far, there was no going back now.

After their couple days of rest, they started back on the trail again. "Wagons, roll!" seemed to have new meaning for Trudy. Their journey was about to get rougher, Ellis had said. They had been very fortunate so far. The Lord had truly looked out for them. Trudy increased her nightly prayers to the point that sometimes she fell asleep before she said "amen." But she knew God understood as surely as He was watching out for them.

"What is all that?" she asked Ellis as they walked along. Molly was safely ensconced in the cave that Ellis had built for her. He constructed it so that she had room to play with the paper dolls she had brought along.

He scanned the land around them, littered with all sorts of items, food, fabric, even beautiful furniture had been left to bake in the hot summer sun. "I think most of the wagons are getting heavy."

"But what if they need the supplies later?" she asked, staring in awe at a ten-pound package of bacon lying next to a broken crate.

"There'll be a couple more places to buy supplies on down the road."

"And will it be like Fort Laramie?" The prices there had been nearly two hundred times more than the cost back East.

"Hard to say. But it won't matter much if you can't make it there because your oxen have all collapsed from exhaustion."

"I suppose." In times like these she felt helpless, at the mercy of the trail. But that didn't mean she would give up. She had started this journey and would see it through to the end.

〰️

"Independence Rock." The murmur went through the travelers as they neared the landmark. It was the day after July Fourth. And they had been on the trail for just over two months. Trudy was still shocked and surprised as people dumped out their precious cargo or turned and headed back home. The wagon ruts were such that these days a guide was not needed to navigate the trail, but the thought of coming this far then going home was as foreign to her as the land she now stood upon.

"That's it up ahead." Ellis pointed toward the large rock formation. It was huge and round, like the rubber ball of a giant, half buried in the earth. Wagons were veering off the trail to travel in for a closer look.

"I hear it's good luck to write your name there." Ellis's voice was so close that Trudy whirled around to find him mere inches from her. "What do you say?"

"What? About what?" She could scarcely think with him so near. He was just so big and masculine and capable.

"Do you want to write our names there?"

"On the rock?"

He shot her a small frown. "That is what I've been talking about. It's a few miles out of the way, but it's not every day that you get to pass through as beautiful a place as this."

"I would love to." Together they got Molly from her play cave and walked her between them as they made their way to the big rock.

It was even bigger up close and surrounded by a multitude of people with the same plan as the three of them: write their names on the rock for future travelers to see.

"Here." Ellis handed her the ink. "You do it. I'm sure your penmanship is much better than mine."

She took the ink and approached the rock, not quite certain what she wanted to say. Finally she wrote, *Ellis Hardy, Trudy Johnson, and Molly Johnson were here July 5, 1851. God bless America!*

She stood back and admired her handiwork.

"Perfect," Ellis said.

Molly nodded in agreement.

Trudy smiled, then together the three of them headed back to their wagon.

〰️

Five miles west they caught site of Devil's Gate. It was a fitting name as far as Ellis was concerned. Rising dangerously from the ground, the rock formation appeared to be cleaved in two by the hand of Satan himself. He had heard the rumors floating around about the area, and he prayed that none of them got back to Trudy and Molly.

They headed around the rocks, not taking the time to trek over on foot to visit the mountain range. Something in Ellis wanted to keep going, and the women he escorted readily agreed.

They pressed onward until they reached the South Pass.

"I thought it would be smaller," Trudy said, gazing around them at the vast valley. "Didn't you?"

"I heard word before we left Independence. A man's got to be prepared."

She shot him a grateful smile, and he had to exhale a long breath to keep from puffing his chest out in pride.

Most travelers believed the South Pass to be a narrow split through the mountains with rocks and cliffs looming high above on either side. In truth the pass was open and grassy measuring nearly twenty miles wide.

But the pass held a different charm. "Did you know we're in Oregon Country now?" he asked.

Trudy's eyes grew wide, and her face lit up like the sun. "Really? So soon?"

"I mean, we're in Oregon, but we still have many miles to go."

"Oh." Her smile fell faster than a spring downpour. "Well, at least we can say we made it to Oregon."

"Yes," he said, but he got a funny feeling in his gut. If he left her now, he could say that he got her to Oregon, but he was staying at least until Parting of the Ways. That was still a few weeks away, but the thought didn't sit any better with him than leaving now.

But what choice did he have? She and Molly, his favorite girls, belonged to another.

—∞—

"Look there."

Trudy swung her gaze around. Ellis pointed toward huge floating rings in the sky, like smoke rings blown from a huge mouth in the earth. "What is it?"

"We're at the springs," he said.

They had been traveling down the banks of the Bear River for the last twenty miles. Talk had been running through the travelers, rumors and tales of the springs up ahead that tasted like soda straight from the drugstore fountain. Trudy was beyond skeptical. How could such a thing exist?

But God was wondrous and mysterious she reminded herself. He could do anything, whether it fit into human logic or not.

And the springs defied all logic she could comprehend. She could hear them roar like a steamboat, belching big vapor rings into the air. The land was laced with them, all different sizes and depths. Some smelled suspiciously like sulfur, but others were a treat.

"Can we try it?" Molly asked. She stared at the bubbling springs with eyes full of wonder and awe.

"Sure." Ellis nodded toward the spring, then as if remembering that he wasn't completely in charge of Molly's care, he looked to Trudy for confirmation.

"Are you sure it's safe?" She stared at the water with distrust in her eyes.

"As can be," Ellis replied. "But I hear that just like regular soda water, you shouldn't drink too much or it'll give you a bellyache."

"Yes, sir." Molly lifted her skirt and ran to the water's edge, her ankle long since healed. She knelt down and, like those around her, scooped some of the water into her mouth. She turned back to look at them, her eyes wide. "It does! It does! It tastes just like the sodie water Pa got for us that time, Trudy."

She smiled at her sister. "That's great, Molly Sue."

"Come try it. Please," she added when neither one of them made a move toward the water. "Pleasepleaseplease."

Trudy turned to Ellis who merely shrugged. Then he grabbed her hand, and together they ran to the water's edge.

"It's amazing," she said after swallowing the first mouthful.

She laughed and turned to Ellis.

He was laughing and smiling as well.

They looked at one another, and time froze. Somehow they were the only two people there on the banks, perhaps in the whole world. How easy it would be for her to lean in and press their lips together. Not that she could be as bold to make that first move. But she wanted to. Oh, how she wanted to.

She looked into his eyes and saw that longing there, the desire to see what a kiss between them would be like. But he thought she belonged to another. Ellis Hardy was a gentleman. Despite their crude and rough surroundings, he would remain a gentleman, honorable and true.

He cleared his throat, and the moment vanished.

"I, uh. . ." Trudy coughed and pushed to her feet. She needed to put some distance between them and fast. Not for him, but for her.

Lord, why am I here? Why am I with a man who believes I am something that I'm not? A man who has vowed never to marry. Father, please take these feelings from me. Help me move on. Help me remember that soon we will part, never to meet again. Help me remember, Lord, and help me get over the pain that will follow. Amen.

Trudy wasn't positive, but she thought Ellis was starting to avoid her. They spent three nights at Soda Springs but managed to dodge any bellyaches. Others around them weren't so lucky.

It was no easy feat to keep Molly from dipping into the springs every chance she got, but once little JJ Kelley fell bellyache victim to his overindulgence in the springs, Molly tempered herself. She might be only six, but she was smart. It didn't take more than once for her to see the perils of overindulgence.

But there was more there than the bubbling water. There were cold springs, hot springs, and some that smelled worse than a public outhouse.

Yet once they left the springs, Ellis became as distant as the moon. The easiness that had developed between them evaporated like a quick summer rain.

"I'm going on up ahead for a bit." He untied the horse from the back of the wagon without even looking in her direction.

"Fine," she said. She took up the stick and started to lead the team of oxen.

She knew they were nearing Fort Hall and not long after that came Parting of the Ways. If the talk was correct, most of the wagons were turning south toward California.

But the remaining ones would head on north, deeper into Oregon. She still had to find a new driver, and Ellis had to find a wagon to hitch to in order to make it to the goldfields.

But the look in his eyes at the springs. That look like there might be something more growing between them...

Once again she was faced with the gravity of her lies. What would happen if she told Ellis Hardy the truth? What if she explained her fears, the reasoning behind her falsehoods? Would he understand? Forgive her even? Would things between them change? Would he consider going on into Oregon with her and Molly? Maybe join their lives together forever?

A sense of peace descended upon her. That was all she had to do. She could tell him the truth, tell him there was no husband. That Molly was her sister and she, Trudy Johnson, was deeply in love with him.

She had to take that chance. It was beyond forward, but they were on the trail. Social decorum had faded away long ago. She was a frontierswoman now, and she had to embrace that adventuresome spirit that would see her through the trials she was about to face in Oregon. And with any luck, her risk would produce something wonderful and righteous.

From up ahead she heard not one but two gunshots ringing through the dusty air. It was a common occurrence, gunfire on the trail. Many of the drivers carried loaded guns at the ready. Indian attacks were rare, she had discovered, but still possible all the same. *The Lord favors the prepared,* her father always said, so she understood the need for the protection.

She tapped the goad against the oxen's wooden yoke and wondered how soon before Ellis would return. She really hated driving the team by herself. Yet, she didn't mind so much when he was walking by her side. Just one more reason why she had to tell him that she loved him. Perhaps there was a future for them after all.

"Mrs. Hardy! Mrs. Hardy!" Joseph Kelley galloped toward her, his hat flying off in his haste.

Great, she thought. How come it was every time Ellis left her alone, their unwanted trail companion showed up to torment her?

But there was something different about his posture today, something she couldn't quite name.

He dismounted without even stopping his horse, running alongside the beast as he continued in her direction.

"What is it?" she asked. "What's wrong?"

"It's Ellis," he panted, taking the goad from her and prodding the team off to the side of the trail. He took a gulp of air trying to gain back his breath and speak all at the same time. "Ellis has been shot."

The words buzzed in her ears like an angry bee. She heard wrong. She had to have heard him wrong. There was no other answer. She had just seen Ellis. He'd left only half an hour ago. He'd just rode ahead, and she had decided to tell him that she loved him. This couldn't be happening.

Mr. Kelley hobbled the team.

"Where's Molly?" he asked.

She pointed toward the wagon. He gave a quick nod, and before she knew it, JJ was there to stay with Molly while Mr. Kelley slung her in front of him on the big black horse and headed toward the front of the wagon train.

As they jostled along at a terrifying speed, the truth of the matter settled over her heart. Ellis had been shot.

She closed her eyes and bowed her head, only the grace of God keeping her on the horse as she prayed and prayed for him to be all right.

But she knew the chances were against him—even if she couldn't allow them to invade her own thoughts. They were miles from any civilization, no doctors, no fresh water.

She was starting her prayer a second time, when Mr. Kelley pulled his mount to a stop and hoisted her to the ground.

She opened her eyes to see Ellis prone, face white, a bloom of red covering one shoulder. Thankfully it was his right one and far from his heart. But the dark stain covering his upper right thigh was just as worrisome.

She ran toward him, tears streaming as she brushed his hair back from his face. He was still breathing, steady but shallow. His wounds themselves didn't appear to be an immediate threat on his life, but it was infection that would be their main concern.

His blue eyes fluttered open, glassy with pain and hardly focused, but somehow he knew she was there. "Trudy?" he whispered.

"I'm here, my love." She tried to hide her concern, not let him see how worried she was. She gave a small chuckle that convinced no one. "This is a heck of a way to get off the trail, Ellis Hardy. If you wanted to stop all you had to do was ask."

He gave her a small smile in return, but it turned to a grimace as a pain hit.

Then his eyes rolled to white and closed once again.

Chapter 6

The light was brighter than he could ever remember seeing before—white, blinding, otherworldly.

He tried to move but felt as if he'd been pinned down like a butterfly in a little boy's bug collection.

The relentless white light continued. Then he remembered. Riding ahead on the trail, feeling the burning in his shoulder, then a twin sear in his thigh as he fell from his horse.

Was he dead? Is that what the light was about? Was he heading to heaven? As much as he wanted to see the beauty of heaven as told to him in God's own Word, he wasn't ready to go yet. He had to talk to Trudy just one more time and tell her the truth.

"Trudy," he managed to rasp. Was that his voice?

"I'm here," a sweet voice said in return.

Was that her?

He managed to force his eyes open. The light came from the sun, through a window with a real glass pane, but he couldn't manage to hold his eyes open against the glare.

He moaned and closed them once again.

Then the light was gone, and a sweet smelling shadow took its place.

"Ellis? Are you awake?"

It was her! He forced his eyes open once again.

And there she was. "Trudy."

Her meadow-green eyes filled with tears. "Dear Lord, thank You. Thank You." Her fingers trembled as she traced the lines on his face, the curve of his eyebrows, and the length of his beard.

Beard? How long had he been unconscious?

"Five days," she said, dashing the falling tears from her cheeks.

Five days? "But the wagons." He tried to push himself up from the bed. Bed. Where had she gotten a bed?

"The wagons are gone, Ellis."

"But Oregon," he said. "And your husband." That wasn't what he wanted to say, but his head ached and his mind wasn't completely his own.

"*Shh,*" Trudy shushed, once again trailing her fingers through his hair. "We'll talk about that another day."

From outside the window, Ellis heard birds chirping, men talking with strange accents, what sounded like a flag fluttering in the wind. He opened his eyes.

He was inside a building for the first time in months. He was lying in a bed. A cot really. And he was alone.

He pushed himself up a little on the mattress, his head swimming with the motion. His shoulder ached and his leg felt as if it had been blown in half, but a quick assessment showed that he still had possession of all his limbs. He had been riding his horse ahead on the trail trying to put some distance between him and Trudy when suddenly he was on the ground, shot twice.

But how had he gotten here? And where exactly was *here*?

If he had to guess, he was probably in Fort Hall, the British outpost just this side of the Parting of the Ways. He'd been shot and dumped here while the train went on without him. The wagon train and Trudy.

Oh, the mistakes he had made. She had gone on, and he'd never gotten to tell her the truth. That he loved her with all his heart and always would.

He was at least two weeks behind the train if not more. There was no way he could catch up by himself. No possible means for getting there on his own.

"I guess I'm here until spring next year."

"We're here." The door to the small room opened. In came Trudy with a steaming bowl of water and a rag, Molly on her heels.

"You're awake. You're awake. You're awake." Molly rushed forward and would have bounced on the bed next to him had Trudy not stopped her.

"Sit over there, Molly Sue," Trudy said, indicating a wooden chair in the far corner of the room. "Mr. Hardy still needs his rest."

Reluctantly, Molly obeyed, though she dragged the chair across the floor and sat at the edge of his bed.

"What are you doing here?" he asked.

"I'm nursing you back to health."

"But the wagon train," he protested.

"Is probably halfway through Oregon Country by now."

"But you're here."

"That I am." She crossed to the bedside table and poured him a cup of water. Then she held the cup to his lips and braced his head as he drank. The cool liquid trickled down his dry throat like milk and honey.

"That's good," he said.

"And that's a good sign. Are you ready for something to eat?"

At the word his stomach rumbled. How long had he been abed? "Yes." An appetite was a good sign, yes? But not nearly as good as the fact that Trudy had stayed with him. She had let the wagons move on and stayed with him instead.

"Molly, run go tell Cookie that Mr. Hardy is awake and hungry."

"But—" the child started to protest then stopped. She slid from the chair and raced to the door. "Don't go anywhere," she warned Ellis.

He smiled, his leg throbbing with pain. "I won't."

The creak of the door punctuated her exit, then the two of them were alone.

"I need to tell you something." They both spoke at the same time then laughed at their own folly.

"Ladies first," Ellis said.

"I'm not married." The words tumbled from her mouth as if they had been waiting there all along.

"I know."

"I'm sorry I lied to you, I never meant to—what do you mean you know?"

He gave her a quick smile. At least no part of his face hurt.

"When did you figure it out?"

"At Soda Springs when Molly called you Trudy."

"And that's all you needed to know that I had been lying to you for months?"

"It was all I needed to give me hope that you had been not so truthful with me. Then Molly let it slip. Tell me something. Why's a nice Christian girl like you telling lies and traveling the Oregon Trail?"

Ellis leaned back against the pillows as Trudy explained how her father had died, leaving her in charge of Molly—and how the mismanagement of their inheritance and the creditors who had taken almost all that she had sent her running for a fresh start in the West.

"So you forgive me?" Trudy asked.

Ellis smiled. "Forgive you? It's the best news I've heard all day." He loved the smile that lit up her face.

"What did you want to say?" she asked. She wet a rag in the basin and wrung it out as she waited for his answer.

"Just that I love you."

The rag made a plop as it splashed back into the bowl. She whirled around to face him. "You. . .you love me?"

"I love you," he repeated. "And I want to marry you and be a father to Molly."

"I—I—thought you had vowed never to get married."

"Can't a man make a mistake?" he grinned.

"Say yes," Molly called from the hallway.

"I thought you went to get Mr. Hardy something to eat."

Molly beamed at him. "Do I have to call you Mr. Hardy when you two get married?"

"You can call me anything you'd like." *Just as long as we join lives.*

She seemed to think about it a second. "Poppy," she said with great conviction.

Oh, how Ellis loved that little girl. "Poppy, it is," he said in return.

"Now go get him something to eat," Trudy instructed. "Sorry." She shot him an apologetic look as she pulled Molly's chair even closer to the side of his bed.

"You never replied," he reminded her.

"Yes," she said. "Yes, I will marry you."

"Does this mean you love me?" he asked.

Tears filled her eyes, and he reached up to dash them away with the backs of his fingers. He never wanted to see her cry again. "More than you will ever know."

"How long before Molly gets back?" he asked.

"Ten, maybe fifteen minutes."

"What should we do until she returns?" he asked with a sly smile.

"I could wash your face and give you a shave," she suggested, but the light in her eyes said so much more.

"Or you could scoot over here a little closer and give me a kiss instead," he said.

The feel of her lips on his, knowing that she loved him as much as he loved her was more than enough to heal his wounds. God was good, and He brought them together, but more than that, He showed Ellis the truth in love lies within the heart and not the words.

"What about California?" she asked, once their kiss ended.

"I've been thinking more about someplace a little farther north."

Before she could respond Molly bounded back in. "Cookie's on his way. Here, this is for you." He took the pillow from her, only then realizing that it was covered with the sampler Trudy had been working on while they were on the trail.

A good name is rather to be chosen than great riches, and loving favour rather than silver and gold. PROVERBS 22:1"

And what he had there with him was as good as gold. Even better.

He smiled at his two favorite girls and thanked the Lord for the healing miracles of love.

Daughters of the Wind
by DiAnn Mills

Acknowledgments

Tom Morrisey for your endless knowledge of firearms and willingness to help writers. Lauraine Snelling—Thank you for your expertise. Love you, my friend.

Chapter 1

June 1851

I didn't mind leaving Independence, Missouri, for Oregon Territory, but I hadn't realized the journey would steal my spirit. In the beginning, all of us on the wagon train sang about the rich, black earth and the thick forests that would be our new homes. We danced to the tune of a lively fiddle and told stories around crackling fires. But that was then, and this is now.

We've been hungry, thirsty, bone-tired, and frustrated. Eaten enough dust to plow a field and displayed tempers in a fit of rage. When I think about all who've died from sickness and accidents, my heart aches. Those who are gone had dreams, and I no longer have any. Except to escape the memories and perhaps find peace. The original two thousand miles stretched on endlessly, and yet it was the Rocky Mountains that terrified me. I must keep walking west, for to dwell on things I cannot change means death.

And above all things, I am a survivor.

The sun began its slow ascent to sunrise, and I crawled from beneath the wagon, swinging my gaze east. The fiery shades of orange and yellow lifted the curtain on a new day. Sometimes angst twisted my heart for the unknown, but a new day meant leaving yesterday behind and moving forward.

I shivered in the early morning chill, and my stomach complained of the little food I'd eaten the night before. Pa had offered me his plate of beans, but I told him I'd had enough. That's why Pa and the boys had risen early to fish and hunt before the wagons were readied to pull out. We were all feeling poorly, and he didn't want to lose any more of his family.

A small hand slipped into mine, and I knew without looking it was Nancy. She sought me at every opportunity, most likely to escape her family since her baby brother had died of fever barely a week ago. I'd held him once, probably a mistake.

She smiled, and I wanted to hold her tight against life's ugliness. "Miss Deborah, I dreamed about my baby brother again last night."

"And what happened?" I squeezed her hand gently, but I couldn't look into her pale face.

"He said I was going to make it to Oregon 'cuz he'd sent an angel to watch over me."

The lump in my throat thickened. Nancy had grown so thin, and her brown eyes had lost their sparkle. "Then it must be so."

"My pa wants to have a farm next to yours. Then I'd get to see you 'most as much as now."

"I'd like that, sweetheart." I hoped she made it—I hoped not one more person died.

The wagon train's scout rode toward us. He wore his usual scowl, evident before the sun took its place in the sky.

"He scares me." Nancy gripped my hand.

"Mr. Walker's not so bad. I think he's more concerned about our welfare than making friends." That's what Pa had said. Whenever I studied the scout, he was helping someone or barking orders. Never stopped to rest.

"Listen up." Mr. Walker must have a religion about not wasting words. "Stay put this afternoon and rest."

"Yes, sir."

"Tell your pa we're having a meetin' at sundown. Might want to bring your brothers."

"What about me?" I shouldn't taunt him, but I couldn't resist. The women already outnumbered the men, and those who'd lost their husbands deserved to know what was ahead.

"Suit yourself." He nodded, and I caught a glimpse of amber eyes before he rode on. The man might be pleasing to look at if he ever smiled. Not that I'd notice. I was accustomed to Pa's kind mannerisms and the way he always made me and my brothers feel special.

"What are you going to do today?" Nancy's bubbling voice mirrored my thoughts, eager for a day different from the others.

"Wash clothes and fix a pot of beans."

She tilted her head. "Could we take a walk later?"

I understood how her family grieved, and the sadness wore at the little girl. "Ask your ma if she can spare you midafternoon."

Nancy dropped my hand and sped away. I doubt if her ma would let her go, which relieved me. I wanted time alone to explore the rock hills about a mile away. Wildflowers bloomed there, and I wanted to write in my journal. Weariness when we bedded down and chores in the early morning stopped me from keeping track of the trail to Oregon, and my mother had wanted me to record everything.

Pushing aside the darkness that could snatch me into its clutches, I promised myself to write only beautiful things today. Maybe I'd sketch a flower or the purple peaks in the distance. Whatever it took not to think about how I'd failed to keep my precious mother alive.

Hours passed, and with the wash hung from every peg on the wagon, I stretched my back. Five men and myself made a mess of dirty clothes, even if none of us had much. Beans simmered over the fire for dinner, and the noon meal of freshly caught fish long since ended. Pa and the boys rested up for the hard trail ahead. I pulled my journal and my mother's quill pen and ink bottle from the chest in the wagon and dropped them into a pail. Maybe I'd spare a little honey and fix a cobbler tonight. Pa and the boys had brought down a couple of rabbits, and that meant a feast for dinner. I straightened the provisions, mentally keeping track of the journey ahead. At Fort Laramie, we'd prepared for the mountains—gathered extra provisions and greased the wagon wheels. Oxen and horses were shod, and women mended and washed. Everything breathing tried to regain their strength.

"Deborah, your brothers and I want to do something special for you today."

I looked up at Pa. Lines formed around his eyes, but his smile filled me with love. "What's that?"

"Beans are on, and we got a couple of rabbits to skin. We'll roast 'em up. No need to come back until dinner."

The freedom soothed me. "Are you sure?"

He kissed my forehead. "Go, my sweet girl."

I nodded and started my walk toward the low hills.

"Miss Deborah, are you ready?"

I would not let Nancy see my disappointment. She needed me, and I couldn't refuse her. But when I greeted her, a sea of faces smiled shyly. "What's this?"

Nancy blinked. "I. . .I told 'em about our walk, and they wanted to come along."

Childlike innocence stared at me. How could I turn them away? My insides sunk to my toes. I'd been young once, and my mother always made time for me. These girls' mothers were tired, yet they didn't deny them a few hours reprieve—even at my expense.

"Miss Deborah," Nancy said, "can they come with us?"

I counted seven of them including Nancy. "Give me a moment." I hurried back to my wagon, placed my personal belongings back into the trunk, and latched it.

We fell into step toward the rocks in the distance. Not much green or vegetation, but a few sparse wildflowers. Most of the girls sang to pass the time. Late afternoon sunlight mirrored in their eyes, and a few still had polished apple cheeks. I envied them. Even in the midst of hardships, their childhood glistened.

A couple looked sickly, like Nancy, and I blinked back a tear. The air would be good for all of us.

"Shall we race?" I said.

Seven giggly girls ran with me to our destination. My sides ached, and the wind blew my hair back as though I were flying atop one of the horses we'd left in Missouri.

I spotted wild berries and knew they were not poisonous but a treat. We ate two for every one we dropped into our pails. Watching the girls reminded me of my mother's words: *Children are the legacy for tomorrow, and they must be loved and protected.*

We wove wildflowers into wreaths for our hair and played chase, told stories and made up songs. Hours drifted by with so much joy.

I didn't pay attention to approaching changes of weather until a crisp breeze from the north picked up leaves and debris. A chill settled on my shoulders, and the scent of damp earth met my nostrils. A navy-blue sky moved our way faster than we could race back to the wagons. A jagged path of lightning like a wicked sword told me we needed shelter now. Thunder crashed before I could count to three.

"Beneath that rock ledge," I shouted above the oncoming storm and pointed to a lower slab of overhanging rock that could protect us from nature's fury. "Hurry, girls. Squeeze yourselves as far back as you can."

"I want my mama," a little girl cried.

When a second girl sobbed, another told them to hush.

I ignored the questions and cries while shepherding them to safety. Temperatures dropped, and I suspected hail would soon be upon us. Lightning grew closer, slashing the sky with its power. When the girls were safely positioned, I sat in front of them where Nancy wept quietly. Wrapping my arms around as many trembling shoulders as I could reach, I assured them we'd be fine. But the hammering against my chest revealed my fright.

Hail pelted the stone roof above us. Huge balls of ice lay within feet of where we huddled, and lightning flashed its demons. Would it ever stop? My stomach curdled with thoughts of all the wagons exposed to the storm.

The remaining afternoon and evening, we huddled together as the storm raged around us. Hours passed and nothing changed. In the veil of night and the continuous downpour, I sought to comfort the others.

"Look, Miss Deborah," Nancy said. "The sky's turning from dark blue to green. What is happening?"

I knew, but I couldn't tell her. . .death wind.

"I see something," a yellow-haired girl named Grace whispered. Like me, she must fear if she uttered the words aloud they would be real.

In the distance, a beast whirled across the plain, churning black smoke, spitting all that got in its path, and it whirled straight for our loved ones. The funnel hovered over the wagons, sucking up life and hope and dreams.

Chapter 2

Lane Walker stood under a rock ledge with one hand on his mare's reins to calm her. While scouting ahead to avoid alkaline waters, the late afternoon had churned to gray with a violent storm that lasted for hours. The fury ushered in a burst of thunder and lightning that struck like a knife piercing the earth. Nature's rage was more horrifying than anything man could do. For who controlled it but the hand of God?

He watched the storm, willing it to cease. He'd been too far from the campsite to warn the others. Or ride fast enough to lead them to safety.

The mare wanted to run, and so did he, but he held on tight. The sky blackened and finally turned a hideous shade of green. There was no escape from a whirling mass of roaring wind that drew everything into its path with a violent shake. Looked to him like nearly a half-mile wide. Caution wove logic through him, but it was hard to do nothing.

How long would it take to repair the wagons and move on? A day? Two days. Time wasted when they were already behind. The mountains seemed to heckle. The treacherous inclines and sharp curves took hours, sometimes days, and early snows could make the mountains impassable. Another delay brought on the winter storms. Lane had made the trek once with the wagon master, and the dangers ahead didn't subside until they pulled the oxen and horses to a halt in Oregon City.

Who was he fooling? The twister could destroy everyone in its path, including good men, women, and children.

When Lane signed on to learn how to lead a wagon train, the wagon master told him if half the people survived, they were lucky. He'd warned the folks anxious to get to Oregon the same thing, but it didn't stop those eager to leave Missouri for new homes.

Lane understood their lure of a better life, as though a force stronger than any of them pushed them west. Since fourteen, he'd been searching for purpose, and he believed he'd found it helping folks reach new homes.

The wagon train had journeyed three days beyond Fort Laramie. Since leaving Missouri, they'd lost folks to sickness and accidents. Cholera had snuffed out the lives of over a hundred folks, taking a third of them.

Images of the men, women, and children he'd vowed to lead to Oregon refused to leave him alone, faces and smiles, fears and doubts. Ever since he was orphaned at fourteen, he woke each morning with a sense of responsibility to help others. The one part of him that fought what the good Lord expected of him was his preference to be alone. Seemed easier that way.

As hard as he fought to be alone, one young woman stayed fixed in his heart—Deborah Ford. Her huge robin's-egg blue eyes and a splattering of freckles kept him looking for excuses to visit her pa and brothers. Her smiles were rare, and he lived for them. Earlier he'd seen her with a group of girls carrying baskets for berry picking. The little ones loved her gentle spirit. He'd wanted to ask her pa proper about courting her, but he hadn't found the right time. Her brothers were protective, too, and Lane fretted he might not be good enough.

Was she among the survivors? He prayed so. He prayed for all those caught in the twister.

———

Through the blackness, I attempted to see what the twister had drawn into its funnel. The beast had devoured its prey and moved on, lasting only a few minutes. The rain had stopped, and all was calm, but I failed to see any fires from the wagons. I fretted to stay or leave. Yet, I couldn't move, as though I were paralyzed. Later we'd find our loved ones.

Our families and friends would be protected under the wagons, and I clung to that hope. Some of the girls were crying. I wanted to weep, too, but as always, I shoved aside my feelings.

Grace touched my arm. She held the hand of her younger sister, Ruby. "What do you think happened to the wagon train?"

I read the fear in her eyes. "If we don't hear from our families, I'll check on them in the morning. I think it best we sleep under the ledge."

"We could pray," Grace said, her voice trembling. "They could have escaped the wind."

I nodded. "Peace comes from God." But He didn't care about any of us. Only in the grave could one escape life's tragedies.

Most of the girls fell asleep.

I shivered and snuggled close to the girls, but I couldn't sleep. I kept waiting for Pa or my brothers to find us.

I thought of each girl by name. Grace was eleven years old, and her sister Ruby was seven. Nancy was ten. Abigail and Faith were nine-year-old twins. Hope and Beth were eight-year-old cousins. Of all the girls, Nancy had the poorest health. All needed their families. I often ached for my mother who died before we left Missouri, and I was seventeen. Imagine losing a mother at these girls' ages. No, I refused to think of the worst.

I was foolish fretting over each one as though they were my own charges. But fear consumed me. I'd heard what twisters could do. . . .

When morning came, I'd find our loved ones.

Chapter 3

I woke to singing birds and a burst of sunlight in a clear sky. Unusual for me to sleep past early morn, and I should have felt alert, but I only ached. . .in my body and heart. The unknown was worse than facing a fear in front of me.

None of the girls mentioned food or water, but they needed both. I'm sure they'd grasped the truth about the twister, but I would not speak of it. I made sure they were all right, giving them each a hug and urging them to eat some of the berries from yesterday. Water trickled from a mountain stream, quenching our thirst. All the while, I wrestled with how to prepare them for what lay ahead.

For that matter, how did I prepare myself?

A wagon had dropped from the sky during the storm and crashed several yards away. It shattered into kindling. How many could live through such fury?

I gathered them and placed Grace in charge. She was the oldest in her family as well as with the girls. "I'm going to the wagons," I said. "I'll be back soon."

"Why can't we go with you?" Nancy swiped at her eyes.

These girls were not strangers to misfortune. Oh, but I wanted to spare them. "I don't know what I'll find, and after the long night, your parents will want to fetch you."

"You think they're dead?" Nancy said.

My spirit sunk to near tears. How did I postpone what she believed in her heart?

"Miss Deborah, your face shows fear," Nancy said.

"Some of our friends might be hurt. Good reason for all of you to stay here."

Nancy pointed to what was left of the wagons in the valley. "Nothing's moving down there, and everything looks broken."

I lifted her chin with my palm. "Listen to Grace. She might need help with the younger girls."

I walked away from them with the hope I'd soon see life. Odd how walking into the valley took so long when yesterday we raced to the site where berries and wildflowers flourished. This morning, each step focused on the inevitable. I sunk into the soft earth from the rains. Four horses grazed several yards from me. Six oxen moved within the rubble. One wagon stood. Another needed much repair. The rest were in pieces. Not a single person walked. No one called for help or moaned. Only silence.

Sometimes folks don't want to see what they're afraid of, and that was me. I blinked and realized the bodies. . .and parts of bodies were strewn everywhere. Vacant eyes would haunt me forever. Friends who'd lost their lives were positioned like rag dolls. Children with no future. Adults with crumbled aspirations. I tore my gaze from them, but the sight would remain with me until the day I died. What was life if it could be snuffed out like a candle?

What would happen to my little girls?

I walked through the carnage, trying to make sense of what I saw. Were any alive? I checked, but no one had a pulse. Not a single chest raised. How could I bury them? And how could I sort out missing arms and legs? Where were Papa and my brothers? Was I being a child to think they might have survived? In that instant, I saw a familiar gray homespun shirt. My oldest brother with the same empty stare. Another brother. Pa. My stomach revolted until there was nothing left in me. The tears began like the torrential rains from the day before. Alone, I'd never felt so incredibly abandoned. And the truth was, I wanted to be with them.

I stared at the blood on my hands. Numbness swept through me, and I forced myself to continue to look for signs of life. The children were the worst. Many sheltered in their mother's or father's arms. Soon the stench of death would rob my breath as well.

What a wicked cruel monster to claim the innocent. Where was God in this tragedy?

"Miss Deborah?" a familiar male voice shook me as though one of the bodies had risen from the dead. I whirled around to see Mr. Walker several feet away. He appeared uninjured. "Are you ill?" he said. "Hurt?"

"I'm not sure." My mouth tasted of bitterness from my stomach's retching. What did he expect? Then I remembered the blood on my hands was now on my face.

"I saw you walk down from the rocks. Were you safe there?"

"Yes." I wasn't sure words would even come to me. "I didn't expect this."

"Neither did I. You have blood on your face and hands."

"It's not mine. I'll wash at the river." I swallowed the vile taste in my mouth. "What are you doing?" An insane question, but I wanted someone to blame, to fix these poor people with lifeless eyes.

He walked closer, weaving by bodies and examining the pulse of each one. My heart thumped against my chest until it hurt. I repeated my question.

Mr. Walker's amber gaze bore into mine, troubled eyes brimming with sadness. "I'm thankin' God for the time He let me know these fine folks."

Anger roared through me like the twister's vengeance. "How can you say such a thing when they're dead? And how did you escape the twister?"

"I was away from camp when it blew in." The helpless sound of his tone echoed my heartache. Did he feel as though he should have been there with them, too? He pointed to his horse. "We were out of its path."

I sunk to the ground, my anger useless. "Me, too."

"You have no need to be afraid of me."

I hadn't been conscious of my shaking body. I slowly panned the destruction. "What do we do now?"

"Head back to Fort Laramie."

"What about burying these people?"

He blew out a sigh. "Miss Deborah, it would take days to dig graves for all of them."

He was right, but we were civilized people. "We're not animals."

"But if we stay here, the heat will take over. The smell unbearable," he said. "Then we'll be fighting vultures and wolves."

I understood, and my stomach rolled again. "I have a problem."

"What's that?" His words were curt, as though finding me alive were a burden.

"Never mind. I'll tend to it."

"Miss Deborah, what's the other problem you speak of?"

I hesitated. "In the foothills where I took refuge from the twister, I wasn't alone. Seven little girls are awaiting word on their families."

He removed his hat and wiped his brow. "More of a reason to get back to Fort Laramie."

I refused to think of turning back. Not now. Not with the devastation around us. "But we've come so far, and the journey behind us was hard." I took a deep breath. "Going back seems wrong, as though we gave up on our parents' and friends' dreams."

"Do you have any idea how hard it'll be with children?"

"The girls offer a future that's better than this. Going on to Oregon means the others didn't die for nothing." How could I make him see?

He shook his head and stared at me. "That means we can't tarry but head on to the mountains before the snows set in. We're already behind."

"Could we take two days to bury who we can?"

His shoulders lifted and fell. "I suppose. But how do we choose which ones?"

"The babies and children first." I bore sincerity into his face. "More than one child per grave."

"I have to think on it. Foremost I have to plan how we can survive."

"But you've done this before."

His brows narrowed. "If we're to head over the mountains, then I need to salvage food, provisions, weapons, tools, and such. Two milk cows were unharmed and a few chickens."

I also wanted a plan to bury all of the dead proper. Could I convince him? I glanced toward the hills where my girls waited for me to return. How could I nurture them through this nightmare? Who would help me?

"If we do this thing," he said. "We have to work together. It's a terrible journey for adults. I don't see how little girls could make it."

He could very well ride out of here and leave us behind. Who'd blame him? When I glanced into his face, I saw grief, and my heart softened. "How many times have you taken wagons over the mountains?"

"Once. . .as a scout for this outfit. The wagon master was like a pa to me. Can't even find him."

"I'm sorry." Apprehension swept over me. "Do you know the way?"

"I have the map." He crossed his arms over his chest. "Is this really what you want? Are you sure this is best for the girls when we could turn back? Shouldn't you pose the question to them?"

I hesitated. Pa believed in Oregon. Said we'd all be happy there. Ma begged us to go in her dying words. Was I being selfish? "I'll ask them. Explain the dangers and hardships."

"Thank you."

"How old are you, Mr. Walker?"

"Near twenty."

He wasn't any older than my middle brother. Panic seized me. A boy to do a man's job. . .and a girl to mother seven little girls.

"I'm a man, Miss Deborah."

Dare I believe him? "Mr. Walker, will you promise not to leave us?"

His gaze bore into mine. "Never. But Miss Deborah, I know nothing of how to care for little girls."

I nodded. "We can do this together."

"Yes, ma'am. I reckon we have to try."

Chapter 4

Lane strode beside Miss Deborah to see about the girls, seven of them. The number repeated in his mind like a bad omen. He led a horse carrying food, a few blankets, and an extra musket. In his other hand he carried a milk pail and was comforted that a stream flowed from nearby rocks. His heart sank each time he thought about them being orphans. Worse yet, how would he get them over the mountains?

"Are you always this quiet?" she said.

"You're used to me shouting orders."

"Yes." She sighed. "When I think about what's behind us, I'm afraid I'll weep and not be able to stop."

"I understand." When he considered what lay before them, he feared the girls and Deborah would die before they reached their new homes.

"Will we live to see Oregon?"

How did he respond to a question for which he didn't have an answer? He'd seen the strongest of men and women fall. "I promise I'll do my best. Right now getting to Independence Rock before July Fourth would keep us on schedule."

She nodded. "Mr. Walker—"

"Lane, ma'am."

"Of course. First names befit the circumstances, and I'm Deborah. How will we do this?"

"The girls will have to learn how to be grown women. If they're not strong, they won't make it."

Her face shadowed. "They can't be children. They'll need to learn how to cook, mend, wash, and clean. Most have been helping their mothers with the same chores."

"Even more important, I want them to learn how to drive a wagon, hitch up the oxen, hunt, team up to use a musket, and grease a wheel."

"Will we run into hostile Indians?"

He sobered. "Possibly. And if we do, everyone has to be prepared."

"I'm a fairly good shot. I can help teach the girls to shoot."

Up ahead, the band of girls ran toward them. "Miss Deborah! Is everyone all right?" a girl called.

"Lane, this will be difficult," she whispered. "They'll want to see their loved ones, but that means they'll see the nightmare, the twisted and mangled bodies."

"We can't let that happen. It will never leave them for as long as they walk the earth."

"Then you and I will bury those we can alone." Deborah reached out her arms. "Girls, we have much to talk about. Wait there."

She hurried toward them, but Lane lagged behind a few feet. His own memories of finding his family dead surfaced. He'd guard the way in case any of the girls attempted to run past to the wagons.

She asked the girls to sit. "I have something important to tell you." She touched the cheeks of those closest to her.

"Where are all the people from the wagon train?" a girl said. "They aren't with you."

"Nancy, that's what we're going to talk about. The twister was powerful and mean. I'm sorry, but our friends and family are gone."

"Gone?" a taller girl with blond hair said.

"Yes, Grace. I'm so sorry, but we are the only ones who survived the storm, and Mr. Walker."

The girls looked at him, many with tears streaming down their faces. Much too young to endure such heartache.

"I'm going to lead you to Oregon," he said, sounding braver than his curdling insides seemed to say.

"All by ourselves?" Nancy said. "How? I want to see my ma."

Lane nodded at Deborah, silently pleading for help. He'd rarely spoken to a child since his little sister died. Didn't have any words. Didn't want to feel the pain of loss again.

Deborah smiled, but her lips quivered. "What is the best way to show our love for those who were killed in the storm?"

Grace stood and brushed yellow curls from her face. "Be very brave. My pa and ma wanted a new home in Oregon. They won't be able to do that, but Ruby and I can."

"Right," Deborah said. "I want to be brave, too. Mr. Walker suggested we return to Fort Laramie and then back to our original homes. What do you want to do?"

"Oregon." Grace's face tightened with determination. "We sold everything we had for this trip. There's nothing behind us, no family either."

The other girls wanted to continue on, too. Surprise worked through him. He expected the girls to turn back.

"Can all of you help each other?" Deborah said. Through their tears, the girls agreed. "Let's hold hands, and I'd like each of you to tell us what you loved the most about your family." She glanced at Lane.

"While you're talking about your families, I'm going to gather food, blankets, and provisions for our trip," he said. "Promise me none of you will follow me."

They nodded through tears. Glancing west to the mountains, worry needled him. They wouldn't be lowering any wagons over steep cliffs, and he prayed early snows waited for them to pass. Rivers were treacherous to cross, and they'd be slowed with the children. His attention rested on each of the girls. How would he ever guide them safely to Oregon? God help him. He was in charge of this small band of female children. Not the wagon master with his abundance of wisdom. Not the grown men who'd banded together in determination to make the journey. Not the women who supported their men. The realization punched him in the gut.

Lane walked toward the valley's devastation. The bodies haunted him, one of the many decisions of God that he'd never understand.

One wagon stood intact, and another needed its hickory bows replaced. He could use the wood from the other broken wagons to repair it when they camped in the evenings. Perhaps he could salvage some of the canvas to cover the bows and keep the wagon's contents protected from the elements. Rain and snow would be the worst as they headed into the mountains. With all the flour, beans, and bacon along with other needed items, he fretted about weight. Not enough meant they starved, and too much weight wore down the animals. When they left Independence, each person needed 150 pounds of bacon, 10 pounds of coffee, 20 pounds of sugar, and 10 pounds of salt. Those were for adults, and granted they'd fished and gathered wild berries and greens to provide a variety in their diet, but he had no idea how much the girls would eat. He'd found three chickens and a rooster and would attach their cages to the sides of the wagons.

Oh, God, this is more difficult than I ever thought. Thank You for Your guidance.

The girls would have to walk and sleep outside. A task they'd already done. The image of little Nancy entered his mind. She was the most frail and sickly, and he'd found little medicinal herbs among the wagons.

Strange how the fierce wind could take what it chose and leave other things untouched. They had oxen to pull the wagons and a few extra to carry all the provisions he could rummage. Horses could be ridden. If needed, he could trade with the Indians for food or safe passage. He'd piled a few good pieces of wood to craft into bows and arrows fittin' for smaller hands. Another chore while the oxen and horses rested on the trail.

Deborah would be heartbroken with what he had to tell her. The thought of disappointing her sliced at his heart. But it had to be done. They'd figured around 120 days to get to their destination, but the journey was usually two to four weeks longer. The wagon master had pushed them to accomplish fifteen miles on good days, but disease and accidents slowed them, and now they had the worst of ground to cover. Burying all those people was impossible, but he'd not discuss it until later. Didn't matter how she reacted to his decision, or how he felt about her. She could hate him from here to Oregon, but he'd stand his ground. The girls would not survive lingering another day here, and even now he feared the worst. The wagon master told him right from the start that those who finished the journey were what mattered. Not how many men, women, and children who hated him, but people who reached Oregon strong to build new homes.

Chapter 5

I spent hours talking to the girls about their families. Some of them shared light-hearted times, and others wished they'd been better daughters and sisters. We cried and laughed and cried again. Our tears were cleansing, and I wept, too, thinking about my mother who died before we left Independence and my pa and brothers whom I'd never see again.

The sun shone warm against a cloudless blue sky, but it had yesterday, too. Weather and life. . .each could change without warning.

We ate some of the food Lane and I had brought. Nourishment was vital for all of us, but my stomach threatened to get rid of every bite. I ached for all who were gone.

"Eat up, girls," I said. "We need to be strong."

"I don't feel like it," Nancy said. "My tummy hurts."

"Your mother would tell you to do everything Mr. Walker and I ask of you."

She bit her lower lip and reached for a biscuit and honey. "When will Mr. Walker be back?"

Already Nancy had attached herself to him. He was most likely digging graves and preparing to bury as many as possible. "He's working very hard so we can leave soon for Oregon."

"How will we remember our families?" Grace said, my little somber child.

Such hard questions when my own heart grieved those I loved, too. "In our hearts they'll live forever."

"I don't ever want to go back to Missouri. My pa said Oregon was like heaven." Grace took Ruby's hand. "Like I said before, we're going."

The afternoon slipped to evening, and I built a small fire to fight off the cold. I fretted about Lane, not that he might be hurt, but would he leave us? The thought troubled me, and I shoved it away. The girls helped me lay out a couple of blankets in the caves where we'd taken refuge yesterday. They were exhausted from dealing with the tragedy, so needy and fearful. In truth, I was, too.

I waited outside the cave where the fire burned. As darkness touched the ground, Lane stepped into the firelight. His mere presence gave me hope this small group would see Oregon. His features tightened, most likely from the burden on his shoulders. He sat on the opposite side of the fire and peered into my face.

"How are you holding up?" he whispered.

"As best I can. Some of the girls are asleep."

"Good. We need to talk, Deborah. Do you feel up to a walk?"

I heard the worst in his voice, but what more could go wrong? He helped me to my feet, and we moved away from the caves.

"I loaded the wagon with all the food, provisions, firearms, gunpowder, and lead I could find. Much was left over, so it's ready to pack on the extra oxen. We have four horses, healthy animals." He pulled out a leather pouch and handed it to me. "I searched around the wagons of the girls' families until I could find a little keepsake for each of them. A few are for you. A trunk inside your wagon held a journal, pen, ink, and perhaps this is a picture of your mother."

His kindness overwhelmed me, and I was thankful for the darkness to hide my tears. "I'm very grateful, and they will be, too."

"Also, in my saddlebag is a pouch of gold from each of their families with a piece of paper showing how much is due each one."

I hadn't considered what would happen to them once they reached Oregon.

"Now they won't arrive penniless and be forced into families who only want them to work," he continued. "They'll have a chance with good people."

Another thought nibbled at me. "What about the gold from the other people?"

He hesitated. "I feel like a thief, but I have their money separately. I couldn't find a list of the families to return it. Not sure what the good Lord would have me do once we get to Oregon."

"A decision you can make later."

"The rest of what I have to say will be hard." He paused, and I shivered at the sound of his voice. "We must leave at first light. I need you to lead the girls around to the west side, where I'll be waiting with the two wagons and animals. That way, they won't see the bodies."

Fury washed over me. "What about burying at least the women and children like we talked about?"

"The task would take days, and we don't have any to spare. The accidents and cholera epidemic have already slowed us down. We were over a week earlier on the last trip and still got caught in the mountains in a blinding snowstorm."

How could he be so cruel? "You'd leave good people to be eaten by wild animals? You're no better than heathens. I won't go, I tell you. Neither will I allow these girls to experience such barbaric treatment of their families."

"Deborah"—his voice was low, frightening—"if any of those people were able to talk, they'd tell us to leave them behind. Their souls have gone to their final resting place, and only their shells remain. I know you want to bury them, but in doing so, you'll kill the girls you want to protect." At the sound of a wolf, he stared out into the night and wrapped his hand around his musket. "This is the way it will be, and I need your word you won't fight me on it. Wake them at six, and I'll meet you at six thirty." He handed me a pocket watch.

The truth pierced my heart. He was right, but I hated him for his cruelty. Honest folk deserved a decent burial. . .especially the women and children.

Without Lane, we'd perish, and I owed it to all I loved to make it to Oregon. Pa claimed it was the richest land on earth, where crops grew bigger and a man grew richer right alongside them. We had to obey Lane or surely die. No choice and no discussion. He was a hard man. The only reason he'd gathered the items in the leather bag for the girls was to pacify me with his ultimatum. His amber eyes that emitted warmth earlier now reminded me of a predator.

—⁂—

Lane accepted how Deborah felt about him. Her face showed contempt in how she viewed his decision, but leadership was a lonely position. He left her alone with the girls and made the trek back to the wagon, ready to hitch up to the oxen and pull out at daybreak. He'd have preferred mules for putting miles behind them. Why think on it? God had spared him and the others for something more powerful than he could ever imagine. Like Deborah and the girls, he sensed they were to go forward.

He'd repair the broken wagon by firelight so it could be driven. Sleep would come later. Probably once they were over the mountains. At the wagon site, he lit the wood ready for him to begin the work. One thing good about the night was he didn't have to look at the bodies. If anything at all pushed him to Oregon, it was the graveyard around him.

Early morning, he hitched up the oxen to the two wagons and tied a rope between them to keep them moving toward Deborah and the girls.

He left the valley behind, a once beautiful respite from the long journey, and drove the slow oxen over rock and sand to meet his charges. The sun lifted its flames of light into the western sky. Always the same, regardless of what happened the day before. In the distance, he saw Deborah carrying the musket, and the girls each with a small load. Deborah had won a couple of shooting matches while her brother held the weight of the musket. Lane hoped she didn't turn it on him.

Deborah.

His heart longed for what he could not have. For in pacifying her, she and the others would be as those left in the valley. He pulled the oxen to a halt. "Morning."

The girls mumbled the same, but not Deborah.

In the faint light, Nancy's shoulders slumped. The younger cousins appeared too tired to walk. "Miss Deborah, would you drive the other wagon and let Hope and Beth ride with you?"

"I will." Her words were cold.

"Nancy, I could use your help driving the oxen," he said, and the girl beamed. "The rest of you will need to walk. At noon, we'll see how all of you are doing. I'll be teaching you how to drive the oxen because at times I need to scout ahead." He turned his attention to Deborah and removed his hat. "Let's have a word of prayer for the good Lord to protect all of us."

All said amen but Deborah. Didn't she know without the Lord's help, they'd not make it through the days ahead?

Chapter 6

When the sun was high, Lane signaled for us to stop and eat. It also provided time for the cattle to graze, as the wagon master had instructed each day at noon. While the girls and I bustled about putting together a quick meal of bacon and biscuits from our morning meal, he added new bows to one of the wagons. He never rested, much like one of my brothers.

Although I hadn't spoken to Lane all morning, I now carried food and water to him. Nancy hadn't left his side. A bit of jealousy wove through me, when I'd often found her a nuisance.

He obviously didn't notice my approach. "This is for you," I said.

Sweat dripped from his brow. "Thank you. My stomach's been rumbling since before sunup. Smelled the bacon and biscuits." He took the tin mug of water and drank it down.

Alarm spread through me. "You didn't eat breakfast?"

"No, ma'am. Wasn't time."

What if he got sick? What would we do then? I was selfish, but I couldn't help myself. We needed Lane to survive the journey. "You must eat and drink, and we have plenty. From now on, I'll make sure you take care of yourself."

He hesitated. "In every way I can, I will ensure my health stays strong."

His words sounded sad, and I studied his weary face. "Did you sleep last night?"

"No. Too much to do." He bit into the biscuit. "These are very good, Deborah."

As much as he'd angered me, I had to share in the responsibilities. "I could have helped you. We agreed to this journey together. You can't do this alone, and that means I'll do guard duty tonight."

"When will you sleep?" he said.

"Grace can drive the wagon while I rest tomorrow. You're exhausted."

He glanced away, and I wished his thoughts were words.

"I'll let you watch for a few hours tonight," he said. "One thing you can do in the next few days is mend the canvas." He pointed to the wagon's top. "When you're finished, I'll cover the bows."

"Grace and Nancy can help sew. Not sure about the others."

"Appreciate it."

He finished the biscuit with bacon tucked inside, and I sent Nancy to fetch two more. I watched her scamper to the others. Awkwardness crept over me at being alone with him.

"Deborah," he said, "I'll bear my own sin for not burying those folks. I did pray over all of them and willed their souls to heaven."

I frowned, my face hot with anger. "I'll never understand."

"I imagine not, unless you see a child frozen to death."

I gasped. No response came to mind. Death in any form was horrid.

"Tonight, can we talk about what's ahead?"

"Yes, of course," I said.

"The journey over the mountains is dangerous, and I have much to teach the girls, and I'm not sure how to figure out what's first."

"Teaching them to shoot and such?"

"And how to drive the oxen and lead the horses around treacherous curves. I plan to carve a couple of bows and arrows, ones that will fit small hands. They also need to learn how to throw a knife with accuracy. Build a fire. So much, and so little time."

"I see." I wasn't sure if I'd ever see inside this man's heart. In one breath, he uttered cruelty and no respect for the dead, in the next, the girls' safety came first. "All I want is to get to Oregon. I'll sleep then," I said. "You can count on me for whatever's needed."

His amber eyes softened, and I saw a hint of something indistinguishable. "I have no doubts about your strength."

Nancy joined them and handed him one biscuit dripping with honey and another filled with bacon. "Thank you, little one," he said. Her face lit up with his approval. He smiled at me. "Once we stop for the evening, I'll hunt for fresh game."

"Wonderful. Full bellies make the going easier." I walked away but not before I heard Nancy cough, a deep, tight sound that seemed to come from her toes. Spinning around, I watched her clutch her chest. "Are you ill, child? I have ginger and peppermint for tea."

"Maybe so, Miss Deborah. My head's hurtin' something fierce."

"Please, brew some tea. I thought she looked flushed," Lane said. "I'll have her rest in the wagon this afternoon."

———

Lane cleared a spot atop boxes and used blankets to make a mattress for Nancy. She slept all afternoon. Repeatedly he checked her breathing and felt her head. Fever soared despite the tea. He prayed for the child while helplessness settled in his bones.

His little sister died of fever and cough, the same age as Nancy. His parents had been ill, too, and while he hunted for healing herbs, they all died.

A good broth would help, and he scanned the area for rabbit or deer tracks. A buffalo would be a blessing, but many had disappeared. As dusk approached, he spotted three buffalo nibbling at the sparse grass. He pulled the oxen to a stop and grabbed his musket.

"Stay back," he said to the girls and hurried toward the animals. Fresh meat would help Nancy regain her strength and keep the others strong. He raced, hunched over, until he was close enough to have a cow in his sights. Dropping to his knees, he poured gunpowder down the musket barrel and rammed a lead ball. Aiming, he held his breath and fired. The cow fell while the other buffalo scattered.

Finally, something had gone right. Evening drew in, giving him time to skin and gut the buffalo, and they had plenty of salt to cure it. They were short on buffalo grease for the wheels. God had provided.

Vultures circled above, but he ignored them. He called to the girls and enlisted their help.

"Miss Deborah is tending to Nancy," Grace said. "We prayed for her fever to break."

"Miss Deborah, too?" He didn't look up from gutting the buffalo.

"Only us."

"Has Nancy wakened?"

"No, sir. Deborah couldn't wake her. But she's breathing."

Chapter 7

I rarely left Nancy's side that evening. When buffalo stew bubbled over the fire and Grace started biscuits, I left the remainder of meal preparations for the girls. When not dabbing Nancy's face with a wet cloth, I mended the canvas. Lane worked on the other wagon's bows with the girls gathered around him. He spoke gently, and I appreciated it. Yet I was still angry for the mass of bodies left behind to endure nature's vengeance. My journal entry was filled with mixed emotions. Maybe by the time we reached Oregon, I'd better comprehend what he'd done. . .and why.

I was supposed to take the watch tonight. I'd enlisted Grace's help to stay by Nancy and immediately regretted the burden I'd placed on her. But did I have a choice? Closing my eyes, I listened to Lane talk to the girls.

"Little ladies, the journey over the mountains will be a test of your courage," he said. "There's much you must be able to do. Tonight we'll have our first lesson. Every spare minute will be more lessons. I expect by the time we get to Oregon, you'll know more than me."

A few girls giggled, and I smiled despite my ruffled feelings and weary body.

"In a couple more evenings, the wagon will be fixed. Miss Deborah and any of you seamstresses will be needed to finish the mending, so we can cover your things on the inside. Grace and Nancy will drive the front wagon on those times I'm scouting the trail."

"What about us?" Abigail, one of the redheaded twins said. "Can we help?"

"Sure." Lane laughed, and I'd never heard him merry about anything. "The buffalo hide needs to be scraped clean of all the flesh, and I can show you and Faith how it's done. When you're finished, I'll stretch it out over one of the wagons to dry. It will feel warm in the cold mountains."

They clapped, making it sound like removing buffalo flesh was a picnic.

"Beth and Hope, I think you two could make sure the cows are milked and eggs gathered. The rooster can be cantankerous, but let him know who's in charge. My guess, he's afraid of your spunk."

"Yes, sir," the two said.

"Who wants to get up early in the morning to learn how to load and shoot a musket? You'll be learning in pairs."

Little voices chorused.

"Any of you help shoot one before?"

"I have," Grace said. "Pa held it for me, but I still fell backward. Oh, and I've used a bow and arrow, but my aim's not too good."

"Your pa's bow is most likely heavy. I'll see about getting a couple made that will fit smaller hands."

"Any of you know how to throw a knife?" A pause. "All right, I'll have you fixed up there, too."

He continued on about the lessons to come and how important for them to pay attention. "We'll pray for Nancy to feel better and for sickness and accidents to leave us alone."

"Will we have trouble with Indians?" Grace said.

"Not usually. That can be a matter of prayer, too. If hostile Indians step into our path, the good Lord will fight for us. I wish we had time for you to be children, but I don't see how," he said. "Guess you can play when we arrive in Oregon."

"By then we won't want to," Grace said. Wisdom seemed to pour from the girl.

"Maybe not, but growing up too soon is not what your parents wanted for you. I was left an orphan at the age of fourteen, and it's not easy. Listen up, girls. I know your parents discussed rules and such, but I want to go over a few. Rule number one: obey me and Miss Deborah. No questions. Rule number two: always look out for each other and pray. The wagon master had Bible reading and prayer early on Sunday morning before we broke camp, and we'll do the same. Rule number three: Accidents and drownings killed a lot of good people and children before the twister. Stay clear of the wheels. We'll talk about how to handle the muskets soon enough. In the meantime, all will be unloaded except mine. Rule number four is to be frugal in everything."

"Yes, sir," they said.

"What I have to say next is for your own good. If something happens to me or Miss Deborah, you have to go on to Oregon. In my pocket is the map. I believe in each one of you. You're strong and smart. All of you escaped the cholera outbreak, and from here on out, we should be free of it. That's why I'll be teaching you everything to survive."

Again they agreed. I wasn't so sure any of us would make it, but I'd been the first to champion going on. Conflicting thoughts whirled in my head. Perhaps I was simply tired and afraid, grieving for so much loss. Sometimes the grave sounded easier.

Lane's voice broke into my thoughts. "I could tell a story," he said. "Do you like David and Goliath?" Off he went, telling the biblical account of the shepherd boy who killed a giant with a slingshot. Made me wish I believed the Bible and in God. "David became Israel's hero and later their king. Know what I think?" He paused, and I envisioned him staring into the girls' faces. The fire cracked and sputtered, and I too waited for what Lane would say next. "Each one of you is like David, and the mountains are your Goliath. They look beautiful from here, but they're steep, and when it rains or snows, they're slippery. If you're frightened or don't feel well, pray. In fact, I have something for you. In my hand are seven smooth stones, ones like David used. Put one in your pocket, and whenever you touch it, remember God is on your side. He is bigger than any Goliath."

I marveled at how he'd encouraged the girls. . .and me. He knew the right words to capture our attention and make us feel brave. They loved him for it, trusted him, too.

I wanted to respect his decision to help us, except his horrible deed settled too fresh in my mind.

Nancy moaned, and I touched her cheeks. Hot as a fire poker. I lifted her head and forced tea between her lips.

"Drink, sweetheart."

Tea trickled down Nancy's chin. I leaned back, searching my mind for a way to soothe the child's feverish body.

"Deborah," Lane whispered outside the wagon, "stay with Nancy. I'll keep watch tonight. Grace needs her rest, too."

I should have protested, but relief overcame me. "Thank you. I'll keep watch tomorrow."

"We'll see. The girls are bedded down."

"You did a fine job with them tonight."

"Never talked to children much. Strange how life walks a man where he least expects."

Was Lane as evil as I thought? Or did he have more wisdom than I'd ever imagined?

—m—

Lane fell asleep during his watch that night. Guilt consumed him when he woke at the break of dawn. Far too many things could have happened. The first thing he did was check on Nancy. Her fever had broken, and Deborah had fallen asleep with her hand entwined with the child's.

If only the days ahead would pass as peacefully as the two sleeping. But they wouldn't, and that's what gripped him. Every morning when he looked to the mountain peaks, more snow covered them.

Each day became like the previous one. Each sunrise brought new challenges and brought them a little closer to their destination. Thunderstorms beat down hard against the wagons, and he chained the two together so neither would topple over. The waterproof canvas kept the supplies and travelers mostly dry. But the crack of thunder and the whip of wind frightened the girls, and he didn't reprimand them. Gave him cause to watch the skies for black turning to green.

The wagons inched up the incline, and it was easier to walk than ride inside. Some nights he allowed Deborah to take watch, and he'd catch a few hours of precious sleep. Nancy slowly recovered, but she still perched her small body beside him on the wagon.

The identical twins, Faith and Abigail, had Irish tempers to match their fiery red hair. They did well with the buffalo hide. Every time he brought down game, they wanted to help tan the skin.

Grace mothered them all. Little Ruby, a blond like her sister, did all she was told. The cousins, Hope and Beth, were determined to keep the rooster in line. Both had dark brown hair and green eyes.

Deborah never complained outwardly, yet Lane saw a sadness from deep within, as though her soul cried out for help. Such emptiness could only be filled with God's Spirit living inside her. But she refused talk of God. Every night she wrote in her journal, and he prayed it gave her comfort to put her feelings into words.

By the time they reached Independence Rock on July 8, about 250 miles from Fort Laramie, they celebrated the near halfway point of the journey. The girls had mastered loading the musket. The last two nights had been filled with target practice showing them how to brace the heavy musket inside the wagon. The weapon was too heavy even for Deborah to lift, and each shot sent her and the girls on their backside. If Indians or drifters chose to attack, they'd need plenty of lead balls and good aim.

Lane drove them harder than he wanted, but the girls didn't complain, even when they had to gather buffalo chips when timber and twisted grass were sparse.

He focused on the unseen—signs of Indians. Last year, the Bannock, a tribe of the Shoshone, attacked a wagon train. Several people were killed. Lane and the girls had little chance against them, easy prey, and the children would end up as slaves or worse.

His map took a winding climb toward South Pass, which led them to the best camping spots near water. If the water was mostly mud and insects, he had them boil it to get rid of the wiggly-tails. The map also marked the poison springs that killed animals and people.

"Lane, you're frowning again," Deborah said one morning as she walked alongside him and Grace drove the second wagon.

With Nancy riding next to him, he had to be careful what he said. "Just thinking about tomorrow and being alert." No point to alarm her. "What are your plans when you reach Oregon?"

She shrugged. "Make sure the girls are with good families. Find a job. Maybe teach school."

"You'll do fine, Miss Deborah, and God will be with the girls." They were close to passing by the destruction from an Indian raid the last trip, and he veered away from it.

"Indians," she whispered.

"We have two horses we can trade if need be."

Nancy pointed. "Are those broken wagons, Mr. Lane?"

"Sure thing. They didn't make it." *Lord, if the worst comes, help me defend those who might seek to hurt my girls.*

Chapter 8

We plodded on day after day, steadily moving upward, and every night the temperatures grew colder. I kept our days in my journal, but sometimes I wondered why. By noon we were always exhausted, and from the looks of Lane and the girls, they were ready to camp for the night. But every step brought us closer. We were lucky to have fresh eggs and milk. Lane called it a blessing. I was simply grateful.

He and I crossed the Sweetwater River more than once, but each time we made sure our charges and the supplies were safe. I'd ride by horseback with a girl, and Lane would do the same. Finally we drove the oxen across.

Lane told me the wagons would venture across the river nine times before reaching the Continental Divide at South Pass, Wyoming, and I counted each one. About eighty miles west of Independence Rock, we stopped at Ice Slough, a natural bed of ice. Lane told us we'd come to the highest point of the trail, the Continental Divide. They all enjoyed the ice, but I was too tired to pay it much mind.

The higher we climbed, the colder the mornings and evenings. We continued northwest along the steep canyons of the Snake River, a part of the climb I didn't want to consider. I no longer cared for much of life, except the girls. Once when Beth suffered a scratchy throat, and I told her she didn't have to tend to the animals, Lane called me a she-bear. And I guess I am.

Today Nancy walked with Abigail and the twins. She'd grown stronger and didn't depend so much on me or Lane. I sighed with relief that all the girls were doing well and learning so much. Lane stopped the oxen and interrupted my thoughts. Then I saw the narrow path.

I climbed down from the wagon and made my way to his side. A blue spruce lay across the path and over the cliff. The sky darkened, and a thread of lightning burst in the distance.

"The storm's moving this way." He picked up loose branches and tossed them over the cliff. "I'll cut it at the roots and shove it over."

I searched in his wagon for the ax, wishing there were two, but I could pull back the smaller branches. We had no shelter, and taking cover beneath trees or against bare rock increased the danger. Lane didn't need to mention the lightning's power. The girls cleared what they could, and he asked them to stand back. From the lines around his eyes, he feared the danger, too. It hurried toward us, faster than we could move aside the tree. Even if we were able to get through, where could we find shelter from nature's fury? Grace, Nancy, Abigail, and Faith calmed the horses. The other three leaned close to the wagon.

I tugged on a limb and lost my balance, falling backward. My head spun as I managed to get to my feet.

"Easy," he said. "No—"

Sawtooth lightning flashed so close the hair on my neck prickled. Thunder roared like a demon.

"Deborah, are you all right?" His words sounded distant, and my ears rang. I nodded so he'd not worry. "Why don't you stand with the girls instead of out in the open?"

"And leave you to move the pine? We'll get this done."

I looked to see if the girls had the horses under control, and they held firm to the bridles. No one wept, and they kept their attention on him. Lane was an excellent teacher—by focusing on him, they could fight the terror around them. The horses snorted then pawed sporadically. Their heads jerked as though they wanted to run. I didn't blame them, I'd run too in a weak moment.

A burst of light, like a sword, struck the rear wagon sending the canvas into a raging fire. I stumbled over the tree with energy I didn't have a moment before. Food, provisions, and, worst of all, gunpowder were stored there. Lane was already at the wagon, battling the flames to pull out the gunpowder.

I took the heavy boxes from him and rushed them out of the way. Back again for food and anything else that could be salvaged.

"Deborah, stay back," he shouted, but I didn't listen. Didn't he know by now we were in this together?

And in that moment in the midst of fear and fire, I realized how much I cared for Lane Walker. The bodies left behind and my confusion about his decision were of the past. He was our leader. I'd fight to the end to help him get the girls to Oregon.

"Girls, pray for rain!" He continued to jerk out sacks of flour, including one that he used to smother the flames, while the fire licked at his hands. I cringed at his pain. His face blackened, and I took the sack from him no longer feeling the flame's heat or weariness.

"Deborah, listen to me."

I ignored him.

Heavy sheets of rain fell as though a waterfall had broken from the clouds. Little voices cried thank You to a God I didn't believe in. Within moments, the fire was out. Lane's hands were singed, and so were mine.

We were all drenched. But we were saved. Lane was on his knees, water pouring from his hat. The girls followed. All but me.

A miracle? I wasn't sure. I listened on Sundays when he read from the Bible. Much I didn't comprehend. I stared into a blue-gray sky and let the rain wash my face. Someone or something created the earth. But how could a good God cause the sun to shine—and the storms to blow?

Lane huddled around a crackling fire with the girls. Finding dry wood had taken awhile due to the fierce rain. But now the small group dried and relished its warmth. Half the blankets and the buffalo hide had been stored in his wagon, and they'd used all of them. Two of the blankets had been burned. The others smelled of smoke, some with holes. But when one was cold, any covering helped.

He'd shoved the pine tree over the cliff, and in the morning they'd set out again. Steadily dropping temperatures brought the realities of a bitter cold night. In the morning, he'd switch out oxen again. Having the extra animals was a true blessing. He studied each girl's face and his Deborah. Every day he loved her more, but he dared not dwell on anything but getting them all to Oregon.

He sighed and summoned divine help to encourage all of his girls. Their welfare was above everything else, as though their loved ones had instructed him to make the ultimate sacrifice as they had done. Wind blew in around them, whistling like a ghost, and he drew Hope and Beth closer, wrapping his thin blanket around their small bodies. A wolf howled. Then another. He despised the animals, and vowed to keep the fire going all night.

"Girls, we tasted death again today, and God preserved us," he said. "You were brave and did exactly as I'd taught. I'm proud of you." He prayed for the right words, not to scare but to prepare them for the upcoming trials. "I've said before, we're late starting through the mountains. Early snows threaten to stop us, but we won't let anything get in our way. The path will be slippery, and at times we'll need to move the snow out of our way. We've had a few difficult times in the past, but the trail ahead is worse. The elements of nature must not deter us. Sleep two or three together to stay warm."

Tonight he wished he'd forced them back to Fort Laramie after the twister. Maybe he should have taken the time to bury those people and then gotten the girls to safety. Foolishness for dragging these girls and Deborah through the mountains settled on him worse than the damp and cold. Back then, going forward seemed right, but—

"Mr. Walker, what's wrong?" Grace said. "Are we going to freeze to death?"

Her little voice, usually the one of inspiration, startled him from his concerns. "Grace, I promised you when we started that I'd do my best to get all of you to Oregon, and I will." The weight on his shoulders seemed too heavy to carry. "Because I care about you, which is strange for me 'cause I haven't been around children since my little sister died, I. . .I'll sound harsher going forward. Mean. Cranky. I'll make you walk when you want to stop because walking prevents a person from freezing to death. You'll help me hunt for food. You'll do without sleep until you can't move. Do you understand?" They looked so small and fragile around the fire. He refused to lose any of them.

"Mr. Walker is our leader." Deborah's teeth chattered. She swallowed, and his attention focused on her face, wishing he could see her orange-brown freckles and robin's-egg blue eyes. "We all must obey even if we don't understand." She smiled at him. "If you think he's demanding, later on you'll see his wisdom."

Was this her way of saying she'd forgiven him? He hoped so.

"Thank you. I s'pect by morning we'll have more snow and bitter cold. Are we ready to show these mountains they can't stop us?"

Their response wasn't so robust.

Chapter 9

Three days later, with temperatures plummeting to an unbearable cold, Hope and Beth informed me the three hens had frozen to death. The girls had tried to sleep with them, but the birds weren't enthusiastic about snuggling. Hope and Beth shed tears, fearful of disappointing Lane. He held them both, told them they'd done better than an adult. The rooster still strutted, but he'd be cooked when food grew scarce. At least in the cold, the chickens wouldn't spoil.

"One of the horses froze, too," he said. "I know how you feel. It's sad, but there's nothing we can do."

I walked and let Grace drive the wagon since it was chained to Lane's. The terrain had evened a bit, but the stretch wouldn't last long.

Cough and cold plagued my girls. I'd brew tea until it disappeared. We held blankets around us to help fight the biting wind.

Lane called to me. "I'm stopping to cover the oxen's feet. Their feet are too sore to go much farther."

Grace and Nancy helped find pieces of leather that Lane had kept for this reason, and we tied them around the hooves. Two extra oxen allowed us to give the animals a rest. Unless they froze, too.

The other girls sat in the snow watching.

"Get up. Now," Lane said in an ugly voice. "See about the animals. Keep moving. Get that rooster into a cage or a wolf will fill his belly with him."

Abigail opened her mouth to protest, but Faith stopped her. The oxen's feet were wrapped in short order, and we plodded on.

At noon, I stared at the cliffs of the Snake River. Just as Lane had described, they looked impossible to climb. He reached inside his jacket and studied the worn map.

"This looks impossible," I said. "Is this where wagons are broken down and raised?"

"Yes, but I know of another trail we can take. Will be a day or so longer." He shook his head. "Don't have much choice."

I touched his arm. "Lane, don't fret so about things. Share with me your concerns. I can listen. Maybe we can find a solution."

His amber eyes softened, and he touched my face with a gloved hand. "When we get to Oregon, I'd like to speak my heart."

He wasn't talking about snow or ice or fear of one of us going over a cliff. He meant us together. I sensed it to my cold toes. I wanted to step into his arms, but that was brazen. Closing my eyes, I let myself think of Oregon and hardships behind us. And time to spend with Lane.

His lips brushed against my forehead, and happiness flooded through me. To think

I'd despised the man for his harsh decision. Now I see he did what he believed was best, what our families would have wanted. Going back meant defeat. The untamed wilderness would have won, and we'd all have looked like cowards. He'd taken time to search for the girls' keepsakes and their family's gold. Honor moved him to collect it from the other wagons and possibly find a way to return the funds. The girls were stronger mentally and even physically with his teachings. They'd left their childhood behind and now were little women, and because of this, they'd stare adversity in the face for as long as they lived.

This man cared for me, and I for him.

Was I strong enough to ponder a life with him? His faith made him strong, and I often envied it. Maybe I was too stubborn to trust God, especially when He'd caused tragedy after tragedy. The God of Sunday morning Bible reading and prayers couldn't possibly be the same One who'd sent a twister.

I missed my parents and brothers, the comforts of home, dear friends, and not fearing death. In the darkness of night, I wept for them and the day-to-day suffering. The girls did, too. Lane had to hear, but he never said a word. Once when Grace failed to hush Ruby, he took both girls and moved them beside him until morning.

Lane Walker showed love in every breath. But would his devotion get us to Oregon?

—⁓—

Lane walked beside the oxen, guiding the animals every step of the way. The trail ambled straight up over snow and a layer of ice beneath. Once they reached the top, two more peaks faced them. From the map and what he recalled, they'd then leave the worst of these mountains behind.

A scream pierced his ears, and he whipped around, his heart pounding like a war drum. One of the horses slipped, toppling over the cliff and dropping Beth with it. He raced to the edge, expecting to see his sweet girl plunged to her death.

The horse had dropped to the floor of the canyon, but Beth had fallen onto a narrow rock ledge about twenty-five feet down. Her small body lay sprawled, quiet.

"Beth!" His words echoed off the cliffs.

Her head moved.

"Stay still. I'm coming after you."

"My leg," she said.

The twisted limb indicated it was broken. If only the bone didn't protrude the skin and leave her a cripple.

"Is she alive?" Grace covered her mouth as though the truth were in her doubts.

"Yes, and I need to get her off that rock." Deborah handed him a rope, and he wrapped it around an aspen, one of the few remaining trees at this elevation.

"Mr. Walker's coming," Grace shouted. "I'm praying for you, Beth."

What would he do without his girls? "Hold on to the rope, all of you." He secured the other end to his waist and started down the cliff. The blowing air cut through him like a knife, and he could only imagine how cold his Beth must be. Once his feet touched the ledge, he called her name, and she opened her eyes, a lock of red hair covering most of her face.

"I knew you'd come," she whispered. "I have my David rock in my pocket."

He brushed the tears from her cheeks. She'd come so close to falling to her death. "Sweet girl, in carrying you to the top, you're going to hurt powerful. Cry. Scream. I don't care."

"I'll be brave."

"There's no need." He studied her leg, figuring the best way to carry her. Glancing up, he drew courage from Deborah and the girls peering down. "Beth, I need you to hold to my neck tight. Promise me you won't let go."

"I won't," she said. "I'm afraid."

"Deborah, you and the girls have to pull us up. I'll try to scale the rock with my feet." He scooped her up in one motion and nearly lost his balance.

The slow ascent up the treacherous rock sent Beth to trembling and shouts of agony. He'd gladly take her place. "Don't let go," he said. "Think about happy things."

A cry erupted from her throat. "It hurts."

"I'm sorry. We're almost there."

"Can you make my leg better?"

"I'll do my best." His typical response to challenges beyond him.

He planted his toes into crevices to make the going easier, but still she whimpered. Once he finally scaled the top, and Deborah helped them over the cliff, she hurried to clear a space in the wagon. Deborah's pale face mirrored his concern.

He carried Beth to the wagon and waited while Deborah made a bed of blankets. The child gripped his arm as though warding off the pain. "Beth, I'm right here," he said. "Deborah is, too."

"Make it better, please."

How did he respond to such a plea? He laid her gently onto the blankets. The wagon master had shown him how to set a broken bone. He'd also talked about the time he'd cut a man's leg off to save his life.

The others were gathered around the wagon. "Girls, fetch buckets of snow. Any ice that you can. Grace, can you find anything to use for bandages?" The wagon train's supply of laudanum was depleted during the cholera epidemic as well as any whiskey. All they had to ease the pain was the cold.

Inside, Deborah spoke gently. "Beth, I have to see your hurt leg." She tenderly removed the girl's outer garments, dress, and stocking until an exposed bare leg stared awkwardly at them. Bloody scrapes and bruises would heal. Tears filled Deborah's eyes. "The bone hasn't pierced the skin."

He stepped back to avoid Deborah seeing his own tears of gratitude. "Keep her warm while I look for splints. Have you ever set a leg?"

"No. Never seen one done either. What can I do?"

"Start icing it as soon as the girls bring buckets of snow. Later I'll need you to hold her."

She nodded and held Beth's hand. He grabbed an ax and cut down the same aspen that had held him firm while he fetched his little girl. With numb fingers, he fashioned two straight pieces. Providing he set Beth's leg straight, the splints would ensure she walked again. He secured rope from his wagon and took determined steps to Beth and Deborah while praying for guidance.

"Mr. Lane, will Beth be all right?" Hope struggled with a bucket of snow.

He glanced at the child and then to the others. "We never stop praying for each other."

He took a breath and climbed into the wagon. His attention focused on Beth, who'd bitten her lip until it bled. Her leg was packed with snow, and her eyes squeezed shut. "How is she?"

Deborah held the small hand. "The bravest girl I've ever seen."

He moistened his lips, thankful Beth's eyes were shut and she couldn't see his consternation. "Beth, what I have to do now will hurt worse than anything else. But for you to walk and run again, it's necessary."

Her eyes fluttered open. "I don't want to be a cripple."

"Me either. I'll work fast to straighten your leg. Miss Deborah will hold you tight. She can't let you move. Afterward, we'll keep it in place with splints. You scream clear to Oregon. We don't care."

"Do it quick, please, Mr. Walker."

He offered a prayer and gazed into Deborah's eyes. "Are you ready?" Robin's-egg blue eyes gave him confidence. She positioned herself at the little girl's head, leaned over her, and pinned her at the waist. "On the count of three. One. Two. Three." He swept back the ice and snow then gripped the twisted leg. Holding his breath, he slipped it into place.

Beth screamed, a cry sure to scare the devil.

Deborah held her firmly.

The child passed out. A blessing in his opinion.

The broken leg looked normal and even with the other.

"We got it." He let out a breath. "The worst is over."

Beth slowly surfaced from unconsciousness while he wrapped torn petticoats around the splinted leg. Sweat dripped from his brow despite the bitter cold.

"Thank you," Beth said between tears.

Deborah kissed her cheeks, telling her repeatedly of her bravery. He swallowed a lump along with a fresh commitment to make sure his girls found proper homes in Oregon, people who'd love them. . . Like he did.

Chapter 10

I talked to Beth all the while the wagon crept up the icy path. My gloved hands tightened on the oxen's reins until they hurt. She moaned, and I cast my own discomfort aside. I was so selfish to fret over sore hands. Beth's leg pained her something fierce, and the jostling in the wagon made it worse. Neither of us had slept much last night. My purpose was to calm her, and my constant reassurance kept my mind off the precarious incline.

I'd grown used to the cold, and if I allowed myself to look, really look, at the world around me, it was breathtaking. White so vast and open that I felt small and yet protected. Deer skirted, and rams picked their way over rock. Animal prints of all sizes in the snow filled me with a beauty I'd never seen before and hoped I'd never forget. Up this high, I rarely saw a pine, mostly aspen. Occasionally bite marks of an elk or moose rose up the slender trunks. Stillness impressed me as the best way to live and breathe. Once on an opposite cliff, a grizzly rose on its haunches. I held my breath, but the bear was a long way off.

"Do you sing, Miss Deborah?"

"Haven't for a long time."

"My ma used to sing when I was sick."

She laughed. "Not sure anything I could do would make you feel better. What did your ma sing?"

" 'Oh, Susanna.' That was her name."

I smiled. "What else?"

" 'Laura Lee.' Hymns, too."

Deborah recalled her mother singing hymns. "My ma liked 'Amazing Grace.' "

"Can you"—she drew in a quick breath—"sing it for me?"

"I sound like a bad splatter of rain." So I called to Nancy, "Would you see if Mr. Walker can sing 'Amazing Grace'?"

The girl scurried to him. A moment later, a rich sound rose around them.

"Amazing grace, how sweet the sound. . ."

The others joined in. But I listened with Beth. I wish I had faith, but the well was dry.

Days later we left the mountains. I looked back at the rocky peaks, a barrier intended to keep us from a new life, but it hadn't stopped us. For sure I respected them, and for sure I never wanted to make the trek again. My charges were safe, and I remembered what Ma had said. *Children are the legacy for tomorrow, and they must be loved and protected.*

Lane pulled his team to a halt beside a sparkling river. He jumped from his wagon and waved his hat. "We're in Oregon Territory. It's a long way yet to go, but we're here in God's country."

The girls hugged each other, and some shouted. I loved seeing everyone so excited, especially Lane who reminded me of a little boy. Beth shouted from her bed behind me, a little girl tired of staying inside the wagon. Slowly she grew stronger, and my heart lifted.

"Deborah, are you feeling well?" Lane said.

I was incredibly tired and my body ached, but I'd felt like that for days. "I'm fine." I smiled. "Can't believe we're in Oregon. Will it be easier now?"

Lane's chiseled face frowned. "I wish I could tell you yes. We'll make it." He pointed southwest. "At Fort Bridger we could buy fresh oxen and supplies. It makes the trail longer, but—"

"What are you thinking?" I said.

"The wagon master preferred to take out across Sublette's Cutoff. It saves miles. About fifty miles without water until we get to the Green River. It's a desolate stretch." He leaned on his saddle horn. "Do you and the girls need a few days' rest?"

"No," Beth said from inside the wagon. "Can't we tote the water we'll need?"

"Yes, little lady," he said. "I'm going to carve you a crutch. You need to walk like the rest of the girls."

She giggled. "Yes, sir."

"Lane, I don't want to take any extra miles if we can help it," I said.

He looked at me, tarrying a bit until I blushed. When he laughed, I realized I'd caught a humorous side of him.

"And what has you in such merriment?"

"My birthday. I'm twenty today."

My heart danced, and I wasn't sure why. Getting older didn't get us to Oregon City any faster. "Let's make tonight special."

The other girls crowded around and wished him a good birthday.

He winked, and warmth crept up my cheeks. "Every moment with you is special."

"Are you two getting married?" Beth said.

My eyes widened as the other girls laughed with Lane. What dared I say when my heart had been stolen? "You shouldn't speak of such things," I said to Beth.

"And I haven't asked her." He tipped his hat and hurried to the oxen. "She might turn me down and break my heart."

Never had I heard such shameless talk from him. Oh, I loved the ring of his laughter.

"We can stop for midday," he said. "Load up on the water and fill our bellies before crossing sagebrush. Cold beans and biscuits sound good to welcome Oregon."

The Green River looked inviting, and if it wasn't for freezing to death, I'd love a bath. The girls needed one, too. That nicety would come days from now. I stopped the oxen and led them to the water's edge. We all drank in deeply. Nothing tasted better than cool water. I stood, and pain stabbed into my eyes and head, blinding me. I startled. Lane's questions about my health repeated. I could not get sick. The girls depended on me, and I believed Lane did, too.

—⁂—

Lane had pushed the oxen to the Green River in four days. He breathed in relief to have cut so many miles off the journey. The girls were tired, but at the sight of the river, they'd perked. What bothered him was Deborah. The last two nights, she'd left supper fixings to the girls and gone to bed. When he checked on her the previous evening, she had a fever.

No herbs for tea. His Deborah would have to suffer through the illness, and he prayed she'd be strong and endure it. Life without her seemed. . .meaningless.

This evening he let the oxen graze and looked in on her. Grace had driven the wagon the last two days while Deborah rested beside Beth.

"She's not good," Beth said. "Sleeps all the time, and she's hot."

Lane carried her from the wagon to the riverbank, leaving Beth alone, but she didn't stir. "Girls." He fought to stop the panic in his voice. "We need to pray for Miss Deborah."

Nancy gasped and raced ahead of the others with him. "She won't die, will she?"

He couldn't look at any of the girls. "She's in God's hands, like we all are."

Lane tore himself from Deborah's side long enough to tend to the animals and reassure the girls. What a falsehood when he couldn't comfort himself that Deborah would recover. He forced water and broth between her lips. At times he simply held her and prayed.

At nightfall, he carried her to the wagon. There he sat by her side until dawn. Waiting. Trying desperately to believe.

She failed to get better.

When the girls wept, he refused to scold them. His own grief clawed at his heart. He'd sworn when his family died that he'd never love again, but he'd ignored his logic and given his heart to Deborah and seven little girls. Why love if death awaited those he cared for? First he fussed with God, and then he asked forgiveness. Mental and physical exhaustion pelted him.

After breakfast the following morning, he hitched up the oxen and pulled out toward Soda Springs. Seventy miles of desolate land. Seventy miles of worry over Deborah. He couldn't imagine a day without her.

Chapter 11

I woke to the rocking of the wagon and Beth staring at me. When I gazed upon her angelic face, she shouted to the others that I was awake. Weakness held me a prisoner, but I attempted a smile. Moments later, Lane bent at my side and took my hand.

His amber eyes watered. "Thank God, you're awake. You gave us an awful scare."

"I only remember being tired. How long have I been ill?"

"Five days. We're nearly to Soda Springs."

So many days. I closed my eyes. "Who took care of me so I can thank them proper?"

"Mostly Mr. Walker," Beth said. "He was afraid of us getting sick."

I thought about what that entailed, and humiliation settled on me. I couldn't look at him.

"It's all right." He squeezed my hand. "I don't want you to feel uncomfortable."

I probably would have died if not for him. "Thank you."

"He cried," Beth said. "Grace told him tears didn't help you get better. Then we all cried."

"I'm not as strong as you think. The thought of losing you made me want to give up."

"But we loved on him." Beth wrapped an arm around his shoulders.

My dear girls and Lane. Love and gratitude washed over me. "How can I ever repay you when you should have left me behind?"

"There's only one way to thank me."

Peering into his face, I wondered what he might require.

"Marry me when we get to Oregon City."

I was too weak to laugh. "Yes, sir. I can do that."

He kissed my forehead and left me alone while the wagons moved ahead. When I asked Beth about what happened while I slept, she told me the rooster had been cooked days before. The obstinate creature pecked Abigail, and Lane decided it was time the rooster met his maker. I was fed the broth.

In and out of sleep, I attempted to remember any awake times during my illness. Muted voices. Prayers. Lane reading the Bible.

He told me of his love.

Yes, I would marry him, but I must do something else first. "Beth, would you see if Mr. Walker can speak to me? It's important."

I drifted back to sleep until I heard his voice whispering my name. "Lane, I want to know more about Jesus," I said. "Only God could have saved me. But I don't see why He causes so much misery."

"My sweet Deborah, I don't have all the answers. But we can study the scriptures together."

"Yes," I smiled. "We're in this together."

My strength returned much faster than I anticipated. Or maybe God blessed my decision to trust Him instead of my own stubbornness.

At Soda Springs, Lane introduced us to bubbly springs. We added a little sugar to it and enjoyed the treat.

"We never celebrated your birthday," I said, enjoying the water that tickled my throat and stomach.

"Yes, we did. When you recovered and became a Christian." He glanced around to see if anyone was watching and stole a kiss. "That's for agreeing to be this man's wife."

We hitched up the oxen and continued on to Fort Hall, a ten-day journey. The fort was low on supplies, but we were all right. Lane hunted and fished when he could squeeze it in, and the girls followed him like puppies.

Another huge stretch had to be crossed along the canyons of the Snake River, and we'd have to cross it two more times. I despised that river, claiming it got its name because it rolled and spit the venom of death. One of our oxen drowned there.

Steep cliffs shot straight up alongside the Snake River for mile after mile. Monotony best described it, that and snakes. Abigail and Faith had a contest to see who could spot the most of those nasty critters.

One evening while beans bubbled and a rabbit roasted, a rattler crawled around a wagon wheel. I didn't see it, too busy patching a hole in Hope's dress.

"Would you look at that?" Faith said. "Sister, can we make it into something?"

"Mr. Walker would know." Abigail sighed. "Which one of us is going to rid the earth of this thing? I'll jar him off his resting place."

I pondered their conversation while tying a knot in the thread. Scorpions came out at night. "What are—"

"That's the finest kill I've ever seen. Good job, Faith."

My heart leaped, and I whirled around. Faith had sunk a knife into a rattler's head. Lane rounded the corner, his laughter easing my fear of what the deadly rattler could have done.

"Are you proud of me?" Faith said, revealing a missing tooth.

"You proved me wrong," he said. "All this time, I thought you were the quiet one."

"Papa used to say the same thing."

Lane picked up the snake. "Ever eat rattlesnake meat?"

"No, sir," the twins echoed.

Surely he didn't want us to cook that thing when we had plenty of other food.

"I'll skin it and show you two how to cook it up."

"Some of us might not be interested in eating it," I said.

He grinned, that lovable sweet turn of his lips. "Now, Deborah, where's your spirit?"

"In the pot of beans and bacon, where it's safe."

Grace and I didn't touch the snake meat, but the rest claimed it tasted good. In my opinion, they'd have agreed with Lane no matter what it was like.

— ⁓ —

Lane spent the evenings reading the Bible to us. I began to see the ugliness of life was not what God wanted. Not sure why he couldn't wipe away the evil when He was God, but Lane claimed some of it was our own doing, and some he didn't understand either.

"Explain to me about all the deaths. All along the trail, the accidents and cholera. The twister and why the girls are orphans." I didn't mention my mother. Having an explanation of the tragedies since leaving Independence was enough to satisfy me.

"Deborah," he said, and I appreciated the tender way he said my name, "I only know the things God does is part of a plan, and we may never see why things happen like they do. Maybe when we get to heaven, we'll get our answers. When my family died, I was bitter, despised God. Then a neighbor talked to me long and hard about God's will. I didn't like it. Still don't. But without God, I have nothing now or eternally."

"Is it wrong for me to ask Him why?"

He glanced into the fire with only the sounds of insects and spitting flames. "I do it all the time. David in the Bible questioned God. To me, it's when I try to tell God how to run his business that it's a sin. Faith is acceptance of the things I can't see and belief He knows best."

Lane said more to me about God than ever before. The girls listened, too, while the fire crackled and warmed us. I'm sure their minds raised doubts. His confession made me feel better. I could trust God and the sacrifice of His Son and still be confused.

—⁂—

Lane guided the wagons around the swamps of the Grande Ronde River Valley, beautiful but treacherous, and now he urged the oxen up the slow climb to the Blue Mountains. Evergreens grew all around them. The first time over, he thought the peaks were worse than the Rockies.

The wagon master claimed everyone was just plum wore out.

Nancy had driven the oxen for a while until Lane saw an incline that needed his hand. The girl walked, but Beth rode beside him. Her restlessness showed her renewed strength.

"I'm going to cook supper tonight," Beth said. "Then you and Miss Deborah can go for a walk."

He chuckled. "How are you going to cook on one leg? You'll fall into the fire and be in a fine mess."

She lifted a pert nose. "I know how to balance myself."

"Tell you what," he began, "get Grace and a few of the others to help, and I'll ask Miss Deborah for a walk."

"You gonna marry up with her?"

He feigned annoyance. "For one little green-eyed girl, you sure do ask a lot of questions."

"Do you love her?"

"Beth." He touched her nose. "Have you always asked so many questions?"

She smiled, revealing another lost tooth. "Yes, sir."

"What am I going to do with you?" It occurred to him how very hard it would be to part with his girls when they reached Oregon City.

Weariness stalked him, but no more than any of the others. Deborah walked most of the day. She laughed again, and her cheeks tinted with color. Only God could have healed her, and now she recognized His power.

He longed to talk of the future with her, but most days they were too tired to form words. He'd not take this trail again. Once he drove the oxen into Oregon City, he'd head right into the Pacific Ocean before ever heading back East.

Two days later, they climbed a mountaintop, and he spotted the winding Columbia River. He wanted to share the sight of the magnificent river with Deborah, but all he could do was point. Grace, Abigail, and Hope walked beside the wagon.

"Will we cross the river?" Grace said. "It looks mighty big even from here."

"No, we'll take the Barlow Road. Too dangerous to take a raft down the Columbia."

"Beth might topple over," Hope said.

"No, I wouldn't." Beth leaned over to glare at her cousin. "Just you wait till my leg is mended, I'll outrace you."

He sealed times like these in his memory. One day when they were grown, they'd remember how they became little women through adversity.

The wagons eased down the trail to a grassland reprieve. Nancy and Grace drove the oxen, allowing him to walk beside Deborah.

"If I stole a kiss, would anyone see?" he said.

"Only takes one."

She laughed, and he treasured the sound. "I might have to ask you to marry me. Oh, I already did."

Whirling toward him, her eyes clouded. "But you lead wagon trains from Missouri to Oregon, maybe down to California. I know you love me, but would you be happy?"

She was right. "Neither a wagon master's wife nor a scout's wife is fitting for a woman. I want to settle down in Oregon."

"Are you sure? You're a leader, a fine wagon master."

"I'd rather be your husband—"

Up ahead, riders caught his attention. That's when he saw three Shoshone Indians heading straight toward them.

Chapter 12

I covered my mouth to stifle a scream. The three Indians rode toward us. "What can we do?" The moment the words escaped me, I had an answer. We'd be strong. Lane had prepared us for this.

"Stay calm and do not show fear," Lane said. "Deborah, get back to your wagon with the other girls. I'll see about talking our way out of this. The Shoshone may be in a bartering mood." He lifted Beth down from his wagon, handed her the crutch, and sent her to me.

"All of you inside my wagon," I said. "Now. We'll be fine." I wished my trembling spirit could believe my own words.

They scurried in quiet obedience, and I took Grace's place as driver.

"We're all like David from the Bible, and we're not afraid," she whispered.

I wrapped my right hand around the musket beside me on the wagon bench. A few days before, Lane had loaded it, saying the driver needed to be prepared for danger.

Since leaving Fort Laramie, I'd lived in paralyzing fear. I did my best to rely on God, but right now He seemed so far away. The shirtless men riding on spotted ponies had been the subject of a few campfire discussions. The closer they came, the more frightening their appearance—ruthless heathens. The stories of what they did to wagon trains marched across my mind.

"Easy," Lane called to all of us. "Remember all I've taught you. Show your strength."

"And pray," I added, surprising myself. How many times had I heard him instill those instructions into the girls' hearts and minds? The Bible stories of God delivering those who trusted in Him flashed in and out of my mind. My senses were numb, but one thing I knew for sure is I wouldn't allow anyone to hurt those I loved.

Lane spoke to them in their language, and I marveled at this man who had an abundance of resources. Was there nothing he couldn't do? Then I remembered his tears when I was so ill. He carried so much responsibility.

I heard rustling behind me, and a clanging of metal. "What are you doing?" I whispered.

"Preparing to fight," Beth said. "My leg doesn't stop me from taking aim and firing."

"Please, girls." I wanted to scream. "Let Mr. Walker talk to the Shoshone. Maybe we can give them a rifle, and they'll leave us alone."

"Why give them something so they can hurt other people?" Grace said.

Her logic held far too much truth.

"You're supposed to be praying," I said.

"We are, while loading the muskets," Grace said. "Ruby, Mr. Walker taught you how to load it, now do it right. No reason to be shakin' when we have God."

Out of the mouths of children. . .

The Indians sounded angry, but Lane's voice was calm. *If only I understood what was being said.* I forced myself to look straight ahead while my heart threatened to leap from my chest. The girls were quiet, and I was too fearful to find out what they planned. I wanted to peer into the back of the wagon, but my sudden movement might alarm the Indians.

Lane jumped from the wagon and walked back past me. He neither looked at me nor spoke a word. *If God really heard the prayers of the oppressed, now was the time to show His power.*

—m—

Lane took a deep breath. He told the Shoshone he had a horse for him, but the Indian demanded a musket. Fetching the musket and exposing the girls worried him. He'd reach inside, grab the musket, and rely on his teachings that the girls wouldn't show any signs of fear. The one speaking wanted gunpowder and lead balls. The idea of turning over a weapon to Indians who'd kill others wrestled with his conscience. But Deborah and the girls' lives were in the balance.

The Shoshone rode their ponies beside him. Every step brought dread. He should have used his musket on them instead of trying to deal peacefully.

Not a sound came from inside the wagon.

He pulled back the canvas. Four muskets balanced on the boxes, aimed at the Indians. Grace, Nancy, Beth, and Abigail had their fingers on the triggers.

Beth fired, narrowly missing one of the Shoshone. His pony startled. Another shot went wild, and the Indians fled, leaving a trail of dust.

"How's that, Mr. Walker?" Beth said, pulling herself up from the wagon. The jolt of the musket had sent her onto her backside. "We aimed high so not to kill 'em, just scare 'em off."

"I think you were better than an army," he said. "Fine job. All of you."

Nancy had fallen backward when she fired, and Grace helped her up.

Lane blew out a long breath and removed his hat. "I don't think they'll be back. Is everyone all right?"

Little voices chimed in. Lane glanced at the disappearing dust. Not sure what to say. Deborah joined him. He glanced at her and saw a hint of amusement.

Had they all gone mad?

"You're stone pale, Mr. Walker." She laughed.

Maybe it was the fact death had escaped them, or the sight of his girls scaring off the Shoshone, or all the hardship of the journey, or that they'd gone insane, but he laughed until his sides ached.

"Girls, drop your weapons and give me a hug," he said. "You saved our hides today."

"You taught us what to do," Nancy said. "We poured gunpowder down those barrels and rammed the lead with a piece of cloth to cushion it." She nodded. "I'm not going to ever be afraid of anything again."

"I think you girls will do just fine in Oregon. In fact, I feel sorry for anyone who gets in your way."

Chapter 13

I eagerly looked forward to ending our journey, and the Barlow Road near Mount Hood was the last stretch before reaching the Willamette Valley.

"We have a toll to pay before taking the road," Lane said to me. "The men who opened the trail a few years ago make their money from people who want to avoid the Columbia River."

We had money, and the wagon master had indicated a toll would be charged to cross the Cascades, but I'd forgotten the cost. "How much will it cost?"

"We'll need five dollars per wagon and ten cents for each animal." He must have noted my shock at the toll. "I've never been on the Columbia River. Neither do I want to risk our belongings and lives with the rapids. Heard too many stories of drownings."

"But we're so tired. What price to take the river?"

"Fifty dollars. We'd need to sell most of our belongings before boarding a raft."

I startled. His sentiments were all I needed to reach into the trunk that held our treasures and pull out gold. Embarking across the Cascades, over a trail laden with trees and rocks increased our chances of survival, and I'd seen enough death and threats of it to last a lifetime. "Then we'll pay to take the trail."

Nearly forty miles later, we headed our wagons toward Oregon City where the Columbia met the Willamette River. Sadness settled on me as I considered the girls. . .and what their future held. At noontime, I asked Lane if we could talk privately. We walked ahead several yards.

"Where do I look for the girls for a proper home?" I said.

"I think you mean we." He took my hand. "I think we should talk to a preacher first. He'll know of good people who'd love the girls."

"Do you think Grace and Ruby or Abigail and Faith will be separated?"

He shook his head. "They've been through so much already."

"Where would their new families live? The thought of not seeing them again breaks my heart, and imagine how they must feel."

He glanced back to where the wagons stood hitched to the oxen. "They've been quiet since we started the Barlow Road."

"Last night I heard Hope and Beth crying," I said. "Their whispers told me they were afraid of being separated. Cousins. . . Ignoring their fears seems wrong. But what do I say?"

"We'll think of something." He held me tight. "Answers will come when we find proper homes for them."

We'd gone through so much to get here, and for what? To see the girls miserable?

By noon the following day, we saw the outskirts of Oregon City. It had been so long since we'd been around other folks or even looked presentable. Shyness overtook me. Lane suggested we all have baths at one of the boardinghouses, and we agreed. The price of such luxury was worth it. Never had warm water and lye soap felt so good.

We kept our wagons outside of town where the animals could graze and rest while we tended to business. The one that weighed heaviest on our hearts was to visit the preacher about the girls—and also to marry us. My heart should have been merry to take wedding vows with Lane. But I didn't sleep at all. The girls were restless, too. Was it wrong to want to keep them close to me when I had so little to offer?

Chapter 14

"We're here," Lane said, holding fast to my hand. "Hold your head up high. You've walked where many have perished."

I heard no enthusiasm from him or the girls.

The streets were busy, sights and sounds that should have been exciting for all of us after the months of hardships. Our charges were quiet, and I looked at them. Their little faces were sad. My spirit sank, too.

"Why aren't we happy?" I said. "God brought us here. We're alive."

"I don't want to leave you," Grace said, the first time I'd not heard optimism from her. "Or any of you. We're like sisters. We love each other." She touched Ruby's cheek. "I'm afraid I'll never see any of you again."

"Family," I whispered.

Lane squeezed my hand, and we faced the girls. "Can I have a word with Miss Deborah?"

They nodded, and we walked a few feet away for privacy. He swallowed hard. "I love you. And I love those girls." He took a deep breath. "I know I'm asking a lot. But instead of finding families for them, can we homestead together? Could we give our girls a home?"

Tears flowed from my eyes, and I wrapped my arms around his neck. I didn't care what others might have thought. "Lane, you're the finest man this side of heaven. You showed me how to survive. You nursed me when I was ill. You love me. You showed me Jesus and helped me find God. I want to be your wife and never leave your side. Let me help you raise our girls." I blinked back the wetness. "They're already little women."

He kissed my forehead. "You've made me one happy man. Maybe I can start a lumber mill." He glanced around. "But we can't file a homestead today."

"Why not?" Hot and cold flowed through my body.

He grinned. "We have to be married first to claim the 640 acres."

"Where's the closest preacher?"

"Oh, you've grown bold." He took my shoulders and pointed down the street. "There's a church. Shall we take our family and do this proper?"

"Will you tell them what we plan to do?"

"I will. Not sure we'll ever earn the title of ma and pa, but they're ours as sure as God brings up the sun."

We walked back to where the girls waited. Lane smiled. "Would you girls help us?"

"How?" Nancy said.

"Miss Deborah and I are going to get married today. Would you join us?"

Smiles met them.

"Here's the hard part," he said. "We're going to claim a homestead, but we're going to be powerful lonely. Would any of you want to live with us?"

The girls rushed him, nearly knocking him down. Lane reached for my hand, and we all walked toward the church.

A new life.

A home with our girls.

What more could we possibly ever want?

—⁂—

Five Years Later

I walked the short distance from our home to the edge of town where our lumber mill flourished. The scent of freshly sawed timber filled the air, and I hurried to bring Lane his lunch. He'd left before sunrise, and I knew he'd not eat unless I brought him food. When that man had work on his mind, he forgot to take care of himself.

When I thought about how far we'd come with the girls since the twister, I could only thank God for His provision. Who would have ever thought seven girls and two young people could make it to Oregon? The girls' money from their families wasn't a substantial amount, but we'd save it until they married or were twenty years old. The land company in Missouri insisted Lane keep the money he'd found after the twister. After three years, I persuaded him to start the lumber mill. I think it was God's way of blessing us.

"Papa working?" Three-year-old Effie tugged on my hand. She had my light blue eyes and Lane's thick hair, bringing his total to eight girls. Nine counting me. Perhaps the little one in my womb would be a boy.

He stepped from the busy lumberyard and waved. Every time I saw him, my stomach flitted. His wide shoulders, amber eyes, and wide smile made everything around me sparkle. I hoped those feelings never changed.

He hugged me and bent to pick up Effie. "How are the others?"

"Busy. Grace is washing, and Ruby's helping."

He laughed. "Grace just wants to be hanging clothes to dry in case the Emerson boy stops by. I told him last night she was too young for courtin' until she was fifty."

I laughed. "Did you now, Papa Bear? What did he say?"

Lane shook his head. "Told me he'd wait. Reminded me of how I felt about you. I never got the nerve to ask your father about courtin' you."

"God took care of it."

"So He did. So what's the rest of my little women up to?"

"Abigail and Faith plan to cook supper, so they're picking vegetables for dinner. Beth and Hope are berry picking."

"And Nancy?"

I shook my head at our girl who wanted to do the same things as a boy. She'd come a long way since her sickly childhood. "She insists upon riding your wild mare. Every time she's thrown, Nancy gets right back on."

"Don't have to worry about boys with her. She'll run them all off." He kissed her deeply while holding Effie. "Love my girls. Love you more."

"Any regrets?"

"Nope." He touched her stomach. "I imagine this one's another girl, and I don't mind. We're in this together."

His Frontier Family
by Anna Schmidt

Chapter 1

That boy needs a family of his own," Ginny Hastings announced.

"That boy is nearly thirty years old, and you are not his mother," her husband replied. "And why are you so concerned about him when there are half a dozen other officers who are not yet wed serving on the grounds?"

"Jason Campbell has the maturity and kind, gentle soul to make an excellent husband and father. Some of the others are still far too rowdy and self-centered. I'll get to them in time."

Major Martin Hastings drank the last of his coffee, set the china cup back on its saucer, checked his uniform in the mirror over the sideboard, and then kissed the top of his wife's gray head. "There's a wagon train coming today," he told her. "I'll not be home until later."

"Be sure you eat something," she said. She stood at the window and watched him stride across the compound. Life in Fort Laramie was not luxurious by anyone's definition, but it was home—their home—for the foreseeable future. Ginny fully intended to do what she could to see that it was populated with young families so that when the day came that it was no longer needed by the government, it would be a thriving community set on the banks of the Laramie River. When her husband, Major Martin Hastings, had assumed command of the former-trading-post-turned-military-outpost to protect settlers headed to California or other points west, they had lived in a tent. The government had refused to approve funds for housing for married officers and their families, even though it made much of the importance of families living on the post for purposes of morale.

Her husband had gotten around that by requisitioning funds and materials for four field kitchens, and then he had turned those structures into houses for himself and his two married officers. Ginny had plans for that last house—plans that included Captain Jason Campbell. In the meantime, she had turned the dwelling that she and the major occupied into a haven for the single officers and the enlisted men by hosting dinner parties. She also planned balls and celebrations that were held in the larger two-story Victorian structure that housed the bachelor officers.

She watched as Martin conferred with the young captain who had spent many an evening in their company and shared many a meal at their table. Jason Campbell was tall and broad shouldered. He dwarfed her short, stocky husband. He had hair the color of rich black coffee and the most beautiful hazel eyes that Ginny thought she'd ever seen on a man. She might not be his mother, but she cared and worried about him as if she were. The fact that he was still unmarried at his age concerned her. His every waking moment seemed to be focused on fort business—keeping the surrounding territory and its residents as well as the increasing number of settlers that passed this way safe. At the same time, he worked to gain the trust of the various tribes who were understandably unnerved by the increase in traffic across what had once been their land.

Through the open window, she heard the shout of a soldier standing watch in one of the guard towers. He had spotted the approaching wagon train, and that meant that she had work to do. The emigrants would stay for several days while the wagons were repaired, the sick recovered, and everyone enjoyed some rest as well as food that did not have to be created from supplies that could last the trip across the plains and mountains.

Since Ginny had appointed herself the social director for such visits, she could not spend any more time worrying about Captain Jason Campbell. On the other hand, she thought as she cleared the breakfast dishes and smoothed out the lace cloth covering her mother's dining room table, a visiting train of emigrants always held promise for Jason. There could be a family with an eligible daughter. There could be three or four such eligible young women—there had been before. Not that Jason had paid them the slightest mind. Ginny had practically had to force him to ask the last one to dance at the party she always organized for the night before the train was to set out again. For this group of travelers, the party would be extra special as it would fall on Independence Day.

Two days earlier, the train's scout had arrived at the fort with the news that the emigrants were on their way, but at the same time, he'd delivered disturbing news that a boy traveling with his widowed mother had run off. Jason and two enlisted men had joined the scout for the search, found the boy—sunburned and parched—hiding in a thicket of scrub brush several miles upriver and decided to hold him at the fort until his mother arrived. The scout had ridden back to give the boy's mother the news, and Jason had taken the boy by the scruff of the neck and steered him directly into the holding cell where soldiers awaiting court martial or punishment for lesser offenses stayed. It was seeing him take the boy in hand that had given Ginny the thought that he not only needed a wife—Jason Campbell needed a family.

—⁂—

After making sure that everyone had their orders for the day's preparations to receive the arriving train, Jason went to check on the boy.

"You can't keep me here," the kid snarled as soon as he saw Jason. "When Mama gets here—"

"Seems to me you ran away from your mama, so what makes you think she wants anything to do with you now?"

"I ain't broke no laws," the kid countered.

"You're changing the subject." Jason pulled a wooden chair closer to the cell and sat down. "Your mother and the others will be here later this afternoon, and here's what you are going to do in the meantime. One, you are going to wash that dirty face and the rest of your scrawny self as best you can. Two, you are going to change out of those wet, filthy clothes into something presentable for seeing your mother." He pushed a stack of military-issue clothing through the bars. "Three—"

"I ain't wearing no uniform."

"Three," Jason continued, "when you do see your mother, you are going to apologize for causing her—and everyone else on that wagon train—unnecessary worry."

"And if I don't?"

The kid had bluster. Jason would give him that. In fact, young Ben Carson was a lot like Jason had been at that age—sullen, rebellious, mad at the world. He held up the ring of keys. "If you don't, you will be held here indefinitely. For all I know, you were aiding and abetting the enemy."

"I didn't do nothing but strike out on my own. I have friends back in Iowa, and—"

"Ah, if you were headed for Iowa, which is east, why were you found several miles west of where you left the train? No, the way I see it, you're covering something." He jangled the keys and turned to leave.

"Wait, mister."

"It's captain," Jason said.

"Captain." The boy spit out the word as if it were something foul-tasting. Then he fingered the stack of clean clothes that Jason had set next to the basin of water and towel just inside his cell. "What if I do what you said? Wash up and change clothes."

"And apologize to your mother and to everyone else, especially the scout who had to take time to find you, and—"

Ben's eyes went wide with indignation. "You didn't say nothing about apologizing to nobody but my ma."

Jason shrugged. "If you keep trying to make bargains with me and refusing a direct order, I have no choice but to continue to add to the terms of your release."

"You can't do that."

Jason pointed to the cell indicating Ben's position locked inside and his own standing free. "Seems like I can, kid. Think about it."

He left then, ignoring the shouts from the boy that were definitely insulting and bordered on offensive. When he emerged into the sunlight and heat of the summer midday, he was chuckling. He felt sorry for Ben's mother, but then given the boy's actions and his complete lack of respect for his elders, it seemed to Jason that the woman had done a poor job of bringing the boy up. The scout had told him that she was a widow traveling alone with her son. Sounded to Jason like the apple didn't fall far from the tree when the scout chuckled and said, "She's a stubborn one, that's for sure. Won't hardly let nobody help her out, determined to go it alone." He suspected that meeting the Widow Carson would explain a lot about why Ben Carson had decided to strike out on his own in the middle of nowhere.

—๛—

Emma sat on the edge of the hard wagon seat, mentally pleading with the team of oxen she was driving as well as all the teams ahead of her to move faster. Randy Miller, scout for the group, had returned late the night before with the news that Ben had been found and taken to Fort Laramie to wait for them.

"But why didn't you bring him back here?" she had asked.

Randy had removed his hat and scratched his thinning hair. "Well now, ma'am, we had a hard enough time corralling him at all, and the captain was sure he'd try to run again, so he—"

"This captain has no right to make such decisions. Ben is my son, not one of his soldiers."

"Well, ma'am, you ain't gonna like this news either, but it needs to be told. Captain Campbell is holding Ben in the fort's jail."

She was speechless, but the expression on her face must have spoken volumes, for Randy continued. "Now, he said it was for the boy's own safety, and I'm inclined to agree. Your boy fought like a wildcat when we come upon him. The captain had to wrestle him to the ground and—"

"This man attacked my child?"

"No, ma'am. I wouldn't say that. Beggin' your pardon, ma'am, but young Ben has been a bit of a handful from the day we left."

The truth of that only made Emma more upset. "How long before we reach this fort so I can free my son, Mr. Miller?"

Randy stared up at the sky. "Barring any weather or other problems, we should get there sometime tomorrow."

So from the moment they set out at sunrise, Emma had been mentally pushing the wagons along, willing them to move faster even as she prayed for the bank of clouds that had appeared on the horizon to stay put. Rain was the last thing she needed, even if it would be good for the land.

The truth was that she partially understood why Ben had run away. She had to admit that she was having her own doubts about her decision to move west. At first it had seemed the perfect solution for handling Ben's growing anger and restlessness and her fears that he was falling in with a rowdy group of boys back home in Iowa. When he had stopped attending Sunday services with her a year earlier, she had thought that it was just part of the process of growing up. But not going to church was followed by disappearing for hours and then barely answering her when he returned. Then he'd been arrested with a group of boys for vandalism. That's when she'd decided she needed to take action.

At first the trip had been exciting, and even Ben had seemed like he was coming around. But then it had begun again—the snide comments about the other children on their train and the constant harping on his friends back home. By the time the group had passed Chimney Rock—marking only one-third of their journey—Ben had been in three fights with other boys, had talked back to the wagon master, and had been caught by Randy the scout trying to spook the horses one night. No wonder Randy had not questioned the captain taking Ben in hand.

She caught her first glimpse of the fort midafternoon and was surprised at how busy it was—a little like a small town. Men riding in and out the open main gate, smoke rising from the campfires of a cluster of teepees set up outside the fort's adobe walls, a couple of small children racing about, and cattle grazing nearby as men in uniform sawed boards, hammered them in place, and climbed ladders to continue their construction on a small house at the end of a row of houses that looked brand new. The fort and the houses were situated on a bluff that overlooked a curve in the Laramie River—a beautiful, peaceful setting that was a relief after the weeks of life on the trail fighting storms and mud and breakdowns and always the fear that they might be attacked by savages or be in the path of a buffalo stampede.

The wagon master signaled for them to circle their wagons near the river just outside the high adobe walls of the fort. Some soldiers came out to help with the unhitching of the oxen, leaving Emma free to go in search of this captain who had taken her son prisoner.

She lifted her skirts and trudged across the grassy area outside the walls of the fort. Above her she saw a central watchtower and two smaller square bastions where soldiers kept watch. In addition to the cluster of teepees and the row of homes, she saw a cemetery. Once inside the main gate, she had to dodge soldiers as they went about their duties, but she got her bearings fairly quickly as she identified housing for the enlisted men, better housing for the officers, a dwelling at the far end of the fort she assumed to be that of the commander, a bakery, a surgeon's quarters, a commissary, and something with a faded sign that announced ENNY THING U NEED FER THE TRIP.

A man wearing a blacksmith's apron conferred with Randy Miller—the two men seemed to be old friends. Just as she was about to approach them to ask directions, a gray-haired woman with a welcoming smile called out to her.

"Hello, and welcome to Fort Laramie. I am Virginia Hastings. My husband is Major Martin Hastings—the fort's commanding officer. You and the others in your party will be meeting the other officers and their wives—those who have wives—later, but right now I—"

"Beggin' your pardon, ma'am," Emma said interrupting the welcoming speech. "My son, Ben. . ."

"Ah yes, my dear. You must be so worried, but I assure you that young Ben has been well cared for. Come with me, and we'll find Captain Campbell right away."

"I don't wish to see the captain, Mrs. Hastings. I wish to see my son."

"Now then, before we get too taken up with business, let's understand that we don't stand on ceremony here—at least among us women. I am Ginny, and you are. . .?"

"Emma, but. . ."

Ginny Hastings hooked her arm through Emma's. "Come along then, and let's go find that young man. I expect he has had some time to consider the foolishness of his act, and I hope he has the good sense to apologize for putting you to such worry."

She headed toward a door that stood open and stepped inside, pulling Emma along with her. The soldier at the room's lone table leaped to his feet. Emma knew by his uniform that this was not the captain.

"This is young Ben's mother," Ginny explained. "She'd like to see her son."

"Yes, ma'am. The captain's back there with him now."

If that man has laid a finger on my son, I will. . . Emma pushed her sunbonnet off her head, wanting to be sure the captain was aware of the full extent of her fury when they met. She followed the guard and Ginny Hastings through a second door.

The first person she saw was Ben. He sat on a cot. He was dressed in clean clothes, and his hair glistened with a recent washing and combing. He did not meet her gaze, but at a murmured order from the man standing outside his cell, Ben stood up.

The second person she saw was the man in uniform, and she knew enough about the military to know that here at last was the captain who had held her son captive. His back was to her as he unlocked and opened the cell door, the jangle of the ring of keys and the protesting squeal of the metal door the only sounds in the room. He stepped aside, murmured more words to Ben, and had the audacity to place his hand on her son's shoulder as he led Ben forward.

"How dare you?" Emma managed to choke out even as she grabbed Ben into her embrace and held on tight.

"Mama, I—"

"You may be an officer, sir, but you had no right to place my son in jail." The captain was staring at her as if he had never before seen a woman, or maybe it was that he had never seen a woman who dared to speak out to him. He was good-looking to be sure and probably used to the female of the species falling all over themselves to please him. Well, in that case he was in for quite a rude awakening.

Beside her she was aware of Ginny Hastings fighting to hide a smile. Was this all some big joke to these people? Ben had turned to face the captain as well, and he was also wearing a smile—a smile of triumph.

"And you, young man," she said turning the full force of her fury and the fear she'd gone through these past few days on Ben, "you have nothing to smile about. Do you have any idea what you put everyone in our party through?"

"I think you will discover, ma'am, that your son—"

"Captain Campbell." Emma released her hold on Ben and stepped closer to the man. He was tall, but then so was she. Her eyes were level with his mouth, and she was momentarily taken aback by the dimple that was so embedded into his cheek that he didn't need to smile to have it come to life. "Captain Campbell, you have overstepped your authority. Still, I thank you and your men for the help you gave in finding Ben and in keeping him safe until I could arrive. Now if you'll excuse us. . ."

"Begging your pardon, ma'am, but I'm afraid it's not that simple. Ben here has a debt to pay, and I plan to hold him to it even if you don't."

The man was questioning how she was raising her own child? How dare he? "Do you have children, Captain?" she asked, forcing her tone to one of sweetness and genuine interest. It worked. She saw the spark of confusion that crossed his features.

"That's not the point."

"Oh, but it is, and I assume that the answer to my question is that you do not yet have children of your own."

"He'll have to take a wife first," Ginny Hastings murmured. The woman was still smiling as if this were all some bit of staged entertainment.

"Ma, the captain and me have been talking, and—"

"The captain and I," she corrected automatically.

"Your son and I have worked out an arrangement, Mrs. Carson. While your party is encamped here over the next few days, he will take responsibility for some maintenance chores—"

"Such as?"

"Mucking out the stables and grooming the horses."

"And in return?"

"The captain's going to teach me how to shoot a gun," Ben interrupted, his eyes glinting with excitement.

Torn between the first sign of excitement about their journey she'd seen in Ben's eyes and her horror that this man had thought for one minute she would approve such madness, Emma swallowed the only words she could find. But they were in her eyes as she stared directly at Captain Campbell, and she sincerely hoped he was understanding her message as clearly as if she had shouted: *Over my dead body!*

Chapter 2

Jason was positive that he had never seen a more beautiful woman. Emma Carson was tall and as slender as a girl. He would have taken her more for Ben's sister than his parent. Her son had clearly inherited the same fiery red hair—disaster for a boy his age. The teasing he must have endured. He and his mother also shared the same large, deep green eyes. And like Ben, she had a sprinkle of freckles dashed across her nose and cheekbones. As furious as she obviously was with him, there was no denying her loveliness. Even her voice was attractive. It was not the high-pitched whine he might have anticipated, but rather was deep and calm in spite of her anger.

In those green eyes—turned to hard emerald stone when she looked at him—he read her message loud and clear. She would not approve of her only child handling firearms. But a deal was a deal, and as long as Ben lived up to his end of things, Jason intended to do the same.

"You and Ben are no longer in Iowa, ma'am," he said hoping to reason with her. "The frontier is—"

"Is my son free to go, Captain?"

"Yes, ma'am, he is, but rescuing him doesn't come without consequences. It's for the boy's own good, ma'am."

He could see that his repeated use of *ma'am* was irritating her and realized that she thought he was mocking her. He glanced at Ginny, and as usual she stepped in to help.

"Emma—may I call you by your given name?"

Ben's mother nodded but kept her glare focused on Jason.

"I wonder if I might offer a compromise in this matter?"

The Carson woman turned to Ginny. "Please do," she said.

"You and Ben will be here for several days yet, and from what I've been able to learn, this young man is not especially pleased with the way his life is going."

"I want to go back to Iowa," Ben said, sensing that at last he might have an ally.

"Yes, well that is unlikely to happen, young man," Ginny said, her voice as kind as that of a loving grandmother's. "Do you not have friends among the other young people on the train?"

Jason waited to see what the boy would say. Ben had confessed to him that the other boys his age on the train had teased him about his small size and his red hair and had generally excluded him from their circle. Jason understood the cruelty that could come from boys that age. He'd lived through a similar boyhood, only in his case the bullying had come from his father and brothers.

"No, ma'am," Ben replied. "They don't like me."

"They don't know you," his mother added, wrapping her arm around his shoulders.

"Ben is a good boy—a hard worker," she told Ginny.

"I'm sure he is. It seems to me that what Captain Campbell is attempting to do here is teach your son a lesson that may stand him in good stead over the years to come and at the same time give him some status among the other boys. Besides, you must agree, Emma, that his actions cannot go unpunished."

"Yes, but—"

"My husband, Major Hastings, has instituted a unique system for dealing with lesser infractions committed by the enlisted men here in the fort. In his view, simply locking a man up only feeds whatever the problem might have been that led him to trouble in the first place."

"But those men are soldiers. My son is a boy. . . ."

"A boy on the brink of manhood, my dear. And one you are now trying to manage alone. Captain Campbell could provide some guidance over the coming days that just might help Ben see himself as the fine young man he will be one day."

Jason saw what Ginny was doing. She'd tried it before more times than he could count. Ginny was matchmaking. She cared about the boy, but what she really saw was a wife for him. It happened every time a wagon train came through the fort. Ginny would meet the train and size up the prospects. It was pretty evident that she'd settled on Emma Carson as the perfect match for him.

"Ginny, Mrs. Carson has a point. Ben is not one of the men—he's her son, and—"

"No," Emma interrupted. "Mrs. Hastings—Ginny—you make a strong case for turning this situation into a chance for learning."

Ben groaned. His mother tightened her grip on his shoulders.

"My concern is that he will try to run away again."

"Ma, I promise—"

"You promised to give our new life a chance once before, Ben, and look what happened. Do you have any idea what could have happened? There are Indians and poisonous snakes and who knows what all out there. That's why we travel with others."

"There are Indians camped right here at the fort," he argued.

"And what did I tell you about that?" Jason asked.

Ben hung his head and muttered, "Not all of them are bad."

"And?" Jason prompted.

"And some that seem bad are just trying to protect their homes and families. They're scared."

Jason looked at Ben's mother, seeking approval for the lessons he had taught her son already. She scowled at him. Once again Ginny came to his rescue.

"As you can see, Emma, your son and the captain have formed a bond of sorts. Why not allow Ben to stay with the captain in his quarters while you stay with the major and me? That way you can get some much-needed rest without having to worry that you need to keep watch over your son."

"Ma!" It was a bleat of pleading.

Jason faced Emma Carson and waited.

"Very well," she said, and he could not have explained the way his heart raced with relief. "But no guns."

"Ma!" This time the protest was loud and clear.

"Well now, the boy is going to have to know something about hunting if you're planning to homestead, ma'am."

He could see that she hadn't thought of this. "Very well, some basic hunting skills and perhaps fishing, but nothing that involves that." She pointed to the pistol holstered on his hip.

"Excellent," Ginny said, pressing her hands together in a gesture of delight. "Our bargain has been struck."

"But. . ." Ben protested.

"Oh, stop that," Ginny chided, ruffling Ben's shaggy mop of hair. "Guns, fishing, working as Captain Campbell's top aide? You'll be the envy of every boy on that wagon train out there, not to mention the object of every young lady's interest."

Jason saw Ben blush and then allow himself a half grin as this idea sunk in. The boy looked up at his mother. "If you think it's for the best," he said, his eyes wide and innocent. The kid was a scamp and a conniver—just like Jason had been at that age. He felt a little sorry for Emma Carson and wondered if her son had always been able to get around her or if that had just started now that the father was no longer part of his life.

—⁓—

Emma walked back across the compound and out to the wagons where Ginny orchestrated the unloading of the trunk that held her extra clothes and Ben's. Around her the other officers' wives were extending similar invitations to some of the women on the train in greatest need of rest—the old, the infirm, and the wagon master's pregnant daughter, who was due to give birth any day now. Once Emma realized that the wagon master's wife and daughter would also be staying with the major and his wife, she relaxed. But moments later as Ginny led the way to her house, Emma was all too aware of her stained and dirty dress, her mud-coated shoes, and her hair coated with dirt and grime from the trip so far. Inside the house, she remained frozen in the doorway with her arms crossed tightly around her, afraid to set foot on the polished wooden floors or risk brushing against any of the numerous items that filled the small tables and shelves in the sitting room.

"Come in. Come in." Ginny directed the soldiers to carry the trunk upstairs. "Second door on the left," she called up to them. She repeated the instructions when the soldiers brought the other women's trunks. "The larger room across the hall from the first one," she said then waited until the two men had come back downstairs, thanked them, and turned again to Emma and the other women. "Ladies, why don't you go up and wash some of that trail dust off your faces and change out of those clothes while I make us some tea?"

"Please don't go to any bother," Emma protested, although the other two women were already halfway up the stairs. "You've already—"

"Now understand this, Emma. The arrival of a wagon train is cause for celebration for everyone living in this fort—from the enlisted men to my husband and especially for us women. It breaks the monotony and gives us something we can do for a few days. It's you doing me the favor here. Now scoot."

Emma smiled and climbed the stairs. The bedroom she'd been given was small with a single narrow bed, a single side chair, some hooks on the wall for hanging clothing, and a washstand. Across the hall, the pregnant woman and her mother were sharing the larger room and had spread out their things, leaving their trunks open. Emma's trunk barely fit at the foot of the bed. She opened it and began laying out fresh clothing and personal items—her hairbrush, the bar of lavender soap she had brought with her from Iowa, and her Bible, which she placed on the windowsill next to the bed.

When she heard Ginny come up the stairs, she slipped out into the hallway to thank her. "Everything is so lovely—and clean," she said and laughed. "I never thought about how much dirt and dust there would be on a trip like this." She untied the streamers of her sunbonnet and, in pulling it free, caught the pins holding her hair in place so that it came down and lay against her neck and back in a tangled mess.

Ginny was carrying a kettle that steamed, and she moved past Emma to fill the pitcher on the washstand. "You wash up and change," she said, "then come on down to the kitchen and we'll wash that lovely hair and have our tea. By suppertime you'll feel like a new woman."

After Ginny left to attend the other women, Emma washed and changed and then sat on the chair and picked up her Bible. As was her habit, she let it fall open on her lap and then read the passage. She had adopted this practice when nothing in her life had seemed to make sense. She realized that she did not know where to find solace following the death of her husband, or balm for her terror that she could not raise their son on her own, and that in her zeal to get Ben away from possible trouble, she had perhaps made the worst decision of her life.

The worn leather cover and the crisp tissue-thin pages fell open to Exodus, the twelfth chapter. Emma scanned the page, and her eyes came to rest on the second verse: "This month shall be unto you the beginning of months: it shall be the first month of the year to you."

She knew the words referred to the exodus of the children of Israel from Egypt, yet they seemed to speak to her circumstances as well. She and Ben were setting off into a kind of wilderness as those Israelites had so many centuries earlier. She closed the Bible and clutched it to her chest as she stared around the room. A calendar on the wall reminded her that today was Tuesday, the first of July.

The gathering round the major's table was not unusual. Whenever a wagon stopped at the fort, Ginny Hastings turned the entire affair into one ongoing party. Jason, along with the other officers and their wives—or sometimes just the wives if their husbands were on duty—regularly joined the major and his wife for supper. It was a good time for the men to talk and share ideas. The number of wagon trains was increasing, so that during the summer there was hardly a break in the comings and goings of them. It was tradition for Ginny to invite the wagon master and his family and anyone staying in her home and their families to share this first meal. On the evening before the train left, she would organize a large party with food and music and dancing, which was usually held in the common area of the unmarried officers' quarters—a building the men had nicknamed Bedlam because it was so often the scene of such gatherings.

No, the only problem with this particular meal was that Ginny had made sure that he and the Widow Carson were seated directly across from each other—another of Ginny's usual matchmaking tricks. The trouble was that this time she'd found a woman who had made it perfectly clear that she did not care for him. That should have made things easier, but the truth was that he had done his best with her son. Obviously she'd been having trouble with the boy well before Jason met him. He'd think she'd be grateful, but even after she had accepted his terms, she had added terms of her own.

As Major Hastings pulled out the chair for her, Jason stood as was proper. She glanced his way, frowned, and then turned the sunbeam that was her smile on the major. "Thank you, sir," she murmured as she settled herself into the chair. She had changed her dress from the faded blue made gray by trail dust that she'd been wearing when they met to a rose-colored gingham that highlighted the pink in her cheeks. Ginny had seated Ben at the far end of the table next to the major. Ben's mother was seated between Ginny and the wagon master.

Ginny introduced Jason to the wagon master and his wife and their two daughters—one of whom was in the advanced stages of pregnancy without a husband in sight. "And of course you have already had the pleasure of meeting Mrs. Carson," she added.

"Yes ma'am, we've met."

He made sure to keep his focus on her until she was the one who looked away. She made polite conversation with Ginny as the meal was served by two enlisted men. He did the same with the wagon master's wife and daughters, laughing—perhaps a little too loud—at their tales of life on the trail, answering their questions about what they might expect for the rest of their journey, and in turn entertaining them with details of life in the fort.

"It must get terribly lonely for you, Mrs. Hastings," the wagon master's wife said.

Ginny shrugged. "One can be lonely in a crowded city as well." She glanced at Emma Carson.

"How is your son?" The way the wagon master's wife delivered the words reeked of disapproval—of the boy and his mother.

Jason felt an unexpected urge to come to Ben's defense. "It's not that unusual for a boy—or even a girl—to try what young Ben did," he said, addressing the wagon master and his wife. "Young people like that can feel as if decisions are being made for them, and sometimes they rebel." He became aware that Ben's mother was staring at him intently. "I speak from experience," he added.

Soon the others were plying him with questions about his own youth, how he had run away to join the army, how he had been fortunate enough to come under the command of Major—then Captain—Hastings, and eventually Ginny.

"Yes, Jason has been like a son to us," Ginny said, smiling fondly at him.

This led to a question of whether or not the Hastings had children of their own. They did not, but Ginny quickly steered the conversation to the wagon master and his family.

Jason was aware of Emma Carson quietly eating her supper, smiling or nodding now and then but taking no active part in the conversation. He did not miss the fact that her polite smile never seemed to reach her eyes, and he wondered what she would look like if she laughed—a true laugh. The sadness in her eyes seemed to have rooted there like some pesky weed in the garden. Its tendrils had found their way deep into the soil of her very being, twisting themselves around until removing them would take hours—and patience. He suddenly felt quite sympathetic toward her. He might not agree with her decision to leave everything and everyone that she and Ben had known behind to strike out for what surely had to be a vast unknown, but at the same time he could not help but admire her spunk and courage in doing so.

"Jason?"

He realized that Ginny had asked a question, and tore his eyes away from Emma Carson. "Sorry," he murmured and saw by the look on Ginny's face that he had just given her all the ammunition she needed to continue her mission to get him and Emma Carson together.

Chapter 3

After supper the wagon master—who had also acted as their spiritual leader on the journey—invited the Hastings, the officers who had dined with them, and any enlisted man not on guard duty to join him and the emigrants for evening vespers. Emma wrapped her arms around Ben's back and shoulders as they stood around a campfire, listening to the reading of scripture followed by the sharing of thanks and blessings and finally a benediction and prayer for their safe arrival at their destination.

"The space is small, but there's room in the bedroom I'm in at the major's house for you, Ben. We could make you a pallet on the floor." Ever since the encounter with the captain in the jail, Emma had had the oddest sense that she might be losing her son. The news that Jason Campbell had also once run away had not calmed her fears in the least. She had seen how Ben hung on every word that Ginny's husband and his aide said during dinner, his eyes shining, his expression so eager to hear more. Far from rescuing her child, she feared that the captain had only led him further afield.

"I promised, Ma. It's part of the deal me and Captain Campbell made, and before supper when I was out in the compound and wearing these soldier clothes, you shoulda seen how the boys from the wagon train were all of a sudden wanting to talk to me. And when I told them that while we're here I'll be working for the captain, they couldn't believe it—wouldn't believe it until Captain Campbell called out to me and told me to get back to work. Then they believed me, and boy were they impressed."

Ben's enthusiasm did nothing to ease Emma's fears. "Ben, it's important that you not get too—"

"Ma, I know we'll be leaving in a few days, but please let me do this for now. I promise I won't give you no more trouble."

"Any more trouble," she corrected him and smiled as she ruffled his hair. "I expect I may have to remind you of this promise in the days to come, but all right. I guess it won't hurt, but no guns, understood?"

"But you said hunting would be—"

"I changed my mind. There will be time enough for you to learn such skills once we are settled."

"But—"

Just then Captain Campbell came alongside Emma. "A good soldier follows orders, Ben, no matter whether or not he agrees. Now it's past curfew, so time for bed." He motioned toward the quarters where he and the other single officers slept. "Mrs. Carson, I wonder if we might have a word?"

Ben glanced from the captain to his mother and, with a heavy sigh, trudged away.

Emma was far too aware of the fact that she and the captain were now alone with the exception of the soldiers in the towers keeping watch. "I should be going in," she said.

"I wanted to apologize," he said at the same moment.

"There's really no need."

"Yes, ma'am, there is. I might have overstepped in my dealings with your son. I should have consulted you before making that bargain with him. The truth is I only wanted to scare him just enough so that once you left here he would think twice before trying anything so stupid again."

"Perhaps I am partly to blame. I was so frightened by him just taking off like that, and then when I heard that he was being held in a jail cell. . ."

Jason chuckled. "He was not all that happy with that part of his rescue, either—I can tell you that. How long since his pa died?" The question came out of nowhere, and he heard her sudden intake of breath. *Way to mess up a fragile truce, Campbell.*

"Ben was five when his father died."

"He was ill?"

"He was shot. He challenged another man to a duel. He lost. Good night, Captain."

Well that explained a lot about why she didn't want Ben anywhere near guns.

—⁓—

Lying awake long after the house had gone still, Emma thought about what the wagon master and Major Hastings had been discussing when she went back to the house after her conversation with the captain.

"Of course, the worst of the trip is still ahead of us," she heard the wagon master say. She paused by the stairs, openly eavesdropping on the conversation. "There's the mountains we have to get over, and that won't be easy. We're already behind schedule."

"Still, if you leave on the fifth, you should be at Fort Bridger within a week—two at the most."

"I don't know, Major. Some of those wagons out there aren't in the best shape now, and once we hit dry air, you know how it goes—wagon wheels can shrink and might even fall off altogether."

"I'll have my men do a thorough job checking each wagon and making sure it's in the best possible shape for your journey."

Emma heard the rustling of the men rising from their chairs and making their way to the front hall, and she scurried up the stairs to her room.

Now she lay awake going over the conversation. She had thought the trip grueling already. How much harder could it get? But she had seen the mountains, and even from a distance, they seemed forbidding. The truth was that she did not fully trust the wagon master. He was a good man, but there had been times when she—and others—had questioned just how much he really knew about leading them to their destination. They had lost valuable time when he had hesitated in his decision of where to cross the Platte River, and rumor had it that it was not all that unusual for there to be snow in those mountains in the middle of summer. In any case, the higher altitudes would pose problems when it came to finding grazing pasture for the animals.

And then there was Ben. He was clearly becoming infatuated with life here in the fort. When they had to leave in a few days and he was once again faced with the tedium of life on the trail, would he try to run away again?

But the thoughts that kept her awake until the first streaks of dawn lightened the room had nothing to do with the dangers of the journey or her fears for her son. What kept her awake was the feeling she'd had the minute she entered Ginny Hastings's kitchen and felt herself enveloped in all the trappings of home. She had been taken back to the early days of her marriage when she and her husband, Max, had shared a lovely little cottage on the edge of town and supported themselves running a general mercantile. Ben had spent his first five years playing in that store while his parents worked. There he had first crawled and then walked and spoken, read and written his first words.

If only. . .

That had been her plea for years now. If only Max had not doubted her love for him. If only he had known that he was as worthy as any man of her devotion. If only he hadn't been so jealous of any man who dared to joke with Emma or compliment her. If only Willie James hadn't enjoyed sparking that jealousy until one day the two men came to a decision of no return—a duel. Max had shot first and missed. Willie's bullet found its deadly mark, and suddenly the life that Emma had lived for five happy years was over. She had struggled on alone, but between running the store and raising Ben, she had always seemed to be neglecting one or the other. Then a year earlier she had been cleaning out Max's desk and discovered a stack of letters tied with the twine they used to wrap packages at the store. Reading those letters from a woman she did not know, she had learned that her happy life had been a lie. Max had loved this other woman—someone from his boyhood—and kept up a correspondence with her for all of the years he and Emma were married.

Unable to face the familiar pieces of a life she had thought perfect, she had sold the cottage and the business and paid far too much to be outfitted for the trip west. She knew Ben didn't understand. And the truth of the matter was that neither did she. Once she and Ben reached Oregon, she had no earthly idea what they would do—where they would live or how.

She heard voices outside and threw back the covers as she sat on the side of the bed and looked out the small open window. Captain Campbell was saddling his horse, and to her surprise, Ben—who she had to roust out of bed every morning—was standing next to him, fully dressed in the clothing he'd been given the day before and carrying on an animated conversation with the captain.

Emma strained to hear their words—Ben's high-pitched and pleading and the captain's a low calm bass.

"But I could help you," Ben said.

"Not this time, kid. Too dangerous. Besides I need you here to take charge of the stables since Buster will be going with me." Emma saw an enlisted man already mounted and waiting patiently for the captain's orders. The soldier grinned at Ben.

"All right. . .sir."

The captain smiled and gave Ben a sharp salute before mounting his horse. "We'll be back by supper." His words seemed to hang in the air as he and the soldier rode away from the fort.

For the rest of the day Emma heard those words—*back by supper*—and as the day wore on and she busied herself washing clothes and conferring with the blacksmith about the state of their wagon, she found herself watching the entrance of the fort. Around four o'clock, she went to the stables in search of Ben. He had not come to the major's house for lunch, but then neither had the major or any of his men.

"There's been some trouble," Ginny had told her and the other women. "The colonel sent one of the men back for some tools, and he reported that another wagon train had encountered problems trying to cross the river. It happens more often than you might think. An axle breaks or one of the oxen loses its footing and pulls the wagon over altogether. I just hope no one was hurt."

The other women agreed, and the wagon master's wife suggested they hold a moment of silent prayer for the safety of those travelers. Emma bowed her head but realized that her thoughts went immediately to the safety of the captain and the soldier who had left with him that morning. Weren't they likely to be in danger, as well? And as she crossed the compound to the stables, she could not resist scanning the horizon for any sign of a dust cloud that might indicate horses coming her way.

Ben wasn't in the stables. He had obviously worked hard, for everything was pristine—stalls cleared of manure and restocked with fresh hay for the horses, the tack hung on hooks, the two horses occupying the stables brushed to a high sheen. She heard Ben's laughter and followed the sound, stepping through a narrow doorway in the fort's thick wall to the area where the teepees were set up and dozens of native women and children were going about their day—the women preparing an evening meal while the children played.

She saw a boy about Ben's age dressed in buckskin pants and wearing no shirt. His long, sleek black hair was held back from his face with a string of leather. He was showing Ben how to use a bow and arrow.

"Ben!" It came out sharper than she had intended, and she saw the arrow fall to the ground as Ben startled and released the bow string. As he turned to face her, she saw the expression he had worn for the entire journey until they reached the fort. He was scowling at her, and his lips were pressed into a thin line of resistance.

"You said no guns, Ma. You didn't say nothing about bows and arrows."

"Anything," she corrected as she reached them. "Hello, I am Ben's mother, and you are?"

"Flying Hawk," the native boy said proudly.

"Well, Mr. Hawk, my son and I have an agreement about his use of weapons, and—"

"Ma. . ." Ben moaned. "It's Flying Hawk—that's his name like my name is Ben, and I let him help me work with the horses so he's teaching me how to shoot an arrow."

"You let him?" Emma had trouble hiding her smile. Somehow Ben had connived to get this boy to share the work that he'd been left to do. "Did the captain give you permission to take extra help?"

"He won't mind none. He and Flying Hawk's pa are friends. That's how we met. It was. . ." He turned to the other boy. "Could I just call you Hawk?"

The boy shrugged.

"Hawk's pa was the one who came to tell the captain about the wagon train breaking down trying to cross the river."

"I see." It did not escape her notice that Ben had avoided the question. "Still, this is a dangerous weapon, and. . ."

"It is our way of gathering meat for our meals," the boy interrupted. "Ben wanted to shoot a rabbit for your supper."

"Do you fish, Flying Hawk?"

An expression of disdain passed quickly over the boy's features, but he smiled up at her. "Yes."

"Then perhaps you could take Ben fishing for our supper?"

"The river is high and rapid in this season. Shooting a rabbit is far easier."

"Fishing is safer," she replied and heard Ben's sigh of pure mortification.

Flying Hawk studied her for a long moment, and she did not allow herself to look away. It was a match of strong wills, but she believed—based on what she had heard about tribal cultures—that she would win because she was the elder. Suddenly the boy grinned.

"We will fish," he said. "Wait here." He ran off toward a teepee several yards away and emerged with a long spear.

"What is that?"

"It is how we fish," Flying Hawk replied as he pretended to study the ground as if it were a river then suddenly thrust the spear into the dirt.

Visions of her only child accidentally impaled by the vicious-looking weapon nearly overwhelmed Emma.

"If I were you, ma'am," she heard Jason Campbell say softly, "I would choose the bow and arrow."

She wheeled around both surprised and inordinately happy to see him. "You're back," she said softly.

"Yes, ma'am. That's the way of it. We go out on patrol, and hopefully we come back."

The boys forgotten, she looked at him for a long moment, taking stock to be sure that he was not injured. His shirt and especially his hat showed signs of dampness, his boots were coated in mud, but otherwise he looked fine—better than fine.

"I'm glad," she said.

He was the first to look away. "Put that spear away, Flying Hawk, before your father gets back. You know you aren't supposed to have that unless your pa is with you." Flying Hawk grinned sheepishly and left to return the spear to the teepee. The captain held out his hand for the bow and arrow Ben was holding. "You want to learn to shoot something?"

"You told Ma that I should learn about hunting and stuff. We was just gonna get a rabbit for supper."

"Our bargain was that I would teach you."

Emma cleared her throat since they both seemed to have forgotten she was still there. "Our bargain, Captain, was that there would be no more talk of weapons while we are here." She looked from Ben to the captain and saw in both faces that they thought she was being far too strict. "On the other hand," she added choosing her words with care, "if a certain young man were to go an entire day without mangling the English language—a language he knows perfectly well how to speak properly—I might—*might*—be inclined to reconsider."

The smile that lit Ben's face, as well as the captain's look of surprised pleasure, was worth any price. "Of course," she continued, "I would need to have proof, Ben—someone we could both trust to be with you and report any infraction."

"I think I might just be up to that assignment, ma'am," the captain volunteered. "That is if we limit the time to from now until dawn tomorrow."

Ben rocked from one foot to the other, his eyes filled with hope. "Is it a bargain, Ma?"

For an answer Emma offered the captain her handshake. He hesitated for a moment, and then instead of accepting the gesture, he gave her the same sharp salute she had seen him give Ben earlier that morning.

Jason could not say why he had substituted the salute for the handshake. He tried to tell himself it was just ingrained in him, but that was a lie. The truth of the matter was that something about touching Emma Carson in any way told him he wouldn't be able to stop. Never in all his days had a woman affected him the way she had. He'd barely slept the night before, and the whole time he was rescuing the travelers in the wagon train that was even now limping its way toward the fort, all he could think about was what if this had been Emma's wagon? What if Emma had gotten caught in the swift current and swept downstream?

Such thoughts were pure nonsense. In two days her train would leave, and he'd never see her or the boy again. And what was he thinking anyway? There had been plenty of pretty available women that had passed through this fort—and his life. He had danced with them and even kissed a couple. But once they'd moved on, he'd barely thought of them again. Meeting Emma Carson had been like getting struck by lightning, and the worst part of it was that he couldn't talk to anybody about it. If he said anything to one of his fellow officers, word was bound to get back to Ginny Hastings, and she would no doubt move mountains to make it all work out.

He stopped dead in his tracks.

Would that be such a bad idea? After all, if anybody would tell him the truth, it was Ginny. The woman was more of a mother to him than his own mother had been. What if he admitted that he felt something more than the usual passing fancy when it came to Emma? Ginny would either tell him to hold his horses—that he was moving too fast—or she would see the rightness of a match between them and help him make that happen. Ginny Hastings talked big when it came to the subject of finding him a wife. Well, maybe it was time to see what she could do in the forty-eight hours left before Emma and Ben moved on. The way Jason saw it, he won either way. If Ginny pulled off a match, it would be with a woman of his choosing, and if she didn't? Well, he doubted she would try matchmaking—at least for him—ever again.

Chapter 4

Ginny could hardly believe what she was hearing. "You want her to stay?"

Jason nodded. "The boy, too, of course. He's a good kid. I see a lot of myself in him, and he seems to have come around to liking me some."

"And your plan is to convince her in the next two days?"

"With your help."

"Well then, we'd best get busy. This is not going to be easy. The two of you just met, and we have no idea if her late husband is still someone she grieves deeply for, even after all these years."

"Yes, ma'am." He hadn't thought of that.

"Do you have any idea at all what her feelings for you might be?"

"No, ma'am." He was an idiot thinking this had any chance of working out.

"Well, fortunately I do," Ginny said. "Any woman who spends most of her day finding chores she can do with one eye on the gate you'd have to come riding in through must be feeling something more than idle curiosity."

"You're saying that Mrs. Carson—Emma—was keeping watch?"

"Like a ship captain's wife walking her widow's walk back in Nantucket where I came from before I married the major. So we have established that there is a mutual attraction. The thing we have not established is how to keep her here. She's a proud woman used to making her own way and too proud to accept charity from me and the major once those wagons pull out of here."

The more Ginny talked, the more Jason was certain that there was no way this could ever work out. "Look, forget I said—"

"Hush. I need to think."

They were sitting outside the bachelor officers' quarters. Ginny had come over to appropriate various items from their kitchen that she needed for the Independence Day party. She stood at the top of the veranda steps and surveyed the fort. Then she smiled. "I believe I have an answer."

Jason was afraid to acknowledge the hope that suddenly filled his chest. "Really? What can I do?"

"You can concentrate on spending as much time as possible with Emma and her son and leave the rest to me." And without another word she walked down the stairs and straight to the trading post run by the same man that had managed it before the government bought the property and turned it into a military outpost.

—∽—

"Ezra Watkins," Ginny called out as soon as she had cleared the door of the crowded store.

"Right here, Miz Hastings. What can I do for you today?"

"Oh, Ezra, it is not what you can do for me but rather what I have come to do for you."

The shopkeeper eyed her warily. "Now, Miz Hastings, that sounds a might suspicious. My prices are firm. You know that."

"Yes, everyone knows that, Ezra. And we also know that you raise those prices at will if you spot some poor immigrant in desperate need of something you have to sell. So let's get down to business. Do you still wish to leave here and join your sons in California?"

"Well now, those boys could use my help, that's certain, but I'm not seeing how that's. . ."

"What if I told you I might have a buyer for this place?" She swept her hand around the store, filled with merchandise and decades of dust. "It would be strictly a barter deal."

Ezra squinted at her. "I don't get your meaning, ma'am."

"A barter—your business in exchange for something other than cash." Ginny realized that Ezra would never agree to the barter she was about to suggest. There would have to be cash. She wondered how much money Jason had managed to put aside from his pay. "Only in this case," she amended, "it would be in exchange for goods plus cash."

"I'm listening."

She was moving too fast. She had no idea if Emma would even consider staying, much less staying to take over the trading post. Of course, she had skills in that area. She'd told Ginny all about how she and her husband had run a mercantile back in Iowa. From the way her expression had softened at the memory, Ginny was sure that Emma had enjoyed her work. "I can't say more just now. But if you are truly interested in selling out and going, then I will get back to you."

"I can't say you haven't got my attention, Miz Hastings. The answer is yes. I am interested in hearing more." He sounded almost gallant but spoiled the moment by spitting tobacco in the general direction of a half-filled spittoon and missing.

—⁓—

Emma was mystified by Ginny's behavior the next morning. As she and the other women helped the major's wife prepare for Friday's Independence Day party, Ginny's focus seemed to be on her.

"Do you ever miss running your own business, Emma?"

"Sometimes. It was not just the exchange of goods and money and the life that afforded us. It was the socializing. I liked seeing people and hearing their news. I liked being in touch."

"Are you thinking of opening another business once you reach—where are you headed again?"

"Oregon, and no, I used what money I have to make this journey. I'll have to find work once Ben and I get settled."

Ginny was quiet for so long that Emma thought the conversation was over. Then she asked, "I don't suppose you'd think of staying here."

"Here?"

"In Fort Laramie."

Surely Ginny was teasing her. "You mean because Ben seems to like it? It's just the excitement of being with the soldiers and the natives. He's seeing that perhaps moving west might not be so bad after all."

"He sure has settled in. Seems downright happy compared to how he was when Jason first brought him to the fort."

Emma laughed. "Well, the captain placed him in jail, so that might explain why he was a little upset."

"Oh that boy was more than a little upset, Emma. He was lashing out at anybody who came within two feet of him, even though Jason had a hold of him. At least until your boy bit him."

"He did not."

"I'm afraid he did. Broke skin and drew blood."

"But the captain never mentioned that. Surely he knows that I would have punished Ben."

Ginny shrugged. "Jason has a soft spot for that boy. I think your Ben reminds Jason of the boy he was at that age. Took the army to straighten him out, and look at the man he is today. If you and Ben were to stay here. . ."

"Ginny, we're headed for Oregon."

"You might want to think on what you expect to find once you get there, Emma." She picked up a pile of red, white, and blue fabric. "I've got to get this bunting over to the Bedlam so the men can get it hung."

Emma continued preparing crusts for the pies she and the other women would make later, but Ginny's strange conversation had found its mark. And the fact that Ben had actually wounded the captain? Well, that called for an apology—from Ben and from her. She finished rolling out the last crust, fit it to the pie pan, and covered it with a tea towel before setting it on the counter with the dozen other crusts she'd made that day.

Outside she spotted Ben talking to Flying Hawk. The two of them were grooming the captain's horse. "Ben, come here, please."

Both boys looked her way. Apparently her tone had given her away, for Ben walked slowly toward her, his head down. He was still holding the grooming brush. "Yes, ma'am."

"When Captain Campbell brought you here, is it true that you bit him?"

"Yes ma'am, but—"

"Did you apologize?"

"No ma'am, but—"

"And where is the captain now?"

Ben jerked his head toward the unmarried officers' quarters where Emma saw the captain talking to Ginny. "Come along then. You need to apologize."

———

For knowing Emma Carson less than two days, Jason was astounded at how he seemed to know instinctively when she was around. He had his back to the major's house, yet he somehow knew she was coming his way. Maybe it was Ginny's smile that gave him the clue. Whatever it was, he could not resist turning to watch her. She had Ben by the arm and was marching the boy his way. "Captain Campbell, Ben has something he needs to say to you if now would be convenient."

"Any time is convenient, ma'am."

She nudged Ben forward, but her eyes seemed fixated on his forearm, exposed because he had rolled back his sleeves to help install the bunting. He realized she was looking at the bandage that the surgeon had applied a couple of days earlier. Instinctively he started to roll down the shirtsleeve.

"Sorry I hurt your arm," Ben muttered. He obviously was offering the apology under duress.

"And I apologize as well, Captain," Emma added, stepping forward and lightly touching his arm to stop him from hiding the bandage. "This looks serious, yet you said nothing even when I berated you so."

His mind went blank, and all he seemed capable of was feeling the rush of warmth that came from her fingers on his arm. "That's all right," he managed.

"It most certainly is not," Emma declared, breaking contact to once again push Ben forward. "And that is not much of an apology, young man."

"Does it hurt much?" Ben asked. He too was now staring at the bandage. "I mean, I guess I didn't realize. . . ."

"You were scared," Jason said. "And no, it's no more than a scratch. I don't know why the surgeon insisted on such a serious-looking bandage."

"Still it was wrong of me to hurt you, Captain." He thrust out his hand. "No hard feelings?"

Jason gave him a sharp salute. "We're square, soldier." Then he turned to Emma. "As for you, Mrs. Carson, I'm remembering now that I hadn't had a tongue-lashing like the one you gave me since the last time Ginny here got upset with me. I expect I might just have to exact a higher penalty from you."

He liked the way the color rushed to her cheeks and her eyes went wide with surprise. If she'd agree to stay he was determined to make sure her life was full of surprises—good ones.

"But. . . ," she sputtered, looking to Ginny for support.

"I was thinking you might save me a dance at tomorrow's festivities."

"Oh, you're teasing me, Captain," she said with a half smile and obvious relief.

"No, ma'am. I'm dead serious. Now if you plan on resisting, then we'll just have to change that to two dances."

"Really, Captain Campbell."

"Three, and when it's just us and folks we know, you drop this 'captain' business and call me by my name."

"I. . ."

"Four," Ben crowed, getting into the spirit of things.

"I was about to say that I don't know your given name, and. . ."

"Five," Ben shouted.

"It's Jason, ma'am, and I'm hoping at least while we're dancing—which it appears we might be doing often—you'll agree to let me call you Emma?" Now the rosy color of her cheeks had crept down her neck, and she was the one looking again to Ginny for support. *Say something,* her eyes pleaded.

Ginny took pity on her, cleared her throat, and announced, "Well, no one will be dancing or doing much of anything else if we don't get this bunting hung and the tables set up." She turned to Ben and handed him one end of the striped fabric. "Take hold of this, young man." When Ben did, Ginny picked up a hammer and nail and tacked the fabric to the railing.

"Let me do that," Jason said.

"Well, if you're sure you can hammer a nail—you being wounded and all," Ginny teased.

Ben snorted with laughter, and even Emma was smiling.

"What can I do to help?" she asked.

"Supervise these two. Men are hopeless when it comes to decorating. I have work to do back at the house." She winked at Jason and left.

"I guess you've had some experience with this," Jason said as Emma began gathering the fabric and draping it in swags as he tacked it in place and Ben trailed along feeding the fabric to them off the bolt.

"Because I'm a woman?"

"Not at all. Because Ginny told me you once had your own store—you and your husband."

"Oh. That's true."

"And so I assumed you must have done some decorating for holidays and the like."

"I did."

Jason frowned. Talking to this woman was like finding his way in a blizzard. Maybe it was best to just shut up and be grateful for the fact that Ginny had found a way to put them together at least for now.

"Ma?"

"Yes."

"Once we're done here, can I go see Flying Hawk?"

"You may."

"Can I ask him and his folks to the party?"

"I expect they've already been invited," Emma replied as she stood back to make sure the distance between the swags was even.

"Yeah, but I was thinking if maybe they could sit with us—eat supper with us?"

"They may prefer to—"

"How about you ask if you can sit with them?" Jason interrupted.

Ben rolled the last of the fabric off the bolt. "What's the difference?"

"Well," Emma said before Jason could form an answer, "I think what the captain is saying is that we are the visitors here. This is their home, so they need to invite us not the other way round."

"So I can go now?"

Emma laughed and took the empty cardboard from him. "Yes, but watch your words. Be polite and respectful when you discuss this with Flying Hawk, and if he thinks it's a good idea, then let him take it from there."

"Sounds pretty complicated," Ben said as he ambled away.

Jason stood next to Emma watching as the two boys walked back toward the teepee encampment together. "It is their home," Jason said. "Unfortunately it's not going to be that way much longer."

"Surely we can all live in peace," Emma said.

Jason stared at the horizon, imagining the steady parade of covered wagons that would keep coming. "Not likely, Emma. It might have worked if there had been fewer emigrants, but with the gold fever and the promise of cheap land and a fresh start, I'm afraid there's no stopping the invasion."

She was looking up at him now. "That's how you see it? As an invasion?"

"Invasion. . .conquest. . ." He shrugged.

"Surely there's something we can do for the natives."

"Not your problem, is it? I mean in a couple of days you'll be back on the trail. Besides, the problem is bigger than anybody can imagine, and it's going to get a lot worse for both sides."

She clenched her fists. "Why do there always have to be sides? Why can't everyone get along the way God intended? I mean, isn't that why God put us here?"

"You can't save the world, Emma."

"Maybe not. But we have to try."

The next words that came out of his mouth shocked them both. "Did you try with your husband?"

Chapter 5

For a moment Emma felt as if she couldn't breathe. How dare he? "You did not know my husband or me," she challenged.

"I know he was shot in a duel. Was it over you? Is that why you've punished yourself all these years?"

They were questions she had framed in the middle of many lonely nights but refused to face in the light of day, choosing instead to focus all of her attention on Ben. She looked up at Jason. She should be furious at him for opening this door, yet she found that she wanted someone to understand.

"Yes," she answered. "The duel was about me—he thought another man was paying me too much attention. The other man enjoyed aggravating my husband, although his attentions to me were innocent."

"Are you sure?"

"Of course. Why would it be otherwise? We were all good friends. He just went too far, and Max—my husband—issued the challenge, and well, you know men and honor or what they think is their honor at stake—my honor at stake. . . ." Her voice trailed off. She'd never allowed herself to admit that, because to do so would be to admit how furious she had been that Max had decided for her, had refused to listen when she tried to convince him to call off the duel.

"You're just a woman, Emmie," Max had said. "You must leave such matters to me. I know what's best."

But had it been best for him to risk his life over some foolishness? Had it been best for him to get himself killed leaving her to manage alone? Had it been best. . . ?

"Emma?"

She pulled herself free of the memories and looked up at Jason. "Sorry," she murmured. "I should be getting back to help Ginny."

She started to go, but he took hold of her arm. His touch was gentle. She could easily have pulled free and kept walking. But she stayed. "I don't want to talk about my husband or his death anymore," she said.

"All right. Let's talk about Ben." He sat down on the top step as if he had all the time in the world. He looked up at her and patted the place beside him.

She sat. "What about Ben?"

"If you are determined to make a life for the two of you on the frontier, the boy deserves to know how to use a gun."

She felt an involuntary shudder race through her body in spite of the stifling heat of the afternoon sun.

"I could teach him," Jason offered.

Emma searched for an excuse. "The party is tomorrow, and we leave the day after. There's no time."

"Don't go." He spoke the words so softly that she thought perhaps she had misunderstood.

"What?"

"Stay for a few more days—or a week. There'll be another wagon train coming through—probably five or six before it gets too late in the season to make the rest of the journey. You and Ben can join any one of them."

"But I heard Major Hastings and the wagon master talking last night, and the major said we were already late and taking a risk."

"Do you trust this wagon master?"

"He's a good man. A man of strong faith."

"Faith won't be enough to get you the rest of the way, Emma."

"But waiting for another party to come and restock and such before they move on doesn't make sense, either."

Jason stared out at the land beyond the walls of the fort. "No, I guess not." He looked defeated, as if something he'd wanted badly was impossible. Had he come to care for Ben so much in such a short time?

"Ben will be all right," she assured him, although she had no basis for believing that.

"And you, Emma Carson? Will you be all right, as well?"

Was he doubting her as Max had? Was she in fact "only a woman" in his eyes? She bristled. "I've had seven years to learn how to manage on my own, Captain."

To her surprise, he grinned. "Not questioning your ability to take on anything that comes your way, Emma. Just wondering if you'll be happy."

"Why?"

He shrugged and stood up. "Not sure. Seems like it's important that you should be." He picked up the hat he'd left on the newel post at the foot of the steps and put it on. "I've got to check in with the major, if you'll excuse me." He tipped his hat to her and started walking across the compound but turned back. "Don't think for one minute you're off the hook for those dances just because we seem to be getting along so nicely and all. We're up to what—seven?"

"Five," she corrected, but she was laughing, and as he walked away, so was he.

Ginny had asked Emma to go to the trading post for several things she needed for the party. Emma had made her own list of supplies she and Ben would need to replenish for the remainder of their journey. But she was completely unprepared for the prices the store's owner was charging.

"That's twice what I paid for the same thing in Iowa," she said when he started tallying up her bill.

Ezra Watkins grinned, exposing his tobacco-stained teeth. "Well now, missy, you're always welcome to shop someplace else. Of course the next trading post is at Fort Bridger—a week's journey at least—and that old buzzard will charge you more than this, but if that's your pleasure. . ." He started to take back the items she had selected.

"No. I mean, leave the rice and the cornmeal and. . ." She mentally calculated what else she could afford. "And the stick candy. It's my son's birthday next week, and I want to surprise him with something sweet."

She may as well have been talking to the wall for all the interest Mr. Watkins showed. He chewed the nub of the pencil as he added up the total. His nails were black with dirt, and the shop had an odor that she realized came partially from him.

"I'll put the major's goods on account as usual," he said. "You need to pay cash," he growled as if she had tried to cheat him.

"I know." She was fishing for the money when the bell over the door jangled, and Ezra looked up and frowned. "Captain," he muttered.

Jason ignored him and spoke to Emma instead. "Ginny said you might have more than you could carry, so I came over to help."

"You should have sent Ben. I'm sure you have far more important things to do than carry groceries for me."

Ezra was watching the two of them, and he let out a snort and then a yelp of protest as Jason reached for the bill and studied it.

"I think you might have made a mistake here, Ezra. Seems to me a pound of rice was half this just two days ago."

Ezra shrugged. "Prices keep going up. Nothing I can do about that. I got bills to pay same as the next fella."

"Just as long as you're charging everybody the same. You are, aren't you? I mean, I was speaking with Moon Hunter's wife the other day, and she said—"

"That squaw's got no business running her mouth. I give them the same service as anybody else. You and the major seen to that."

"Yes, we did. And the definition of 'same service' includes same prices."

Ezra grabbed the sales ticket from Jason. "Let me see that." He studied it for a long moment and then laughed. "Oh I see my mistake now. I was reading my own figures wrong. This here looks like a seven when it ought to be a one, and—"

"Just settle up with the lady, Ezra, and we'll be on our way."

"That man is a cheat." Emma was still upset knowing that if Jason had not come along she would have paid the inflated price for her order.

Jason chuckled. "Yes, ma'am, he is. We do our best to keep him in line, but he gets away with more than he should."

"Taking advantage of people who he knows are struggling and need to watch every penny. How can he do that?"

"What he tried with you is nothing compared to what he pulls with the natives. He trades with them. Used to be this was a trading post for animal pelts and furs. Ezra has kept that idea going when it comes to dealing with them."

"Who is Moon Hunter?"

"Flying Hawk's father. Once the government took over the post, he organized a council of elders to meet with Major Hastings. That's when things changed for Ezra, and he has not been happy since. He keeps threatening to leave, but so far it hasn't happened."

"Well, it is no way to run a proper business," Emma grumbled.

They had reached the back door to the major's house. She held the screen door open for Jason to enter with the packages, which he deposited on the kitchen table. The house was quiet—empty.

"If you ran that store, what would you change, Emma?" he asked.

It was a preposterous question, so she answered him with a laugh. "Well, the first thing I would do is drag everything off those shelves and out of that building and give the place a thorough cleaning. If he would just wash the windows, there would be so much more light in the place and his customers could actually see what they were buying."

"I think that's exactly why he doesn't wash the windows. He doesn't want people looking too close." He leaned against the kitchen table and studied her. "What else?"

"This is a ridiculous conversation, Captain."

"I thought we agreed on Jason when we're. . .at times like this."

And suddenly she was aware that they were alone and that the way he was looking at her—and she was looking at him—surely was not proper. She turned away and busied herself opening the packages and putting things away. "Well, Jason, thank you for looking out for me—and the others who may not be able to bargain effectively with Mr. Watkins. Perhaps one day he will make good on his threat to leave and you'll have someone running the trading post who—"

"You could be that someone, Emma."

"Oh, sure. I could just pull out whatever exorbitant price Mr. Watkins asks and hand it over," she protested, glancing back at him over her shoulder, certain that he must be teasing her. But his expression was serious.

"What if you didn't need to pay out any money?"

"Oh, he would just give me the store?"

"No. There might be another way. And if it could happen, Emma, would you consider staying? I mean you and Ben?"

"Jason, this is a frivolous discussion, and I have work to do. I would imagine you have duties that need your attention, as well?"

He smiled and pushed himself away from the table, but as he did, he took hold of her hand. "Promise you'll give the idea some thought. If things don't work out, you and Ben can move on come next summer."

He raised her hand to his lips and kissed her knuckles then brushed a strand of her hair away from her face. "Seven dances, right?"

His teasing brought her to her senses, and she moved away from him. "Five," she replied firmly.

He was laughing as he left the house.

Meanwhile Emma was shaking with a rush of emotions she had not felt in years. A rush of emotions she had never expected to feel again.

———

That evening Jason made an excuse not to have supper at the major's. Emma needed time to figure out Ben and her future, and he didn't want her to think he was pressuring her. After all, even if she stayed, things might not work out. It was important that she see some way that she could go on to Oregon if she decided that was what was best. But the more he thought about it, the more sense it made to him that they should at least try. As he'd told her, she could always go on to Oregon later. The truth was that he was worried about the wagon master's ability to get them through the worst of the trip before the weather changed and trapped them. The scout, Randy Miller, was the best in the business, but he could only offer his advice based on experience, and he'd already told Jason about a couple of situations where the wagon master overruled him and everyone paid a price. The idea of any settler who had made it this far being endangered because of their leader's inexperience or foolhardiness was unacceptable. The idea that Emma and Ben might pay that price was unthinkable.

"Campbell!"

Jason looked back as he strode across the compound on his way to speak with the soldiers on guard duty and saw Ezra sitting outside the trading post. He had reared the wooden chair back on its two hind legs and was glaring at Jason.

Jason walked toward the man, and as he did Ezra spit a long stream of tobacco that landed just in front of Jason. "You want something, Ezra?"

"That's a pretty little thing you got your eye on, Captain. Be a real shame if something was to happen to her—or that boy of hers."

"Do not threaten me, Ezra."

The shopkeeper rocked the chair forward and stood up. "Why I ain't threatening you, Captain. No, sir. That would be downright foolish. But you know how it is out here. All sorts of dangers—snakes, Injuns, accidents."

Jason took another step forward. His fists were clenched.

Ezra held up his hands as if preparing to protect himself. The man was a bully and a coward. "Just passing the time of day, Captain. No need for you to get yourself all worked up now." He spit again and went back into the dungeon that he called a store.

"The only snake I worry about is you," Jason muttered as he once again headed off to check with the guards.

—⁂—

If it wasn't enough that Jason had planted the ludicrous idea that she and Ben might actually make a home in the fort, running the trading post, Ginny had apparently joined the campaign.

"There's nothing for us here," Emma protested as she helped Ginny peel potatoes for the salad.

"And what is there in Oregon or wherever it is you're headed? Do you even know for certain where you will end up? Is there a town, a job, people you know?"

"I know the people on the wagon train," Emma protested.

"Those folks will scatter to the four winds once you reach Oregon, Emma."

"Ben has—"

"Do not tell me Ben has friends on the train. He has some boys who taunted him mercilessly until Jason took him in hand and gave him some status."

"Well, he has no one here."

"He has Flying Hawk. From what I've observed, the two of them have become pretty tight. Would be a real shame to separate them. I mean, wasn't that part of the problem you had taking him out of Iowa?"

"It's not the same."

"It is exactly the same. He might have had several good friends there, and it's true that he's only made one here—in just two days I might add. But do not fool yourself. It is the same."

"But. . ."

"And then there's you. Do not think I haven't heard the talk. The women on the train don't like you because they're afraid of you."

"Why on earth. . ."

"Have you looked in a mirror lately, Emma Carson? You are one of the most beautiful women ever to travel west. It doubles their jealousy that the hardships of the trip don't seem to dampen that beauty even one little bit. They worry about their men seeing you and you seeing them and—"

"I can hardly be blamed for—"

"No one is blaming you. Well, maybe they are, but as long as you don't have a husband, they are going to keep their distance."

"I should marry so the other women aren't jealous?"

Ginny sighed. "I did not say that. You should marry for love and nothing else. Life is too hard and too short to go any other way."

The two women worked in silence for several minutes. Then Ginny wiped her hands on her apron and patted Emma's forearm. "Don't mind me, Emma. The major will tell you that I never saw somebody else's business but that I wanted to get in the middle of it. The truth is I like you, and it seems to me you've been carrying this load of providing for Ben and trying to find your way long enough. Wouldn't it be nice to have somebody to help you with the totin'?"

Emma thought of Jason carrying the supplies back to the house for her earlier that day. She closed her eyes as tears welled, and she thought of the warmth of his lips touching her knuckles. It had been so long. . . .

"I've been here barely two days, Ginny, and you've done so much to make it feel like home, but it's just a resting place. We both know that." She laughed and touched Ginny's wrinkled cheek. "Besides, if you go adopting every lonely widow coming through here, what would the major say?"

"He would throw up his hands, but he wouldn't turn one of them away no more than he's turned away that tribe of natives camped outside the fort. He was given an assignment to keep the peace, Emma. Natives and settlers are going to have to find a way to live together because those wagon trains are going to keep coming. If you stayed here, you could be a part of figuring that out. Besides, what's your hurry? It's not as if you've got friends or family waiting for you out there." She scraped the last of the onions into the bowl of potatoes and added, "And don't be thinking this is only about you. The other officers' wives and I get awful lonely between wagon trains, and pretty soon they'll stop coming until next year. It would be mighty nice to have another woman."

"I'll think about it, I promise. But Ginny. . ."

Ginny grinned. "Stop right there. No *but*s until you've thought this through."

Outside they heard the laughter of the other women who lived permanently in the fort, and soon the kitchen was filled with chatter and the sounds and smells of a feast in the making. Emma couldn't deny that she felt more like a neighbor with these women than she had with any of the women she'd met on the trail. And she couldn't deny that the comments she'd overheard about the qualifications of their wagon master and the travails they might face on the journey to come were disturbing. Ben seemed happier and more content here than he had in months. But still. . .

Chapter 6

The celebration started bright and early with a review of the fort's troops decked out in full uniform as the flag was raised at first light. Major Hastings invited the wagon master to lead those gathered in prayer, and then he gave a short speech. The day was already almost unbearably hot, and everyone was relieved that the major had obviously heeded his wife's admonition to keep his comments brief.

Emma spent the rest of the morning making the arrangements necessary for Ben and her to continue their journey. She carefully folded their freshly washed clothing and bedding as she packed the wagon, adding the supplies she'd bought from Ezra's store along with several items Ginny had insisted she no longer needed and distributed among the women on the train. Emma had been glad not to be singled out by Ginny's generosity.

Ben had been helpful if glum. It was clear that he dreaded leaving the fort and the new friend he had found in Flying Hawk. But he seemed to accept that they would leave. His lack of protest made Emma nervous. He'd been just as quiet and cooperative right before he ran away from the wagon train. She thought about asking Jason to speak with Ben, but perhaps that would only make matters worse. Besides, Jason had been out on patrol for most of the night before—some disturbance at a settlement some miles away. According to Ginny, he and the men who had gone out with him might not make it back in time for the festivities. Emma did not want to consider how disappointed that idea made her. She had been looking forward to dancing with Jason.

The noon meal was the feast of the day and included the troops stationed at the fort, the Indians from the encampment outside, the emigrants traveling west on the wagon train, and even some people—farmers, trappers, so-called mountain men—who had come to the fort for the occasion. After the main meal, there were races and contests of skill. Ben surprised her by insisting she be his partner in the three-legged race.

"I'll slow you down," she protested.

"Come on, Ma. Hawk's mother is doing it."

She looked over and noticed the Indian woman she'd seen only from a distance watching her. The woman smiled, and her eyes seemed to say, "They're only young once. You don't want to miss this." So Emma agreed, and once Ben showed her the trick of it, they hobbled their way to victory. The major awarded them with a ribbon that Ben promptly pinned to his shirt.

The races and contests were followed by music. A small military band made up of a bugle, a drum, and a flute played patriotic songs. Then several braves from the tribe performed an intricate dance while the women stood in a circle drumming and chanting out the rhythm. And finally the trio of soldiers were joined by a banjo player and fiddler, and the dancing began.

But Jason had not returned. Emma could not shake the feeling that he might be hurt or in danger. It was similar to the feeling she'd had the day Max went off to duel with Willy. She had prayed that day for their safe return—that they would realize their friendship was too precious to throw away. She had imagined them shaking hands and then wrapping their arms around each other's shoulders and laughing as they returned home. But none of that had happened.

Now she could not seem to shake the feeling that Jason needed help. The longer the festivities went on with no sign of him, the more anxious she became. Suddenly the lively gathering of people seemed oppressive, and she could only think of her need for somewhere quiet—somewhere she could pray. Making sure that Ben was happily occupied with Hawk, she slipped away and walked down to the river.

The sun was setting, and the sky was streaked with shades of purple and orange and pink. She eased down to the edge of the water and dipped her hand in the rapidly running river. The water was cool and fresh, and when she saw a fish jump a few feet away, she smiled, remembering how she had suggested that Hawk and Ben go fishing instead of playing with the bow and arrow. How shocked she had been when Hawk ran to his teepee and returned with the spear that his people used for fishing.

She wished there had been time for Jason to take both boys fishing. She wished that there had been time for her to get to know Hawk's parents. She wished that. . .

A soft cry in the underbrush a few yards down the shore from where she sat interrupted her thoughts. She stood up, saw the bushes rustle as if perhaps an animal was there, then heard the cry again followed by the unmistakable sound of a man's angry voice and something that sounded like a crack. She thought about calling out for help, but with all the laughter and music coming from the celebration, no one would hear. So she picked up a large rock from the shore and slowly edged her way toward the sound.

"Who's there?" she said.

Silence. Then a rustling. Ezra Watkins stood up, pulling his suspenders into place as he did so. "Well, look at this," he said, slurring his words. "Two squaws. Must be my lucky day."

Behind him, Emma saw Hawk's mother pulling her deerskin dress back onto her shoulders. Her eyes were wide with fear as she shook her head violently as if to warn Emma. She had a cut on her cheek that was bleeding.

"What are you doing?" Emma demanded of the storekeeper.

He lifted a jug and drank as he kept his eyes on her. "I'm getting paid," he said. He tossed the jug into the brush and started toward her. "Come to think of it, I didn't get the full price of the goods you bought, either. So time to pay up, little lady."

He lunged for her, and Emma dodged, sending the man stumbling into the river. He swore and tried to stand but then was swept under by the rapids. She realized the music had stopped, so she screamed for help as she ran along the shore, keeping sight of a panicked Ezra.

Seemingly from nowhere, Jason was there, pulling off his uniform jacket and his boots and thrashing into the water. He grabbed Ezra by his shirt, but Ezra fought him, pulling them both under the rushing water. Emma saw Ezra climb on top of Jason and force his head underwater.

"No!" she screamed and turned to Hawk's mother who was now standing next to her. The two women held on to each other as they both watched, helpless to do anything except pray.

"Please," Emma prayed. "Oh please, not again." And in that moment she understood that she had feelings for Jason that went beyond what she would have imagined possible for knowing him only a few days.

Just as several other soldiers waded into the river, Jason rose above the current, and his fist found its mark on Ezra's jaw. Ezra fell backward, his head hitting a boulder, and as Jason struggled to regain his footing, Ezra sank beneath the water. Still Jason went after him, fighting exhaustion and the rapids to save the storekeeper. Two of the soldiers that had waded into the water helped Jason back to shore. Two others went to get Ezra's inert body.

"Get him back here," Jason sputtered. "He's going to answer for what he's done here."

"No harm, Captain," Hawk's mother said softly. "He didn't. . . ." She let the words die on her lips and turned to Emma. "Thank you, Ben's mother," she said.

"Too late, Captain," one of the men said as two other soldiers dragged Ezra's limp body onto dry land. "He's gone."

Emma stared at Jason, realizing that this was a side of him she did not yet know. This was the protector, the man of duty who did not see a difference between whites and Indians. This was a man sworn to serve and protect—both sides.

Suddenly the tall, invincible man before her crumpled to the ground.

"Jason," she cried as she knelt next to him.

He smiled weakly. "Tell one of the men to go for the surgeon," he said, his voice a whisper. "I got shot while we were on patrol."

Emma turned to seek help and saw the doctor running toward them. "Durn fool," he growled as he bent over Jason. "Why didn't you come straight to me?"

A soldier hovered nearby. "He was on his way, Doc. But then he heard the ruckus, and he took off like one of those wild horses we seen out on the trail."

Relieved that the doctor had arrived, Emma sat on the ground and cradled Jason's head in her lap as the doctor tore one leg of Jason's trousers. She gasped when she saw the blood.

"It's a scratch," Jason murmured.

"Then how come I'm seeing a hole the size of a nickel?" The doctor reached for his bag and opened it. "If you don't mind, I'll do the doctoring here."

He handed Jason a stick. "Put that between your teeth and bite down," he instructed, and when Jason did as he was told the doctor took a bottle of alcohol from his bag and poured a liberal amount of it on the wound.

Emma stroked Jason's hair as he bit down hard on the stick to get through the burning pain. "Wouldn't it be better if we moved him to your quarters?" she asked.

"Trying to keep him from losing this leg, ma'am."

Jason was looking up at her, and he removed the stick and offered her a weak smile. "Doc tends toward the dramatic, Emma. Pay him no mind."

"Stop your gabbing and bite down on that stick," the doctor ordered as he probed the wound with a long, thin pair of forceps. "Got it," he muttered as he carefully twisted the forceps free of the wound and held them up. At their tip was a bloody bullet. "You're saying you rode all the way back here with this stuck in your leg? Where the devil did those savages get Winchesters?" he asked.

"From Ezra Watkins," the soldier who had stayed to watch said. "He was trading guns for buffalo hides then selling those."

Emma recalled that the one thing she had noticed in the trading post was the high stack of hides and the sign above them: GIT YOUR BUFFALO ROBE NOW OR FER SUR YOU'LL FREEZE AFOR YOU KIN REACH CALLYFORNYA. The price he'd put on the robes was equal to a month's profit when she and Max had owned their store.

"What's going to happen to the trading post now?" one of the settlers who had come for the party demanded.

Major Hastings had arrived leading a party of men carrying a stretcher. "Now folks, let's just all calm down," he said. "We've had some excitement and some tragedy here, but it's all over now. Mrs. Hastings and the other ladies have prepared some mighty fine-looking pies for us, and it would be a shame to see them go to waste."

The children instantly lost interest in the dead body and the wounded captain lying on the banks of the river and took off for the fort, their mothers trailing after them. The men stayed to help get Jason on the stretcher and to wrap Ezra in a blanket before carrying both back up to the fort. As the stretcher was lifted, Jason reached out and took hold of Emma's hand. "Do not think for one minute this means we won't be dancing, Emma Carson. I aim to collect on all five."

Relieved to see him looking so much better and with tears running down her cheeks, she squeezed his hand and said, "I thought it was seven dances you promised me."

Jason laughed, and the sound of it was like music to her ears.

—m—

The following morning, Jason was stiff and sore, but he insisted on getting up. Using a cane the doctor loaned him, he limped outside. Beyond the opening of the fort he could see the emigrants preparing to continue their journey. The wagon master called out the order to move on, and slowly the train of canvas-covered wagons passed by. He was too late. He'd run out of time. He'd thought he would have the whole day of the celebration to convince Emma, but then there had been that skirmish with the renegade braves who thought they could turn back the tide of white people.

Even once he was settled in the surgeon's quarters for the night, he had wanted to talk to her, convince her. Ben had come by to bring him some supper.

"We're going," he'd said. "I heard the wagon master tell Ma to be packed up and ready by sunup."

"Go get your ma. Tell her I need to see her."

"You'll make her see that we should stay?"

"Go get her."

But Ben had returned later to say he couldn't find her and that Miz Hastings had told him to leave her be—that she needed to think.

Jason couldn't fault her. What woman would throw up all her plans on the whim of a man she'd just met? Maybe he should have asked her to marry him. No. That would have scared her off for sure. Besides, what had he been thinking? Jason was not a man who acted rashly.

So now, as the wagons lined up and lumbered away from the fort, he leaned on the cane, willing himself to accept what he was sure he could not change. Even if he could run, would it do any good to try and stop her? He had to respect her decision, respect that she had no doubt put Ben's future ahead of her own happiness. What kind of life was there for them here with him running off to put down frontier skirmishes, with the harsh winters and the unbearably hot summers, and with only a few other women and youngsters for company? No, as much as he hated to admit it, she'd made the right choice.

He turned to hobble back inside and discovered Emma standing not three feet away.

"You didn't go," he said.

"How could I? You owe me those dances."

He held out his arms and nearly lost his balance. She reached for him and helped him to a bench. "Sit down. We've plenty of time for dancing once that leg is healed."

"What happened? Why?"

She shrugged. "I took a long walk last night and talked to some very wise people—Hawk's mother for one. She told me that Flying Hawk had developed a hatred of all white people mostly because he knew of Ezra's harassing her whenever her husband was away. But then Ben came along, and he began to see what she had been trying to teach him all along."

"And who else did you talk with?"

"The major asked me if I might consider staying to run the trading post. With Ezra dead and winter coming, somebody needs to step in until Ezra's sons can be contacted. He said if they didn't make any effort to claim the post, then it would be considered abandoned and taken over by the government."

"Anyone else?"

"The wisest of all. I prayed for a long time."

"And how did you know God had answered?"

She smiled. "I listened."

"I don't understand."

"It's the only way I know. 'Be still, and know. . . .' It works for me. It's how I came to the decision to sell the business and head west. It's how I knew that there was something very special about this place, these people—you."

"You heard all that?"

"Well, some of it I read." She told him of her habit of sitting with her Bible and letting it fall open to God's message for her at any given time.

He saw that she was carrying her Bible, her forefinger marking a page. "And what was the message this time?"

She smiled and opened the Good Book. "It's from the fifty-first chapter of the book of the prophet Isaiah," she said. "The third verse says, 'He will make her wilderness like Eden, and her desert like the garden of the Lord; joy and gladness shall be found therein, thanksgiving, and the voice of melody.' I think it's pretty clear, don't you?"

"You can always move on next season if things don't work out," he said, suddenly afraid of the sheer happiness that filled his heart.

"Now don't you go trying to wriggle out of this, Jason Campbell. Ben and I are fully prepared to give this thing a fair chance, and besides, don't be thinking this is all about you. Ben wants to stay because of Hawk, and I've gotten attached to Ginny, and. . ."

He grinned. Standing before him was the spitfire who had faced off with him that first day at the jail. Standing before him was a woman strong enough to abandon a safe and comfortable, if not happy, life and travel halfway across the country to find something better. Standing before him was a woman he could love—if he didn't already—a woman he could build a life with, a family with.

"Now if you think you can manage to not fall down or get hurt again, I'll go get you some breakfast," Emma said.

"Not sure I knew you could be this bossy," he replied.

"Oh, you knew," she said with a toss of her head. "That's why you couldn't stay away. It must be a long time since you met anyone willing to call your bluff, Captain."

He let her get down the steps and halfway across the yard before calling out to her. "Hey, Emma, here's something for you to be thinking on—how about marrying me?"

All around him, work stopped as his men turned to stare, their mouths hanging open. "Get back to work," he instructed as he hobbled back to the bench, prepared to wait for his breakfast. He grimaced as he straightened his wounded leg, but he couldn't remember a time in his life when he'd been happier.

Chapter 7

Three Years Later

"Wagons!"

Ben raced down the steps that led to the yard from the guard tower and over to the trading post. "Miz Hastings, they're coming, and there's a whole lot of 'em."

His ma and the major's wife stepped outside the door of the store. Ma was holding his baby brother—born just a month before. His little sister was hanging on to her skirts. "I'll go tell the captain," he shouted.

"No need," Jason said as he emerged from the major's office. "The entire fort, not to mention everyone living around this place, can hear you, Son."

Ben grinned. He liked the captain a lot. He could be strict, and he talked a lot about how a man needed to be honest and respectful and such, but he also made Ben feel proud about stuff. Like when Ben had helped Flying Hawk and his family reset their teepee after a storm or like when he'd stood up to a boy of a train passing through the previous summer when that boy tried to pick a fight. Ben hadn't fought. Instead he'd found a way around fighting the way he'd seen Jason do when he was dealing with some of the tribes that still wanted to fight. Truth was, Jason was the only pa Ben could remember. He'd been only five when his real pa died, and those memories were pretty faded.

"Well, young man," Miz Hastings announced, "we've got work to do. You go help those soldiers unhook the wagons and send the women and children over here to the store, all right?"

Ben grinned. This was one of the best parts of welcoming any newly arrived wagon train. Ever since his ma had taken over the trading post, all the women and children were sent there first thing. The women were treated to a length of ribbon for their hair and each kid got a small piece of peppermint to suck on while the wagons were unhitched and camp was set up. It always made Ben smile to see how surprised the women and kids were with the treats.

Of course there would be a party. There was always a party. That was the very best part. There would be music and great food and games and races, and he and his best friend Hawk would square off to see who was the fastest runner. Hawk usually won, but Ben didn't mind.

He stood at the door of the trading post, passing out the candy as the women and children filed in.

"You live here?"

Ben looked up to see a girl about his age staring at him. She had about the bluest eyes and the blondest hair he'd ever seen. Unable to find his voice, he nodded.

"All the time?"

He nodded again.

"Aren't you scared?"

This question shocked his vocal chords into action. "Of what?"

"The Indians?" She glanced nervously over her shoulder, looking at the teepee village.

"They're just folks—same as us," he replied mystified by her obvious fear.

"But they aren't like us. Their skin is darker and their hair is so black and. . ."

Ben frowned. "You and me are different, too. You've got yellow hair, and my hair is red. Your eyes are blue, and mine are green. And as for skin—well, when I first got here my skin was light like yours, but living here with the sun and the wind and all. . ." He pointed to his tanned forearm and shrugged. "Nothing to be afraid of, miss," he said. "At least not when it comes to the folks you'll meet here."

She didn't look convinced, and Ben really wished Jason were around. Jason had a way of explaining stuff that made it seem right and proper. "Tell you what," Ben said, "let me finish handing out this candy, and then I'll take you to meet my friend Flying Hawk."

She hesitated and then grinned. "Okay. Here let me help you with that," and just like that Ben was standing next to the prettiest girl he'd ever seen in his whole life, laughing and talking like they'd known each other forever.

—⁂—

Emma could not have been prouder of Ben. From the day she and Jason had married—Christmas Day, the first winter after she'd decided to stay—he had settled into life in the fort. In addition to Hawk, he had made friends with several of the younger soldiers—many of them little more than boys themselves—and he had accepted Jason as his father with an ease that made her wonder if all along he hadn't been missing that male influence in his life.

She, too, had settled into the daily routine of Fort Laramie. Almost as soon as the wagon train she and Ben had been traveling with had left the fort, she set to work cleaning and reorganizing the trading post. With the help of the other women, she had washed and scrubbed, discarded spoiled goods, and set up displays until the trading post had become a popular gathering place for off-duty soldiers as well as the Indians. The post was often filled with laughter or the serious discussion of politics and other news.

And through it all, she and Jason had spent every free minute together, until finally, as they walked along the banks of the river one snowy December morning, he had dusted the dry snow off a rock and led her there. "Sit," he had ordered, and when she had started to protest, he had added, "and listen."

She had folded her hands primly in her lap and waited. He had paced up and down and up and down, wearing a path in the snow. The more he paced, the more she was certain that he was about to admit that her staying had been a mistake—that he wasn't the marrying kind, that he loved the adventure of his life far too much to ever settle down with a wife and family.

Mentally she had been planning her next move. It would be hard, but she would stay on until the first wagon train came through in the spring, and then she and Ben would make the rest of their journey to Oregon. She would—

"Marry me, Emma."

He had asked her only once before, and then she'd known he'd been teasing because they had barely known each other at all. In all the hours they had spent together since then, he had never mentioned the subject again.

She was speechless—certain that she had not heard him correctly, for he was frowning. Actually he was scowling at her.

"Why?"

He threw up his hands and resumed his pacing. "That's your answer?"

"That's your proposal?" she shot back.

"You can't say you haven't been expecting it," he argued.

"Expecting and receiving are two entirely different things, Jason Campbell, and frankly. . ."

He dragged her up from the rock and into his arms. He kissed her with a passion she had never known before. When he was done after what seemed like an hour and at the same time mere seconds, he held her away from him and whispered, "Marry me, Emma Carson, because I love you and because I cannot imagine living one more day without you as my wife and because I want Ben to have brothers and sisters and because without you my life has no meaning." He kissed her again then pulled away and grinned. "How's that for a proposal?"

"Better," she said primly, but then she laughed and she wrapped her arms around him, and this time it was she who kissed him—and did not let go.

Ginny and the other wives arranged everything, and they were married in front of the fireplace in the major's house. Ben walked Emma down the aisle that separated the soldiers from the Indians and the settlers from the trappers who had come to the fort for Ginny's traditional Christmas celebration. They stood together with Jason as Major Hastings performed the ceremony. The reception that followed was a noisy affair, with Jason's fellow officers raising glasses of fruit punch as they made toasts, while the women seemed to disappear.

When she and Jason left the reception and walked to the house she had seen being built the day the wagon train had arrived, Emma understood where the women had gone. Lamps glowed in the windows, and a wreath had been hung on the door.

"Welcome home, Mrs. Campbell," Jason had murmured as he scooped her high in his arms and carried her inside.

"Jason, put me down. Ben. . ."

"Ben is staying the night with the major," he told her. "Listen."

At first all she had heard was the wind howling through the trees, but then she had heard the distinct sounds of a fiddle and a flute. The music floated in through the windows as the musicians stood on the front porch.

Jason held out his arms to her, and she went to him without hesitation. They danced until long after the musicians had slipped away, until the sky grew light with a new dawn—a new life for them both.

State of Matrimony
by Ann Shorey

Chapter 1

St. Joseph, Missouri
April 1858

Diantha Bowers dropped a wet rag next to a bucket of dirty water. After glancing around to be certain she was unobserved, she shifted her weight from her knees to her heels and dug her fingers into the small of her back to massage aching muscles. Fresh water, more lye soap, and she'd have the floor of the Litchfield & Golden Mercantile cleaned to Mr. Golden's satisfaction. She hoped so, anyway. His moods were as unpredictable as the spring rains that turned the streets to mud. Mud that customers tracked over the floors during the day. The same mud she spent her evenings scrubbing.

She tucked an errant lock of black hair behind her ear and headed for the alley to refill her bucket. Although the sun had begun its descent to the west, the street beyond the store remained busy. Echoes from boots clomping by on the boardwalk bounced from the narrow walls between the mercantile and saloon next door.

Craning her neck, she studied the horses hitched to a rail next to the walk. One day, she'd have a horse and buggy of her own. And a house. And a family. But not now. Not while she worked as a scrubwoman. The kind of man she dreamed of marrying would never notice a girl like her.

"Daydreaming again?"

Diantha jumped. For a big man, Mr. Golden moved as silently as a cat. She took several steps back to open a space between them. "You startled me, sir. I apologize. I'll be done in a few minutes."

He leaned against the doorway, one side of his mouth twisted in a frown. "I expect you will, but that's not why I sought you out. There's a matter I need to discuss with you." His frown deepened. "I'd hoped to do it this evening, but my brother hasn't arrived as planned."

Heart hammering, she gaped at him. Surely he wasn't going to dismiss her for taking too long to clean floors. As for him having a sibling, this was the first she'd heard of a brother.

She fought to control the quiver in her voice. "Sir, if not this evening, when do you want to talk to me?"

"Tomorrow, soon as the store closes. If Michael's not here by then, I wash my hands of him." He spoke the last sentence under his breath then glanced up as though surprised to see her still standing there. "Go on about your chores, Diantha. It's time you finished."

"Yes, sir."

He entered his small office and closed the door. As soon as he was out of sight, she dropped to her knees beside the bucket, grabbed the rag, and splashed cleaning solution over the floorboards with quick strokes. Her mind tumbled between worry and prayer. *Lord, You know I need this job. Help my work please You and Mr. Golden.* The man could be a stern taskmaster. If he decided to dismiss her, she'd lose her small salary as well as the room and board he provided at Mrs. Wilkie's.

She scrubbed her way to the rear entrance, telling herself the tears she wiped from her cheeks were due to the eye-stinging odor of lye soap. She'd learned long ago that crying helped nothing.

———

When Diantha entered Mrs. Wilkie's house, her landlady bustled through the cluttered sitting room and met her at the door. "You're just in time. Supper's ready."

"I don't think I could eat a bite, but I'll sit with you to keep you company."

"Not hungry?" Mrs. Wilkie pressed her fingers against her plump cheeks. "Harold Golden works you too hard. I've told him time and again that you don't have a strong constitution. Your parents never dreamed you'd end up—"

"I'm grateful for my job." Diantha shook raindrops from her cloak and hung it on a peg behind the door. "I'm especially grateful to live here with you. If Mr. Golden hadn't known my father, I don't know where I'd be." She swallowed as her brief encounter with her employer filled her mind. "Now I don't know where I'll be tomorrow."

"Come to the kitchen with me this minute. A little food will put you right, and you can tell me why you think I'm going to turn you out on the street."

Diantha followed her to the snug room where the aroma of baked beans laced with molasses rose from a covered pot in the center of the table. A bowl of pickled beets and a plate of corn bread sat next to the beans. She settled into her usual place. "Maybe I'll just take a little bit."

The lines on Mrs. Wilkie's face fanned out in a smile. After blessing the food, she filled two plates then pinned her sharp blue gaze on Diantha. "What happened today to worry you so?"

"Mr. Golden said he had something to discuss with me, then he couldn't do it because his brother wasn't there. I didn't know he had a brother, and I certainly don't know why he needs to be present when Mr. Golden talks to me." She paused, knowing she was speaking too fast. "I'm afraid. What will I do if I lose my job?"

"You'd stay here with me, of course."

"I couldn't do that. How would I pay you?"

Mrs. Wilkie reached across the table and patted Diantha's hand. "I was a lonely old woman until you came. Your home is here. If your worries are real, I'll manage somehow until you find another position."

"You're very kind. Thank you." Warmth heated her neck, and she lowered her head to hide quick tears. Living with Mrs. Wilkie was part of her salary. To remain if Mr. Golden no longer paid her room and board would be accepting charity.

She'd do anything to avoid such a fate.

———

The following evening, chores completed, Diantha waited at the back door for the summons to Mr. Golden's office. The few times she'd glimpsed him during the day, he'd been preoccupied and took no notice of her. A tiny part of her mind hoped he'd forgotten about the matter he wished to discuss.

At the front of the alley, a rider dismounted from a broad-chested black gelding and wrapped the reins around the hitching rail. She watched, mesmerized, as he whipped off his hat and wiped his forehead with the back of his arm. Setting sun lit his wavy hair with streaks of gold. A handsome horse and a handsome rider. He had to be new to St. Joseph, otherwise she'd have remembered him.

Oblivious to her scrutiny, the rider strode south on the boardwalk and disappeared from view. She sighed. A man who could afford such a fine horse would never be interested in someone like her.

Floorboards creaked, warning her of Mr. Golden's approach. At least on this occasion he'd caught her daydreaming after work hours.

"I see you've finished for the day. Excellent. Please come with me." He walked a few steps ahead of her, opened his office door, and directed her to a chair inside.

A desk sat beneath a small window, and an additional two chairs were pushed against a bookshelf. She drew in a sharp breath. The rider she'd seen a moment ago occupied the seat nearest to Mr. Golden's desk. Up close, she noticed his hazel-brown eyes and a dimple in the center of his chin. Her heart fluttered. Was he the brother Mr. Golden mentioned? No, it couldn't be possible. This man was only a few years beyond her own age. Mr. Golden must be near forty.

The stranger gave her a brief nod then turned his attention to her employer. "Get on with your announcement, Harold. I canceled my plans to be here this evening."

"Formalities first. This is Diantha Bowers, the girl I mentioned. Diantha, this is my brother, Michael."

Eyes wide, she dipped an abbreviated curtsy before taking her seat. "Pleased to meet you." She cut a glance to her hands, hoping the men hadn't noticed her surprise.

Harold Golden settled behind his desk. "You both need to know. I've made plans to travel to Dalles City in Oregon Territory to open a mercantile. There's been talk in the legislature of statehood. I want to be there when the bill is approved. Michael, once we're established, you'll manage the store."

Diantha gripped the arms of her chair as the room spun around her. If Mr. Golden left, she'd have no job.

Chapter 2

Michael Golden sprang from his chair. "You can't do this to me! I'm not going to spend months driving a wagon across the country to end up in some forsaken outpost."

Diantha sat stunned as he stamped toward the door. How could anyone dare defy Mr. Golden's orders?

"You'll do what I tell you. Sit down." The older brother's voice carried an edge of steel. "Our father made you my ward until you're thirty. Three more years. After that, do what you want."

Michael remained next to the door, dimpled chin raised. "Three years and one day, and I leave you and your mercantile—assuming we ever reach Oregon. People die on that trail every day."

"You won't die, and you won't drive a wagon. I'm hiring a mule skinner to manage the team. Now sit and pay attention."

Diantha squirmed. She shouldn't be listening to a family squabble. With her job ending, she needed to make plans. Maybe she could—

"This concerns you, too, Diantha." Mr. Golden's voice intruded on her thoughts.

Here comes my dismissal. She straightened and squeezed her hands into fists. "Yes, sir."

"My wife refuses to travel unless I hire someone to do the cooking and camp chores. I know you're a hard worker. Can you cook?"

Was he asking. . . ? A pulse drummed in her throat, threatening to choke her. "Yes, sir. My mother taught me."

"Are you interested in signing on with us?"

"I. . .I don't know. I was born here. My parents are buried in the cemetery east of town." She shook her head. "Can I think about this?"

"You're eighteen now, am I right?"

Diantha nodded.

"Old enough to make your own decisions. I'll give you until morning. Whatever you decide, know this." He turned his head to view both her and his brother. "The arrangements have been made. We leave in three weeks." He focused on Diantha. "With or without you."

His words struck like the tolling of a bell. Three weeks. But less than one day to make a decision affecting the rest of her life.

—⁂—

Blind to Friday-night activity on St. Joseph's main thoroughfare, Diantha hurried toward Culver Street and the sanctuary of Mrs. Wilkie's house. As she passed one of the saloons, two men planted themselves in front of her. Piano music tinkled from beyond the saloon's swinging doors.

"Where you goin' in such a hurry, pretty gal? Come on. We'll have us some fun." The smell of stale sweat and beer filled her nostrils. One of the two men clamped his hand over her arm and tugged her toward the entrance.

She jerked away. "Let me be."

"Aw, don't be that way. We just want to be friends."

A tall man wearing a wide-brimmed hat stepped between her and her assailants, towering over both of them. "Maybe you should find some new friends." His voice growled from deep in his throat. "I'll wait here until you're out of sight."

The men disappeared inside the saloon, and Diantha turned to her rescuer. "Thank you." She bit her lip to stop the trembling. "I wasn't paying attention to where I was going. Normally I—"

He held up his hand to stop her. "You don't need to explain yourself. Glad I was able to help." His hat shaded his face, but not enough to hide his dark eyes and thick mustache. Smile lines creased the sides of his mouth. "Want me to see you safe to home?"

She blew out a breath. She knew better than to show a stranger where she lived. "That's kind of you, but I'll be fine. Thank you again." She whipped around and sped down the boardwalk. At the corner of Mrs. Wilkie's street, she paused and looked back.

Her rescuer was gone. For a moment she didn't know whether to feel relieved or disappointed, then chided herself for her foolishness. She had far more important concerns pressing on her mind this evening.

Diantha found Mrs. Wilkie sewing by the sitting-room hearth. A table lamp sent a circle of light over her needlework. At the sight of Diantha, she dropped her embroidery onto the table and jumped to her feet.

"What did he say? I've been on pins and needles all day."

"He said. . ." She drew a ragged breath. "He said he's going to Oregon Territory to open a new store. He asked if I was interested in going with them as a cook."

"What? Take that dreadful journey? Of course you told him no."

She shook her head. "I want to think about my decision. More than think, I need to pray. I have to tell him yes or no tomorrow morning."

"What is there to decide?" Hands on hips, Mrs. Wilkie faced Diantha. "You could die out there. I've heard stories about Indian danger, bad water, and I don't know what all."

"Well, I've heard about rich farmland, thick forests, and rivers wider than the Missouri." She surprised herself with her defense of Oregon. A short while ago she was frightened at the very idea of the journey, now a door in her mind opened to reveal the promise of a new beginning. But then the enormity of the prospect overwhelmed her.

Mrs. Wilkie's eyebrows shot toward her hairline. "You've made up your mind already?"

Diantha plopped onto a rocking chair next to the fire. "No. I haven't decided anything. This is all too sudden."

"I should say it is. Just tell him no." The older woman turned toward the kitchen.

"Come eat your supper. I'll make us a cup of chamomile tea. I know it's your favorite."

"Not tonight, thank you." She crossed the room and pushed open the door leading to her small bedroom. "I need to be alone to sort out my thoughts."

Tears shone in Mrs. Wilkie's eyes. "As you wish. I'll just eat by myself." Shoulders slumped, she walked into the kitchen.

Sympathy tugged at Diantha's heart, but she'd lived with Mrs. Wilkie long enough to recognize the woman's manipulative tricks. She'd watched her coerce her son into running unnecessary errands. And Mrs. Ellis, her next-door neighbor, dropped by once a month to take her to a quilting bee, even though Mrs. Wilkie was capable of traveling the distance on foot.

Diantha closed the door gently behind her. Fond as she was of her landlady, she couldn't allow tears to influence a decision this important. She dropped to her knees next to the bed and rested her head in her hands. *Lord, please make Your way clear to me. Help me decide.*

"Make a list."

She heard the words as though they'd been audible. *A list, Lord? What kind of a list?*

"List your choices."

She leaned back on her heels and rubbed her temples. Maybe she should have eaten supper. Hunger and fatigue must be clouding her thoughts. For a moment, she considered joining Mrs. Wilkie in the kitchen, then the clouds cleared. *Of course, list my choices.*

A copybook rested in the top drawer of her bureau. Diantha gathered the book and a pencil, lit a candle, and sat on the edge of the bed. She headed one column "Pluses" and the other, "Minuses."

News had come back from settlements out West. Wives were needed. Communities lacked the civilizing influence of women. She'd heard it said that a person willing to work could succeed at almost anything they tried. Some women actually homesteaded on their own.

Tickles of excitement filled her as pluses flowed from her pencil to the paper:

A new beginning.
Fresh opportunities.
Passage paid for the journey.
Freedom to choose where she'd live.
A better chance for a home and family.

She leaned on her pillow for a moment, tapping the pencil against her teeth as she considered the minus column. Maybe never seeing her parents' graves again could be a minus, but they were not there anyway. They were in heaven with the Lord.

Despite being born in St. Joseph, she had no real ties here. Yes, Mrs. Wilkie would miss her. However, Diantha knew the woman wasn't as lonely as she pretended.

Work on the trail would be hard, but she was used to hard work.

The minus column remained blank. She raised her eyes to the ceiling. "All right, Lord. I'll go!"

First thing tomorrow, she'd give Mr. Golden her decision.

—⁂—

The next morning Diantha left the house after avoiding Mrs. Wilkie's probing questions about her decision. What happened next was between her and the Lord.

She marched along the boardwalk, heart hammering. Suppose Mr. Golden had changed his mind and decided to hire a real cook or perhaps convinced his wife she could do her own cooking. She shook her head at the thought. She had never met Priscilla Golden, but the woman was known in St. Joseph's gossip circles as "difficult." Rumor had it she'd come from a wealthy family in St. Louis and barely tolerated rustic life along the Missouri River.

Wagons carrying Saturday shoppers filled the wide main street. Business would be brisk. For once, the muddy road didn't fill her with dismay at the thought of scrubbing floorboards that evening. Today was her first step toward a better life.

Diantha ducked into the alley and entered through the mercantile's rear door. She hurried to Mr. Golden's office before she lost her courage.

A dark-haired woman dressed in a jewel-toned purple plaid silk dress, trimmed with lace at the wrists and collar, stood beside Mr. Golden's desk. She raised an eyebrow when Diantha stepped into the room.

"How is it you enter my husband's office without knocking?" The woman spoke with a mosquito-whine of a voice. Her gaze swept Diantha's simple indigo dress and acorn-brown apron.

The difficult Mrs. Golden, Diantha assumed. She dipped a half curtsy. "The door was open, ma'am. I work here. Mr. Golden is expecting me this morning. I. . .I have a message for him."

"He's quite busy at the moment. Perhaps you could give me your message and get back to your tasks."

Diantha had a strong feeling that her decision would never reach Mr. Golden if she left the message with his wife. She backed toward the door. "I'll just stop by later. Thank you." She whirled to leave and bumped into her employer.

"Oh, gracious. Excuse me, sir. I didn't know you were behind me."

"No harm done." He flicked a glance at his wife then focused on Diantha. "What have you decided? If you're not willing to sign on, I need to interview other possibilities."

"Yes! That is, yes, I've decided to make the journey as your cook." She couldn't stop the smile that lifted her lips. "Thank you for the opportunity."

Mrs. Golden's skirts swished as she crossed to her husband's side. "When you said you'd hire a cook, I thought you meant a chef, not a mere girl." She looked down her nose at Diantha. "What do you know about menus? Have you ever prepared anything more complicated than beefsteak and beans?"

Diantha's dream of a new opportunity withered beneath the woman's superior attitude. She had no idea how being a chef differed from regular cooking, but knew she could prepare everything necessary to feed a family. At any rate, if Mrs. Golden didn't want her, there was nothing more to be said. Determined not to reveal her pain, she faced her employer.

"Thank you anyway. I need to start my chores now." Tears stung her eyes.

He held up his hand. "One moment. I have a list of supplies you'll need to order for the journey. You may add anything I've forgotten in the way of groceries. My brother will help you when he's not busy loading the merchandise wagon."

Diantha reeled. "You still want me? I'm a plain cook, sir, not a chef."

"Overland travel requires plain food, not trout amandine." He directed his remark toward his wife.

She huffed and turned her head away.

Uncomfortable at being in the midst of another squabble, Diantha focused her eyes on the toes of her boots. Apparently Mr. Golden treated his family with the same brusque manner he used on his employees.

He shuffled through a drift of papers on his desk until he found what he sought. "Here's the list you'll need, Diantha. In a few minutes I'll have Michael drive you down to the riverfront. Look for a bookstore run by a fellow named Holbrook. Ask him for the newest guidebook about the Trail, then use that to be sure we have all the necessary supplies. Tell him to add the book to my account."

"Excuse me, sir, but what about my duties here?"

"I told you we're leaving in three weeks. Outfitting our wagon is your new duty. Let me worry about the store."

"Yes, sir." As she left the room, she shivered under Mrs. Golden's icy glare.

Chapter 3

Diantha found her way to a quiet corner of the storeroom and sat on a packing crate to review Mr. Golden's list while she waited for his brother. In addition to foods she would have expected, like bacon, canned butter, and sugar, she found unfamiliar items. Pressed vegetables and something called "cold flour," a mixture of cornmeal, sugar, and cinnamon.

Mr. Golden promised his brother would help her. Her insides tickled at the thought of sharing this task with the handsome young man she'd met yesterday. But how to address him presented a problem. Calling him "Mr. Golden" would be confusing, yet no other name presented itself. After pondering a moment, she decided to think of him as Michael and call him Mr. Golden when she spoke to him. Maybe over time, he'd ask her to use his given name. Three weeks of working side by side then months on the trail. Who knew what might happen?

She gave herself a little shake to rein in her imagination. One thing at a time. Her first step was a visit to Mr. Holbrook's bookstore. The riverfront area was an unsavory portion of town, but early in the day she should be safe enough, particularly with Michael Golden as her escort. After gathering her shawl and reticule, she reentered the crowded mercantile.

Women browsed along an aisle containing fabric and notions, while their husbands studied farm implements, horse collars, and firearms. Next year at this time Mr. Golden would have a similar store in Dalles City—and she would have a new life. She closed her eyes and drew a satisfied breath. She'd made the right decision.

"We meet again." Her eyes flew open at the sound of an unmistakable deep voice. The man who'd rescued her last night grinned down at her. When he removed his hat, she had a full view of his rugged features. Smile lines feathered out next to his coffee-colored eyes. His skin was tanned to a leathery brown, marking him as a man who made a living outdoors.

"Yes, yes, we do." She hated the way her voice stammered, and cleared her throat. "You were very kind to come to my rescue last night. Thank you."

"Always glad to help a lady. Now maybe you can return the favor."

"You need rescuing?"

The grin reappeared. "Some. Do you know where to find Mr. Golden? I'm supposed to sign a contract here today."

"He should be in there." She pointed over her shoulder at the closed door to his office. "He's my employer."

"Well, that's a coincidence. I'm going to look after his livestock on the trail." He lowered his voice into a deeper growl. "You knew he was leaving, I hope."

"I'm going, too, as the cook."

"Ah. Then we'll be seeing more of each other. Name's Charles Griffin, by the way."

"Diantha Bowers."

"Pleased, Miss Bowers." He nodded farewell and strode toward the office.

Charles Griffin looked strong enough to handle the most stubborn team. Mr. Golden made a wise choice for his mule skinner.

The office door opened before Mr. Griffin touched the handle. Michael marched past him toward Diantha, his face flushed. "Here you are. Harold said I'm to drive you to a bookstore on Front Street. You ready?"

"Yes." As she followed him from the mercantile, she glanced over her shoulder and noticed Mr. Griffin watching them. He touched the brim of his hat to her before entering the office.

She subdued a pleased flutter in her throat then hurried to match Michael's swift strides.

———

Charles Griffin paused on the threshold of his potential employer's office. He couldn't remember when he'd seen a girl as fetching as Miss Bowers. The shadows around her deep-set green eyes hinted at a story behind her willingness to leave Missouri. Everyone who went west had a story—he knew he did. He dragged his attention back to the mercantile. Wool-gathering about a pretty girl wouldn't help him return to Dalles City.

Mr. Golden stood next to his desk and watched him enter, a frown creasing his forehead. Unlike the first time they'd met, today the man wore no jacket. Buttons on his waistcoat strained over his barrel-shaped chest. He faced Charles and extended his hand. "Wondered what happened to you. Thought you'd be here earlier. I have a couple of questions before I sign you on."

"Took me a minute to find your office." Charles gave the man's hand a brief shake. "What do you want to know? Thought we covered everything the other night."

"I've heard stories about drivers signing on with travelers, then when the feller gets where he aims to go, he deserts the wagons." Mr. Golden stalked behind the desk and thumped his bulk onto a high-backed armchair. He steepled his fingers under his chin. "So, how do I know you intend to travel all the way to Dalles City?"

"Told you, I was at Fort Dalles with the army. When my enlistment was up, I had to come east to settle family business but never planned to stay here. I got someone waiting in Dalles City." He squared his shoulders. "If you've changed your mind, say so. Plenty of travelers need a hand with their teams."

"Never said I changed my mind. Wanted to make sure, is all."

"And are you?"

"What?"

"Sure."

By way of answer, Mr. Golden pushed a closely written page across his desk and pointed to a pen and a cone-shaped bottle of ink. "Sign on the bottom. I'll pay you half now and half when we reach Dalles City."

The pen scratched as Charles signed his name. He rolled a blotter over the damp ink and handed the document to his new boss. "When do you want me to start?"

"I'm meeting with a mule trader Monday at eight. I'll expect you then, Mr. Griffin."

"Call me Griff." He tipped his hat and left the office, his mind lingering on Miss Bowers's smile.

The journey across the country in her company would be pleasant, despite the often harsh conditions they'd face. *Whoa there, Griff. You're already committed.*

—∽∾—

Diantha stole glances at Michael as he drove the mercantile's high-sided buckboard along the main street. The name Golden fit him well. From his dark blond hair to his dimpled chin, he was one of the handsomest men she'd ever seen. If only he'd talk more. He could have been riding alone for all the attention he paid to her. She smoothed her skirt, hoping he wasn't cut from the same superior cloth as his sister-in-law.

The wagon jolted, and she grabbed the edge of the seat as they bounced down the rutted road. Countless wagons had traveled this way over the last dozen years or so, most of them destined for new homes in the West. She looked across the muddy water at the route she'd soon follow, memorizing the sight. In three more weeks she'd be aboard a ferry, crossing to Kansas Territory and points west.

When they reached Front Street, hundreds of covered wagons fanned up the riverbank above the ferry landing. Strings of smoke from campfires spiraled into the sky. Mules brayed, oxen lowed, horses whinnied. The reek of manure combined with smoke filled the air.

She wrinkled her nose. "My word. Why are all these wagons stopped here?"

"Waiting for grass to grow."

"No. Really. Why are they here?"

Michael slowed the team to a walk and turned to face her. He didn't smile. "Grass needs to be high enough in Kansas so they won't have to carry so much feed. Too heavy. Takes up space. That's the Boyer Immigration Company waiting. Someone goes over every day or so and measures the growth." He must have noticed her astonishment because he smiled. His dimple deepened. "Really."

"Will we be part of a company when we leave?"

"My brother thinks that would hinder our progress. A company can only travel as fast as the slowest wagon."

"I never thought of that. There's so much I don't know." Her shoulders sagged. "I hope his trust in me isn't misplaced."

"Harold doesn't make mistakes. Just ask him." Bitterness laced his tone.

She pressed her lips together and pretended interest in a ferry moving across the river. The last thing she wanted was to be between two warring brothers.

After a moment, Michael broke the silence. "Where's this bookstore?"

"I'm not sure. Somewhere along here. The owner's name is Holbrook."

He grunted and turned the wagon toward a row of businesses. They passed a hotel, a blacksmith shop, and a harness maker before she spotted HOLBROOK'S painted on a weathered storefront.

She tapped his arm. "There it is."

He guided the wagon to an open space at the side of the street. After he tied the team to a hitching post, she waited for him to help her down. Instead, he headed toward the door of the bookstore. "Aren't you coming?"

Heat burned her cheeks as she scrambled from the wagon. For a moment she'd forgotten her position as scrubwoman for his brother. She wouldn't make that mistake again.

A bell on the door tinkled when they entered. The shop wasn't much bigger than Mrs. Wilkie's sitting room, with book-laden shelves rising to the ceiling on three walls. A man stood with his back to her, brushing a feather duster over one of the shelves. A faint beam of light shone through a square window at the front of the space.

The memory of her father's library washed over her. After his death, his possessions had been sold to satisfy debts. She'd set aside a half dozen of her favorite volumes, including his Bible, but the rest went to auction.

Michael's nudge brought her back to the present. "We don't have all day. Ask him for the book Harold wants."

The man turned at the sound of Michael's voice. "You folks have a certain book in mind?"

His youthful face and voice surprised her. Somehow she'd expected a dusty man to own a dusty bookstore. This fellow wore a fashionable plaid waistcoat under a tan jacket. His dark hair was combed back, with a soft wave over the forehead. In all respects he looked as well-turned-out as Michael. "Are *you* Mr. Holbrook?"

"Indeed I am. How may I help you, miss?"

"I. . .that is, we need a copy of the most current Oregon Trail guidebook. My employer, Mr. Golden, said you would have one."

"In fact, I have several." His eyes sparkled with humor.

She smiled back. How nice to be treated as someone other than a scrubwoman.

Mr. Holbrook reached onto the shelf next to him and handed her a slim volume titled *The Overland Trail: 1857 Handbook for Pioneers.* "This should have all the information you need. Tells you what to pack, best routes, how to make repairs—anything you can think of, it's in here. Fellow that wrote it claims he's been to Oregon Territory and back three times."

Her fingertips tingled when she grasped the book. "Thank you." As soon as she returned to Mrs. Wilkie's house she'd study the contents cover to cover so Mr. Golden would have no reason to regret taking her on the journey.

The shop owner walked to a table under the window and opened a ledger. "Am I to add this to Mr. Golden's account?"

"Yes, please." She clutched the handbook to her chest, its promise burning beneath her heart.

—⁂—

One week before departure, Diantha leaned forward in Mrs. Wilkie's sitting-room chair to review the supply list. A grocery across the street from the mercantile had promised delivery that morning of most of the necessary foods. She made a mental note to be at work early.

Mr. Golden had stationed the wagons for the trip in the alleyway behind the store. They'd been fitted with canvas covers, custom-made boxes for supplies, and tools for any emergency. Every inch of space inside had been spoken for. Excitement bubbled up at the thought of adding her few possessions to the load.

Mrs. Wilkie entered the room, frowning when she saw the list spread over Diantha's lap. "There's still time to change your mind. After you've loaded everything, tell him you're not going. I'm certain fancy Mrs. Golden will learn to cook rather than starve."

"I'll never have another opportunity like this. I don't plan to change my mind."

"Please." Mrs. Wilkie sank into a chair next to Diantha's. Tears glittered in her eyes. "For these past two years, you've been the daughter I always wished I had. I can't bear the thought of you taking that dangerous journey." She sniffled.

Diantha sighed. Much as the landlady's tears distressed her, she knew Mrs. Wilkie to be a resourceful person. She placed her hand on the woman's arm. "We've been over this before. I believe this opportunity is the Lord's leading. When we reach Dalles City, I'll send word back. Besides, you know your son and his wife would be pleased to have you live with them if you get too lonely."

"I'm not ready to go live with my son like some old lady. My home is right here."

"Then you'll soon find another girl to rent your spare room. With me gone, Mr. Golden's partner will need someone to keep the store clean. You could pay a call on Mr. Litchfield this week to let him know you have a room available."

"I don't want another girl." Mrs. Wilkie clasped her arms across her middle, jaw set in a firm line.

Diantha folded her list and rose. "I expect we could go around and around all morning, but I need to be at the store. Let's both pray for peace about this." She gentled her voice. "I'll see you this evening."

She left the house with her thoughts in turmoil. The Lord's leading had seemed so clear when she made her decision. What if Mrs. Wilkie's words were His message telling her to stay?

Chapter 4

In the wagon nearest the street, Diantha recited her inventory to herself as she rear-ranged their food supplies. Michael was supposed to be working in the merchandise wagon, but when she peeked out, he sat in the shade with his hat covering his face. She shook her head. She'd seen him charm his way past Mrs. Golden, but if his older brother saw him slacking, there'd be fireworks.

"Need some help, Miss Bowers?"

Diantha turned toward the front when she heard Charles Griffin's voice. "Mr. Griffin. How kind of you to offer. I was just struggling to move this medicine chest out of the way of my cooking utensils. Lord willing, we won't need medicine at all, but I do have to cook every day." She chuckled.

The wagon creaked as Mr. Griffin climbed inside. "Show me where you want the chest."

"Over there. I'll put bedding on top for Mrs. Golden."

He lifted the heavy wooden chest as though it weighed no more than an empty birdcage, pivoted, and lowered it to the space she'd indicated.

"Anything else you need?"

"No. Thank you, Mr. Griffin."

"Call me Griff. We'll be spending too much time together to be so formal."

"Then you can stop calling me Miss Bowers. My name's Diantha."

Footsteps thudded outside, and Michael appeared at the front of the wagon. "Checking to see if I have to fetch anything more from the grocer."

"Yes, thank you. The hundred-pound sacks of beans and rice can be loaded now." She pointed to an open space. "I saved room right there." Her cheeks warmed when she noticed his gaze travel between her and Griff. She lifted her chin. If their mule skinner offered his help, why shouldn't she accept?

Michael groaned under his breath before facing Diantha. "Hundred-pound sacks. Right. Hope the grocer has a cart."

Griff stepped forward. "Want a hand?"

"No thanks." Michael crossed the street with brisk strides. Diantha watched him leave, sensing he was putting on a show for her benefit. His older brother was too hard on him. With a little encouragement, once they started across country he'd learn to do his fair share.

"One more day." Diantha sang the words as she carried two bulging satchels toward the camp wagon. She'd filled one satchel with extra clothing—a linsey-woolsey dress for cool weather, and two calico wash dresses for every day. Her warmest cape. Underthings, nightgowns, and an extra pair of boots took up the rest of the space. The smaller satchel held her father's volumes and her copybook to use as a journal. Her mother's wedding ring and green glass earbobs were sewn into the lining, tucked away in a carved wooden case. She'd have reminders of her parents to share with her hoped-for children.

Her shoulders ached by the time she reached the alley behind the mercantile. She left one satchel on the ground and climbed inside the wagon using the spokes of the front wheel as a ladder. In the dim light beneath the canvas, her reflection stared back at her. She dropped her burden and blinked at the sight of a tall cheval mirror standing where she'd planned to store extra feed for the mules. Her pots and pans now sat crowded between two trunks in the midst of their supplies. This would never do.

She hurried into the store and stalked straight to Mr. Golden's office. He turned when she entered. "Everything ready for tomorrow?"

"Not quite, sir. Didn't you say we weren't taking unnecessary items?"

"That's so. We need the space for supplies."

Her pulse pounded. The mirror could belong to only one person. She cleared her throat, praying he hadn't been the one to add the fragile item to the wagon. "The cheval mirror takes up the area I've set aside for the mules' grain. Plus the glass is sure to break if it falls over. The shards—"

He held up his hand. "Cheval mirror? That's staying behind. I'll send my brother out to remove it immediately."

"I'm sorry to cause difficulties. It's just with space so tight. . ."

"You're not the one causing difficulties." His mouth clamped into a thin line. "Don't concern yourself. This will be settled by morning."

She plodded back to the wagon, certain she hadn't heard the end of the issue.

—*m*—

Once Michael removed the cheval glass and added the sacks of grain, Diantha busied herself arranging her kitchen goods where they'd be readily accessible. She hummed while she tucked her satchels next to her bedroll. The wagon held everything recommended in the handbook, and nothing that should be left behind. With the Lord's blessing, they would have a successful journey.

The wagon swayed when Mr. Golden climbed aboard. He smiled at the sight of the crates, barrels, and boxes. "You have a knack for fitting things together. I'd never have thought we'd have room for everything on that list. Good work."

She hugged his compliment to her heart. Praise from his lips was rare indeed. "Thank you, sir. I'm grateful for your confidence."

"Looks like we're ready to depart at daybreak." After one more glance around, he climbed off the wagon.

"I'll be here," she whispered to his retreating back.

She jumped to the ground, heading to Mrs. Wilkie's for one last night. As she reached the mouth of the alley, a buggy rolled to a stop next to the boardwalk.

"One minute, Diantha. My husband's brother returned my mirror a short while ago.

Apparently you objected to its presence?" Mrs. Golden's sharp voice knifed through the dusk.

Diantha sucked in a breath. If the woman decided to blame her for every mishap along the way, the trip would be a long one indeed. She stepped close to the buggy. "I beg your pardon, ma'am. Your mirror is too lovely to risk on such a rough journey. According to the handbook Mr. Golden suggested I use, the wagon must be filled with practical items."

"A looking glass is practical. How is one to know when one is properly attired?"

"For our clothing, the handbook says—"

"I know what the handbook says! Mr. Golden has been quite helpful in that regard." The peacock feathers on her hat swayed when she glared down at Diantha. "He actually expects me to dress as drably as you do."

She eyed the woman's royal purple grosgrain dress with its contrasting lilac overskirt and suppressed a desire to shake her head. Instead, she stepped away from the buggy. "I'm sure you could never look drab, ma'am."

"Well. . .thank you. I suppose I can manage with no mirror for a short time. Harold can buy me a new one when we reach Dalles City." She fluffed her overskirt, then released the brake and gave the reins a slight flick.

Diantha blew out a sigh as the horse moved forward. A scripture verse she'd learned as a child came to her mind. *If it be possible, as much as lieth in you, live peaceably with all men.* Living peaceably with Mrs. Golden promised to be a challenge, but nothing could subdue her excitement over tomorrow's departure.

Come daylight, she'd be on the trail for Oregon.

—∿—

Diantha lay awake staring at the ceiling. An owl hooted in the darkness outside her window. She curled into her favorite sleeping position, mounded her pillow beneath her cheek, but her tumbling thoughts drove slumber away. So much to consider. Had she ordered enough food to last until they could resupply? Would her cooking please Mrs. Golden—and Michael? Would Griff remember his promise to help build the cook fires? How could she. . .

The pearly light of dawn brightened her room, jolting her wide awake. She jumped from the bed and hastened into her new tan and maroon calico dress. In moments, she'd combed her hair and twisted it into a knot at the nape of her neck. As she rolled her stockings over her feet and ankles, she heard a thud.

Mrs. Wilkie must have dropped something. Odd to have her up at this hour, but perhaps she arose early to wish her well on the journey. Diantha finished with her stockings and shoved her feet into her boots. Leaving her satchel open on the bed, she hurried to the kitchen for a quick bite of breakfast.

"Thank goodness you're up." Mrs. Wilkie's raspy whisper came from somewhere nearby.

"Where are you?" Diantha scanned the shadowed room and discovered an overturned chair. Mrs. Wilkie lay on her side between the table and range, hands cupped around one ankle.

Diantha dashed across the kitchen and knelt beside her. "Gracious! Are you hurt?"

"My leg. My ankle. My foot. I'm not sure. I tried to stand, but the pain is too great."

"What happened?"

"With you leaving, I don't need my large griddle, so I tried to get the small one from the top shelf. Then the chair tipped out from under me." She clasped Diantha's hand, wincing at the movement. "Come sunup, could you please fetch Doc Rowan?"

Sunup. Diantha shot a glance out the window. Early rays gilded a black walnut tree growing next to the cottage. Her stomach clenched. She needed to leave now or risk Mr. Golden's wrath.

But she couldn't abandon Mrs. Wilkie.

Chapter 5

Diantha rubbed her temples and tried to think. With the sun rising higher every minute, she had no time for dithering. Only the most hard-hearted person would leave an injured woman and run off to satisfy her own desires.

Hot tears stung her eyes as she slipped her arm under Mrs. Wilkie's shoulder. "Let me help you to a chair. If I hurry, I can stop at Dr. Rowan's house and then go to the ferry dock to retrieve my things before the Goldens depart." Despite her efforts to avoid self-pity, her voice quivered.

"Bless you, dear. I'm so glad you're here to help me." She settled onto a chair with her injured leg extended. "I won't move until you get back."

After tucking a blanket over Mrs. Wilkie's shoulders, Diantha donned a shawl and set off for the street where Dr. Rowan lived. Morning fog rose from the river to curtain the western sky. She drew a shuddering breath and bade farewell to her dreams. Tomorrow she'd go to Mr. Litchfield to ask for her job back. For today, she'd grieve.

Fighting tears, she climbed the steps of Dr. Rowan's house and knocked. A slim woman wearing a flounced wrapper opened the door partway and peered at her. "If you're seeking my husband, he's out delivering a baby." She took a second look at Diantha and opened the door wider. "You don't look well. Are you the patient?"

"No. I'm Mrs. Wilkie's boarder. She fell and hurt her leg this morning." Diantha sniffled. "Could you please ask the doctor to call when he returns?"

"Of course." The woman stepped away from the door and pointed toward the interior of her home. "Would you like a cup of tea? That's my remedy for most anything."

Her kindness threatened to undo what little control Diantha possessed. She pivoted toward the street. "Thank you, but I must run an important errand before it's too late." Her new boots clattered as she dashed to the boardwalk and hurried toward the river.

A large group of wagons waited near the crossing in a scene similar to the one Diantha had observed when Michael drove her to the bookstore. On the opposite shore, a ferry was tied at the dock while a wagon, followed by a single rider on a black horse, disembarked. Her eyes widened. It couldn't be. The sun had barely begun its ascent.

She spun around, searching for wagons with "Golden's Mercantile" painted in large red letters on the canvas covers. Some of the conveyances read "Oregon or Bust," but none had the store's name on their sides. Maybe her employer was farther back in line.

Her heart pounded in her throat, threatening to choke her. All her possessions were in the Goldens' wagon. She dashed toward the waiting line of travelers, ignoring curious glances as she panted past wagon after wagon. Eyes blurry with tears, she tripped over a patch of bunchgrass. Putting her arms out to break her fall, she stumbled two steps forward then landed in the dirt.

Strong hands clasped her waist, drawing her to her feet. "Miss Bowers. Diantha. Are you all right?" Griff's gravelly voice rumbled beneath the noise of bawling oxen and shouting children.

"Griff. Praise God, you're here. Where's Mr. Golden's wagon?"

"Let's see to you first. Hold out your hands."

She looked down at drops of blood oozing from scrapes at the base of her palms. "This is nothing, really. I just need to find his wagon." She tucked her bleeding hands behind her back.

He grunted and drew a bandana from his pocket. "Here. You don't want to soil that pretty dress."

"Thank you." She raised an eyebrow and clasped the folded cloth between her palms, surprised he would think about keeping her dress clean. "Now, where's the wagon?"

"Left at daybreak, like he said he would. Wanted to get ahead of the rest of the folks so he'd have the best grass."

Her heart plummeted. *I should have come here first then gone for the doctor.* "Then why are you still here? Didn't he wait for you either?"

"Thought the store goods would be safer if I traveled in a company of other wagons."

"Mr. Golden can handle a mule team?"

"Says he can. We'll see soon enough." He grinned at her. "He was plenty upset when you didn't get here. His missus was even more wrathy—now she's going to have to cook." His grin reappeared, then he sobered. "I was surprised, too. Thought you wanted to go to Oregon Country."

"I did. I still do, but. . ." She swallowed the lump that rose in her throat. "All my possessions are in that wagon. I came to fetch them. I wasn't that late. He could have waited."

"Fetch your gear? Why?"

"I can't go with you." Her voice wobbled. She glanced up at the sound of harnesses and hoofbeats then jumped to one side to avoid a wagon jostling for position. The few closest to the dock would be next to board the ferry for the slow journey across the muddy river. She'd come so close to her dream. And now. . . She bit her lip to prevent useless tears.

Griff tucked his thumb beneath her chin and tilted her head to face him. His brow furrowed. "Want to tell me what changed your mind?"

He was the last person she'd expected to show an interest in her plans. "My landlady fell this morning. She can't walk. It wouldn't be right to go off and abandon her."

"Can't someone else stay with her?"

"Her son, maybe. But even so, the Goldens would be well into Kansas Territory before she made arrangements."

On the shore below, a ferry scraped against the bank, dark smoke billowing from its stack. Three wagons rolled aboard. Shouts of "See you in Kansas!" rang from the waiting company while the rest of the drivers moved forward to take their places in line.

Griff took Diantha's hand. "I'll see to it your belongings get on the ferry back to St.

Joe." His dark eyes were pools of regret. "Wish I could wait for you."

She tightened her hold on his rough palm. "Thank you, Griff. God bless you. Safe travels." Her voice cracked. She dropped his hand and hurried toward Mrs. Wilkie's without a backward glance.

—⁂—

Warmth remained where Diantha had wrapped her small fingers around Griff's palm. He watched her slight figure disappear up the slope, wondering how she'd worked her way into his heart after he'd promised himself never to care for anyone again.

He kicked at a dirt clod and walked to the lead mule in his team. By the end of the day, he'd be on the ground in Kansas, headed for Oregon Territory. Running his hand over Jasper's white muzzle, he focused on the opposite side of the river. Harold Golden had a half-day's start, but Griff felt sure he could follow close behind and meet up at suppertime. Harold would have delays contending with his wife's whims.

Griff had no wife to slow him down. That's the way he'd wanted things—no complications.

Wheels creaked as a wagon rolled to a stop beside him. The driver leaned down. "You're goin' to lose your spot in line if'n you don't get moving. You was ahead of me, so I'll wait." He pushed his hat up his forehead. "Some of the folks behind us might not be so kindly."

A pretty woman next to him smiled down at Griff. "Is your wife inside the wagon? Maybe we could share chores on the trail."

"I'm without a wife, ma'am."

A puzzled expression crossed her face. "But I saw—"

"An acquaintance." He bit off the words then turned to her husband. "You go on ahead. I'll hold my team and fall in behind you."

The man tipped his hat and slapped the reins over the backs of his oxen. The white canvas covering their wagon billowed as they passed. For a moment, Griff pictured himself on a wagon bench with Diantha at his side, traveling to Oregon. He blinked away the image.

He had to face Dalles City alone.

—⁂—

Diantha's steps dragged as she approached Mrs. Wilkie's street. White canvas and green-painted wheels colored her memory of the wagons waiting their chance to cross the river. Strange how weeks of planning could be swept away in a few minutes' time.

She tucked her shoulders back. Instead of weeping over spilled milk, she'd focus on the blessing of finding Griff still on the Missouri side of the river. She remembered his broad hand clasping hers, and warmth rose within. His promise to send her carpetbags back to her was a blessing, too. In another day or so, she'd have her father's books and her mother's earrings safe in her possession. Small comfort, but a comfort nonetheless.

Upon reaching Culver Street, Diantha noticed a horse and buggy parked in front of Mrs. Wilkie's house. She picked up her pace, eager to hear Dr. Rowan's diagnosis. When she opened the front door, Mrs. Ellis, the next-door neighbor, waited in the sitting room. "Good morning, Miss Bowers. How nice to see you."

Her jaw dropped. Mrs. Wilkie's leg must be worse than she'd feared. "Good of you to come, Mrs. Ellis."

The woman blinked. "It's the day our quilting circle meets. You know I always take Frances with me."

"But her leg—"

"I'm ready to go." Mrs. Wilkie hustled into the room, her flowered sewing bag hanging over one arm. Her face flushed when she saw Diantha. She slowed her pace to an exaggerated limp. "I completely forgot this is the second Friday of the month. Even though my ankle hurts dreadfully, I can't miss the quilting circle." She patted Diantha's shoulder as she limped her way to the door. "See you at supper. When Doc Rowan gets here, tell him I'm much improved."

The snap of the latch echoed in Diantha's ears.

This can't be happening. Perhaps I'm dreaming. She turned her back on the entrance and hastened toward the kitchen. A quick search revealed a half-finished cup of tea on the table, an empty peg on the wall where the landlady's shawl had hung, and the large griddle resting on the stove.

Her jaw tightened. This was no dream. She'd been duped.

Chapter 6

Diantha stamped into her bedroom, heart slamming with hot anger. How could she have fallen into Mrs. Wilkie's trap when she knew the woman's nature? One thing was certain, she'd never spend another night in this house.

She spied her *Overland Trail* handbook on her night table. The image of canvas-covered wagons lined up at the river's edge floated into her vision. Perhaps some members of the company hadn't yet crossed.

She grabbed her satchel and stuffed her nightgown, hairbrush, and toiletries inside—everything she'd need until she caught up with the Goldens' wagon. She'd ask someone to take her across then worry about finding her employer once she reached the other side. The door banged behind her as she raced for the river.

She sped along the boardwalks through town and down to the waterfront, grateful to see a ferry tied at the landing. Ropes held the craft to stanchions onshore while workmen loaded firewood into the hold. The steamboat dipped as wagons rolled aboard. She looked up the bank, observing that many travelers had crossed during the time she'd wasted returning to Mrs. Wilkie's. No matter. She changed direction, determined to join the first people she saw.

She gripped her satchel and headed across the sloping ground, glancing toward the water when the wagons rolled forward. The ferry crew had begun to gather the ropes anchoring the craft to shore when she spotted red letters spelling "Golden's Mercantile" painted on one of the conveyances boarding the ferry.

"Griff!" Her shout went unheard amid the commotion raised by livestock and the hollering of the crew. She lifted her skirts above her boot tops and raced for the landing. "Wait! Please!"

One of the men onshore grasped a rope in both hands and tugged it around a stanchion. Digging his heels into the sandy earth, he strained to hold the craft. "Run, lady! You'll make 'er."

Diantha sprinted the last few yards and leaped onto the gangplank. She gained a foothold, and the man onshore released the rope. The ferry swung into the muddy river, its paddlewheel chuffing against the current.

A crewman wearing an official-looking cap approached her. "Fare's ten cents, miss." He leered at her and raised an eyebrow at her travel bag. "Don't look like you plan on staying in Kansas long—or you got plans once you get there." He stepped closer.

"I'm traveling with the Golden's Mercantile wagon. The fare the driver paid covers me as well." She gulped, praying she was right. "Would you please direct me to the hold?"

"Sure you don't want to stay up here in the fresh air?"

The air in the hold would be fresher than his noxious breath. She moved away, trying not to inhale. "I'm quite sure."

He jerked his thumb toward his left. "Down them steps over there. You'll hear the racket."

"Thank you." She descended to the cargo hold, assailed by a cloud of doubt. Missing the departure time this morning may have sealed her fate with Mr. Golden. He hired her as cook because of her dependability. What if he'd already discovered someone to take her place?

She lifted her chin. Worrying about tomorrow was the thief of today, her mother always said. For now she'd be grateful for crossing the river. Tomorrow could take care of itself. Swinging her satchel, she crossed the deck toward the hold.

Wagons crowded the space inside. It took but a moment to spot the Golden's Mercantile wagon at the far side of the area. The mule team was secured with the others. None of the animals had been unhitched. She picked her way through the pungent-smelling hold. Griff stood beside one of his lead mules, stroking the animal's muzzle.

Diantha's courage faltered. She wasn't Griff's responsibility. He didn't have to deliver her to Mr. Golden. Through openings in the hold she watched the water flowing past the ferry, felt the gentle up-and-down motion as the craft traveled toward her goal in the West. Taking a deep breath, she raised her hand and waved. "Griff!"

His head jerked up. "Diantha?" He hastened toward her, a grin creasing his face. "This is more than a surprise. Thought I'd never see you again. How'd you get here?"

Relief melted her bones. "It's a long story."

—⁂—

Diantha watched with admiration as Griff directed their team around the wagons assembled on the Kansas shore. His broad hands never let up on the reins, keeping the mules moving at a brisk pace. By early evening they spotted the Goldens' wagon ahead, parked several yards off the trail. A pale wisp of smoke rose from the remains of a campfire nearby.

Her insides prickled at the prospect of facing her employer. She half stood to get a better view of the camp. "I don't see anyone."

"Turned in early, maybe." Griff tugged the reins to the left. "Haw!" The team moved off the trail, harnesses jingling.

Within moments, Mr. Golden boiled out of his wagon and stomped toward them. "Griffin! Thunderation, man, where've you been? I hired you to take care of the stock." His eyes widened when he noticed Diantha on the wagon bench. "And you! When I say first thing in the morning, I mean first thing. Not whenever you feel like it. If I could've found someone else today, I would have."

Diantha squared her shoulders. "I can explain, sir."

"Never mind. Tell me later." He whipped his attention back to Griff. "We got us a little difficulty. The mules ran off. Wouldn't have happened if you'd been here."

Griff set the brake and jumped from the wagon. "How'd they pull up their stakes?"

"Didn't think I'd have to stake them. Plenty of grass here. No reason for them to leave." Mr. Golden frowned, as though the mules had made an error in judgment.

"They're not trail broke yet. Bet they thought they'd make their way back to the stable."

"I don't care what they thought. Find them."

While the men faced each other, Diantha climbed down with her satchel and stood beside a wheel. Thankfully, Mr. Golden had bigger worries than her tardiness, but she knew her time would come. *Lord, please give me this chance. Don't let him send me back.*

Griff stood next to his team, face set in hard lines. "Why didn't you send your brother after them soon as you saw the mules take off?"

"Don't question me!" Mr. Golden shoved his hat back on his head and huffed out a breath then spoke in a calmer tone. "Michael's out looking now. Fact is, we didn't notice right away. Too busy trying to get a fire going so we could eat."

Diantha shrank back against the wheel when Mr. Golden's eyes met hers. He nailed her with a glare. "Figured you lost your nerve. Stocked us with food and left us."

"No, sir. I'll start cooking as soon as you're ready."

"He's ready now." Mrs. Golden picked her way toward them over the uneven ground, holding her flounced skirt above her boots. Several burned holes decorated the ruffled hem. "My dress is ruined from that dreadful fire. I can't believe I'm saying this, but I'm ever so thankful to see you."

Diantha couldn't hide the pleased smile that lifted her lips. "Thank you, ma'am. I'll cook supper right away." As she followed Mrs. Golden to the wagon, she caught Griff's wink. She winked back.

—◆—

At dusk, Diantha stood near the campfire and watched as Griff and Michael returned, the mules strung out single file behind them. "Thank You, Lord. We can be on our way tomorrow," she whispered.

While Griff staked the team, Michael ambled over to the fire. "Griffin told me why you weren't at the dock this morning." He took a tin mug out of the cook box and poured a cup of coffee from a pot resting on the coals. "Lucky thing you caught up with us. We'd have starved if we depended on Priscilla." His eyes held a mischievous glint.

Diantha glanced over her shoulder, hoping Mrs. Golden hadn't heard his comment.

Michael lowered his voice. "Don't worry about her. She's probably in the wagon, dressing for dinner." He snickered.

The glow from the fire highlighted the dimple in his chin. Aside from the ride to the bookstore, the two of them had seldom been alone. Her heart drummed when he moved a step closer. He saluted her with his mug.

"I'm glad you're here—and not just because of the food, although it smells mighty good."

She dropped her gaze, suddenly shy. "Thank you, sir."

"No need to 'sir' me. I'm not my brother—I'm Michael."

"Yes, sir—I mean, Michael." She flashed him a quick smile then lifted the lid on a dutch oven. A puff of steam rose from browned biscuits inside.

He leaned over her shoulder. "Mmm. I could eat the whole batch."

"If you'd tell the others supper's ready, you'll get your fair share." A tickle ran through her. Here she stood bantering with her employer's brother—something that wouldn't have happened in St. Joseph. Things were definitely different on the trail.

—⁓—

The next morning Diantha prepared breakfast, put up the lunch, then cleaned and packed their cookware in a sturdy wooden chest. She looked around to ask Michael's help with the chest but discovered Mr. Golden coming her way instead. Traces of sunlight slipped through the trees and striped his blue flannel shirt.

"Sun's up already. We need to get rolling. Why are you standing here?"

"I'm waiting for your brother, sir. He said he'd lend a hand with the camp box. It needs to be stowed in the wagon."

"Michael left soon as he finished eating. Didn't you see him ride off?"

She bit back a sharp retort and shook her head. Between scrubbing charred bits of batter from the skillet and washing their tin plates, she'd had no time to keep an eye on Michael.

Mr. Golden glanced at the bulky wooden box. "I'll get Griff to put this in the wagon. You'd best get in, too. We're traveling fast so I can stay ahead of the St. Joseph company."

He strode away, and a couple of minutes later Griff approached. He smiled down at her. "Mighty fine breakfast, Diantha. This the box you need loaded?"

"Yes, please, and thank you for the compliment. I'm still getting used to cooking over a campfire, so I'm afraid the flapjacks were a little burned."

"Tasted fine to me."

He grabbed the rope handles on the chest. The wagon bobbed when he climbed up and thunked the box inside. Mr. Golden trailed his steps.

"We're burning daylight. I'll leave first. You bring the merchandise wagon along behind."

Griff vaulted to the ground and paused next to Diantha. "Come get me when we stop for the day. I'll help you with the box." He removed his hat and rubbed the back of his head. "Maybe I can find a way to nail it to the outside of the wagon."

She studied the rough wooden sides of their conveyance. The pick, ax, and shovel were mounted horizontally between the wheels. There might be room next to the water barrel if they moved the tools toward the rear. A smile bubbled up from inside. "That would save so much time when we're stopped. What a good idea."

His face flushed red beneath his tan. "Hold on now. Didn't say it could be done."

"I believe you'll find a way." She thought about what she'd said, and her cheeks warmed. It wasn't her place to give Griff orders. "I mean, if you want to. That is, if you have time." Oh, dear. She was making things worse with every word.

"Griff!" Mr. Golden barked. "You going to drive that team or not?"

With one eyebrow cocked, Griff matched his employer's glare. "Just waiting for you. Soon as you roll out, I'll go." He strolled to the merchandise wagon, climbed to the seat, and gathered up the reins.

Diantha slipped on her Shaker sunbonnet so Mr. Golden couldn't see her grin beneath the elongated brim. One thing about Griff, he was a good man who knew his job. He also knew Mr. Golden needed him to tend the mules. She wished her own position were as secure. They'd have no tasks for her if Mrs. Golden ever decided to do the cooking.

She settled beside her employer and his wife on the wagon seat. With a flick of the reins, Mr. Golden guided the team onto the trail, and soon the jingling of the harnesses and clopping of hooves drowned out the birdsong. The wagon swayed from side to side as they rolled ahead over uneven terrain. Mrs. Golden perched ramrod straight beside her, silent as a stone and seemingly unaffected by the bumpy ride.

At first Diantha didn't mind the motion, but as the morning wore on her stomach rebelled. Her palms grew clammy. She gulped in several deep breaths. She couldn't be sick. Not now. She clapped her hand over her mouth.

Mrs. Golden turned toward her, red silk flowers fluttering on her straw bonnet. "Can't you sit still?"

"I'm sorry, ma'am. I don't feel well." Her stomach rocked in rhythm with the wagon's jolting. "Could I please get down and walk?"

"Oh, for heaven's sake." Mrs. Golden tapped her husband's arm. "Harold. Stop and let Diantha down. She'd rather walk than ride in this miserable wagon."

He pulled up on the reins. They came to a halt not a moment too soon. Diantha jumped down then stepped away and waited for the dizziness to pass. Mr. Golden leaned around his wife.

"If you can't keep up with the team on foot, you'll have to ride. Can't have you lost on the prairie."

"Yes, sir." With solid ground beneath her feet, she already felt better. As the wagon rolled forward, she pulled off her bonnet while she walked and removed the wooden slats supporting the brim. Without them she could see on all sides.

The prairie opened up before her. A jackrabbit bounded away through tall grass that undulated on both sides of the trail. A meadowlark dipped and circled above. Diantha drew a deep breath then sighed with pleasure. Her feet were on the road to Oregon.

Although the trail ahead appeared flat, the grassland rose and fell like ripples following a riverboat. Gradually Diantha lagged behind. The wagon rolled over a swale ahead and then disappeared. Glancing back, she couldn't spot Griff either. She increased her pace. Even if she had to trot all the way to Oregon, she wouldn't ride in the wagon again.

Chapter 7

Diantha froze. A man on horseback galloped across the prairie toward her. Warnings of renegade Indians pierced her mind, but the Goldens were too far ahead to hear if she cried out for help. She had no idea where Griff might be. Running was useless.

So was standing still like a frightened rabbit.

She bent over and picked up the heaviest rock she could carry then increased her pace, jaw thrust in the air. The rider, whoever he was, would have an unpleasant surprise if he accosted her. The hoofbeats came closer.

Without looking back, she marched up a rise in the trail. A hundred yards ahead the wagon's white canvas covering shone like a swaying beacon. Diantha held her skirt up with her free hand and ran.

Hoofbeats, then the horse snorted close behind her. She tightened her grip on the rock.

"Diantha. Why are you out here alone?"

She dropped the rock and spun around at the sound of Michael's voice. "You frightened me. I thought you were in front of the wagons."

"Duke needed a run. He's not meant to poke along with mules." He guided the horse off the trail and dismounted. "Now tell me why you're walking."

"Riding in the wagon made me ill. Your brother said I could walk as long as I kept up with them." She glanced forward as the wagon crested another swale. A prickle of alarm shivered through her. "I need to hurry on. They're too far ahead."

"I can fix that." He pointed to the horse. "You can ride in front of me. We'll catch them in no time."

She stepped close to Duke and stroked his lathered neck. Ride with Michael on this beautiful horse? What would people say? A chuckle escaped. Out here, no one would see her. She met his inquiring gaze.

"I'd like that. Let's go."

"Excellent." With a swift motion, he gripped her waist and lifted her, supporting her in front of the saddle. "You'll have to ride astride."

After a brief hesitation, she hitched her skirts enough to straddle the horse's neck. Michael swung into the saddle, put one arm around her, and tapped Duke's side with his foot. "Giddap."

She'd never been this close to a man. Diantha held her back straight, praying Michael couldn't feel her heart thumping beneath the pressure of his arm. She raised her face to the wind. *So this is how it feels to be held. Maybe someday. . .*

He leaned forward and spoke in her ear. "Want to gallop?"

"Yes!"

They flew down the road.

—⁓—

Griff topped a rise in time to see Michael lift Diantha onto his black horse and ride away. A bolt of jealousy took him by surprise. He had no claim on Diantha. Far from it. Yet the sight of the two of them together rocked his vow never to care for another woman.

His fists clenched when the animal broke into a gallop. What could Michael be thinking to risk Diantha's neck with his reckless horsemanship? If he wanted to ride like a fool, let him do it alone.

He'd been holding back to stay out of the Goldens' dust, but now he shook the reins, urging the mules to a faster gait. If she were to fall off, he wanted to be there to care for her. Not that he was interested in courtship. Not at all.

Michael reined his horse to a stop when he approached Golden's wagon. Mr. Golden apparently didn't see them. The wagon kept rolling while Michael set Diantha on the ground. Griff slowed his mules.

She turned to Michael and said something, but try as he might, Griff couldn't hear her words. Then Michael remounted and rode away.

Diantha glanced over her shoulder when Griff tugged his team to a stop. Her cheeks pinked.

"You saw me?"

"Yup. Could've broken your neck, the way he rode that horse."

"Well, he didn't. I'm safe."

"Good." He tried to think of something else to say, but his brain failed him.

Diantha pointed at the Goldens' wagon rolling down the road. "Riding made me ill, so I'm walking, but I fell behind. Michael happened by." She raised her eyes to his.

An odd tingle filled Griff. She cared enough to explain herself. Emboldened, he leaned forward. "Don't suppose you'd like to try riding with me. I don't usually drive the team as fast as I did that first day."

"That would be fine. My feet are a little sore." She pointed downward. "New boots."

He helped her onto the seat then flicked the lines. "Get up." The mules plodded forward.

After a couple of minutes, Diantha smiled up at him. "You're right. This is much better." She settled back on the seat.

"Nothing to it. Just takes practice." He squared his shoulders. Better be careful. He could get used to having her beside him.

—⁓—

Several evenings later, Diantha crept into her little tent after supper, tired to the bone. Whether walking or riding, the constant travel took some adjustment. She exchanged her work dress for a flannel nightgown, sank onto her bedroll, and tucked a quilt around her shoulders. Mr. and Mrs. Golden slept on a feather bed in their wagon. Michael and Griff shared space with the merchandise. The tent gave her welcome privacy to dress and undress, but unfamiliar noises outside the canvas walls prevented her eyes from closing.

The night was black as a cavern. Wind snapped at the sides of the tent, tugging at the ties that secured the entrance. The sky lit with a brilliant flash, followed by a burst of thunder. Diantha sat up, clutching her quilt to her chest. She tried to remember the rules about being in the open in a thunderstorm. "Don't stand under a tree" was all that came to mind before another flash and roll of thunder.

She slipped her feet into her boots and stood trembling while the storm reverberated around her. *Lord, be with me.*

"Get the mules between the wagons," Griff shouted. Mr. Golden and Michael yelled at each other between thunderclaps. Lightning flared incessantly. The tent rocked on its stakes as the wind tore around the canvas.

Diantha dropped to her knees on her bedroll, certain she'd be carried away in the next gust. The entrance tore open. She shuddered and huddled in a low crouch as rain sprayed over her.

Griff pounded through the opening. "I've got you. Come with me." He threw a waterproof poncho over her shoulders then lifted her to her feet. "Run. You're going to the Goldens' wagon."

He gripped her hand, and they splashed past the terrified mules. A jagged bolt of lightning illuminated the white canvas top as he clasped her waist and swung her aboard. "Get inside where it's dry."

"Aren't you coming, too?"

Water dripped from the brim of his hat. "I'm staying with the teams. Can't risk them running off." He disappeared into the darkness.

She wiggled through the opening in the canvas. A shadowy figure at the rear moaned when the wagon swayed under Diantha's weight.

"Harold?" Mrs. Golden's shrill voice rose an octave.

"It's me, ma'am. Griff brought me out of the storm."

"Where's Harold?"

"Helping with the mules."

"I need him here. Now."

Diantha felt her way around barrels and chests until she touched a corner of the feather bed. "I'm sure he'll come as soon as he can."

Mrs. Golden shrieked when a peal of thunder shook the wagon. "I want to go home! I hate this wagon, and I hate this journey. We never should have left Missouri."

"We have storms in Missouri, too, ma'am." Now that she was safe in the sturdy wagon, she forgot her earlier fear. She sat on a chest next to the bed. "Listen. Thunder's moving away. The rain will let up soon."

"Not soon enough." She groped for Diantha's hand. "Promise you won't leave me."

"I'll be with you all the way to Oregon, I promise you that." Once they were settled in Dalles City, she would get on with her new life. And so would Mrs. Golden.

Chapter 8

Mr. Golden's wracking cough broke the morning air. A week had passed since the storm, but they'd traveled only as far as the Big Blue River before he collapsed and had to be carried to his bed.

Diantha stirred the fire to life, and Mrs. Golden paced back and forth nearby, wringing her hands. "I knew we should have turned around. Now Harold's sick and there isn't a doctor for at least a hundred miles." She whirled to face Diantha. "How do I know your remedy will work?"

"My mother always gave me pleurisy root tea to stop a cough." Mrs. Golden's distress revived Diantha's feelings of helplessness in the face of her mother's final illness. None of the remedies the doctors tried were enough to save her. Now Diantha clung to the memory of warm tea and her mother's soothing hand on her forehead. With the Lord's help, Mr. Golden would recover.

The wagon jolted as Griff jumped to the ground carrying the medicine chest she'd insisted on including when they set out for Oregon. He placed the chest on the ground below the spot where he'd mounted the cooking-utensil box. "Anything else you need?"

"Not right now."

"I'll gather more wood for the fire. Shouldn't take long."

She smiled into his caring eyes. "Thank you, Griff. I don't know how we'd get by without you."

After he left she busied herself combining powdered roots with heated water in a small pot. Mrs. Golden sidled next to her.

"I noticed how you looked at Griff. You should know he told Harold that he has someone waiting for him in Dalles City."

"He's been a great help, is all. Michael has, too." Nevertheless, her heart plummeted. She looked away rather than give Mrs. Golden the satisfaction of seeing that her comment hit its target.

When she turned back, the woman narrowed her eyes. "Well, don't think you can go after Michael either. He comes from a good family—not servant class."

Diantha sprang to her feet. "I have no expectations of making a match on this journey. For your information, my father was a professor at Spencerhill Academy. He came to St. Joseph with plans to write a book. I may work as a servant now, but I know the Lord has better plans for me in Dalles City." She grabbed the pot, poured some of the yellow-brown liquid into a mug, and thrust it at Mrs. Golden. "Have him drink some of this every hour." She deliberately left the "ma'am" off her statement.

Mrs. Golden raised an eyebrow. "I hate to see you pining after someone out of reach. I only meant to be helpful."

"Of course you did." She folded her arms across her middle and glared at Mrs. Golden until the woman walked toward the wagon. Servant class, indeed. She blinked back stinging tears. Thankfully her parents would never know how their deaths had diminished her standing in St. Joseph.

Footsteps crunched over the grass beside the trail, and she looked up at Griff approaching, arms laden with firewood. A quick dash with the back of her hand removed the evidence of tears from her cheeks.

He dropped the wood near the fire and settled his dark eyes on her face. "Everything all right?"

"Just fine, thank you." She took in his rugged features, smile lines, and broad shoulders. No wonder he had someone waiting in Dalles City. She gave herself a little shake. He was a helpful companion, that's all.

Pointing a thumb at the wagon, he asked, "You worried about the boss?"

"Not worried, exactly. I just pray he gets better." Diantha frowned as another coughing spell struck. "He may have pneumonia."

"D'you have sassafras in the medicine chest? It'll break the fever."

"Oh mercy. I should have thought of that myself." She hurried to the wagon and rummaged for a bottle of the healing bark. "When the tea is ready, would you mind taking it to Mr. Golden? It's not proper for me to attend him."

"Sure. Faster he recovers, the faster we'll be on our way. Dalles City's waiting."

And so is the girl you left behind. She swallowed a lump in her throat.

Crying helped nothing.

—〰—

Late the following afternoon Diantha faced east in wonder as dust clouds rose in the distance. Buffalo? A stampede? She took a step back, ready to run to their camp with a warning, when a wagon crested a rise in the trail. Astonished, she watched as a full company of emigrant wagons rolled toward her. Creaking wheels and lowing oxen shattered the quiet of the meadow. Rather than be caught gaping when the travelers came close, she sped back to the shelter of the Goldens' wagon.

Griff stood by the fire, tin mug in hand. "Looks like all our rush was for naught. We'll be sharing pasture from here on."

"Not if I can help it," Mr. Golden hollered. He climbed down from his wagon, nightshirt tucked into his trousers. He wobbled toward them. "Those folks will need a day or two by the river to rest their stock. We'll move out at first light tomorrow." He drew a rasping breath then braced his hands on his knees as he bent forward in a fit of coughing.

Wagons flooded the meadow around them, spreading from the riverbank through the lush grassland. Ten, twenty, dozens. Prairie hens flew from their hiding places to wing across the river. A jackrabbit shot past.

Diantha touched Mr. Golden's shoulder. "Perhaps we'd best wait until you're better. Let them get ahead."

He straightened, looking like his former commanding self. "You see all that? What do you think will be left for our teams if we follow those wagons?" His glance slid to

Griff. "Get us hitched up at daylight. We're leaving." He took a few steps toward his wagon then staggered to one side.

Griff caught his arm before he fell. "Sir—"

"Let go. I'm fine." He covered the rest of the distance and climbed to the seat. After drawing several shallow breaths, he leaned toward them. "Send Michael to me soon as he comes back from wherever he went. His horseback days are over. He'll be driving the wagon from now on."

A small smile flitted across Griff's face. "Yes, sir."

Diantha poked up the fire and added more wood to the coals. She'd bake extra corn bread tonight so she'd have a quick breakfast ready. By adding bacon and beans, they could be far down the trail before noon. She'd learned the hard way that Mr. Golden meant every word when he said they'd leave at daylight.

—⁓—

Michael and his horse were silhouettes against the sunset when he rode into camp. As soon as he dismounted, Diantha hurried to his side.

"Your brother is asking for you."

"Griff told me." His jaw set in a tight line, he ground-tied Duke then leaned toward her. The smell of sweat and leather swirled close. "After supper, would you like to walk by the river? I hoped we'd have more time here, but brother's word is law." The last rays of sun bathed his face with a ruddy glow.

She hugged her arms around her middle. "A walk would be pleasant. Thank you."

"I'll come looking for you later."

She watched him as he loped toward his brother's wagon. She didn't care what Mrs. Golden thought—if Michael wanted to court her, who was she to resist? In a new territory, old class distinctions had no value. She wished she'd thought to say that to Mrs. Golden.

After the evening meal she hurried through her chores then ducked into her tent to grab her shawl. When she stepped back out, she collided with Griff.

He put his broad hands on her shoulders. "Steady there."

"I'm sorry! I wasn't looking where I was going." Heat climbed her neck when he didn't release his hold.

"Running into you is a pleasure. Don't apologize." He dropped his hands to his sides. "Wondered if you'd like to walk down to the river with me. Be awhile before we're stopped in a place this pretty again."

"I forgot, you've been here before."

"Twice now, but how'd you know?"

"Mrs. Golden mentioned something about you and Dalles City." Her pulse pounded when she remembered the woman's words. Griff had somebody waiting for him. She forced herself to look away from his heart-melting coffee-brown eyes.

"She mentioned me, eh? Well, maybe you should hear my side of the story. Let's take that walk."

"I'm sorry. I already promised Michael."

Griff's expression hardened. "I see." He tipped his hat. "Good evening, Diantha."

She bit her lip and watched as he walked away, knowing in her heart that if Michael hadn't asked her first, she'd have gone with Griff without thinking twice. Just as a friend, of course.

—⚭—

Mrs. Golden's voice grated on Griff's ears as he passed their wagon on his way to check the mules. He didn't mean to eavesdrop, but her whiny tone was unescapable.

"Why can't we go back tomorrow instead of this incessant hurrying on?"

"Not another word about turning back. D'you hear me?" Harold Golden's voice rose. He coughed and then continued. "We're going to Dalles City, and that's—"

Griff passed beyond the sound of their argument. He'd never met a more mismatched couple than the Goldens. If he had to listen to that woman's voice day in and day out, he'd go mad.

On the other hand, he could listen to Diantha's gentle tones forever.

He stopped short. Where had that thought come from? Forever? He'd promised that once, in Dalles City, and life betrayed him.

Maybe it was time to give life another chance, as his sister had urged him before he traveled east. The expression on Diantha's face when she mentioned Mrs. Golden's comments left him feeling defensive. What had the woman said?

His lead mules, Jasper and Jackson, snorted when they saw him coming their way. He checked their stakes then draped an arm over Jasper's neck. "I said I'd tell Diantha my side of the story. Do I risk telling her all of it?"

The animal sidestepped and bent his head for a bite of grass.

Across the meadow, Diantha took Michael's arm as they walked toward the riverbank.

Griff tightened his jaw. He couldn't compete with a man who had a secure future waiting for him in Oregon Territory.

—⚭—

Diantha gripped Michael's elbow for support as they crossed the uneven ground leading to the Big Blue River. Oaks, sycamores, and cottonwoods lined the bank, lending a feeling of seclusion in spite of the many wagons camped in the area. The watery smell from the river mingled with wood smoke from campfires. She drew a deep breath.

"I've always loved the smell of rivers. Something about all that water, traveling to new places."

He tipped his head toward her. "You're a poet. I never give rivers a thought, unless I have to ford them."

"We've forded a few already. Thankfully with no upsets."

"Yes. And we'll cross this one tomorrow." He rested his hand over hers. "Let's not talk about the trail. I'd like to know more about you."

Her heart trip-hammered. "There isn't much to tell, I'm afraid. You know I work for your brother."

"That's not who you are, it's what you do. I'm curious why you're willing to risk this journey all alone."

"My parents both died two years ago, when I was sixteen. I have no other family.

Oregon will be a new start for me."

"So you really are all alone." He stopped beneath the spreading branches of a sycamore tree and touched her lips with his forefinger. "Maybe we need to do something about that."

She stepped away, feeling the rough bark of the tree against her shoulders. Her heartbeat filled her throat. "It's getting dark. Let's turn around."

"Ah, Diantha. I apologize for frightening you. Of course we'll go back. We'll have plenty of time for walks. Oregon's a long way from here."

She swallowed hard. "So it is."

Perhaps before they arrived, she'd listen to Griff's story from his lips. That's what friends were for.

Chapter 9

At daylight the next morning Michael drove the family's wagon into the water of the Big Blue River. Mr. Golden rode alongside on Duke.

Diantha sat on the seat of the merchandise wagon, while Griff paced back and forth watching the crossing from the bank. She gasped when the wagon wobbled in the current. "Are they going to upset?"

Griff pivoted to look at her. "Not if Michael doesn't lose his head. Driving a mule team's different than riding a horse." He cupped his hands around his mouth and hollered, "Don't slack on the reins! Keep 'em moving."

Diantha slumped against the seat back. This was the biggest river they'd had to ford thus far on the journey. "I thought there'd be ferries."

Griff joined her, released the brake, and picked up the lines. He angled a glace in her direction. "Not much in the way of ferries from here on. Just have to know how to read the river."

"And you do?"

"Yup."

On the opposite shore, Michael's team of mules tucked their heads down, shoulders straining, and hauled the wagon up the muddy bank. As water poured from the mules' bellies, Duke shied and then crow-hopped. Mr. Golden flew off the animal and landed on his back in a rocky shoal.

Diantha pressed her hand to her throat. "He'll drown!"

Griff shook the lines. "Git up!" The mules descended the sloping ground and plunged into the water.

Michael waded into the river and dragged his brother to shore. The older man lay unmoving. Mrs. Golden ran to him, screaming his name, then her frantic gaze found Griff and Diantha. "He's bleeding! Help me!"

"Git up! Git up!" Griff half stood, muscles in his forearms distended as he urged the team forward.

Diantha clutched the edge of the bench as they rolled into the river. Ripples in the mules' wake swept over the wheels, brushing against the front. Halfway across, the wagon rocked as it lifted into the current. Without thinking, she grasped Griff's arm. "Mercy sakes! We're floating away."

He shook his head. "Mules aren't swimming. We'll be across in a couple minutes." The animals found a foothold and pulled, climbing the bank and drawing the wagon onto dry land. Griff stopped the team and jumped down.

Diantha clambered over the wheel and dashed toward Mr. Golden's still form, her boots slipping in the sandy soil.

Mrs. Golden ran to her, grabbing her arm, tugging her forward. "I don't know what to do. He'll bleed to death if you don't help him." The woman's hair tangled loose around her shoulders. Naked fear shone in her eyes.

Michael stood off to one side, his expression stony. "Told him that horse was too much for him, but he wouldn't listen. He never does."

Heart pounding, Diantha knelt next to Mr. Golden. His barrel chest rose and fell in the faintest of movements. Blood stained the pebbles near his head. She lifted her eyes to Michael, who'd moved next to his brother. "Turn him, please. I need to see how badly he's hurt."

He slid his hands under the man's shoulders, rolling him onto his side facing away from her. Blood streamed from a gash in the back of his head.

She probed the edges of the wound, relieved to find a tear to the scalp but no apparent injury to the skull beneath. *First thing to do is stop the bleeding.* Her mind skated over remedies she knew. Comfrey. Yarrow. She couldn't remember seeing either plant on their journey. Pressing the torn edges of his scalp together, she decided on the only solution close at hand.

After wiping her bloody fingers on her skirt, she lifted the calico garment over her ankles and tore a strip from her petticoat. She wadded the cloth into a square and pressed the makeshift poultice against his wound. He moaned, stirred, and flopped onto his back while she followed his movement, keeping the cloth against his scalp.

Griff knelt next to her. "D'you need the medicine chest?"

She shook her head. "Comfrey leaves would be a godsend though. As soon as he wakes up, I'll search along the riverbank. Might be some plants in the damp soil."

Mrs. Golden hovered nearby, wringing her hands. "No. You stay with Harold." She directed her attention to Griff and Michael. "Take him to the wagon then find the plants Diantha needs."

Diantha sought Griff's eyes. "Mind you keep his wound covered."

She stood, watching while the two men lifted Mr. Golden and crossed the uneven ground to his wagon. Her limbs trembled. They'd come so close to disaster.

Thank You, Lord, for being with us this day. As she thought of Griff's calm steadiness, she added, *And thank You for Griff.*

⁓

That evening, Diantha slumped in one of the two folding camp chairs from the Goldens' wagon. Coals from the dying campfire glowed in the dusk. Her mind circled the events of the day, reviewing Mr. Golden's accident over and over. She'd washed the wound after a comfrey poultice stopped the bleeding. He'd awakened and sipped a mixture of cold flour stirred into a generous amount of water. Now he seemed to be sleeping normally. Had she done enough? She wished she knew.

She rose and paced past the fire to stand facing the shadowed grassland. The picketed mules were dark silhouettes against the pink and coral wash of color in the western sky. One of the shadows separated from the herd and came toward her. Her heart quickened when she recognized Griff's purposeful stride.

"I thought you'd be sleeping by now." His deep voice rumbled in her ear. The fragrance of wood smoke and leather enveloped her. She inhaled deeply, savoring his nearness. "I can't seem to settle down. Perhaps I should remain by the wagon, in case he awakens during the night."

"If Mrs. Golden needs you, she'll summon you." He extended his elbow. "Come, let's take a walk. We can watch the stars come out."

"That sounds lovely." She tucked her hand over his arm. Everything about him set her senses fluttering. For once, she decided to cast aside thoughts about his Dalles City commitment and simply revel in his nearness.

Grass whispered against their legs as they strolled in companionable silence. When a bright star appeared on the horizon, she stopped and pointed. "The evening star. See?"

"Venus."

"What?"

"That's a planet named Venus."

Ready to comment on his knowledge of the heavens, she looked into his eyes. Instead of speaking, she felt herself sinking into their depths.

He moved closer.

Then bent his head.

His lips met hers.

Heat traced a path down her body. She slid her arms around his muscular back and rested her head on his chest. "Griff. . ." The word was a sigh.

He placed his hands on her shoulders, moved her a step away. "I'm sorry—I had no right."

Cold awareness jolted her to her senses. "Of course you don't. I'm the one who should apologize. Mrs. Golden warned me."

"That's not what I meant. Let me explain."

"There's no need." She turned and fled.

"Diantha, wait!"

She ignored him, her feet pounding over the hard soil. Of all the foolish things, to let him kiss her when she knew he was promised to another. Tears knotted her throat.

Tears don't help. Nothing would help the shame she felt.

⁓

Griff stamped across the grassland toward the spot where he'd tethered the mules. The man must be mad. Two days ago Harold Golden had been near death, and now he insisted they continue west. The emigrant party they'd left behind would pass them at any time if they remained where they were.

For once, he hoped Mrs. Golden's pleas would have some effect, but so far they hadn't. Harold was determined to reach Nebraska Territory ahead of the St. Joseph Company.

"Another week won't make any difference. He's not well enough to travel," Griff said to Jasper. The mule pulled back his lips in a conspiratorial grin. He stroked the animal's neck and began the process of hitching his team to the merchandise wagon.

One good thing about moving on—he'd have Diantha with him on the wagon seat while they continued along the trail. She'd avoided him since he'd kissed her. Why shouldn't she? He'd been cowardly about telling her the truth, and Mrs. Golden's words had hanged him without a trial. He shot a glance at the campsite. Diantha leaned over the fire frying bacon, judging from the aroma that drifted his way. Rising sun shone on her glossy black hair. For a moment he imagined those silky strands beneath his fingers.

The image shattered when Michael walked to the fire and said something to her. She smiled at him and replied.

Griff narrowed his eyes, cursing the moment he'd allowed his emotions to run away with him. A girl needed to feel safe, not threatened. Would he never learn?

Chapter 10

Diantha blew out a weary breath and surveyed the sterile countryside before entering a new-looking stone building beside the trail. Here and there a few cottonwoods stood in clusters marking the presence of a creek or water hole. Rock Creek Station was the first sign of civilization they'd seen since reaching Nebraska. Clutching the handful of coins Mr. Golden gave her, she entered the low-ceilinged single room.

"Wondered when one of you folks would come in. You're welcome to camp here, but 'course I hope you'll buy something." A middle-aged man with a grizzled beard leaned on a makeshift counter fashioned from two parallel boards balanced on barrels. "I'm Ernie Wagstaff, by the by. Merchant wagon just come through last week. I got a good stock right now."

"We've run low on salt." She cringed, remembering Mr. Golden's tirade when he discovered she hadn't stocked enough.

"Salt." Mr. Wagstaff took a box from a shelf behind him and plunked the package on the counter. "That all?"

"I need some powdered charcoal. My employer is ailing, and our water has become stagnant."

"Wise choice. Water out here is chancy at best." He rubbed his beard. "If he don't perk up, there's a doctor at Fort Kearney, about a week's travel northwest."

"Thank you." She prayed Mr. Golden would "perk up" much sooner than that. Every day on the trail drew his energy down further.

Mr. Wagstaff pushed her two parcels together and gave her an expectant look. "Anything else?"

She shook her head.

"That'll be one dollar."

"A dollar?" A pulse throbbed in her temple. Mr. Golden would be livid.

"Costs money to bring freight out here. Can't give things away just 'cause you're a pretty gal."

Hot, dusty, and perspiring, she felt anything but pretty. She gave him a dollar coin, promised to send someone for the purchases, and hurried back to camp. Mr. Golden was waiting.

When she neared their wagon, Mrs. Golden raced in her direction. "Harold sent me to find you. What took so long?"

"I was only gone a few minutes." She strove to keep her voice calm. Bad enough to have to face Mr. Golden without also enduring his wife's scolding.

Michael strolled over. "Relax, Priscilla. She's here now." He offered Diantha his arm.

"I'll walk you to the wagon."

"I'm to go inside?"

He drew her a few steps away from Mrs. Golden then lowered his head to speak close to her ear. "Harold's failing. Did you buy the charcoal?"

Her heart skipped at his warm breath on her neck. "Yes, of course."

"Then I'll start filtering soon as I fetch the packages. Fresh water should help." He put his hands on her waist and lifted her onto the wagon, then crossed to the supply station.

Surprised at the change in his attitude toward his brother, she watched him walk away. Weeks on the trail had mellowed his defiant behavior. She liked him better now, but still. . . Her eyes searched the camp for a glimpse of Griff. Then she gave herself a little shake. Mr. Golden was suffering. The last thing she ought to be doing was mooning over someone promised to another.

She poked her head inside the canvas covering and recoiled at the stench of rotting flesh. Until now, she'd spoken to her employer outdoors where constant wind kept odors at bay.

"Diantha?" Mr. Golden raised himself onto his elbows. His voice wheezed. "You bought what we need?"

She picked her way around the contents of the wagon. "Yes, sir. Here's your change."

He looked at the coins. "Salt and charcoal powder cost a dollar? I should open my store right here." He tried for a chuckle but ended up choking.

Grateful he wasn't angry, she leaned close, trying not to inhale the cloud of putrefaction that surrounded him. "May I check your wound, sir?"

"Just don't touch it. Hurts like blazes." He leaned forward.

When she saw the back of his head, her stomach clenched. The edges of the gash were red and swollen. Greenish pus oozed into his hair. She took a step backward. "Good gracious. Why didn't you tell me about this sooner?"

"Figured it had to hurt to get better."

She drew a shallow breath. "As soon as our water is clear, I'll clean the area and add a new poultice. Would you drink another cup of cold flour?" The cinnamon-flavored mixture was the only food he'd tolerated for the past several days.

"Yes." His voice faded as he reclined on the bed. "I'll sleep now."

Diantha crept from the wagon, shocked at the change in him over the past twenty-four hours. She had no other options beyond keeping him clean and nourished. A headache pounded her temples.

She hadn't felt this helpless since her parents died.

―∾―

Griff stood next to the merchandise wagon and studied the muddy water of the broad Platte River. Above him, Diantha perched on the edge of the seat. The Goldens' two wagons took up most of the space on a log flatboat as ferrymen poled them slowly toward the opposite bank. The crude vessel tipped. Mr. Golden moaned, the sound loud over the gentle lapping of the water.

Fear contorted Diantha's face. Griff stepped nearer, wishing he could wrap his arms around her and hold her close against his heart. Day after day she'd worn herself to exhaustion nursing their employer while cooking and tending to all of them. And it seemed Michael was at her side every moment that he wasn't driving a wagon.

Griff silently cursed his cowardice. He'd confess his past and let her decide if she could love him. He would. As soon as they reached Fort Kearney.

The flatboat scraped bottom, and he climbed back onto the wagon. "We'll be on dry land in a minute."

Diantha gave a weak chuckle. "This river's so shallow in spots, it felt like we were on dry land half the time."

"A mile wide and a few inches deep, some people say."

He waited while Michael drove the Goldens' wagon onto the shore, Duke tied behind, then followed.

A few miles beyond the river they saw the square outline of Fort Kearney straight ahead. In the center of the parade ground a large American flag waved from atop a tall staff. He smiled at the familiar sight of the fort, protecting settlers on their way west.

Diantha touched his arm. "The first thing we must do is find the doctor. I'm grateful Mr. Golden has held on this long."

He rested his hand over hers. "Thanks to your care." Her face flushed, and she drew her hand away.

Today. I'll tell her today.

Flicking the lines, he drove alongside Michael's wagon and pointed to a one-story wooden frame building at the left of the parade ground. "There's the hospital. I'll help you take him inside."

—∿∿—

Diantha moved aside to give Griff and Michael space as they supported Mr. Golden's weight between them. They maneuvered him from the wagon into the hospital then eased him onto a couch placed against one wall. A table, two wooden chairs, and a cluttered shelf beneath a fly-specked window also furnished the reception area. The remainder of the hospital hid behind two closed doors.

Mrs. Golden trailed them inside, her once-elegant purple gown stained and tattered. She stared around the room with wild eyes. "Where's the doctor?"

One of the doors swung open, admitting a short man sporting a brushy mustache and a beard trimmed to a dagger point.

"I'm Dr. Irving." He crossed the room, stopping beside Mr. Golden. He wrinkled his nose. "How long's he been like this?"

Diantha stepped forward. "Eight or nine days. He fell off a horse and hit the back of his head. I've tried everything I know, but nothing's helped." Her voice trembled.

"You his wife?"

"No. I am." Mrs. Golden tipped her chin up. "She's a girl my husband hired."

Heat flamed over Diantha. After all her efforts, she was just the hired girl? She dipped her head and backed toward the entrance. Wood smoke and leather. Griff stood behind her. He rested his hand on her shoulder for a brief touch, long enough to share his strength.

Dr. Irving bent over Mr. Golden and turned him onto his side. When he probed the edges of the wound, the injured man jerked and gave a ragged moan. After another moment, the doctor straightened and looked at Mrs. Golden.

"I'll have orderlies take him to a bed in there." He pointed at the second door. "He's feverish. The infection's probably spread. I'll do all I can for him, but I don't hold much hope."

She clapped her hand over her mouth. "Harold. . ."

The doctor's stern expression softened. "Why don't you get some sleep? One of the soldiers will come for you if there's any change."

"Thank you."

Diantha waited until Michael led Mrs. Golden from the room. As soon as the door closed, she faced Dr. Irving. "I cleaned the wound the best I could, and used comfrey poultices. What else should I have done?"

"You said he fell off a horse?"

"Yes. The animal threw him into a shoal on the banks of the Big Blue. He shouldn't have been riding—he'd been sick."

"You couldn't have changed this outcome, miss. Mud, algae, foreign matter, any of those would infect a wound." He glanced at Griff. "The two of you might rest a bit before returning to your duties. I suspect the past week has been trying."

Thankful for his compassion, Diantha released a long sigh. She'd done all she could. Mr. Golden's fate was now in the Lord's hands.

~~~

After situating the wagons behind the enlisted men's quarters and turning the mules loose in a corral, Griff joined Diantha beneath one of the trees bordering the parade ground. "There's a little piece of grassland east of the fort. Will you walk there with me?" He knew his timing couldn't have been worse, but he wouldn't let another day go by without clarifying whatever Mrs. Golden had told her. He held his breath while he waited for Diantha's response.

She looked at the ground, fiddled with a loose strand of hair, then nodded. "It would be nice to get out of sight of the hospital. I can't stop thinking about poor Mr. Golden."

"No one could have done more than you did. Dr. Irving is well known as a healer. Don't lose hope."

"I keep forgetting you've been here before." She gave him a wan smile before taking his elbow. "Show me this patch of grass."

They walked west between the commanding officer's house and the sutler's store, past the laundress's quarters, and out onto an open plain. When they reached the pocket-sized meadow, Griff stopped and turned Diantha to face him.

"Mrs. Golden told you something about me and Dalles City." He poked the toe of his boot against an orange poppy. "What did she say?"

Diantha jammed her hands on her hips. "She said you have someone waiting there. She thought I should know."

"I should have told you myself a long time ago, but I was afraid of what you'd think."

"What is there to think? You're promised to another. It shames me to remember I let you kiss me."

He bowed his head, rubbing his mouth with his fist. *Lord, give me the words.* "She's partly right."

Diantha bristled. "You brought me out here to tell me something I already knew?"

He lowered himself onto a clump of grass and held out his hand. "Sit a minute and listen to me."

She humphed, but settled near.

"That someone waiting for me is my little daughter, Bets—Elizabeth." He kept his eyes on the grass at his feet. "When her mother died, I promised myself I'd devote my life to caring for her. Then the army sent me back East, and I had to leave Bets with my sister—but only until I could get back to Dalles City, which is where I'm headed now."

He dared a glance at Diantha's face. She stared at him, wide-eyed.

"Why didn't you say something sooner?"

"I thought I had no right to involve you in my tangled past. But I couldn't force myself to stay away from you. You've been in my heart ever since I rescued you in St. Joe."

"Oh, Griff." Tears shone in her eyes. "I didn't dare hope. . ."

He took her hands in his and drew her to her feet. "Neither did I."

He kissed her waiting mouth, and she tightened her arms around his neck and kissed him in return. Her soft lips lit a fire inside him. He held her tight against his heart, where she belonged.

"Diantha! Griff! Where've you been?" Michael raced toward them across the parade ground. "Harold passed on about twenty minutes ago."

Diantha sagged against Griff. "No. Please, no."

Michael leveled his red-rimmed eyes on her. "Please come with me. Priscilla needs you. We have to find the chaplain and arrange for burial."

"Yes, of course I'll come." She squeezed Griff's hand and then stumbled after Michael.

Harold Golden, gone. Griff watched as Michael and Diantha covered the distance to the parked wagons, his mind jumping to the days ahead. He pushed his hat higher on his forehead, wondering who'd be making the travel decisions—Michael or Mrs. Golden.

Jaw clenched, he marched toward the corral. No matter. He was going to Dalles City, even if that meant waiting for the emigrant train and traveling with them.

Chapter 11

Diantha and Mrs. Golden lingered in the post cemetery following the burial. Michael had excused himself after the chaplain read scripture over the grave. Griff didn't attend the brief service. Diantha caught herself puzzling over his absence when she should have been listening to the chaplain's words.

When the burial detail dropped the last shovelful of dirt over Harold Golden's coffin, Mrs. Golden took Diantha's arm and led her away from the cemetery.

"I have something to show you."

"Where are we going?"

"The sutler's store."

A team of mules hitched to an army supply wagon waited outside the wooden building. On the driver's perch, two soldiers tipped their hats. "Miz Golden. The captain gave permission for you to come with us to St. Joe. We leave tomorrow. That suit you?"

"Perfectly. I'm not traveling another mile west." The feathers on her black silk bonnet rustled when she looked at Diantha. "Michael will transfer our things to this wagon."

Diantha gaped at her. "*Our* things? I'm going on to Dalles City. Griff—"

"An unmarried girl traveling with two men? Out of the question. My husband was responsible for you, and I'm assuming his role."

"You have no right."

"I have every right." The woman pointed toward the commanding officer's home. "Captain Harlow's wife has kindly invited us for an evening meal."

Diantha spun away from Mrs. Golden's grasping fingers. "I'm not hungry."

Griff. She had to find Griff. She sped toward the wagons, stopping short when she saw one wagon instead of two. Michael lounged on a camp chair next to a pile of trunks, boxes, and her carpetbags.

"Where—where's the merchandise wagon? Where's Griff?"

"Priscilla sent him on ahead. He left when we gathered for Harold's burial."

Shock fired through Diantha. Two nights ago she'd believed Griff cared for her—loved her as she did him. *Griff left. Without explanation. No good-bye. Just. . .left.* She swayed, devastated at his betrayal.

Michael sprang to her side and steadied her. "I know you're surprised. Things have happened so quickly."

"To say the least," she murmured, trying to accept Griff's departure.

"Priscilla thought it best that you travel with her to St. Joseph, while Griff and I open the mercantile in Dalles City. I'm leaving in the morning." The look he bestowed on her was more a smirk than a smile. "The store will be mine. She wants no part in Harold's Oregon scheme."

"You said you didn't want to go to Dalles City."

"That was before I owned the business. Things are different now."

She stared up at his triumphant expression, wondering how she could ever have thought him handsome.

She turned her back on him and plodded toward the sutler's store. Unshed tears stung her eyes. Her dream of Oregon. Her dream of love with Griff. Both buried with her employer in an army cemetery. *Lord, I was so sure of Your leading. You brought Griff into my life. Now this.* She sniffled. *You must have a future planned for me, but what is it?*

—⁂—

The next day Diantha sat on her carpetbags inside the supply wagon watching the western trail unroll behind her. With every mile traveled eastward, conviction grew in her heart. She was meant to go to Oregon. With or without Griff, she'd get there.

When they stopped on the banks of the Platte River, she dropped her bags to the ground and jumped out of the wagon. Mrs. Golden stamped toward her.

"What on earth are you doing? Put those back."

Chin jutted in the air, Diantha gripped the handles, lifted the bags, and faced west. "I'm going to Oregon."

"On foot?"

"I'll wait at the fort for an emigrant wagon, and hire on as a cook." She sent the woman a crooked grin. "Thanks to you, I have experience."

"But I'm responsible—"

"No, you're not. I'm eighteen. I make my own decisions." She nodded at the wide-eyed soldiers. "Have a pleasant journey."

She hefted her bags and stalked west along the rutted trail. Within minutes she topped a rise and the supply wagon disappeared from view. She half expected one of the soldiers to come after her. When no one did, she drew a relieved breath. She'd reach Fort Kearney before nightfall.

Mourning doves cooed in the grass surrounding the trail as she approached, then broke cover and flew away. Her spirit soared with them. Free of Mrs. Golden, free to make her way west. Part of her dream was in her grasp. She tried not to think about Griff.

A dust cloud billowed behind an approaching rider. Gauging from his speed, he'd gallop over the top of her. She stepped off the trail.

Horse and rider stopped before her. She gasped, unable to believe her eyes. "Griff?"

A broad grin creased his face. He jumped from the horse and swept her up, covering her face with kisses. His lips settled on her ear. "Thank the Lord, I found you."

She snuggled into his embrace. Wood smoke and leather. Her heart threatened to beat its way out of her chest. After a lingering kiss, she leaned back in his arms. "Michael said you'd gone ahead to Dalles City."

"They told me you'd be in the other wagon. It wasn't until Michael caught up with me that I knew they'd lied." He curled his mouth in a half smile. "You might say I persuaded him to loan me his horse."

The joy that filled her spilled out in laughter. When she sobered, she placed her hand on his cheek. "Oh, Griff. I thought you deliberately left me behind."

"Not for the rest of my life—if you'll have me."

"Yes! A thousand times, yes."

"In that case, we need to find the chaplain at the fort. Mr. and Mrs. Griffin have a long journey ahead of them. We need to get started."

He lifted her into his arms and settled her in front of Duke's saddle. "We'll come back for your things after the ceremony."

Holding the reins with one hand, he kept his free arm tight around her waist. She rested her head against his chest.

Griff and Oregon together. The Lord had answered every prayer.

Sioux Summer

by Jennifer Uhlarik

Dedication

To Dave,
I love standing shoulder to shoulder with you on this journey of life.
Thank you for your love, gentleness, and understanding.
You exemplify Christ, and I am proud to be your wife.
Ephesians 5:25

Chapter 1

The pungent scent of stale sweat mingled with something wild and musky, knotting Ellie Jefford's stomach. Coal-black eyes locked with hers as a foul-smelling Sioux warrior circled her, clad in only a breechclout, leggings, and moccasins. Her heart raced, and sweat snaked across her skin. The sweltering summer heat didn't help matters.

Do not let on that you're afraid, Ellison.

Guttural words broke the stillness, and she turned toward the two braves behind her. Ellie forced a slight smile. "Have you found something you want?" She formed the stilted sign language gestures that Frank had taught her, and after a moment, the three men laughed.

Wrong word, Ellie. It must have been. Yet knowing it was wrong and being able to fix it were two very different things. Using the right signs was of utmost importance. Their little business couldn't survive if she agreed to trades that would benefit only the Sioux.

"Where. . .Frake?" The one named Wise Eagle labored over the English pronunciation as he signed the question in fluid motions.

"Frank is busy. I will help you today."

Lord, forgive me.

It wasn't *really* a lie.

Wise Eagle's brow furrowed, and Ellie stumbled to sign the answer. He frowned at the trade goods she'd draped over the front porch railing. He and the other man, Kills Many, spoke quietly in their native tongue. Ellie's skin crawled. They could be plotting anything, and she'd never know. If only she understood their words.

Something stirred the damp tendrils of hair that tickled her neck. She swiped at it, and her hand contacted something solid. Ellie spun. The third warrior stood behind her, his malformed hand, devoid of the last two fingers, poised as if to touch her hair. Her stomach clenched so tight a wave of nausea swept through her.

"Don't touch me." She adjusted her stance to see the other two men, who had turned to watch.

Broken Hand signed the word for *trade* then pointed in her direction.

"What do you want?" Her throat went dry as she signed the question.

Again he reached toward her hair, grasping a loose tendril near her ear while producing something from a pouch at his waist. He pressed the small item into her palm, and Ellie held it up. *A bear claw—for her hair.* Tremors rolled through her, and she stepped back, pulling her hair free from the man's grasp.

"No. No trade." She held the claw out to him on her open palm.

Wise Eagle spoke, and all three looked toward the horizon. Broken Hand snatched the bear claw and returned it to his pouch before the three scurried toward their horses. They swung onto their mounts and rode away without a word.

As their hoofbeats faded into the distance, Ellie's knees trembled. She searched the horizon. *Nothing.* Yet something had spooked the warriors. The horses in the nearby corral all focused on the same distant point. She squinted. Faint plumes of dust colored the sky, and a few wagons appeared in the distance.

More emigrants.

"Lord, thank You for more customers." She sighed and gathered the goods she'd brought out to show the Sioux. After she'd stashed the items on the counter, she slipped through the blanketed doorway that separated the storefront from their residence and hurried to Frank's bedside.

Her aging father-in-law slept, his stubbly cheeks damp with sweat. Ellie wet a clean cloth in the nearby basin, sponged his face, and placed the folded cloth on his fevered forehead. He barely stirred. A knot clogged her throat, and her lower lids stung for the hundredth time that day.

"Father, please. This place has claimed my husband and child. I can't bear to lose Frank, too. Make him well." She adjusted the blankets and laid a gentle hand on his too-warm shoulder. "Frank, there's another wagon train coming. I'll be just outside if you need me, all right?"

He didn't stir.

Ellie straightened and headed toward the doorway again, though she paused to smooth her skirt and tuck the stray wisps of blond hair in place. She checked her appearance in the tiny mirror above the washstand. Far from perfect, but it would have to do. She exited the trading post to stand at the edge of the rickety porch.

She shaded her eyes and perused the long line of wagons, horses, and livestock. Quite a group, this one. At about the fourth or fifth wagon, her eyes scanned past then returned, resting on a single familiar silhouette sitting tall atop a large black horse. At the sight of him, her pulse quickened and a smile parted her lips. A tendril of hair fell loose and tickled her jaw, and her fingers strayed to it.

Mercy. Had she known *he* was coming, she would have taken the extra minute to make herself more presentable.

—⁂—

Teagan Donovan looked to either side and marveled. It didn't matter how many hours or days they'd been traveling, at the first sight of civilization, every wagon in every train he'd ever led west sped up. This one was no different. The wagons and stock hurried toward Frank Jefford's trading post as if it were the gate to heaven itself. And maybe it was.

Leastways, Frank's widowed daughter-in-law was pretty as any angel.

Pretty she might be, but probably a little touched in the head to stay on with old Frank all these years. The man's bad temper was well known up and down the Trail. It hardly seemed to bother her though. Teagan chuckled and spurred his big black gelding into a canter to reclaim his place at the head of the line.

Teagan squinted at the lonely little outpost as he passed the first wagons. The corral held several horses and a pen farther on had cattle. Behind the trading post, he could see the corner of a large garden. Looked like they were prospering.

Leaning against the porch railing, a single, shapely figure waited to greet them. The hairs on the back of his neck prickled. In the five years since they'd opened the solitary trading post, he'd never seen Ellie greet the newcomers. It was always Frank. Teagan nearly spurred his gelding into a run but thought better of it. If he did, every wagon would follow suit and descend on the place at full speed.

He drew to a halt ten feet from the porch and swung down. A wide smile tugged at his lips, and his heart rate quickened. "Howdy, Ellie."

The first of the wagons rumbled up behind him as the young woman stood tall. "Teagan Donovan. You're later than usual. I didn't think you were coming back." Her tone was scolding, and a stern expression etched her face, though a teasing glint lit her pretty blue eyes.

He chuckled. She'd thought of him. Now that was a comfort. He'd certainly pondered on her plenty, especially since Christmas. "Told you I would. We got out of Independence on time, but we were delayed by heavy rains along the way."

Her harsh countenance cracked, and a soft grin replaced it. "It's good to see you."

"You, too."

A pretty blush colored her cheeks as she shifted her attention to the wagons stacking up behind him. "You've brought a large group this time."

Yep, prettier than an angel. Though. . . Always slender, she looked too thin. Dark circles rimmed her eyes. "Ell, where's Frank?"

Her smile faltered if only for a moment. She quickly recovered and motioned to the families who began to gather. "Welcome to Jefford's, everyone. Please make yourselves at home. As you can see, there's plenty of land for grazing, and there's a well out back for drinking water. I'm sure the journey's been long and you might need some supplies before you carry on. While I cannot promise we have everything, I'll do my best to accommodate your needs. I can accept gold, cash money, or barter."

Ellie beckoned the weary travelers inside and disappeared. Teagan looked toward the tiny graveyard to the left of the house. *Still just two crosses.* He exhaled.

Teagan's younger brother approached, also on horseback, and stopped beside him. "Need you to get everyone settled, Cody. I got some business to take care of."

Cody grinned and nodded at the trading post door. "Is that her?"

"I told you it was."

"You ain't joshing. She's *real* pretty."

Teagan huffed. "You think I'd lie about that? Now git. Do what I asked." After Cody rode off, he tied his gelding to the railing and bounded through the door.

Despite the lanterns scattered throughout the room, it took a moment for his eyes to adjust. Once they did, he found Ellie behind the counter arranging items on a shelf. At his approach, she scooped a couple of blankets from the counter and scooted away. Again he followed, catching up to her as she stashed the blankets in the far corner.

"You didn't answer my question. Where's Frank?"

"A bit under the weather." She met his eyes, a fragile smile forming on her lips. It crumbled the longer she held his gaze.

"How long has he been sick?"

She looked at the floor.

He settled his hands on her shoulders. "How long, Ell?"

"Ten days." A sob convulsed her delicate frame, and she fell into his arms.

Chapter 2

"*Shhh*. It'll be all right."

Teagan's words rumbled softly in Ellie's ear as she leaned into to his thick chest. She twined her fingers into his shirt and let the tension ebb for the first time in more than a week.

Lord, thank You for sending Teagan.

She took in the scent of him—of sunshine and sweat and manliness—similar, but oh so different from Broken Hand's foul odor.

Don't let him too close, Ellie. You know this can't work. The old niggling thoughts battered her, but for once, she swept them aside and allowed herself to drink in the comfort of his presence.

The old porch creaked, and the excited chatter of a child filled the room.

"Oh, pardon us," a woman's startled voice called out. "Children, come."

Ellie's cheeks flamed as she pulled out of Teagan's arms, avoiding his probing green eyes. "No. Please, stay." She choked down the knot clogging her throat, dabbed her eyes dry, and turned.

Foolish woman. She knew better than to let Teagan Donovan distract her. *Don't get your heart involved, Ellie. It's foolishness indeed.*

"Please forgive me." She mustered a smile and approached the dark-haired woman. "How might I help you?"

The woman held the hands of two children. The girl, probably about seven years old, stood silent but alert, her blue eyes perusing the interior. The other child, a little blond boy no older than three, tugged at his mother's hand as he reached toward an apothecary jar filled with rock candy.

"Candy, Mama?" He tugged at her until the woman released her daughter's hand and scooped the boy into her arms.

"Not now, Caleb." The woman smiled. "I didn't mean to interrupt." She shot a sheepish grin in Teagan's direction as he looked at the selection of cans lining a high shelf.

Ellie peeked his way, and heat once more crawled into her cheeks. Even Teagan's tanned face seemed a bit redder than usual.

"It's no trouble." She kept her tone confidential. "I'm Ellie."

"It's nice to meet you, Ellie. I'm Laura Pritchard, and these are my children, Caleb and Dorothy."

"A pleasure, Laura."

The woman grinned. "My husband and I are out of flour and sugar, and if we can come to an agreeable trade, we may want more coffee and a few other items. I'd like to look around, if I might."

"Of course. Once you're done looking, we can discuss a trade."

Little Caleb pitched sideways toward the candy jar. Laura righted him and shifted the boy to her other hip. "I'd be willing to trade this rascal if he doesn't behave." Laura winked.

Ellie grinned, though a knot tightened her chest as she looked at the chubby-armed boy. His hair, bleached nearly white from the sun, stuck up all over his head, his big blue eyes focused completely on the candy.

So like her own son, Gideon.

"Would you mind if I. . ." She motioned to the jar and nodded toward Caleb and Dorothy.

Laura shook her head. "We haven't the money for such luxuries."

"My treat. Your son reminds me of someone very special."

She hesitated. "It's a kind offer, but I would prefer you not."

Ellie forced a smile. "Of course. I'll gather the items you requested."

Other travelers had filtered inside, and she told them to look around. She turned toward the back to retrieve Laura's goods. However, Teagan strolled past carrying the items.

"I can get those," she whispered, trotting along after him.

He smiled. "Now you don't have to."

"It's *my* job." Ever since Teagan's first visit after her husband's death, he seemed to look for ways to lighten her load. Whether carrying heavy supplies or quieting her inconsolable baby, Teagan Donovan had proven himself to be a godsend.

He deposited the items on the counter, caught her elbow, and led her toward the doorway separating the store and residence. "Would it be all right if I went back to see Frank?"

"He's sleeping. I'd prefer you not wake him."

"I won't."

She bit her lip. Teagan was one of the few people Frank liked, and it would be a comfort to have someone else look in on him. She glanced behind the blanket at her father-in-law. He hadn't moved. "All right. Quietly, please."

Teagan smiled. "Yes, ma'am." His green eyes locked with hers, and he gave her hand a gentle squeeze. "I've missed you, Ell."

The urge to burrow back into the safety of his arms swept over her, though she resisted this time. "I've missed you, too."

He turned toward the doorway, but before he stepped through it, hurried footsteps pounded through the front door of the trading post. "Teag? We got trouble."

———

Heart pounding, Teagan jerked toward the front of the building where his brother's silhouetted form filled the doorway. It wasn't like Cody to sound an alarm for no reason. With an apologetic glance, he brushed past Ellie and crossed the room. Cody stepped outside to stand beside his horse, and Teagan barged after him. "What's the matter?"

"Ezra and Silas Benton just spotted three Sioux watching the trading post. They—"

"Watching the trading post?" Ellie's voice broke in from the porch. "Where?"

Teagan swung to face her, noting that several members of his wagon train spilled out of the building to listen as well. "Let me handle this. Please?"

"Just before your wagon train rolled up, I was trading with three Sioux braves. It's probably them, though why they'd be watching us, I can't explain."

"They haven't done this before?"

"No."

"Teag. . ." Cody's voice grew urgent. "Ezra and Silas are going to confront 'em."

The Benton boys. He spun back in the direction Cody pointed and saw the two young men riding off in the distance. It didn't matter what the circumstance, those two were always on the lookout for what mischief they could find. And this could turn into far more than mischief if he didn't hurry.

Three long strides carried him to his horse's side where he loosed the reins from the hitching post and swung into the saddle. As he turned the big black in the direction of the trouble, Ellie stepped up beside him.

"Take me with you." Her blue eyes locked with his.

Take her? "No. Too dangerous. Besides, it's my problem."

"Maybe Ezra and whoever are, but I can help with the Sioux. I know them."

Teagan swallowed hard, his stomach roiling with the choice. "No. There could be an ambush or fighting."

"Do you know how to speak the Sioux language?"

"No."

"I can sign. Not fluently, but I can get a message across. Let me help you."

His thoughts warred. He'd never forgive himself if something happened to her. Yet. . . He turned to Cody. "Stay here and watch the store for her."

"What?" His brother's expression twisted in confusion.

"Do it!" Teagan removed his foot from the stirrup and offered Ellie his hand. She scrambled up behind him and threaded her arms around his waist. He spurred the black into action.

Lord, please, keep us safe. Especially Ellie.

She held tight to him and molded her body against his as he bent low over the black's neck. The big horse's stride gobbled distance, and in a couple of moments Teagan made a wide loop around the brothers. Ezra and Silas drew up as Teagan stopped in front of them.

A quick scan of the area showed three retreating Sioux a short distance off. Teagan shot a glance heavenward. At least they were withdrawing.

He turned on the brothers. "Just what in blazes do you two think you're doing?"

Ezra gestured toward the three Sioux. "Saw we had some unwanted visitors, so we figured to scare 'em off."

"Those are hardly unwanted visitors, sir." Ellie's voice took a sharp tone. "They are my customers, and I'll thank you to leave them alone."

"They're *Injuns*, ma'am. . . ." Silas piped up.

"Yes, and I trade with whites and Indians alike. Those three were just at my trading post moments before the wagon train came into view. At the sight of it, they spooked and rode off without completing their trades." She glared at the two before she plowed on. "Indians are curious sorts, so my guess is they were inquisitive and circled back to watch."

"I don't trust 'em." Ezra glared after the retreating braves.

Teagan cleared his throat. "Despite the fact it was stupid and irresponsible, you boys did what you set out to do. The Sioux are leaving. Now go on back to camp."

Silas eyed Ezra, who in turn watched the disappearing braves. When Ezra turned his horse, his brother fell in beside him. Teagan hung back a moment, watching the Bentons leave, then checking again to be sure the Sioux were truly gone.

He glanced over his shoulder at her. "Do you really believe the Sioux were just curious, or was there something more to this?"

She hesitated. "I'm not sure. Frank has always insisted he be the one to deal with the Sioux. He's been even more protective of me lately. A few times in the past couple of months, he's asked me to wait in the residence until they've gone."

Teagan roughed a hand over his face. "Have you had trouble with 'em?"

"None."

Lord, something isn't sitting right with all this. . . .

"I reckon I need to keep an eye on those boys for a bit, make sure they don't run off on another adventure. But you and I need to talk. Can I call on you later?"

Chapter 3

The sun sat low on the horizon as the last customer departed. Ellie rubbed the knots in her neck and shoulders, surveying bare spots that peeked from between the canned goods and textiles. After the tension with the emigrant men, what seemed like half of Teagan's wagon train came to buy provisions in a few short hours. Before she slept, she'd need to take stock and replenish from the extra supplies in the barn, a task Frank usually took care of.

She paced to the front door. Near the circled wagons, a group of children played in the slanting rays of the setting sun. Horses and oxen grazed in the distance, and fires dotted the landscape inside the circle. The scent of cooking meat wafted toward her on the evening breeze. Her stomach growled.

It was always a welcome sight, the yard filled with wagons and emigrants. Under normal circumstances, when the evening meal was finished she and Frank would sit outside and talk with some of the settlers, listening to their stories and telling a few of their own. Rather, she'd tell a few tales, and Frank would grumble about whatever came to mind. She chuckled. For all his irritable ways, her father-in-law was a sweet man, and she loved him.

Ellie shut and locked the door, stifling a yawn. There would be no visiting with the emigrants until Frank improved. She was looking forward to the agreed-upon chat with Teagan, but even that would have to be cut short so she could accomplish everything needing her attention. *Lord, give me the strength to carry on. There's still so much to do yet tonight.*

After turning down the wicks to each of the oil lamps, she slipped through the door into the residence. Sometime since she'd last looked in on him, Frank had burrowed deep under the covers. The quilt was drawn up around him, as if he'd thrashed and writhed until he'd bound himself tight in a cocoon. He groaned in his sleep. Heart in her throat, Ellie hurried to his side.

"Frank?" She jostled his shoulder gently. Heat radiated through the covers. "Can you hear me?"

His eyes fluttered open and blinked a couple of times then closed again. She rolled him gently to loose him from the bedclothes.

"Frank?" *Lord, please. . .let him answer me.*

Again he blinked, and this time locked glassy brown eyes with hers.

"There you are. . ." A wobbly grin spread across her face, and her lower lids burned. *Be brave, Ellison.*

"Water?" His voice was a gravelly whisper.

She swallowed hard and reinforced her smile. "Of course."

Ellie grabbed the cup from the table and hurried to the washstand only to find the pitcher was empty. She hated to leave him, even for a moment, for fear he'd slip back into unconsciousness. If she could go quickly, maybe. . . She snatched up the pitcher. "Frank, I'll be back. Please stay awake."

He gave a faint nod.

Ellie flew out the back door toward the well, but stopped short at the sight of several emigrants standing around the well pump, each holding buckets or canteens. All eyes turned on her, and she approached more slowly as her cheeks warmed.

"You all right, ma'am?" It was the same handsome young man who'd warned Teagan of the trouble earlier in the day.

"Yes, I just need to get some water for my sick father-in-law."

The man took the pitcher, positioned it under the spout, and pumped the well's handle. Once filled, he held it out to her with a smile. "Hope your kin gets to feeling better."

"Thank you." She scrambled back through the door, water sloshing over the sides of the pitcher. Inside, she poured a cupful of the cool liquid and sat down beside her father-in-law.

"Frank? I brought you water."

His eyes opened, distant and groggy, but he quirked a small grin when his focus settled on her. He was so weak. Her hands shook as she lifted his head and tipped the tin cup to his lips. He slurped a little, coughing and sputtering, so she eased him back to his pillow until the fit passed.

Ellie wet a cloth and wiped Frank's face. "More?"

He groaned and rolled away, his back to her.

She rubbed his arm through the quilt. *Lord, he's getting worse.*

A sharp knock came at the back door, and Ellie jumped.

"Who is it?"

"It's Teagan."

Just the sound of his muffled voice quieted her jangling nerves. She rose and opened the door to find Teagan leaned against the door frame, hat in hand and dark hair curling over his ears and collar. She resisted the urge to tuck the unruly locks back in place.

"Heard you were having some trouble." His eyes strayed to her father-in-law. "Everything all right?"

If he would hold her, maybe—

Stop it, Ellison. You know better.

She shrugged. "I probably looked like a fool, running out there like I did, but Frank was asking for water, and I didn't have any." *I was afraid he'd slip away again before I got back.*

She looked away as a knot threatened to choke her.

"Can I come in? You promised me a talk."

—⁂—

Ellie hesitated then motioned him inside with a sweeping gesture. He stepped through the door and glanced around the room. The tiny kitchen sat against the wall separating the home and storefront, a stone fireplace situated in the corner. Frank's narrow bed inhabited the left side of the room, a single chair stationed beside it. A square table and three more chairs filled the center of the space. And to the right, two tall armoires sat side by side, forming a partition that blocked that side of the room from view. Probably Ellie's sleeping quarters.

"You said Frank is awake?" He headed toward the man's bed.

"He's very weak." She caught his arm. "I don't think he's up to a visit right now."

He stared down at her delicate features, creased with worry. "This ain't a social call." He gingerly peeled her small hand from the crook of his elbow. "I'm worried about you two." Especially with the Sioux watching the trading post.

He eased into the chair beside the bed and tossed his hat aside. "Can you hear me, Frank?" The man didn't stir. He touched Frank's shoulder. Heat radiated from his body like the sun reflecting off the salt flats at high noon.

The old coot had aged a fair bit since last year's visit. His thinning hair was now completely gray. Deep-set wrinkles lined his ashen face, and his formerly sturdy frame was frail, withered. Teagan roughed a hand over his stubbly jaw as the ever-present ache in his chest swelled.

This is too familiar for my liking, Lord.

She hovered just over Teagan's shoulder. "Please, can't you see he's in no condition to talk?"

Teagan rose and motioned her to the far side of the room where he leaned a hip against the kitchen counter. "Do you know what he's sick with?"

Ellie shrugged, and her big eyes misted. "Fever, weakness, no appetite." She fidgeted. "I got him to eat some broth last night, so maybe he's getting a bit better."

"This isn't some passing illness." Teagan spoke the words as gently as he could. "He's bad sick."

"No. He *will* get better. He just needs more time."

The desperation in her voice sucked the air from his lungs. He gingerly took her by the shoulders. "Have you thought about what you'll do if he doesn't?"

Chapter 4

Had she thought. . . ?

A deep sob rumbled out of her, and Ellie buried her face in his chest. She melted against him. *Of course* she'd thought. It was all that occupied her mind. She had begged God's mercy. Surely He would comply, wouldn't He?

You have to, Lord. . . .

Teagan held her close as she cried, and when the storm of her emotion finally slowed and ceased moments later, she pulled back, hanging her head a little as she wiped her eyes. He tucked a finger under her chin and tipped her face up.

"I didn't mean to upset you."

She swallowed. "I know."

He cupped her cheek in his big hand, and his gaze intensified. Ellie's heart pounded as he bent and brushed her lips with his. A stuttering breath escaped her.

"I love you, Ell. I've loved you for a very long time."

Her heart seized. *He couldn't.*

Teagan claimed her lips softly. Protests clanged in her mind, though her body melted against his once more. His hand trailed down her side until it settled at her waist, drawing her nearer still. He kissed her sweetly, tenderly, and like a fool, she clung to him as if he were life itself, and kissed him in return.

Finally he broke the kiss and pushed her back a step, though his hands lingered at her waist. "Reckon we should stop that."

Unable to meet his eyes, she nodded.

An awkward silence fell, and Teagan released her as he straightened. "Um. . .have you eaten anything yet tonight?"

"No."

"All right then. I'll be back in a few minutes." He eased past her, grabbed his hat from Frank's bedside, and slipped out the door without another word.

Trembling, Ellie slumped in the nearest chair. *He loved her? He couldn't love her.* She didn't deserve it. Not after. . .

Lord, this can't be. It just can't. Please help me fix it.

She cared for Teagan—deeply. Under other circumstances, perhaps they could make a life together, but the circumstances weren't different. She didn't deserve his love.

Her nerves jangled and muscles jumped with pent-up energy. She rose and checked on Frank then hurried back through the door to the trading post. Ellie lit the nearest lamp and grabbed a paper and pencil from a drawer behind the counter. She always could sort through her thoughts better when she was busy. Only she couldn't quiet her mind enough to think about the inventory. Instead, her thoughts slipped back over the years.

It had been exciting, leaving her old home with Anson and Frank, joining the wagon train that would head into the unknown on a grand adventure. It was there they'd met Teagan as he led their train into the wilds. They spent many nights around the fire after a hard day's travel, laughing and spinning yarns.

But when she discovered she was with child, the excitement waned, marred by the difficulty she had carrying Gideon on the grueling journey. Teagan did all he could to help them, choosing longer routes if it meant smoother traveling, or planning for more days to rest. Despite such a troublesome time, Ellie was heartbroken when Anson and Frank decided to stop on this spot, rather than going on. She cost them their dream.

Not only that. . .

Ellie clamped her eyes shut to block the memory of the fateful day, yet it battered her strongest defenses.

She'd followed Anson into the barn, watching as he climbed into the loft for supplies to replenish their shelves. "Teagan Donovan should be returning soon," she'd called from the floor below. It was hardly the first time she'd broached the subject.

"Ellie, don't do this." Anson's voice sharpened as he hoisted a bag onto his shoulder and set it at the loft's edge.

"If we pack now, we could finish the journey with him and settle in California like we'd planned."

"No." He turned away from the loft edge.

"Please, Anson. Let me give you back your dream."

"Woman, how many times do I have to say it? We've made our choice. We're doing fine right here." He disappeared from her view as he bent to retrieve something from the loft's floor.

"We're *not* doing fine!" Not so long as guilt gnawed at her.

Anson stomped toward the loft's edge again. "I've had enough. The answer—"

His foot caught the corner of the bag he'd set there, and he pitched forward over the loft's edge.

—⁂—

"I'm back, Ell," Teagan called softly as he reentered her little home. The room was still except for Frank's soft snoring. "Ell?"

When she didn't respond, he set the plate, utensils, and the pouch he'd brought from camp on the counter and peeked into the trading post. Faint lamplight lit half the room. Ellie faced the back wall, her arms wrapped tight about her body.

He hurried to her side. "You all right?"

She inhaled sharply and turned on him.

"What's the matter?"

She swallowed hard. "Just. . .tired." Her voice rasped.

He searched her face. "Looks like it's more than tired. You're. . ." *Beautiful.* He smiled. ". . .plumb tuckered."

She nodded.

"C'mon." He reached for her hand, but she pulled it just out of reach.

"Teagan, I know I said we could talk, but could we postpone this until morning?"

"Postpone?"

"I'm sorry. I still have things I need to do tonight in order to be ready for the morning, and I'd like to get some rest while Frank is sleeping comfortably."

His chest tightened. After almost a year apart, he ached to be near her. He'd gladly go without sleep for days—and *had* in the anticipation of seeing her—if it meant being with her.

"Look, I brought you a plate of food, and I brought some herbs to see if I can't help Frank. Why don't you sit and eat. I'll do what I can for him. Anything else you've got to do, I can help you with once you're done." He nodded toward the residence.

Ellie hesitated before she gave a curt nod and shuffled through the doorway. He extinguished the lamp and hurried after her, scrambling to hold out the nearest chair for her. Once she was seated, he set the plate of beans, potatoes, and biscuits, plus the utensils he'd brought, in front of her.

"Did you make this?"

He shrugged. "If you listen to talk around camp, I'm a half-decent cook." He grabbed a biscuit from the side of her plate and handed it to her. "Eat. You're too thin."

She sighed and took it, nibbling a corner. Teagan shifted his focus to the pouch full of herbs he'd brought with him. The leaves or bark of a few well-chosen plants might help bring Frank's fever down. He was under no illusions that it would have any lasting effects, but perhaps he could give the man a little relief.

"Mind if I kindle a fire to heat some water?" He hooked a thumb toward the fireplace in the corner.

She settled an elbow on the table and rested her cheek in her hand. "I don't mind."

More than once while he built the fire, he felt the weight of her gaze, yet when he glanced her way, she averted her eyes. Not quite the response he'd hoped for, but perhaps she was even more tired than he knew. Teagan put water on to boil. Then he pulled wild mint leaves from his pouch and chopped the aromatic leaves with the knife he kept at his waist. Before the water boiled, he busied himself with refilling the pitcher and gathering another armload of wood from outside.

Done with the short errands, he found the water was ready. He emptied Frank's cup, dumped the freshly cut herbs into the bottom, and poured the steaming water over them. He carried the cup toward the table.

"This needs to steep a few min. . ." A grin tugged at his lips.

Head still cradled in her hand, Ellie slept in her chair. He chuckled. *Plumb tuckered. And beautiful.*

Teagan set the cup on the table then crossed to the far side of the room where the two armoires partitioned Ellie's private quarters. A dressing screen draped with two dresses stood on the open end of the space, folded back partway. Careful not to knock the clothes off, he opened it wider and stepped inside. Heat crept up his neck as he noticed a petticoat spread over one corner of her bed. Averting his eyes, he moved it to the other corner and turned down the quilt before returning to her.

He lifted Ellie into his arms. Her cheek settled against his shoulder, and her breath stirred against his neck, sending a little shiver across his skin. He smiled. This was where she belonged. In his arms. He drank in the faint scent of something flowery lingering on her hair or skin.

Teagan eased her onto the bed and reached for the quilt but hesitated. With nimble fingers, he slipped her shoes from her feet and grinned as he covered her. For another instant he stalled, drinking her in.

The night hadn't gone how he'd hoped. Surely tomorrow would be better.

Laying aside her shoes, he bent over her and pressed a gentle kiss to her forehead. "G'night, Ell."

Chapter 5

Ellie stretched and blinked heavy eyelids. She lay curled in her own bed, still fully clothed, a corner of her quilt pulled across her body. Now, how had she. . . ?

Teagan.

As if struck by lightning, Ellie bolted up, senses alert. On the other side of the screen, something sizzled and popped, and the scents of bacon and coffee filled the room.

Her stomach knotted. He was still here. Had he stayed all night or left and come back this morning?

She rose, and on cat feet crossed to the dressing screen, peeking around the edge of the screen. Teagan squatted at the hearth, his back to her as he poured a cup of coffee. She bit her lower lip.

Not good. She had a large wagon train camped in her front yard, and the train captain kept disappearing into her home. She had no desire to be fodder for the rumor mill, particularly when she would *not* entertain any further advances from him.

Ellie closed her eyes. If only she could climb out through the small window above her bed without him hearing. Far easier than facing him.

But face him she must. Hands straying to her hair, she found that half of it had come loose from its pins and hung down one side of her head in ropes. The last thing she needed was to step out from behind the screen looking as if she'd just stumbled out of bed.

Ellie pulled the yellow dress down from the screen and changed into it. After extracting the pins from her hair, she brushed and rebraided it, letting it fall down her back. She crammed her feet into her shoes and smoothed her dress one last time before she slipped out from behind the screen. Teagan rose and turned from the hearth at the same moment, the two nearly bumping into each other in the tight confines of the corner.

"Morning." A grin played at the corners of his mouth as he brushed past her. "You're looking more rested this morning." In one hand he held a plate of bacon and scrambled eggs, and in the other, the coffeepot.

Her cheeks burned. Blast him. He was too pleased with himself. "Did you stay all night?" The words croaked out.

He shrugged. "You fell asleep while you were eating, so I tucked you in bed and sat up with Frank." He set the plate down.

She balled her hands to keep them from shaking.

"You want some coffee?" He retrieved a mug from a neat stack of dishes on the counter.

She stepped closer. The plates and silverware were clean. Every last one of them. "You didn't. . ."

"I had to have something to do. I didn't know where to put 'em though. Sorry."

Ellie closed her eyes, a hand straying to her forehead. *Lord, I know he's trying to help, but. . .*

"Coffee?" He asked again, holding up the cup.

Her stomach rumbled its agreement, but she ignored it and sat at Frank's bedside. "No, thank you." No sense encouraging him. "I have too much to do. I would guess you do as well. Doesn't the wagon train need you?"

"Don't start this again. You've got to eat something. And you fell asleep before we could talk last night."

"About what?" She touched Frank's forehead, his cheek, and drew her hand back quickly.

"His fever's down some." Teagan grabbed another chair and sat beside her.

Not just some. Frank's temperature felt quite a bit lower. She spun to face him. "What did you do?"

"I bathed his skin with a mint tea. It's got a cooling effect that can help to bring a fever down."

Laughter bubbled out of her. She grabbed his large hand between both of her own. "Thank you. You don't know how many remedies I have tried." She turned again toward her father-in-law. "Frank?"

"I can't promise it's permanent." He laced his fingers between hers, caressing her hand with his thumb.

"It's a good start." If the fever would just break, maybe his body would have the strength to fight whatever else was going on. She untwined her hand. "Frank, can you hear me?"

Teagan caught her arm as she reached to jostle his shoulder. He folded her hand inside his much larger one.

She stilled, looking first at his large hand covering hers then to his perfectly chiseled face. Deep green eyes stared back at her, and her stomach fluttered.

"I did this in hopes he'd be strong enough to travel. I want you two to come with me when we pull out."

Her blood chilled in her veins, and she stared. "What?"

"If you'll say yes, I'll get a few of the men. We'll help you pack your wagon today and still be ready to pull out early tomorrow morning, right on schedule."

Her jaw went slack, and her mind scrambled for a safe response. "This is our home, Frank's and mine."

"Yes, but I was hoping you'd consider making your life and home with me. I told you last night that I love you, Ellie. I want you to be my wife."

She gasped. *His wife. . .* She pulled her hand out of his. "I. . .um." She shook her head. "I can't."

"Can't—" He hung his head. "Didn't I make it clear how much I care about you?"

"Care, yes, but. . ." Why was he even asking her this? His life was unsettled. He spent the bulk of his year traveling the Oregon Trail before rushing back to winter with his ma and younger brother in the mountains of Tennessee. What kind of a life could he provide for a woman?

"But what?"

"Frank and Anson gave up their dream of seeing California for me, to keep me alive while I carried Gideon. This place became Anson's new dream. I can't waste that. I can't waste his life. He deserves better."

"Anson's been gone for four years. The way you kissed me last night tells me you have feelings for me. Can't you find room in your heart to let me in?"

Oh, God, I don't want to hurt him, but this can't happen.

He waited, his expression full of anticipation.

Trembling, she darted out the door into the yard without answering.

—⁓—

"Ellie." Teagan rose as she raced outside.

Tarnation.

He'd wanted to ask her to marry him for years, but he'd waited to give her ample time to grieve for her husband and son. In the intervening time, he'd saved his money to provide for her. Between his own change in circumstances and the discovery of Frank's failing health, it had seemed the right moment.

A snort rumbled out of him. "Wouldn't seem so, after all." Teagan walked outside, coffee in hand. He took a sip of his lukewarm liquid, which turned to acid in his stomach. He tossed the dark brew out. "Can you convince her, God?"

The barn was still closed up tight. Doubtful she'd gone there. He paced to the corner of the house. In the distance, the camp buzzed with activity, though she wasn't likely to have gone there. He shifted toward the small cemetery. Ellie's golden hair was just visible above the short fence surrounding the two graves.

Of course. She'd run to Anson.

Lord, her husband was my friend, and I mean no disrespect to the dead, but I don't understand. How could she kiss me like she did last night if she's still in love with him?

He blew out a breath. Maybe sitting out there would clear her head and she'd return ready to talk. In the meantime, he could bank the fire and clean up the breakfast mess, meager as it was. He paced back to the house.

As he entered, Frank stirred on his bed. "Ellie?"

He slid into the chair. "It's Teagan Donovan, Frank."

Dull brown eyes blinked. "Donovan. What're you doing here?"

"Leading another wagon train through."

A slight smile curved Frank's lips, revealing yellowed teeth. "I'm glad."

"Ellie's outside. I can get her for you."

"Not yet." Frank shut his eyes and lay still for nearly a minute before he reached a hand out. "Donovan?"

"I'm right here." He clasped his friend's feeble hand.

"The Sioux. . ."

Yes. . .the Sioux. They'd weighed heavy on his mind since the previous afternoon's encounter.

Teagan waited for him to go on, but the old man went silent. The sharp image of

Ma lying in her bed, too weak to move, flashed in his mind. His belly knotted. *Lord, I gotta tell you, I don't like this.*

Frank's eyes fluttered open, and he furrowed his brow as if he were lost.

"Hey, Frank." The man looked at him. "You were going to tell me something about the Sioux. Remember?"

He hesitated then nodded. "They're bold."

He'd never known Frank to mince words. Perhaps his thoughts had become addled. "Yeah?"

"Growing restless. . ." The man went silent again.

"Have they caused you problems?"

"Not rightly, but. . ." He wheezed for a few seconds.

Teagan's gut had told him the treaty signed three years earlier between the American government and the Indians was a temporary fix. Even in his very limited interactions with the Sioux, he'd sensed a tension bubbling beneath the surface, just ready to boil. The stories of what they did to neighboring warlike tribes chilled him to his core.

Frank wheezed on. "The one named Broken Hand. . .he concerns me. Keeps asking to trade for a piece of Ellie's hair. Three times now."

Her hair. . . That was no addled rambling. It was specific. "Does she know about this?"

"Didn't want to scare her." He paused. "I ain't got much longer, Donovan."

Unable to find his voice, Teagan nodded.

"Wouldn't be good, Ellie being here alone. Promise me you'll take her with you."

"I've already asked her." If she would just agree. "I will do all I can to take care of her."

"She won't convince easy. Ellie's pulling a wagonload of guilt." A sad smile creased the man's face. "Don't let her tell you no." His eyes closed, and his gaunt frame shuddered.

"Why does she feel guilty, Frank?"

A moment ticked by, and a smile parted the old man's lips. "She loves you."

Chapter 6

Ellie huddled at the foot of Anson's grave, knees drawn to her chest and her arms wrapped around them. *Leave the trading post. . .leave Anson and Gideon behind. . . marry Teagan.*

Her stomach roiled right along with her churning thoughts.

"Lord, I cost Frank and Anson their dream of going to California, and I begged You to help me give it back to them. I begged You to let us leave here, but Anson died fighting to stay. Fighting *me*. If the trading post was so important to him then, how am I to walk away from our home now? How am I to leave behind my husband, my baby, and everything we worked for?" Her eyes strayed toward Gideon's grave. Always sickly, the boy had lived only nine months longer than Anson before another illness claimed him far too soon.

She settled her chin on her knees and squeezed her eyes shut.

From behind her, someone cleared a throat. Ellie clambered to her feet and spun, expecting Teagan. Her brows arched at the sight of the young man who had drawn her water from the well the previous night.

Hat in hand, he shot her an apologetic smile. "Don't mean to intrude, ma'am, but it's important. I was wondering if you know where I can find my brother?"

"Your brother? I don't believe I know who that is."

"Well, sure ya do. Teagan. . ." He arched his brows, and his voice rose a little, as if encouraging her to remember something.

Ellie gasped. "You're. . .you're Cody?"

He grinned. "Yes, ma'am."

Why on God's green earth hadn't Teagan told her that? She let herself out through the creaky gate as she looked him over. Same build, same chiseled face. Hazel eyes rather than green ones, and his hair a lighter shade of brown, but the resemblance was strong. Both handsome as the day was long. "I'm Ellie Jefford. It's so nice to meet you in person. Teagan's spoken so highly of you across the years, I feel as if I know you."

"Likewise, ma'am." He gave that same sheepish look his brother did when he was uncomfortable. "Forgive my rudeness, but I really need to find Teag. There's a bunch of Sioux headed this way."

The Sioux. It was unlike them to return two days in a row, particularly when her yard was filled with wagons. "Where?"

He tugged his hat on and pointed to the far side of the trading post. Ellie marched off to the front of the building. Still a fair distance away, the mounted group appeared larger than usual, five or six in all. She shaded her eyes, squinting to bring the individuals into focus. It looked to be Wise Eagle, Kills Many, and Broken Hand, along with two others whom she wasn't as familiar with.

"Ma'am, my brother?"

Ellie sighed softly. "This way." She beckoned him to the back of the building and through the open door into the residence.

From beside Frank's bed, Teagan looked up.

"Nice of you to introduce me to your brother." Ellie nodded in Cody's direction as she tramped past him. With both men watching her every move, she poured a cup of coffee and stalked into the trading post. She would need it in order to deal with the Sioux.

—·—

"What's going on?" Teagan cast a quick glance after Ellie before he rose to face his brother.

"Figured you'd want to know about the Sioux riding this way."

His thoughts spun. Teagan glanced at Frank, who had drifted back to sleep. The man couldn't have known they were coming, but their conversation was perfectly timed. Teagan spun toward the front. "Ellie?" He kept his voice quiet for Frank's sake

"Hey." Cody caught his arm. "Where are you going?"

"To talk to Ell."

The younger Donovan jabbed a finger toward the trading post. "Teag, I think it's about time you talk to the folks out front. They listen to me a little, but they hired *you* to lead them. I know for a fact some of 'em are scared right now, and it wouldn't surprise me if the Benton brothers try to stir up more trouble."

Teagan huffed. Blast the Bentons. They were becoming a thorn in his side.

"Teag, you've told me this whole journey how a good captain not only leads the train west but keeps the folks he's leading from getting into hazardous situations, too." Cody's voice dropped to a confidential tone. "I know you got some hopes and plans for you and Ellie, but—"

"Hold your tongue." Teagan gritted his teeth.

His brother shrugged. "I'm just saying. . .that's important, but right now, I need your help."

Of course Cody was right. He was getting *paid* to lead the wagon train. But he *loved* Ellie and promised Frank he'd look after her. If one of the Sioux was taking too much of an interest in her, he'd see to it that stopped today.

"Come on."

Teagan barged through the doorway into the trading post, Cody on his heels, just as Ellie scooped a stack of goods and turned toward the door.

"I don't want you trading with the Sioux." He waved a hand sharply, as if shooing an irksome fly. "Tell 'em to go away."

Her eyebrows shot up as she faced him, and her delicate features hardened. "I don't recall that being any of your business."

"I'm *making* it my business. I don't have a good feeling."

"This is what Frank and I do. While he's sick, the full weight of running this place falls on my shoulders, so I *have* to trade with them." She stomped toward the door, unlocked it, and flung it wide. "I can't afford to turn them away."

"Sure you can." His sharp voice ratcheted louder. "Come with us tomorrow."

A derisive huff nearly exploded from her. "I told you. . .this was Anson's dream, and I'm keeping it alive. How would you feel if someone walked into your life and demanded you leave your home, your business, and the last ties to your family behind?"

The familiar ache rolled through him. "I understand those things more than you know, Ell."

"I don't think you do. If I leave here, the trip will kill Frank. Then what do I have?"

"You'd have *me*!"

"Teag?" Cody broke in. His younger brother turned from the window where he stood watching the yard. "The Benton brothers. . ."

He crossed to the door. Silas and Ezra Benton, rifles in hand, had walked to the front of the crowd of emigrants that had gathered to watch the approaching Sioux. He shook his head. Guns and the Benton boys tended not to mix well.

"Excuse me, Ell. I gotta take care of something." He brushed past her, Cody on his trail.

"As do I, thank you very much," she called after him.

Stubborn. Hot-headed. Mouthy. Ellie Jefford could be all those things, but until he was sure the Benton boys were under control, he couldn't worry about her.

He eyed Cody. When his brother looked at him, Teagan jerked his chin toward the Bentons. "That's kind of exasperating, you being right."

Cody snickered. "Now you know how I felt growing up, always hearing about how good you were. For the longest time, I didn't reckon you knew how to do wrong."

Teagan crossed the distance, taking in the scene. To the left, the Sioux approached, horses held to a walk. Halfway between the nearest wagons and the trading post, a knot of emigrants watched, talking among themselves. And in the middle of things, stirring them all up, Ezra and Silas Benton.

"Ezra, Silas, you two are starting to test my patience," he spat as he drew near enough to be heard. "Put your guns away. And the rest of you, go on about your business. There's nothing to see."

"I ain't putting my gun away, Donovan. Not so long as them Injuns come back for more." The man pointed to the approaching Sioux with the barrel of his rifle.

Teagan's nerves zinged. Last thing he needed was one of the braves getting the idea they were preparing to shoot. "You trying to start a war?"

"Silas and me are just trying to protect ourselves from the likes of them sorry Injuns."

Teagan stepped closer, locked eyes with Ezra, and dropped his voice to a snarl. "Put the gun away, or you will deal with me."

"Why don't you two listen to him?" someone else called. "He hasn't steered us wrong yet."

Seconds ticked by before Ezra broke eye contact and rocked backward.

Silas cleared his throat. "How do we know we can trust them savages?"

Teagan flicked a glance over his shoulder to see the Sioux had dismounted, and

Ellie was talking to them in sign language. "Doesn't appear they came to see you, Silas. I guess it doesn't really matter if *you* can trust 'em."

The group chuckled, and Silas Benton's face reddened.

"You got a real smart mouth, Donovan." Ezra spat.

"And you've got a hot head. I'm just trying to lighten the mood. Fact is, Frank and Ellie Jefford trade with the Sioux about once a week, and they haven't had any problems." Not exactly the truth, but these two rascals didn't need to know that. "I'll not have you stand in the way of the woman doing her job."

"We ain't standing in her way," Silas chimed in. "We're keeping an eye."

"I can respect that. But the longer you two stand around with those guns in your hands, the more likely there is to be shooting trouble. Go put 'em away."

Both the Benton brothers looked from him to the Sioux and back. Silas relaxed a little but eyed his brother.

Ezra cradled the rifle in the crook of his elbow. "I still don't trust 'em."

Nor did Teagan, but at least he'd try to keep a level head. "Tell you what. Go put your guns away while I keep a closer eye on things."

He'd just invite himself to the party.

Chapter 7

The five Sioux perused the various items Ellie had brought out to the porch. *"I want a knife,"* White Thunder signed.

"What do you have to trade?" She carefully formed the signs so he could understand her question.

He held up a leather bag with a brightly colored porcupine-quill design on the front, leather and horsehair fringe hanging from the bottom. A wide, quilled strap finished the piece, looking as if it would be long enough to hang at waist level. Ellie reached to touch it, but he pulled it away. White Thunder signed. *"Can I see the knife?"*

Ellie lifted her chin. *"I need something more than that bag for a knife."* She stumbled through the hand motions.

The man eyed her, looked at the bag, then crossed to his horse. From a similar pouch tied to his saddle, he produced something black and shiny. He turned to show her. A buffalo's horn.

He tucked the horn under his arm. *"Good trade?"*

"Good enough to think about it." Ellie motioned for him to wait.

She strode into the trading post and walked behind the counter. The door darkened, and she turned as Teagan entered.

"Ell—"

"Not now. I'm in the middle of something."

He followed her behind the counter, stopping near her. *Very* near. "Please don't do this." He hissed the words.

"Don't do my job? Is that what you're asking me?" She snatched two different knives from under the counter and unsheathed each. After a momentary inspection, she resheathed them and stashed one under the counter again.

Teagan blocked her path, his right hand on the counter, left braced against the wall. "I mean, don't trade with th—"

"I heard you clearly enough." She ducked under his arm and scrambled toward the door before he could stop her. "Please don't interfere, Teagan."

Ellie darted back through the door and stopped in front of the man. She drew the blade and held it out to him, handle first. He took it, along with the cover, and handed her the beaded pouch and the horn.

The Sioux warrior ran his finger across the blade's edge. Ellie checked the seams of the bag, and tested the soundness of the quillwork. Good quality. It would bring a nice price. She turned her attention to the buffalo horn, inspecting the flawless piece.

After a moment, White Thunder replaced the knife and tucked it under his arm. *"We trade?"*

"*Yes.*" She tucked the horn inside the pouch and turned toward the trading post door again. Only Teagan stood in the open doorway, broad shoulders filling the narrow space.

She marched up to him and thrust the bag into his hands. "If you're determined to be a nuisance, at least make yourself useful. Put this on the counter, please."

His dark eyebrows shot up. "Nuisance. . . ?" Teagan glared but took the newly acquired item and disappeared inside.

She turned back to the Sioux as the other newcomer, Iron Bear, pointed to the plug of tobacco she'd brought outside. "*Trade?*"

Ellie dickered with him just as she had with White Thunder, and this time bartered for a freshly tanned deerskin. Wise Eagle also requested tobacco, and she slipped past Teagan to retrieve it, casting him a warning glance as she did. Thankfully this time he stayed in the doorway watching the Sioux. When she returned, the man offered her another deerskin, which she looked over and accepted.

"*Trade?*" Broken Hand asked.

Ellie resisted the shiver that threatened to overtake her. "*Trade for what?*"

The man retrieved a small pouch from his horse and held it out to her. She cautiously looked inside as he shook it, the contents rattling. Upward of twenty oddly shaped yellowish-white pieces filled the pouch. Elk teeth. She glanced back to him when he shoved it toward her with a nod, as if encouraging her to take it.

"*What do you want for those?*"

He caught her hand, deposited the whole pouch in it, and reached behind her to grasp her thick blond braid.

—◊◊◊—

Teagan launched himself at the Sioux warrior with the missing fingers, driving him back a couple of steps.

"Don't touch her."

The warrior's brown eyes widened for an instant, but he schooled his expression quickly. The other four Sioux circled them.

"Teagan. Stop it." Ellie pawed at him.

"You put your hands on her again, and you will answer to me for that."

"*Teagan.*" She hissed his name and tried to shove him out of the way. Her attempt barely moved him.

The Sioux snarled something in return, his tone sharp and threatening.

"Stop it! Right now. Both of you." Ellie darted between them and drove a sharp elbow into Teagan's chest. With eyes locked on the warrior, he stepped back.

Everyone's attention snapped to her. A motion in the corner of his eye caused Teagan to look away for a second. The Benton brothers and Cody approached, both Silas and Ezra still toting their guns. He held out a hand, hip level, and discreetly motioned them to stand down. Thankfully Cody stopped and cautioned the others to follow suit.

Ellie deposited the pouch into the warrior's hand. "I already told you *no trade.* I'll keep my hair, thank you."

Teagan darted a glance at the warrior. *And just when had that happened?*

She jabbed a finger at their horses. "Now go. All of you." In a flurry of sharp gestures, she translated her words.

For a tense moment, they eyed one another.

"I mean it. Go!" Again she signed the words.

One of the other Sioux moved toward his horse first, the rest following suit. Finally the brave with the missing fingers moved on, snarling something at Teagan as he departed. Teagan watched him until the group had turned their mounts to leave.

"What in the names of Peter, James, and John did you think you were doing?" Ellie hissed quietly, her blue eyes flashing.

He turned to her, his own ire flaring. "Trying to protect you."

"I am plenty capable of taking care of myself." She glanced off to her right, where Cody, the Bentons, and several other emigrants were again approaching. She stabbed a finger toward the trading post. "Go inside. We need to talk. Alone."

He spun and walked inside.

Before the first of the approaching group reached the creaky porch, she shut the door and locked it then spun to face him. "How dare you undermine me while I'm conducting business."

How dare he? "He wanted your *hair*, Ell." He spat the words as if they burned his tongue.

"Yes. They use hair to decorate their clothes and other things." She jabbed a finger at a bag she'd traded for, touching one of the many clumps of colored hair mixed into the fringe.

"Yeah, *horse* hair."

"Which they dye different colors, including yellow." She shook the bag at him. "I don't know. Maybe he was trying to save his woman a step in the process by buying some that is naturally yellow."

Teagan clenched a fist to keep from grabbing her by the shoulders and shaking some sense into her. "You're being naive. When the Sioux go to war against the Cheyenne or other tribes, they scalp their enemies and keep the hair as trophies." She was touched in the head if she thought this was a normal request.

"Frank and I have never been considered enemies of the Sioux, but thanks to you and that reckless act"—she jabbed a finger toward the front—"I'm not sure what relationship I'll have with them. Or if they'll even come back to trade with us again."

"Good." The word exploded out of him. "All the more reason for you and Frank to come with me tomorrow."

She loosed a frustrated screech. "That's what all this is about, isn't it? You're doing everything you can to make me leave my home."

Something stilled within him. She was scared, and no amount of shouting was going to set her at ease.

He started again, his voice calmer. "Ellie, if I leave here without you tomorrow, I'm afraid I'll never see you again."

"Hogwash. Each year, you lead a wagon train safely through to its destination then ride hard for Tennessee. You stop back through here every time."

"Not this time." He took off his hat and ran a hand through his hair. "Not anymore."

She snorted. "Oh? And why *not*?"

He crossed his arms. "Cody and I lost Ma just before Christmas. She took sick with pneumonia. Lingered for weeks, getting to where she couldn't fight it, just like Frank in there. She and Cody were the only reasons I went back."

Her perfectly shaped lips parted, and her blue eyes glistened. "Oh Teagan, I. . .I'm so sorry." The news seemed to suck the wind out of her.

He stepped closer, cupped her face in one hand and stroked her cheek. "I wasn't planning to come back this way again. Last year when I was in California, I found the perfect place to settle, build a house. . . I'm planning to go on to California and put down stakes."

Her face paled. "I see."

Hand still lingering on her face and neck, he caressed her soft skin again. "Marry me, Ellie."

She closed her eyes. Teagan drank in the dotting of tiny freckles scattered across her nose, the long lashes that rested against perfect cheeks, the curve of her soft lips.

Goodness, but she's beautiful, Lord.

Her lips beckoned him, and he bent, his pulse racing as he angled her face toward him. Ellie's eyes flew open when he pressed his lips to hers. She stiffened, tried to pull away, but he circled her waist with his other arm. An instant later, she softened, and he sought to draw her into the kiss. Instead she twisted her face away, his lips settling on her cheek.

"Please stop." She braced her forearm against his chest, forcing space between them.

His shoulders slumped. Surely she could see how much he loved her. He rested his forehead against hers.

"Quit thinking for a minute, and tell me what your heart *feels*."

Her body shuddered in his embrace. "My heart is broken."

Chapter 8

Teagan released her. Breathless, she stepped back a few paces, smoothed her dress, and ran the back of her hand across her mouth.

"I don't understand. I'm pledging my life to you, and you're heartbroken?" Pain twanged in his voice.

A knot the size of a boulder clogged her throat. "Teagan, I lost my pa when I was a baby. Frank is the only father I've ever known. He's so weak right now, making a journey like that will kill him." Her voice faded. "I can't be the cause of his death, too."

"Frank's already dying, and he knows it."

Her stomach knotted. "No. He's better. His fever is down."

"We just talked, and he said as much to me. He said the Sioux are growing too restless and to take you with me when I go. To look after you."

She shook her head, panting. "You're lying. He wouldn't say that. We've never had problems with the Sioux." Besides, Frank was too ornery to resign himself to death.

Teagan stepped nearer, but she backed up a step. Confusion clouded his green eyes. "I'm telling you the truth. You're going to find yourself all alone here real soon, and I fear what the Sioux may do then. Come with me so I can protect you. Even..." He shrugged. "Even if you don't want to marry me."

She folded her arms. "If it's so important to you to look after me, why don't you stay here?"

"You know I can't do that. I have a duty to the wagon train." He motioned toward the wagons out front.

A sharp laugh erupted from her lips. "So? I have duties here. Are your duties more important than mine?"

"I didn't mean—"

"Why do you think it's all right for you to ask me to turn my back on everything my family has built?"

"That's not what I—"

"That's exactly what you're asking of me, and I don't appreciate it."

Silence reigned in the room for a moment before Teagan held up his hands in surrender. "I give up. I've tried every way I know how to help you and Frank since I arrived. I came, intending to ask you to be my wife, but I'm told I'm selfish for thinking you'd want to leave your home to be with me." He clenched his jaw. "You don't have to worry about it anymore. I'm done asking. Go ahead and stay."

Teagan spun and stomped to the front door. When it wouldn't open readily, he twisted the key still stuck in the lock and eased the door open a crack. Without turning he said, "This place obviously means far more to you than I knew. I'll make sure we're out of your hair come morning."

He jerked the door open and stalked out.

— m —

"What's the matter?" Cody asked as Teagan stomped off the porch.

"Nothing. I'm fine." He barged past his younger brother and headed toward camp. "Things all right out here?"

Cody shrugged. "Reckon so, excepting that folks are probably buzzing about what happened with the Sioux back there. You might want to set their minds at ease some."

Teagan heaved a sigh. He was in no frame of mind to set anyone at ease. How in heaven's name had he misread Ellie so completely? He'd been certain she loved him, certain she'd agree to spend her life with him.

She'd made it all too clear that she wasn't interested.

"A few of the folks have been asking if the trading post is gonna open today. Not everyone got their supplies yesterday, and they don't want to miss their chance."

"Yeah, we need to restock a few things, too." He produced a wadded paper where he'd scrawled a list of items, plus a little money, and handed both to his brother. "If she opens today, get the things on the list. If not, we'll make do until we get to the fort."

"You don't know if she's opening her shop?"

"Not rightly, no." At this point he questioned everything he thought he knew about Ellie Jefford.

"Well, don't you want to handle this business? I mean, she's your—"

"Just do what I tell ya. I got other things on my mind at the moment."

"Teag?" Cody trotted along beside him. "You sure things are fine? You seem kind of mad."

He shot his brother a sidelong glance. "Go call everyone together. I'll talk with 'em for a minute."

"All right." Cody headed toward the nearest wagon as Teagan continued toward their campsite. Not far off, his black gelding grazed contentedly with Cody's bay. He grabbed his saddle and bridle and turned to the horses. At his sharp whistle, both horses' heads came up and their ears pricked forward.

Teagan walked to his horse. "You ready to stretch your legs?" The black nudged his chest, eliciting a melancholy smile from him. "Good. Let's get you saddled up."

It took only moments to bridle and saddle the black. He settled his rifle in the scabbard and tied his bedroll behind his saddle. By then, about half the wagon train had gathered. He swung onto his mount's back and walked his horse toward the growing crowd. As he drew near, the questions started.

"Are those Injuns gonna be a problem, Mr. Donovan?"

"Were they trying to hurt Mrs. Jefford?"

"Is the trading post going to open today or not?"

"You all right, sir?"

He held up a hand, and the group quieted. "I'm not of a mind to repeat myself today. Let's wait for the rest to gather, and I'll tell you what I know."

Within minutes, Cody and the last handful of settlers straggled up. The soft murmuring died when he again held up his hand for silence.

"I'm sure you all saw the scuffle with the Sioux." The murmuring returned. "It's nothing for you to worry about."

"What happened?" someone called from the midst of the crowd.

"A misunderstanding. There shouldn't be any further problems." So he hoped.

"Sure hope you're right, Donovan," another voice rang out.

"Yeah, that looked like quite a dustup from where we stood," someone else chimed in.

Worse from where *he'd* stood, though he wasn't about to confirm that for his critics. "It's been handled. We'll be pulling out at dawn tomorrow. Be packed and ready to go. I'm heading out to scout our trail for the morning. You have any problems while I'm gone, Cody's the man to see."

"What about the trading post? Is that woman opening up today or not?"

His eyes strayed toward the porch. "I reckon she will. If not, barring any trouble, we'll make Fort Laramie by late tomorrow, and you'll be able to get what you need there. I'll be back in a few hours."

A few continued calling out questions, but Teagan turned his horse and walked away. Once he was beyond the circle of wagons, he clucked his tongue at the black and moved into a canter along the rutted path.

Out of sight of the trading post, he turned toward Bordeaux Creek, where Ellie's nearest neighbor lived. Frenchman James Bordeaux, also a trader, was married to two Sioux women and tended to know what was brewing with the tribes. Maybe he could gather some information before the wagon train pulled out.

Chapter 9

Ellie woke slumped over the table, her head resting on her outstretched arm, the appendage tingling from fingertips to shoulder. Pain jolted her neck and back from the awkward position. She gingerly pushed herself up, working her fingers to restore blood flow to her limb. With her other hand, she rubbed at the worst of the knots in her neck. Blinking several times, she twisted toward Frank, lying peacefully under the quilt. *Lord, please let him be better today.* When she reached to touch his forehead, a ray of bright sunlight warmed her cheek.

She swayed to her feet and peered out the window above Frank's bed. *No.* It was hours past dawn. She had not meant to sleep so long. Heart pounding, Ellie burst through the blanketed doorway into the trading post and scurried to the front window. Emptiness as far as she could see. No wagons in sight. She unlocked the door and stepped out on the rickety porch. Her head spun until she grew nauseous.

Gone.

They'd probably left hours ago. Teagan always made sure his wagon trains got started as close to sunup as they could. He also made a point to say good-bye to her each time. Except *this* one. Her heart heavy, she turned back toward the residence.

He'd made himself scarce the day before, going so far as to send Cody in to purchase their provisions. His avoidance had cut her to the quick. She'd kept watch on the camp the rest of the afternoon while she helped the remaining customers, but even the big black gelding he rode was nowhere to be seen.

Ellie slipped through the blanketed doorway, eyes straying to her father-in-law's bed. She stopped short. "Frank?"

He offered a feeble wave and a tired smile. "Morning."

She slid onto the chair beside his bed and touched his forehead. *Cooler.* Teagan's mint tea remedy was working. She grasped his feeble hand as he reached for her. "I'm glad to see you awake. How are you?"

"Ornery." He closed his eyes. "Tired of being in bed."

Ellie chuckled. "Ornery is good." Particularly if it meant he was getting back to normal. "How about I make you something to eat, get your strength up some."

Frank squeezed her hand. "Not hungry."

"Just a little broth, maybe? That won't sit too heavy on your stomach."

He shook his head.

"C'mon, Frank, if you hope to get better, you have to—"

"I'm not hungry. . ." He forced a little more volume. "Don't figure I will be."

"Of course you wi—"

"I won't, Ellie." Dull brown eyes locked on hers. "You know that, don'tcha?"

Ellie looked away, and the air seeped out of her lungs. Teagan had tried to tell her yesterday, only she hadn't wanted to hear the truth. Her eyes misted.

"Don't do that." Frank jiggled her hand. "A fractious old man don't deserve a young gal's tears."

"I'm hardly a young girl, Frank. I'm a twenty-six-year-old widow, and you're my family. So I'll cry over you if I feel like it."

He loosed a small huff. "Stubborn."

She lifted a quivering chin.

"That's why you put up with my guff, ain't it, girl?"

Her vision blurred again, and she swallowed. "I don't put up with anything. You've always treated me right." She hung her head, and her voice dropped to a whisper. "Particularly since I killed your son."

"No!" The word burst out of Frank's mouth. "Look at me, girl."

She peeked at him, though it was a battle to maintain eye contact.

Brows furrowed, Frank heaved a shaky breath. "I've said it before, but you *hear me* this time. Anson's death was an accident."

"But if we hadn't been arguing—"

"It was his time."

The statement stopped her.

Voice gravelly, Frank pushed on. "If you hadn't argued, he'd have still fallen. Or God might've taken him another way. It's not your fault."

"I want to believe that, Frank. I do." But. . .

She slid out of the chair to kneel beside him, resting her head against his shoulder.

Frank laid a feeble hand on her hair. "I've never blamed you, Ellie, and neither has God."

Her throat knotted. Could it be true. . .not even God blamed her? After years of believing the opposite, it would take time for that truth to sink into her soul.

After a long while, Frank stirred a little. "I talked to Teagan."

Her heart seized as Teagan's words returned to her. He had said he'd talked to Frank, but she had accused him of *lying*.

"Asked him to take you with him when he moves on."

And she'd driven him away. *Lord, how much more of a fool can I be?* She caught his hand and squeezed it. "I can't leave you, Frank."

"You have to. I'll rest easier knowing you're taken care of." He tightened his grip again and caught her eye once more. "Stop by Bordeaux's place on your way. Tell him to look in on me in a couple days. Tell him to bury me next to my son."

Her stomach clenched. "I don't want you to go, Frank."

"It'll be all right, darling girl. When I get to glory, I'm gonna expect God to let me see my wife and son, hold my grandson again." He stroked her hair again. "You're gonna be fine, too. You get shut of this old place and make a life with the man you love."

Ellie clung to him. *The man she loved was gone for good.*

———

From atop a small rise, Teagan scanned the horizon for the hundredth time. Nothing but rolling hills, a few trees, and a bright blue sky ahead. The heavily loaded wagons rumbled along, women and children walking beside the wagons. A man had to have his pride and self-respect. He didn't need to be talked to the way Ellie had the day before.

If all that was true, why did his chest ache with every breath? He should have knocked on her door and begged her one last time to come along. Only he said he wouldn't ask again.

It was clear she had no desire to leave. She'd driven the point home when, for the first time in the years he'd known her, she didn't stand on the front porch and wave good-bye as they pulled out.

Yep, a man had to have his standards.

But a man was only as good as his word, and he'd promised Frank he'd look after Ellie.

"So which one is better? Having your standards or keeping your word?" He huffed. *Leave the past in the past, you fool.* Reliving every detail wasn't going to change a thing, and it only made his chest ache worse.

He searched the horizon again. No sign of the Sioux, thankfully. That had helped to silence the emigrants who were critical of the previous day's scuffle. During his visit to James Bordeaux's place yesterday afternoon, the Frenchman hinted that there were rumblings and unrest in the Sioux camps. Many disliked the flow of white settlers into their territory, and they hated the restrictive rules of the treaty they'd signed three years earlier. Bordeaux said the Sioux were starving, and the money promised to them by the American government was slow in coming. But according to the Frenchman's account, the Sioux chiefs were managing to keep the young warriors' discontent from spilling over into violence.

He scrubbed his stubbly jaw. He should have forced Ellie to come.

"Teag?" Cody's voice sliced into his thoughts. The younger Donovan rode up from among the long line of wagons. "There's dust off in the distance."

Teagan noted the large plume coloring the sky almost directly ahead. "Good eye."

Apparently his thoughts were still firmly rooted with a pretty young lady five miles behind, rather than on the journey ahead. If he didn't find a way to remedy that, it could turn deadly.

"So who do you reckon it is?"

"If it was another wagon train, we'd have been seeing that dust for a while now." He pulled his telescope from his saddlebags and focused in on the dust cloud. As yet, he couldn't see the source. "Who or whatever it is, it must be coming toward us."

"Have we got reason to be concerned?"

Teagan glared. "How many times do I have to say it? Out here, until you can prove otherwise, there's always reason to be concerned." So why had he let his mind become so preoccupied with a woman who didn't want him when there could be danger about? He handed their packhorse's lead rope to his brother. "I'll ride ahead and see what I can find out. Stay on your guard. Keep the wagons moving to the northwest." He pointed. "I'll be back after a while."

Cody took the rope, and Teagan drew his rifle and clucked his tongue at his big black.

"Be careful," Cody called as he started down the sloping grade.

He waved and urged his horse into a canter. It took little time to pass the plodding wagons, and once he was safely beyond them, he headed toward a rise about a half mile off. Atop it, he dug his scope out and looked through it again, a grin spreading on his face. Soldiers. Twenty-five or thirty, with a few familiar faces among them. Good, maybe while they were on regular patrols, he could get them to look in on Ellie. Teagan tucked the scope away and moved out in the direction of the detachment.

He met up with the group nearly a mile farther on. An unfamiliar young second lieutenant spoke to Sergeant Bill Litchmore beside him, who in turn called for the soldiers to halt. Litchmore grinned his way, as did Corporal Max Willits, who sat behind the lieutenant and sergeant.

"Lieutenant Grattan, meet Teagan Donovan. That man there is just crazy enough to lead a wagon train all the way to California and turn around and ride back to Tennessee every year so he can do it all over again the next."

Teagan chuckled as he turned to the lieutenant. "Good to meet you, sir."

Grattan nodded. "Likewise."

"Sir, would you allow the men a ten-minute rest?" Litchmore asked.

"Five, Sergeant. We still have to get to the Sioux encampment and arrest that heathen, and I'd like to get back to the fort before dark."

"Five minutes, sir." Litchmore gave the command, and the soldiers broke formation and dismounted.

Teagan also dismounted and shook the sergeant's hand. "How are you, Litchmore?"

"Ah, you know how this soldiering job is. Doesn't change much from day to day. How're things with you?" His friend looked toward the wagon train off in the distance as he led Teagan away from the crowd, their horses trailing. "You got quite a group this year."

Teagan filled the air with small talk until they reached a safe distance. Then Litchmore dropped the act and rolled his eyes.

"Things not going so good, Litchmore?"

The sergeant snorted. "The bigwigs in Washington figure it shouldn't matter which fresh-faced graduate they stick out here to run the fort. Between the senior officer, who happens to be a lowly first lieutenant, and Grattan over there, we've got a heap of problems."

Teagan looked discreetly in Grattan's direction. "What was he saying about arresting someone?"

"Oh, a Mormon wagon train came through here a day or two ago, and one of their cows wandered off. An Indian by the name of High Forehead killed the cow, probably wanting something to eat. So now we're involved, trying to sort it out."

"Doesn't sound like the type of thing the army should be tangling with. Where's the Indian agent?"

"Whitfield's on his way, but for all we know, it could take him a month to arrive.

Grattan decided he'll handle the matter in Whitfield's stead."

From over the back of his horse, he studied the lieutenant. "Be careful, Bill. You don't want on the wrong side of things with the Sioux."

A grim expression crossed Litchmore's face. "Agreed."

"Speaking of. . . You know that trading post about seven miles back? Frank and Ellie Jefford run it?"

"Yeah?"

If *he* couldn't watch over Ellie. . .

"You think you can keep an eye on that place?"

Chapter 10

Ellie set the last of the supplies in the rickety wheelbarrow. A shiver raced down her spine as she thought of the multiple trips she'd made into the barn loft. After Anson's death she'd sworn she'd never go up there again, and Frank made sure she never had to. But she'd forced herself tonight.

She eased the brimming cart out of the barn and secured the door, thankful to be shut of that place. Lantern in hand, she secured the door, her eyes straying to the black sky dotted with thousands of twinkling stars.

"Father, thank You for helping me face the barn again, and especially for letting Frank wake up. I've missed him." She breathed deep of the dewy night air and bit her bottom lip. "Could I make a selfish request, Lord? Be merciful to me and don't take him. I wouldn't know what to do."

Particularly now that Teagan wouldn't be returning.

A leaden shroud cloaked her heart, black and heavy. To lose either one was hard enough, but to lose both. . .

Lord, I wouldn't know how to go on.

The lonely yipping howl of a coyote carried across the distance. A moment later others answered. Another shiver gripped her. She grabbed the barrow handles and hurried around to the front of the trading post and eased the wheel onto the creaky porch. Leaving it in front of the door where she could easily reach the goods, Ellie slipped inside.

She unloaded the wheelbarrow quickly, depositing the supplies on the counter, then pushed the barrow out of the path of the doorway and locked herself in. She could put the cart away in the light of day.

Her neck and back muscles ached from her awkward sleeping position the previous night. Propping a hip against the counter, she leaned her head back and rubbed at the tense muscles with both hands.

The memory of Teagan's big hand cradling her cheek and tipping her head back washed over her. The feel of his arm circling her waist, drawing her close, his lips on hers.

Her heart raced. She'd *wanted* to respond to his kiss, just as she had the night before. With every fiber of her being, she had wanted to. How easily she could have gotten lost in the safety of his strong arms as he showered her with kisses. On the lips. The neck. The collarbone.

She sank into a puddle on the floor. "Why, Ellie? Why didn't you?"

Because the guilt she felt over Anson's death had bound her tight.

Because she didn't deserve to leave this place when her husband was forever trapped here.

Because she felt unworthy of love.

"I've never blamed you, Ellie, and neither has God." Frank's words echoed in her mind. Could they be true?

Lord, if Frank is right, then would You help me to forgive myself? The weight of this burden has nearly crushed me. Please take it from me.

Throat aching, she rubbed at her stinging eyes. Ellie heaved a sigh and crumpled, cheek pressing against the rough floor planks.

Lord, please help me. What do I need to do?

She lay there for a long time. With every breath, her chest loosened a little, and the shame she'd felt seeped away. Perhaps not completely—not yet—but enough to know that God had heard her and was easing the ache in her heart.

After a long while, the weight eased, and Ellie finally pushed herself up from the floor and set about putting away the supplies. Tins of biscuits, bags of coffee, sewing needles, spools of thread, ribbons, and various textiles. She stashed them in their rightful spots, though making them look neat and organized would require a fresh eye and some sunlight. It would do for tonight. She circled the trading post to extinguish the lamps.

Father, thank You. You have been gracious to me today, answering my prayers for Frank to get better, in helping me conquer my fear of the barn, and now this. If I could make one more selfish request. . .please, give me another chance with Teagan.

Hope filled her heart, and a smile parted her lips. God had heard her other prayers. Surely He would answer this one positively, too. Perhaps Frank would be awake again so she could tell him of the answered prayers.

She slipped through the doorway and moved toward his bed but stopped a few feet from him.

Frank's lifeless eyes were fixed on the ceiling, a hint of a smile parting his bluish lips.

—⁓—

"He's so weak right now, making a journey like that will kill him. I can't be the cause of his death, too."

With gray light etching the predawn sky, Teagan rolled his bedding as Ellie's words churned in his mind. Somewhere in the night, upon the thousandth replay of the conversation, his mind had snagged on those words. What had she meant, being the cause of his death, *too*? Whose death?

He tossed his bedroll aside and stood. Morning cook fires dotted the area inside the circled wagons. Outside the circle, Fort Laramie was awakening. A few windows in the various buildings showed flickering lamplight, and shadowy forms moved across the parade ground as soldiers reported to their guard posts or other early duties.

Cody approached and handed him a steaming cup of coffee. "I reckon you can use this."

"Yep." He blew on it before he sipped.

"Get *any* sleep last night, or did you just pace the whole time?"

Darn that boy. Hard to keep secrets when his hawkeyed brother paid such close attention. Teagan looked off toward the eastern horizon. "Slept a little." Unfortunately his thoughts had swirled over and over the situation with Ellie, and a *little* was all he'd gotten.

"*I can't be the cause of his death, too.*" He huffed. *Lord, what did she mean by that?*

"Never did tell me what happened back there."

"Nope." Teagan sipped his coffee again. "Don't reckon I did."

"Well, don't you think I deserve some kind of explanation? I mean, you been talking about Ellie Jefford for at least three years, saying how you planned to marry her one day. I figured you were gonna ask her this time around."

He stared into the steaming cup. "I did ask."

"You did?" Surprise tinged Cody's voice.

He rubbed at the ache building between his temples. "I did."

"And?"

Teagan bit back the sharp-tongued response that threatened to erupt, and instead shrugged. "She's not here, is she?"

"She said no?"

A thick lump filled his throat.

"I'm real sorry, Teag. . . ." Cody fell silent and took an awkward swallow of his coffee. "So why'd she turn you down?"

"I'm not rightly sure. She said she didn't want to leave the trading post. It was her husband's dream." He sipped his coffee. "And she was afraid Frank was too weak to travel. Said she didn't want to kill him, too."

Cody's brows furrowed. "What does that mean?"

"Hanged if I know."

"Well, are you gonna go back and talk to her, find out?"

"I'm not gonna beg, Cody. A man's got to have his pride."

"Blast your fool pride. Do you love her or—"

Several sharp bugle blasts rang out across the parade ground, followed by distant shouts. Teagan came to attention, his heart hammering.

Shadowy forms on the parade ground set off in a run, heading toward the commotion. Across the way, the door of the big white two-story building flew open, light spilling from the doorway as men flooded onto the porch. More blasts from the bugle and the fort came alive.

Teagan's nerves sizzled as if lightning coursed through his veins. Something was very wrong. He dumped the coffee and shoved the empty cup toward his brother. "Stay with the wagon train. Keep everyone together, and try to keep 'em calm. I'll see if I can't figure out what's going on."

Wide-eyed, Cody nodded.

"And. . .keep a close eye on the Bentons. Last thing we need is them getting stupid."

"I will." His brother also dumped his coffee and tossed both cups toward their pack.

Teagan grabbed his rifle and, in long strides, hurried toward the source of the unrest near the guardhouse. Soldiers ran past, and ahead a tight knot of men gathered around something.

"Someone get the post surgeon. This man's hurt bad."

He broke into a run.

"Move back! Give us room." The voice rose above the din, and the cluster of bodies widened a little.

"More. Back up. Give him some air." The group spread out as Teagan reached its edge.

"Stay quiet now, Willits."

Max Willits? The corporal had been with the detachment of soldiers he'd come across as they headed out to arrest one of the Sioux yesterday. Taller than many in the group, Teagan craned his neck and peered over the heads of the soldiers, yet he couldn't see the injured man.

Pounding footsteps approached, and a young man in trousers and a white shirt, his face half covered in shaving lather, ran up shouting orders. A second, older man arrived, black bag in one hand, blanket in the other.

"Make room!" the half-shaven man growled, pushing his way into the crowd. The group scattered a few feet, finally allowing Teagan a glimpse of Willits.

The first rays of dawn illuminated the man's unnaturally pale face, now bloodied. Several arrow shafts protruded from his torso, each broken off inches from his body. The man's uniform glistened with fresh blood.

Lord God, have mercy. He's not long for this world.

The doctor knelt beside Willits, checking his wounds, while the half-shaven man bent near his head.

"What happened, Corporal?"

Willits tried to speak, but whatever he said was lost in the murmur of the crowd. The half-shaven man spoke again, and this time bent low to hear.

"That's enough, Lieutenant. We need to get this man inside now. You"—the doctor threw the folded blanket, hitting Teagan and a baby-faced private with it—"spread that out on the ground beside him."

Teagan laid his rifle aside and helped the other fellow shake out the folds. As the doctor directed, they placed Willits onto the blanket. Teagan and the young private gathered the corners nearest the injured man's head, and two others mirrored their actions at his feet. The lieutenant stationed himself near Willits's head.

"What about the other soldiers, Corporal?"

Willits squeezed his eyes shut. "Sioux got 'em. All dead."

The lieutenant swore.

"Flemming," the doctor called, "we *must* get this man to my operating table."

The officer looked Teagan's way. "Step out of the way, sir. This is an army matter."

Teagan stepped back, allowing the lieutenant to take over, and they spirited Willits across the parade ground. He snatched his rifle from the ground and hurried back to the circle of wagons, headed straight for his horse.

"What's going on?" Cody fell in beside him, matching his long strides.

He dropped the rifle and grabbed his bridle and saddle instead. "Near as I can tell, about thirty soldiers are dead by Sioux hands."

"What? What happened?" Cody's voice was etched with surprise and disbelief.

"I don't know."

"Where are you going?"

His heart hammered. "I'm putting aside my *fool pride* to check on Ellie and Frank."

Cody glanced back at the circle of wagons then headed for his own gear. "I'll get saddled, too."

"No. I need someone I can trust to look after the wagon train until I get back." He dropped the saddle beside his horse and eased the bridle over the black's nose.

"Teag, you shouldn't go alone."

His mind churned. As usual, Cody was right. He'd be far safer with a few extra pairs of eyes—and guns. And he knew just the men.

"Tell the Benton boys if they want a fight with the Sioux, they'd better get saddled up."

Chapter 11

Bleary-eyed and exhausted, Ellie stared at the ground. Perhaps she should just ride to James Bordeaux's place and ask for his help. Perhaps, but the idea didn't sit well. Frank and Mr. Bordeaux tolerated each other at best, though much of their dislike struck her as two old men trying to out-bellyache each other. The least she could do was try to bury him on her own. She owed Frank that. Yet the midmorning sun glared down on her, and the air clung thick and heavy, causing perspiration to form on her skin before she began. With a sigh, Ellie donned a pair of leather work gloves and picked up the shovel.

Lord, please help.

Those words had been her only prayer, the only words she could find. They fell agonizingly short in expressing the feelings lodged deep in her soul.

Please help.

Would He? After Frank woke the previous morning and was able to talk with her more than he had in days, she'd believed God was going to heal him, but He hadn't.

She positioned the shovel's edge even with the end of Anson's grave and dug in. Only a small chunk of earth came up. She tossed it aside and attacked the same spot. Bits of dirt broke loose, not whole shovelfuls like when Frank and Anson used to dig. She chiseled away at the spot, widening the hole until it was roughly the same length and width as Anson's grave, but mere inches deep, rather than feet.

Ellie paused for a drink, a faint sound rattling in her ears, distant and nearly unnoticeable at first. She looped the canteen strap over the fence post and took up the shovel again. She turned back to the shallow hole, and the sound grew louder. *Hoofbeats.* A quick scan of the skyline indicated no dust of an incoming wagon train, nor was the pounding like any wagon train she'd ever heard. Wild horses, perhaps. Or buffalo.

She listened again. The sound was coming from the west.

A ghostly scream split the air, and Ellie gasped. A band of Sioux warriors rode at her, maybe fifteen in all, their faces painted in ghoulish masks. Thundering hooves churned the ground. Their inhuman cries pierced her eardrums. They raced past the small cemetery on either side. Heart hammering, Ellie backed up a step and tumbled onto her backside. She scrambled up, clutching the shovel handle, and spun. The mounted men wheeled around for another pass.

Lord, help me!

Before she could move, they charged, turned, and crisscrossed around her. Several men broke off and stormed toward the trading post. A few circled the fenced graveyard, and one dived from his mount's back over the fence and ran at her.

Ellie screamed, tried to run, but he was on her. A strong hand caught her hair and dragged her up and over the fence. Her feet tangled in her skirts, and she went down face-first. Lightning shot through her jaw, her shoulder, her hip. He let go, stumbling past her.

Despite the pain, she climbed to her feet. The mounted Sioux circled. The warrior faced her and lunged. Shovel still in hand, Ellie jabbed the long handle between his legs, and he sprawled flat on his belly. Missing no chance, she swung the other end at his head. It connected with a loud metallic clang, and he went limp.

The nearest rider's horse shied, and Ellie darted past it. If she could get inside, she could lock herself in. There was a rifle not far from the door. Maybe she could stave off the attack.

—⁓—

By the time they got within a mile of the trading post, Teagan had seen plenty of Sioux, stripped down to their breechclouts and smeared with war paint. They moved like ants, crawling across the countryside in fast-moving lines, weapons in hand and horses ready to run. More than once he and the Benton brothers had been forced to hide in the brush along the riverbank or find what cover they could while a war party passed. It was God's providence they hadn't been found, hadn't run headlong into a fight with one of the bands. However a ride he'd hoped to make in little more than an hour had taken several.

Lord, I need You. Ellie needs You. I tried my hardest to provide and care for her, keep her safe these last few days. I reckon I've been trying to do Your job, and I'm sorry for that, Lord. If You'd be so merciful, keep her and Frank in Your hand, and don't let the Sioux or anyone else hurt 'em.

"Donovan." Ezra Benton's voice broke into his thoughts. "Look."

He traced the direction of Benton's pointing finger to a gray haze coloring the sky in the direction of Ellie and Frank's place.

Smoke.

His stomach dropped. *This is what I mean, Lord. Keep her safe.* From his saddlebags, he retrieved his Colt Dragoon pistol. Gun in hand, Teagan spurred his horse into a run, the Bentons falling in behind him. The savage cries of the marauding Sioux reached his ears before they could see the attack. Coherent thought became impossible, and his heart nearly beat out of his chest. They dipped into a depression and rode onto the next rise, the trading post coming into view.

Horses and riders swarmed. A couple of warriors ran across the trading post's roof, torches in hand, and flames licked at the corners of the building. Black smoke billowed from the structure. A woman's piercing scream rose above the noise.

Ellie.

"Fan out!" he shouted.

Both Bentons picked a direction like they'd rehearsed the tactic before.

Teagan crouched over the black's neck. As if the horse understood, it bounded forward, hooves thundering over the terrain. From his left a gun roared, and the warrior on the roof pitched to the ground. Another shot sounded to his right, and a mounted warrior twisted sharply on his horse's back. Teagan leveled the pistol and fired on a third one just as the Sioux drew his bow in their direction.

Lord, help me find her. She had to be there. He could hear her. And Frank, had he awakened, gotten outside? An arrow hissed past Teagan's ear. He aimed and fired again, and this time, his target tumbled from his horse. Teagan raced headlong into the fray.

Ellie ran into view from around the corner. One of the mounted braves bore down on her and leaped, knocking her to the ground. Teagan veered toward them just as gunfire erupted from somewhere behind. Indian ponies, some still carrying their riders, raced around him, but his focus stayed on Ellie. Feet from her, he pulled his horse to a sliding stop and vaulted from its back.

Facedown, she struggled against the Sioux straddling her back. Sunlight glinted on a knife blade as the warrior's hand arced toward her. Teagan launched himself at the man. His shoulder slammed into the Indian's side, and they both toppled into the dirt. Teagan's pistol skittered out of reach.

Nose to nose with Ellie's attacker, Teagan recognized the man despite the war paint. *Him.* The one who wanted her hair. The Sioux slashed with the blade, but Teagan rolled free and lunged to his feet. The Indian also scrambled up.

Before the Sioux had his legs under him, Teagan landed a crushing fist to the warrior's jaw, once more sending the man sprawling. "I told you not to touch her."

The brave stared, obviously rattled, his brown eyes settling on Ellie. She faced him, Teagan's pistol leveled at his head. Hoofbeats pounded toward them, and the Sioux lurched to his feet and burst past Teagan. A charging horse raced by, and the rider caught the warrior's arm, swinging him onto the back of the horse. The remaining Sioux retreated, the Bentons giving chase.

Once they were gone, Teagan turned to Ellie. Without a word, she pressed the pistol into his hand and slipped into his arms, her body shaking with silent sobs.

Behind them, the roar of flames and the groan of weakening timbers registered. He pushed Ellie back a step, every nerve zinging. "Where's Frank?"

Her eyes brimmed. "Inside."

"No." Teagan spun toward the door, watching the flames dance through the small window beside it. He stumbled toward it, but she caught his arm.

"He died last night."

The words took a moment to make sense. She slid back into his arms, and he pulled her close. "I'm so sorry, Ell."

She shuddered.

Silas and Ezra Benton returned, stopping a short distance off. "It's clear, Donovan. For now."

The building groaned again, and part of the roof gave way with a crash and a spray of glowing embers.

Teagan wrapped her tighter in his arms and dipped his mouth toward her ear.

"You gotta come with me now. It's not safe here. We've got to get to Fort Laramie before the Sioux return."

Chapter 12

Evening, Ell."

Ellie looked up from the sleeping face of young Caleb Pritchard at Teagan's quiet greeting. She mustered a smile. "Evening."

Outside the circled wagons a couple of soldiers passed by, talking and laughing. Teagan glanced their way as he squatted near her. He tore a couple blades of grass from the ground. "You doing all right?"

"Better. I slept some." It had helped to freshen up and change into a dress she'd borrowed from Laura Pritchard.

"Good." He grinned, though the smile was tinged with sadness. "Would you be up to a short walk with me?"

She had hoped for that all afternoon, though Teagan had kept himself busy elsewhere. "That would be nice."

He helped her to her feet and glanced at Laura Pritchard. He motioned to the blanket she'd been sitting on. "Could we borrow that, ma'am?"

"By all means."

Teagan folded the blanket under one arm and tucked Ellie's hand in the crook of his other.

For several minutes, they walked in silence, a slow, ambling pace with no particular destination. When the silence stretched on, Ellie cleared her throat. "Are we just walking, or were you thinking we'd talk some, too?"

Hopefully the same things were on his mind as hers.

He veered off their chosen path, heading toward the shell of an old building. The stark white walls nearly glowed in the last vestiges of sunlight. He stopped just outside of it. "Would you sit with me?"

"Of course."

Teagan spread the blanket and offered her his hand as she found a comfortable position. He sat across from her, though he kept his focus on the blanket between them and picked at some imaginary dirt.

"I figure I owe you a mighty big apology for leaving the way I did yesterday. I acted like a fool. The least I could've done was say good-bye."

Her heart swelled, and she longed for the safety of his arms. "If you owed me anything, Teagan, I think you made up for it when you came back this morning." Ellie grasped the fingers of his left hand. He looked up, almost startled. "I'm sorry that I hurt you. It was the last thing on earth that I wanted to do."

"I was trying to push you into something you didn't want."

"It's not that I didn't wa—"

He held up a hand, silencing her. "It's all right. You don't have to explain. I understand."

"Do you?"

"I'm more concerned about what you're going to do now, what with the trading post getting burned and. . ."

"And Frank dying," she finished for him.

"Yeah." His left hand still entwined with hers, he picked at the blanket again with his right. "I don't think it'd be wise for you to rebuild the place. After this morning—"

"I don't plan to rebuild."

He jerked his head up. For a moment he was silent. "All right. You don't have family, leastways not parents or brothers and sisters, right?"

"No family. Ma and Pa are both dead, and I was an only child. I have no contact with any of my aunts or uncles."

Teagan pondered a moment. "Have you thought on where you want to go or what you want to do?"

Her stomach fluttered. "Is your marriage proposal still open?"

His shoulders slumped as he pinned his gaze on the blanket yet again. "You shouldn't marry me. Not if you don't have those kinds of feelings."

"Teagan?" She squeezed his fingers gently.

"I've already talked to Lieutenant Flemming, and he's going to arrange an army escort so we can see if there's anything left at the trading post. From there, I'll do all I can to help you find a place and get on your feet. I won't leave you on your own. I am responsible to get this wagon train to California, but once I'm done, I'll take you anywhere you—"

"*Teagan.*"

He looked up, brow furrowed. "What?"

Before she could second-guess herself, she swung up onto her knees, grasped his shirtfront, and kissed him.

Teagan stiffened, drew back, his eyes wide. She twitched a smile at him and brushed his lips again, lingering. He resisted but then allowed himself to be drawn in. His rigid muscles relaxed, and her grip on his shirt loosened until her hands flattened against his broad chest.

Now this felt right.

—⁓—

"What was that?" Teagan asked, pulse pounding, when Ellie finally sat back.

A coy smile parted her lips. "It's called a kiss. You tried to give me one yesterday. . . remember?"

Oh, he remembered. "I seem to recall it wasn't well received."

"I'm sorry for that. It wasn't you. I, um. . ." She paused. "Do you know how Anson died?"

Teagan shrugged. "Frank said that it was some kind of an accident."

She nodded. "He fell from the barn loft. . .during an argument with me." She twisted the fabric of her dress. "I was pushing him to pack up and go on to California."

"Oh, Ell." Suddenly it all made sense. Frank's statement about her wagonload of guilt. The strange comment about not costing Frank his life, too. Teagan reached for her hand. "Please tell me you don't think you were to blame. . . ."

"I did." Ellie wrapped her arms tight around her waist. At her whispered confession, he scooted closer and drew her into his embrace. She rested her head on his shoulder. It was a long moment before she continued. "I was so eaten up with guilt I couldn't allow my heart to love. I thought I needed to stay at the trading post and live out the life Anson never got to."

He laid his cheek against hers. "I'm sorry. I didn't know."

"I made Frank promise never to speak of it to anyone." She sighed. "We barely talked about it ourselves all these years. Until yesterday."

"And what happened yesterday?"

"God gave me a gift, one more good conversation with Frank. He said that Anson died because it was his time to go, and whether we had argued or not, God would've taken him. I'd never thought of it that way, but after that, I spent a long time praying, asking God to help me forgive myself and move on."

Teagan smoothed her hair. "Have you?"

She nodded against his shoulder. "I think He helped me through a whole lot of it last night. I still feel tender about it, but it's not got me so bound up anymore. I can finally admit that I love you, and I'd like to be your wife if you'll still have me."

For years, he'd loved her and longed to take care of her, but. . .

Teagan released her, and she sat up. "Ell, I've waited a long time to hear those words, and I certainly don't want to mess up a good thing, but I've got to know. Are you saying this because you've got no one else, or are you saying it because you truly love me?"

Though he fully expected a flash of anger in her blue eyes, she smiled softly. "Do you remember the first time you came to the trading post after Anson died?"

How could he forget? It had been a hard visit for all of them. "Yeah."

"Gideon had been crying for three days straight. I was so distraught over Anson, I couldn't comfort my own baby. You walked in, took Gideon out of my arms and held him to your chest. In minutes, you had him asleep in his cradle, and for the next couple of days, you helped me pick up the pieces and figure out how to carry on. My feelings for you began to change then, and I fell more in love with you every time you came back. I just didn't feel worthy to have you."

"It about killed me, leaving you there that year." And every one since.

"I know."

Teagan pulled her close once again, bending to claim her lips. He drank in her sweetness, and she responded in kind, melting against him with a quiet moan. One hand strayed upward to cradle the back of her head, and his mouth ranged across her jaw. He breathed deep, getting lost in her scent, her warmth, her softness.

He dipped his mouth next to her ear. "Marry me, Ellie."

"I will."

"Tonight. Right now."

She pulled back and looked up at him, blue eyes full of love and perfect lips curved in a little smile. "Do you know where we can find a preacher?"

"Laura Pritchard didn't tell you?"

"Tell me what?"

Teagan grinned. "Her husband's a preacher. I reckon if you say it's what you want, we can be married right away."

Her smile widened. "Well then, what're we waiting for?"

Epilogue

Ellie Donovan's stomach fluttered at the pungent scent of sawdust mingled with something familiar and masculine. She stood tall and pinned her focus on her husband's long shadow as he approached. Her heart raced as strong, familiar arms circled her bulging waistline, and Teagan kissed the back of her neck, sending a little shiver down her spine, despite the sweltering summer sun.

"What're you doing out here in the heat, Ell?"

She smiled at the small fenced plot blooming with poppies. In the center of the bright flowers, several stones jutted up, each with a name carved across its face. *Frank. Anson. Gideon.*

"Reminiscing."

"You miss them."

"Every day." Not a day passed that she didn't think of each of them fondly.

Teagan exhaled, stirring the loose tendrils of hair tickling her neck. "Do you ever wish you'd stayed and rebuilt the trading post?"

She chuckled as she faced him. "Goodness, no. God knew what He was doing when He burned that place down. By letting it go, it freed me to remember all the good things without the guilt eating at me."

He tucked her deeper into his embrace. "Are you happy here?"

She hugged him tight and laid her cheek against his chest. "I've never been happier."

"You mean that?" His deep voice rumbled in her ear.

Ellie tipped her face up to look at her handsome husband. "With all my heart."

He grinned and brushed her lips with his, lingering there for a moment. "Cody and I finished building the cradle. He's carrying it into our bedroom now. You want to see it?"

She twined her fingers between his. "Silly question, Teagan Donovan."

Dear Reader,

Thank you for reading my debut novella *Sioux Summer*. I hope you enjoyed getting to know Ellie and Teagan as much as I enjoyed writing their story.

While this is a work of fiction, several of the story's minor characters were real, and the conflict between the Sioux and the army was a historic battle. The engagement is known as the Grattan Massacre. The conflict started when a single cow wandered from a Mormon wagon train and was killed by one of the Sioux. When an amicable agreement couldn't be reached between the Sioux and the Mormon emigrant, Lieutenant John Grattan led a detachment of thirty soldiers to the Sioux camp to arrest the offender. The Sioux asked French trader James Bordeaux to translate, but still, no agreement was reached. The situation turned deadly when a young private got nervous and fired his gun, fatally wounding the Sioux chief. In retaliation, the twelve hundred Sioux warriors at the camp attacked and killed Grattan and his men. Only one survived the immediate attack but died soon after. For several days after the massacre, the Sioux raided the countryside, even ransacking Bordeaux's trading post. This conflict was the first battle in a decades-long war between the white settlers and the Sioux Nation.

Thank you, again, for reading. I hope I have earned a spot on your bookshelf.

Sincerely,
Jennifer Uhlarik

About the Authors

Amanda Cabot's dream of selling a book before her thirtieth birthday came true, and she's now the author of more than thirty-five novels. Her romances have appeared on the CBA and ECPA bestseller lists, have garnered a starred review from *Publishers Weekly*, and have been finalists for the ACFW Carol, the HOLT Medallion, and the Booksellers Best awards.

A popular speaker, Amanda is a member of ACFW and a charter member of Romance Writers of America. A Christmastime bride, she married her high school sweetheart who shares her love of travel and who's driven thousands of miles to help her research her books. After years as Easterners, they fulfilled a longtime dream when Amanda retired from her job as Director of Information Technology for a major corporation and now live in Cheyenne.

You can find her at www.amandacabot.com.

Four-time Carol Award winner and bestselling author of twenty books, Melanie Dobson is the former corporate publicity manager at Focus on the Family and owner of Dobson Media Group. To research for this novella and *The Journey: A Legacy of Love Novel*, Melanie and her two young daughters drove a thousand miles from Wyoming to the Willamette Valley, creating their own Oregon Trail adventure via car. Because of her husband's work in the film industry, their family has lived in multiple states, as well as Germany, but the Dobson family is settled for now in a small town near Portland, Oregon. Melanie loves connecting with readers via her website at www.melaniedobson.com.

Award-winning author Pam Hillman, a country girl at heart, writes inspirational fiction set in the turbulent times of the American West and the Gilded Age. She lives with her family in Mississippi. Contact Pam at her website: www.pamhillman.com.

After several years away, native Texan and award-winning author Myra Johnson is happy to be back in her home state enjoying Hill Country wildlife and real Texas barbecue. Myra is a three-time Maggie Awards finalist, two-time finalist for the prestigious ACFW Carol Awards, winner of Christian Retailing's Best for historical fiction, and winner in the Inspirational category of the National Excellence in Romance Fiction Awards. The Johnsons share their home with two very pampered rescue dogs who don't always understand the meaning of "Mom's trying to write." They've also inherited the cute little cat (complete with attitude) their daughter and family had to leave behind when they moved overseas. Visit Myra online at www.MyraJohnson.com.

Amy Lillard is a 2013 Carol Award–winning author who loves reading romance novels, from contemporary to Amish. She was born and raised in Mississippi but now lives in Oklahoma with her husband and their teenage son. Amy can be reached at amylillard@hotmail.com, and found on the web at www.amywritesromance.com.

DiAnn Mills is a bestselling author who believes her readers should expect an adventure. She creates action-packed, suspense-filled novels to thrill readers. Her titles have appeared on the CBA and ECPA bestseller lists; won two Christy Awards; and been finalists for the RITA, Daphne Du Maurier, Inspirational Readers' Choice, and Carol award contests. She is the director of the Blue Ridge Mountain Christian Writers Conference, Mountainside Marketing Retreat, and Mountainside Novelist Retreat with social media specialist Edie Melson. Connect with DiAnn at DiAnnMills.com

Anna Schmidt is the author of more than twenty works of fiction. Among her many honors, Anna is the recipient of *Romantic Times* Reviewer's Choice Award and a finalist for the RITA award for romantic fiction. She enjoys gardening and collecting seashells at her winter home in Florida.

Ann Shorey has been a full-time writer for over twenty years. Her latest releases include *Love's Sweet Beginning* and a novella in *The Mail-Order Brides* collection. Ann's great-grandparents came west over the Oregon Trail as part of one of the last wagon train migrations. According to her grandfather's memoirs, "there were thousands of covered wagons on the road." This novella is the story of one of those wagons. Ann and her husband live in southwestern Oregon. She may be contacted through her website, www.annshorey.com.

Jennifer Uhlarik discovered the western genre as a preteen when she swiped the only "horse" book she found on her older brother's bookshelf. A new love was born. Across the next ten years, she devoured Louis L'Amour westerns and fell in love with the genre. In college at the University of Tampa, she began penning her own story of the Old West. Armed with a BA in writing, she has finaled and won in numerous writing competitions, and been on the ECPA best-seller list several times. In addition to writing, she has held jobs as a private business owner, a schoolteacher, a marketing director, and her favorite—a full-time homemaker. Jennifer is active in American Christian Fiction Writers, Women Writing the West, and is a lifetime member of the Florida Writers Association. She lives near Tampa, Florida, with her husband, college-aged son, and four fur children.

JOIN
US
ONLINE!

Christian Fiction for Women

*Christian Fiction for Women is your online home
for the latest in Christian fiction.*

Check us out online for:

- Giveaways
- Recipes
- Info about Upcoming Releases
- Book Trailers
- News and More!

Find Christian Fiction for Women at Your Favorite Social Media Site:

 Search "Christian Fiction for Women"

 @fictionforwomen